THE Scavenger's Daughter

A novel by

WILLIAM G. THOMPSON

To my reader:

This novel deals directly with the subject of human trafficking and the personal suffering endured by innocent lives caught up within the unending nightmare of its grip. While, to the best of my knowledge, its characters are entirely fictional and its story neither based on any actual or specific events nor even unique to the location in which it is set, its graphic depiction of sexual activity, violence and torture along with its use of coarse language is designed to provide you, my reader, with an intimate yet accurate portrayal of the victims of those whose chosen trade is the buying and selling of men, women and children.

For more information, here are some websites that may be of some interest:

- *www.humantrafficking.org* for information to combat human trafficking through prevention, prosecution and victim protection.
- *www.endhumantrafficking.org* for information on The Project to End Human Trafficking (PEHT), a non-profit organization that was founded in 2004 as part of a global anti-slavery movement.
- *www.polarisproject.org/human-trafficking/overview* for information about advocacy programs in providing assistance to those directly in need.
- *www.stopchildslavery.com* for those interested in researching ways to help bring an end to human trafficking.
- *www.endslaverynow.com/?goto=underground&section=take_action* for information on volunteer organizations, facilities and service professionals.
- *www.catwinternational.org* is the Coalition Against Trafficking in Women-International (CATW) which promotes women's human rights worldwide by working to combat the sexual exploitation of women and young girls.
- *www.traffickingproject.org* for an online community working to raise awareness of human trafficking and modern day slavery.
- *www.acf.hhs.gov/trafficking/rescue_restore/fed_efforts.html* for a list of federal agency programs that protect and assist victims of human trafficking and their efforts to apprehend and prosecute their traffickers.
- *kristof.blogs.nytimes.com/tag/human-trafficking* for articles and writings from New York Times columnist Nicholas Kristof on finding ways to confront 21st-century slavery.

With your understanding, then, this novel has been written for the mature reader only.

~ WGT

For Bridget,
without whose selfless devotion and attention to detail
none of this would have been possible,

and to Eva,
whose life of implacable strength and courage
proved to be this novel's deepest inspiration.

Part One

And Jesus called a little child to him and set the child in their midst and said, "See that you not despise even one of these little ones; for I tell you, their angels in heaven always behold the face of my Father."

MATTHEW 18: 2, 10

"For whosoever causes one of these little ones who believe in me to sin, it would better for him if a great millstone were hung about his neck and he were thrown into the sea."

MARK 9:41

2004

Prologue

THE YOUNG WOMAN sitting on the damp cement of the open-air parking garage's fourth floor seemed in a world all her own as he approached her slowly, deliberately, quietly. She was leaning back against the concrete column, her arms wrapped around knees up against her chest, bathed in the dying light of another unusually warm and muggy mid-July Chicago evening. Her eyes closed, she rocked her head softly back and forth as she listened to her iPod through earbuds. Her voice, though barely audible, still echoed softy throughout the spacious if sparsely populated floor as she sang unevenly along, lost inside lyrics that recalled a time that was now just a shrouded memory.

When all that you've known has been taken from you,
When you're frightened and trembling, and its' pain all that's true,
When all your prayers go unanswered while your world's torn in two,
In your darkest hour of your darkest days, somehow I'll find my way to you...

She seemed so much older than nineteen.

She opened her eyes as if on cue, looking up to find him walking toward her. The receding cigarette butt glowed brightly as she took one more drag before rising to her feet. She was athletic and toned, maybe 5'7", attractive and shapely. Her streaked brunette hair was pulled back in a ponytail. Her clothes were clean, her jeans fashionably torn at both knees. She wore a soft pink midriff cotton tank top that sported the aging remnants of a tastefully small Cubs logo. The summer sun had been kind to her, leaving her skin a rich, tantalizing milk chocolate. The thin straps across her square shoulders revealed no tan lines. She wasn't wearing a bra. He had trouble hiding that he'd noticed.

She pulled out her earbuds, turned off her iPod and placed them inside her purse.

"So," she said, dismissing any pretense, "you wanna do this here or what?"

He recognized the distinctive aroma of cannabis.

"No," he replied quietly, "my car is right over there. Why don't we –"

She dropped the remnants of a burning cigarette butt to the floor and snuffed it out with a twist of her right high-heeled shoe, partially hidden by the cut of her jeans. He enjoyed watching how gracefully she moved.

"It's this way," he said, motioning her down a semi-populated row of angled cars toward a weather-bleached brown 1996 Toyota Corolla.

She seemed angry, her mood darker and more distant than he remembered.

"I didn't know you're a Cub fan," he said awkwardly, reaching for conversation.

She ignored his unimaginative effort at small talk as she walked slightly ahead of him toward his car, not noticing he moved with a slight limp. He'd worked to keep himself in shape, barely carrying 185 pounds on his 6'1" frame, but his back was acting up again. At fifty-three, he knew it was becoming chronic. But his career depended on him remaining active, at least those aspects of it he loved most. So he'd stepped up his ibuprofen routine. It was providing diminishing returns.

He noticed her rigid posture. She seemed tense, more so tonight than any of the other times they'd been together. He wanted to reassure her, help her relax, to say something clever, maybe make her laugh, to let her know it would be all right.

He just wasn't sure he could be that convincing.

He followed her to the passenger side of the car and opened the door. As she slid into the bucket seat, he waited for her to acknowledge his gesture. He was disappointed. Closing the door behind her, he tried to ignore the pain shooting down his left leg as he maneuvered around the car to the driver's side. As he slowly got in, he noticed her trying to light another cigarette.

"Would you mind?" he asked hopefully.

She glared at him in response. Cigarettes were her only real vice though backing down was not in her nature. Her eyes drilled through him, then drifted condescendingly to his scraggly beard, as gray as it was ash brown, the predominant color of what hair he had left on his head. Both were in desperate need of a trim. The unlit cigarette remained extended from her lips, held stiffly between her fingers while the flame from her disposable lighter danced conspicuously, awaiting a verdict. Her look tightened in anger as she watched his brown eyes soften, hoping to avoid meaningless words between them that would only get in the way. She was in no mood. Her thumb twitched, acquiescing.

The flame disappeared.

"Thank you," he said appreciatively.

She turned her head forward, then just as quickly out the passenger-side window. He sat there waiting, unable to take his eyes off the back of her head. She tossed her cigarettes and lighter onto the dashboard.

"I don't know if I can do this without a…" she warned him.

He took a moment to consider his next words carefully.

"Do you think you were followed?" he asked, regretting what he'd said as soon as he heard himself say it. Her head snap around, her expression angry and scathing.

"How in the fuck would I know?" she said, her voice gaining emotion. "Just how in the fuck would I *ever* know? Christ, you ask me that *every* god… damn… time!"

He waited for her to finish.

"I'm here, aren't I?" she rhetorically asked. "I wouldn't be talking to you if they knew where I was, now would I? Jesus, give it a fuckin' rest."

"Ok, ok, I'm sorry, I'm sorry," he said, backtracking. "Look, this will have to be the last time we can meet for a while. I've got to –"

Her body language said she seemed something less than disappointed.

"I was supposed to be in Baghdad at the end of last month, my editor's all over what's going on at Abu Ghraib. But I've put her off so I could see you and –"

She couldn't have been less interested.

"I mean," he started again. She finally ran out of patience.

"You're goddamned right this is the last time!" she interrupted, "I can't keep doing this! I can't keep –"

She stopped and swallowed hard, turning to look at him.

"If he even –"

She stopped again, closed her eyes and took a deep breath. Her chest heaved noticeably. A tear escaped down her cheek.

He dropped his head and waited patiently.

"Look," he said, talking quietly into the steering wheel, "I told you I know someone. She's a fed, FBI. She does this kind of thing. She can help, really. She's —"

He turned toward her and noticed a sadness veiling her face. He knew she had her doubts, whether she wanted to believe him or even if she could afford to. He'd hoped they'd spent enough time together over the past few months to believe him if not trust him. But, most of all, he wondered if he could deliver on his word, to make the risks she continued to take worthwhile which, up until now, had only benefited his curiosity.

"I'm leaving day after tomorrow."

"Lucky you," she said with equal doses of sarcasm and jealousy as her long fingers slid again across her face.

"Please," he pleaded. "I won't let you down. I'm not sure how long I'll be there. But, before I go, I'll bring her up to speed on everything. I'll do it tonight. I promise!"

She searched his eyes and saw what she remembered sincerity could've looked like. Her mood suddenly changed, as did the callous tone in her voice.

"Ok, here's the deal," she stated firmly. "If we do this again – this one last time – you have to promise me…"

Her eyes welled up with competing emotions of hope and fate.

"No matter what happens to me, you have to promise…"

She swallowed hard to get out the last words. Her gray-blue eyes glistened.

"…I, I don't care about me, I just… I just want —"

Her voice trembled as her eyes collected welling tears. He turned and looked out across the darkening garage floor. Her voice suddenly changed.

"Fuckin' promise me!" she demanded. "Look at me and promise me, damn it!"

Each of her words took on a force all their own.

He looked back at her. He wanted to say something – anything – that would comfort her. He just couldn't help wondering if the truth made any sense right now.

"Say it, goddamn it," she repeated. "Say it right now or I'm outta here!"

She impatiently grabbed her purse and conspicuously reached for the door handle. She felt his hand touch her arm.

"We do this one more time," she said in a nervous calm, without looking at him, "and you promise me you'll find her. You promise me you'll find her and get her out!"

He finally relented, nodding slowly.

"Yes, of course, yes," he said softly, "you have my word. I promise."

She looked back toward him as she again wiped her face again.

"We'll get you out, you and your sister, we honestly will," he said, pleading in tone that seemed more an effort to convince himself as it was her. "We'll help you –"

"I don't *want* your fuckin' help, "she insisted, understanding the difference.

"Christ, you don't get it! I want your word! That's all I want! And get her *out*!"

She swallowed again, taking a moment to compose herself.

"That you'll get her out…"

Her anger subsided as she let herself believe he not only meant what he said but that he could actually do it, ignoring the reality that she had no real choice.

"I still have the photograph you gave me," he said slowly, reminding her she'd trusted him enough before. "It'll be a big help."

She nodded, fighting a losing battle to control the emotional torrent flowing beneath her next words.

"It's the only one I could get so –" she said softly.

She turned her head and searched out the passenger-side window. She waited a moment, took a deep breath and dragged her lean fingers across her cheeks. She felt herself in a freefall. She tried breathing normally. Her heart was racing. She had trouble swallowing. Her vision was still clouded.

"Ok," she said. She tried to smile, her expression almost fateful, as the tension finally began easing from her face. She took another deep but halting breath then shifted in her seat. He began to relax as well.

"Ok," he affirmed. "So…"

She leaned back, her head meeting the headrest.

"Yeah, well, let's get this over with," she said, with all the enthusiasm of awaiting a dentist's drill. "I gotta get back before –"

"Ok, ok," he agreed. The last thing he needed was to be reminded of how he'd continually placed her in harm's way. He felt bad enough about that already.

But not that bad.

He leaned toward her and reached across her lap.

"Excuse me," he said politely.

He unlatched the glove compartment door.

"What, you remembered to bring your own this time?" she asked caustically.

He smiled.

"I deserve that."

He pulled out a microcassette tape recorder then snapped the hinged door shut.

She laughed a bit.

"You gonna to tape us this time?"

"Would you mind?" he asked with a boyish grin.

"Sure, why not?" she replied mordantly, without turning her head. "At least you'll have something to remember me by when you get to that fuckin' desert…"

"Just a sec," he said.

Leaning back, he reached behind the passenger seat and grabbed a thick, small and well-traveled spiral notebook from beneath some old sweats and a pair of running shoes that had long ago seen better days. He settled back in his seat, pulled a pen from his shirt pocket and clicked it into operating mode. Finally, he was ready.

"Ok, I just have a couple of questions about some things you told me last time…"

She watched the Corolla's only working brake light disappear down the parking garage's exit ramp before turning toward the stairwell to make her way back down to the street. Fighting the inclination to second guess herself, the details she'd provided him over the last ninety minutes or so left her feeling more nervous than before, strangely uneasy, almost frightened. Whatever she'd tell Carlos about where she'd been this time, she'd find a way to make him believe her. He *would* believe her. He *had* to.

After all, she could be very convincing. And he enjoyed being convinced.

Maybe it was because she simply refused to believe this could be the sum of the rest of her life. If she accepted that, it meant believing that everything she'd endured, everything she'd survived, was all there was left, for her and for her sister. It meant giving up, quitting, admitting they no longer mattered, that their lives no longer counted and their only value was determined by those who would use their bodies for their own sadistic pleasure if not personal profit. And it meant that everything her sister now knew – all the shame and worthlessness, the unrelenting pain and unending hopelessness – was all the promise the world would ever hold for her.

Or maybe it was that, over the last few months, she'd proven to herself she would literally risk *anything* to find her sister – and get her out. She knew when she first decided to talk to him – to tell him what she knew, what she'd been through, what she'd seen – that she'd mentally crossed a line and that, with what she said tonight, it all might finally come to an end. For a moment, she actually let herself believe he could make it happen, that they'd find her sister, that she'd be alive, even reasonably well, all things considered.

And they'd get her out, that her life might finally be hers again. And hers alone.

She reassured herself, once he told his FBI friend about her, it really could work out. *It really could.* But no matter what would come of her own life, whatever the cost, it would all be worth it to know her sister would have her life back. Any price she'd pay would have been worth knowing that.

Still, if Carlos even suspected…

The thought caused her to abruptly stop, to look around and listen. She heard the sound of her footsteps recede. She waited. And wondered.

She recognized the distinctive aroma of cannabis as she pressed against the bar of the heavy metal door, the sound echoing loudly throughout the stairwell as the door swung open. She reached the first step and suddenly stopped, frozen by the sight of the heavyset man waiting for her at the bottom of the first flight of stairs.

Their eyes met. Her heart stopped. And her world began to crumble.

She heard the heavy metal door closing rapidly behind her. As she frantically turned to escape, a hand reached around from behind her, gripping her firmly across her mouth. Another hand curled around her waist as she fought her way through the half-opened door. A second set of hands quickly joined the first. Her muffled screams were lost within the fading echo of the exiting Toyota's squealing tires now floors below her. Everything went dark as an old ragged blanket was dragged over her head. Together, the two young men pulled her back into the stairwell.

The door slammed hard after them.

Maria, however, would not go quietly. Not this time. If they insisted on having their way with her, it would come at a price. She bit the hand that had first covered her mouth, then, twisting around, her knee found the groin of her second attacker. Her nails tore at a pair of eyes and cheeks. She fought herself out from under the blanket and slipped from their grip. She pushed toward the door, forcing her way forward.

Then, from out of nowhere, a fist landed against the side of her face. Maria's eyes rolled back in her head as her body immediately slumped into the arms of her assailants, her lip cut, her cheek sliced open and bleeding. Carlos watched her collapse as he calmly repositioned the two ornate rings on the fingers of his right hand.

Still conscious, she heard herself make a sound as they threw her to the floor. She desperately struggled to think, to crawl, to move, to do anything but lie there. But she felt a swift boot stomp into her side followed by another to her stomach and then another. She struggled to find air to breathe. One more kick sent her head up against the first step of the stairwell's ascending staircase. Gasping, she shifted her weight, reaching around, trying to crawl her way up. Just then, she felt a hand curl her ponytail around his fingers and pull her head up then shove it backward. She tried to raise her one free arm to fight back, to protect herself, but it hardly mattered. As she succumbed to the final time her head was slammed against the sharp edge of the unforgiving metal staircase, she saw a man standing above her, his dark, green eyes hard and cold, a recent, dime-size scar on his right cheek. He took a newly-lit cigarette from his mouth and handed it to Carlos.

"Get video," he said cryptically.

Carlos returned eye contact and took a drag before handing the fag off for the young men to share. He said nothing as he pulled a scrap of paper from his pocket and handed it to his boss. The man glanced at the license plate number scribbled on it and shoved it in his pocket. He offered no reaction.

"Make sure they clean up," he said, placing a reassuring open hand on Carlos' shoulder, who kept his feelings to himself.

As she fought to remain conscious, she watched as the man turned and walked back up the stairs without another word or even looking. Maria whispered her sister's name and imagined her face, her image now as clear as that last Albuquerque afternoon they'd been together. Her flailing arms and legs had finally conceded, leaving her defenseless. The waning voices of laughing couples, two, maybe three, floors below her in the stairwell, on their way out of the garage swirled around her head. She knew they were leaving her to them, walking away – unconcerned, not to be bothered – like so many before them had done so easily. No one would be coming to help her. Again. But why should they? It's hard to see anything when you're in the dark.

And she knew it no longer mattered. Not anymore.

Two harsh voices, their Spanish vulgar and crude, besieged her thoughts. She felt a set of hands tear open her shirt, another pull at her jeans. She groaned her objections but only at first. She turned her head and tried to open her eyes but blood streaming from the gashes on her forehead and temples left focusing on anything impossible. The pounding in her head drowned out their laughter. She saw Carlos standing back toward the door, his cellphone open and seemingly trained on her and the second young man removing his pants. She felt a hard, viscous slap across her face as her legs were forced apart. Something was shoved into her mouth, a tee-shirt that tasted of sweat and grime, smelling of engine oil and gasoline. The first young man moved to climb on top of her.

Then, without warning, a lightening bolt of excruciating pain screamed from below her abdomen, sending a scorching sensation searing through her body. It was as if her every nerve ending had been set on fire. She sucked in a deep breath, the horror of her torture blazoned in her eyes. Her body convulsed into a single burning spasm, making it impossible for her to move let alone cry out. But they'd pressed the cigarette for too long against her tender, delicate tissue; paralyzed by the agony and drenched in sweat, Maria finally blacked out.

Silently, she acquiesced as her legs were hoisted into the air above her.

She had hated her life, at least the hellish existence it had become. It was hardly a surprise that this was the path she would have to walk to embrace her freedom. After all, her body hadn't been her own since that one summer day almost three years ago. But as she lay there now, unconscious, beyond even their most brutal intentions, she was with her again, together one more time. Smiling. Laughing. Hugging. Crying. The pain, the blood, the fear – it was all gone. An overwhelming sense of serenity bloomed inside her.

Her sister's arms were safe and secure. They looked into each other's eyes. She wore a bright, welcoming smile. They brushed away each other's tears. They exchanged "I love you's" in trembling, broken voices. She heard her sister say she was ok, she was fine, she would be alright. Then Maria heard her say, "it's ok, it is… it really is. I'll find a way to home, I promise I will… And we'll see each other again one day. We will…"

"I promise."

And then she was gone.

Once they'd finished taking their turns avenging her defiance, Carlos motioned to one of them who carelessly tossed the old ragged blanket again over her bruised, bleeding and battered naked body. This time she offered no resistance. The two young men then picked her up and carried her to the open trunk of the waiting Chevy Impala. Their inexperience showed as they struggled awkwardly with her dead weight. Despite her slender build, she was heavier than they expected.

It took them three tries to heave her torso into the trunk.

The ratty blanket fell to the garage floor but, having finally succeeded, they congratulated themselves before shoving her arms and legs in after her. Maria lay sprawled and lifeless over empty liquor bottles, a couple of used shovels and some old hand tools. Carlos walked up from behind, stepped between them and slammed the lid closed. He had to remind them to go back for her clothes and shoes. As they walked back toward the stairwell, one laughed as he noticed the other had yet to zip up.

If the fifteen year-old wasn't the boss's nephew and the thirteen year-old the kid's cousin, Carlos would've shipped both their worthless asses off to work the border route long ago.

The fluorescent lights throughout the parking garage floor cast a shadow across Carlos' face, hiding the scar that ran from his cheek down the right side of his jaw. He was in his early twenties, with a baby face that belied his years working for Raúl, whose orders he followed liked sacred writ. If he'd worked for anyone else, betrayal such as Maria's would have gotten her killed long ago. But the way tonight played out would still serve its purpose. Once word got around, the video's stark images would make Maria a valuable example. The lesson would be learned. That was the important thing.

Raúl was nothing if not an opportunist. He knew that staying in business meant flying beneath the radar and that meant killing was always a last resort. But he himself had given Carlos the green light tonight. Maria just hadn't left him any good options.

Ordinarily, dead bodies didn't solve problems; more often then not they created them. Even when it came to someone like Maria who still dared to believe there might remain a way out. To Raúl, running a successful business was all about ensuring the maximum return on his investment, both for him but also for his investors.

And losses only served to reduce his profit margin.

No, Raúl had originally decided he would be rid of Maria's troublesome nature while still turning a profit. She would be sold overseas. In twenty-four hours, she would literally be out of the country. In seventy-two hours, she'd have been bought and sold, changing hands like so much auctioned livestock. And in less than a week, she'd most likely disappear into some foreign land, perhaps into some remote area of some god-forsaken part of the world, rendering services for her new employers that would make as many people as much money as her young, firm, supple body could provide. And when she had outlived her usefulness – who knows, within a year, maybe two at the most, when someone with significantly less patience and foresight than Raúl possessed would find her stubborn and indefatigable nature much more trouble than she was worth – she'd be put down like some contentious farm animal no longer able or willing to pull it's weight. To Raúl, the reality was that Maria – and countless others like her – were simply casualties of how the world truly worked. Accepting this life as it was left only finding ways to make it turn a profit. Raúl made no apologies for being a good businessman.

He never worried about serving two masters.

Carlos took the expressway north. Miguel, Raúl's nephew, and Miguel's cousin, Enrique, sat in the back seat, talking shit like the wanna-be hoods they saw themselves, satisfied the boss himself was there to see their work. They'd even gotten laid – sort of.

All in all, a good night.

Raul's instructions were to head upstate, just over the Wisconsin border, to a secluded cabin not far from a private lake just south of Delavan. They'd probably have to stay there until tomorrow. He expected their work would keep them there quite late.

There would be no trace of Maria Engañada after tonight.

*   *   *

Four Years Later

Chapter 1

THE DEMONS ALWAYS came in the morning. They were as reliable as the dawn breaking through the casement windows above his bed. Each morning. Every morning. Weekends. Holidays. It didn't matter.

The only comfort they offered was that they did not disappoint.

They would greet him with a wicked, inviting embrace and usher him down a well-worn path into the darkest recesses his fears had spent so much of his life forging.

Sleep seemed only to encourage them, his dreams only to welcome them.

He watches her carefully as she has stands alone, eight, maybe ten feet in front of him, her naked back to him. It takes a moment before she slowly turns to notice him. She tilts her head slightly, her soft hair falling across the gentle curve of her face. She smiles that so very familiar smile. He moves toward her, amid a deafening white noise, but she gets no closer. She looks directly at him as her lips part slowly, delicately, invitingly. She excites him all over again. He's captivated by her deep, piercing brown eyes. They resurrect in him memories of their last time together, when he was submerged in the immense pleasure of her. And just as he begins to feel her all over again, her features, so clear and distinct a moment earlier, inexplicably begin to fade. He stumbles in his desperate attempts to reach her as visions suddenly explode like mines all around him: a brother, holding his sister's lifeless body, wails as his heart fractures; a child screams in desperation for his mother,

3

though she is nowhere to be found; a young woman lies resistant beneath her rapist as his friends' laughter competes with her cries for mercy.

His head spins as his attention is drawn in every direction at once. The confusion batters his body and his mind. He hopelessly tries to decide who to save, convinced he still can. He looks back to where he last saw Carmen, to ask her what he should do. But she's gone. All that remains is a heavy fog around a growing darkness. A cold mist envelops him, penetrating him, invading his bones. He sees his breath. He shivers violently. The screams now fill his head. He yells out Carmen's name but he cannot even hear his own voice. He searches around for her, first walking quickly then, panicking, he begins to run. But his legs are heavy, tight, tired and sore. They soon refuse to respond. The voices are debilitating, and they've been joined by others. So many others. In almost every language and every dialect. He hears himself pray. And he never prays. He lifts his head and raises his eyes to heaven. He pleads with God to take him; anything to make it all stop.

Suddenly a blinding column of white light splits the clamor and reveals a single child, a girl of nine or ten huddled beneath a sky-blue mantle, kneeling solemnly on the ground, her head bowed, her lips moving in prayer, her eyes closed. A ring of flowers, white roses tinged in pink, adorn her hair. In the stillness he can finally hear his own thoughts. And something about her is familiar, so very familiar. Yes, he does know her. He smiles. It was so long ago but he could not ever forget her. The memory of her was vivid and very much alive. He calls out her name in a stammered voice.

Annie! It's you, isn't it? Remember me? Please, tell me you remember me...

The child's eyes open. She stops praying and slowly raises her head in response.

Her expression is vacant, her eyes empty. She owns a look of deep sadness, an inconsolable melancholy. Tracks from her tears glisten in the unforgiving light. Her once-curly brunette hair now lies flat against her head. Blood first trickles, then runs, from the thorns in the rose entwined in her hair, which is now a deepening ruby. Heavy streaks of red now hide her delicate features. Blood pools around the floor where she kneels. She extends her arms to him. But her wrists are bound together, tightly ensnared by a pearl white rosary, dangling from her reach. Perspiration mixed with crimson cascades down the worn amber beads, dripping constantly from its crucifix. The cloak falls from her shoulders. Her naked body is bruised and battered, tortured and bleeding. He looks away in shame and guilt. He begins to sob uncontrollably. Fighting through halting breaths and falling tears, he hears himself speak.

Forgive me, Annie... I'm so sorry... Please, please forgive me...

He raises his head and turns back toward her. Carmen is standing beside

Annie, her arm draped across the child's shoulder. Storm clouds gather quickly behind her. Thunder rumbles as lightening flashes crackle. The winds pick up, a driving rain ensues.

"How many more, Jack?"

A soft, humid breeze stirred him this Friday morning as 5:30 AM had come and gone some time ago. How he hated summer. What intolerably shitty weather Mother Nature couldn't squeeze into July she'd found a way to put to good use during this first week in August! Why he still lived in the suburbs remained a mystery to him, at least that's what he told his friends and colleagues. The truth was hardly so intriguing. He'd been born and raised in the suburbs northwest of the city. His mother – 84 years young, thankfully, and still active – still lived in the house he grew up in. Almost unbelievably, it had been more than seven years since his dad had passed, though he remained grateful the old man had gone six months before September 11th. A World War II veteran, his father's patriotism had only been matched throughout his 76 years by his deep and abiding Catholic faith. And whether it was his insistence in observing meatless Fridays or monthly Sacred Heart devotions, long after both traditions had fallen out of favor, his father's faith and his religion had proven as immutable as they'd been indistinguishable.

Now, as he lay there, sweating without moving a muscle, he found himself envying his father's devotion if only for the order it brought to the chaos. He wouldn't deny that his own faith – or was it his religion, a difference he, too, saw no reason to acknowledge – had become part of a growing list of casualties in a life now littered with former absolutes. He'd long ago settled on a compromise, making an uneasy peace with holy righteousness masquerading as truth. He'd left behind the God of his childhood, whose infinite wisdom and boundless mercy allowed that everything not only happened for a reason but always for the best. The void that remained in its wake he filled, to the extent that he could, with his career, as much now a mission as a vocation. And however unsettling his daily existence had become, he could at least take solace in knowing that the choice had been his and his alone. No deity had made it for him.

It remained cold comfort.

He rolled over onto his stomach, the damp top sheet sticking to his naked torso, again to find no one there to disturb. There hadn't been for some time. He instinctively shifted the pillow between his knees, a habit he'd developed after listening to his chiropractor some years ago. The persistent warble of a nearby cardinal sliced through what little was left of his will to sleep. As much as he enjoyed the often quiet and mostly peaceful setting of Chicago's southwest suburbs, it did have its drawbacks. And, right now, all he wanted now was for that damned bird to shut the hell up.

He reluctantly forced his eyes open. They were sore and crippled. He felt like he hadn't slept at all. Again. The late hours were grinding him down; there could be no denying that. The nightmares seemed to be getting more vivid, more intense. And, as much as he wanted to believe otherwise, he had begun wondering if he was still in control. He hated himself for not being able to let it go. But it seemed that every night, when he was able to find what little rest waited for him, he would fall asleep focusing not on the countless women he had located or the children he had rescued or the families he had reunited. No, it would be the demons who would call on those who were still out there, defenseless and subjugated, still waiting for him to save them. Crying out for someone to care, praying to be delivered from the evil that had devoured them. And he would respond. Nothing would stop him. His will, his conscience, his faith in himself would not allow him to believe otherwise.

If only that were enough.

The scourge that is human trafficking had done more than simply define his work or even his career. It had consumed him, becoming his purpose, perhaps even his sole purpose. He'd come to despise that it had replaced what passed for his life. It was his failures that now defined him. And it was one more reason why he found himself alone again this morning. And every morning he could remember since Carmen.

He knew he was not falling back to sleep. A low, distant mumbling distracted him. He felt the remote beneath the pillow. He raised his head and turned to look over his shoulder. Once again, he'd left the television on all night. Or was it only since the last time he'd gotten up? This morning, it greeted him with a couple of infomercial actors selling the benefits of the latest all-natural herbal concoction designed to cleanse your colon and provide you with the added benefit of losing up to ten pounds almost instantly. *That's a lot of shit,* he immediately thought. He grinned in response, not quite smiling. That seemed to him to be the one way he knew his sanity still had a pulse.

The condemned can at least still laugh; the dead, not so much.

He felt a stiffening soreness grip his lower back as he rolled across the damp fitted sheet. He took a moment to stretch, then slowly rolled out of bed. He carefully steadied himself against the stationary bike that stood next to the queen-size bed. He rode almost every morning, usually twenty-five miles, sometimes farther. It helped loosen him up while giving his mind some other place to go.

It was time well spent. On both counts.

He straightened up and stretched again. He stood just under 6' 2" tall, with lean, muscular legs and an upper body that displayed evidence of the time he'd spent the last few months lifting free weights again. And, other than a clandestine weakness for all things chocolate, he remained committed to his routine. Now two months past his forty-fifth birthday, his doctor wanted him under two hundred pounds. This year, it appeared, she would finally get her wish.

He stepped past the stationary bike and walked gingerly out of the bedroom toward the attached master bath. He noticed the standing water in the sink. A crumpled washcloth, still wet from a couple of hours earlier, lay on the countertop. His memory was as vague as the remedy was ineffective. He stared into the mirror. He rubbed his eyes with the palms of his hands. He was desperately tired.

The blinking light on his answering machine, positioned on the nightstand beneath the room's single lamp, momentarily caught his attention as he returned to his bed. He bent slightly to pull on a worn-out pair of gym shorts and drop a threadbare sleeveless tee-shirt on over his head. He turned and walked slowly through the hallway, into the second, smaller bedroom that now served as his office.

Boxes were still stacked in all directions. And though it had been more than six months since he had left the Bureau, most of his things still needed to be unpacked. One item he'd intentionally left buried in one of those boxes – he couldn't be sure which – was the framed photograph of himself with the former Attorney General. Pro forma kind of stuff, really. It had been taken not long after the Senate had confirmed the Attorney General's appointment in early 2005. But there was no need reliving those memories.

At least not voluntarily.

He had pulled one item out of the remnants of his public service career, though. A group photograph taken with the President, now prominently displayed on the shelf above his computer workstation. Taken after a hastily arranged press conference with the White House press corps, it was part of a formal albeit private ceremony held in the Roosevelt Room of the White House to honor the field agents responsible for the success of the FBI's Operation Homeward Bound. For Jack, it was a signature moment, not so much for him – he disdained such political photo ops – but for his team. To him, the Operation's success was due more to the skill and professionalism of the team he'd help assemble than any direction he'd given as its coordinator. That it resulted in real men, women and children being rescued and reunited with their families was reason enough to tolerate what he viewed as the insufferable political nature of the job.

The photo was of the entire team posing with the President although whenever Jack noticed it – which was only every time he entered the room – his attention was invariably drawn to one face in particular. And despite the months that had passed since he'd last seen her – now that his heart's initial freefall had been reduced to a constant dull ache – he still felt the need to welcome her memory every chance he knew he'd regret.

Special Agent Carmen Eyas was recruited into Bureau right out of the University of Illinois, where she had been pre-law. A veteran of more than ten years with the FBI, she ultimately decided to forgo law school for a career in federal law enforcement, where she succumbed to the thought of working for the Treasury Department, specifically as a member of the Secret Service. Had she not been so disarmingly attractive, her career choice may have been taken more seriously and encountered significantly less resistance.

In her early thirties, she's worked diligently to keep herself in top physical condition. She was slender, stood 5' 6" tall, athletic and shapely. Blonde highlights streaked through her shoulder-length brown hair. She understood that her looks could either work for her or against her. Working successfully undercover as she had on more than one occasion was one thing; gaining acceptance as an agent on equal footing with her male counterparts was – no surprise here – quite another. As with most workplace circumstances, being a professional woman meant working twice as hard to be entitled to half the credit. But being an *attractive* professional woman, at least where the feds were concerned, made advancement all but impossible. Glaciers could disappear in less time. Yet she was determined not to allow her dedication and commitment to be questioned or, worse yet, compromised. The Bureau seemed a reasonable, even acceptable, alternative.

Enter Senior Special Agent Andrew Jackson Sturdevant. They first met at a Nuclear, Biological and Chemical – in local parlance, an NBC – terror symposium sponsored by Homeland Security. It was held at a downtown hotel in Alexandria, VA over the Martin Luther King, Jr. weekend in 2006. The attraction between them was as instantaneous as the sex was uninhibited. But his tendency, as had been displayed too often in his past, was to lead with his heart. And while it wasn't long before the "L" word was in play, they both knew their careers came first. It wasn't so much a matter of priorities. It more often than not was the price he paid for who he was. And he knew that, as real as his feelings were for Carmen, his mission remained. And whether she was there – whether anyone would *ever* be there – the life that, in many ways, seemed to have chosen him would always be there.

Still, they had been very diligent at being discreet. They often joked, lying in bed, his arm cradling her closely, that their relationship technically qualified as a conspiracy. To their knowledge, though, there weren't even rumors. And, where he could, he made a point not to be responsible for any team assignments she had drawn. On that they had both agreed.

But Operation Homeward Bound had proven to be somewhat different.

For the last twelve of his nineteen years with the Bureau, Jack had served as liaison to the Criminal Section of the Civil Rights Division within the Department of Justice. And in what would turn out to be his last assignment, he acted as coordinator of the eight month long undercover investigation that infiltrated and, ultimately, disrupted a major human trafficking artery supplying the country's east coast.

Literally hundreds of people were rescued, most illegally transported immigrants who'd been bought and sold into one form of human slavery or another. Some were men but many more were women and almost as many were children. They had worked in deplorable conditions, under the most dreadful and desperate of circumstances.

Still they were the lucky ones.

The less fortunate were there for sex. Plain and simple. Most often it was the younger women, especially the girls, but boys, too. In some cases, they spent up to ten hours a day, every day, in the service of paying off the "indebtedness" they unknowingly incurred for having been brought to this country. They were there to meet their clients' demands, as often sadistic as not, and were constantly being turned over, sent to work one day here, another day there. And the Internet had only made sales skyrocket.

The web had created a completely new world of commerce. The venue had made it possible for purveyors to make an almost unlimited amount of money off their indentured servants. It offered instant access to a virtually insatiable demand of the most deviant appetites. And it didn't matter if you were posting individual jpegs, producing streaming videos or filming live sex shows complete with online requests. The exploding number of subscribers willing to pay $29.95 a month to view or download these images made it a win-win situation. For everyone, of course, except those who were cast in starring roles.

But in only the most recent example of political gamesmanship, Jack found himself accepting responsibility for overseeing the Operation when the original lead agent-in-charge, a former prosecuting attorney from the Civil Rights Division named Laura Kallinger, was abruptly and inexplicably reassigned. A close friend and colleague of Jack's – and the mutual friend who had introduced him to Carmen that holiday weekend in January –, she was one of more than two dozen agents that had either been reassigned or summarily dismissed by direct order of the Attorney General. Jack's sources deep inside the Department of Justice confirmed for him what he had long suspected: that the Attorney General, at the expressed direction of and in apparent complicity with the White House, had begun systematically removing key players throughout the DOJ for failing to carry out the Administration's political agenda.

It proved to be an insurmountable conflict for Jack. So, against every instinct he had, he allowed himself to be used as a third-party anonymous source for a series of stories that ran in the New York Times detailing the White House's reach into the DOJ's "reorganization." A Washington Post blogger termed the Administration's covert efforts "Watergate without the… bag men." In an effort to control the damage and reduce their widening exposure, the Attorney General was eventually asked to fall on his sword.

But if his years in the Bureau had taught him nothing else, Jack knew retribution would follow as surely as the cherry blossoms bloomed each spring on the Mall. And while he was no stranger to such headwinds – he had certainly navigated political waters before – he was under no illusions. He understood the fate that awaited those whose names surfaced during the DOJ's internal investigation into the leaks.

Witch hunts seldom relied on the rules of evidence.

But the post-9/11 world environment was different then any he'd witnessed throughout his career at the Bureau. The DOJ itself was now under siege, one that was all the more insidious because it was so effectively organized. Jack watched as strategists and operatives alike, both inside and out of the White House, seeking to convert their voting constituencies' fear as well as their political enemies' timidity into an unassailable power base, infiltrated the Department's culture intent on legally affirming the same paranoia they'd sown in framing the public's perception of patriotism.

Jack's father had taught him at a very early age that simply being right was a poor substitute for doing right. And Senior Special Agent Sturdevant was about nothing if not doing right. But what he couldn't have anticipated

– what he never saw coming – was the role Carmen had played in the way things went down. For that he was sorry.

But that all seemed like a lifetime ago. In the six months since his resignation, Jack had struggled to continue his work. He'd taken a part-time teaching position at a local junior college. He'd used contacts he still had at cable news' shows, NPR and other radio outlets and accepted virtually any request to speak on the subject of human slavery regardless of where he had to travel. He was not above using his connections to get published in the Op-Ed sections of newspapers, both locally as well as nationally, in print and on the web.

Still, he knew all of it was a poor substitute for being where he missed most, where he knew he could do the most good – on the front lines.

As he slumped into the worn office chair in front of his workstation, he remained lost in his thoughts of Carmen, the work he had loved, the politics he so loathed and the personal political action committee that the Department of Justice was becoming. He ignored the icons that flashed across his monitor as his computer finished booting up then swiveled around to find himself lost in history.

The custom wallpaper serving as his desktop's background was imported from a jpeg file that Laura, an equally devoted Cub fan, had found for him online. The image captured perfectly the complete – some might say, even divinely ordained – seemingly endless futility that awaited those who loved the Cubs. The frozen moment displayed on his screen would secure the fate of one fan, in particular, whose name would unfairly become synonymous with – even, in the minds of some who were there, responsible for – continuing a century-plus of incessant heartbreak and maddening frustration.

The game would come to be known simply as "The Bartman Game."

It was October 14, 2003. Wrigley Field, Chicago. Game six of the best-of-seven National League Championship Series. It's the eighth inning. There's one out. The Cubs, winners of three of the Series' first five games, lead the Florida Marlins this night 3-0. Thanks to Mark Prior holding the Marlins to just three harmless singles, the Cubs are literally five outs away from their first appearance in baseball's Fall Classic since 1945 and, with it, a chance to win their first World Series championship since 1908.

But fate occupies a front-row seat down the leftfield foul line alongside the aforementioned Mr. Bartman, faithfully wearing a Cubs cap, a sweatshirt for the traveling youth baseball team he coaches and a set of headphones. The irony, of course, is that he's undoubtedly listening to the Cubs' radio broadcasters describe the very history he is about to make.

He is leaning across the brick and mortar wall that rises on an angle toward the leftfield corner. His hands are awkwardly open. He's just missed his chance to catch the baseball that's descended out of the clear, chilly mid-October night sky, its path having vacillated between the stands and the foul territory of the playing field. The right hand of the Cubs' leftfielder has found the wall, having braced his leap. His left arm remains extended skyward, his reach straddling the brick divider. His glove is now closed as his pursuit of the ball has ended. He's not yet aware that an unexpected pair of bare hands – a fan excited at the prospect of catching a playoff game ball if not the heady thought of the Cubs finally in a World Series – understandably if inexplicably has gotten in his way.

A second later, the ball will fall harmlessly away from them both. The moment is still in creation, the ink not yet dry on another chapter being written about the curse that only true Cubs fans know all too painfully well. The rest of the inning, as well as the game, plays itself out as the living nightmare to which every devoted Chicago baseball fan is now accustomed, perhaps even entitled, to expect. The Cubs go on to surrender eight runs in the inning and lose the game. Game seven the next night isn't even close.

And, to add insult to injury, the stunned and silent Wrigley Field faithful can only watch as the Marlins celebrate on the field after winning the National League pennant. *After winning CHICAGO'S National League pennant!* Twenty-four hours earlier, "next year" for the Cubs was a possible five pitches away. And living through it, excruciating as the experience had been, was the only way to believe it had actually happened.

But the baseball gods had spoken. In the literal blink of an eye, Mr. Bartman had become to Cub fans what the axe was to Lizzie Borden's parents. But in the true Chicago tradition of trying to make chicken salad out of chicken shit, the event was not without its up side: the casual dress of the now vilified fan, complete with headphones and Cubbie blue baseball cap, provides gallows-humored Chicagoans with what would become the most popular costume at Halloween parties all over the city just two short weeks later.

And another infamous moment is added to the lore that fertilizes the sacred ground upon which only true Cub fans dare tread. Still, when it came to their Cubs, Laura and Jack's masochism seemed to know no bounds.

And they wouldn't have wanted it any other way!

He caught himself grinning as he recalled the life he'd once known with Laura, now an almost unbelievable five baseball seasons ago. Her commitment to the same ideals he'd built a career pursuing was what first drew him to her. But it was her deep, penetrating blue eyes that left him imagining the salacious nature of every curve of a body he had come to know so intimately – and so often. Despite her conservative Catholic upbringing – or, perhaps, because of it – Laura nourished an almost untamed wild spirit that defied the nature of all things conventional. She possessed a sense of style and grace that belied her blue collar Pittsburgh roots. The very thought of her now – as it had so often then – brought a smile to his face.

Despite the years it had been.

His mood having lifted, his attention wandered to the words of Edmund Burke, a favorite quotation that hung on the wall just to the side of his workstation. Carmen had the saying of the 18th Century Irish statesman replicated by a professional calligrapher. It was matted horizontally in a 15" x 12" frame made from American black walnut, which sported a hand-rubbed, dark carnauba wax finish. She had given it to him one New Year's Eve as a belated Christmas gift. It meant the world to him then, as it still did now.

Especially now.

All that is necessary for the triumph of evil is that good men do nothing.

His Internet connection loaded his home page automatically. Jack remained a web novice, by any definition of the term, though he had intuitively climbed a steep learning curve thanks to Carmen's insistence. Almost without thinking, he opened his email. Only two pages of messages appeared this time. The spam filter seemed to be doing its job. Most of it was still junk or, at best, correspondence he had no interest in responding to. He briefly reviewed the incoming mail, selected "all" and clicked delete.

The page refreshed. One new incoming message displayed.

It was from Laura.

Jack opened it and noticed she had a new contact number not to mention a new department address. He did a double take then reached for the cordless phone.

"Department of Justice, Office of Tribal Justice, Ms. Kallinger's line, how may I help you?"

He was surprised that anyone was there so early.

"Good morning. Is she available, please?"

"Whom shall I say is calling?"

"Jack Sturdevant."

"One moment, please."

The Office of Tribal Justice? What the f–... Shit, she didn't get demoted, she got exiled! Only seconds past before he heard her familiar voice.

"Jack?"

"Laura, what the hell are you doing in the –"

"Jack, I tried calling you last night. Didn't you get my message?"

He thought back but couldn't recall the phone ringing. The blinking light on his answering machine testified otherwise.

"I don't recall the –"

"Never mind," she hurriedly interrupted. "Listen, do me a favor. I shouldn't have sent you that email last night from my Blackberry. Call me back on my cell phone, ok?"

"Sure, not a problem, Laura. Everything ok?"

"Give me a couple of minutes to get out of the building so we can talk? You know what? Better yet, I'll call you as soon as I'm outside. Will that work?"

"Sure, I'll be here."

"I'll call on your land line."

"Ok."

"Thanks." And she abruptly hung up.

Jack spent a minute lost in wondering about her email, which other than her new phone number, simply read, "call me!" He grabbed the phone, plugged in his headset and hooked it to the back of his gym shorts as he headed downstairs. He stepped forward as he reached the base of the stairs into an almost empty living room. He walked over and began opening the blinds that adorned the aging bow window. Its eastern exposure drew his attention to the light show unfolding before him.

He watched the vast expanse of a deep bluish gray sky relinquish its hold to a slow luminance gaining strength with each passing minute. He was back in Washington State, with Carmen, on their return trip from ten days hiking British Columbia two Octobers ago. They'd spent their last night on vacation in Cle Elum, near Roslyn, where the television series *Northern Exposure* was filmed. After dinner, they drove outside of town and found a dark, secluded spot on the side of the road. They got out of the car and were awe-struck by the wondrous light show occurring in the blackness above them. As they stood gazing into the heavens, they watched in an almost reverential silence as the constellations and shooting stars seemed to open up the absolute magnificence of life itself. And heaven it most surely seemed to be. It remained a moment that still breathed life into his memories of her.

He smiled as he recalled being up early that next morning. He'd wanted to bring Carmen her morning coffee before they headed out to Sea-Tac International Airport to catch their return flight home. As he walked across the vacant street to the coffee shopping just opening its doors, he remembered stopping to watch the watercolors unfold and paint the slowly stirring daybreak sky. Streaks of crimson, pink and purple merged with splashes of blue and orange reflecting the emergence of brilliant yellow rising above the horizon. It was as if a rainbow had left behind colors it didn't know what to do with. He simply stopped and watched. And, thinking back, the peace he'd felt those days, the happiness he'd known, maybe even found with her, was his again. He remembered, even now, thinking all he wanted was to forget his life and everyone who had a piece of it. That what he wanted most was to take Carmen and head back into the mountains.

And stay there. In truth, to hide there. Leave everything and everyone. Just to be. For themselves. For each other. And, for just that one single moment in what had seemed like a lifetime of moments since, his heart was whole again.

Seconds later, he flipped down the microphone arm on the headset and pressed the call button on the ringing phone.

"Laura?"

"Jack, hi… Listen, I've got…"

"Laura, seriously… the Office of Tribal Justice? What the hell did they do to you? I mean, shit, wouldn't taking a package have been better than…"

"Jack, just shut up for a minute and listen, will you?"

Her tone was sharp, cold and immediate. In an instant Jack shifted gears.

"Yeah, sure, I'm sorry. What is it? What's going on? You ok?"

"Yes, I'm fine. It's not me. It's Carmen."

His instincts told him all he needed to know.

His stomach dropped. The events of three nights ago on a deserted highway outside Chicago were only details now.

"Jack!" she said into the silence. "Jack, you there?"

He wanted to speak but no sound would form his words.

"Jack?"

"Yeah," he stammered out resignedly, his eyes clouding. "Yeah, I'm here…"

He gazed off into the waning sunrise as his heart began to fracture all over again.

* * *

Chapter 2

OF THE SEVERAL discs he'd loaded into the digital CD player it was Toby Keith's turn he'd anticipated most. The singer's signature anthem proudly declared his undying, boot-up-your-ass, love of God and country patriotism into the warm, humid night through the open windows of the late model midnight blue Mitsubishi Spyder. Its' single passenger waited in the darkness on the side of a lonely stretch of Interstate 80, about 35 miles southwest of Joliet. His attention alternated between his cell phone and the desolate highway running infinitely into his rear view mirror. Tonight it was a white extended-cab van heading east with three Mexicans up front. They'd be heading eastbound on their way to Chicago, in from Denver via El Paso, with a full cargo. The van would display only a temporary license plate and there would be some front-end damage he could see from the side of the road. A crumpled bumper accompanied by a broken passenger-side parking light.

He checked the dashboard clock.

This first Tuesday night in August was about to become it's first Wednesday morning. He wondered out loud why there were three this time.

He slowly turned his head. His deep blue eyes made contact with his reflection in the rear view mirror. He hadn't shaved in days. His growth was dark but thin. He liked the rugged look it offered, attractive in an Eddie Bauer outdoor catalogue sort of way. The burnt red baseball cap of soft cotton twill he wore

17

was turned backwards, the dark embroidered image of a Maine black bear on the side of the cap barely visible from his angle. Sewn above the bill was a patch, the logo for the State of Maine's Department of Inland Fisheries and Wildlife. Bear hunting season was roughly from Labor Day to Thanksgiving. He was looking forward to getting back there, maybe mid-October this time, tracking along with his band of brothers, not unlike their tours together in Iraq.

What new?

Detective Bobby Colavito, a thirty-four year-old plainclothes detective and a veteran of the Chicago Police Department's violent crimes unit for a little more than three of his eight years on the force, had been waiting patiently on the shoulder of the road just over two hours, long enough to regret that last beer though not the shapely bartender who drew it for him. The steak fajitas, though – those he could have done without.

His fingers drummed the leather-bound steering wheel as his attention turned to his favorite lyrics. He sat up and listened, as if for the first time, how justice would be served while the battle raged on. He shook his head slightly, hardly believing it had been almost seven years since September 11th. He mumbled along about how the biggest dog on the block would finally fight when they rattled his cage, how sorry those sneaky rat bastards would be that they screwed with the US of A.

And how that boot up their ass had Bobby's name written all over it!

The song had been his anthem in Iraq, his and his platoon's. It was no less now. He'd still considered the times he spent in Iraq to be some of the best of his life. He'd served three tours, volunteering to go back each time. There was no whining about stop-loss or about how unfair the rotations were. Duty didn't allow for such petty, selfish bullshit! Answering his country's call was all that mattered and he'd made his move before the crater had cooled in that heroic farm field in Shanksville. And though he'd left the service as only a Second Lieutenant, the pleasure he took in commanding the squads that reported to him – thirty-two of the roughest, toughest field-savvy bad asses that fucking hellhole of a country would ever hope to see – remained the best part of all his tours. He thought of it as his legacy. And, truth be told, he'd do it again in a heartbeat.

Because that's what you do for your brothers.

"Rock" – what other nickname would a young, good-looking and athletic Italian named Colavito and the son of a lifelong Cleveland Indians fan have? – had been with the CPD about five years before enlisting right after 9/11. He'd admired Pat Tillman for doing the same thing just weeks earlier. Tillman was a man's man, what a real American's response should be. He'd left a multi-million dollar professional football contract on the table to become an Army Ranger, that much was true. How could you *not* respect that? In the wake of the attacks, Tillman walked away from all of it. His country needed defending and that was that. And his love for his country would lead him to become the media's patriotic darling. The ultimate example of American self-sacrifice, as the Army would be only too ready to ensure, the truth notwithstanding. But Bobby Colavito would look to do Pat Tillman one better. He would make certain that, unlike Tillman's tour of duty, Bobby's would survive his comrades' friendly fire.

His first rotation in country that summer found him at Abu Ghraib. Ridiculously brutal, and not just the heat, either. Not hard to imagine how things would get so out of hand. And so what if they did? Who could blame them, seriously? After everything America had suffered through, did anyone *really* think payback wasn't coming? Besides, the inmates weren't the only ones locked up in that god-forsaken shit hole of a country. Surviving in that place, one day after the next – the heat cooking you during the day, camel spiders the size of your fuckin' helmet feasting on you at night – was anything but assured. You didn't have to be behind bars to know that. Sleep was a luxury few grunts ever experienced for more than a couple of consecutive hours at a time. For every soldier stationed there, Abu Ghraib tested the most basic and fundamental of human instincts.

Survival.

But the treatment the guards there received once those pictures got out was just goddamned wrong. The inmates, they got what they deserved. They were there for a reason despite what people back home may have heard. Any male over the age of ten was considered a potential threat. Period. But the guards, they got fucked over, hung out to dry – by the press, their own commanding officers, even some who broke rank, like the son of a bitch who leaked the photos. A deeper shit hole did not exist anywhere in Iraq, that much was true; but it was especially true for the guards. Yet, as things played out, nobody seemed to take that into account once the New York Times got wind of the story.

His attention wandered to the seemingly endless emptiness into which the lonely stretch of road behind him disappeared. It reminded him of the desert, just outside of the prison. He could still recall his amazement at how black the darkness actually was there. The only light came from the stars themselves. There was more nothing there than any other place on earth he'd ever seen. Everything was so isolated, so abandoned, so coldly nothing; a place where death itself lived, almost certainly before the invasion but just as much since, that much he'd seen for himself. The nights it was his turn, the trip into the desert left him grateful that he, at least, had a better than even chance of coming back.

Unlike the detainees he was burying.

He looked to make certain that his odds were at least that good tonight.

As he reached to turn up the volume to the next song, he felt his cell phone vibrate once. He grabbed it from the passenger seat and opened the incoming text message.

"n5"

Just as quickly, he flipped it shut and returned it to the leather pouch clipped to his belt. He turned on the ignition and waited. It wasn't long before he saw headlights in the distant horizon break through the darkness three or four miles down the road. A moment later he made out the one headlight flanked by a dim yellow glow. He switched on the digital radar mounted on his console. He straightened up and watched the vehicle slowly growing in his side view mirror. He noticed three heads dimly silhouetted in the van's front seat.

This wouldn't be like last time. That's why he was alone. He was still answering questions about what he saw that night, about how the trooper from the second car on the scene ended up with a knife through his neck. It wasn't surprising that the board of inquiry didn't believe him; shit, *he* didn't believe him!

No, this time, and every time from then on, would be different. No more mistakes. No more stupid chances. Shaking down coyotes was one thing. They move bodies, pure and simple. Smuggling illegals – "trafficking" had such negative connotations – had long been a simple business opportunity, at least to those who recognized one when they saw it. Players ranged from organized cartels to local gangs and independent drivers, each filling the economic void to grab their share of this American dream. And, in a twisted sort of way, that's exactly what it was: quintessentially American. For all successful business models had three things in common: Meet your customers' needs. Return a profit for your investors. And, one way or another, if you can't minimize your competition, eliminate them.

Detective Bobby Colavito took that maxim to heart.

But working directly with scavengers – "*carroñeros*", as they were known – was quite another. The money was significantly better than guaranteeing a coyote's safe passage but it came with greater exposure. In reality, *carroñeros* were more like pirates than scavengers. They would let the coyotes set up the routes, find the product, supply the transportation and move the cargo. Then they would just step in on some deserted stretch of highway and hijack the truck. It wasn't rocket science. It was fringe work. Dangerous but very lucrative.

And business, after all, was business.

The *carroñeros* had increasingly come to rely on off-duty assistance. That's where Bobby came in. He met no one, talked with no one. Everything was arranged through third parties, who most often simply relayed messages they themselves were given. Everything was done in the shadows. His instructions almost always came through short, coded text messages. They contacted him. He knew tonight one of the three Mexicans was a *carroñeros*. He just couldn't be sure who it was. That's why texting made sense. Tonight, the one who texted him would be his guy. The other two would be casualties of the business plan.

Call it downsizing.

The system was meant to be loose so any mistakes would lead nowhere. The way Bobby saw it, if they didn't get their end right, that wasn't his problem. And it didn't really matter to him if these guys stole from each other. He thought of himself more as a mercenary, anyway. A part-time hired gun in a war of attrition. His only loyalty was to his payday. The rest was up to them to sort out. The less he knew, the more he could deny knowing. Who ended up getting bought or sold – or dead, for that matter – made no difference to him.

The radar's numeric display caught his attention as it jumped to life when the van finally came within range. It quickly came to rest. Eighty-five. They had no sooner sped passed him than the unmarked car pounced. His headlights flooded the four-lane road as his siren split the night's pristine silence. His tires spun amidst the scrambling and flying gravel. Swirls of red, white and blue emerged from a thickening cloud of dust.

The van immediately accelerated, then seconds later, began to slow. It's only working brake light lit up, then dimmed. It was obvious what was happening. Their first reaction is always to panic. He accelerated, quickly closing the distance between them, then decided to give them a couple more seconds to think about it.

A moment later, the submissive glow of the brake lamp reappeared. And stayed lit.

The van pulled over onto the side of the road. Bobby drove up from behind in close proximity. The shoulder was ten, maybe twelve foot wide at most with a narrow drainage ditch, at most two feet wide and eighteen inches deep, running parallel to it. Beyond the shoulder an open field of mature cornstalks ran off into the darkness. He turned off the siren but left flashing the visor-mounted lightbar. A good fifteen feet remained between his car and the van. No rear license plate was visible. A heavy link chain, bathed in the headlights that enveloped the width of the shoulder, swayed from the rear door handles. A padlock dangled where the heavy links met. He reached across the console, switched on the digital dashboard camera then opened the glove compartment, pulled out a second set of handcuffs and clipped them to a belt loop. He turned off the ignition, glanced into the rear view mirror and immediately pulled off his cap. He tossed it into the back seat then reached for the navy blue CPD ball cap on the floor behind the passenger seat. As he stepped out of the car, the revolver strapped to his ankle brushed against the inside of the opened door.

The limestone crunched beneath his trail boots as the detective walked deliberately toward the driver side of the van. He stood just over six foot tall. He'd boxed light-heavyweight during his hitch in the service as he did while training at the Police Academy. And though he'd gained a few pounds and a couple of inches around the middle since his discharge some eighteen months ago, he could still handle himself. He was no less an imposing presence in plainclothes as he'd been in olive drab.

He unsnapped the leather strap across his sidearm and secured it behind the holster. He focused his attention on the cracked sideview mirror as he approached the driver's side of the van. He noticed the young driver was agitated. He was just a kid, really; maybe late teens, early twenties but no more. And clearly nervous. Fuckin' coyotes; they'd use anybody they could buy cheap.

After all, anonymous help made for dispensable labor.

The window was rolled down. He watched in the mirror as the driver made quick eye contact with him. The reflection was confused, scared and desperate. He heard arguing. He saw the driver's shoulders slump as his body leaned to the right, out of his view. Movement, rustling, then the sound of the glove compartment snapping shut. The Spanish was excited, nervous and unintelligible. They talked over each other.

Bobby placed his hand on his sidearm as he heard muffled voices rising from deep inside the van, more of a din actually. He heard movement behind the padlocked rear doors. As he approached the driver's side door, he could still hear them arguing.

The driver shot one more glance into the side mirror but, this time, saw no one. Suddenly, he froze. The arguing in the cab stopped. The driver turned slowly toward the road to find Bobby standing there, his detective's badge hanging from his shirt pocket, both hands training his Glock 22 directly at the driver's forehead.

"Chicago Police! Keep your hands where I can see 'em, all of you."

The young driver was sweating profusely. Sitting three across the converted bench seat, his two companions remained equally still. Behind the extended cab back seat appeared to be chain link fencing in front of a secured sheet of plywood. Holes had been drilled in the wood at eye level.

"Turn it off! And gimme the keys."

Confused, the kid turned toward his friends. The man sitting in the middle looked back quizzically. The other, a woman in her early thirties, reached across and turned off the ignition. *At least one of them spoke English this time.* She handed the keys to the driver, mumbled something in Spanish and motioned for him to hand them to the officer.

Bobby took the car keys through the open window. He pulled out his badge and, along with the keys, placed them both inside his shirt pocket.

"Alright, let's go. Outta the car. Slowly..."

The detective stepped back, the hinges creaking cheaply as the driver opened the van's door. With a slight wave of his wrist, he motioned for him to line up against the van. One after another, they slid across the bench, out the door and onto the shoulder.

"Turn around, hands in the air. Face the van. Feet back and spread 'em. Now!"

Bobby slammed the door shut. He walked carefully past the last two and started with the kid. He kicked the driver's feet further apart and out, then forced his arms higher on the van. He frisked him quickly, found nothing, then grabbed his arms, one at a time and forced his hands to the back of his head.

Keeping a watchful eye on the remaining two, he grabbed the driver and stepped back, turning him around so he was facing the road.

"On the ground, dumbass. Now!"

The butt of his gun landed squarely into the young man's lower back, dropping him to his knees. The detective gripped the back of his neck like a vise, then shoved him to the ground, onto the limestone, perpendicular to the van.

"Keep those hands behind your head!"

He lay there in pain, his back in spasm.

The routine was repeated for the next one, this one maybe early to mid-twenties, slender build and unshaven. Unlike the driver, his eyes were steady, almost cocky. He'd been here before. He sported a tattoo running the length of the left side of his neck and down his arm, prominently displayed beneath his sleeveless tee-shirt. An uncoiled cobra with bulging eyes, its hood flared beneath a crown of thorns. The handle of a dagger protruded from the top of the snake's head. After the frisk, Snake-Eyes voluntarily assumed a similar position, parallel to the young man on the ground.

Finally was the woman, a Latina. At least she appeared to be. He was taken back by her look. Slender but athletic, shapely and inviting with blonde high-lights running through her shoulder-length brown hair that was tied behind her. She wore loose jeans over her hiking boots and a cotton olive-green tank top over a black sports bra. She moved deliberately as she turned toward the van. He stepped up behind her and forced her arms higher against the van. He kicked her feet farther apart and started frisking her. He kept the two men on the ground in his peripheral vision. All he needed was a helmet, some body armor and his M16. He could have been on any roadside checkpoint in Iraq.

He started at her hips. He bent down and ran his hands down the outside of her jeans' left leg when he felt the strap around her ankle. He pulled up her trouser leg and tore the Velcro apart. He pulled the knife from its leather sheath. He'd seen this type before. It was military, the kind issued to specialists, underwater demolition teams and SEALs. The six-inch blade was stainless steel with a flat black finish and a double-edge point. He held the solid steel butt cap in his hand, felt the non-slip resin grip and serrated back. It was worn. It'd seen action. It had great balance, very light.

It brought back memories.

He looked up from his crouch.

"What branch were you in?"

She turned her head slightly and spoke softly with a Spanish inflection.

"Special Ops."

He wondered what a former member of a Special Ops Command unit was doing running with this crowd.

"Really?" he asked snidely.

"Yeah, really," she replied indignantly.

"What branch?"

She looked back toward the van and didn't respond.

"This is special issue," he continued.

Again, nothing. He wasn't buying it but there wasn't time to argue.

"So, what is a former Special Ops doing running with this shit?"

"Girl's gotta make a living."

He laughed, not believing a word. He wondered about the coincidence. He returned the knife to its sheath and shoved it into his back pocket.

He stood up and pressed himself against her as he ran his hand up into her crotch and squeezed. She tightened up but only a little. He started massaging her slowly but roughly. She violently turned her head and glared at him. He moved his hand up to the back of her jeans methodically. He found the cell phone in her right back pocket.

He flipped the phone open, punched up the last outgoing text message. "n5"

They sent a woman this time. Nice touch.

He closed the phone and stuffed it back into her front jeans pocket, reaching down as far as he could, toward her crotch. She mumbled something in Spanish and shifted her hips, pulling away from him.

He shoved her forward against the van. She could feel him through her jeans. She smelled the last cigarette on his breath. She felt him reach around her waist, trying to force his fingers inside her pocket.

She pushed him backwards and turned sharply around to face him. Her eyes were riveted to his. He liked that she fought back.

"Ok, *señorita*, hands behind your head and lace 'em."

She didn't move as she glared at him in response.

"Now, *chica*," he said arrogantly, turning his gun sideways and pointing it directly between her eyes. "I won't ask you again."

He watched as she slowly raised her arms, placed her hands on the back of her head and laced her fingers together. He cautiously moved forward and slowly patted her up one side and down the other. His eyes never left hers as he ran his hand across her chest and fondled her slowly. Her sports bra kept the moment from somehow rising to the level of excitement he might otherwise have anticipated.

Satisfied she was clean, he stepped back and motioned her toward the other two.

"Over there, with your *amigos*."

The woman moved slowly toward the prone men. Movement from inside the van again caught his attention.

"How many in the van?"

None of the three acknowledged him.

"I'll only ask you once more," he said. "How many in the goddamn van?"

Again, nothing.

He handed both sets of handcuffs to the woman.

"Hook 'em up. Now!"

She motioned to the other two men to get to their feet.

"No, they stay down. Hook 'em down there. Lock their arms and cuff 'em."

He watched carefully as she told the two on the ground to sit up, back-to-back. As she bent down, he noticed that she knew to have them intertwine their arms behind them. She then secured their wrists and applied the cuffs. When he heard them ratchet up, he approached the three of them. He pushed her over onto the gravel. He grabbed Snake-Eyes by the arm and pulled them both to their feet. He inspected the cuffs, then motioned to the woman to go before them. She slowly came to her feet, her eyes focused directly on him. She led them around the front of the van, through the glare of the burning headlights, and around to the other side. He walked the cuffed pair to the side of the drainage ditch and shoved them in.

He turned and motioned to the woman to the back of van.

"Open it."

"I need the keys," she said with a discernable accent.

The detective pulled the set of keys from his shirt pocket and tossed them at her feet. She glared back at him briefly, then bent down and picked them up. She searched the half dozen keys on the ring as she walked into his car's headlights toward the back of the van. He checked back on the two in the ditch then followed her at a safe distance.

She unlocked the padlock securing the doors and threaded the heavy chain through the door handles, then dropped it to the ground. He stepped back as the rear doors swung open. He scanned the human cargo through the makeshift chain link gate, seated equally on both sides of the van. He quickly counted the heads.

"Twelve?"

The woman simply nodded in response.

Nine women, ranging in age from what looked like their early twenties to maybe as young as ten. The three others were just boys, none older than eleven or twelve. They were all dressed for the Texas heat. All had the same vacant, frightened expression.

His attention was drawn to one young woman, a girl actually, seated just inside the mesh fence to his left, next to an older but decidedly less attractive woman. One of the smaller boys was sandwiched in between them, barely noticeable. The girl could hardly have been more than twelve though her features seemed much more mature: deep brown eyes, raven-colored hair, round lips and a body no twelve year-old had a right to possess. Her look served his purpose well. She was wearing cut-off jeans, just below the crotch, open-toed sandals and a loose-fitting peasant blouse. A beaded bracelet rested on her right wrist and a small, simple gold cross around her neck stood out against her brown skin. A strand of beads from a homemade rosary was wrapped tightly in her hand.

He watched her lips subtly move. His eyes widened. The beginnings of a lecherous grin betrayed him.

She looked right at him. She'd been crying. Her nose was red, her cheek discolored and deeply scratched. Her lip was swollen. Old, dried blood smeared the inside of her thigh. Her stomach was in knots. Her memory was as fresh as her wounds.

He couldn't help himself.

"What's your name?" he said, more demanding then asking.

Instinctively, her eyes shot to the floor. She said nothing. He was not dissuaded.

"What's your name?" he repeated.

The boy pushed himself forward.

"Leave Ana alone. She doesn't have to talk to you."

The boy glared at Bobby.

Ana released the rosary from her left hand and reached around the boy, drawing him to her. She winced in pain. His eyes never left the detective.

It was getting late. He turned his attention to the woman standing next to him though his eyes did not leave Ana.

"You have my money. Where is it?"

"In the glove compartment. I'll get it."

He felt for the sheathed knife in his back pocket.

"No. You wait right here. And stay in the light."

Ana rested her head against the boy. The detective wished he had more time. His head moved slowly in the direction of the woman's voice, his eyes trailing.

"I'll just be a minute."

He turned and started walking back toward his car.

"Are you done here?" the woman asked him.

Bobby ignored her and kept walking.

The woman reached around to close the swivel the doors. Ana took one last breath of the stale warm and humid air as the doors shut out her last look at freedom.

Bobby walked back to his car and opened the front passenger-side door. He leaned in, turned off the dashboard camera and the visor-mounted light-bar, then reached below the passenger seat and opened a box of latex gloves. He pulled out a pair and snapped them on, then reached under the seat a second time and pulled out a small, heavy burlap bag. He removed a Beretta Tomcat 32 Automatic along with two clips and tossed the bag onto the seat. The piece was a gift from the *carroñeros*. It was unregistered and supposedly untraceable. It hardly mattered, though. Any fingerprints wouldn't be his. The gun, the clips, the bullets, he'd been very careful.

It was all good.

He stepped back and closed the car door. As he walked toward the woman, he inspected the first clip, counted ten rounds, then shoved it in his back pocket. He then checked out the second clip. Ten rounds, five each. These people were known for their overkill. He slid the clip inside the handle and snapped it in place. He made eye contact with the woman waiting for him at the rear of the van. She watched him carefully as he walked toward her, the loaded gun confidently in his right hand.

"Get the money," he demanded.

"What's that for?"

"Just shut up and get my money! This has taken too long as it is."

She walked over to the passenger side of the van, reached through the window and opened the glove compartment. Bobby walked directly over to the two prone men and stepped down into the ditch. They were on their sides, back-to-back, with Snake-Eyes facing the van. He grabbed tat-man by the throat, just beneath his chin, and glared into his frightened eyes. Bobby watched as they suddenly darted to the woman walking towards them. He released his hold on him and let him drop into the ditch. He secured his footing then racked the slide of the gun, loading the chamber. He reached down, grabbed a fistful of hair with his left hand and twisted his head until he was face-down into the ditch. He pointed the gun barrel at the back of his head.

The woman's voice broke his concentration.

"Freeze, you dumb sonuvabitch!"

He looked up to see the woman standing there, feet shoulder-width apart, both hands training her weapon directly on him. Her Spanish inflection had given way to something with a much more native Midwestern flavor.

"Drop your goddamned weapon. NOW!"

His face was expressionless. Any semblance of surprise was conspicuously missing. She repeated herself.

"I will shoot you where you stand, asshole. Drop your weapon. Now!"

"Are you kiddin' me?" he answered softly, more to himself than to her.

He heard the click as she pulled back her gun's hammer.

"Do I look like I'm kidding, dumbass? Toss me your weapon!"

He gripped his pistol securely. She could tell he was considering his options.

"You can die right here, right now, or not. You choose, officer. Right now!"

He tried to buy some time.

"Show me your badge."

"Shut the fuck up and do what you're told!"

He looked directly at her and smiled a cocky grin.

"Last time!" she commanded. "Drop your weapon. NOW!"

He took his time tossing the pistol aside, up on the shoulder, a few feet away.

"Now, the other one… slowly, with two fingers of your left hand."

He reached across his body and carefully removed the sidearm from its holster. He tossed it up onto the shoulder in the opposite direction.

"Now, get up here! Hands behind your head, lock your fingers."

He stepped up onto the limestone, raised his hands behind his head and laced his fingers together. Confused, the two prone men in the ditch spoke frantically in Spanish.

"Over here, on your knees."

Bobby moved as he was told, taking a few steps toward the van, then dropping to his knees. She held the gun in her left hand as she removed the cuffs from her back pocket and cautiously circled around behind him.

"Where's your backup, right or left?"

With a nod of his head, he motioned to his right.

She kicked the outside of his right ankle and felt the holstered weapon.

"Face down. Kiss the gravel. Now!"

She turned her head slightly to see the men in the ditch behind her, struggling to get up. She said something to them in Spanish, telling them not to worry.

Suddenly, she felt a foot land inside her right knee. The pain shot up her thigh and into her lower back. She instinctively cried out as her knee buckled. She collapsed to the limestone. Her gun fell to the ground as she reached toward the pain.

The detective reacted, raising one knee up from the ground and pulling her knife from the sheath in his back pocket. True to all he'd learned in survival training, he immediately pivoted and, in a single motion, impaled it deeply into her stomach.

An army of one.

Her eyes were wide as she slumped onto her back, staring into the oblivion that now awaited her. She coughed up blood. Her body convulsed with her remaining breaths, which were loud and labored. The detective got to his feet and kicked her gun into the ditch. He calmly walked over to retrieve his Glock and returned it to its holster. He then turned back and picked up the Beretta. He walked over to the woman and watched her spend her last moments on this earth wrestling with death. He noticed her hands struggling to reach inside the waist of her jeans, finding it amusing if not inexplicable. But time was short. He rolled her over with his boot as she started choking. He bent down on one knee and calmly fired five rounds into the back of her head.

"My cellphone," he heard a voice yell from the ditch, "get my cell phone!"

Bobby reached down and across her body. He pulled her cell phone from the front of her jeans. The keys to the van fell out onto the ground. He shoved them both into his front pocket then stepped back down into the ditch and raised his weapon.

"Did you get my phone?" Snake-Eyes asked him.

Bobby looked down at him.

"This is *your* phone?" he asked almost incredulously.

"Yes, yes…" he repeated, desperately trying to roll away from him. His breath left him as he tried to scream not to shoot him. His heart was racing.

"Shut the fuck up…" Bobby told him calmly.

He stepped over Snake-Eyes and positioned himself as he had before, this time over the young driver. He reached down, grabbed the young man's hair and twisted his head to one side. He started to cry out as Bobby lowered his weapon and emptied the five remaining rounds from his clip into the back of his head. Blood and brain matter splattered across Snake-Eyes' clothes. Bobby shoved the gun behind him inside his waistband against the small of his back.

"You got my cell phone, right?" Snake-Eyes reassuredly asked in broken English.

Bobby turned in response and glared.

"Shut the fuck up…" he repeated just as calmly.

The young man's tattoo was trembling noticeably as the detective bent over to remove his handcuffs. He scrambled out of the ditch and onto the shoulder, trying in vain to wipe the remnants of his companion's head from his clothes. He almost tripped over the woman's body as he staggered up onto the shoulder of the road. He paused for a moment and tried to catch his haltering breath. He suddenly darted for the side of the shoulder by the drainage ditch where he fell to his knees and vomited. Bobby just shook his head. The young man took a moment, then gradually if shakily got to his feet. He slowly started heading in the direction of the van when Bobby called out.

"Hey, *chico*," Bobby started, "where the fuck you think you're going?"

Snake-Eyes stopped and looked back.

"Get her back into the van," Bobby instructed.

Understandably jumpy, Snake-Eyes words were broken.

"I can't take her with me. What if I get stopped again? Besides, she's gonna stink up the fuckin' truck!"

"That's your problem. We can't leave her here. Stop and bury her some-where, I don't give a shit. But you're not leaving her here."

Snake-Eyes considered his options quickly.

"Ok, ok, I think I've got something we can wrap her in."

"What's this 'we' shit? Get me my money so I can get the fuck outta here."

Snake-Eyes took one more look at her corpse then walked carefully over to the van. He opened the car door and pulled a thick envelope from among the maps stored in the door's side compartment. He walked over to the detective and handed it to him.

Bobby cracked open the back of the envelope and flipped through a wad of hundred dollar bills. A thousand per; he'd count it later. Without changing expressions, he folded the envelope in two and stuffed it in his back pocket behind the second clip.

Snake-Eyes had already dragged her body to the van's open passenger-side cab door. He reached behind the front bench seat and pulled a heavy-gauge clear plastic tarp onto the shoulder. The lower half of her shirt was drenched in a combination of blood and her last meal. Her hair was matted and wet and had now started changing colors to a dull reddish-brown. Loose gravel and limestone dust was glued to her clothes.

The detective joined him as Snake-Eyes quickly stretched the plastic out on the shoulder. He helped rolled her over and shoved her forward. She landed face down on her left side in the center of the tarp.

"Wait a minute," Bobby cautioned.

He pulled the unused clip from his back pocket and bent down on one knee. He shoved the clip into her back pocket then reached across her body and placed the Beretta in her right hand. He carefully wrapped her index finger around the trigger and tightened her remaining fingers around the gun handle. No loose ends.

Together, they then rolled her up into the plastic.

The tarp was slippery as they each grabbed an end. They lifted her body and maneuvered her onto the floor of the cab. Snake-Eyes jogged around to the other side, opened the driver's side cab door and pulled her dead weight toward him. He folded the excess plastic over her head. Her head banged against the door as he slammed it, her torso shifting slightly. He returned to the passenger side, reached in and shoved her legs forward, pinning them up against the back of the bench front seat. He stuffed the remaining plastic behind the bench seat. She wasn't going anywhere anytime soon.

He turned and motioned toward the ditch.

"What about him?"

"Your choice – you're the scavenger! How many passengers do you want?"

Snake-Eyes looked oddly at Bobby.

"Fuck 'em. Buzzards gotta eat, too," he said, slamming the passenger cab door shut. "One stiff's enough."

He then patted his back pockets.

"Hey, you got my phone?"

Bobby pulled the cell phone from his front pocket. He flipped it open and checked for any outgoing calls. None. Then he checked for any outgoing text messages. Nothing, though she could have sent one and not saved it. Company could be coming.

"Yours?" he asked. He tossed Snake-Eyes the cell phone then the car keys.

"Why the fuck didn't you say something?"

"I didn't know she was FBI. How the fuck would I know that?"

"She's FBI?" Bobby's curiosity displayed a leading edge.

"How'd you know that?"

Snake-Eyes took a moment and looked directly into the detective's eyes.

"I figured she must be some kind of Fed, right?" Snake-Eyes responded.

Bobby calmly returned his look without expression.

"What the fuck was she doing with your phone?"

"She told me to give it to her, when you pulled us over. She said you wouldn't find it on her."

"And you believed her?"

It didn't make sense. She could have left with the van. She had the cargo. Why wouldn't she just take off? One guy's a coyote, the other's *carroñeros*. Arresting them is hardly worth losing your life over. Maybe he was right. She *had* to be some kind of Fed. And she could be Bureau. That would explain it. But, still, to move without backup? Always a risky choice and never a smart one, even if she didn't end up dead. There simply isn't any room for heroes in this business. Not live ones, anyway.

Still…

Snake-Eyes'd had enough. He turned and headed around the front of the van to the drive's side.

"Just let me get the fuck outta here, man."

He knew he was behind schedule. Bobby leaned in the open passenger-side window as Snake-Eyes got in the driver's side.

"Get your brake lights fixed."

Snake-Eyes just grinned.

"*Adios, gringo.*"

He stepped back from the van as it peeled away from the shoulder of the road, headed east. It left him standing in a thin fog of rising dust. He took a couple of steps back and waved his hand from side to side in front him. He recognized a scent of antifreeze in the air. As the cloud dissipated, he looked carefully up the shoulder and saw the damp spot. His investigative instincts got the best of him. He walked over to the area and bent down. He reached over and dabbed his gloved fingers in the wet gravel then rubbed his fingers together. He raised them to his nose. He stood up and stepped back, shifting the gravel around with his feet, covering the spot.

No loose ends.

About a quarter of a mile down the road, Snake-Eyes, still shaking nervously, flipped opened his phone and punched up a preset number. The voice on the other end was irritated and impatient.

"Where the fuck you been, Sandy?"

He so hated that name. "Snake-Eyes" was so much more his game.

"Got some unexpected company. I'm on 80, just outside Joliet."

A long moment of silence greeted the news. He knew they were waiting for an explanation.

"Don't worry, Cool, nothing I couldn't handle. I should be there in about an hour and a half, maybe two, depending on –"

"Call when you make the neighborhood, assuming you don't have any more 'unexpected company'."

"Don't worry, everything's –"

He found himself responding to a dial tone.

Shit!

Sandy Delagarza checked his rear view mirror and quickly accelerated. He flipped the phone shut and tossed it onto the passenger side of the bench. It slid across the vinyl seat. He settled in. He had learned he was able to talk a good game. He'd find a way to deal with it all when he finally got there.

He always did.

Still perspiring, his smile slowly broadened. Truthfully, it could hardly have worked out any better. You actually *could* kill two birds with one stone.

He noticed he was up around 80 miles an hour. He let up on the accelerator and turned to admire the quiet summer evening.

Fuck 'em. I'll get there when I get there.

Detective Colavito watched the one working taillight slowly disappear into the horizon. He walked back to his car without a thought in his head. The

Army's psychiatrists had termed it a "depersonalized disorder with periods of dissociative amnesia." He had little choice but to accept their diagnosis. It was either that or a general court-martial. And who wanted to roll those dice? Even loyalty had its limits. Besides, the Army had no interest in allowing what little press coverage the incident had received to get beyond the scope of its control. While he hated the thought of leaving the military – and it pissed him off it was on their terms –, he took the deal and never looked back.

He opened the passenger-side door and snapped off the bloodstained latex gloves. He stuffed them into the small burlap bag and shoved it back under the seat. He'd burn them later. He closed the door then turned toward the ditch and relieved himself.

Once he'd finished, he walked around the car to the driver's side and slid in behind the wheel then took a moment. He tossed his cap into the back seat then pulled the folded envelope from his back pocket, removed the bills and fanned through them. He could tell just by looking it was all there. At this rate, that cabin in Idaho was closer than ever. He missed the fishing. It wasn't the same rush he got from hunting black bear in Maine. But the separatist politics of what the mainstream press labeled as "extremist," popular with northern Idaho militias, was more in line with his views on social policy.

And, as he'd learned in Iraq, family wasn't just everything. It was the only thing.

He pulled out his cell phone and settled in. He searched his address book for the number with the 202 area code he wanted, listed under "WM. D." The irony was never lost on him. A moment later, the connection was made.

"It's done," he said.

"Any doubt?" the male voice asked.

"None!"

"Good."

The call lasted precisely four seconds.

He slapped his phone shut and returned it to its leather pouch. He leaned forward and reached for the ignition. The Spyder roared to life. He pressed the remote on the steering wheel. The CD player lit up. He fished tailed away from the shoulder and headed west. Headlights sliced through the darkness. He pressed the volume remote on the steering wheel, raising it to an ear-shattering decibel. He could hardly hear himself singing along.

Toby never sounded so good.

It brought him back to his regiment one more time. Every once in a while, he'd let himself think back and miss the days when he felt he was among real friends. Truth be told, it wasn't really the friendships so much. No, it was the loyalty born of mutual survival that he missed most. Each watching the other's back. The "all for one, one for all" shit, that's what he missed. Police work was similar, maybe the closest thing there was in civilian life. But there was a bond borne of survival that only those who lived through a war zone could understand, could ever appreciate. He missed that most of all.

What could civilians know of that?

He'd been on the road about ten minutes when he decided he was hungry enough to head back to that pub just outside Morris, maybe another five miles west. It wasn't that late, they should still be open. Only, this time, he'd skip the fajitas. What he really wanted, what he really needed, was to get a drink. And his hands on that bartender.

Jamie, wasn't it? He smiled, as if he cared.

His thoughts of her surfaced in a widening grin as he recalled how the young woman displayed herself. Long, slender legs. Soft, smooth lines. That richly tanned body accented by that all-too-tight, snow-white midriff tank top. The whisper thin straps dropping off those well-defined shoulders. Her soft, blonde hair, streaked almost white, from the summer sun. The frigid air conditioning. Those hard nipples.

The rpm's raced as he shifted gears. Yeah, tonight would be her lucky night. All night.

He lay there, perspiring slightly, covered only by the crumpled sheet stretched across his groin. The naked young woman to his left rested comfortably on her side, her back to him. A familiar aroma hung in the humid air. He took another long, slow hit and stared a hole through the ceiling. The street lamps cast soft, gray shadows against the wall of her second floor apartment. The sound of an occasional passing car through the bedroom's one open window intruded on his solitude. Sleep was too elusive.

He thought back through the night's events. The dead kid in the ditch. Killing him was necessary. And the Fed bitch. That couldn't be helped. What bothered him most was that she got inside. It exposed him. Somebody'd gotten careless. His only recourse was to take some time off. Problem was, if he stopped answering his text messages, eventually they'd stop sending them. And there'd go his paydays. There was nothing that could tie him to the *carroñeros*. Nothing he knew of, anyway. He'd been very careful from the very start. But that someone had let the Feds get inside now made it a problem. Maybe even his problem. He'd find out.

But someone, somewhere dropped the ball. And killing her? Seriously, what choice did he have? Still, it was unexpected. He hated surprises. Too many loose ends to tie up, too many chances to fuck up. And it only took one.

Just one goddamned time.

The young woman rolled over, stirring slightly. She curled up against his chest and dragged her knee up his thigh beneath the sheet. Still half-asleep, she reached for the joint in his hand. She took a short hit, followed quickly by another longer one. Her eyes stayed shut. A soft smile emerged. He took it from her hand, and toked one last time before placing it carefully in the ashtray on the nightstand.

He rolled over on his side and slid down toward her. She fell back into the crook of his arm, her expectant smile having now widened. He took her face in his hand and kissed her deeply. Their tongues danced eagerly as she moaned agreeably. He fell back over as she rolled deliberately to her knees, her eyes still closed, feeling her way. She pushed the sheet away as she dragged her wet tongue across his smooth, sweaty chest then slowly down his stomach. He laid back, content in anticipation, caressing her hair. She knew what he liked. It's what they all liked.

He felt the warmth of her mouth engulf him, her tongue encircling him. He loved her tongue. Reality slowly blurred. His eyes closed, his mind wandered. He was back at the ditch, standing over the hero bitch, listening to her die, watching as she drew her last, noisy breaths. He was dispassionate, unemotional, almost disinterested. He watched as she shook uncontrollably. Her shirt was soaked and discolored. Blood trickled from both sides of her mouth. It pooled around the wound in her abdomen, spurting upwards like a fountain each time she inhaled. It flowed through her fingers, over her hands, across her wrists. The handle of the knife was almost indistinguishable from the...

His eyes shot open.

Shit!

The fuckin' knife!

* * *

Chapter 3

ANA MORÁLES HAD finally fallen asleep when the van suddenly changed lanes, waking her back to the world that was now hers. It had been more than an hour since she'd heard the gunshots while they waited on the side of the road. She was sore and beyond tired. She'd been in that van for longer than she could remember. She repeated a silent prayer that this journey would mercifully end, one way or another. Then again, if mercy had anything to do with it, she wouldn't be here at all. She wouldn't know the constant fear her trembling hands betrayed. She wouldn't have been victimized, time after horrible time, by men two, three, four times her age. She wouldn't have been beaten. Or humiliated. Or lost inside a world she could not comprehend let alone escape.

Or left wondering why.

A tingling numbness ran through Ana's left arm still wrapped around the shoulder of the young boy curled up next to her sleeping. As she slowly took it back, he began to slide forward toward the floor. An older young woman, no more than nineteen and seated next to them, reached quickly around to hold him. He stirred, naturally shifted positions and, without waking, proceeded to curl up against her.

"I will hold him for awhile," the young woman said gently.

Ana nodded in return as she brought her arm forward and began rubbing feeling back into it. She tried to smile but her lips barely moved. Her still-disbelieving eyes searched the few vacant expressions she could make out in the wan and pallid darkness. She feared for herself but also for them, each of them. She wondered how many of them had been treated like she had been. She trembled as she fought to control her tears.

"How long have you been here?" the older woman quietly asked.

Ana looked back at the woman now cradling the boy as if he were her own. She really didn't want to talk. She wanted to be home. She wanted to hear her mother's singing. She wanted her innocence back. She wanted her life back.

"I don't know, I'm not sure," she replied softly, "a few days, maybe a week."

"Me, too."

Ana retreated and moved her gaze toward the rumbling floor. It seemed like a lifetime ago when she left her family. She felt her stomach tighten as she thought of her mother, her sisters, the barnyard animals at her grandparents' hacienda where they lived. She was grateful that none of them knew. That none of them *could* know. It wasn't much to be thankful for but it was the only the peace her soul could reach for.

Now, anyway.

Her thoughts insisted on returning to her memories of the farm. And though her life there had never been easy, she would give anything to be there now. She closed her eyes and took a deep breath. When she opened them again, she wanted to see San Miguel de Allende again, off in the distance. Though only a small colonial town, to Ana it'd been paradise. Rising against the backdrop of the Bajío mountains of central Mexico, it was more to her than simply a world away. It held the sum of her dreams, a lifetime of promise. She'd wondered so often about the fun she would have there, the times she would enjoy there, the boys she would meet there, the love she would find there. She would imagine everything that waited for her beyond the world of her grandfather's farm.

But she never could have imagined this.

Yet, that day – the one that changed her life forever – when the beautiful stranger came to visit, the woman who told her mother of the opportunities that waited in America for someone as pretty as her oldest daughter, Ana was captivated. There were jobs there, good jobs, working in hotels, at resorts, wearing clean uniforms, working for important people, traveling to exotic places. Even weekends off. There was good money to be made, plenty of money to be made, for those who were willing to travel to America get it. Money she could send home to her mother to buy the family new clothes, fresh fruit, good food, clean water. She could finally help her family in the most important way. And even though she wouldn't turn thirteen for some months yet, Ana wanted nothing more in this world than to help her family find the better life they deserved.

Because for everything they so desperately needed, it was hope they needed most. And it was that hope Ana was so excited about providing now.

Her younger brother, Martín, had been sick for so long. But there had been no money to pay for his care. Her mother had borrowed a cart and a mule from Ana's grandparents and had taken him to the town's local church. She remembered helping her mother place Martín gently into the cart, helping her pack up some meager provisions and watching her walk the mule off into the distance. Her mother's faith was the family's strength. And as rugged as the journey to town promised to be, Ana knew her mother would be undeterred. Like her, Ana had hoped for something, anything, that would help him get better, that would spare his life. But, in the end, while there was no shortage of people willing to help, there was little anyone could really do. She returned with him some days later, with a local priest. Her sadness broke Ana's heart.

Springtime would always hold his memory for Ana. And though it had only been weeks since he'd died — from some kind of fever, Ana's mother knew little else to help her understand — the emptiness was getting harder to bear. Along with her sisters, Ana had watched him lie there, day after day. They took up his share of the work around the farm during the day. At night, they tried to sleep as he moaned in pain. She watched her mother stay up with him, after working all day, every day, seeing to him, comforting him.

Her mother knew he was dying. And she knew she was helpless to stop it. She had given all she had and Ana hated that it could not be enough. How could it *ever* be enough? That her mother also knew made it hurt that much more. And her mother, who would be there for her? Their father had disappeared years ago. In truth she had very little memory of him at all. And what she did remember, she loathed.

It was shortly after Martín had passed that the beautiful stranger first arrived and only a couple of days later that she'd returned. It had taken Ana all that time to convince her mother to let her go. Strangely, the woman must have somehow known that Ana would succeed. She'd already purchased a bus ticket for Ana along with a new dress to wear. They would travel from San Miguel to Guanajuato, where they would meet another woman who would take Ana to Mexico City. From there, Ana would fly to Ciudad Juárez, then take a bus-ride across the border to El Paso. She would pay the woman back from her earnings once they had found her work, a little at a time. At each stop, she had met others just like herself.

She remembered wondering if there would be enough jobs for all of them.

Ana leaned back, uncomfortably resting her head against the wall as it rattled rhythmically behind her. She tightened the grip on the homemade pearl white rosary wrapped around her right hand. She closed her eyes. She envied her younger brother.

She straightened her lower back, sore from sitting on the plywood boards that passed for seats, then gingerly leaned forward. She placed her hands behind her and rubbed. It didn't help much. The more vivid the memories of El Paso became, the more trouble she had breathing. It was there – in El Paso – that it happened for the first time.

And had so many times since.

She felt again the consuming fear surrounding her like a dark veil. She wiped away the tears now trailing slowly down both her cheeks. There'd been four or five of them in the room when she first got there. Maybe more, she couldn't be sure. As soon as she had entered the room, someone slapped her. Hard. And she remembered falling to the floor but little else after that. There were lots of voices. She was so frightened.

And there was so much pain.

She jumped as the young woman's hand rested gently on her arm.

"Are you ok, *querida*?"

Ana leaned forward and hung her head, teardrops falling from her raw, red eyes. The young woman reached over and caressed the back of her head. Ana tried to inhale but it was getting harder for her to breathe. She rubbed her eyes again, the rosary entwined within her fingers swinging back and forth. The sounds of El Paso intruded.

Images flooded in torrents across her memory, spasms of short terrible clips that ran together like some unbroken tortuous highlight reel. Waking up, without her clothes, lying bound on some dirty mattress on the floor, her arms pulled above her head, her hands taped together so tightly she couldn't feel her fingers. Her legs had never been so sore. Her stomach and chest hurt. The mattress was moist and sticky with blood. The sound of men's voices – congratulating themselves on finding a virgin – grew louder as they pushed each other aside to take their turn with her. Again. And again.

She heard herself screaming, crying, pleading. And always their laughter.

The woman gently rubbed the back of Ana's head, caressing her hair. She felt her heart breaking as she watched Ana visibly tremble, knowing firsthand the horror that this young girl was reliving all over again. All she could do was listen as Ana tried to speak.

Her voice cracked as she spoke.

"I just gave up," she said ashamedly, "I saw them there. And I just gave up."

"Saw who, *mija*?" the young woman asked.

"The others. There were others. Some were older than me, others were maybe the same age as me. They were standing on the other side of the room, just watching them, what they were doing to me. They listened. They heard. They watched…"

"And they did nothing…"

Ana's voice submerged under a tide of emotion. She was so tired. Her head ached. She still had trouble believing her own words. That it had actually happened.

She took a moment, swallowed hard, then started again.

"…They didn't even *try* to help. They didn't try to stop them. They just stood there. They just stood there and watched."

Her voice grew stronger. And angrier. She looked up at the

"Why didn't they do anything to help me?"

The young woman recalled all too vividly her need to forgive, too.

"Maybe they were scared, *mija*."

Ana looked directly at her and paused for a moment.

"Maybe I was, too," she said slowly.

Ana dropped her head, her eyes focusing again on the floor.

Throughout it all, she wondered where God was, where Jesus was. Nothing made sense anymore. She didn't understand. She couldn't understand. Her world had been ripped inside out. All she knew was the pain of what living now meant. She had asked Him to take her. She admitted to herself – and to Him – that she didn't have the courage much less the strength to bear this cross. She desperately wanted to sleep but only if it meant not waking up again.

Her mother had taught her that God answers every prayer, maybe not in our time, but always in His. And sometimes His silence was His response. But Ana found herself demanding more of Him than that now. Yet, once the screams and the tears and the pain had retreated, however momentarily, she found that was all she had left to comfort her.

His silence. And her fear.

* * *

Rolando Raúl-DeJesús snapped his flip phone shut and checked the cell window for the time. But as he looked to the opposite side of the bed, seeing her slip back into her panties, the incoming cargo was rapidly becoming the farthest thing from his mind.

It'll take Sandy at least another hour.

He dropped the phone on the floor, rolled over and wrapped his arm around her. She giggled as she fell back on top of him.

"Raúl, what's gotten *into* you to –" she started playfully in a shy, childlike voice she knew made him crazy. Her words became muffled as he firmly planted his mouth against hers, the taste of cigarettes and tequila on his tongue as it rushed to explore her's once again. She sighed in response as she felt his calloused hand fondling her, then slide down across her flat stomach. Her young, firm body responded quickly to his efforts. She pushed him back then peeled off her panties and flipped them at him, laughing. She pulled away the damp sheet that separated their bodies and locked her eyes on his.

That he wanted her was no surprise anymore. She understood so much more now.

He lay back to get comfortable. His eyes grew wide watching her move toward him. Straddling him, she deliberately crossed her arms in front of her then slowly raised the silken, snow-white camisole up over her face. Her rich, creamy brown flesh, made only more stunning by the symmetrically thin tan lines etched by the summer sun, made him ignore his normally cautious nature for the exquisite pleasure her body promised.

Enticingly moist, warm and glistening, savory and tender to the touch.

She reminded him of a Thanksgiving turkey Martha Stewart would be proud of.

She felt his eyes on her as she paused with her arms extended above her head, a generous grin betraying her intent. She brought the satin lingerie down and dragged it across his chest, then let go as he roughly grabbed it from her and threw it to the floor. She acted surprised at his impetuousness, his impatience at having his way. Her eyes lit up as her smile widened, offering her desire. First teasing before retreating, resisting, even fighting, before submitting, her acquiescence was something he took, not accepted.

He would have it – he would have her – no other way.

She leaned forward and reached beneath her, between his legs. She stroked him against her, forward and back, her wet anticipation signaling she was ready for him once more. He closed his eyes, raising his head then dropping it back into the lumpy pillow. Her mouth opened slightly as she directed him slowly into her. She started to whisper his name as she felt his open hands press down on her shoulders, his size already shoving forward, pushing upward, selfishly demanding she take him in – all of him – at once.

She closed her eyes tightly and swallowed hard.

Caridád Engañada had not always been so cooperative. It had been eight years since she and her sister, Maria, had been abducted from an Albuquerque outdoor mall. Caridád was all of ten years old at the time. And she hadn't seen her sister since.

When she was fourteen, Caridád had been given as a gift to Raúl – a payment, actually, for a debt that he'd been far too long in collecting. At first, like all the others, she had to be taught the way Raúl's organization ran. He preferred not to think of it as gang rape. To him, it was more of an initiation – a bizarre rite of passage –, an effective if somewhat crude way of introducing her and those like her to their new livelihood as now dictated by the gospel of the street's only "Cool" Raúl.

But, not unlike her older sister, Caridád had a spirit that was as resilient as it was rebellious. It was one of the first things that Raúl noticed about her, that and her inviting meadow-green eyes. From the moment he took possession of her, he realized there was something different, maybe even special, about her. She had a survivor's instinct that he couldn't recall seeing in most, if any, of the others he'd seen come through.

She reminded him of himself.

The reality was that most quickly learned to give in, to abandon any hope that their lives would return to any semblance of what they'd once been. Raúl's approach was as ruthless as it was brutally simple and it demonstrated that accepting their new life was their only real hope to survive. His years in the business had taught him that it was their fear of their own vulnerability, maybe even of their own weakness, as much as it was their fear of him that made their surrender a virtual certainty. He'd watched that fear welcome their despair. And it was in that desperation that their hope would evaporate.

It was one of the first lessons Raúl had learned early on. Hope must be the first casualty. Their hopelessness was his strongest weapon. It undermined their resistance and any doubts they had about their futures. His control over everything they did – every place they went, influencing every thought they had – depended upon it. He'd come to rely on it as a most insidious, though highly effective, form of brainwashing.

In Raúl's world, the ends *always* justified the means.

At the time she was given to Raúl, Caridád was already a veteran of the business. And in the intervening years with him, she'd shown significant signs of recovery from the physical and emotional humiliation that had become her new life. She had only recently begun to speak of it to Raúl though she offered few details. She remained a mystery to him. He never learned where she'd come from; he didn't ask, she never said. Her accent was maybe southwestern United States, but he couldn't be sure. No matter, he could hardly have cared less. But despite his better judgment, he found himself strangely attracted to her. And while he wasn't so naïve as to think that her interest in him was based on anything more than her own self-preservation, he didn't care. The familiarity she offered Raúl each time he reached for her brought with it a comfort level he began to find measured beyond just the sex. That Caridád had become even more striking than when he first took her in was simply an added bonus.

When Raúl was fifteen, he'd already been in the business for almost four years. Now, at twenty-eight, he looked considerably older. He'd been taught early on how things should run. When he organized his own group, he'd already come to understand how his piece of the process *must* run, what running smoothly meant for him financially – and physically. You didn't get fired in this business. You were either trusted or you were eliminated. And, in the end, trust only took you so far. Everyone knew everyone was, ultimately, expendable. At least at this level. It was something he didn't spend much time thinking about, at least he tried not to. Still, in his neighborhood, it wasn't as if there were a lot of other career options available to him or people like him.

Certainly none that were as lucrative.

The organization was very loose and intentionally so. Groups worked as stand-alones, as separate cells, individual units. People vouched for one another and brought each other in. They'd be told only what they'd be doing, never why. It wasn't important that *they* understand, Raúl believed. What's important is that *he* not be misunderstood.

Misunderstandings almost always proved fatal, usually for the misunderstandee.

But what made this business so profitable – selling boys, girls, men and women of almost any age to anyone who could use them – was that nobody wanted to admit it was actually happening. Especially in America. That's why they could use houses like this one, right in the middle of some sleepy neighborhood in the shadow of the Sears Tower.

Because nobody wanted to know.

So, when one or two or even more people would end up dead in some ditch somewhere, it was unusual for it *not* to be chalked up to, and later dismissed as, "gang activity." And the murders remained unsolved for a reason. The police didn't really want to know. The politicians certainly didn't want to know. And, most importantly, people busily going about their daily lives absolutely didn't want to know.

In his experience, only three kinds of people cared.

Those who got paid. Those who got careless. And those who got delivered.

From her knees, Caridád buried her face into the dank mattress as she cried out. She instinctively reached behind her and pressed an open hand against his groin, though she knew it didn't matter; he would not let up or even slow down. Experience had taught her that helplessness only fueled his rampant, almost insatiable, desire. But as she felt the coarse, numbing rhythm intensify and heard his breathless groans escalate toward another moment's approach, her pain confirmed that her submission had again served its purpose.

A hard, cold look – born of a punishing anger – settled over his dark green eyes. Harder and faster, the dull wet thud from their crashing bodies became louder as his grip on her hips tightened. She seized the stale sheets with the undeserving hope of a trembling penitent. Turning her head, she moaned her surrender, crying out his name and begging him to stop, repeating "no" time and again, the way she knew he expected.

And each time it was Maria's voice she'd hear.

Well over an hour later, a sleep-deprived Raúl stepped out the back door of the south side brick bungalow into the warm, humid Chicago night. He could still taste her, even smell her, as he yawned and walked across the cracked concrete patio and down the long, narrow walkway that ran parallel along the length of the house. The yard was separated from the neighbor's driveway by only a small width of grass. He walked across the front yard and into the driveway. The attached 1½ car garage was set back from the street and was virtually hidden behind the back of the house. It served to make things that much more discreet.

He walked down the driveway toward the sidewalk to wait for Sandy. A stocky figure, he carried a few extra pounds on his 5'9" frame. He kept his hair trimmed short and sported a pencil-thin mustache that matched the beard running along his chiseled jaw line. The scar, a remnant from an old lesson learned – a bullet had entered his mouth but had, somehow, exited his right cheek –, had diminished. Still visible, it looked more like a mole he might've had removed. The hump who'd pulled the trigger wasn't as lucky.

His faded jeans and previously white sleeveless tee-shirt, now discolored from another day's heat, was just one more indication the neither he nor his clothes had been clean for some time. The pigmentation on his left arm was still vibrant, the subject matter still menacing. Careful inspection revealed a cobra whose tail began at his wrist and coiled around his forearm and bicep to just below his shoulder. Magnificent work, really, and quite artfully done. Worth every penny. It looked poised to strike, its hood flared, its eyes focused on its prey. And while he was initially flattered by the imitation Sandy had inked on his own arm, Raúl often found himself wishing, especially lately, that Sandy's desire to be like him didn't simply end with a tattoo.

Raúl reached the sidewalk and looked up the street. He noticed a familiar aroma wafting through the slight breeze as he lit another cigarette. Though cars lined both sides of the narrow two-way street, his attention was immediately drawn to the Chevy with the primer painted quarter panel. Three heads remained silhouetted, illuminated by one of the few working street lamps burning brightly a few yards behind them. They hadn't moved, still parked on the opposite side of the street, keeping a watchful eye.

Or so he imagined.

Sandy maneuvered the van slowly down the south side neighborhood's narrow streets. Always too many goddamned parked cars. And always on both sides of the fuckin' street. He was thankful at least there wasn't any snow! He'd learned from experience that the only thing worse than driving through a Chicago neighborhood during the summertime was being fool enough to try driving through one during the winter!

Deliveries to these areas always made him grateful for the portable GPS he had placed on the dashboard. And even though he hated the early morning drops, they just made too much sense. Never anyone around. The streets were always dark and almost always quiet. Just made things simpler. And no one he knew argued with simpler.

A soft breeze blew through the cab's open windows. Despite all of the hassles of making the trips up here, he really did enjoy Chicago, especially during summer. Most guys didn't care for the heat and humidity. But he didn't mind it so much. Getting up here during the summer always meant one thing: baseball. He would take the Chicago route every chance he could. Most of his friends were die-hard soccer addicts but not him. No, he loved baseball. And the White Sox were his team.

When he'd get up here during the season, he'd try to make it to at least one game. He'd followed them since he was a kid but 2005, that was somth-ing special. The baseball gods had seen to that. He'd actually made it to two playoff games that year, one against the Red Sox and the other against the Angels. He was there the night Pierzynski's "dropped third strike" made playoff history. His friends had long ago tired of hearing him tell of it. But it had seemed so magical, the way they'd won it all that year. Chicago wasn't known as the "Second City" for nothing; losing seasons, whatever the sport, were as much a tradition as buying elections. But, ever since 2005, as he told his friends, even if it never happened again, he could always say it had at least happened once during his lifetime.

Unlike the masochistic Cub fans who he still thought of as his friends!

Yes, he had come to love the city; he just hated driving in it. Almost as much as he despised his given name. And "Sandy", what his former girl-friend called him – one of the many reasons why she was a *former* girlfriend – was hardly an improvement. He thought "Snake-Eyes" suited him much better. The artistry that covered his left arm up to his neck was more than just creative expression. For Sandy, it was a declaration.

The idea for the tattoo came from his half-brother, Raúl. Sandy had looked up to him ever since he was eight. The truth was he was never certain that they were really related at all. Sandy's mother left him with Raúl's family one day and simply never came back. For that matter, Raúl's mother wasn't around that much either to say nothing of Raúl's father. That left Sandy in the care of Raúl and his younger sister, Teresa, who was only a couple of years older than Sandy. And even though they moved around a lot – sometimes by choice, sometimes not –, Raúl somehow always made sure that the three of them had something to eat, a safe place to eat it and a dry if not comfortable place to sleep. It was never easy but what Sandy learned about survival, he learned from Raúl. What he learned from Teresa proved equally valuable, if somewhat more intimate. But it was when she went missing one late hot August night that the course of Sandy's life, to say nothing of Raúl's, would be permanently altered.

It was on an evening out with friends at a local dance club that brought the world they knew to a jarring end. Teresa had been out celebrating a birthday with friends at one of the popular cantinas in the neighborhood when she stopped at a local bodega to pick up a few things on the way home. It really wasn't that far from the apartment, just a couple of blocks up and one block over. But as she left the bodega, witnesses would later recall, a group of skinheads began following her.

The police were only able to identify three of the bangers and even then only one of them ever got charged, a nineteen year-old punk Nazi-wannabe named Steven Vourteil. Rumors flew that there were as many as six or seven men involved. Teresa's body was eventually found in an alley not far from the bodega, naked, face-down inside a large, broken wooden crate hidden behind the dumpster which held her torn clothing. Bruised and discolored, her hair shorn, her eyes left open wide, she was all but unrecognizable. Streaks of dried blood mixed with semen remained smeared across her thighs and chest.

They apparently had taken their time.

The word "putta" – a misspelling of *puta*, Spanish for "whore" – had been carved across her torso with an unidentified sharp object. She'd also been violated with a foot-long piece of construction rebar the killers had left in place once their fun had subsided. Her wrists had been tightly bound with what seemed at first to be a string of cheap plastic beads, connected by metal clasps, which met together at the top of a small oval medal. A single, broken beaded string hung emptily – meaninglessly, worthlessly – from the bottom of what was later determined to be her rosary's center piece.

The crucifix was never found.

The neighborhood convulsed. Local activists and politicians alike stumbled all over each other getting themselves in front of any camera or live microphone they could to express their outrage and demand a stronger police presence. A local minister hosted a town hall meeting which even the mayor attended, who struggled in a losing effort to reassure the community. The murder investigation became a topic for the mayor's press secretary during daily City Hall press briefings. And the morning, noon and evening local newscasts were littered with sound bytes from administration and other city council leaders reminding the community to just let the police do their job.

The case's notoriety even catapulted one resident, a postal worker and community organizer named Maria Sanchez, into the city council. Her only son – Raúl's best friend, Estéban – and Teresa had been close, even dating for short time. Estéban was devastated by her death and had a difficult time accepting it. His mother's concerns for him eventually led her to send him to live with relatives in Denver, where he stayed until he enlisted in the Marine Corps.

But as these things inevitably do, when the news cycle eventually ran its course, the media coverage slowly dissipated which, as it turned out for the kind of justice Raúl had in mind, was a good thing.

Of course, it was never proven that Raúl had anything to do with it. But, less than a week after Steven Vourteil's lawyers arranged for his bail, he and six of his Aryan brothers began being discovered, one by one, in alleys around the neighborhood. Each was found in a dumpster, a piece of rebar protruding from his rectum, with the correct spelling of the word *puta* carved in his forehead. And each had his testicles separated from his penis though they'd been reunited inside his mouth. The coroner had found that each mutilation was performed with a similar if not the same dull serrated blade and that they had been inflicted premortem. His report concluded that each of the deceased had known the taste of his own genitalia before he slowly bled out.

Raúl was naturally questioned and more than once as bodies began showing up in dumpsters all around the neighborhood. And it was even rumored that charges were all but imminent. But, somehow, the cases were never made. And while he would find some satisfaction in knowing the neighborhood appreciated he had brought justice to those who'd so savagely mutilated and butchered his sister, the vengeance done on her behalf ultimately did little to fill the gaping emptiness that had assailed his very core.

But while Raúl had been inconsolable, Sandy had suffered no less a broken heart though he could not help but believe that Raúl had gotten it all terribly wrong. And the warm, summer nights like tonight were the worst. Sandy's heart would ache while his thoughts turned to quieter, more peaceful moments with Teresa. When it was too warm and humid to sleep, they would sit outside on the fire escape, the front steps, wherever they happen to be living at the time. And, when they could, they would listen to Selena.

Teresa loved Tejano. Its blend of folk and popular music suited her personality perfectly. And Salena's music spoke to her in a way none other ever did. They would watch the evening's sunset turn into the night's starlight and sing the lyrics of Selena's most endearing love songs. And though Teresa had no compunction whatsoever about her own singing voice, Sandy often needed more encouragement. But when Salena's "Dreaming of You" or "I Could Fall In Love" would play, he would simply listen and cherish the way she would embrace every word. Those were their two favorite songs, though he struggled to live with the reality it was for completely different reasons.

Which is why Sandy came to believe that Raúl's measure of neighborhood justice had completely missed the mark. He knew Teresa, in some ways maybe better than even her brother did. And he'd certainly come to know Estéban. She'd confided to him that she was breaking things off with Estéban, that she'd had enough. She'd heard the stories Estéban was telling about her around the neighborhood, about the things he said she would do with him. And *to* him. He'd also tried to get her to use drugs, cocaine mostly. And the cash he always had with him made her suspect he was dealing as well. But it was soon after he first became aggressive – when his anger finally graduated from simple verbal abuse to physical violence –, that Teresa finally would take no more.

In the days after she went missing, Estéban was stoically right there at Raúl's side. After all, that's what best friends do, right? But Sandy wasn't buying it. And while Raúl didn't want to hear about it, Teresa's feelings lived restlessly in his thoughts. He couldn't get past everything Teresa had told him, the bruises she had showed him and fear her eyes revealed whenever she spoke of him. The day Estéban left for Denver, Sandy watched any chance to hold him accountable for Teresa's murder go with him.

There was so much that Sandy missed about Teresa, even today. But it was her love of poetry – T.S. Eliot, in particular – that still made him smile in wonder. *And he didn't even know who the fuck T.S. Eliot was!* None of it made much sense to him. But listening to her recite the poet's words, watching her eyes light up as the excitement in her voice painted worlds beyond the reality of their own decrepit neighborhood, he could almost hear the sound of a young woman's dreams taking flight. That was Teresa.

His heart seemed to grasp what his mind could hardly reach.

Their conversations were seldom about how tough things were, about how difficult life in the neighborhood had become or even how impossible the odds might be that they'd ever get out. No, Teresa was constantly a wellspring of optimism. Where it came from, Sandy never really knew. But, sitting outside on those summer nights, she would have Sandy gaze up at the stars and make a wish or talk about how different, how better, life would be for all of them when they got older. She would talk about people in the neighborhood and how kind they were, how they looked out for one another. She believed in the goodness of people. Her heart simply knew no other way.

And as much as he now wanted to believe her ways were those of a foolish girl, choosing to ignore the world as it is, he couldn't bring himself to deny how she had touched him. And he often wondered what she would say about what he was doing now.

Sandy checked the approaching street sign at the upcoming intersection then glanced at his GPS. He started searching the houses on his left for the address when he noticed a dim glow coming from a parked car up on his right. For a brief moment he saw what he thought were two, maybe three heads in the car. He recognized the aroma immediately. It had been a long night. He wished he could join them.

Just then, he heard his cell phone vibrate. He reached across the passenger side, groping for it in the dark but found nothing. Leaning over, his reach strained to find the still vibrating phone while he struggled to keep one eye on the dark, crowded street. Finally, he switched on the overhead cabin light and glanced down at the bench seat.

It was nowhere to be seen. *What the fuck…*

Looking back toward the street, he noticed a stocky figure that he recognized at once to be Raúl, who looked to be on his phone. A moment later, the garage door rolled up its rails and a cone of light flooded the long, empty driveway. Raúl crushed a cigarette beneath his shoe as he snapped his cellphone shut.

The van creaked noticeably as it climbed over the curb and up the cracked and fragmented concrete drive. He rolled slowly past a distracted Raúl and into the garage, stopping just shy of the workbench standing against the back wall while gently nudging a rubber garbage can with the bumper. He turned off the ignition and noticed Raúl in his rear view mirror, back on the phone, now facing the house. He took one more look around the cab for his phone, then opened the door. The single glaring brake light went out.

The garage door waited to roll shut as Raúl walked deliberately toward the back of the van to find his adopted brother waiting.

"Everything ok?" Sandy asked.

"We may have some company," Raúl responded calmly, unemotionally.

"Seriously?" Sandy responded inquisitively. "Did you see something?"

"Just up the block, parked on the other side of the street, by the street lamp." Raúl answered. "You see 'em, there?"

"Yeah, now that you mention it, I did notice something." Sandy thought for a moment before saying anything more.

"Just some mules or idiot gangbangers, maybe?"

Raúl took a drag from his cigarette.

"Could you tell how many?"

"I don't know, two, I think. Why? Who do you think they are?"

Raúl ignored him for a moment then turned and looked directly at him.

"Your phone working?"

Sandy thought quickly.

"Yeah, I think so. I've been having some problems but nothing major, why?"

Raúl grinned a bit as he took another drag.

"Lemme know if we need to get you a new one. C'mon, let's get them moving. We're expecting more later."

Sandy pulled keys from his pocket and removed the padlock securing the twin doors, threading the heavy chain back through the handles and dropping it to the floor. He opened the twin doors and unlocked the makeshift chain link gate. He mumbled something in Spanish and its human cargo awkwardly began to file out.

Raúl stood off to the side, showing little reaction as he took another drag. He looked each of them over as they passed in front of him and lined up along the passenger side of the van Working in such small numbers as this required too many resources. Too much risk, not enough reward. But managing his exposure was the key. He'd take what he could get – literally and figuratively –, no question. But he was hoping for bigger scores, maybe a tractor-trailer. Less overhead. Greater return.

As the last one found her place in line, Raúl's nineteen year-old nephew, Miguel, and Miguel's seventeen year-old cousin, Enrique, entered the garage through the home-made screen door at the far corner of the garage. Both thin, each standing maybe 5' 10', Miguel's recent work with free weights was about the only way to tell them apart from a distance. But as far as Raúl was concerned, though, of the two of them, Enrique had shown much more potential.

Raúl gestured toward the twelve frightened strangers now grouped off to the side.

"Ricky, get them inside," he commanded. "Miguel, you stay with me."

Enrique retraced his steps, opened the screen door and instructed the twelve, in both English and Spanish, to follow him into the house.

"Where do you want them?" Enrique asked Raúl.

"Put 'em in the bedroom down the hall from the bathroom."

The group followed Enrique through the open down, shuffling slowly down a short hall that led through a small mudroom into the kitchen. The young woman, with her arm around Ana, brought up the rear. The boy remained sandwiched between them.

Miguel acknowledged Sandy with a nod and a smile.

"Head on in, we'll take care of things out here. Get yourself something to eat. There's still some pizza left, I think."

"You don't need any help?"

Miguel looked at Raúl, who shook his head while crushing his cigarette beneath his sandal on the garage floor.

"I don't think so."

Raúl looked up and into Sandy's eyes. Sandy'd seen that look before.

"What was the holdup? Any trouble?"

"You might say that," Sandy said proudly.

Raúl was not amused. Sandy's expression immediately changed.

"Some undercover Fed hitched a ride," he said. Then he grinned.

"Not again, though."

They walked together toward the front of the cab.

"Where is he?"

"You mean, 'she'..." Sandy corrected him. "...she's in the cab, on the floor."

"She?"

"Yeah, some *chica*. Fed, I think."

Raúl's mind raced. His expression remained unchanged as his head turned back in the direction of the street and the three mutts in the Chevy. His gut told him something more than coincidence was happening here.

"You sure you don't need any help out here?" Sandy halfheartedly offered.

Miguel jumped in as Raúl remained thinking about the connection.

"Naw, we got it. Get on in before the pizza's all gone," Miguel said with a smile.

Sandy stopped on his way into the house and turned back toward the van. It had been a long night. And already a long morning. He wondered about that last phone call. He almost mentioned to Miguel to look for his cell phone. But he thought better of it, what with Raúl standing there. Besides, he was hungry. Deciding he would check back with Miguel later, he turned and disappeared into the house.

The passenger door creaked loudly as Raúl opened it, revealing that the heavy, clear tarp was no longer transparent. Miguel looked, uninvited, over Raúl's shoulder.

"What do we have here?" Miguel offered.

"Other side," Raúl directed him.

Miguel jogged lazily over to the extended cab's driver-side door and opened it. The agent's blood and stomach contents had seeped through the plastic tarp that now seemed cemented, along with her clothing, to her body. And, as an added bonus, she'd become wedged on the floor between the bench and the cab seat. The front bench had moved forward a bit, but was lodged tight. It wasn't going anywhere.

Miguel stepped back at looked at Raúl across the inside of the van for guidance.

"Ok, so now what?"

Miguel closed the door and walked around to the other side. Raúl studied the corpse for a moment. Miguel offered his usual unsolicited analysis.

"Blood's all over the floor of the cab."

Raúl ignored him. He took a long drag from a newly-lit cigarette.

"Dump the fuckin' thing…"

"The truck?"

"Yeah. And make sure you douse it good. I want nothing left. Nothing…"

Miguel nodded in response.

"Any idea where?"

"Some place quiet. Get Ricky to go with you. Just leave it clean."

"No problem, uncle," Miguel responded confidently. "Have I ever let you –"

Raúl shot him a steely look.

"Nothing can be left on this one," he said as he walked away.

Miguel knew things had to go better this time. This wasn't some nameless, troublesome delivery that simply refused to understand her new life. Or some former associate who always seemed to be in the wrong place at the wrong time when the heat turned on. No, Miguel could be forgiven some indiscretions, some mistakes. Family, after all, was family.

But business was business. This was too important. Raúl realized he needed someone with experience for this job. He decided he'd have Carlos meet up with Miguel and Enrique north of the city. Carlos knew what to do. The job would get down right and maybe the two of them would actually learn something.

As Raúl entered the house through the screen door, he felt his phone vibrate. He stopped as the door closed behind him. His expression didn't change as heard the news.

"No, he said there may have been three of them."

He listened intently to what happened.

"You have them both back there now?"

He'd learned to expect complications.

"I'll be right there."

He snapped the phone shut and shoved it into his back pocket. He thought of Caridád. A smile tried in vain to crack his expression.

Miguel knelt awkwardly on the seat in the extended cab, still stuffing the edges of a worn, heavy wool blanket as best he could around the hardened plastic. It would ignite quickly and accelerate rapidly, if properly saturated. Being tucked that tightly around the tarp, the intense heat would melt the plastic and make it all but impossible to identify her. And as searing as this van was likely to get, it would be like cremating her.

Just as he finished with the blanket, an intermittent buzzing caught his attention. His first thought was a cell phone. He searched the cab bench seat he was kneeling on but saw nothing. He turned himself around, shoved his fingers in the crevice where the perpendicular back and seat cushions met and ran his hand inside the vinyl cushion line

Nothing.

The vibrating continued. Convinced he was looking for a cell phone, he leaned forward and scanned the front seat. Still nothing. He then looked at the body. He wondered if someone was trying to call her, if the phone was on her body somewhere. *Sandy would have been smarter than that. He had to be! Right?*

He pulled the blanket back off the agent and tossed it to the corner of the seat to his left. He ran his hands around where he thought her hips would be, thinking it was still in her jeans somewhere. He felt around through the brittle plastic. Something hard, small but oblong, something that didn't belong there, got his attention.

He turned to the back of the van where Enrique had been loading the gasoline canisters through the open back doors.

"Ricky, get me a knife."

"Here." Enrique pulled a switchblade from his back pocket and tossed it more at him than to him. Miguel flipped the blade open and sliced through the thick, brittle tarp across her waist. He tore the plastic open in both directions and looked in. The color, let alone the smell, was approaching the vomit threshold. He heard the vibrating again. Whatever he had discovered, it wasn't making any noise. His attention started following the vibration when he noticed the agent's left hand inside the waist of her jeans.

"Toss me a clean rag."

"Jesus," Enrique responded, "what's next, wiping your ass?"

"Just get me a clean fucking rag, will you, please?"

Enrique had moved to the workbench, where he was filling the remaining containers. He looked around and picked up what was actually an old, torn flannel shirt. He shook it out and walked over to the open passenger side cab door.

"C'mon, man, we gotta get this thing movin'." Suddenly, the pungent odor hit Enrique. "Shit, what *is* that?"

Miguel ignored him as he reached out of the back seat and took the rag. He placed it over his mouth and nose. He then slowly pulled the agent's half-exposed left wrist from her jeans' waistband. A small, rectangular, metal device was wedged between her thumb, index and middle fingers. It looked to Miguel like a computer's flash drive. One end was solid while the other, the end near her fingers, blinked green intermittently.

Miguel slowly removed the device from her cold, stiff fingers and examined it. He noticed that the end that was flashing was actually divided into two separate pieces. One side looked to be solid while the other appeared to be a push-button.

"What the fuck is this?" he said quietly to himself.

Miguel turned and looked over to Enrique, who had less of a clue than Miguel had. Enrique returned Miguel's "what the fuck" look with one of his and just shrugged.

"Whatever it is," Enrique sarcastically concluded as he went back to work, "it ain't gonna do her any good anymore!"

Miguel's curiosity overtook his common sense. He slowly depressed the push-button once and, as he removed his thumb, the blinking light stopped.

Suddenly, Miguel heard the cell phone vibrating again. He quickly pushed the device into his front pocket and shoved the rag from his face into the open space left by the torn plastic. He pulled the plastic over the rag and tucked it under. He pulled the blanket over and again tucked it securely over the agent's body.

Miguel kicked open the door and stepped out of the rear cab. He opened the front passenger-side door and knelt down next to the seat. He saw nothing on the floorboard. With his right hand he reached under the seat as far as he could. He regretted that decision almost immediately.

He navigated through a swamp comprised of, among other things, the remnants of a crumpled fast food bag, molded aging French fries in various stages of decomposition, the remains of a couple of Chicken McNuggets and something his touch immediately recognized but didn't want to believe he'd found.

He pulled his hand back, his fingers pinching a used condom.

"Jeee—sus fuck—ing..."

He leaned back and called for Enrique.

"...Dude, bring me a flashlight. And a goddamned towel!"

Enrique was headed toward the screen door to find Snake-Eyes to get the keys to the van when he heard Miguel call to him.

"What the fuck, dude, how am I gonna get anything done being your bitch?"

"Just bring me a goddamn flashlight? And get me the rag, I left it in the back."

Enrique just laughed as he walked over to the workbench and opened a drawer. He flipped the switch to make sure it worked then walked over and handed it to Miguel.

"Whaddya break your leg or something?" he inquired.

Miguel held his hand out like it had leprosy.

"Where's the fuckin' rag?"

"What am I, your goddamn butler?"

Miguel reached for the flashlight and wiped his hand on across Enrique's pants. He took the flashlight from him and grinned.

"Dumb ass, eh?"

Enrique decided against telling him he was wearing Miguel's baggy shorts!

Miguel turned and bent over inside the van and across the passenger-side floorboard. He pointed the flashlight under the seat and scanned the floor. He still saw nothing, and now he heard nothing. If it was a phone, whoever was calling had given up.

All the more reason to find the goddamned thing, he thought.

His eye caught something that reflected the flashlight's beam.

"What the fuck?" Miguel asked himself out loud.

He set the flashlight down so it shown beneath the seat and reached into the track that allowed the bench seat to slide forward. Wedged between the outside track of the bench seat and the contour of the floorboard, just inside the open passenger door, was a flip-up cell phone. From what Miguel could figure out, the phone must have slid off the seat and down the space between the rounded edge of the bench and the passenger door. Combine the rattling of the old van with Chicago's infamous potholes, sprinkle in Sandy's unique driving style, and there you have it.

"Well, I now know why the goddamn bench won't move!" Miguel said with a sense of accomplishment.

"Why's that?" Enrique asked without interest.

"Hand me a screwdriver, Ricky."

"Dude, seriously…"

"Would you just shut up and get me a goddamn screw driver! Jesus!"

A moment later, Miguel was removing the cell phone from its lodged position with all the precision of a battlefield surgeon. He noticed the message "2 Missed Calls" displayed through the scratched and the heavily scratched cell window.

"No shit," he responded rhetorically.

Miguel stood back away from the van, shoved the cell phone into his back pocket and slammed the van doors.

"Get the keys from Sandy and let's get out of here." he said. "I'll get the car."

His head shaking, Enrique mumbled a response as he disappeared behind the screen door and into the house. Miguel left through the garage door, leaving it opened him. As he walked down the long driveway toward the street, he reached into his front pocket for his keys. He pulled out the device he'd taken off of the agent's body. He noticed that the one end that had been flashing green was now illuminated a solid red.

"Whatever it is, it don't mean shit now."

Miguel started to toss the device into the front yard then stopped. He shoved it into his back pocket as he reached the sidewalk and turned up the street.

"The sooner we get out the hell out of here, the sooner I get to bed…"

A faint but familiar aroma still hung in the heavy, early morning air. He walked past a row of empty cars on his way to his down at the end of the block. The fading smell of cannabis made him horny.

Raúl walked determinedly into one of the back bedrooms and closed the door behind him. It was empty except for two standing lamps in opposite corners and the five muscular men standing guard over two younger black men, one in cornrows, the other with a dangling right-handed black fist earring – ala Tommie Smith –, seated back-to-back, secured with duct tape to their chairs which were also taped together. They were, maybe, in their late teens and both showed visible signs of an interrogation that had stopped only minutes before. Thus far, efforts at motivating either young man to talk had met with limited success.

Raúl stood before the young men and looked to two of his guards standing on opposite sides of the chairs. Each grabbed the head of the young man seated in front of them and twisted it forcefully to one side until they faced Raúl.

"Who knows?"

Neither said a word.

Raúl made eye contact with a third man, who held a solid piece of construction rebar, about 3/8" in diameter and about eighteen inches long. He walked around to the one in cornrows seated to Raúl's left. With one forceful swing, he landed the heavy metal bar against the black kid's right kneecap. The teen shrieked in response to the splitting sound.

Raúl looked to his second guest whose kneecaps were both still functional.

"Now, who knows?" Raúl calmly asked again.

Earring boy swallowed hard as his friend's labored breathing grew stronger.

"I don't know nothin'," came the response. "I don't, I swear I –"

"How many are coming?" Raúl interrupted sternly.

He waited a long moment for the home boys to assess their options then nodded to the man with the rebar, who stepped forward and positioned himself within striking distance. Raúl reached over and grabbed earring boy by his hair, twisting his head back and his face forward. He bent over and glared directly into the teenager's eyes.

"For the last time," he asked again slowly, "how many are coming?"

Raúl counted to three then turned his head and made eye contact with his friend.

"Ok, ok!" earring boy finally cried out.

Raúl let go of the kid's head and tossed it forward.

"Maybe five," the young man said, "maybe more, I'm not sure."

Raúl appreciated the young man's newly found spirit of cooperation.

"How soon?" Raúl demanded.

"I don't know. 'Cue knows, you have to ask him. Ask 'Cue!"

Raúl reached down, curled the young man's tee-shirt in his right hand and pulled him forwarded.

"Who?"

"I dunno his name," the frightened kid responded, "he was here tonight, in the car with us, but then he left. I don't know who he is! I only know his name is 'Cue. Honest, that's all I know!"

Raúl looked up and made eye contact with anther of his men then returned his attention to his suddenly responsive friend.

"How soon are they coming?" Raúl demanded.

"I dunno! I swear to Christ, I don't fuckin' know!"

Raúl let him go, then nodded to the fourth man standing next to him, also holding a similar length of rebar. A moment later, a second shriek emanated from behind the closed door. Raúl glared at the seated young men, then looked up and met Carlos' eyes.

"Who's got their phone?"

Carlos dutifully pulled a small cellphone from his back pocket and handed it to Raúl. He flipped open the phone and examined the keypad. His attention returned to the two newly crippled young men still seated in front of him.

"How do I find the last number you called?"

Neither responded.

The men with rebars each moved in front of their other knees. Through his tears and throbbing pain, Cornrows started talking first. A moment later, Raúl was looking at the last number dialed on the phone. It had been called twice tonight, both times since around midnight. Raúl's eyes grew very cold. Seconds later he had the phone to his ear, waiting for the recipient to pick up. A voice answered before the fourth ring.

"Hello?"

It sounded strangely familiar.

"Who is this?" an angry Raúl demanded.

"Raúl?" responded a familiar voice. "Uncle, is that you?"

"Miguel?"

"Yeah!" he yelled into the phone. "Whaddya want?"

"What are you doing?"

"Whaddya mean, 'what am I doin'?' I'm talking to you!"

"That's not what I meant, dumbass!"

"I'm dumping the thing, just like you said. Ricky's with me, he's following me to the place. We're just leaving now. Why are you calling? And on this phone?"

"Is this your phone?" Raúl asked.

"Hell no, I'm surprised the damn thing even works." The call was breaking up.

"Where did you get it?"

"I found it on the floor of the van. It was shoved in the track. It's why we couldn't move the seat, remember?"

"So this isn't your phone?"

"Shit, no! I don't know whose it is. Maybe Sandy's? Did you ask him?"

The connection was dropping in and out. Raúl couldn't wait for Miguel to finish. He looked directly at Carlos.

"Miguel, get your ass back here now! NOW!"

"What?"

"Just shut and listen to me, Miguel. Get with Ricky and get your ass back here."

"But I still got her in the cab!"

"There isn't time. She'll have to keep. Just get back here. NOW!"

Raúl flipped the phone shut and shoved it in his back pocket. He nodded to Carlos then turned and walked out of the room. Carlos followed him out and closed the door behind them.

Raúl glared directly into the man's eyes.

"Get rid of those two. Get everyone packed up. We may not be able to wait for them. And find Sandy…"

Raúl placed his right hand on Carlos shoulder and griped it firmly.

"…and bring him to me! NOW"

* * *

Chapter 4

FBI SPECIAL AGENT Marc Cauldwell sat alone in one of the utilitarian plastic chairs that dotted the sterile hallway of Chicago's Northwestern Memorial Hospital's third lower level, his rapt attention paid to yet another game app he'd freshly downloaded to his new iPhone during a "working" two-for-one drink lunch special at the pub across the street. His Fridays were not typically spent in such morbid places. He had planned to get away by this time today, to be on the road heading north to his cabin for a long, relaxing weekend with – he still had trouble remembering her name.

That was, until this thing got in the way.

It was quiet. Empty. Tomb-like. He sat in a silence he completely ignored. The overhead fluorescent lights cast an cold, eerie pall across the eggshell linoleum floor and equally generic whitewashed cinder block walls. Hidden from his view, around the corner at the opposite end of the hall, was the reception desk. It sat across from a bank of elevators, one of which had just announced its arrival. As the doors opened, a young woman, curled brunette hair resting gently just past her shoulders, late-twenties and still cheerleader cute, stepped off the elevator with an armload of manila folders, her scrubs providing an unflattering service to her slender build.

She conversed softly with the receptionist, an older somewhat obese woman, who welcomed her warmly. Their conversation quietly echoed throughout the barren halls. The young woman followed the older woman's pointing finger in the direction of the morgue. As she turned the corner, she noticed him. Her perfume subtly announced her approach but it wasn't until she had walked past him that her fragrance had done its job.

"DAMN IT!" he suddenly exclaimed.

His concentration ruined, the game ended. His hands fell into his lap as his head dropped backward against the wall behind him, frustrated by the distraction.

At least temporarily.

He stood up and walked a couple steps in her direction as she continued down the hall ahead of him. He quickly found the view was worth the disruption. A lecherous grin crawled across his face, a look he personally believed even sober female acquaintances found so inviting about him. Despite standing just shy of 5'10" and living with strawberry blonde hair that did little to serve his more romantic inclinations, Marc Cauldwell lacked for nothing when it came to self-confidence. He considered himself still in game shape, especially now that he was crossing the bridge approaching forty. He'd come to accept, however reluctantly, that his rugged, outdoor persona – whether real or imagined – gave him an inside track that allowed him license to view any unexpected opportunity as more of a challenge toward conquest than an invitation to an engaging relationship. More to the truth, his shelf life concerning the latter, not unlike his stature, had more often than not proven disastrously short. And though he was recovering from yet another annual summer bout with allergens that had left his eyelids swollen to the point of almost legal blindness, he seemed to have no trouble focusing on the slender figure now disappearing into the file room at the end of the hall.

He shook his head and, with a lascivious grin, imagined the possibilities before turning to find Jack's look of dull surprise waiting for him to finish leering.

Cauldwell smiled shamelessly then immediately extended his right hand as he shifted into his professional mode. He displayed a dispassionate expression that he'd hoped resembled that of a stranger. Having lost the glasses in favor of contacts and added a goatee to go along with a renewed weight training regimen, Cauldwell felt comfortable Jack believed they were meeting for the first time.

"Jack Sturdevant?" Special Agent Cauldwell asked inquisitively.

Cauldwell subtly searched Jack's eyes for any indication he might remember him.

"Yes," Jack responded, accepting his hand. "Special Agent Stephen Cauldwell?" He hid a sigh of relief.

"Uh, *Marc* Cauldwell, yes," Cauldwell corrected him with a smile.

"Nice to meet you."

"Same here. Ok, what do you say we get this over with?" he said, still thinking he could make it north in time for his favorite Friday night all-you-could-eat fish fry.

They walked together down the hall until they reached the set of double doors just opposite a vending machine of snacks. Cauldwell pulled the temporary card key from his pocket that he'd been given by the receptionist and slid it through the electronic meter on the wall. The small light flipped immediately from red to green. The doors slip apart.

Jack followed him into the refrigerated room where the temperature was noticeably colder, easily twenty degrees, maybe more. The heavy, wide doors slid closed quickly behind them, the insulated overlapping strips sealing themselves shut. The room was big, vacant and sterile. Lining the wall to their right were six vertical rows of four secured stainless steel freezer doors, running from the floor to the ceiling, perhaps two-and-a-half feet square. The contents of each compartment were identified by a 2" x 6" tag that slid into a holder attached to the front of the door. These were bodies awaiting autopsy. Jack's showed no emotion as he followed Cauldwell toward the opposite end of the room. There, in a room having more in common with a walk-in closet than an office, seated amidst a sea of paper and manila folders, sat the county coroner, Dr. Amir Haziz.

"Excuse me, Dr. Haziz?" Special Agent Cauldwell inquired, entering uninvited.

A balding, somewhat overweight Middle Eastern man of sixty-two raised his head out of his paperwork and looked up from behind his bifocals.

"Yes, how may I help you?" Vestiges of his education and his early days practicing forensic medicine in Cairo as well as elsewhere in and around Egypt and the Arab world still distinguished the accent in his voice. He was a veteran of death in virtually all of its forms and under the worst of circumstances. Spending much of his career in the Middle East had offered him many opportunities to perfect his skills.

"I'm Special Agent Marc Cauldwell of the FBI. This is Jack Sturdevant, my associate. We're here to identify the body."

Dr. Haziz stood to shake hands with both Cauldwell and Jack.

"Yes, I've been expecting you. Allow me a moment to find her file. I left it out, expecting that you would be here."

Dr. Haziz thumbed through a couple of small mounds of unkempt paperwork on his desk, then walked over to a file cabinet in the corner opposite his desk. He pulled a conspicuously thin file from a third group resting on top.

"Yes, here it is."

He read from the file cover, as if expecting confirmation from either man. "20080806-IL-002-03-DOE. Yes, here we go. This way, please."

Dr. Haziz moved awkwardly past the two men as Jack coldly acknowledged Carmen's numeric fate, fighting the urge to react as they exited the doctor's office and followed him toward another set of double doors. Dr. Haziz leaned forward and ran the access card hanging around his neck through the electronic reader to the right of the door. Immediately, the glowing red light flipped green and a heavy metal click opened the doors automatically in front of them. They walked through to find the temperature had dropped yet again.

To their left lie maybe half-dozen cadavers on immaculate stainless-steel tables in various stages of autopsy. To their right were more multiple stainless steel freezer doors, a replication of the room they had just left. Dr. Haziz walked over to the compartments and begun searching the tag on each of the doors until he found the matching one. Without uttering a word, he released the lever and swung open the heavy metal door. The rollers beneath the metal rails spun discourteously as he pulled the frame holding her body out from it's temporary sepulchral. He extended the railings until the toe tag on her left foot was visible. He matched the numbers on the tag to the cover of his file. A thin white sheet covered her from her head to her ankles.

Dr. Haziz took a couple of steps to the front of the extended frame and looked directly at Special Agent Cauldwell.

"Are you ready?"

Cauldwell turned, looked at Jack and waited a moment.

Jack's attention was fixated on the shroud, his mind racing, trying to imagine anyone else but her lifeless body beneath it.

Cauldwell turned back to Dr. Haziz and nodded. He pulled back the sheet, laid it to rest just below her shoulders and stepped back. Jack's eyes glazed over.

Cauldwell indifferently turned to him, looking for his response. Dr. Haziz waited a respectful moment then inquired.

"Perhaps she has a birthmark or some other distinguishing feature that might –"

Jack's head slowly moved from side to side.

"No," he said in a soft, stoic voice.

"It's her," he admitted as much to himself as to the medical examiner.

He realized he hadn't really believed it – he *couldn't* really have believed it – until right now. No memories flooded his mind; no feelings ached to be expressed. All he felt was an emptiness, a vacuum of pain that was sucked through the hole in his heart where the scab had once been.

He looked up at Dr. Haziz and nodded.

"It's her," he repeated.

Dr. Haziz made eye contact with Cauldwell.

"There's some paperwork for you to sign back in my office."

Jack interrupted.

"She'd signed up to be an organ donor, doctor."

Dr. Haziz, looking decidedly surprised, responded matter-of-factly.

"There's little chance of that, at this point," he said. "This long after her death, without being properly maintained, her organs would no longer be viable for transplant."

"I see." Jack thought for a moment. "What about donations to research?"

"That may still be a possibility, yes," Dr. Haziz said, comfortable with that conclusion. "Very good, I'll make a note of that. If you leave me your number, I'll get back to you to see what appropriate arrangements can be made."

Special Agent Cauldwell felt ignored. Again. It was his turn to interrupt.

"If you would, doctor, please contact me instead. I'll leave you my number. This agent was killed in the line of duty and, as such, the Bureau may still be interested in the disposition of her remains. And there may be open evidentiary issues that require resolution before any decisions can be finalized."

Jack ignored Cauldwell's attempts at being impressive.

Dr. Haziz's eyes met Jack's. He waited for confirmation but saw only the resignation of one still in mourning. Still, Jack nodded, as if his approval mattered to Cauldwell.

"Very good, then."

"If you're ready, Jack," Cauldwell impatiently said.

Jack didn't hear him. Cauldwell turned and walked toward the secured doors. He pulled his suit jacket tightly around himself as the chill penetrated him. Dr. Haziz dragged the sheet carefully back over her head and began to slide her body back into the compartment when he felt a Jack's left hand on his forearm.

He stopped and looked up at Jack then stepped back.

Jack pulled the sheet back off of her face. He gently stroked her cheek with the back of his hand. The cold sensation was foreign to the countless times he'd touched her before. It still felt like yesterday. Or last night, for that matter. He ran his fingers over her forehead and across her hair. He wanted to say good-bye. He had to say good-bye.

But it wasn't in him.

"Jack?" Cauldwell impatiently called out.

Dr. Haziz looked at Jack for a response that wasn't coming. Instead, Jack turned her head slightly, then bent over next to her ear.

"All that is necessary," he whispered, his voice halting with growing strain, "for evil to triumph…" He closed eyes and touched her forehead with his. He took a deep staggered breath then opened them again. Tears clouded his vision. "…is for good men to do nothing."

He moved her head back then leaned forward and kissed her on the cheek. He cleared his throat, looked into her shuttered eyes and, with his hand still stroking the icy strands of her hair, whispered once more.

"I will always love you…"

He wanted this moment to seer into his consciousness. He prayed that this pain would galvanize his determination. He demanded that her memory – *their* memories – give rise to the necessary means that could result in the only end that now mattered.

The sound of the heavy metal doors closing echoed throughout the room as they slammed shut behind Special Agent Cauldwell. Jack straightened up and looked back at Dr. Haziz, expressionless.

He nodded toward the doctor and, without a word, turned and walked away.

They waited in silence as the slow-moving elevator approached the parking garage level.

"Where you parked?" Jack asked brusquely.

"Down a bit," Cauldwell vaguely offered, "not too far from –"

Jack wouldn't wait for him to finish.

"I want in on this case," Jack said as Cauldwell moved toward the opening doors.

Cauldwell ignored him as he stopped at a soft drink vending machine just outside the elevator bay. He reached into his pocket for change as he considered his choices.

"Cauldwell?" Jack demanded.

Cauldwell turned around deliberately.

"Jack, with all due respect to your relationship with Special Agent Eyas and to your years of service in the Bureau," he prefaced coldly, "what you do or do not want has no bearing on our investigation."

"Listen to me, goddamn it! Carmen was murdered working undercover on a trafficking assignment. No one knows that turf better than I do. 'Homeward Bound'…"

Cauldwell interrupted him.

"Don't go giving me chapter and verse on 'Homeward Bound,' Jack, I know all about it. Everyone knows about it! You were a fuckin' hero, ok? You put a dent into their East coast operation all the way from Miami to fuckin' Bangor. But that was then, Jack. And, in case you hadn't noticed, that was before you decided that going outside the change of command was more important than doing your goddamned job!"

Cauldwell wasn't quite finished.

"You don't have many friends left in the Bureau, Jack, to say nothing of the DOJ. The best thing you can do is take the consulting gig we've offered you – generously, in my opinion – and let it go at that. And you should consider yourself lucky you got that!"

Jack stepped up closer to him and looked deeply into his eyes. Cauldwell knew nothing of "Homeward Bound" let alone of Carmen, of Jack or their years of service with the Bureau. He knew Cauldwell was nothing but an errand boy sent to baby-sit him for as long as the ID process would take. And he knew that Cauldwell assumed Jack would simply acquiesce and settle for the scraps that might fall from their investigation's table.

But what *really* pissed him off was that Cauldwell hadn't earned the right to call him "Jack."

"Perhaps you didn't hear me, Special Agent Cauldwell," Jack said slowly, "I said I want in on this case."

Cauldwell just laughed and wagged his head as he dismissively turned his back and dropped in three quarters. Jack gripped him by the shoulder, spun him around and shoved him backward. With one motion, he reached in with his left hand and removed Cauldwell's service revolver from its holster while securing his right forearm against the agent's chest, just beneath his chin. He pushed forward and up, lifting Cauldwell against the vending machine.

Jack glared into Cauldwell's eyes and spoke in an unmistakable whispered tone.

"Listen to me, you stupid fuck. *This* is what you are going to do…" Jack leaned forward for emphasis. "…you will not only recommend that I am put on this case immediately, you will authorize me to have full and complete access to everything from itineraries and plane schedules to confidential emails and any communication given 'Top Priority.' And you *will* grant me need-to-know authorization and you will *not* hinder my efforts in any way in solving her murder."

He pressed forward, his forearm now securely planted beneath Cauldwell's chin and up against his throat.

"Do I make myself clear, Special Agent Cauldwell?"

Cauldwell tried to regain his composure despite his frightened expression.

"Are you out of you're goddamned mind? Assaulting a federal agent, you stu–"

Jack shoved up and forward a little harder and higher, lifting Cauldwell off his feet and tipping the vending machine up against the wall.

"I said," Jack repeated slowly, hesitating for effect, "*do I make myself clear, Special Agent Cauldwell?*"

Choking, Cauldwell struggled to speak.

"How the fuck am I supposed to –"

Jack wouldn't wait for his excuses.

"How you do it is up to you. Or Wallace. I couldn't care less. But I expect to hear from you by the end of business today that I have agent status on this investigation."

Cauldwell refused to relent.

"You are fuckin' crazy, man! There is no –"

Jack looked wildly into Cauldwell's eyes.

"You're goddamn right I'm crazy, you arrogant little prick. And if I *don't* get what I want by the end of the day, I will make two phone calls: One to your boss here in Chicago and the other to my friends at the New York Times – yeah, I'm still somewhat of a celebrity there – and I will give them both the same name."

"So fuckin' what, asshole, you think giving 'em my name means anything?"

"Not your name, dumbass."

The smirk on Cauldwell's face could not have set the table any better.

"I know all about Anderson Scott. And I know," Jack said, pausing for effect, "what Wallace knows…"

Cauldwell suddenly blinked, then gulped hard.

"…and *doesn't* know!"

There's no fuckin' way Jack could know anything about…

Jack leaned forwarded and whispered roughly into his ear.

"I know everything," he said. "I know about the women. About the families. I know about the desert. And about the bodies. I know it all, you stupid little shit."

Jack tightened his grip across Cauldwell's chest. Cauldwell exhaled with a burst but couldn't inhale.

"And I promise you this, Special Agent Cauldwell. When I get finished with you, you won't be able to get work as a fuckin' security guard."

"Assuming, that is," Jack added, "you're ever granted parole!"

Cauldwell found himself out of options.

"Ok, ok," Cauldwell conceded. "I'll talk with Wallace and get you on the case."

"I don't give a shit if you talk with him or not, you stupid fuck. I expect to be a part of your inner circle no later than close of business today. That or your boss will be reading about his impending indictment in Sunday's paper."

"Ok, ok –"

Jack pulled his business card from his shirt pocket and tucked it into the front pocket of Cauldwell's rumpled suit jacket. He then stepped back and released his grip. Cauldwell dropped to the floor as the vending machine rocked back to level ground. Jack looked him dead in the eye and offered him back his service revolver.

Cauldwell took the gun from Jack and returned it to its holster.

"Excuse me, please," Jack said, motioning for Cauldwell to step to one side. He reached down into the vending machine and pulled a Coke from the dispenser bin.

"I believe this belongs to you."

Cauldwell accepted his purchase along with an unsolicited admonition.

"And I hope, for both our sakes, Agent Cauldwell..." he said deliberately.

"...that you're a lot smarter now than you were the last time we worked together."

* * *

Alejandra Montoneros – "Alex" to everyone but her parents and her ex-husband's attorney – sat in the warm mid-afternoon downtown sun as the weekend rush hour showed distinctive signs of erupting. From her seat on a recently painted wooden bench across from the Park Restaurant just outside Chicago's Millennium Park she watched as, almost on cue, Michigan Avenue converted from shoppers, tourists and those enjoying the last days of summer to a virtual tsunami of commuters heading home in every conceivable direction. One wave after another of suits in wing tips, dresses with high heels, khakis, pantsuits and other creative combinations of what now passed for the latest corporate interpretation of business casual inundated Chicago's Magnificent Mile.

She released the straw from her lips after taking a long sip from her raspberry smoothie before returning to her laptop. She was organizing photos from the almost two months she'd recently spent in the Middle East, specifically Jordan and Syria. Her article on the ongoing Iraqi refugee crisis and the socio-economic impact it was having on these two countries was maddeningly still in editing. She remained hopeful the magazine would commit to a publication date before she left to cover the Democratic National Convention in Denver at the end of the month.

She'd accepted an invitation to stay with a childhood friend while visiting the city she grew up in. The woman lived on the Gold Coast, an historic neighborhood just north of the downtown area and, literally, two blocks from Lake Michigan. Being within walking distance of North Avenue beach helped her decide to take her friend up on her offer. Alex traveled light, always had, and presented little inconvenience. She found the luxurious furnishings of her friend's two-bedroom apartment, along with the balcony's panaramic view of the city's picturesque lakefront, a study in stark contrasts to the somewhat humbler accommodations she'd left behind just days before.

Alex's laptop kicked into gear with a high-pitched whine, the hard drive spinning rapidly in response to the multiple jpeg files she was opening. She quickly realized it had taken her far too long to organize the file folders of uploaded photographs with the drafts of copy she'd developed for all the articles she'd written. As she basked in the warmth of another glorious Chicago August afternoon, today seemed as good a time as any to begin making progress. She placed her almost half-empty smoothie on the ground, twisted her hair back it into a bun and secured it with a hair stick then got to work.

As cascades of the digital photographs dominoed across the flatscreen before her, memories of her assignments actively vied for her attention. A soft smile graced her lips as thoughts of Timothy St. James Elliot – her colleague, mentor, best friend and lover for more than fifteen years – jealously insisted on occupying her thoughts. The work they'd published, the continents they'd traveled, the adventures they'd shared, the narrow escapes they'd made. Fifteen years her senior, "Jimmy", as he eventually acquiesced to her calling him, had taught her how to develop her skills as a writer to match her instincts and the gifted eye she had for photography. And while Alex had risen among the ranks of independent photojournalists to where her work now commanded the attention of news organizations everywhere, she knew none of it would have been possible without him.

Her choice of park benches allowed her to remain in the sunshine while dusk, still some four hours away, had already begun to hint its arrival as the high-rise buildings lining Michigan Avenue prematurely cast shadows in her direction and around the Park. The inviting weather justified her procrastination. She put her down her laptop and removed her thin, white linen blouse to

reveal a soft, modestly-laced pastel yellow camisole that gracefully compliment-
ed her smooth, provocative shape and matched her cuffed khaki shorts. She
slipped out of her sandals, drew her limber, tanned legs to her chest and pushed
her sunglasses up onto her head. At thirty-eight, she remained as desirable as
her college days at Loyola's Lake Shore campus, where, as a student, she'd first
met Jimmy when she enrolled in a photography course he was teaching.

She stood 5'6", cordovan brown hair the summer sun had compliment-
ed with natural blonde highlights that ordinarily fell elegantly just past her
square shoulders. She had deep, piercing green eyes. Her soft, olive-skin com-
plexion she owed to her mixed Hispanic-Italian heritage. And even dripping
wet, which was often the way Jimmy preferred her, she seldom reached 120
lbs. She almost never worked out, as if she ever had the time. She always responded to those who would ask that her job was her exercise and, of course,
she was right. At Jimmy's insistence, though, she did have some formal training in various martial arts. It only made sense, given where they traveled.
Taking care of herself often meant using more than her wits.

Alex enjoyed a figure both men and women openly admired, some less
discreetly than others. Her inquisitive nature, fueled by an active imagination,
often led her wild side to experiment, to explore the exciting if uncertain ter-
rains of both physical and emotional intimacy, although her inclination was
that she preferred the utility of men. But while her career provided her with
no shortage of opportunities, she had, for most intents and purposes, remained
steadfastly loyal to Jimmy. Not that she didn't find her attributes convenient
when the right occasion called for it; no one would ever mistake Alejandra
Montoneros for naïve let alone a fool. But when it came to matters of the heart
– to the one love her heart always came home to –, her true north was Jimmy.

Which only made losing him that much more difficult to accept.

Jack started walking over to Michigan Avenue after leaving the hospital,
then headed south. Acceding to the mid-afternoon heat and humidity, he
removed his suit jacket and slung it over one shoulder, then rolled up his
sleeves. As he loosened his tie, he mumbled again – if for no other reason
than to remind himself just how right he was – how much he hated summer.

He'd been sweating for almost twenty minutes when he finally reached
the Chicago River, crossing over on the Michigan Avenue Bridge, leaving
the Magnificent Mile behind. Deciding to seek the shade offered by the
Park, he walked over to one of the vendors and purchased an artic frost Gatorade. He checked his cell phone.

It was almost 5:00 PM.

He made his way through the growing crowd toward the only partially-shaded bench situated across from the outdoor restaurant just outside the Park. Already seated at the one end still in the sunshine was an attractive woman, who appeared to be in her late twenties, preoccupied with her laptop. He looked around and gratefully realized she occupied the only bench that shade had begun to breach. To him, this was a no-brainer.

"Excuse me, but would you mind if I sat here?"

She looked up from behind her sunglasses then, almost rudely, returned to her computer screen without saying a word. She started to say something but then stopped.

"I'm sorry," Jack said, retreating, "you're expecting someone. I can find some place else to sit." He took her silence as all the answer he needed.

She looked up again then, oddly, one more time back to her laptop.

"I'm sorry to have disturbed you," he said as he moved away.

"No, wait, I'm sorry," she said, apologetically. "Please, have a seat... please." And, even though there was plenty of room, she instinctively moved over a bit for him.

"Great," he replied. "Thanks."

He immediately noticed that she continued to look at him, at his profile, while seemingly grinning at her computer screen.

"Forgive me," he interrupted her, "but I couldn't help noticing that you were... Do we know each other from somewhere?"

She smiled and removed her sunglasses as the sun gradually disappeared. "No, but I think he does."

And, with that, Alex swiveled her laptop around to show him a photo on her computer of Jack with, of all people, one Timothy St. James Elliot!

Jack was stunned. He hadn't thought of Jimmy in forever.

"Where..." he finally asked, "where did you get that?"

"I work –" She hesitated then corrected herself. "I mean, I worked with him."

"Seriously?"

"Yeah," she responded proudly, "for quite a few years. How do you know him?"

Jack could hardly take his eyes off the screen. The picture had been taken of him and Jimmy at one of their favorite D.C. bars, though he drew a blank on the name. It had to have been years ago, maybe five or more. They were standing at the bar along with their friend and trusty bartender, who'd joined them in the photo. He couldn't remember the server's name who'd taken it but he did remember that she'd used Jimmy's camera, which was, in itself, unusual since Jimmy was paranoid about anyone using his equipment. This was the first time he'd seen the picture taken that night.

"Oh, my gosh," he said modestly, "Jimmy and I go back quite a ways. I don't remember where or how we met but he did some good work for us."

"For us?"

"Oh, yes, I'm sorry, when I was with the Bureau," he said, before realizing he hadn't yet introduced himself.

"Forgive me, my name is Jack Sturdevant."

He extended his hand and she graciously accepted.

"Very nice to meet you, Jack. I'm Alex. Alex Montoneros."

"Montoneros?" he asked. "Any relation to the Argentinean rebels?"

"Excuse me?"

"Montoneros, your last name," he said, about to demonstrate once again his dismal skills at small talk. "It was the name of a left-wing militia guerrilla group during the late 60's and throughout the 70's. They supported Juan Perón's return to power."

She had the look of someone who had just be given too much information.

"You remember 'Evita', right?"

She was still paying enough attention to nod her head.

"Madonna, right?" she replied.

"Yeah, right. Well, the musical was based on the life of Juan Perón's wife during his first reign as president of Argentina throughout the late '40s and early '50s."

She shook her head and laughed.

"Well, there ya go," she said. "Who knew?"

He looked back at her and smiled.

"I take it this all comes as news to you."

"Yes, I'm afraid it does… But, thank you for the information. Should I ever need it going forward, I'll be sure to give you credit."

Jack chuckled and sat back.

"Not necessary, I assure you."

Somehow, Alex was intrigued.

"You mentioned you were with the Bureau?"

"Yes, I was with the FBI for almost twenty years. I worked in the Criminal Section of the Civil Rights Division for the Department of Justice."

She nodded her head, then ask almost incredulously.

"What kind of work did Jimmy do for you?"

Jack smiled as memories of Jimmy opened up like a file cabinet. But, unsure of who he was talking to, he kept his thoughts generic.

"Jimmy was good people. He was someone I came to trust. I could always count on him to get it right. And he was well connected. He helped a great deal when I was still with the Bureau."

Puzzled by his response, Alex's journalistic instincts kicked in.

"You're no longer with the FBI?"

"No, I left them some months ago."

"Interesting, you didn't make your twenty years?"

"No, things didn't quite work out the way I had planned."

"And did Jimmy have something to do with that?"

"Indirectly," Jack responded, trying to remain vague without being impolite.

"Ok... indirectly?" she said, now intrigued. "You can't just leave it there."

"Well, it's been a long time since I've seen him and..."

He no sooner had started than he felt his cell phone vibrating.

"...Excuse me, Alex, please, I'm expecting an important call."

She smiled, acknowledging his politeness as well as his good looks, and feigned turning her attention back to her laptop as Jack stood up to walk a short distance away.

"This is Jack Sturdevant."

"Jack, Special Agent Marc Cauldwell here," he said with a great deal more self-assurance than when they'd parted company earlier in the afternoon.

Alex looked up and watched Jack's body language as he alternated from strolling in an aimless pattern and standing rigidly still. She noticed he was in shape, well-toned and someone who seemed her age if not younger. She couldn't hear his conversation nor could she tell just yet what was happening. But that she was interested in learning told her all she needed to know. Her instincts had already kicked in and taken things to the next level. A few long seconds later, it appeared the conversation was coming to an end.

She pretended to focus back on her laptop. She heard Jack's flip phone snap shut as he walked back to the bench. She looked at him as he took his seat.

"Everything ok?"

Jack took a moment then turned to her.

"You mentioned you worked with Jimmy."

"It was a while ago but, yeah. Why?"

"I was wondering, Alex... Do have any plans for dinner this evening?"

His dimples were irresistible. She pulled out the stick from inside her bun and ran her fingers through her falling hair. He simply smiled.

"I think I do now..."

* * *

The world of twenty-four hours ago seemed like a lifetime away. After giving Jack the news this morning, Special Agent Laura Kallinger found herself calling on every ounce of energy she had just to make it through her scheduled meetings. Telling him about Carmen was the most difficult thing she could remember doing in a very long time. The one saving grace this evening held was the weekend that lay ahead of her and with it maybe a chance to make some sense of everything that had happened. She left her secretary a voicemail during lunch saying she was leaving for the day and headed home. The last thing she needed today was to spend another day rendering valueless judgments from worthless reports for a meaningless job as a resident of the federal government's version of the Island of the Damned.

Just after four o'clock, Laura and her three year-old Alaskan malamute, Bo, had completed a grueling if not mind-clearing eight-mile run throughout her neighborhood and surrounding cobblestone streets of greater Georgetown. She sweated profusely as she walked up the tree-lined sidewalk past the charming Queen Anne style brownstones toward the building she'd called home since relocating to D.C after her transfer from the Chicago office. Feeling both invigorated and exhausted – her body already testifying to the tortuous nature of her workout – it seemed Bo was ready to pick up their pace even as she had to beg off until next time. She hoped he'd understand.

Even today, his almost limitless exuberance brought a smile to her face. Even today.

His tail reacted predictably as she bent down, rubbed his head roughly and promised him they'd go again soon, though perhaps not tomorrow. She stroked his neck and up and down his back, her damp hands catching shedding hair from his thin summer coat of fading gray that had changed colors into more distinguishable patterns of white and black. Graciously, if not reluctantly, he accompanied her up the concrete staircase and through the heavy security door on their way to her two-bedroom apartment on the third floor.

Bo scampered ahead of her through the opened door as he recognized his favorite pet sitter from the second floor, an attractive silver-haired woman in her late sixties. Having risen from her entry-level secretarial position to become Allegheny Life's first woman senior executive vice president before retiring in the past year, Fran Segeve was a reliable choice for watching both Bo and Bo's stepbrother, Barney, an afghan hound. Her fashion sense impeccable, Fran was on her way to meet friends for an early dinner and then to the theatre. As she bent down to greet Bo, she mentioned that she'd be available anytime to take care of "da boys," as her Chicago roots still allowed her to call them. And while walking both dogs could prove challenging even for her, she'd made no secret how much she enjoyed their company. Still quite active, "Aunt Fran," as she preferred Laura call her, had no plans to travel until later in the month – it seems Italy had come calling once again. She was looking forward to spending some time with her four-legged friends before the cruise set sail just before Labor Day.

A perspiration-drenched Laura begged off giving Aunt Fran a grateful hug, saying "good night" instead with a strong smile and bright eyes, then met Bo at the top of the remaining stairs to enter her apartment. She followed him through the front door and walked through her tastefully appointed living room, across the wood plank floor, and into the kitchen. She tossed her house keys into a small wicker basket next to her recharging cell phone on one countertop. She ignored a second larger wicker basket on the dining room table that held exactly one week's worth of mail, including today's, which she'd dropped off before they went running. Bo proceeded to trot triumphantly past her and into the family room off the kitchen in search of Barney, who shared Bo's age if not his interest in exercise. Barney was comfortably positioned on the couch, having prepared himself for a relaxing Friday evening in hopes of adding the final touches to his tirelessly lazy and contently uneventful day.

Bo jogged around the couch and strutted between it and the heavy, dark oak coffee table and began nuzzling Barney, in truth more to pester him than anything else. Having lived with Bo for almost three years, Barney seemed to instinctively know where this was headed. He snapped back, exerting more energy than perhaps at any other time during his day. Bo ignored him, seemingly comfortable in the knowledge they both knew who the alpha dog was.

Laura had brought him home from the shelter first followed soon thereafter by Barney a couple of months later. She'd been to the rescue shelter only twice since relocating to D.C. And neither time could she leave empty handed! And from that very first day she adopted them – or, perhaps, it was they who adopted her, it was sometimes hard to tell – everybody in this household knew who was in charge. Laura included.

Across from the couch was a quaint, historically reconditioned stone fireplace, one of the more magnificent aspects of this apartment that had sold Laura almost immediately. Before it laid a flagstone hearth, designed in a semi circle pattern, which dovetailed nicely with the room's beige shag carpeting. In one corner, to the left of the fireplace, sat a pre-plasma, pre-widescreen era 34" television. Beneath it in the custom-designed cabinet was the stereo component system. In the opposite corner was a soft, comfortable wing chair. Next to it, a down-filled love seat upholstered in a warmly off-setting dark earth-tone fabric sat perpendicular to the matching couch that Barney continued to commandeer. This evening's cloudless sky welcomed the setting sun which cast the day's dying light through the windows on the wall opposite the love seat, a large center window flanked by two casements that provided Laura with an impressive view of the neighborhood lying just outside of Georgetown's historic district.

Laura gave her boys fresh water and checked on their food. A long hot shower and a Cobb salad later, she was ready to relax. She'd thrown on a pair of old sweats and a matching blue and gold sweatshirt from her undergraduate days at Clarion, a small private university outside of Pittsburgh. Her father used to kid her that she chose to attend law school at Pitt because they had the same colors. Whenever she thought of her dad's teasing, the memory of her father's gentle baritone voice once again left her smiling, if missing him.

When her father moved the family to Pittsburgh from the north side of Chicago, he brought with him three great loves: his wife and family, an uncompromising if inexplicable devotion to his beloved Chicago Cubs and an undying commitment to his Catholic faith that found its most fervent manifestation not on Sunday mornings but, rather, on Saturday afternoons, living and dying with his beloved Fighting Irish football. But when it came time for college, Laura felt compelled to turn down her scholarship at Notre Dame to be near her mom, whose love of life and for her family could only be extinguished by a long, difficult fight with breast cancer. Laura chose to attend Clarion University as much for it's small size as its location. She didn't realize until her dad pointed out later that the Fighting Eagles shared their colors with Notre Dame.

But when it came to the Cubs, there would be no such compromise. And if it's true that baseball doesn't develop character so much as reveal it, then the six-plus sun-drenched if not insufferable decades since the Cubs last played in the World Series, never mind the century it's been since they actually won one, spoke directly to the nature of her father's patient ways. And Laura was simply helpless when it came to her dad's passion. That Jack shared her love of the Cubs was not just one more thing they had in common. With Jack, though, it helped frame what defined the man he was, much as it had with her father. For Laura, it was one more insurmountable obstacle she'd encountered in trying to leave Jack behind when her promotion to the D.C. office came through, a career move that would amount to the calm before the Office of Tribal Justice storm.

She poured herself a glass of pinot grigio and grabbed her laptop from the kitchen table along with the AC adapter. She shoved aside her matted, damp shoulder-length chestnut hair as she bent down to plug it into the outlet next to the loveseat before settling in. She grabbed the CD remote. It wasn't long before Mick and the boys' distinctive sound soon filled the family room, singly softly about being blinded by rainbows, one of her favorite Stones' songs. It matched her mood perfectly tonight. She booted her computer from its sleep mode and almost immediately found herself online. An instant message flashed across the corner of her screen.

It was from him, swoopeagle_mxm.

She really wasn't up for conversation, electronic or otherwise.

Sorry, not really in to chatting tonight... she typed and then entered.

Tough day? came his response within seconds of hers.

Yeah, about as tough as they get...

Sorry to hear that... Anything I can do?

She paused for a second.

Not unless you can raise the dead, she wrote cryptically.

A few seconds passed.

Jesus I'm not, sorry to say...

She felt badly.

Sorry, that was dumb...

She waited a few seconds, trying to decide where she wanted her evening to go.

I found out last night I lost a dear friend, had to tell someone very close today...

I'm sorry... came the reply.

She was killed, murdered actually, in the line of duty a couple of days ago...

She paused before completing her thought. She saw he was typing a reply.

Sometimes, I really hate this fucking world... she added.

A few seconds passed before his reply came through.

Maybe you need a drink...

Laura laughed out loud at his lack of tact. His game needed work.

Way ahead of ya, dude...

Barney groaned, exerting more effort than he expected was necessary to change positions. Bo remained quietly at her feet, comfortable just being near her. She looked for something mindless to occupy her time while her body continued to decompress. She decided, since she couldn't remember the last time she had, to check her personal email. She downloaded her messages to find it had been a little over a week since she'd cleaned out her inbox. And though the spam filters she'd recently updated seemed to be working, there remained enough incoming email to make her begin dreading her decision almost immediately. She quickly scrolled through the alphabetical list of senders and found a couple from her dad, another from her sister, one each from her younger brothers and one from a friend from law school she'd only recently reconnected with. Of the forty or so messages that remained awaiting the delete key, one other grabbed her attention. It was sent from a phone number. And one she did not recognize. It was dated three days ago.

Tuesday.

Laura hesitated opening it. Her last bout with a system virus, she'd been told by her FBI geek friend, was introduced to her system from an incoming email. His advice to her was simple: never open anything if you don't recognize the sender. Leaving the ones she recognized, Laura highlighted then deleted the rest, which, in effect, simply moved them from her Inbox folder into her Delete folder. But instead of right-clicking on that folder's icon to empty it, she inadvertently double clicked on it, opening it. The incoming message sent from the phone number was the first displayed in the long list of emails waiting to be removed. And though the message didn't open, the preview window displayed the only two lines it contained. It appeared to be a text message.

And it was from Carmen.

It was sent the day she died.

A sudden rush of emotion closed her throat and locked up her chest. She heard the slight jingle of the tags on Bo's chain as he raised his head from between his paws, sensing something was wrong. She slowly maneuvered the mouse's pointer over the message and double-clicked. Tears collected in her eyes as she tried to inhale. She hovered over every written word.

Laura, it's me. Haven't much time. Sending u this from a private #, my #'s not safe. Mailed u docs, get them to Jack. Wallace is dirty. Call u l8r. Carmen

Laura pushed forward out of the love seat and placed her laptop down on the coffee table. Bo jumped to his feet, reacting in a flash to her sudden movement. She momentarily lost her balance as she rushed into the kitchen. She rifled through the mail.

Nothing.

She pulled a handful of envelopes from the large wicker basket and started searching each, carefully examined them for any sign one might be from Carmen.

Still nothing.

A thin, green postcard fell from within the next handful of envelopes. She bent down and turned over the card to learn the envelope was too large to be delivered, that a second attempt would be made tomorrow to deliver it. The postcard was dated Tuesday, the day Carmen had sent her text message.

Three days ago.

She quickly went through the rest of her mail and found the follow-up postcards. Delivery was attempted again Wednesday and once more on Thursday. On Thursday's postcard, it revealed that, since three unsuccessful attempts to deliver the envelope were made, it was being returned to sender on Friday.

Today!

"God *damn* it!" she yelled out. She slumped forward against the countertop. She began to cry. Again. She felt Bo nuzzle up next to her. She turned and slid down until she sat on the floor, her back pressing up against the dishwasher. Bo moved forward and starting licking the tears that had begun spilling down her cheeks. She drew him closer to her. He sat down and let her hug him.

She didn't know what to feel. It seemed so incredible, so unbelievable. Carmen was gone and whatever she'd sent Laura was God only knows where. What were the documents her message talked about? And Wallace being dirty? What was that all about? And could he have had anything to do with her murder?

And how would she ever be able to tell Jack?

The questions multiplied, circling within her head. And she couldn't help but wonder if the answers were now lost because she hadn't taken the time to *check her fuckin' mail!*

A moment later, the phone rang. It was her landline. She made no move to get up. Whoever it was, it didn't matter. She didn't want to talk. To anyone.

Two rings later, she heard the click from the answering machine in her bedroom as it picked up. A moment later, a familiar voice drifted down the hall.

"Laura, good evening, I hope I'm not disturbing you…"

She raised her head and held her breath. Bo's ears perked up alertly as he stepped back out of her embrace.

"…This is Deputy Director Wallace calling."

* * *

Chapter 5

DETECTIVE BOBBY COLAVITO sat with growing impatience at the watermarked oak veneered table in what had become a de facto conference room on the fourth floor of Chicago Police Department's Area 1 District headquarters in the 1700 block of South State Street. Truth be told, it was a retired commander's former office and one whose décor was in serious need of being introduced to the 21st century. And other than a half-hearted paint job that had brought the room up to the institutional gray business standards in vogue during the Reagan Administration, the room had been left virtually untouched going on three decades.

Ordinarily, by this late on a Friday afternoon, Bobby was already stepping into his weekend plans. But even he recognized this would be no ordinary weekend. He punched up his cell phone's voice mail again, only a few minutes since the last time he'd checked. Still nothing from Cauldwell. He'd given that FBI mutt more than enough time. Shit, it'd been almost seventy-two hours since they'd found her. How much time did he need, for Christ's sake? The crime scene had to be processed by now.

What the hell was he waiting for?

The knife was really all he cared about. Forensics on the five hollow-point rounds in her skull would quickly take them nowhere. But leaving his prints was a probie mistake. And the way he'd instinctively gripped it, he'd be surprised if he didn't leave a clean set. Full or partial, though, it wouldn't matter.

They wouldn't need a ten-point match for it to lead back to him; six or seven points would be more than enough. He couldn't have any explanations that would work in his favor. It was like goddamned DNA. He had to get his hands on that knife, to wipe it down, before the Bureau ran tests.

He knew it would take a while before they'd run his prints against any law enforcement databases. That would actually buy him some time. But someone would eventually recognize that the knife was military issue. And once they ran it against the government's databases, the game was over. Nothing bothered him more than being sloppy. And nothing was sloppier than leaving loose ends. He'd left a fuckin' trail of breadcrumbs. He was smarter than that.

His hole card – the one ace he held on Cauldwell – that would get him access to the knife was what he knew and the evidence he had about the FBI's stealth al-Qaeda investigation into Iraq. For Cauldwell, it had become just another field op that, officially or unofficially, had led nowhere. And while it had succeeded in ridding the world of more than a handful of eventual suicide-bombers, the intelligence the operation had provided left them wondering why they'd bothered. "Dead-enders" became the term of choice that agents had begun using to describe such an intense waste of resources. It was a term originally coined by the nation's previous Secretary of Defense whose concise if cavalier approach to the Administration's pharisaic global war on Islamic extremism had given rise to its adopted use. But it came to denote the sardonic appreciation of those lucky agents sent to the "fun in the sun" paradise that was Iraq during the summer months as well as their gratitude for all the amenities that life in the Green Zone had to offer.

What Bobby knew about the FBI's work there and what he'd done on their behalf, especially Cauldwell's, during their time in the desert was enough to at least get him a chip in the big game. And, with one phone call, he knew Cauldwell could get him into the loop on the FBI's investigation into her murder. Bobby also knew Cauldwell was stalling him. He had to be. Still, Cauldwell knew better than to ignore him.

Something must be up. For Cauldwell's sake, something had better be.

Across from Bobby at the conference table sat his Police Benevolent Association lawyer who seemed lost amid more paperwork than Bobby thought this situation could possibly warrant. Every law enforcement officer – LEO, in the local parlance – was entitled to representation throughout the internal inquiry process. Should eventual charges be levied against an officer, usually outside counsel would be retained. The open secret about PBA lawyers was that they had a foot in both camps. They were arbitrators as much as defenders. Perhaps that was why, even though he had met him only minutes ago, for a thousand dollars cash, payable on the spot, Bobby could not remember the man's name. But watching the man deftly maneuver between contrasting piles of paper reminded him of a quote he read somewhere about people creating their own need in order to justify their own existence.

That and Shakespeare's opinion about lawyers.

And it would have been funny were the consequences not so serious. But becoming a person of interest in any Internal Affairs Division investigation was a matter even the most seasoned officers would not laugh off. IAD generally worked under the unofficial assumption that investigations were only requested when they were warranted, not unlike juries who'd find defendants guilty because, after all, why else would the cops arrest them? Or the DA prosecute them? And where those investigations were warranted, action was expected. Action required reports. And reports required paperwork. Seemingly *massive* quantities of paperwork. Which, itself, of course, then demanded *more* action.

It was the viciously circular nature of that argument which gave rise to that bureaucratic (and often career-ending) black hole which, somehow, seemed to support the very reason for the goddamned investigation in the first place!

But, just as importantly, being presumed guilty until proven innocent served another very critical end of the investigation. Or, more precisely, the administrative interest in the end of that investigation. And that, of course, was politics. An underlying premise as basic as its very presence was constant, only the ignorant or the truly naïve underestimated the political end game of an IAD investigation. And to the extent that they did, it was at their own considerable peril. It reminded Bobby of that Pink Floyd video for "Another Brick in the Wall", the one where the school kids enter the grinder on one end and exit as hamburger on the other.

Bobby had no intention of allowing that to happen. He wouldn't make the mistake of thinking he was smarter than they were or that he somehow knew something they didn't. And he didn't know how much, or even if, he could trust his PBA lawyer. But what he did know was that his intuition helped him survive three tours in Iraq. That and simple street smarts. He figured if he could survive suicide bombers, roadside IEDs and a civil war based on nothing more than whose Allah was greater, his career could somehow survive the rigors of a bureaucratic political hack job. All he had to do was remain focused, tell them the truth to the extent they could determine its veracity and, above all, *not* allow them to get into his head. He realized that what his time in the desert had in common with this investigation was that you could never be certain exactly who the enemy was. He came back without the need of a body bag by trusting only those who had earned it. He saw no reason to alter that approach now.

Bobby got up from his seat at the table, shoved his hands into his unpressed suit pants pockets and walked to the window facing Lake Michigan. Though he could not see the lake from his fourth floor vantage point, he imagined being out there on such a warm, beautiful summer's day, fishing, drinking, relaxing, screwing. It was a world away from the bullshit this whole thing was shoveling his way.

Never mind what they didn't know!

He turned and looked at his PBA lawyer busily writing away.

"Where the hell are these guys, anyway?" he finally asked.

No sooner had he spoken then two large men in baggy suits walked past one of the glass walls that flanked either side of the office's open door. Bobby turned and watched through the open blinds as they entered the room followed by a decidedly unattractive if not equally obese younger woman. Briefcases and heavy gusset folders filled with more manila folders landed on the table.

"We apologize for being late. I'm Lt. George Williamson, IAD and this is Det. Henry Jorgensen. We're expecting one more, a representative from the IRB, who, hopefully, will be joining us shortly."

Bobby shook each of their hands in turn. His PBA representative stood and repeated the gesture. Bobby halfheartedly listened for the man's name but still didn't get it. Lt. Williamson motioned to the young woman setting up her equipment on the table while Det. Jorgensen closed the door to the conference room.

"This is Karen Samuelson. She's our stenographer and will be keeping a formal record of this follow-up meeting."

She raised her head while simultaneously looking for an electrical outlet. She smiled briefly but said nothing.

"Shall we get started?" Lt. Williamson suggested. With that, everyone took their seats. Amidst a reshuffling of notes and documentation by everyone at the table except Bobby, Lt. Williamson waited for her to give him the go-ahead.

A moment later the stenographer looked up and nodded.

"Should we wait a few more minutes?" Det. Jorgensen asked.

The lieutenant checked his watch and grinned broadly.

"I'm sure he'll be along shortly. Let's get started, he'll catch up…"

Karen nodded she was ready.

"Ok, we are here today, again in the matter of Detective Robert Colavito of –"

Just then, the final member of the group walked past the window and knocked quietly at the door. Det. Jorgensen turned and wheeled his chair to open the door.

"Forgive me but this is the IAD inquiry, isn't it?" he asked in a tone that seemed to already presume to know the answer. The burly Lt. Williamson swiveled around and immediately recognized one of the senior members of the Independent Review Board.

"John, how are you? C'mon in, we're just getting started."

A quick smile flashed across the late fifty-something man's face as he entered the room, shook hands all around and quickly found a seat, not coincidentally, at the head of the table. The Reverend Monsignor John Stuart Miles displayed the shape of someone whose morning regiment included jogging five miles, rain or shine, along the lakefront's bike path. He was dressed in a comfortable open collar maroon knit shirt and khakis.

Monsignor Miles was one of the Mayor's first choices to serve on the panel with full authority to investigate CPD police-involved shootings. One of the original members of the IRB, he had served on the Board for the last eighteen years after the City Council first created it as the civilian offset to the Department's Office of Professional Standards. From its inception, he was one of the Board's ranking members. Lately, he'd played a less active role, most often in the role of a consultant, as his increasingly demanding travel schedule for the Archdiocese required him to scale back his duties.

The Monsignor's reputation had preceded him. He'd performed tirelessly on behalf of his childhood friend over the course of the Mayor's career that was now in its third decade. From appearances at political fundraisers to mentoring programs and community projects to serving on various advisory committees deemed critical to the Mayor's unbroken string of reelections, Monsignor Miles had proven himself to be the power if not the conscience behind the throne. And while his appointment to the IRB initially created some controversy, in the end the City Council offered up only token resistance, hailing him as a fair-minded man and one whose opinions influenced decisions that seemed, for the most part, above the patronage for which the City Hall machine was so universally known.

In truth, everyone understood the unspoken language of Chicago partisan politics. Only the most jaundiced and cynical observers believed it was more than simple coincidence that the Board's work had successfully provided the Mayor's administration with precisely the means it needed to strike a balance between the city's rapidly growing minority voting blocks and the equally powerful rank-and-file union, the Fraternal Order of Police. Certainly, from time to time, community perception being what it is, "professional misconduct" occurring in certain neighborhoods made it necessary for the CPD to serve up one of it's own. It was an open secret that when – and how – that would occur was largely a matter of politically convenient, or inconvenient, timing, depending on the officer's ultimate fate. What did – and, just as importantly, what did not – constitute such situations was precisely the reason why inquires like this one took place.

And that's where the Reverend Monsignor's opinions always mattered most.

"Ok," Lt. Williamson began again, "if we're all set to get started…"

Det. Colavito felt his cell phone vibrate. He discreetly pulled it from his back pocket and flipped it open. He pressed two buttons and the text message appeared.

"kavenaughs 8pm don't be late"

His efforts did not go unnoticed.

"…I'm sorry, Det. Colavito, if you're ready?"

Bobby flipped shut his cell phone and shoved it into his back pocket.

"Yes sir, I'm sorry. Of course…"

"Alright, then… Karen, let's try this one more time…"

Her fingers were poised on the stenograph machine as Lt. Williamson began one more time.

"…All right, then. Once again, we are here in the matter of…"

* * *

The small back bedroom was dark and dank. The air was heavy and the odor was unmistakable. Thick curtains on the room's two shuttered windows prevented Ana from knowing whether it was day or night. She felt tired and nauseated.

And no longer like a child of twelve.

The mattress she was lying on was filthy and smelled. Or it could have been her. She couldn't remember the last time she'd bathed. Once awake, she rose carefully to her feet, feeling a bit dizzy. She had trouble focusing on the objects around her.

But she felt the unmistakable presence of someone else in the room.

She stood still for a moment, trying to get her bearings and wondering what she should do now. What she *could* do now.

"I was hoping you weren't dead," a thin, soft voice said out of the darkness. Ana jumped.

"Who is that? Who are you?" she said quietly.

"It's me, Daniel."

The little boy from the van! Ana's racing heart almost kept her from speaking.

"Shhh! Not so loud, *mijo*," she said in a loud whisper. "Where are you?" She reached out into the darkness without any sense of direction.

"I'm over here, in the corner."

She stumbled as she took her first steps toward his voice.

"Daniel, don't stop talking. Say anything; just don't stop talking, ok? And just not too loud."

"Uhhhh, ok. But what do you want me to say?"

Ana struggled with even trying to speak.

"Ummm, just start spelling your name and keep spelling it until I find you…"

"Ok," he responded. "Should I start now?"

"Yes!" she exclaimed, now almost in tears.

"Ok, here I go. D-A-N-I-…"

Ana put one hand on what she knew was the wall and decided to walk around the perimeter of the room. She moved slowly, her eyes still adjusting to the blackness and, though she was careful with each step she took, she stumbled after only a few steps.

"…Are you ok, Ana?"

"Yes, *mijo*, just keep spelling."

She passed the curtains on the first window turned the corner and headed down the length of the room. A few seconds later she found him. She fell to the ground, reached for his head and pulled her to him. She couldn't stop crying.

"Daniel, are you ok? Are you alright?"

The boy tried to talk but he was still being smothered. Struggling, he was finally able to pull back from her grip.

"I'm fine, Ana, I am. Are you ok?"

"Thank God," she exclaimed, instinctively saying a silent prayer of thanksgiving.

"What are we going to do, Ana?"

"I don't know, *mijo*, I don't know."

She embraced him again. He felt her trembling.

A long moment later Daniel heard something outside.

"Listen," he told her.

They sat holding one another, very still. Voices came from outside, maybe the yard. There were two of them and they sounded like men. Neither Ana nor Daniel could make out what they were saying, other than a word here and there. But the voices were definitely male.

"Shhh," Ana commanded him. "Be very still, *mijo...*"

They sat there in silence, frozen to one another. Ana heard her heart beating.

A minute or two passed, maybe more, before, without warning, a latch clicked and the bedroom door opened. Light flooded in and blinded them both. A large but silent figure walked into the light and stood silhouetted before them in the doorway. A few seconds past, then, whoever it was, stepped back and closed the door. Another click.

Ana heard voices again but this time they were coming from outside the door, maybe down the hall. She had trouble understanding everything they were saying. Her English was a little better than Daniel's, though neither was by any means fluent. It could be the same two men, she couldn't be sure. She only knew they were no longer coming from outside. No, they were definitely coming from inside the house.

And this time there was a third voice, a girl's, maybe even a woman's. And though she still could not make out exactly what she and the men were saying, it sounded like they were arguing or at least disagreeing. She held Daniel even tighter. She found herself praying again. She wondered if this time God would be listening.

Once again, the door opened but, this time, the figure was smaller.

"Hello?" It was a young woman's voice this time. "Are you guys ok?" Ana nodded as if her expression could actually be seen.

"Where are you? It's so dark, I can't see you." There were no light bulbs in ceiling fixture. Ana put her hand over Daniel's mouth and continued to stay silent.

"I have some soup here for you. And some bread. And water. I'll leave it for you over here by the door."

Still no response.

She bent down and placed a tray on the floor just inside the opened door.

"Do either of you need to use the bathroom?"

Daniel shoved Ana's hand away from his mouth.

"I do!" he exclaimed.

The young woman smiled.

"Ok, come with me. Just be careful, watch your step..."

Ana struggled to overcome her fear while Daniel had already decided he was going, with or without her. She rose with him and held his hand as they moved slowly along the walls toward the door.

Caridád Engañada waited patiently for them. As they approached the door, Ana placed her arm around Daniel.

"This way," Caridád said gently and led them both a few steps down the hall.

Forgetting his manners, Daniel spoke up.

"I have to go first!"

Ana nodded and began to follow him into the bathroom. She quickly looked around the cramped room and saw no possible means of escape.

"No, you can't come in with me. You wait out there!"

She bent down, placed her hands around his neck and drew his ear close to her.

"Don't say anything but, if you can find anything we can use to hurt them," she whispered quickly, "to get out of here, hide it in your pocket and bring it out with you."

Daniel looked directly into her eyes.

"Like what?" he asked her hurriedly, his voice unintentionally rising.

"Anything you can find," she responded sharply, her eyes telling him to be quiet.

The boy nodded as she straightened up and stepped back.

"Ok, now go!" Daniel excitedly said.

Ana nervously complied after looking inside the bathroom, making sure no one else was in there.

"I'll be here when you're done, *mijo*. Don't forget to wash your hands."

"I won't!" he said to get rid of her and the door closed between them.

Ana stood in the hallway with her head down, choosing not to make eye contact with Caridád.

"Are you alright? Has anyone hurt you?"

Ana hardly knew where to begin. She knew Caridád's accent, that she was some form of Spanish or Mexican though she couldn't place it. Deciding against saying anything, Ana merely shook her head without looking up.

"Is there anything I can do for you, anything I can get for you?"

Surprised at the question, Ana looked up, an expression of amazement on her face. She looked deep into Caridád's eyes. And in a clear, strong voice, with a conviction no twelve year-old should yet have, she spoke.

"You can let us go home."

Caridád looked at her and saw her own past. It wasn't that long ago she stood where Ana was now. She felt a chill, remembering the journey she was forced to travel just to simply survive. She sensed a strength, a courage in Ana that reminded her of herself. And what it had taken to endure it all. Caridád had no one when she was brought north. She owed her survival as much to luck – her good looks proved to be as much a curse as a blessing – then anything else. She believed Ana could survive, too, that she would overcome all of this. Somehow.

Or maybe she just wanted to believe.

It hardly mattered now anyway, not really. Her world, just like Caridád's, had changed forever. There was no going back. Survival was all that mattered now. It still beat the alternative though most that passed through houses like these might argue with that. Where Caridád had succeeded was in accepting that fact and then turning their strengths against her captors. It was something her sister, Maria, would have done.

Strange as it sounds, Caridád had been in the right place at the right time. It turned out to be her good fortune that the man who laid claim to her – the brother of a friend of Miguel's, actually – owed Raúl more money than he could pay. The drug business was a volatile one, to be sure. Most players don't have what it takes to keep out of their own way. They either sample too much, skim too much or talk too much. Or create a fatal recipe from the three. Raúl knew he shouldn't get involved but Miguel was his nephew and, after all, family is family.

So, against his better judgment, Raúl reached out to Miguel's friend and offered to cover the short delivery. As a result, Raúl succeeded in gaining access to a much needed, if not somewhat risky, revenue stream. Intentionally maintaining a low profile, over time he was able to gain greater control over the distribution of drugs throughout the south side. For the brother of Miguel's friend, however, in the end, Raúl's generosity didn't much matter. The guy apparently just couldn't learn a lesson. He was eventually found with neither hands nor feet when he was pulled from a discharge pipe near a makeshift pond just outside Milwaukee's industrial district. It was later determined that the cause of death was drowning. But the fluid that filled his lungs wasn't water.

It was toxic waste.

Regardless, the price for Raúl's original largess was Caridád. At the time, it could hardly have mattered less to her. They all looked alike. And they all treated her pretty much the same. And, like virtually all of the others, she was made available at any hour of the day, any day of the week. Paying customers naturally got priority but girls like Caridád could be handed out whenever an occasion warranted it. Any occasion. And her life with Raúl had shown few signs of changing. That is, until the night she suffered a horrific beating at the hands of a small group of affluent though surprisingly young white commodities traders – *whettos*, in Raúl's neighborhood – who apparently didn't quite get the memo regarding the intrinsic value Raúl assigned to his property. Within forty-eight hours, Raúl was present when the misunderstanding was cleared up.

Caridád's internal injuries required her to spend time in the hospital. To her amazement, Raúl would come by and see her, once even bringing her flowers. But even such unexpected treatment could not comfort her. Because of the way she'd been repeatedly violated, Caridád learned that she would be incapable of having children. Having not yet reached her 18th birthday, Caridád seemed a distant bystander to the life she had always planned. From her hospital bed, she watched as whatever future she still found reason to dream about dissipated within the confines of a world where nothing she said, nothing she did, nothing she felt, mattered.

She couldn't help wondering if her past lay in Ana's future.

Why Raúl began treating Caridád so well was as much a mystery to her then as it was now. And as much as she welcomed his increasing attention, she was uncomfortable becoming comfortable with expecting it. Every day she spent with him, every night she lay with him, she refused to let down her guard. Despite how she may have come to feel for Raúl, in the end, she could not escape the single truth that all that really mattered was she wanted her life back.

Hers and her sister's.

The bathroom door opened and Daniel walked through it into the hall.

"Ok, your turn," he told Ana.

She turned to Caridád.

"Would you please watch him for me?"

Caridád nodded.

"Thank you," she replied and, inexplicably, politely excused herself to use the bathroom. Caridád placed her arm around Daniel and stood quietly in the hall. She let out heavy sigh. Daniel looked up at her.

"Will we be able to go home soon?"

She looked away and started to think. She watched as a heavyset young man walked up the hall towards them. He had a pronounced scar running across his cheek down the right side of his jaw. His eyes were hard. His presence was frightening.

"Why are you out here with him?" he demanded.

"She's using the bathroom."

"Who said she could do that?"

Caridád glared back at him. Carlos was no match for that look. He respected her influence with Raúl.

"Just hurry it up," he said in retreat. And with that, he turned and walked back down the hall.

They heard the toilet flush and the water run. A moment later, Ana joined them in the hallway. Caridád watched Ana's eyes, then stepped past them and walked into the bathroom. She opened the door to the medicine chest. She turned looked directly at Ana and reached out her hand.

"Give them back to me," she told Ana. "Believe me, they'll only get you hurt."

Ana just stood there, her arms around Daniel, who stood in front of her.

"This isn't the way. You don't know who you're dealing with."

Caridád looked at Daniel then back at Ana.

"Please… If you care what happens to him, give them back to me."

Ana reluctantly pulled a pair of four-inch trimming scissors out from her pants pocket then slowly reached across and placed them in Caridád's open, outstretched hand. Caridád shoved the scissors into her back pocket.

"Thank you," she said softly, making eye contact with Ana.

Ana returned a slight smile.

"C'mon, let's go," Caridád said, leading them back into the bedroom.

"Have some soup and bread," she said. She bowed her head as she turned to leave. "I'll be back to check on you in a little while," she whispered.

Ana looked puzzled but nodded in return. She stood perfectly still as the room darkened again. Daniel looked up at her as they heard the latch turn, locking them in.

She carefully helped Daniel sit down then sat down next to him. She moved the tray in front of them and gave him the soup as she ate a little bread. They shared the bottle of water. It was still cold. And refreshing.

They heard voices outside again. The two men they recognized. The third voice sounded like Caridád's. They were excited, maybe arguing. It sounded like she was insisting that they go do something, though what she couldn't quite make out. By the tone of the conversation and the vulgar Spanish, Ana understood Caridád was not getting her way.

A loud roar unexpectedly drowned them all out. A car's engine revved up and, a moment later, seemed to slowly drive off down the street. The conversation ended.

A couple of minutes later, the door to their room opened again. Ana and Daniel looked up from their seat on the floor. It was a different man this time, maybe younger but definitely thinner. He wasn't wearing a shirt, only shorts. The day's heat and humidity apparently had taken its toll. He looked lean but strong. He scanned the room. It confirmed for him what he already knew. This girl and the boy were the last two. All the others that had arrived with them a couple of nights ago had been delivered. And these two would be heading out soon, hopefully in the next couple of hours. Nothing put his boss in a better mood than moving the product on time and in working condition.

Raúl hated loose ends. The way he smelled that raid coming the other night was amazing. He figured it out like some detective on one of those cop shows. True, they didn't have time to dispose of the dead agent's body. But leaving it in the abandoned van on one of the expressway's exit ramps probably worked out just as well. Less attention was never a bad thing. And finding this place on such short notice was completely due to Raúl's connections. The man knew what he was doing. Just being able to get everyone out of there before the feds showed up was a credit to the man's organizational instincts.

And the two dead black guys left in the back room? No worries. Actually, it worked to their advantage to leave them there, especially with their broken kneecaps. All they had to do was sprinkle enough powder residue around and it would look like just another south side drug deal gone bad. And who'd burn a lot of calories worrying about more dead gangbangers? Certainly not Chicago Police, not in this lifetime anyway. And the dead agent? Nobody could tie her back to Raúl's crew. Shit, they were going to find her anyway. Whoever did her probably wasn't sleeping too well these days but, as for the guys at the house, it all seemed good. By time the feds got there, the only evidence anyone still breathing had ever been there was the cold pizza.

He was just glad he wasn't Sandy!

Ana and Daniel watched the young man standing in front of them and waited without saying a word. He'd spent a moment looking around but now was looking directly at them. He bent over and picked up the tray, then grabbed the water bottle from Daniel's hands. Without a word, he stepped back and closed the door in front of him.

Ana waited to hear the latch click before she helped Daniel to his feet. Arm in arm, they worked their way slowly back toward the corner where she first found him. They sat down, huddled together and waited.

The young man took everything into the kitchen and tossed it onto the countertop near the overloaded sink.

"Caridád," he yelled out. He heard nothing in response. "Caridád, get in here and get these dishes done…"

Hearing no response, he walked out of the kitchen to look for her. He'd been working on his tone. Not enough people took him seriously. At least not yet.

He stopped and shouted down the hallway. "Caridád!" he called out.

Still nothing.

"Fuckin' *puta*," he mumbled as he started looking for her. He started with the living room at the back of the house and worked his way forward. He was walking up the hallway when he noticed the bathroom door was ajar. He heard water running.

He stopped and pushed open the door slowly.

There stood Caridád, facing the mirror. She was dressed in cut-offs so short the pockets extended beyond the denim's frayed edges. A wet, unbuttoned white shirt was all the modesty the heat would allow. She'd pulled the shirttail around and tied it up well above her slender waist. Her toned arms were above her head, stroking her hair now streaked with cool dampness. The contours of her face were dimpled with drops of water. She raised her hair up off her shoulders and turned toward the young man. Her breasts were fully outlined, adhering to her soaked shirt. Her nipples were hard and erect.

"It's just *sooo* fuckin' hot," she said breathlessly, "I just needed to cool off a bit."

She watched him swallow hard. The young man tried to recover.

"The dishes need to get done. The fuckin' kitchen's a goddamned mess."

Caridád dropped her hair down her back and looked him over slowly. She raised her shapely right leg onto the vanity next to the sink and bent over. His eyes zeroed in on her inner thigh.

"I've got a better idea," she said as she looked up, her searing green eyes fixing squarely on his. Her fingers dragged up her shapely calf and past her knee.

"Instead of doin' the dishes," she cooed seductively, "why don't you just do me?"

The young man swallowed hard again. She moved her eyes deliberately so he'd see she noticed the solid form now protruding from his shorts. She drew a short, tight breath, then made eye contact with him as she ran her hand down her stomach and across her crotch. She rubbed herself through her jeans and smiled.

"Wait, I can't," the young man protested, "you're Raúl's girl. I –"

Caridád straightened up, turned toward him and untied her shirttails, leaving them open to fall carelessly to either side past her hips.

"Yes," she said insistently, "but he's not here. And you are. And I want…" she said, pausing for effect, "what I want."

With that, she pushed him back into the hallway and up against the opposite wall.

"And what I want," she said in a low, raspy voice, "is you…"

She reached her hands around his neck and pulled his mouth against hers. Her tongue was warm, soft and deliciously wet. She pushed herself up against him. His resistance melted.

"Fuck me," she whispered excitedly into his ear, "fuck me *now!*"

He placed his hands around her neck and ran them up beneath her hair. He turned her slightly and dovetailed his mouth with hers. He shoved his hips forward. She responded eagerly, wrapping her lips around his tongue. She sucked hard, pulling it into her mouth. He groaned as much in pain as pleasure.

Without warning, she released her grip and slid down his chest and past his abdomen. She gently squeezed him with both hands, then pulled the waistband of his shorts toward her, peeling it over his stiffening response, revealing her objective. As she pulled them down his muscular thighs, she immediately wrapped her mouth around his beckoning, pulsating organ. She closed her eyes and drew him deeply into her mouth.

His shorts fell unnoticed to the floor.

She controlled him completely with her mouth. She moaned loudly, agreeably, and tossed her head to one side. She shoved her hands forward, up his chest until she reached his nipples. His eyes closed. He leaned back against the wall. He placed his hands on the back of her head and guided her motion. She'd long ago learned what works, and when. His hands went from the back of her head to the base of her neck. He gently pushed her unbuttoned shirt off her shoulders and down across her arms, first through the one sleeve, then the other. She sucked on him hard and deep, then released him with a seductive gasp of air. As she slowly stood up, she dragged her breasts against him. Stepping back, her eyes were glued to his as he tried to take her all in. She smiled provocatively and fondled herself, then watched him react.

His look was one she knew very well.

A frantic moment later, they were across the hall in what had once served as a bedroom. An old mirror, maybe 2' by 3' sat undisturbed propped up against one wall. She watched her reflection as he stood behind her, his hands encircling her waist, unbuttoning her cut-offs. One of her hands was hidden between their swaying bodies, massaging his groin. The other grabbed her hair and pulled it down over one shoulder. She watched his open mouth disappear against the tender flesh of her neck. His teeth bit down on her.

She groaned in response.

"Harder," she whispered to him as her moans grew louder. He only too happily obliged. She opened her eyes to see his hands disappear inside her jeans. He reached between her legs and felt her moist desire for him. He watched her expression in the mirror change as she reacted to his touch. She tossed her head to one side. She slipped out of her cut-offs and turned into him. She let him feel the full warmth of her naked body. She felt him flush against her tight abdomen.

She stepped back, out of his embrace. He reached for her but she stopped him.

"Hit me," she said, looking seductively into his eyes.

He looked at her strangely.

"What?" he said, like he hadn't heard her right.

She looked angrily at him.

"Hit me, damn it!" Then she slapped him.

He just stood there, not knowing how to react.

She slapped him again.

"What are you, some fuckin' pussy?" she taunted him.

She shoved him and he staggered backwards.

"You gonna let a girl push you around? What are you now, my bitch?"

She went to hit him again but he caught her forearm before it touched him. He pressed his fingers into her wrist until she relented. Then she spit at him. She reached forward and tried to dig her nails into his chest. He stepped back and brought a thundering right hand across the left side of her face. She staggered to one side, her hair flying behind her. He grabbed her arm roughly with one hand and held her upright. As she straightened up, the back of his hand crashed against the other side of her face.

Blood now flew in the other direction. Caridád fell with the momentum of his slap as he shoved her to the floor. She landed on her side and rolled over on her back.

"You like it rough, eh?" he said, now more aroused than ever.

Her eyes opened and locked on his. Her face was already swelling up. Her lip was cut and bleeding, as was her nose. She moved slowly on the floor. He stepped back and watched her intently. She lay back, placed one arm behind her head and bent one knee. Her one hand slowly moved up her thigh. He watched her with a widening grin.

He saw his image in the mirror bend down in front of her. He pushed her legs aside and slung them over each shoulder. She tried to push him away, using the palm of her hands against his chest. She reached for his face with her fingernails. He slapped her again then punched her once. He placed a strong hand beneath her chin and started choking her.

She reached down and felt him throbbing as he leaned forward toward her.

She guided him against her moist crease, back and then forth, sliding him from one side to the next and back again. She watched his eyes close, his mouth slowly open. She listened to him moan softly. Without warning, she pulled him forward into her. Her sudden warmth surprised him. He couldn't believe how tight she was. She reached to one side, grabbed her cut-offs and tossed them out of their way.

He could not control his desire. He dropped her legs off his shoulders and leaned forward. One leg at a time, he placed his knees outside her straightened legs. He held himself above her as he slid effortlessly into her. Her hips responded in rhythm. Her moans gained strength as their pace quickened. He was already beginning to succumb.

"Harder," she demanded, "fuck me harder!"

He slowly leaned closer. She felt his breath on her neck. Drops of his sweat dripped across her face. She reached around and grabbed him from behind. With each more powerful thrust, she tried to shove him deeper. She cried out each time he slammed into her; she whimpered softly "no" each time he withdrew. A moment later, she began to tremble and shake. She whispered in a halting voice that she was about to come. She wanted him deeper, faster, harder. He drove himself into her.

She heard him groan, quietly at first, then louder, and more often. With each thrust his cries became edgier, more frantic and tense. He lay on top of her as he slipped his hands beneath her. He raised her up slightly. He could hold it back no longer. With one final thrust, he exploded into her. Again and again. And then once more. He closed his eyes and buried his head into her shoulder.

He let out one more loud groan then went limp as he laid on top of her. He convulsed for a moment, maybe two. His muscles twitched. She felt him trembling as his dead weight grew heavier on her.

His blood ran in a thick, random line down the side of his throat and trickled across her chest. She shoved down hard on the scissors one more time, forcing them even deeper into the side of his neck. They were embedded up to the handle.

She rolled him off of her. His eyes were still wide open. Time was short. She had to hurry. She winced as she wiped her own blood from her face. She grabbed her cut-offs with one hand and, placing her other hand between her legs, got up and moved quickly to the bathroom. She reached behind the door for her panties and tee-shirt. She pulled on her underwear, grabbed some tissue and shoved it inside. She then pulled on her cut-offs. She pulled the tee-shirt on over her head. Her blood smeared across it.

She went to the back bedroom and opened the door.

"Quickly," she said, "we haven't much time."

Ana and Daniel were huddled on the floor in the far corner.

"Come here, quickly, out in the hall."

Confused, they stepped carefully through the dark room and into the light of the hallway.

"What's going on?" Ana asked. "What happened to you?"

Caridád reached into her pocket and pulled out what looked like two small coins.

"Never mind," she said, handing them to Ana. "Here, you'll need these."

"What are these?" Ana asked.

"Bus tokens. You'll need them to get on the bus. There's no time. Come, follow me. Quickly!"

Caridád grabbed Ana by the hand. Ana reactively grabbed Daniel's hand. She led them through the house, out the back door, across the small wooden deck and into the backyard. She pointed to a back alley that ran behind a row of houses opposite a series of garage doors.

"Ok, listen to me. Both of you. We haven't much time."

Caridád pointed toward the alley.

"Go down that way. It'll take you to the street. Turn right and head to the first or maybe it's the second stoplight, I'm not sure. Just find Halsted Street. You can catch a bus there. The number 8 bus. Remember that number."

Ana looked like nothing was registering.

Caridád stopped.

"What's the name of the street?" she asked.

Ana couldn't think.

"Halsted," said Daniel.

"Right!" Caridád responded. "And the bus number?" she continued.

Caridád waited a long couple of seconds. She needed to know Ana remembered the bus number, if nothing else.

"Ana! What's the bus number?"

Ana just looked at her, still confused. She tried to remember but she couldn't get it out.

"Eight!" Caridád repeated. "Ana, remember that number. It's bus number 8!

"Yes, ok." Ana finally said. "Bus number 8."

"Right. If you get lost, just ask someone where you can catch bus number 8. And you'll be fine."

"Ok," Ana repeated.

Caridád continued.

"When the driver stops, when he opens the door, get on and drop the tokens I gave you in the metal box. He'll show you where. Tell him you want to get of at 18th Street. He'll tell you when he gets there. At 18th Street, get off the bus, then start walking straight, away from the sun. That'll be east, toward the lake. If you're not sure which way, tell the driver you want to walk to State Street. He'll show you which direction to walk."

"Ok?" Caridád stopped just to make sure.

Ana nodded. As did Daniel.

"Ok, you'll walk for a few blocks, I'm not sure how many. But you'll walk under the expressway and across the river. That's how you know you're going the right way."

Ana was getting more confused. She looked afraid. She wasn't sure could remember everything Caridád was telling her. Nothing she was telling her made sense. She looked at Daniel. All he wanted to do was run.

Caridád couldn't take time to repeat herself.

"All right, when you get to State Street, ask for the police station. There's one right at 18th and State. They'll take care of you. They'll see to it you get home!"

Ana was close to tears.

"Why are you doing this?" she desperately asked her.

Caridád just looked at her.

"Please, just go… now!"

"No," Ana said, "tell me, why are you doing this?"

Caridád started to tear up.

"Because nobody did it for me," she started as her voice began to crack.

Ana reached out and hugged her neck tightly. Caridád winced from the pain.

"Thank you. Thank you so much."

"Just go, *mija*, they'll be here any minute."

Daniel pulled at Ana. "C'mon, Ana, let's go."

Ana pleaded with Caridád.

"Please, you can come with us! You can! Come with us, please!"

Caridád pushed her away. "No, just go. *Now*! *Please*! Before he gets back!"

With that Ana started to run with Daniel toward the alleyway. Caridád stood watching them, wiping a tear away from her eye. She wanted to smile. Her fear would not allow it.

She watched until they disappeared.

Caridád's mind was racing as she turned and ran back into the house. *Had she thought of everything? Could this really work? How would Raúl re-act? What would he say? Would he believe her?* She moved quickly to the back bedroom, removing her clothes as she hurried down the hall. By time she hopped to the back bedroom, her cut-offs were off. She flipped them aside, along with her tee-shirt.

She stood there, naked.

And alone.

When Ana and Daniel came to the end of the alley, they turned right, just as Caridád had told them, and walked quickly up 35th Street. Ana put her arm around Daniel and tried to hurry him along though, in truth, Daniel was already moving much faster. She remembered what Caridád had told them about the sun but she didn't see any buses coming. Ana was desperate, nervous, frightened but undeterred. They passed markets and shops and storefronts of all kinds. It was all a blur. Nothing registered. She was completely focused. They weren't stopping now.

They came upon the first stoplight and searched for a street sign. They looked around, asking anyone who walked by if this was Halsted Street. No one listened or paid them any attention.

Ana became frantic. She didn't know what to do. She had no idea where to go. But one thing she did know. They were free. And, somehow, someway, they were going home. She wasn't going back. And neither was Daniel. She watched the cars go by and waited. A few seconds later, the lights changed. The cross-traffic stopped. She took Daniel's hand and followed a small crowd of people into the crosswalk. She asked everyone that passed her by, coming and going, where is Halsted? Maybe it was her inflection, maybe her accent. Maybe it was simply that no one cared. They got to the middle of the crosswalk and stopped. They stood there, turning around, looking for help.

No one seemed to even noticed them.

She felt her heart racing. She was having trouble taking breaths. She had trouble even thinking. She tried to yell out in as loud a voice as she could muster.

"Won't someone *PLEASE* help us?"

Car horns began sounding as the lights changed. Traffic began backing up. Ana started to cry. No one heard her. No one cared to hear her. She placed her arm around Daniel and drew his head to her. She leaned on him heavily. She was so tired. Daniel hugged her. He held her tightly. They stood, holding each other up, in the middle of the crosswalk of a busy intersection.

They could not have been more alone.

Finally, a young man jumped out of the backseat of an old Buick convertible, seemingly overflowing with teenagers, a few cars down from the intersection and jogged toward them. He bent over and whispered something, then began walking them the rest of the way across the street. The cars still waiting impatiently began moving again

The young man pulled out his wallet and offered her the few dollars he had in it. Ana thanked him as he started to jog back up the street towards his friends. He darted back into traffic. He waited a moment then hopped over the car door and into the back seat of the slowly moving Buick, which then sped away before the light changed again.

Holding three dollars in her hand, Ana looked up and watched helplessly as the world continued to pass by. She pulled Daniel to her and, together, they sat down on the curb. She rocked him back and forth, and started to cry quietly.

"What are we going to do now, Ana?

She was beyond terrified. She knew they were just up the block from the house. Her first thought was to run, though she could not imagine where. They would come looking for them. Of that much she was certain. Staying here, on the street, would only make it easier for them to be found. She prayed. And thought of her mother.

Then she remembered how they would travel to their local church.

"Whenever you don't know, whenever you need help," Ana recalled her mother telling her, "go and see God…" She remembered there were always nice people there. They would talk with Ana and offer their help, to her mother, her brother Martín. They would share what little they had with them. They would listen and do what they could.

Maybe we can find a church, she thought. *Someone there would help us, wouldn't they? That's what they would do, right?*

She looked toward the skyline for a steeple, a cross, anything. She prayed to Jesus. She whispered her mother's name. She no longer wondered how this nightmare could get any worse.

She was so hungry. And so tired. She was having trouble thinking at all, let alone clearly. She knew they needed to move. They *had* to move. They had to go somewhere. They couldn't stay here. She wanted to run. Daniel wanted to know where they were going. The men who'd hurt her, so often and so badly, kept invading her thoughts.

Where are we going? Who will help us? What are we going to do now?

She didn't have the first clue.

* * *

Chapter 6

CARIDÁD STOPPED AND took a deep breath.

Fuck!

She stepped back and moved quickly to the bedroom at the end of the hall. She stood in the doorway of the dark room and listened.

Nothing.

No breathing, no moving, no sound at all... nothing! Maybe he's dead?

No sign of him.

Shit, where is he? Where could he have gone?

She took another deep breath, wincing as she closed her eyes. When she opened them, the room was still empty. The blood dripping from her nose mingled with what was tacky across her swollen lip. She had trouble opening her left eye. It had started to swell almost shut. She wasn't imagining anything.

What the fuck am I going to do now?

She turned and walked back to the bedroom where he'd "attacked" her. That's when she noticed blood streaked the hallway walls. She looked down and realized the cheap carpet was moist and sticky. She saw the trail led out of the bedroom and down the hall. All she could think of was that someone had come to help him, that somehow, when she was in the back yard with Ana and Daniel, someone had come back and found him. She swallowed hard. The possibilities now frightened her. But she had no choice now. She turned quickly and started to follow the path.

Down the hall.

Around the corner.

Into the kitchen.

And there he stood. He was at the sink, leaning over the countertop. Fresh blood was smeared across the pad of the cell phone near his left hand, the one hand he used to steady himself. His right hand was at his neck, vainly trying to stop the profuse bleeding. Caridád reacted quickly. She opened a kitchen drawer and grabbed the first blade she touched, a serrated steak knife. The young man heard the rustling of the silverware inside the drawer and painfully turned to see her.

He slumped backwards against the countertop. She raised the knife and lunged toward his chest. The phone fell to the floor as he grabbed her wrist, first with one hand then with both. She tried to force the knife forward but he still was too strong. She raised her knee into his groin. He turned into her. She hit the side of his leg. He pushed her back. She dropped her knife as she fell hard to the floor. As she turned, her forehead crashed into the metal handle of a lower kitchen cabinet, opening a gash above her right eye. He pulled a dirty butcher knife out of the sink and stumbled toward her. Caridád rolled over and frantically reached for the steak knife but could not find it. He looked upon her naked body, spread before him. He focused on the hair between her legs as he brought a hand back against the side of his throat.

"You fuckin' bitch," he stammered.

He looked up and saw the fear in her eyes.

"You like it hard, do ya?" he mockingly asked her. He slowly raised the dirty blade and watched her eyes follow it. "How 'bout I do you hard with this, huh?"

His eyes wandered up and down her lean, brown body.

"Yeah, I'm gonna do you all right, *puta!*"

He struggled to keep his balance as he stood over her. Blood streamed down his arm and dripped onto her face. He switched the knife to his blood-soaked right hand while his left hand reached down and grabbed her by her hair and twisted it around his fingers. He yanked her head backwards and spit on her.

She spit back at him as he raised the butcher knife.

"Go ahead, you fuckin' piece of shit, go ahead and get it over with."

If it had to end this way, then so be it. She'd done what she could to spare Ana and Daniel the life she'd lived. And she'd already known what hell was like. She'd been there long enough. Since her abduction, she'd lived a life that would challenge even the devil's imagination. She'd been ready for some time for whatever the other life brings.

He blinked continuously and grinned while fighting to stay conscious.

"I'm gonna cut you up, you fuckin' –"

A voice suddenly came from the kitchen's doorway in front of him.

"Ricky, no!" he yelled, "What the hell are you doing?"

Enrique looked up painfully and saw Sandy approaching him.

"Get outta here, Sandy," he replied, breathlessly, "just get the fuck outta here!"

Enrique curled the butcher knife inside his hand and pushed Sandy back with his closed fist. Sandy slipped on the bloody linoleum and fell backwards against the wall.

"Ricky!"

Enrique watched him fall then turned his attention back to Caridád. She frantically turned and looked to Sandy

"Sandy, help me, please!" she screamed, "Please!"

Enrique struggled to raise the knife again.

"I'm giving this bitch what she deserves!" he said deliberately.

"Ricky, stop!" Sandy shouted back, scrambling to his feet.

"You hear me? STOP!"

Enrique ignored him as he staggered for a moment, desperately trying to remain conscious. He twisted Caridád's hair one more time, trying to steady himself. She tried to protect herself with her arms and screamed for Sandy to stop him. Enrique smiled vengefully through clouding eyes.

"Die, you fuckin' little bitch…"

The butcher knife came up one more time then, without warning, dropped loudly, harmlessly, to the floor. Two quick, staccato sounds echoed in succession throughout the house. Blood jettisoning from Enrique's abdomen spattered across Caridád's face and chest. He let go of Caridád's hair and staggered backward. He looked up to see Sandy now standing in the doorway, two hands fixed on his revolver that was still trained on him. A thin but unmistakable pungent odor spread across the room.

Enrique tried to speak but said nothing. His eyes held the look of frightened surprise as they opened wide in the moment just before he collapsed.

Caridád pushed herself up, crawling backwards, propping herself up against a cabinet behind her and bringing her knees to her chest. She was trembling but silent. Her eyes were frozen in fear as she stared at Enrique, waiting for him to get back up.

Sandy shoved his gun into the back of his pants and quickly moved over to her. He slid again on blood and lost his balance as he knelt down next to her to place his arms around her. She made no response, as if she were in a trance.

She was shaking, visibly and uncontrollably. She started to cry but, oddly, didn't – or couldn't – make a sound.

"Ok, ok," Sandy repeated, "it's ok."

"Shhhh, it's over now, it's all over. You're ok…"

Caridád's chest was heaving as she fought to overcome her racing heart just to breathe. Her eyes remained fixed on Enrique, lying motionless on the kitchen floor, his draining blood still openly pooling around his naked corpse. He hadn't moved. He couldn't move. And he wouldn't move. Sandy heard her whimpering. He felt her trembling. Her blood stained his shirt.

"Everything's ok now," he gently reassured her again. "He can't hurt you anymore."

Sandy waited for a few seconds until she seemed to begin settling down. He pushed back from her and put her face in his hands. Her eyes remained fixed on Enrique.

"Caridád," he said, trying to get her to pay attention. "Caridád! Look at me!"

Finally, she turned her attention to Sandy.

"Listen to me, you're ok, you're ok…" he assured her, "he can't hurt you now!"

She searched his eyes for a promise that he was telling the truth.

"Tell me what happened here? Why was he trying to hurt you?"

She looked at him through frightened tears, still trembling.

"Is he dead, Sandy? Is he still dead?"

Sandy looked back at her and gently nodded.

"He beat me, Sandy," she said, trying to talk while swallowing and catching her breath. "Carlos left to go get Raúl. We were alone. He attacked me. He just started hitting me. I didn't want him to do what he did, Sandy, I didn't want him to –"

Sandy had noticed the bruises on her face and the marks on her throat, the bloody nose, the cracked lip. Caridád pulled him forward and placed her head back into his arms. He felt her chest trying to draw air. She swallowed hard once more.

"Did you kill him, Sandy?" she asked yet again. "Is he dead?"

Sandy hugged her back and held her close.

"Did you fuckin' kill him?" she asked, this time more angrily, a sign she was regaining her strength.

"Please, tell me he's dead…" she repeated.

He looked over and saw Enrique hadn't moved. The young man's head was tilted toward him. His eyes were still wide open. Even Sandy was a good shot at this distance.

"Yes, he's dead," he said softly.

"He's dead."

Sandy stroked her hair gently. He couldn't believe what he was saying. Or what he had done. And he hadn't even begun to wonder what Raúl was going to say. Or do.

He wouldn't wait long.

He was still holding Caridád when Sandy heard the screen door open then bang shut. He turned his head and, over his shoulder, saw Raúl walk into the kitchen and stop. Carlos stood closely behind him. He glared at Enrique's body lying prone to the kitchen floor, his blood on the floor already turning shades of a darker crimson.

Raúl looked down at Sandy and a naked Caridád. His eyes noticed the butcher knife on the floor. Carlos walked over to the body then looked to Raúl and, meeting his eyes, barely shook his head.

Raúl shut his eyes and took a deep breath.

"Somebody," he started slowly, "tell me what in the fuck happened here."

Sandy turned back to Caridád.

"Could we get her some clothes first, please?"

Caridád started to say something, to tell them where her clothes were. Raúl ignored her as he looked to Carlos, who was awaiting orders.

Raúl nodded to him.

"Bring her a towel or something, *hermano*."

With that, the young man walked back past Raúl and toward the bathroom just down the hall. Raúl stepped around Sandy and Caridád and walked over to Enríque. Blood that spilled from his neck was becoming sticky, filling the cracks between the linoleum tiles. He knelt down next to him, reached over and gently shut Enrique's eyes. He made a soft fist and brought it up to his mouth.

"*Via con Dios*, Ricky," he said almost reverently.

The young man returned with a bath towel and handed it to Sandy. He wrapped it around Caridád and slowly helped her to her feet.

"Will you excuse me, please?" Caridád said haltingly.

Raúl turned his head slightly as she spoke but didn't watch her leave.

He stood and turned to Sandy.

"What happened here?"

Sandy looked away.

"When I walked in, he had a knife. Caridád was naked on the floor. He was acting crazy, Raúl. He kept saying her that he was going cut her. She was all beat up. He wouldn't listen, he was acting crazy. And he was gonna kill her, Raúl."

"So I shot him."

Raúl waited for Sandy to look him in the eye.

"Did you have to kill him?" he asked, repressing his rage.

"I told you, man, he wouldn't stop coming! I hit him twice but he kept raising the knife. What did you want me to do, let him cut her up first?"

"What were you doing here?"

"I was heading to the Sox game tonight. I knew that all the deliveries hadn't gone out yet so I stopped by to check on things. I knew Caridád was here and I was worried."

Raúl walked up to Sandy and looked hard into his eyes.

"Why were you were worried about her?" he asked deliberately.

Sandy made eye contact with him. He figured now was as good a time as any.

"I was worried," he said softly, carefully choosing his words, "because I'm not sure she's always got your back, Raúl."

Raúl's eyes flared.

"Now, why would you think that, Sandy?"

Sandy wouldn't back down.

"Just a feeling I've been getting lately, that's all. Nothing more, just a weird feeling."

"So," Raúl continued, "was that the same feeling you had the other night when you disappeared on me? You know, when I needed you? When your number was the last one those mutts called, those niggers sitting on the house just before the Feds showed up? Or was it over the last couple of days when I didn't hear a fuckin' word from you?"

Raúl had caught him by surprise.

"Tell me, Sandy, just what kind of feeling was it you were having then?"

Sandy took a breath and decided to come clean.

"Look, Raúl. A few weeks back, I got approached by a guy who wanted to know if I was interested in getting into the business. I wasn't sure what he was talking about but, to be honest with you, I'm getting tired of the hauling. I decided I wanted to have something for myself."

Raúl seemed less than understanding.

"Just as a sideline, ya know, to start," he quickly corrected himself.

"Why didn't you come to me?" Raúl demanded.

Sandy stepped away.

"Because I wanted to *get* it by myself. Christ, I've always depended on you, Raúl, and you've always looked out for me. But I guess I just wanted to feel what is was like to step out on my own."

Raúl remained unsympathetic.

"Anyway," Sandy continued, "it was just a few small shipments to start, nothing big. I didn't want you to think that I was interested in cutting into your business. I just wanted something for myself. That's all, Raúl, I swear to you!"

"So what was with the mutts on the street outside the house?"

"I don't know nothin' about them, Raúl, I swear!"

"Sandy, they had your fuckin' number in their cell!"

"I can't explain that, they had to get it from someone else. I promise you, Raúl, I never gave it to anyone like that! I never would! Why would I? I don't do business with those guys! I swear to you! If you want, I'll find out. I want to know, too, believe me."

"Look, Raúl," Sandy continued in his defense, "whatever you're thinking, you can't think that I would ever turn on you. You're my brother, for Christ's sake!"

He corrected himself.

"You're *more* than my brother. Shit, you were like father to me. You're my family, Raúl, I could – no, I would – *never* turn on you. I'd just as soon have my balls cut off than do that to you!"

Raúl pulled a switchblade from his back pocket and snapped it open. He pointed it toward Sandy and, without changing expression, stared a hole right through him. He motioned to Sandy to take it.

Sandy gulped hard and reached out for the blade. He felt the long, thin, razor sharp edge rest in his sweaty left hand.

But Raúl did not let go. Instead, Raúl wrapped Sandy's fingers wrapped around the blade then reached around and grabbed him around the neck. With a vice-like grip, solid and strong, he pulled Sandy to him. Sandy felt a sting run across his shoulders. Raúl's eyes grew large and his expression became noticeably more intense.

He spoke softly but firmly.

"Sandy, you are my brother. You are my family. And I have trusted you with my life and my livelihood. But if I ever learn that you've lied to me…"

Sandy swallowed hard, blinking constantly as Raúl glared deeply into his eyes.

"…your balls will be the least of your concerns!"

He squeezed Sandy's neck, leaned forward and kissed him hard on the cheek. As Raúl released his grip, he pushed him away. As Sandy stepped backward, he let go of the knife's blade. He looked down and saw the trail of blood the length of his palm.

He never felt a thing.

Raúl reached down and took Sandy's hand.

"Have Caridád take a look at that. See what she can do. Then tell her I want to see her."

Sandy nodded, then started to turn away. Raúl squeezed his hand shut to get his attention one more time. He watched Sandy flinched from the pain. His expression hadn't changed. He *wanted* to see the young man he had literally saved from a life of living out of dumpsters and hustling losers on the street. He *wanted* to see the good-looking kid his sister Teresa had grown so close to. Or maybe the half-brother he'd loved and trusted, the one he had taken under his wing and taught the business.

His instincts told him otherwise.

Raúl lean forward and whispered into Sandy's ear.

"We'll take care of things here," Raúl said softly, "you'd better get going…"

He smiled as Sandy looked uncomfortable.

"You're gonna be late for the game…"

*　*　*

Detective Colavito jogged deliberately down the final flight of stairs on his way past the desk sergeant. He checked his watch. It was almost ten minutes past 8:00 PM. Kavenaugh's was a good ten, maybe even a fifteen, minute cab ride away. And the Friday night traffic wouldn't be cooperating. He thought about grabbing the El as he worked his way through an earlier than usual weekend crowd headed toward lockup. It seemed the heat always brought out the absolute worst behavior in the animal kingdom.

His fought off a widening grin as he walked out into the muggy evening and down the decrepit concrete steps. While he was actually quite pleased with himself and the performance he'd just left behind, he knew a long road lay ahead. True, the IAD meeting had gone better than he had hoped. Nothing they asked was all that unexpected. And they seemed comfortable with his explanation about the trooper from the second car on the scene that night almost three months ago. They did press him about what he saw, what his report had said about how that lone trooper had ended up with a knife through his throat. He did his best to clarify what he'd written without contradicting himself. The PBA suit had hardly been a wellspring of support but he had succeeded in reminding Bobby about that.

If the committee's tone was any indication, they appeared satisfied with Bobby's explanation: the trooper had been attacked from behind and that he never saw it coming. Bobby's account implied that the trooper apparently stumbled onto something suspicious that spring night. A deserted stretch of highway, a guy with a knife, a broken down van. Not much of a surprise there. When Bobby killed the man responsible for the trooper's death, they were comfortable he had no choice. That much seemed clear.

They were less comfortable with Bobby's explanation on how he found himself there in the first place, though. Bobby sensed they didn't seem completely sold. He knew to keep it simple. The less complicated now, the less to trip over later. His story about being with his bartender girlfriend in Morris – a woman whose first name he had trouble enough remembering let alone her last one – made sense enough to them. It just seemed a bit too coincidental, that's all. Perhaps even a bit too neat. Still, they had nothing to say it was otherwise. Besides, she'd been so high that night, she'd have sworn the Pope himself was in bed with them if Bobby had said it was so. He left them little room to work with.

He'd learned a long time ago it was always best, when leading superiors to water, to let them think it was their idea to stop for a drink.

But the reality was it had been too close for Bobby's comfort. It was a combination of bad luck and carelessness that created a situation that almost got away from him. The trooper was uninvited and the goddamned *carroñeros* panicked. Simple as that. Once the trooper lay there dead, Bobby knew he needed a body to go along with that knife. A dead assailant closed the loop. The killer's cell phone confirmed he was Bobby's contact. Which meant the knife-happy idiot's companion would conveniently play the role of sacrificial lamb. The *carroñeros'* Joliet connection provided the plant, a boosted, aging and broken down Dodge Caravan that Bobby's report would identify as the killer's vehicle. And, when the dust had literally settled on the side of the road, the story played itself out. The *carroñeros* left with his intended cargo, Bobby'd dropped himself a cop killer and his lucrative if part-time income stream remained uninterrupted.

The IRB would eventually rule it a good shoot, a clean shoot. And their report recommended that Bobby receive a commendation for heroism in the line of duty.

The man was nothing if not good.

He walked across the sidewalk and decided against the El. He'd catch a cab and get there when he'd get there. He stepped out between a row of parked squad cars and began hailing a taxi that was just coming toward him. He hurriedly opened the back door as it came to a stop and got in. The driver waited a moment for a couple of passing cars as Bobby gave him the address. He felt his cell phone vibrate. He pulled it from his back pocket and flipped it open to find one missed call. A couple of keystrokes later, he was listening to Special Agent Cauldwell's voice mail message. He glanced back toward the stationhouse as the cab slowly began to pull away.

"Change of plans. Vietnam War Memorial. Wabash and Wacker. On my way."

He deleted the message and flipped the phone shut as he gave the driver the new location.

Traffic was pretty much as expected. Bobby exited the cab on Wacker and State Street at 8:30 PM sharp. The last remnants of the evening's sunset gave the city's skyline an almost surreal glow. As much as he would often bitch about it, it still was a beautiful city. He slammed the car door behind him hopped onto the alley-wide sidewalks that lined the river at street level. He turned and entered the park off of State Street. He skipped quickly down the concrete steps.

Vietnam Veterans Memorial Plaza was uniquely designed. It was intended to be a showcase for the city and, as such, was situated on the Chicago River along Wacker Drive with its picturesque drawbridges that span the river's run from Lake Michigan west to its North Branch. Architects visited cities from Pittsburgh to San Antonio to San Diego to give them the kind of perspective necessary to develop the plaza and the riverwalk it served to feature. Located at river level where Wacker Drive curls toward intersecting Michigan Avenue, the Memorial could be seen from the far west end of both sides of the river.

Bobby was no stranger here. He would come here from time to time. But not because he knew anyone who served in that war. And not because it brought him some type of inner peace. No, he would visit whenever he needed to remind himself of how necessary sacrifice truly is in this life, both the kind of sacrifice he'd willingly offered in the desert as well as that which he'd made on behalf of those who were not as willing.

As he reached the plaza, he immediately looked his right. A wall of falling water cascaded down inside a niche, recessed almost a foot inside the concrete wall. Dusk brought floodlights highlighting the water's constant flow down the inner wall. It emptied into a large rectangular pool lying lengthwise a few feet in front of it. Displayed inside the niche, in front of the falling water, was a large stone replica of the Vietnam service medal. A suspended horizontal bridge of black granite ran the length of the wall and across the open niche. The names of just under 3,000 Illinois veterans were carved in it, chronologically by the year in which they fell serving their country. POW-MIA's were listed according to the date they went missing.

A solitary man stood just to the right of the date "1975", his head bowed.

At the foot of the wall was an engraved timeline. It identified significant and critical battles involving both U.S. and North Vietnamese military operations as well as world events that help shape the war's ultimate conclusion. Inside the large rectangular pool was a fountain containing fourteen jet sprayers that would gradually rise in height, each in turn, signifying the varying levels of U.S. troop involvement in the war. Bobby was barely one year old on April 30, 1975. The Fall of Saigon would never mean to his family what it had meant to so many others. Some of his childhood friends had fathers or uncles that served. And so many people found the war to be such a waste.

But not Bobby. He learned from the sacrifice of so many others that, as necessary as war might be, as George C. Scott said in "Patton", wars weren't won by dying for your country. They were won by making the other poor dumb bastard die for *his* country! A lesson he made certain would not be lost during his three tours in Iraq.

He walked slowly past the fountain toward the river's edge. Large expanses of grass on sloped hills flanked him. To his left, the lawn was separated by a wide ascending walkway for handicap accessibility, sloped from the street to the riverwalk. To his right, the lawn ran downhill from the street into the plaza. Large landscaping timbers formed three walls almost six foot high, creating natural breaks maybe three foot wide in the hill where people could stand or sit. Despite being a warm summer Friday evening, it was sparsely populated.

Bobby got to the wrought iron fencing overlooking the river and turned to take a seat at one of the concrete tables that adorned the riverwalk. His attention focused again on the solitary figure that hadn't yet moved, still standing before the expanse of black granite and the thousands of names it held.

He couldn't help but wonder.

"Long time no see, Bobby," a familiar voice said quietly.

FBI Special Agent Marc Cauldwell had approached without a sound, the allergy medication he'd taken just a couple hours before having just kicked in. His suit jacket was slung over one shoulder, his white shirtsleeves rolled up to his elbows. The loosened knot in his predominantly red paisley tie, though clashing with his hair, was at least celebrating that Friday night had finally arrived. He extended his hand, which Bobby accepted graciously if not enthusiastically.

"Same here..." Bobby responded using a similar tone though intentionally not using his name.

"How ya' been?"

"Fine," Bobby replied, ready to get down to business. "I'm hearing you've made a connection between the two crime scenes."

"What, no chit-chat, Bobby? No catch-up time?"

Bobby's dull expression didn't change. He waited for Cauldwell to get on with it.

"Whaddya say we take a walk," Cauldwell suggested.

"Whaddya say you give me what you got?"

"I'm not sure you understand, Bobby. It's not quite that simple."

Bobby's body language expressed contempt for Cauldwell's excuses.

"I'm serious, Bobby, I've got to have a better reason than simply looking to bring in an ol' Army buddy in as a local LEO consultant..."

Bobby's steely glare stopped Cauldwell's sarcasm in its tracks.

"Ol' Army buddy?" Bobby remarked sarcastically. "Go fuck yourself."

"Say what you want, Bobby, my ass is hanging out on this one. I've got four murders to solve here and..."

"Four?" Bobby asked incredulously.

"...yeah, four."

Bobby then nodded his agreement.

"Whaddya say we take that walk now?"

Special Agent Cauldwell turned and started up the riverwalk as Bobby twisted out of his seat. They walked slowly back in the direction where the sun was last seen.

"Talk to me, Cauldwell. How do you count four?"

"You heard me right," Cauldwell said confidently. "We've got two crime scenes here, Bobby, both of which we are now convinced are related. The one you already know about..."

Bobby looked up at him as if to say he should choose his words carefully.

"...the one on I-80 a couple of nights back, Tuesday night, if I'm not mistaken. State Police found the body of a young Hispanic male, early twenties, in a ditch along the roadside with five bullets in the back of his head, execution-style. Ballistics has matched the rounds to a Beretta Tomcat 32 Automatic."

Without looking up, Cauldwell dropped the first shoe.

"You wouldn't happen to have had access recently to a Beretta Tomcat 32 Automatic, by any chance would you, Bobby?"

Bobby failed to find the humor in Cauldwell's typically shortsighted efforts at being funny. He continued.

"We got lucky there, too. There'd been no rain and very little wind the last couple of days. We were able to match tire tracks left at the scene directly across from where the body was found to a van located early the next morning on the southwest side. The same van, as it turns out, in which Special Agent Carmen Eyas was found murdered. There was also the matter of her blood. It was found at the I-80 crime scene as well, though not much good for DNA analysis. The kicker was we found pieces of gravel embedded in the back of her head, her matted hair, gravel which matches size and type from that scene. It seems they excavate that shit from a unique quarry somewhere in Indiana. Who knew?"

He had Bobby's attention.

"Nothing conclusive but certainly more than coincidence."

Cauldwell was feeling very comfortable all of a sudden.

"We may also have gotten lucky another way. We're thinking that maybe one of our perps got sick there as well. Maybe someone not used to killing…"

Bobby looked up quizzically.

"…We found traces of vomit in the ditch near the body. Good thing whoever it was got as sick as they did. Turns out, because it's been so dry, we were still able to get a good DNA sample. We'll know soon enough if it belongs to our dead spic in the ditch."

Bobby turned back toward the river. *Fuckin' Snake-Eyes! Another loose end.*

Cauldwell wasn't finished.

"We got a tip about a safe house being used for running illegals, sort of a drop off point used as a clearinghouse of sorts. We think they would come in large groups of ten or twelve, then stay there until they can be shipped out. It usually works pretty quickly. They're typically not there for more than twenty-four hours. So we moved on it. When we got there, we didn't find any illegals but there were two as-of-yet unidentified black males, also early twenties, with assorted gang tattoos. We haven't come up with a credible theory as to why they were there. Both were shot multiple times, though not with a Beretta Tomcat 32 Automatic – you know, the one you *don't* have? – "

Bobby ignored him, too interested in every word he was saying to indulge in a battle of wits, especially with an idiot like Cauldwell. That time would come later.

"– and their knee caps were broken. Has all the earmarks of torture though, over what, we don't yet know. We discovered a wet spot on the concrete floor in the garage. Assuming somebody didn't get laid there –"

Bobby didn't react, finding another of Cauldwell's ill-timed attempts at humor anything but funny.

"C'mon, that was a little bit – ok, ok. We found a similar spot under the white van some blocks away, the one our agent was found in. Preliminary analysis results indicate a similar coolant-to-water ratio. Again, nothing conclusive but too coincidental to ignore. We honestly don't expect anything more conclusive when the final results come in although I'm told that there's a lot of cool shit they can come up that might just tie those spots to that white van's coolant system. Forensics hasn't finished testing the I-80 crime scene but, if we find coolant there, it wouldn't surprise us."

Bobby kept listening.

"Fuckin' technology, Bobby... Isn't this shit amazing?"

"So," Special Agent Cauldwell summarized, "we've got a stiff spic on I-80 outside of Joliet, two dead home boys in a safe house on the southwest side and one dead special agent in a van we can assume if not positively conclude was at both crime scenes. Let's see, you might wanna check my math but I think that adds up to four."

Bobby was hardly amused.

They had walked up the ramp to State Street, turned around and headed back down the riverwalk toward Lower Michigan Avenue.

"Any leads?" Bobby inquired.

"Nothing serious, no, not yet, but we've got plenty of theories."

Cauldwell stopped for a moment to blow his nose. The antihistamine was wearing off early again.

"One of the strongest comes from our dead agent herself. She was working undercover on a human trafficking ring running illegals across the border for sale into the sex trade. She was wearing a GPS located device at the time she was murdered. In fact – I think I may have left this part out – the device was somehow turned off. We found it on the front seat on the driver's side. We're thinking it fell out of the pocket of whoever had it. I mean, seriously, what kind of moron would leave something like that behind? Especially since we were able to lift a couple of partials. Haven't gotten a hit yet."

"Were they clean?"

"Yeah, it appears we got a good thumb and index finger though how much of a point match we'll eventually get is anybody's guess. The GPS does have her body in the vicinity of that neighborhood when the signal stopped."

"In the vicinity? I thought these things were accurate within feet…"

"Typically they are but Special Agent Eyas was murdered with her own knife."

Ahhh, the knife. Bobby listened carefully.

"It was a fatal abdomen wound. And whoever killed her took the time to unload five rounds into the back of her head, probably trying to make it look like the same execution routine to kill the chico in the ditch. The problem for the GPS was that the blood and stomach contents, particularly stomach acid, exited from the wound and eventually worked its way into the device's battery. The transmission's signal was intermittent for a time until it either shorted out or was turned off. But the lab's still working on that angle. At some point, we're thinking we'll be able to trace her exact whereabouts over her last twelve-to-eighteen hours. Once we get that far, the rest of it should fall into place."

Bobby'd heard all he needed to hear.

They stopped walking and ended up back where they'd started. Cauldwell stood leaning up against the wrought iron fence looking out over the Chicago River. Bobby sat on top of one of the round concrete tables.

"I need two things," he said looking directly at Cauldwell. "I need to be kept in the loop on this investigation – the *entire* investigation –…"

Cauldwell dropped his chin. A smirk grew across his face as he shook his head.

"…and I need access to all the evidence reports as well as the physical evidence."

Cauldwell politely waited for Bobby to finish his speech.

"That's just not going to happen, Bobby, I can tell you right now. Even if I wasn't lead investigator on this case, the best I can probably do is to keep you *unofficially* in the loop on the investigation. I can maybe make the case to my superiors for using a CPD liaison if we can play up the whole trafficking angle. Which could possibly include evidence reports, too, but…"

Bobby waited for the other shoe to drop.

"…there is no fuckin' way I can get you authorized access to the physical evidence, Bobby. That's just not going to happen."

"Perhaps you didn't hear me, Special Agent Cauldwell."

"I heard you just fine," Cauldwell responded. "Perhaps I didn't speak clearly?"

"I'm not sure you understand, Marc."

Cauldwell knew what was coming. He smugly invited Bobby to continue.

"Please, Bobby, enlighten me."

Bobby turned his head and looked out across the river. He spoke in a voice that was strong, clear and firm.

"I know where the bodies are buried," he said cryptically.

Feigning interest, Cauldwell responded.

"What bodies are those, Bobby?"

"The ones you and your *unofficial* investigation had me bury in the desert, Marc. You remember, outside of Abu Ghraib?" Bobby said with emphasis.

"Bobby, now listen, I –"

"Shut the fuck up, Special Agent Cauldwell, it's my turn now."

Cauldwell turned and stood half-bent over the fence looking out at the river.

"Please, continue, Detective," Cauldwell said formally, already preparing his response.

"You and I both know what happened out there. All those detainees your guys' thought might have had something to do with 9/11? Or who you thought maybe *knew* guys who were in on 9/11? Or who you thought maybe *knew* guys who might have *known* guys who were in on 9/11? Christ, man, don't stand there bullshitting me! It was the very goddamned rationale for invading that fuckin' hell hole in the first place!"

Cauldwell shifted a bit uneasily, wondering if anyone else was listening. Bobby was just getting warmed up.

"What was the euphemism that your DOJ lawyers came up with to get around the Geneva Convention? You remember, don't you, Marc? To get around calling it torture? Oh yeah, right... 'enhanced interrogation techniques'... I'm just wondering, Special Agent Cauldwell, do you have any *official* memory of that? Any *official* memory of the information you demanded we get from those mutts? Any *official* memory of the screaming and the blood and the broken bones and the dimming lights? And, of course, you wouldn't have any *official* memory of all those midnight runs we made into the desert to dump all those mutilated bodies."

"I don't have any recollection –," Cauldwell responded confidently, "official or otherwise – of the incidents to which you are referring. And, in case you hadn't been made aware – officially – neither the Bureau nor any of its agents nor any of its authorized or designated personnel ever set foot in Iraq."

He spoke like he was testifying before a congressional subcommittee.

"Besides," Cauldwell added, "even if the Bureau *did* have occasion to visit Iraq, or any other Middle Eastern country for that matter, for any reason, officially or otherwise, it would have done so in compliance with its law enforcement responsibilities and obligations under the PATRIOT Act in its legally constituted pursuit of individual terrorist suspects, suspected independent terrorist cells or groups with established ties to official terrorist organizations in order to infiltrate, disrupt and preempt their collective efforts at designing, developing, implementing and executing acts of criminal terrorism against the United States or its territories."

Bobby was amazed at how mechanical yet fluid it all sounded. He'd obviously been practicing that recitation for some time.

"In addition," Cauldwell concluded, "in the unlikely event that anyone associated with Bureau *had* visited Iraq, or any other Middle Eastern country for that matter, they would have done so with the expressed and prior approval of and in total compliance with the Secretary of Defense and his initiatives in the best interest of national security which are wholly consistent with the specific direction given by the President to the Department of Justice."

Bobby dropped his head and shook it slowly.

"I'm betting that spin might play well with your bosses at the DOJ or even your sympathetic local news coverage. And who knows how it will sound should you end up on CSPAN during one of those dog-and-pony show hearings. But, at the end of the day, when all the corpses had been buried, you and I both know about the covert black ops you conducted there and the 'enhanced interrogation techniques' you guys had us use."

Cauldwell interrupted him.

"The operative word there, of course, being 'us'."

Bobby stood up and leaned across the wrought iron fence next to Cauldwell. He spoke softly.

"You dumb sonuvabitch. You think this whole torture thing is all I got?"

Cauldwell swallowed slowly and looked down into the dark water flowing smoothly west.

"And by that you would mean?"

"It seems the black market was good to you while you were *officially* not there."

He turned and looked at Bobby's bowed forehead. Now he had Cauldwell's attention.

"You want to tell me what the hell you're talking about?"

Bobby looked up without changing expression.

"I'm told you like young girls, Marc, particularly young Middle Eastern girls."

Cauldwell suddenly didn't like where this was headed.

"I don't have the first clue what you're talking about."

"Really?" Bobby continued. "Then I guess I must have you confused with someone else, Marc. It seems someone who looks a helluva lot like you – and who not so coincidentally works for the FBI – spent the latter part of 2004 and the early part of '05 in Baghdad during the height of the Sunni insurgency pursuing some rather creative black market opportunities."

Cauldwell's body language began to sound retreat.

"Yeah," Bobby self-assuredly continued, "it seems your affinity for the fairer, and somewhat *younger* sex, was – how shall I put this delicately – not subject to your usual degree of discretion."

"Just spit it out, Colavito, just say what you came here to –"

Bobby raised his head and looked directly at Cauldwell.

"I know about your involvement in trafficking Iraqi immigrants during the insurgency. And I know that you weren't doing it to satisfy some overwhelming humanitarian impulse you had. The people you worked with, Marc, sold women, children, even entire families, into slavery. They didn't emigrate to Jordan or Syria or Egypt or Palestine or any fuckin' where else. They were bought and paid for – and you helped deliver them!"

Cauldwell stood there, stunned that Bobby could possibly know any of this.

"And *you* knew all about it," he said in slow, long syllables.

Cauldwell shifted uncomfortably and went back to gazing out into the river.

"And not only did you know about it, Marc," Bobby continued, "you *personally* profited from it. And not just financially, I might add."

Cauldwell shot a look of disbelief at Bobby.

"Yeah, I know about that, too, Marc."

Cauldwell started to speak. Bobby interrupted him.

"And before you tell me about how this is all one man's word against another, you should know I have something a bit more convincing."

Cauldwell simply could not believe what he was hearing.

"Of course, I have access to some of the lowlifes that acted as your pipeline over there. I have bank records, wire transfers, account numbers. I have it all. But then…"

As if it could possibly get any worse.

"…there's the matter of those videos. DVD's actually, a couple of them." Bobby couldn't hide his smugness. "The sound quality is actually quite good. And the reproduction amazing clear. Like you said, Marc…"

Cauldwell looked at Bobby and didn't have to ask.

"…that technology shit is amazing stuff. Don't you think?"

Cauldwell offered no response.

"Actually, it's kind of like your greatest hits, Marc, a trilogy of sorts. I have you working a suspect employing those 'enhanced investigation techniques' that your heroes at the DOJ so patriotically embrace. Like I said, the quality is amazing; chilling, actually. I don't know the name of that fuckin' contraption you guys shoved those mutts into but I think, if you look closely, you can almost watch one guy's vital organs fail! I can still see the blood dripping out of his nose, his mouth… and his ears! Jesus! The poor bastard was even bleeding out of his eyes!"

Cauldwell could do nothing but listen.

"But that's just for appetizers. I also have you at various meetings with some rather sinister looking fellows, all of whom have been tied, *unofficially*, of course, to human trafficking and the sex trade, both before and after Saddam, with ties throughout the Middle East."

"And, finally, for dessert, what collection of your greatest hits would be complete without something bordering a bit on the risqué, perhaps dare I say pornographic? Assuming, naturally, that it doesn't constitute rape. Young women, Marc, who not only appear to be well below the age of consent. In some of the more graphic scenes, they don't appear to be very consenting at all…"

Cauldwell was in a state of shock.

Bobby let the moment sink in for a few seconds.

"…And then, of course, there's the matter of that journalist."

* * *

Chapter 7

ALEX MONTONEROS SWUNG her leg around and rolled over onto her side across the queen-size bed. She briefly opened her eyes, long enough to realize she was not waking up this Saturday morning in the second bedroom of her friend's Gold Coast apartment. She brought her hand to her head, which was, fortunately, no longer pounding though the remnants of a headache still lingered. Her eyes darted around the parts of the room she could see from where she was laying.

She slowly turned back over, propped herself up on her elbows and looked around through disheveled hair to find completely unfamiliar surroundings. Then she noticed the stationary bike standing next to her side of the bed.

"Who the fuck rides a bike in their bedroom?" she mumbled to herself.

She sank back into the goose-down pillows and tried to rationalize what little she could remember must have happened last night.

She opened her eyes and stared up at the ceiling, wondering what he – Christ, she couldn't even remember his goddamned *name*! – must be expecting this morning!

"Seriously?!?" she said out loud to herself. "Are you fuckin' *kiddin*' me?"

She heard a gentle knock on the closed bedroom door.

"Yeah?" she regretfully said.

Jack opened the door and brought with him a tray on which sat a hot cup of coffee, and two cups, one with a spoon containing sugar, the other a glass of skim milk.

"Good morning," he said as he stood inside the shadows cast by the morning sun through the windows above the bed.

She quickly checked to see what she was wearing.

"Not to worry," Jack said, almost chuckling, "you're fine. It's an old work-out shirt of mine. It's all I could find in the dark last night."

In the dark? Last night? *SHIT!*

She looked down and realized her sleepwear consisted of a heavy, though surprisingly soft, faded blue men's large sleeveless tee-shirt with the worn letters "FBI" emblazoned across the chest.

"Workout shirt?" she asked suspiciously.

"Don't worry," he responded, "it's clean!"

Alex smiled and ran her hand through her hair, removing the unruly soft strands from in front of her face.

"I don't remember how you like your coffee."

"Ummm, what is it?"

"Starbuck's Morning Blend. I thought you mentioned last night it was one of the things you actually missed when you were traveling outside the States."

She eyed the two containers, which actually appeared to be souvenir cups from, if the message they sported could be believed, Wrigley Field.

"Ok, so, what's in the cups?"

Jack looked down and, without apology, said proudly, "One's sugar, the other one's milk, actually."

"And those were the only containers you had?" she asked cutely.

"Hey," he responded only half in jest, "do you always wake up with such an attitude? I don't usually provide such amenities like this, you know."

Alex retreated and sat up with the pillows propped up behind her back as Jack set the tray down in front of her. He sat down at the end of the bed facing her, pulling a bent knee up onto the comforter. As she carefully added a couple of spoonfuls of sugar she noticed there was no dairy creamer.

"May I have some of your milk?" she politely asked.

He'd just taken a sip but he offered it to her just the same.

"If you don't mind that I just drank from it."

"I've battled worse germs, trust me," she responded and proceeded to add the milk to her coffee. She stirred her coffee with the spoon then took a couple of long sips.

She had no sooner swallowed then she began to cough and gag.

Jack immediately reacted.

"Hey, you ok?"

With one hand covering her mouth, she set down her coffee. The expression on her face said it all.

"How old *is* that milk?" she asked.

"Oh, uhhh, well, it's not exactly regular milk," he acknowledged sheepishly.

"What the hell is this?"

"Well, it *is* milk," he said correcting himself, "but it's skim milk."

Alex feigned her outrage.

"You *are* kiddin' me, right? You spend the night with me and then give me coffee… with skim milk?"

He couldn't help notice how uncomfortable she seemed on that subject.

"Oh," he said, deflecting her tone, "and, by the way, I'm Jack, just in case –"

Alex giggled then lied to him for the first time – at least that she could remember.

"I know that!" she plainly insisted, "What, you think I wouldn't know the name of a guy I sleep with…" She waited a moment to try and spin the reality of her own words. "…after just meeting him on the street?"

"Of course," he said, graciously backpedaling, "and, yeah, about that…"

She pushed the hair back out of her eyes again and started to smile.

"…I didn't exactly spend the night with you. I mean, I guess I did technically but I actually didn't…"

Alex understood what he meant. She thought it was gallant. But she wanted him to finish, to make him say it. He fought off his shyness to look her directly in the eye.

"…what I mean to say is, I slept downstairs last night, on the couch."

"Hmmm, I see," she said slyly.

"Then, tell me," she continued, "if you slept downstairs, how did I end up wearing this?" dropping her chin to point to his workout shirt.

"Hey, I told you. It's not like I gave you something I sweated up yesterday!"

She nodded, acknowledging his accurate correction.

"Well, that's actually not quite true," he said turning away.

"What?" she said in mock horror.

"It's clean, it's clean," he said, smiling in retreat. "I promise!"

She just grinned in response.

"I will admit, though," he continued, "I did help you change – sort of – last night."

Her eyes widened playfully and she waited for his next excuse.

"I mean, I couldn't very well let you sleep in your clothes, especially after you kinda missed your mouth with those last couple of shots of tequila," he started to explain. "I mean, who wants their pillow smelling like some neighborhood cantina, right?"

Alex laughed. She had only a vague memory of that part of the evening. It was around then that the night's festivities tended to blend into one another. She pushed the cup of coffee across the tray and offered an observation as she awaited his explanation.

"Yeah," she responded, "I couldn't help but noticed my clothes are MIA."

"Hey, in my defense," Jack offered as he quickly realized he was undermanned.

He tried getting creative. He decided to start again.

"Ok, you know that baseball movie with Jimmy Fallon – you know, the guy from Saturday Night Live? –"

Alex's eyes widened as if he were telling her something she didn't already know.

"and Drew Barrymore where–"

She wondered where all this was going and how he'd explain her missing clothes. Jack noticed her reaction, that she was apparently neither an avid moviegoer nor – and this one really hurt – a baseball fan.

"Never mind, it's not important," he continued, "besides, other than the scenes shot at Fenway 'Pahhk'," – Jack paused to allow his best though still pathetic Boston accent to take full effect – "it really wasn't all that good."

She wore an expression of someone who wouldn't let him off the hook that easily. Realizing he was in over his head, Jack opted for surrender as the wisest course of action.

"I apologize, Alex, I really do," he offered, "and, yes, I did look but, in my defense, it *was* dark and –"

She smiled appreciatively, grateful that he'd noticed but more thankful he was the gentleman she wanted him to be.

"And, about what you saw?"

He was now officially embarrassed.

"Hey Alex, look," he said valiantly, "you're a very attractive woman. And I'm guessing I'm not the first guy to tell you that. I am sorry, though, it won't happen again."

He could tell he was right. She'd been told a lot.

"Promises, promises..." she kidded before flashing him a big smile.

"But I did only glanced!" he repeated. "And it was *really* dark!"

Alex relented, letting him up off the mat.

"…Ok, you're forgiven," she said, with a tone that offered more than absolution. "Now, about what we talked about last night."

Jack sat up.

"Yes, about last night," he repeated.

"Perhaps you could help refresh my memory just a little bit."

"How much do you remember?" Jack teasingly said.

"Some," she responded, "but, as evidenced by what you see here –," implying that, if her seminaked state failed to jog her memory, perhaps Jack would indulge her one more time.

He smiled and decided to tell her again for the first time.

"Ok, but, on the record or off?"

Alex dropped her chin with a "what kind of dumbass question is that?" look.

He cracked up.

"Ok, well, just one thing before we… you see, it's like this: With Jimmy – when I worked with him and others like him – I was always considered an anonymous source, an unnamed…"

She improved on her look but only slightly.

"…it's just that we've never worked together, Alex, and while think I can trust you – you worked with Jimmy and he never once let me down, even when –"

Now it was her turn.

"No worries, Jack…"

He loved the way she talked.

"…we're cool."

She'd covered this ground as a matter of course for years. But it was always good to get it out there.

"Ok, good. All right, well, I've got to give you a little background. Bear with me if you already know some of this."

"Thank you, I will." She smiled again as she pulled a pillow to her chest.

He took notice and stopped.

"I didn't want you to be distracted!"

He laughed and then began.

"Beginning in July 2003, Amnesty International starts publishing information it has claiming prisoners at Abu Ghraib are being subjected to abusive investigation techniques, including torture. Later that year, in October I think it was, the Red Cross begins making unannounced inspections of the prison and later submits reports to our Secretary of Defense that, essentially, confirm the abuses detailed by AI. It takes the Army until January 2004 to conduct a formal inquiry into the allegations."

Jack's years on the job seemed to instinctively take over.

"Fast forward three months to April 2004. Pictures from Abu Ghraib are splashed over every television screen and newspaper in the country if not the world. Credibly or not, the Administration – including the Secretary of Defense, the Chairman of the Joint Chiefs of Staff as well as the President – all claim this is the first time they've seen any of the photographs. Perhaps, not so coincidentally, a few days earlier – March 31 to be precise – the four contractors from Blackwater are murdered in Fallujah and their burnt bodies hung upside down from the bridge. Our immediate response is Operation Vigilant Resolve, launched by the Marines just days later, in what turns out to be a failed attempt to regain control over the city. Five days after the offensive begins, it is halted, largely due to political concerns. The result? The resistance learns a very valuable lesson. Armed and, more importantly, *organized* retaliation is shown to work against our forces."

"And, as a result, the Sunni insurgency is born."

"Ok," Alex responded listening intently, "some of that I knew, some I didn't, –"

"Ok, good. Now, it's during this time that I learned that the FBI had field agents *unofficially* in Iraq and, specifically, at Abu Ghraib."

"Really?" she reacted. "Hold that thought, I want to get my pad –" She started to climb out of bed.

"Wait, let me finish… we'll go over it all again for you to take notes."

She agreed then pushed herself back up against the down pillows behind her hips.

"Ok, so the FBI is in Iraq and, what's more, they're at Abu Ghraib. They're there to learn anything they can about terrorist plots being set in motion in the States or, just as importantly, isolated sleeper cells that may be waiting a call to kick an operation into gear. Problem is, to move things along, they've begun taking part in and, in some cases instigating, the officially acceptable 'enhanced interrogation techniques,' which now presents a somewhat unique problem."

"Why?" he rhetorically asks. "Because some of their suspects end up dead."

Alex became more interested as he continued.

"Some detainees died in the prison during interrogation, some on the way to being buried in the desert…"

"Being buried in the desert?" she interrupted to ask.

He simply nodded and continued.

"…and others were actually murdered after they brought them there."

Her mind was already working on different levels and at varying speeds.

"One of the field agents that was at Abu Ghraib – and, if my sources are anywhere close to accurate, at other documented retention centers in Iraq as well – was an FBI agent named Marc Cauldwell. I had just left a meeting with him yesterday afternoon when I ended up bumping into you at the Park."

He chose to leave out where he'd met Cauldwell that afternoon – or the reason why.

"Anyway, the group gets their fill of fun and sun in the Iraqi sand, realizes there really wasn't any real strategic importance – what in the trade they term 'high value targets' – or any significant degree of useable intelligence resulting from their time in Iraq and eventually decide to head home…"

"…except for…" she adds.

"Cauldwell!" they said in unison.

"You read my mind!"

Her eyes glistened in agreement.

"Didn't he call you just before we went to dinner?"

"Ahhh, you *do* remember something from yesterday, that's nice to he–"

Another look shot his way, more of a "screw you" this time, though.

He just grinned in response.

"Yes, that was him. Anyway, after the group went their separate ways, Cauldwell took his time coming home. I found out he spent some time in the Middle East. He meets with contacts in Egypt, Israel and Turkey as well as Kuwait and Qatar. He also travels through Europe, stopping in Italy, Romania and Kosovo, locations where the world would eventually learn are destinations for extraordinary rendition, CIA black-op prisons suspected terrorists were being shipped to."

"Right," Alex agreed, trying to ignore a sense of righteous accomplishment from knowing that she was an unnamed co-conspirator in helping the Washington Post publish their series of articles that first exposed the Administration's tactics.

"But here's the thing," Jack noted. "I found out he reached out to connections he'd made in Syria and Jordan, even Palestine, places where no such prisons exist."

"That's true," Alex said. "The CIA would be about as welcomed there as they would be in downtown Tehran."

Jack grinned almost knowledgeably.

"Why," she jumped, taking notice. "What do you know?"

He just laughed again.

"Nothing…" he said, then teasingly adding "…maybe later –"

"Be careful, Jack, I'll hold you to it."

"Anyway," he continued, "It turns out he wasn't alone. Other agents were making similar stops, some alone, some in small groups. Cauldwell eventually makes his way back to the States and is interviewed over a series of weeks by everyone from Homeland Security to CIA to the National Security Administration. Cauldwell is one of a number of agents who collaborates on a classified report that is provided to the deputy director of the FBI, L. Stephen Wallace, with the results of their investigations, who then submits a sealed copy of that report directly to the Attorney General."

"They left the Director of the FBI out of the loop?"

"From what I know, yes, it appears that way."

"Do you know why?"

"Why he was left out of the loop, you mean?"

She nodded.

"Yeah, I think so. Wallace went to law school with Anderson Colton Scott, Special Counsel to the President, and actually worked at Scott's firm for a while after graduating. The open secret across the Beltway was that Wallace was the choice from the President's inner circle for deputy director. I won't say he was promoted to that position to be the Administration's eyes and ears at the Bureau but –"

"Seriously?"

"Seriously, Alex," he responded. "The political shit that's infecting the Department of Justice – and the Bureau in particular – is beyond belief. Richard Nixon had nothing on these guys. I could tell you stories –"

The journalist in her felt a rush.

"I'd enjoy hearing them," she said with a proffering smile. "Maybe later?"

He smiled back, sort of.

"Anyway, now the Attorney General receives the sealed report. He realizes what's happened and immediately contacts Wallace for a sit-down outside of the office. He wants to assess the Administration's legal – and, perhaps more importantly, political – exposure. But he needs to do it carefully. The DOJ, at least under the Constitution –"

"That pesky thing," she sniped.

He grinned in agreement then repeated himself.

"The DOJ, at least under the Constitution, is supposed to be independent of the White House. And, thanks to Nixon and the Saturday Night Massacre, we all know what happens when that independence is compromised."

Alex now has the look of someone engrossed in a legal thriller.

"Given the Office of Legal Counsel's prevailing opinion on Common

Article III of the Geneva Convention…"

"…about torturing prisoners of war," Alex interrupted to confirm.

"…Yes, given that prevailing view, the Attorney General concludes that the Administration has a legal basis for claiming that the United States was neither liable for nor complicit in the FBI's sanctioned interrogations, official or otherwise, as conducted in Iraq. If Geneva doesn't apply, everything's cool, right? He also concludes that there could be no legal ramifications resulting from the fatalities that were reported as a consequence of those interrogations. But he isn't comfortable making that call all by himself. Maybe he knows the legal arguments were nothing but a minefield. Or maybe he just wants to know he has a chair waiting for him when the music stops. Who can say? Problem is, he also knows he can't involve the President directly with what he knows."

Jack waited a dramatic moment.

"So, what did he do?"

"So the Attorney General contacts Anderson Scott directly…" he said slowly.

"…the Special Counsel to the President." She completed his sentence again.

"Yes," he confirmed.

"Ahhh, very clever," she opined. "That way, the Attorney General could convey the report's contents to the President through Scott while the President and his advisors could consistently – and accurately – maintain the President had neither seen the report nor even heard of it."

"Exactly! Except…"

"Huh?"

"The sealed report is *never* opened!"

"What?"

He just nodded.

"To this day, to my knowledge, the seal on that envelope has yet to be broken."

"But, then how –"

"Because if they never read it, they can't be held liable for its contents. Remember what Howard Baker asked out loud about Nixon during the Senate Watergate hearings: 'What did he know and when did he know it?'"

Jack continued.

"If no one can testify that they opened or read the report, everything else is reduced to conversation and hearsay. And it gets better! The Attorney General intentionally chooses to tell the Special Counsel to the President about the FBI's time in Iraq. Why? Because he knows that once Anderson Scott informs the President, that conversation becomes –"

"…privileged communication," she said, again finishing his sentence.

"But not only as communication between a lawyer and his client…" Jack continued.

Alex leaned forward.

"Because Scott, smart lawyer that he is, maybe he brings Owen Sinclair, the President's National Security Advisor, into the loop. And should Sinclair have been the one to tell the President, Sinclair could ultimately claim that their conversation involved information pursuant to ultimately protecting the United States from acts of terrorism, affording that discussion protection as a matter of national security. You've heard of the State Secrets defense, right?"

She nodded.

"It's where federal courts have thrown out lawsuits because the information disclosed during a trial might threaten national security."

"And so it goes," he concluded.

Alex sat back, her beautiful green eyes alive at the titles of all the articles she watched dancing through her head.

"How do you know all this shit?" she asked, unsure she really wanted to know.

"I could tell you," Jack said with a wry smile, "but –"

"Ok, ok," she reacted, "so what do you need from me?"

Alex sat up and crossed her legs in front of her.

"I mean, why are you telling me all of this?"

Jack stood, straightened his lower back and walked around the end of the bed. He knew the powerful resource he had in Alex. And working a lifetime with Jimmy did nothing to dissuade him. But…

He turned and looked at her with an expression of growing mixed emotions.

"Ok, here's what I'm thinking," he started, "and you don't have to commit to anything now…"

She hardly had to hear anymore.

"I'm wondering if you might be interested in researching an article or two…"

Alex immediately thought "series"! Her head began calculating the possibilities. *Print would come first. The New York Times would be her preference but she'd talk to the Washington Post, the Boston Globe, Newsweek (but not the goddamned Journal, not a fuckin' chance!). That would lead to radio, to NPR, then to the networks, maybe even cable, to CNN, MSNBC, even – dare she dream? – Fox News! Christ, '60 Minutes' might even come calling. And she'd always had a crush on Lara Logan!*

She couldn't have cared less about the second shoe.

"…there's just one thing, though…"

"Hmm?" she murmured, still imagining the Times' latest counteroffer.

"...it's just that, well, Jimmy was one of my best sources in Iraq. He put me in touch with a lot of the Army grunts and people in the loop who very quietly pointed me in the right direction on a lot of this. He knew the dangers but he took precautions, he –"

"And you're telling me this because..."

"Because," he said, choosing his words carefully, "he ended up disappearing."

She looked at him with equal parts gratitude for his genuine concern and a "thank you very much, I'm a big girl, I can take care of myself."

"Seriously, Alex," he insisted, "these people are – they're very powerful men and highly connected, which makes them uniquely dangerous. What I'd be asking you –"

"Jack," she interrupted, bringing her slender legs to her chest and wrapping her arms seductively around them.

"I'm hungry... Why don't we talk about this over breakfast?"

She had trouble hiding her enthusiasm at any level.

"Where are you taking me?" she said with a precocious smile.

He relented with a smile of his own.

"You know," Jack offered in rebuttal, "I never had this problem with Jimmy."

"Really?"

"Yeah, really..."

"Well, maybe that's because he never looked this good in your tee-shirt?"

He laughed in agrement. Still, it didn't hurt to err on the side of caution.

"Now, I know you're supposed to be in Denver at the end of the month."

"Not to worry," she graciously responded. "I'm good. I don't need to be in Denver until the 25th, it's a Monday. Nothing ever happens the first day of the convention anyway so I've got some cushion. His acceptance speech isn't until that Thursday."

She looked at him as her eyes grew wide. She swung her long, muscular legs off of the bed and moved slowly if not invitingly between Jack and his stationary bike.

"So, I've got some wiggle room, Jack."

He couldn't help grinning at her double entendré. And he hadn't seen hips like hers in a very, very long time. He fumbled uncharacteristically to say anything at all.

"I, uh, just don't want to throw any kinks into your schedule, Alex, that's all."

She smiled appreciatively.

"Your're really too kind, Jack. But I haven't had any kinks in my schedule for some time," she said, her eyes twinkling. "I kinda miss them."

"I see," he said, smiling in return while he nodded without realizing it.

She stretched out her arms.

"Ok, how 'bout we finally start this day?" she offered. "And, in appreciation for this great story as well as your chivalrous behavior of last evening, I'll even let you take me some place out here to eat!"

"Well, I'm not much of a breakfast eater but, ok."

"Me neither," she said, "but I've *got* to get myself a decent cup of coffee!"

"Yeah, sorry about that. That wasn't the best idea I guess I've ever had."

"No, really, it's ok," she assured him. "I appreciate that you tried. It was sweet."

She looked back at the bike.

"How long you been riding that thing, anyway?"

"Quite a while now. Five, maybe six, years, maybe more."

She walked across the room and decided to investigate what appeared to be his walk-in closet. He turned and watched his tee-shirt, which barely reached the top of her thighs, move in ways he never considered possible. He couldn't take his eyes off the way she walked.

"How far you've gone?" Her voice was muffled as she spoke into the closet.

"I'm not sure," he said in a self-deprecating tone while trying to regain some measure of self-control. "Maybe 40,000 miles or so, maybe more, something like that."

She poked her head out.

"Seriously?"

The more she heard, the more she liked.

"You really should get out more!" He couldn't help but grin and agree.

"Jesus, you may've traveled almost as far as I have."

"Hardly," he said modestly. "But, even if I have, I'm sure your travels have been much more interesting."

She turned her attention back toward his wardrobe.

"Do you think you might have anything else I could wear, maybe something a little less conspicuous than an 'FBI' shirt?"

He happily noticed she seemed to be oddly at home.

"Sure."

"Ok, I'm going take a quick shower. You find me my underwear and my pants, wherever they are, and maybe the most innocuous shirt you can find in there, ok? Something to go with khakis would be nice."

"Innocuous, eh? Hmm, that might be a problem," he quipped.

"I'm sure you'll find *something*," she said.

She flashed him a dazzling smile then turned and walked toward the bathroom, crossing her arms in front of her and pulling the Bureau's sleeveless shirt up over her head. She stopped and stood facing the mirror that spanned bathroom's double sink vanity, the tee-shirt clutched to her chest, watching him still watching her. She smiled once more then, with a swing of her leg, used her foot to close the door between them.

He's seen enough – for now!

Jack could hardly believe what he was feeling. If he didn't know better, he'd have sworn he was alive again. For the first time in a very long time. The heartache and loneliness, the guilt and the hurt had all taken a back seat. At least for the moment.

He heard the water running and the shower almost immediately start up. He thought of finding her something more "innocuous." He started searching through his classier tee-shirts, such as they were.

He hadn't realized how much he missed feeling this good.

Suddenly, the bathroom door opened though only part way. Alex stuck her head out. Unashamedly, the tee-shirt was nowhere to be seen.

"Oh, Jack?"

He popped his head out of the closet, unable to hide his playful interest.

"Umm, why are you wasting my water?"

Alex responded with another playful "go screw yourself" expression.

"I'm, ahhh, just curious, Jack…"

He smiled back. "Uh huh, what?"

"I just looked out the window and, well…" She hesitated for a moment.

"Yeah?" he inquired.

"Where the hell are we?"

* * *

Father Michael Allen Crzyzewski ignored the creaking hinges as he pushed through the solid oak door leading out of the sacristy, just after 8:30 AM, on his way to the front of the altar. He genuflected reverently then walked around the skillfully handcrafted rectangular red oak and black walnut table where he had only minutes before completed celebrating another Saturday morning mass. He walked deliberately up the old marble steps into the sanctuary, stepped in front of the tabernacle and solemnly bowed his head.

His back to the rows of wooden pews silently lined up behind him, the forty-two year-old priest took five steps forward and stood solemnly before St. Jerome Emiliani Catholic Church's original marble altar, the very one where masses had been celebrated every Sunday since the parish was founded in 1933, that is, until the edicts of the Second Vatican Council were enacted during in the mid-1960s changed things forever. Father Mac, as he was affectionately known throughout the southwest side parish, set down on the altar the ciborium he'd just filled with unconsecrated hosts. He placed his hands together prayerfully and bowed his head once again. He then reached into his pocket and pulled out a small silver key from a ring of maybe half-dozen others and unlocked an ornately adorned door to the tabernacle, which was recessed into the stone wall that rose into the rafters behind the immense altar.

The heavy door opened slowly, revealing a vault-like interior. The opening was maybe 12" wide by 18" high and about 14" deep. He carefully placed the gold cup inside, reverently closed the door and locked it again. The unleavened round wafers, each a little smaller than a Kennedy half-dollar coin, were kept in the sanctuary's tabernacle for blessing during mass and distribution during Holy Communion. Attendance at both daily and Sunday masses had been steadily increasing over recent years. He was comforted to think that, where once the number of hosts he'd just secured inside the tabernacle would suffice for an entire week or more, now that same number would probably last only a few days.

St. Jerome's, like countless other Catholic parishes in Chicago, had undergone a seismic shift in recent decades. "White flight" – the choice of a growing number of white families to relocate from the city into the surrounding suburbs – had been a driving force behind the neighborhood's transition. The gradual supplantation of those families by minority populations – in the case of St. Jerome's, predominantly Hispanic – had brought with it an economic impact as well, one that had certainly made itself felt in the weekly Sunday collections.

But what the community lacked in financial resources they more than made up for in ways both large and small. The south side neighborhood had demonstrated, time and time again, a strength and devotion that Father Mac came to rely upon to provide all kinds of support beyond simply money. There was the time he had to turn away more volunteers than they could use to fix a leaky roof on the nearby rectory. Or the time he helped coordinate the tradesmen from the neighborhood's changing cultural mix when the parish grade school was in need of remodeling. Or even when it came to simply organizing schedules for those who took on the responsibilities for the church's ongoing maintenance. And given that the aging structure was approaching its' seventy-fifth anniversary, that was no small task by any measure.

And the community chose to invest more than their time and professional expertise in their church. Most of the supplies they used, from the roofing paper and shingles for the repair work on the rectory to the wallboard, paint, electrical and plumbing supplies necessary for remodeling the school, were either purchased with their own money or donated by area contractors. The neighborhood, even as it was changing, embraced their church as well as their spiritual leader. And, on occasion, even Father Mac was pressed into service, coaching the school's basketball team one day or helping with soccer practice the next. It was a constant source of wonder to him how the community refused to focus on what they didn't have. It always seemed they were simply too busy appreciating what they did. He'd given thanks every day since being assigned to this parish some twelve years ago.

Father Mac circled back around the sanctuary, genuflected once more in front of the aging wooden altar and was walking back toward the sacristy when he first heard what sounded like someone in the vestibule of the church. He turned and stood still for a moment. His first thought was for the donation box. Though the heavy metal box was securely fastened to the wall, a small padlock was all that prevented anyone from opening the slotted hinged top and taking what cash or coins had been donated. Seldom was there more than just a few dollars. And usually he remembered to check on it, especially after the larger gatherings, like Sunday morning masses. But last night, the community meeting ended late and he simply hadn't taken the time.

The meeting had been announced during the four Sunday morning masses in response to rumors, fueled by local news reports throughout the week, that the Archdiocese had recently included St. Jerome's school on its list of those to be closed at the end of the upcoming school year. In addition, the same local stations were reporting that the Archdiocese was about to pay out almost $13 million to settle lawsuits brought by victims of sexual abuse that had come to light during the ongoing scandal, including boys molested by a defrocked priest who had once ministered at the parish.

As Father Mac waited silently, a second sound, like someone moving around, bumping into something, echoed throughout the empty church. He looked up to the choir loft above the vestibule. The sound he heard could have been someone running up the stairs. Instead of returning to the sacristy, he walked quietly up the side aisle toward the church's front doors. He turned the corner into the large, open vestibule and walked over to the donation box.

It seemed undisturbed. He heard footsteps again, coming from upstairs. Exposed stairways were located at either end of the vestibule. He walked over to the staircase where he thought the footsteps had come from. Standing there for a moment, he saw no one. He started slowly moving quietly up the stairs.

It took only seconds for him to be at the top of the staircase. Eight rows of pews, each on descending steps, separated by three aisles comprised the choir loft. In the center, behind an aisle running the length of the loft behind the last pew, was the organ, which hadn't worked properly for some time. From where he stood, there was very little he could determine though a quick scan of the loft showed nothing out of place, nothing unusual. But he knew what he had heard. So he decided to take a seat and wait.

"I don't know how much time you have," he said in loud but non-threatening voice, "but I have all day."

His voice echoed throughout the church.

He waited a bit longer.

"If it's money you want, I don't have much, but I will give you what I have."

He waited again.

"All we want," a child's voice weakly responded, "is something to eat."

Father Mac smiled a sympathetic smile, then said, "Alright then, why don't you and your friend come on out so I can see you and we'll go get you something to eat."

Daniel raised his head slowly from the front middle pew and looked out. He recognized the collar Father Mac was wearing.

"Not to worry, son, you're not in trouble. I won't hurt you." His words were gentle and sincere. Daniel immediately began to feel at ease.

"Are you sure it's ok to come out?" he asked.

"Yes, son, it's alright. And, please, bring your friend."

His eyes remained focus on the priest.

"She's very tired. I think she's still sleeping."

Father Mac leaned forward from his seat in the last row of pews.

"May I came over and see if I can wake her?"

"Ok," Daniel said tentatively, "if you're careful…"

"I'll be careful," Farther Mac said. "Now, you stay where you are. I'm too old to be chasing you around the church, ok?"

"I will," Daniel said.

With that, Father Mac got up and slowly walked down the stairs leading to the front row of pews. He turned and saw the young boy sitting next to a young girl lying prone, lengthwise, across the wooden bench, one arm bent beneath her head. He walked toward Daniel and smiled softly.

"Good morning," he said quietly, extending his hand, "my name's Father Mac."

"I'm Daniel," he said, loosely shaking the priest's hand. He nodded toward Ana. "And this is Ana. I think she's still sleeping."

"It's very nice to meet you, Daniel. Ok, how can I help you and Ana?" he asked.

"We're just really hungry but Ana, I'm not sure she's feeling very well."

Father Mac sat down next to Ana and felt her forehead; she didn't seem warm.

"Let's see if we can wake her up," he said. He smiled again.

Daniel smiled back.

Ana stirred as Father Mac gently nudged her. Daniel was not nearly as patient.

"C'mon, Ana, wake up... the Father's here to help us."

Ana opened her eyes, uncertain of where she was.

"How are you, young lady?" Father Mac asked.

Ana struggled to sit upright.

"Who are you?" she asked in a weak voice.

"I'm a priest here at this church. You can call me Father Mac, all my friends do."

Daniel straightened up at hearing the good news and flashed a broad grin.

"We could sure use your help!"

Daniel and Father Mac helped Ana to sit up. She rubbed her head, then her eyes. Her neck and back ached from sleeping on the wooden pew.

"How long have you two been here?" Father Mac asked.

Ana started to respond but Daniel jumped in, anxious to answer his new friend.

"Just since last night. We saw all the people coming in so we followed them. We figured this would be a safe place to stay. You sure did talk a long time, though."

Father Mac grinned a bit as he ignored Daniel's commentary and focused instead on something else he heard.

"A safe place to stay? Why would you need a safe place to stay? Are you lost?"

"Well, kind of," Daniel replied.

"It's a very long story, Father," Ana replied.

"Well," Father Mac told them, "maybe we can talk about it, if you'd like..."

Despite just meeting them, he sensed something was very wrong.

"...But first, you're both hungry; why don't we go get some breakfast and then we can talk about it?"

Daniel's smile faded.

"We don't have any money for food."

"I see," said Father Mac said, appreciating his honesty.

"That's why I was trying to open the box. It said 'For The Poor' on it and, I figured, 'who could be poorer than us?' so I tried to open it but I couldn't."

Ana shot him a "you did what?" look.

"I understand," Father Mac replied.

"Well, it just so happens, I know of a place where we can all get something very good to eat and it won't cost us any money!"

Daniel perked up, as did Ana.

"Really?"

"Yes, really!"

Daniel's smile returned. Ana nodded her head reluctantly, wanting to believe she could trust the priest. At this point, she understood they were out of options.

Father Mac looked at Ana.

"Are you ok to walk? It isn't far."

Ana nodded her head while Daniel pulled at her.

"C'mon, Ana, we're going to get something to eat."

All Ana could do was try and smile agreeably.

A few minutes and a short distance later, Father Mac, Ana and Daniel walked up the concrete steps into a cozy three-bedroom brick bungalow donated by a parishioner's family for use as the parish rectory some two generations ago. Father Mac announced himself and his guests as they entered.

"Mrs. Lopez? Are you here, Mrs. Lopez?"

A thin, smartly-dressed woman, maybe in her late fifties, entered the foyer from the kitchen, where the aroma of a still cooking breakfast seemed to be everywhere. She greeted them with a big smile.

"Mrs. Lopez, I'd like you to meet my new friends, Ana and Daniel."

"Hello," she happily said in voice much stronger than she looked. She embraced them both as if they were her own.

"Mrs. Lopez, do you think we might have enough breakfast that we could share with these two hungry souls?"

Mrs. Lopez looked up at Father Mac and grinned expectedly.

"If we don't," she said, "we'll just make more."

Daniel's day was made. Ana simply smiled gratefully.

"Come, children, follow me, you can help me set the table," and, with that, Mrs. Lopez put her arm around Ana while Daniel skipped alongside her. She led them into a small dining room just off the living room where a fragrant centerpiece of freshly cut flowers from the garden out back invited them to get comfortable. Father Mac watched them from across the room.

And wondered.

Chapter 8

RAÚL STOOD IN the heat of the early morning sunrise in the kitchen across from where, not twelve hours earlier, Sandy had shot Miguel's cousin Ricky dead. His eyes traveled deliberately down the blood-soaked crevices between the unevenly laid linoleum squares, now stained distinctively darker than the rest of the floor, where the seventeen year-old's body had bled out. His mind spun furiously as his attention wandered away from the voice speaking to him on his cell phone. He turned, made eye contact with Miguel and noticed Sandy standing next to a sleep-deprived Caridád. He shut his eyes, mumbled something in Spanish then snapped his phone shut. He shoved it into his back pocket, stepped next to Miguel and turned toward Caridád to hear it all one last time.

"Now, tell me once more," he started, displaying the collected demeanor of a seasoned defense lawyer whose questions elicited only answers he'd expect.

"What happened to the girl and the kid?"

Caridád was uneasy, nervous, agitated. She didn't want relive it all again. The cuts on her face and forehead were a vivid red, raw and open. Her nose was still tender and sore, her cheek scraped and discolored, her lip swollen from Enrique's enthusiastic albeit necessary foreplay. She ached all over. It hurt to talk.

"I told you, Raúl," she said slowly. "They must've run away when Enrique –"
Her jaw stiffly resisted helping her mouth painfully form her words.

"...when he attacked me," she finished. "They must've heard him and ran out of the house when he..."

She paused to compose herself.

"...when he was – when he was attacking me."

Raúl watched her eyes as she spoke. She swallowed hard and gripped Sandy's hand behind her.

"I don't know where they went," she continued. "What more can I tell you?"

"They just ran out of the house," Raúl asked, his tone incredulous. "Just like that?"

Her body language added emphasis to her insistence.

"While Enrique was attacking you..." he repeated in a redundant monotone.

"Yeah, I told you," she insisted, "why is this so hard for you to understand, I–"

Ignoring her, he turned to see Miguel's reaction as suddenly, in a blur, the side of her face disappeared behind the back of Raúl's powerful open right hand, striking with such force that she felt the slight breeze it made before the inevitable pain screamed from the back of her neck down to the base of her spine. Twisting, she fell in an instant, banging the open wound on her forehead against the metal kitchen wall cabinet, creasing her face against its dull, exposed edge. She felt the moist trickle of blood beginning to drip inside her nose as her cheek quickly began turning deeper shades of crimson.

A stunned Sandy recoiled as the crusted dishes in the overloaded sink rattled with her shifting weight. Silverware spilled across the countertop behind her. She heard herself cry out, yet she could not feel herself making any sound. As she started falling forward, Raúl quickly reached toward her with his left hand. Wrapping it securely around the base of her throat, her soft skin succumbed quickly to the force of his grip. He felt the muscles in her neck tighten. He pushed her upright and, now with both hands, raised her by her throat until her feet left the floor. His dark green eyes were burning, fueled incessantly by the price her betrayal would now cost him.

He should have known better.

And there would be consequences now. As there should be. As there must be.

Stretching her neck required little of the strength in his muscular arms. Choking, feeling her throat tighten, she kept her eyes tightly close, desperately seeking to avoid looking at him. He slammed the back of her head against the cabinet once, then again, his teeth clenching with his effort. He vainly repressed his indignation now taking form with greater vengeance. She covered the grip of his hand with both of hers, instinctively reacting in a useless attempt to pry herself loose.

Miguel visibly enjoyed her struggle as her toes dangled above the floor.

She felt the sharp edge of the countertop scraping her, biting into the small of her back. Raúl's forearms finally began to quiver as his muscles tightened, his biceps spasming, knotting quickly, contracting and weakening his elbows. He suddenly released his grip on her throat, dropping her roughly to the floor.

Sliding, Caridád shrieked as her spine scraped the blunt, uneven edge of the countertop. She immediately reached for her lower back as her toes hit the floor, tripping her up. Losing her balance, she tried to catch herself from falling while reaching for her throat. Her cough was hoarse and constant, fueled by every breath she now felt lucky enough to draw. He reached down and twisted a knot in her hair. Her head snapped back with a sudden yank. She cried out as her neck cracked.

Raúl looked down, glaring at her. He released his grip as he shoved her against the nearest wall. He waited a moment, stepped back and took a breath.

"What have you done, Caridád?" he asked, his voice battling back against the raging emotions her treachery had unleashed.

He clumsily pulled her up by her left arm, jamming it up into her shoulder with such force that she again heard herself shriek in pain.

"I don't know what you mean, Raúl, I swear I –"

Her speech trailed off into an unintelligible mix of tears and convulsive breaths. He shoved her backwards into the wall so hard that the resounding thud drowned out any sound she'd made. Her body crumpled to the floor.

"I should have known better," he said, "than to think I could ever trust you."

Caridád remained slumped in the corner, her breathing stilted, her dead weight propping her up against the wall. A helpless calm started to settle over her, leaving her to wonder how long it would all take. How long it would finally all take.

"You've forced my hand, Caridád," he said, as if passing sentence. "You've left me with no other choice."

He coldly turned and motioned to an already grinning Miguel to help her up. Sandy stepped forward to reach her first but Raúl stopped him.

"Raúl," Sandy asked hopefully, "are you sure? I mean, –"

Miguel's head shot around as he held her up with both hands.

"Sandy, she used you, man," he said conclusively. "She used you to kill him."

Sandy looked at him disbelievingly.

"Don't you get it? She used you! Jesus, wake the fuck up, man!"

He looked to Caridád, thinking it couldn't possibly be true, that he couldn't have been that stupid. It was true he didn't completely trust her; he'd told Raúl that much. But Ricky was going to butcher her. He saw him raise the knife. He had to stop him. He had to shoot him. He had no other choice. Ricky was insane, he was acting crazy. He wouldn't listen. And he just couldn't stand there and watch him slice her up.

Even Raúl would've done the same thing.

It didn't make any sense. None of this made sense. Why would she…

"Raúl, man… this doesn't –" Sandy protested. "I mean, why would she –"

Raúl looked calmly at Sandy, wondering why he would come to her defense.

"Do you know who that was on the phone?" he asked rhetorically.

Sandy remained bewildered, saying nothing as Raúl answered his own question.

"It was Ricky…" he said.

Ricky? Huh? What?

Raúl pulled his cell phone from his back pocket and dialed his voice mail again.

"…or, more precisely, Ricky's voice. He left me a voice mail message yesterday afternoon," he said, "actually, he left two messages."

Raúl waited for Caridád to react. But she moved only to breathe.

"I didn't get them until a few hours ago."

Sandy waited to hear more. Miguel said nothing, just as Raúl had told him to.

"The first one he sent was about an argument he and Carlos had with Caridád about the girl and the boy, about where they were going, how they were being treated."

He turned to Sandy.

"I talked with Carlos a little while ago. It seems, for some reason, she suddenly became concerned about their safety."

Sandy still didn't understand where all this was going.

"But his second call," Raúl continued, "and you might find this particularly interesting, Caridád…"

Miguel had the look of the cat eyeing the canary.

"…he made standing right there," his head nodding toward the kitchen sink, "while he was bleeding out from the scissors he pulled out of his neck…"

Raúl looked down as Caridád slowly raised her head. Sandy listened in disbelief.

"…the same ones *you* stabbed him with, when you thought you'd killed him…"

She refused to even raise her head. He reached down, seized her jaw and harshly pulled it upward towards him. He looked directly into her eyes.

"…right after you took time to fuck him, that is."

Raúl tossed her head aside and reached for his cell phone. He pulled up Ricky's second message, turned on the phone's speaker and handed it to Sandy. Seconds later, they each listened as Miguel's cousin – his closest friend – eerily came back to life, the entire violent, deadly scene from the evening before unfolding all over again.

The young man's voice was hoarse, anguished and splintered. He was struggling for air as he fought to remain conscious. He spoke in short, broken words, trying to make sense, hoping Raúl could somehow still understand him. An abrupt, dull thud signaled he'd put down – or more likely dropped – his phone on the countertop.

Caridád's voice suddenly appeared. There was shouting, cursing, screaming then the distinctive sounds of a physical struggle. When she fell to the floor, the message recorded a solid bang. Ricky's voice became distant but more pronounced as he stepped away from the phone to approach her, the sound of rattling utensils resulting in the rusty butcher knife now in hand. There was more shouting, more cursing, more screaming…

And then they heard Sandy.

The shooting sounded like it happened just as Sandy said it had. Back and forth they yelled at each other, Sandy begging for him to stop while Ricky's vengeance chose to ignore him, a single murderous purpose racing through his mind, determined that if he was going to die because of her, she was damned sure going to die because of him. He was determined to exact his revenge. It would summon the strength he needed, be the reason he remained conscious; it was what now coursed through his veins instead of the blood that still flowed openly from his punctured carotid artery with every halted breath.

They waited as the last words Ricky spoke – "die, you fuckin' little bitch…" – were quickly punctuated by two sharp staccato pops.

Seconds of silence were followed by a deadening crash.

Sandy was stunned! *Could she seriously have set this whole thing up? Could she actually have planned to kill Ricky all along! It was the one sure way she could help them escape! And sunuvabitch if he didn't conveniently show up to finish the job for her!*

He looked at Caridád and couldn't believe she'd almost gotten away with it!

He cleared his throat as he looked at Miguel.

"So, what do you want we should do with her now, Raúl?" Miguel asked.

Raúl motioned to him. Miguel responded by pulling her roughly to her feet again.

Raúl was stone-faced as he stepped forward and placed his open hand against her cheek. She abruptly pulled away.

"I'm thinking we might still be able to make something out of this…"

Miguel reacted quickly.

"Raúl," he said desperately, "no, man, you can't do that… She killed Ricky!"

Raúl locked on to Caridád's eyes.

"Where she'll be going, Miguel," Raúl said confidently, "a day won't go by she won't wish she was spending her time with you!"

Caridád shook her head, tossing her hair out of her face. Then spat at him.

Miguel shoved her backward, banging her head hard against the wall behind her. Raúl calmly wiped the saliva from his face with his fingers and wiped it across her cheek.

And smiled back at her.

"Sandy," he said looking around, "I'll send you the name of a friend of mine. He specializes in overseas deliveries. You call him, tell him I want to see him right away."

Raúl had decided its time to give Sandy a chance to show what he's made of.

"Tell him that I could use his help on something special, something that needs his personal attention."

He looked back at Caridád and smiled ominously.

"Tell him it'll be worth his while."

He then turned to Miguel.

"Miguel, maybe you could keep Caridád company until we can finalize things?"

The young man grinned widely.

"Sure, uncle," he said threateningly, "whatever you say…"

He started to pull her away when Raúl stopped him. He would not see her again after today. And there was one more lasting memory he wanted to leave her with.

Something he wanted her to spend the rest of her life knowing.

"You fooled me, Caridád, and you should know," he said pitifully, "that you've succeeded in being a great deal of trouble to me…"

She raised her head defiantly, almost proudly, looking at him with puffy eyes through tangled strands of matted hair.

"…just as your sister once had been."

Her expression froze, her insolence faded. She didn't – she couldn't – quite believe what she was hearing. He'd never once mentioned Maria…

Once had been?

She looked into eyes now wide with vengeance and ripe with retribution, blazing with anticipation of the satisfaction he'd know when it finally hit her, when she finally took his meaning. When she finally understood.

He wouldn't be waiting long.

Her searing agony paralyzed her, making her momentarily speechless. She collapsed under the weight of her heart tearing in two. Seconds passed before her pain erupted in a window-rattling scream. She sprang to her feet and flailed at Raúl as a now-giggling Miguel stepped between them and began roughly dragging her out of the kitchen. Sandy stepped back, out of the way of her swings, unwilling to help him as he tried to subdue her. He shared her disbelief.

"I'll kill you, Raúl," she cried out from behind her tears, "I'll fuckin' kill you!"

Miguel shoved a rough hand across her mouth.

"Shut your fuckin' mouth, you stupid bit–" he said impatiently.

"I'll see you fuckin' dead, Raúl!" her muffled voice yelled out.

Raúl felt his cell phone vibrate. He pulled out his phone as he looked at Sandy.

"Go with him. Get her out of my sight."

Sandy looked at Miguel, whose eyes were lit with retaliation, then back to Raúl.

"What you want we should do with her, Raúl?" Sandy asked.

Raúl already had the cell phone to his ear.

"Whatever you want, I don't give a fuck."

He caught Miguel's eye.

"Just nothing permanent!"

Sandy watched Miguel reaction as Raúl's stern voice turned commanding. *"No puedo entregar si está muerta."*

"He's right, Miguel," Sandy injected, still not sure why he was grabbing at the chance to keep Miguel from killing her, "he can't deliver her if she's dead."

Miguel grinned and gestured to Sandy as he shrugged.

"That still leaves us a lot of room," he said, his imagination already humming.

"Yeah," Sandy reluctantly agreed, still unconvinced, "maybe we should take some time and think about this for awhile?"

Raúl shot Sandy an odd glance as he turned away and pulled up another voice mail message, this one from an unknown number. Miguel was puzzled, almost indignant, as he tried to pull Caridád along with him. As he left the kitchen with her, he looked over and saw the spot where the cousin he'd loved like a brother – the brother he never had – had died, shot dead like some rabid dog. The spot where he'd found his body stuck to the kitchen floor from the tacky glue of his own pooling blood.

All because of them.

Because of both of them.

Miguel didn't believe a word she'd said, that Ricky had attacked her. *That was bullshit. There was no fuckin' way!* Ricky wouldn't go looking to do her, he knew better. Yeah, he was young but he wasn't stupid. And now way he wouldn't have hit her! Raúl had rules. And Ricky knew them. Just like they all knew them. And followed them.

And Sandy. The fucker had to shoot twice? Christ, twice? He had to kill him?

Something was wrong here. Very wrong. But he would deal with Sandy later. That score would be settled another time. Now, it was Caridád's turn.

He grinned as he watched Sandy walk toward them. He looked to Raúl for approval, whose expression had already evolved to something resembling disinterest. His grin widened as he looked back to Sandy. His look took on a more menacing tone.

"I dunno, Sandy," he said, "I think I've got a couple of pretty good ideas."

Raúl calmly if impatiently waited for his caller to finish before finally responding.

"You're certainly not being very cautious these days, eh, *hómbre*? I mean, I thought you'd be using an untraceable number or something like that, right? Aren't you afraid that–"

"You can't really be this fuckin' stupid," the voice interrupted him, ignoring Raúl's ineffective attempt at enlightened sarcasm. "What took you so long? I called you last night, for Christ's sake!"

Raúl didn't take well to being treated like some migrant farmhand.

"Relax, man, I just got your message, my carrier's been slow, what the fuck do you want?" he responded. "Besides, what's the big deal? We're covered, right?"

The silent response was yet another indication of their disintegrating relationship.

"You should remember who you're talking to, *muchacho*," the voice said.

The truth was Raúl was surprised he was hearing from him again so soon.

"By the way, how did you get this number, *gringo*?" he asked. Raúl made a habit of changing phones as well though probably not as often as his belligerent colleague.

"Perhaps you've forgotten," the voice replied coldly, "it's what I do for a living."

Raúl just wanted him to get to the point.

"We need to talk."

"What do you think we're doing now, *hómbre*, dancin'?"

The voice could not have been less interested in Raúl's pitiful sarcasm.

"You stupid fuck! All the shit that's gone down and this is funny to you?"

Raúl knew that personal is personal but business is business.

"Are you *really* that much of an idiot?"

But breaking balls was still breaking balls.

"You know, *gringo*," he said with an air of gaining control, "you should show some respect. You don't like the way I do things, find another player. But with what I know, what my *amigos* know, could be some things you'd have trouble explain–"

"You don't know shit, dumbass. You get paid when you do what you're told. And you do what you're told or you disappear," the voice warned, "it's that simple."

Raúl waited him out.

"One day you're here, next day you're not. Even you should be able to figure that out. You really blew it with that Fed bitch; you know there's going to be consequences."

"Not for me," Raúl responded, trying to deflect responsibility. "It wasn't me she was after! From what I'm hearing, it's not me who blew it, *gringo*. Word is–"

"How do you know who she was after or what she was doing there?" he asked, knowing Raúl was tap dancing. "Or how long she'd been at it?"

"And do you really think I give a fuck what you think you've heard?"

"Ok, fine, man, whatever you say," Raúl said, giving him some space. "You want to meet? I don't have any plans for later tonight, other than–"

"*Now*, dumbass!"

Raúl's reaction was nothing if not predictable.

"Now's really not a good time," he said, turning to watch Sandy and Miguel half-carry, half-drag Caridád toward the family room floor in the back of the house.

"You don't get it! A couple of your boys haven't been very careful lately. And we have to deal with it. *A-or-ah!*"

Raúl had to admit he just might have a point.

"*Comprende, amigo?*"

Still perturbed that how he got his number, Raúl wasn't motivated.

"Ok, *gringo*, why don't we meet tonight, maybe at –"

"You still don't get it, do you, asshole? 'NOW' doesn't mean tonight."

The conversation was quickly coming to an end.

"One-thirty, the usual place. And don't fuck with me, Raúl. This will get taken care of. One way or the other!"

"I can take care of things on my end without your help, *hómbre*, so –"

Raúl heard the connection drop.

"Go fuck yourself," he calmly if defiantly said into the silence.

With Raúl, it was all about respect. The money, the women, the power.

It meant nothing without respect. He'd worked too hard for too long. He'd been given nothing his whole life. He wasn't some punk spending his nights rolling old ladies for their social security checks. No one kept him down. Maybe it was time to teach that *gringo* a lesson.

And this time make him pay attention!

He flipped the cell phone shut, checked the time and shoved it into his back pocket then walked toward the front door. He knew better than to let his temper cloud his judgment. That's how mistakes were made. But he also knew himself well enough to know how his anger caused him trouble. How it had before. How it could again. And now was no time to get stupid. Rage could not dictate his thoughts. Or his actions.

But on the family room floor, it was a completely different story.

* * *

Jack and Alex walked leisurely to his car he'd intentionally parked under the biggest shade tree he could find. The rest of the parking lot of Zack's Snack Shack and Imbibing Emporium, one of southwest suburb's more colorful eating establishments, was awash in the late-morning sunshine. It was considerably busier now than when they'd arrived a little over two hours ago. And Alex had to admit, just as Jack had predicted, their coffee would have been worth the wait whenever they'd gotten here.

It was a fun place to spend a casual Saturday morning. The décor was equal parts sports bar, family restaurant, beer garden and coffee shop. It featured the usual plasma TV's in the bar though they were also installed in both the men's *and* women's restrooms. It also offered a small gift shop, mostly Southside Irish paraphernalia with intermittent displays of White Sox caps and shirts. Strategically placed signage warned customers as they entered of the perils they could expect should they ask about any items Cub-related.

During breakfast hours, the beer garden served as a quaint but accommodating outdoor café. Despite the midmorning heat and humidity that greeted their arrival, a weather pattern that had shown typical Chicago stubbornness over the past week, Jack reluctantly agreed to be seated on the patio. And while Alex was by no means someone who claimed to "love summer" from the comfort of an air-conditioned office, the tree-lined cobblestone was simply too inviting to turn down. She acquiesced to being seated in one of the more shaded areas where a cardinal's consistent melodic chirp greeted them, hidden somewhere within a nearby crimson king maple. Jack laughed to himself.

He wondered if it that damned bird was following him.

Their meal was predictably good and their conversation proved as revealing as it was pleasant, at least as far as Alex's new assignment was concerned. Truth be told, it wasn't difficult for her to place her work on the back burner for the time she was in town. She'd quickly become comfortable with how handsome Jack was, in the rugged sort of way she'd always preferred. That he was a gentleman. That he was noble. And, most importantly for her purposes over the next couple of weeks, that he was available.

They talked about their careers, about Jimmy and how he'd impacted both their lives, about her travels and adventures around the world and in what direction he felt his life was headed, now that his career with the Bureau had prematurely ended. That subject, Alex noted carefully, was broached delicately with much of it left for another time. Still, the undercurrent running just beneath the surface of everything he'd talked about – what served to endear him to her more than anything they actually discussed – was the passion he so evidently held for his life's work. His quixotic dedication to eradicating human trafficking, if not practical, was at least laudable. She realized they had in common that singular place – that honorable place – their work took them.

As she listened to him quote statistics ad nauseum, she couldn't help but take a step back and see the dichotomy. It did seem true that his vocation was his unrelenting focus, an intense passion. But it seemed just as true that he fell short of being a zealot. He was more than simply an interesting man; Alex had met plenty of interesting men. No, Jack Sturdevant was a *fascinating* man, an uncompromising man, one whose flaws seemed as necessary to his character as his strengths.

Jack's '93 blue Honda Civic hatchback merged smoothly from the on ramp and into traffic heading north on I-57. Before long he was westbound on the I-94 expressway heading into the city. Eventually, traffic came to a virtually standstill a couple of exit ramps south of the 35th Street exit. The White Sox were playing a night game against Boston. It seemed a bit early for game traffic. But, as they sat in traffic, he took advantage of the temporary lull in their conversation just to appreciate that she was there.

Alejandra Cándida María Montoneros – her middle name compliments of her mother's devotion to Saint Cándida María de Jesús, founder of the

Congregation of the Daughters of Jesus – was that rare woman who could make anything she wore look good. And it was a good thing she was. Although her sandals and cuffed khaki shorts were the same she was wearing when they met in the park not twenty-four hours ago, she was now sporting a charcoal gray tank top he'd used during his three-nights-a-week basketball habit that he'd scaled back on only this past spring. On top of the too thin and altogether too revealing tee-shirt she also comfortably wore one of his older tee-shirts, albeit a bit too large. It was purchased two Octobers ago, a souvenir from the time he'd spent in Revelstoke, a quaint British Columbian town nestled within the foothills of the northern Canadian Rockies. It was stonewashed gray with the town's name stitched across the front in a papyrus script sewn with maroon thread. When Alex tried it on, she'd mentioned that it appeared brand new. He'd mumbled something how he had too many other shirts to wear, that he'd just never gotten around to wearing it.

And he hadn't lied to her. Not really.

He just didn't tell her it was one more memory he'd chosen to let die on its own.

Alex'd mentioned again at breakfast how comfortable it wore, how soft and smooth the fabric felt, how beautiful the workmanship was. And while he responded by saying how nice she looked wearing it, he intentionally fell short of offering it to her to keep. His lack of gratuity did not go unnoticed.

He wasn't sure himself why he hadn't. Or maybe he was.

Traffic had slowly begun to move when Jack felt his phone vibrating. He pulled it from his back pocket and smiled.

"Hey, Laura, how are you? How's the weather in D.C. this weekend?"

"Hey, Jack, I'm fine. The weather here sucks but, hey, it's August and it's D.C. What new?"

Jack laughed. Alex watched and listened.

"So, to what do I owe the pleasure?"

"I wasn't sure if you knew, if anyone told you, but Carmen's memorial service is scheduled for Tuesday morning here in D.C. Just thought you'd like to know."

'Uhhh, yeah, thanks. No, I hadn't heard. Thanks, I appreciate you telling me."

"Any chance you'll be making the trip in?"

Jack glanced over at Alex. She could hear Laura's voice even over the air conditioning's low blowing fan. She had an unusually blank expression on her face.

His attention was brought back to the road where traffic had loosened up a bit

"Probably not, no. I was able to see her yesterday. And I said my good-byes."

"Ok, sure," Laura said somewhat coldly.

"Listen," he started, trying to end what was rapidly deteriorating into an uncomfortable situation. "Are you home? Are you going to be around for a little while? I'm in traffic right now and I really can't talk. But I want to call you back. I need your advice on something."

Alex turned and looked out her window.

"Yeah, I'll be home," Laura responded finally able to get a word in. "Not a problem. There was something I wanted to talk with you about, as well."

"Ok, then," he said, "good, we'll connect later this afternoon. I'll call you."

"That'll work for me. Talk with you then, Jack," she said.

He waited a couple of seconds until he heard the connection drop. He flipped the phone shut and noted that it was just past noon.

Alex was predictably quiet.

He started to say something. She interrupted.

"How's things in D.C?" she said distantly.

He understood why she might feel a bit strange.

"Things in D.C. are fine. The weather's a bit shitty there, just like here, but, otherwise, it sounds like things are ok. I told her I'd call her back later."

"I heard," she said, her tone unchanged.

Jack slowly came to a stop along with the traffic ahead of him, then turned to her. He was annoyed yet flattered that he felt compelled to explain.

"Alex, look, Laura's a friend of mine. She still works for the Bureau though I quite honestly don't know why. She called to tell me that Carmen's memorial service is going to be Tuesday morning in D.C."

"You're not going, I take it," she said hesitantly.

"No, I have no reason to. I don't belong there anymore. And, like you probably heard, I've already said my good-byes. D.C.'s got nothing I want and, besides, they'll be nothing going on other than a lot of back-slapping, hand-wringing and political bullshit."

She nodded respectfully.

"Anyway," he said, looking to change the subject. "Where are we headed? Where can I take you?"

"I'm staying with a friend up on the Gold Coast, near Dearborn and Division. You know where that is?"

He looked at her surprisingly.

"Hey, don't look at me. She's some heavy hitter at one of your downtown banks. All I'm doing is crashing there for few days."

"I see," he said, intentionally leaving a trail of discernable interest behind.

She was happy to play the game with him.

"It's not like I have any place else to stay."

Jack smiled. He felt like he should explain, like he needed to explain.

Traffic loosened up significantly ahead of them as they finally inched passed the ballpark. Jack still wondered about the congestion as he started to accelerate. For reasons he wasn't quite sure he wanted to understand, the rest of their ride was quiet.

Jack pulled up opposite a high-rise as he drove north on Dearborn just past Division Street. Alex unfastened her seatbelt and shifted in her seat so she could look directly at him. She finally asked the question he'd left hanging earlier.

"Why do you think she should have left the Bureau?"

Jack looked a bit surprised.

"It's a bit of a long story," he said, trying to ease his way out of the subject. Then it occurred to him.

"Although," he said as he thought out loud, "it probably would help you to have some of the background. What do you have going on later?"

"Ummm, I'm not sure. I think I was supposed to go to dinner this evening with my roommate."

He sensed there was something more to it than that.

"And?"

"And," she reluctantly continued, "I think she's expecting me to meet one of her friends, or maybe it's her boyfriend's friend, I'm not really sure."

"Ahhh, I see," he said, trying to not to let his disappointment color the tone of their conversation.

Alex jumped at the chance.

"But I can beg off," she said hopefully, "I mean, work is more important, right? And I am only here for a couple of weeks. We've got a lot to get done."

Jack smiled, grateful she responded the way she did. He looked at the digital clock on the dashboard. It was almost a quarter to one. He turned and smiled at Alex.

"I dunno, Alex, don't you think its kind of late to be canceling on the poor guy? I mean, he's probably been looking forward to meeting you."

She playfully shot him a "why are you being such an asshole?" look.

"Ok, I'll tell you what. If you want use me as an excuse to get out of meeting the possible love of your life, well, then, who am I to stop you?"

She leaned across the center console and placed his face in her hands. She turned his head slightly and touched his mouth gently with hers. She closed her eyes and kissed him – softly, carefully, invitingly –, her tongue warmly, slowly licking his lips.

She leaned back and looked into his eyes as he smiled.

"Who are you, indeed, Jack Sturdevant?"

She looked into her purse and pulled out a pen and a small pad of paper. She scribbled her number down then tore the paper off the pad.

"Here," she said, "this is my private cell."

Jack reached for it as she placed it gently into his open hand.

"Let me give you mine," he said, his eyes never leaving hers.

She wrote down his cell number, then repeated it back to him.

"Ok, then," she said successfully. "I guess we're all set."

She reached back and opened her car door. She felt how much cooler it was by the lake than in the suburbs. As she stepped out of the car, she looked back, grinning.

"I'll talk with you later," she said comfortably.

The door closed behind her. He watched her walk around in front of the car and across the street. He looked into his rearview mirror to check for traffic. He saw his own eyes looking back.

I'm ready, he thought. And he really wanted to believe he was.

* * *

Sandy stepped out the back door and onto the small wooden deck, dressed for the weather. He wore only a pair of gym shorts in the hot, humid afternoon sun. He took another hit from the joint in his right hand then raised a bottle of Corona to his lips.

It was just past one o'clock. They'd been at it for more than three hours.

Nothing would bring back Ricky. They weren't kidding themselves about that. The reality was he'd gotten careless. Caridád was an attractive young woman and he'd had let his guard down. It always happens when you think with the wrong head. He let himself get played. And he paid the price.

Simple as that.

Sandy knew what he'd done he had to do. The truth was Ricky'd given him little choice. Raúl had called Carlos to help and the three of them – Carlos, Miguel and Sandy – bundled Ricky's body up in some heavy blankets they'd found. Raúl had Caridád wipe up his blood and clean the floor. They'd packed him in the trunk and drove him over to Stroger Hospital, the old Cook County Hospital. They figured, with as busy as that place would be on a summer's Friday night, especially in this heat, who would notice?

And they were right.

Carlos had driven them up near the ER entrance so Miguel and Sandy could carry him to a secluded row of bushes. They removed him from the blankets he was wrapped in and laid him gently on what little green grass had yet to turn brown. Miguel brushed his hair from his face and said a quick prayer. Sandy pulled the gun from behind him where he had tucked it inside the waistband of his pants, the three rounds still missing from the clip. He had taken time to wipe down both the gun as well as the clip, just as Raúl had taught him years ago. He placed the gun inside the front Ricky's jeans. He wanted to leave it in Ricky's hand or at least get a decent set of prints on the gun but rigor mortis had already started setting in. And his fingers were anything but cooperative.

Still, Sandy knew there probably wouldn't even be an autopsy. There'd be no reason for Ricky to be taking up any freezer space, that's for sure. Another dead spic from GSW – gun shot wounds –, like that was news, especially at this hospital. The ER would pronounce him dead on the spot and chances were better than even money that by early next week he'd be in the ground. At state expense.

Case closed.

All that remained was Caridád.

Sandy couldn't help thinking how well things had worked out. Oddly enough, he wasn't concerned about Raúl's reaction over his killing Ricky. That voice mail message had probably saved his life! Plus, he'd told Raúl she wasn't to be trusted. Sandy knew he didn't want to hear it but it certainly appeared he'd been right. Besides, if nothing else, it got him out of Raúl's line of fire, at least for the time being. But he knew he had to be more careful. Raúl was still pissed about the other night, about how his cell phone ended up with those two black guys. He still couldn't be sure how much of that story Raúl had believed. It sounded plausible enough but underestimating Raúl was something few people had the opportunity to do more than once. Only time would tell. He'd keep his eyes – and ears – open. Appealing to their history together had always played in Sandy's favor before. He wanted to believe it was a safe bet it would again.

Still…

But the black guys on the street, sitting on the house. That was just stupid. And sloppy. Sandy wouldn't pay for their fuck-up. He knew 'Cue was smarter than that, at least that's how he saw himself. One thing was certain: "Snake-Eyes" would never be caught up in all that shit. Not a chance in hell. "Snake-Eyes" was *definitively* smarter than them! Than all of them!

Sandy walked past a broken lawn chair toward the short set of stairs that led from the deck into the back yard. The overgrown bushes that lined either side of the staircase had not been pruned once this year. He was out of the shade and standing in the sunlight when he heard Miguel still yelling at Caridád. Raúl had called earlier, just a while ago, to remind both of them to scale it back, not to do her any permanent harm. There was more he might need to know from her. Miguel could enjoy himself – but only to a point.

Caridád understood it for what it was. She knew the risks and what she was doing when she set Ana and Daniel free. It was the one gift she'd wanted so desperately for so long from someone – from anyone! And she hadn't kidded herself, she knew the danger was real. She'd heard enough – and seen enough for herself – to know how those who controlled her future world react to betrayal, real or imagined. What she told Ana was truer than she'd first realized. But what she did for them, how she faced down her fears to do what she knew was right, didn't only just put her life on the line. Having lived the last several years of her life in captivity, it was never death that Caridád feared most.

It was dying.

And the long, slow and imaginatively tortuous ways they would make it happen.

Still, the simple truth was that no one ever had the courage to do for her what she'd done for Ana and Daniel. If they could get away – and stay safely away – what she now had to look forward to would at least be worth it. She thought about her sister.

Maria would have been so proud.

Sandy meandered down the steps and onto the burnt lawn and overgrown weeds that passed for a backyard. He took one final drag from the joint then dropped it to the ground and snuffed it out. He walked over to the one shade tree, a purple ash that may have been there since the house was built for all he knew. It was that big. He looked out across the back alley that emptied out onto 35th Street less than a block away and saw a young boy, probably not even ten, coming towards him in a hurry. He recognized him from the neighborhood but could not recall his name.

"Are you Sandy?" the young boy asked.

"Who wants to know?" Sandy sarcastically remarked as he brought the Corona one more time to his lips.

"My cousin sent me to get you. He says to tell you he knows where they are…"

"Where who are?" Sandy asked.

"The girl. And the boy who was with her."

Sandy froze.

"What are you talking about? Have you seen them?"

"No, but he has. He told me to come get you. He's –"

"Where are they?"

"He's at the –"

"Not him, not your cousin! Them, the girl and the kid; where are they?"

"At the church."

"What church?"

"St. Jerome's," the boy said. "They're at the rectory with Father Mac."

"How do you know?" Sandy asked.

"My aunt works at the rectory for Father Mac. She cooks and cleans and stuff like that for the priests. My cousin overheard her talking with his mom about these two kids Father Mac found in the church this morning. Said they ran away from some place here in the neighborhood. Told them all sorts of bad stuff that happened to them and –"

"Wait," Sandy interrupted, not quite believing what he was hearing. "*His* mom?"

"Yeah, he said that they're only going to be there for a little while longer and then they'll probably be taking them to the cops. That's why he sent me to get you."

Sandy tried to think.

The combination of beer and joints created a maze of confusing options.

"What you want I should tell him?" the boy persistently asked.

Sandy looked at the young man.

"You say they're at the church right now?"

"No," the boy said, frustrated at having to repeat himself, "they're at the rectory, with Father Mac and my aunt."

"Ok, ok," Sandy said, hoping some kind of plan would bypass his brain and magically flow out his mouth. "You go tell your cousin to keep an eye on them. I'll be there as soon as I can. Where is he at right now?"

"He's at the bodega down the street from the rectory. I was there hanging out when he came and got me and told me to come get you."

Sandy knew the place.

"Who's your cousin?"

"Do you know Carlos? He's kind of fat and –"

"Yeah, I know Carlos," he interrupted. "He's your cousin?"

"No," the kid replied, "My cousin's a friend of his, he –"

Sandy had heard enough.

"What's his name?"

"Who, my cousin?"

"Yeah!"

"Manny..." he answered, "well, Manuel, but we call him –"

Sandy was no longer listening.

"Ok, get your ass back to the bodega. Tell him to go to the rectory and keep an eye on them. And not to do anything until I get there. Tell him I'll be there right away."

Just as the boy started to move, Sandy called back to him.

"Wait!" Sandy turned and ran back toward the house. He threw open the screen door and bumped into Miguel, who was wet with the sweat he'd spent working up.

"Dude, where you going?"

"Not now, Miguel."

He ran through the family room and into the kitchen, ignoring Caridád as she lay bound and prone, naked and motionless on the stained, fabric-worn couch. He dragged open a drawer and pulled out a pen and paper. He scribbled down his cell number then just as quickly retraced his steps out to the backyard.

"Here," he said, giving the slip of paper to the boy, "tell him to call me if he sees them leave. Tell him to follow them wherever they go. This is important. Can you remember to tell him all that?"

The boy smiled as he took the crumpled paper from Sandy.

"I can remember," he said confidently.

"What's your name?" Sandy asked.

"Luís..."

Sandy smiled.

"You did good, Luís," he said, "Now, get going!"

The boy laughed out loud as he jumped into action. Sandy watched him run back down the alley from which he'd come. He turned to see Miguel in similar attire, a joint hanging from his lips and a cold beer in his hand, standing on the deck. He jogged up the steps and into the house.

"We may have caught a break, dude..."

"How so?"

"The girl and the kid have been spotted. They're at the rectory, St. Jerome's. I'm going now. You stay here with her. I'm not sure when Raúl's coming back."

"Whenever he does," he said through a grin, "I'll be here."

Miguel followed Sandy through the screen door back into the family room. Even with the windows opened, the familiar aroma had settled in the air. What the boy had told Sandy gave him the excuse he needed to get out of the house. Despite everything Caridád had done, Sandy was still not convinced. He wasn't naïve. He knew what leaving her behind with Miguel meant. But he also knew that, if he stayed, he'd have to be a party to what he was doing. And going to do. Somehow, that seemed even worse.

Sandy understood, as did anyone who had been around long enough, that, to Raúl, loyalty mattered above all else. And what Caridád had done was more than just wrong. It was unforgivable. Whatever misplaced courage it took for her to do what she did, it was very stupid. And Raúl's retribution would not only be punitive, it would set an example. There could be no doubt about that. Miguel's time with her was only the beginning.

There would be no sympathy for her now, not that Raúl was even tempted. To him, she was a traitor or something worse. That he'd shared his bed with her was not that big of a deal. That he had considered her place in his organization was. He'd trusted her to the extent a man in his line of work was capable of trusting anyone. Caridád had betrayed that trust. And she'd killed Ricky as sure as if she'd pulled the trigger herself.

Sandy knew what lay ahead for her. No penance would matter now. It would be brutal. It would be merciless. And, in the end, it would be final. She'd disappear among a thousand other girls her age, some even younger, most likely never to be heard from again. And, if she was lucky, she'd find a way to die a quick, early death that would spare her the agony of living her remaining waking moments in a world where drawing breath only meant being valued for the sexual currency and property she'd become.

But, as he stood there looking at her, the humid air heavy with Miguel's expectant sense of depraved revenge, the decision she'd made to help them, to give someone else the freedom she desired, knowing what it would cost her, seemed all too familiar to him.

He'd known only one other person who would've made such a choice.

And Raúl's overseas specialist had exacted from her a similar price.

* * *

Chapter 9

THE 2006 CYPRESS pearl metallic Lexus GS 430 sedan idled in virtual silence as it sat on Walton Street, pointed west, between the Newberry Library on his right and Washington Park to his left. It was only a couple of blocks north that the meeting was taking place.

The driver's attention was riveted to the multiple windows open on his laptop, which rested on the leather console situated between the front bucket seats. A Nikon 10.2 megapixel resolution digital SLR camera sat in the seat beside him. Inside his camera bag sitting on the passenger side floorboard, wrapped in a soft, protective cloth sleeve, was a 55-200mm zoom lens.

In the aftermath of their somewhat unsettling conversation the prior evening, he realized he could not allow Bobby to be in a position to call the shots. But he couldn't approach Wallace again; he'd gone to that well once already concerning that sonuvabitch Sturdevant. Resurrecting another skeleton from the Iraqi desert could only make him feel more uneasy and, possibly, convince him it was time to make a change. There was no upside to putting the Deputy Director on the defensive. No, the situation with Bobby had to be handled off the books. It had to be done quietly but in such a way that the prick would never try anything like this again.

And it had to be done quickly.

FBI Special Agent Marc Cauldwell considered himself a geek of sorts, though a fashionable one at that, especially now that it was popular to be thought of as one. He was a sucker for "cool" technology. And, like his Mazda MX-5 safely tucked away at his cottage near Sturgeon Bay, this car was loaded with it. From the latest on-board computerized options and its advanced LCD navigational system to its drop-down control panel, he believed in treating himself to the best of everything.

It wasn't that he believed himself to be vain. Or egotistical. Or even pretentious. He simply believed he deserved better. Probably because he thought of himself *as* better. Special Agent Marc Cauldwell seldom lacked for a viable rationále when it came to self-indulgence. He redefined what it meant to be a "dedicated" public servant, for, as he saw it, he unselfishly put his life on the line every day, especially since 9/11. And, in his mind, it was precisely that approach to his job – and to his *career* – that was, in large part, the primary reason why the public was safer because of him.

And that feeling of security quite naturally, like everything else, brought with it a price.

Which is why he had done what he needed to do in order to bring this situation under control. After his face-to-face with Bobby last night, Cauldwell made a couple of phone calls. He'd agreed to provide Bobby with everything he'd asked for: he'd keep Bobby in the loop on this investigation – the *entire* investigation – as well as all of the evidence reports. He'd told Bobby he'd need at least the week to get him clearance to review the physical evidence. After all, he'd told him, Congress could move faster than paperwork through the FBI.

Bobby told him he had until Monday.

Cauldwell had spent the remainder of last night and most of his Saturday morning putting together a read-only CD of all reports, including specific forensic and evidence files, pertaining to the murder investigation of Special Agent Eyas. He'd also downloaded the perp's preliminary profile from the FBI's Behavioral Analysis Unit, standard in the case of a murdered agent. On the CD he included a separate executable file that Bobby would initially be required to open in order to view all of the classified documents. This file contained personalized encryption software which, in conjunction with a secured website, required Bobby to create a password unique to the computer on which the documents were opened. The website time stamped all authorized access and required a seven digit alphanumeric code, changed daily, for viewing the documents. Duplication of any of the files Cauldwell gave him was technologically impossible. And they could only be viewed from the computer onto which they were originally loaded.

Cauldwell did it this way for two very important reasons. Primarily, it was to ensure that, should Bobby wish to look at the CD's reports other than the first day he opened the documents, he would first have to get that day's alphanumeric code from Cauldwell himself, which agents typically received every morning via email. Secondly, and perhaps more importantly, any documents that Bobby opened would be flagged by information cookies embedded in the encryption software which, because it was linked to Cauldwell's account, would then send emails on a per-document basis directly to Cauldwell detailing the viewing activity.

But as impressive as that was, Cauldwell needed to enlist the expertise of a different group of FBI techies this morning to resolve another vexing issue. He had to find a way not only to keep track of Bobby's whereabouts and movements; he needed to know who Bobby was talking to and, just as importantly, about what. And, while the geek squad knew nothing of Cauldwell's reasons or rationale, the guys with the pocket protectors were there with the next generation of answers.

And, in part, it was thanks to organized crime.

In 2003, a U.S. District Court judge authorized the use of what FBI analysts would later term "roving bugs." Wary of conventional techniques such as tailing a suspect or wiretapping, the Department of Justice approved their use against members of a prominent national organized crime family. It was really quite ingenious. The FBI converted the cell phones owned by two mafia captains into listening devices by remotely activating each cell phone's built-in microphone. Subsequent to their convictions, the surveillance technique was itself upheld on appeal. Though it was likely it would not have mattered much to either Cauldwell – or the Bureau – if it hadn't.

The approach he was taking with Bobby was similar. Having neither the time nor inclination to actively listen to every cell phone conversation, Cauldwell had transcripts of all incoming and outgoing calls sent to his FBI email account. Then, using software specifically developed for eavesdropping on al-Qaeda communications within the United States, Cauldwell was capable of automatically searching the transcripts for a predetermined glossary of terms, which he could edit individually. He also was able to pinpoint Bobby's exact location by a process known as cell phone triangulation.

Cauldwell could not count on Bobby's phone having any sort of LDM – i.e., Location Determining Mechanism – since he could not know how recently Bobby had purchased it. So, having provided his support staff with his known cell numbers, they were able to identify Bobby's cellular network operator (CNO), who in turn provides cell network support for his service provider. This was critical since it is the CNO who also maintains a record of cell sites, typically determined by either cell towers or embedded GPS locators, where a specific working cell phone can be located, literally within feet. Thus, by late Saturday morning, Cauldwell was not only enjoying complete transcripts of Bobby's cell phone conversations, he knew precisely where the detective was when he has having them. He began compiling the text conversations into a single document file that allowed him to not only append each new cell phone capture but to search the complete history at any given time. He created an icon to easily open the file.

Special Agent Cauldwell could hardly have been prouder of himself.

The last cell phone conversation Bobby had was a call he made just before 11:00 AM today. He'd apparently given up on using prepaid cell phones; in Cauldwell's experience, the piss-poor coverage and sporadic service outages made what may have once been an appealing alternative nothing more than a troublesome inconvenience. Even so, it appeared that Bobby's call was made to a phantom cell phone. Cauldwell could identify the number but had no way of knowing who its owner was. Maybe Bobby was calling a snitch, maybe some reporter… or maybe he was making a connection.

The way the transcript read, the third option seemed the most viable.

First, there was Bobby's normal (which is to say, extensive) use of profanity, which seemed to imply he was talking to someone from the street. And there was the reference Bobby made to "the Fed bitch." When the respondent replied that "it wasn't me she was after" Cauldwell concluded they were speaking of Special Agent Eyas and, based on that assumption, their conversation seemed to imply some level of knowledge concerning her murder. Later on, Bobby referred to the respondent as "*muchacho*" and then, later, as "Raúl." He also mentioned how "a couple of your boys haven't been very careful lately" which implied gang affiliation. Bobby's open use of a name seemed to seal the deal that Cauldwell had come across a conversation between the detective and a Hispanic gang member, probably a gang captain. Or maybe even *el jéfe*.

Triangulating the coordinates of the cell towers allowed Cauldwell to identify the two callers' locations. Seeing the location of the unidentified cell number was on the city's south side, Cauldwell played a hunch and requested profiles on any high-ranking gang bangers named "Raúl."

Cauldwell grinned like a predator whose prey was completely unaware of his presence. Stalking was always something Cauldwell not only prided himself in doing well; he actually enjoyed it. And he'd become quite good at it, or so he thought. He saw it as nature in all its evolutionary tension, it's most raw, it's most basic, it's most brutal struggle to live, to simply survive.

And Cauldwell was nothing if not a survivor.

But of all it – the game, the hunt, the fear, the kill – it was without a doubt tasting the prey's fear he enjoyed most. The fear. Without a doubt.

The transcript revealed a meeting was set for today, 1:30 PM.

To Cauldwell, that meant only one thing.

He maximized one of the open icons displayed at the bottom of his screen. Bobby's cell phone was on. And according to the grid map, he was at Elm Street moving south on Clark. Cauldwell check the digital clock on the dashboard. 1:22 PM. Wherever he was meeting Raúl, he was meeting him soon. He checked his mirrors then put his car in gear. He slowly approached the "T" intersection ahead of him at Clark Street then turned right, heading north toward them. Elm was still a couple of blocks up.

Cauldwell pulled up to the stoplight at Oak Street. He clicked on the grid map and enhanced the image to show the map's terrain. By virtue of the blinking cursor that acted as the tracking mechanism, he could see Bobby had gone from heading west to now traveling south. It gave him an idea where the meeting might be. Up on the left stood a self-park parking garage in a building that appeared to house an office complex. To the right stood his choice of empty parking spots.

He pulled over and naturally parked across two spaces.

Today being Saturday, Cauldwell's superior powers of deduction told him there'd be no better place to meet. Bobby was no idiot. And it only made sense. Inside a building with layers of concrete flooring and virtually no access via cell phone. Which meant no ability to track a signal. Surveillance would be impossible from the street. And Cauldwell had no means to surveil them from inside the garage.

He measured his options as he watched the map's blinking cursor had come to a stop, which meant they were meeting on one of the floors of the parking garage. Which one hardly mattered. He quickly realized he'd come as far as he could – for now.

If they drove in, he reasoned, they'd have to drive out.

He grinned. Even as he delighted in his own deductive prowess, an approaching car in his side view mirror caught his attention. A metallic cobalt blue vintage, maybe late 80's or early 90's, convertible Chevy Camaro RS with heavily tinted windows was making its way slowly up Clark Street. The engine's RPM's whined conspicuously as it downshifted into second gear and pulled into the parking garage entrance then came to a stop. The driver's side power window came down and the driver, a male it appeared, inserted a card into the electronic reader. The gate's arm swung up as the heavy garage door opened in response. The car slowly disappeared up the ramp. He couldn't tell from his vantage point across the street what kind of card it was. A credit card, a resident's authorized access card or maybe just a monthly parking pass. Little matter. He noted the license plate, the date and time then clicked on one of the opened one of the icons on his laptop to enter the information into his notes. He could find out easily enough later.

Something told him Bobby's telephone friend Raúl had just arrived.

He waited a few more minutes, watching typical Saturday morning traffic pass him by, until he convinced himself he was right. He put his car into gear and slowly pulled into the street. At the end of the block he turned left, onto Maple Street. Ahead of him, a car was turning into the street as another automatic metal garage door up the ramp behind it was closing. He pulled off to the side of the street, the exit ramp and the garage door just in sight ahead of him, and smiled contently.

And waited.

* * *

Jack had been moving in stop-and-go traffic in the expressway's southbound lanes long enough. He looked for the next exit, completely mystified by the enormous backups on a Saturday. One thought did occur to him: Maybe this was the weekend of the Air and Water Show on the city's Lakefront. It didn't really matter. It pissed him off, whatever the reason. Besides, the Air and Water Show was never one of his favorite things to do. The city was home to it every August. The weather was always hot. The crowds were always huge. The planes were always loud. And it was always boring.

But it did make him think of Laura.

He smiled when he remembered how being there was always one of her favorite things to do each summer when she lived here. The event always served to remind her of how fleeting the months had been, how September's autumn chill, then just weeks away, would eventually seal the fate of the warm evenings she so enjoyed. Which only meant that, to Laura, every remaining day held a unique premium she was determined to still, somehow, savor. The show's star attraction, the appearance by the Blue Angels, was what she looked forward to most. Their performance alone attracted about a

million or so of her closest friends to the downtown area was reason enough
for Jack to be miserable. And though he honestly did cherish his time with
her, Jack embraced crowds with the same procrastinating enthusiasm he usually reserved for his annual prostate exam.

His expression faded, though, when it occurred to him his approach was
merely one of myriad reasons he'd given Laura, unintentionally or not, that
would eventually convince her taking the transfer to D.C. was at least in her
best interests if not in theirs.

He approached the Taylor Street exit at a snail's pace. He knew it was
a slow alternative but he figured, making his way to Halsted and then taking side streets, he'd eventually hit Cicero Avenue, the main artery he'd take
south to his neighborhood. On a Saturday afternoon, that meant he'd still
be a good forty-five minutes from home. But, as long as the air conditioning
continued to breathe life, he reasoned he could live with the inconvenience.

It wasn't as if anything – or anyone – was waiting for him there, anyway.

* * *

Sandy headed east on 43rd Street toward the bodega which he knew was just
up the way from St. Jerome's. He pulled quickly into a vacant parking space
that had just opened up directly in front of the grocer. As he got out, he heard
the young boy running up from behind the car, calling to him.

"Carlos followed them to the bus stop on Halsted."

"Get in!" Sandy said definitively.

Luís had no sooner closed the passenger side door when Sandy pulled out
into traffic, did a U-turn and proceeded eastbound toward Halsted Street.

"My cousin called him when I went to tell you he'd seen them…" the kid added.

"Which bus stop?" Sandy asked.

"I'm not sure," the boy admitted.

"Fuck!"

Sandy knew the church was on 39th Street so he figured, when he got to
43rd Street, he'd just go north along the bus route until he found Carlos. It
wasn't long before his plan began to pay off.

"Ok, here's the deal," Sandy told them both. "Here's how we do this."

A minute, maybe two, later, Carlos pointed to the bus ahead of them in
traffic. He remembered the gang symbols spray painted on the Spanish tele-

vision billboard ad adorning the side of the bus. And the unique style with which local taggers had added their own artistic flair to the original features of Telemundo's most popular soap opera couple set the bus apart.

"That's the one," he said, "that's the one they got on."

"You sure?" Sandy asked.

Carlos nodded without looking at him.

"Good," Sandy said.

A moment later, Sandy passed the bus as it made a stop at 31st Street.

"Where do you think they're headed?" Carlos asked.

"I'm guessing they're getting off at 18th Street."

"Why's that?"

"The closest stationhouse is 18th and State. I'm thinking he's taking them there."

Carlos nodded his agreement.

"That's what I'd do."

Sandy was indifferent to Carlos' unsolicited opinion.

Driving with the lights, they reached 18th Street quickly. Sandy kept the bus in his rearview mirror. He pulled over and dropped off Carlos and his brother in front of the intersection. He immediately eyed a vacant parking space on southbound Halsted just across the stoplight. Carlos' brother had no sooner shut the passenger side door then Sandy pulled back into traffic, did another U-turn, and grabbed the open spot. He was now facing the oncoming bus. He watched down the street as the bus approached slowly, making one stop after another, until it finally reached the 18th Street intersection.

The light was green as the bus pulled over and stopped. Sandy's view of the exiting passengers was blocked by the standing bus. Its driver ignored the light changing to yellow and the bus proceeded into the intersection, pulling away. He watched the milling group of people and strained to find the man with two children. He turned around and signaled to Carlos, who nodded approvingly. Carlos watched from the opposite side of 18th Street as Father Mac, having left his collar at home in favor of a knit shirt and khakis, walked hand-in-hand with Ana on one side and Daniel on the other. They moved up the east side of Halsted to 18th Street and turned right, in the direction of State Street.

Just as Sandy had hoped.

A moment later, Sandy watched as Luís ran up to an unsuspecting Father Mac. He watched as the young boy pleaded with the priest to help his mother, who, the boy was claiming, was lying unconscious in an alley up the block from a drug overdose. To ensure that he would leave the Ana and Daniel behind, the boy would claim that her dealer pusher was there with her and wouldn't help his mom. Sandy watched anxiously as the priest's body language said he was torn as to what to do.

Sandy turned a bit to his left and saw Carlos still watching from the north side of 18th Street, now directly across from them. Carlos saw Father Mac take Ana and Daniel inside a small hardware store a couple of storefronts from the intersection then follow the young boy down 18th Street toward the alley. He realized his chance was now.

Carlos waved to Sandy then hurriedly crossed 18th Street.

"Hurry up, you fat sonuvabitch," Sandy mumbled to himself.

The young man disappeared though the door and, within seconds, was half-walking, half-dragging both children onto the sidewalk. Ana twisted and turned, pulling them toward the curb, finally breaking loose. Daniel was wrapped in Carlos' large right arm, unable to break free. She started to run into the street then turned back, screaming to Daniel to come with her. Carlos followed her as the boy struggled violently.

Sandy swung open the car door and stepped out, watching as his plan unraveled before his eyes.

Ana ran on up the curb and onto the north side of 18th Street, then into the crosswalk spanning Halsted Street. Carlos followed her yelling. Traffic began to slow as she kept turning around, screaming for Daniel to get away. The boy continued to fight and struggle but his feet could not reach the ground. As she got halfway across the intersection, she stumbled into a crumbling pothole and fell hard, skinning a knee as well as an elbow, drawing blood. Cars maneuvered around her as if they were avoiding road kill. As she tried to get to her feet, Carlos was suddenly upon her. He gripped her arm with his open left hand and pulled her to her feet. He began dragging them both through the intersection. He turned to look for Sandy as his grip on Daniel finally began to slip.

Daniel dropped to the pavement. Frustrated and only getting angrier, Carlos reached down and grabbed Daniel roughly by the arm.

"Come here, you little bastard," he demanded.

Ana screamed.

Carlos turned his rising temper toward her.

"Shut the fuck up!" he shouted

Just then, he yelled out as Daniel's teeth sunk deeply into Carlos' forearm, cutting through skin and nerves into muscle and tendons. Carlos swung his arm around. Daniel finally let go, tossed to the ground where he rolled to a stop some feet away.

Carlos looked down at the blood and deep red marks now marking his arm.

"Fuck this," he yelled and reached behind him, pulling out his knife, a 4" serrated blade with a jagged edge and a thick contoured handle.

Daniel yelled out her name. Ana started to cry.

Sandy watched all this unfold before him, realizing nothing good was coming of it. He glanced down 18th Street but saw no sign yet of Father Mac. The situation had gotten too far out of hand and was deteriorating quickly. The fat ass had fucked it up. The plan should have worked. It was all Carlos' fault. That's what he would tell Raúl.

Sandy turned his attention back to the intersection where, suddenly, a man approached the three of them, his hands extended cautiously, appearing to try and help. Carlos watched as the man stepped closer and closer. He was finally close enough.

His hold on Ana still firm, Carlos swiped at the Good Samaritan with the knife now firmly held in his right hand. He missed with his first swing but sliced the left forearm of the advancing stranger with a return slash. At the same time, Daniel charged at Carlos, pushing him forward. The man stepped back and used what strength he had to grab Carlos' arm, right where Daniel had bit him, and twist it forcefully. Carlos screamed as he released his grip on Ana and fell to one knee. Daniel kicked him in the leg from behind. The man dropped to the pavement and struggled with Carlos to release the knife. Carlos kicked Daniel out of the way and pushed forward, knocking the man backward and onto his back. Daniel ran around and quickly helped Ana to her feet. They watched as Carlos struggled to get up. He eyed the prone stranger. Daniel tried to pull Ana away but she wouldn't go. She picked up a small but solid piece of loose pavement from the pothole and threw it at Carlos. It hit him square in the temple.

Carlos staggered and dropped the knife. The Good Samaritan dizzily tried to scramble to his feet. Distant sirens seemed to be coming from all directions.

"Fuck this," Sandy said to himself.

He slipped back into his car and slammed the door behind him. He pulled into traffic, heading south, just avoiding the car he hadn't seen coming.

Carlos turned around in time to watch Sandy driving away. He now heard the growing sirens. He swore loudly. His temple now bleeding, he pushed passed Ana and Daniel, knocking them back to the ground, and ran

– trotted, actually – as best he could down 18ᵗʰ Street, westbound, disappearing among a row of houses.

As traffic filled in behind him, Sandy watched in his rearview mirror as Ana, Daniel and that fuckin' Good Samaritan grew smaller.

"Fuckin' Carlos," he practiced telling Raúl, "he just couldn't help fucking it up!"

"There he is…" Daniel yelled out.

Jack pulled his car alongside eastbound 18ᵗʰ Street and stopped as Father Mac, obviously confused, was walking toward them. He stepped quickly out of the car and, standing on one leg inside the open door, he called out.

"Father! Father Mac!" Jack called to him. "Over here!"

The priest followed Jack's voice as he hurried over to the car.

"Get in, please…" Jack requested sternly.

"Who are you?"

"Please, just get in…"

Daniel and Ana were seated in the back.

"Father," Daniel yelled out, "hurry up, we gotta go…"

Hearing Daniel, seeing the children in the back seat, Father Mac hesitated.

"What are those children doing in your –"

"Father, please, I'll explain but we have to get out of here. Right now!"

Father Mac opened the Honda Civic's passenger door and climbed in.

Jack turned, saw no oncoming traffic and quickly pulled out. He headed for the expressway, hoping the congestion had loosened up enough so he could avoid having to come up with a Plan B.

He glanced in the rear view mirror.

"Father, could you help the kids fasten their seatbelts?" Jack asked calmly.

Father Mac twisted around in his front bucket seat and helped the children with their safety belts. He then turned back to look at Jack and waited for an explanation.

"Ok, let's start here," Jack began. "My name is Jack Sturdevant. And I'm a former FBI agent."

A former FBI agent? What…

Father Mac, his confusion fueling his unwillingness to process what Jack was saying, didn't hear him. All the priest cared about was what he'd become – what the kids had become – involved in.

And with who.

"What happened back there?" he insistently asked as he turned to check again on the kids.

"You were set up. That man was there to take back the kids," Jack said.

Father Mac turned back toward Jack with an incredulous look.

"You were lucky," Jack told him. "They only wanted you out of the way."

Father Mac was afraid to believe what he'd just heard.

"Out of the way?"

"They obviously didn't want to harm you," Jack said, "or else you'd be…"

The fear finally began to catch up to Father Mac. The boy who had begged him to help his mother – he'd run away when they got into the alley off the street.

No wonder!

"…you'd be in a lot worse shape right now."

"They?" Father Mac asked. "Who are 'they'?"

Jack's eyes darted from his rear view mirror to his driver's side mirror as he quickly veered down another side street.

"'They'," Jack answered, "are the people who sold Ana and Daniel into slavery."

Slavery?

"It's known as 'human trafficking'," Jack continued. "People of all ages are sold but especially children. They're brought into this country, smuggled usually. They come willingly, many voluntarily, thinking they're going to find work, that there are jobs waiting for them. Many are convinced they'll find work here that will let them help their families back home, often Central America, South America, Eastern Europe…"

Some of what he was hearing already started making sense. He thought back to the conversation he and Mrs. Lopez had just hours ago. She'd spent some time with the children after breakfast, just the three of them, and later when she told Father Mac what she'd learned, he could scarcely believe it. Neither knew much about what Ana and Daniel were talking about. But from what little sense they could make of what the children said they knew something was terribly wrong. And deeply disturbing.

The priest could scarcely believe what he was hearing.

"…they're brought here to work for whatever purpose the buyer has –"

"Whatever purpose…" he interrupted, speaking softly, searching to complete Jack's sentence but stopping short of doing so.

"Yes, Father," Jack said, turning to look at him, "whatever purpose…"

His mood began to change. It all made perfectly horrifying sense now.

"…. and it's a multibillion dollar business."

He turned in his seat and looked sympathetically at the kids as Jack continued.

"The people who do this, Father, who run these organizations…" Jack tried to choose his words carefully.

"…they are ruthless. I worked in a special organized crime division for twelve years when I was with the Bureau that was dedicated to stopping it."

Father Mac listened intently if not unnervingly as Jack continued.

"It's as vile – and as evil – as you can imagine. What happens to these –"

Jack wanted to continue but he knew the children were listening.

Father Mac nodded slowly as he gained a new appreciation for human depravity.

Jack shifted gears.

"In recent years, the industry…"

Father Mac noted Jack spoke of the business of buying and selling people as if it qualified to be a member of the Fortune 500.

"…has given rise to splinter groups called *carroñeros*. It's a Spanish word. It means 'scavenger.' They target – hijack, really – coyote ground transports and –"

"Coyotes?"

"The name given to smugglers, for the people who actually illegally transport unsuspecting immigrants into this country. They use vans, semi-trailers, eighteen-wheelers, anything that can typically move larger numbers of people. And because human smuggling is such a profitable business, it naturally gave rise to the scavengers, who've successfully created a black market *within* the underground trafficking business."

The priest listened without interrupting.

"What they've learned is stealing from the coyotes is itself *obscenely* profitable. They're considered pirates, parasites. In reality, they started as independent splinter factions. But they're becoming much better organized. And, in the process, they've become an increasingly violent problem themselves."

Jack had shifted instinctively into public relation mode, hearing himself repeat the very words he spoke to the press at the conclusion of Operation Homeward Bound.

"Chicago is a well-known destination for both coyotes and *carroñeros*. It is also considered one of the major hubs, along with L.A., New York, Miami, Denver –"

Father Mac's disbelief had become palpable. Jack's passion was taking flight.

"It's a growth industry, one we in this country, even our law enforcement but especially our politics, have been too slow to acknowledge and even slower to react to."

The priest turned to see the children quietly listening to Jack's sermon.

He saw in their eyes something that reminded him of the young woman who'd risked her own life to make their freedom possible.

"Is that what happened to Caridád as well?" Father Mac asked.

"Who's Caridád?" Jack asked, before either child could respond.

"She saved our lives," Daniel jumped in.

"She helped us get away from those men," Ana added.

"Who is she," Jack asked again, "a friend? How do you know her?"

Ana, with Daniel's help, began to explain. Father Mac, having already heard much of their remarkable story between the two of them and Mrs. Lopez at the rectory earlier in the day, filled in the missing blanks. As he listened, Jack began to understand. Somehow, for some reason, this young woman – this Caridád – decided to help Ana and Daniel escape, or at least try to. Without her, they would not have ended up at St. Jerome's nor ever have met Father Mac. But Jack knew her decision to help them escape easily put her own life in danger. If she were somehow found out, she'd be dead before morning. For all anyone knew, she was dead already.

But, if they meant to make an example of her, death would be the moment she would welcome most. Her choice to help them was the kind of selfless heroism, the kind of personal sacrifice, which rose above any altruism he'd seen, in all honesty, since Carmen. Which, in his mind, made the decision simple.

Safeguarding the kids and the priest meant leaving her to them. Or not.

As Jack approached the entrance ramp to the eastbound expressway, leading them south and out of the city, he looked at Father Mac, whose eyes seemed to understand.

And approve.

John Stroger Hospital – the old Cook County Hospital – was simply not an option. That would be the first place they would look for her. Jack had no other choice.

He looked in his rear view mirror and saw the young woman belted in between Ana on her right and Daniel on her left. To them, she was family. And, from now on, he knew she always would be.

Caridád was unconscious but seemed to be breathing steadily. He thought about what he'd had to do to carry her out of there. There'd be time later to prepare for the consequences of what he'd done to bring her out of that house. And now, without the Bureau's network of resources behind him, it would challenge every instinct he'd developed there just to save himself, to say nothing of his passengers.

He looked at Father Mac. There was no need to say a word. The priest's eyes said it all. He knew. They both knew. Father Mac didn't ask him because he didn't want to hear Jack say the words. In all honesty, Jack didn't want to tell him, either. This was no place for a confession.

And Jack had no use for his absolution.

He found the expressway entrance he wanted off of 22nd Street. He would have preferred to get on after 35th Street to avoid running into game day traffic. The White Sox home night game wasn't starting for another ninety minutes but, with Boston in town, it was likely to be a sellout. He was able to maneuver into the express lanes and there traffic flowed smoothly, even as they sped past the ballpark.

Every couple of minutes, Jack checked his rearview mirror.

He was approaching 83rd Street. It was time to formulate a plan. He looked at Father Mac and tried to find the right words to begin. What he had to say had to be said. He spoke quietly but firmly. And with the authority of someone who had spent the majority of his adult life engaging these mongrels.

And learning their ways.

"Ok, here's what I want to do." He had no time for subtleties. "You're in this, Father, whether you wanted to be or not. Are you listening to me?"

Father Mac nodded his head without saying a word.

"I'm not sure who we're really dealing with here. I'll get Caridád the medical attention she needs but, whoever they are, they'll at least want Ana and Daniel back. That was what all that was about back on 18th Street. *And* they know you were with them and that you probably were taking them to the police. No doubt that's why they went after you when they did."

"But *how* could they know, I didn't tell anyone!" Father Mac protested. "There was barely enough time to learn about what they'd been through."

"I don't know," Jack replied, "we can figure all that out later. Tell me, Father, did you call the police? Did the police know you were coming?"

"No," he responded, "I should have, shouldn't I?"

"Maybe," Jack concluded, "we'll see. Maybe *not* calling was the best thing you could have done!"

Father Mac looked surprised to hear Jack say that.

"It doesn't matter. What's done is done. Here's what I want to do now."

"Ok, whatever I can do to help." Father Mac replied.

"I'm going to drop you off at the 95th Street El station. I'm sorry to do this but you can't know where I'm taking them."

Father Mac reacted almost indignantly.

"But I'm responsible for –"

Jack cut him off.

"Father, you've done everything you can for them now. You've saved their lives but all you can do now is make things worse."

Jack regretted he had no time for tact.

"That's what that was all about back there."

Father Mac couldn't argue that point.

"They know you were the last person with Ana and Daniel, other than that guy in the street who tried to help –"

"The one who was bleeding?"

"Yeah, other than him, who they'll probably figure was just in the wrong place at the wrong time."

"Probably," Father Mac concurred.

Jack continued.

"Anyway, like I said, you can't know where I'm taking the kids. In case they try to find you, it's better if you don't know. You can't tell them what you don't know."

Father Mac courageously agreed.

"Ok, now, take the El to Chinatown, which is 22nd Street. It's where we got on the expressway."

Father Mac nodded.

"Get off there and grab a cab to Area 1 District Headquarters, on State between 17th and 18th."

"I know where it is," he said.

"When you get there, tell the Desk Sergeant that you witnessed the incident at Halsted and 18th Street this afternoon. We want them to know that you've spoken to the police. If there's any way you can get the name of the guy who got knifed, do that. Tell the police that you want to reach out to him and thank him for his bravery, shit like that."

Father Mac let Jack's indiscretion slip by without reproof.

"We want these guys to know that, if they have any contacts in the local police, that you've already got something on the record about what happened."

"You mean our own police department might be involved?" Father Mac asked incredulously.

"At this point, Father, we rule out nothing. All we know is that I can trust you, you can trust me and, together, we can trust them," Jack said motioning to the back seat.

"Beyond that, we don't know anything. And we trust no one."

"Ok," Father Mac said.

"Going to police may also help us in another way."

"What's that?"

"We may be able to determine, from what you tell them, if they do have contacts inside the department."

Jack exited the expressway at 95th Street and waited at the stoplight at the end of the off ramp. He searched his rearview mirror intently. The light turned green. He made a left onto 95th Street and, two hundred or so feet down, turned again, this time into the parking lot adjacent to the mass transit station and found a nearby parking space.

Jack watched Father Mac search for a token then check to see how much cash he had on him. Jack pulled out his wallet.

"Here, Father," handing him a prepaid CTA card he purchased some time ago at one of the El stop vending machines. "It's got at least a couple of rides left on it."

Father Mac objected.

"That's very kind of you, Jack, but I can't take your money. Please don't –"

"I wish you would, please, Father."

Father Mac smiled and graciously accepted.

"Ok, I will call you at the rectory later."

"Ok, how can I get in touch with you, if I need to, that is?" Father Mac asked.

Jack thought for a moment. *Shit, how does he reach me?*

He thought quickly then came up with the only solution that made sense. "Here's how."

He opened the glove compartment and reached for a pen. He tore some paper away from the back of an envelope. He pulled Alex's private number from his pocket and wrote it on the slip of torn envelope.

"If you want to get in touch with me, for any reason, call this number, day or night. It's a friend's number. She's works with me. She can be trusted."

Father Mac took the Alex's number from Jack.

Jack started to say something.

"When you call, tell her this."

Jack sat thinking for a quick moment. Then it occurred to him.

He turned and looked into the back seat.

"Ana," he said, "where are you from?"

Ana seemed suspicious.

Father Mac encouraged her. "Please, Ana, it's very important," though he still did not know why.

"I'm from a small town not too far from San Miguel de Allende."

Jack dropped his head. "That's too much. Do you have any brothers, any sisters?"

Ana took a moment. Her first thought was of Martín.

"My brother, Martín."

Jack asked her to repeat his name. "How do you pronounce his name, sweetheart?"

"Mar-*teen*," she said again.

Jack smiled at Ana, who returned a small one of her own. He swiveled around and looked at Father Mac.

"That'll be our password. If you need to reach me, call this number and tell the woman who answers it that you need to get me a message. Tell her you're calling on behalf of Mar-*teen's* sister. Not *Mar*-tin."

"Got it," Father Mac responded. "Mar-*teen*."

"Do *not* use Ana's name." Jack told him. "She'll know if you use Martín's name, you can be trusted. Anything else –"

"Don't worry, Jack, I'll be careful."

"Now, one more thing," Jack said as Father Mac reached to open the door.

"Memorize her number. And, once you have, do *not*, under any circumstances, throw it away. *Burn it! And watch it burn!* This is very important, Father. You cannot let anyone else know this number."

"I understand," Father Mac said.

"Their lives are literally in your hands, Father."

Father Mac smiled.

"And God's," he added.

Jack started to say something then thought better of it.

"Fair enough," Jack responded.

Father Mac shook hands with Jack.

"God bless you, Jack," he said, "and thank you for everything."

Jack just nodded.

Father Mac turned and looked at Ana and Daniel still buckled up in the back seat. Caridád sat silently between them, barely stirring.

"I'll see you all again soon," he said. Then, looking from Jack to the children in the backseat, he extended his right hand and blessed them.

"Go with God, my brave children…" he said. Daniel watched Ana make the sign of the cross then quickly did the same. They both smiled back at him.

Father Mac looked at Jack as he opened the car door.

"…and with you as well, Jack."

Jack nodded again and smiled.

They watched Father Mac walk across the parking lot and disappear into the crowded transit station.

Jack sat silently for a moment. He knew the kind of people he was dealing with. He also knew that there was a better than even chance that neither he nor the children would ever see Father Mac again.

But he had to allow him to return to his parish. The best way to save his life now was to have him work with the police. Jack knew he could not protect them all. Overextending himself put everyone at risk. He knew he could keep Ana, Daniel and Caridád safe, at least for a while. How long that might be would be up to the traffickers and how quickly they coming looking for them. He had no illusions. He knew how this could end. He'd seen it before. He turned around and looked at Ana, then Daniel.

They looked scared. Hopeful. And innocent.

There was no doubt what he had to do.

Jack pulled his phone from his back pocket. He took the slip of paper on which he had Alex's private number and punched it into his cell. She wasn't picking up.

"Alex, its Jack, it's important. Please call me when you get this message. Thanks!" He hoped she would hear in his voice what he couldn't say in the message.

He flipped the phone shut and turned to look at his backseat passengers. Daniel had already started to fall asleep. Ana was pushing the hair from Caridád's face. He shoved his cell phone into his back pocket and headed back out onto the expressway.

He had just exited the expressway and was entering I-57 heading south when he felt his phone vibrate.

That was fast.

He checked the window for the incoming caller, then flipped open his phone as his lane merged far left.

"Laura?"

"Hey Jack!"

"What's up?"

"Jack, something weird's going on."

"Tell me about it," he said sarcastically.

"What? No. Seriously, I just heard from Wallace."

"Wallace? What the –" he stopped himself, embarrassed. "I mean, what did he –"

"That's what I asked him. It's the second time he's called me. Something's up."

"The second time?"

"Yeah," she replied, "he called me last night and left a message on my machine."

"What does want with you?"

"He wants to meet me for drinks this evening."

"What?!?!" Jack tried to keep his attention focused on the road.

"Yeah, no shit… but that's what he said. And the weird thing was –"

"You mean it gets weirder?"

"He asked about you."

Jack took a moment.

"About me?"

"Yeah, about you."

"What the hell?" He cleaned it up this time. "What would he want with me?"

"I'm not sure but he asked if I was still in contact with you, if I knew how to get in touch with you."

"And what did you tell him?"

"I told him the truth."

"The truth? You mean the truth that we used to sleep together or the truth that we just spoke on the phone this morning?"

"No, the truth that I hadn't heard from you since you left the Bureau."

"Oh, *that* truth, ok."

"He didn't believe me."

"Wow, there's a shocker," Jack said.

"Shut the hell up, Sturdevant. I shouldn't even be doing this for you, you know."

"Why, you find happiness at the Office of Tribal Justice, did ya'?"

"You know, *Jack-ass*, I have you to thank for my career rotting away in that cubicle hellhole, you and that big fuckin' mouth of yours." He was glad to hear her tone seemed to have lost any semblance of anger and frustration she'd once so deeply felt.

"And the fact that you believed in what we were doing as much as I did?"

"Yeah," she admitted, "that, too."

"Listen, Laura, I've got something I've got to get to. I'm on the road and –"

"Ok," she said, accepting the brush off. She wanted to tell him about the email from Carmen. About the cryptic message she'd sent from a private cell number because her's wasn't safe. About Wallace being dirty. But especially about the package she'd sent that Laura had unknowingly let get returned.

"Jack, I've got to tell you some –" she started.

"Laura, I'm sorry, but I can't really talk right now. Please, call me tonight, I don't care how late it is. I want to know what's going on. Ok?"

She could tell from Jack's tone something wasn't right.

"Jack," she said, leaving a moment to convey her concern, "you ok?"

Jack smiled.

"Yeah, I'm fine, just got a few things going on. I'll tell you about it tonight."

That worked for her.

"Count on it."

"Thanks, Laura, just be careful tonight. Wallace is a cunning bastard, you know."

"Tell me about it. Take care, Jack. I'll call you tonight."

"Good luck, Laura."

The connection went silent.

Jack flipped his phone shut. He smiled as he leaned forward and returned his phone to his back pocket. He looked into his rear view mirror and noticed Daniel was still asleep. Ana's head was up against Caridád's shoulder. Her eyes were closed as well. He wondered about the last time they felt safe. He thought about Laura, the kids they'd once talked about having and the life they had once talked about sharing. About what they once had together and how – if not why – it had all unraveled. And what role the leaks really played in all of it. For reasons he couldn't quite grasp right now, he wanted more time to think more about her. About them.

But as was true throughout most of his life, more important matters demanded his attention. His focus needed to be on the kids right now. And he couldn't forget about Alex. How she might help. Not to mention how he may have put her in harm's way.

But sorting through all the cascading scenarios rushing through his head, he suddenly felt his mood changing. And his mind wandering. His focus was shifting.

He'd always hated how Laura could do that to him. Or for him.

* * *

His full-time housekeeper, Mrs. Martinéz, had left by her usual time, just before noon, on this Saturday though not before arranging a vase of freshly cut flowers – an assortment of white, red and yellow roses – from the back-

yard's well-tended garden. Their distinctive but subtle fragrances pleasantly
distracted him as he finally decided he'd invested enough of his weekend
afternoon in his work, having spent the last couple of hours cleaning up a
backlog of emails and setting up appointments on behalf of the Archdiocese
for early the following week. With the grandfather's clock in the hall – a
handcrafted Thomas Ross original, he was never shy to point out – now
chiming at half-past four, he placed his Blackberry on the deacon's bench in
the entryway near the custom-designed front door of his North State Parkway home. He'd just started to walk away, toward the kitchen, when he heard
it vibrate once again.

He thought about letting it go.

Deciding against it, perhaps simply because of his innate sense of guilt –
the same guilt over details left undone that had served him so well in forging
a management style that featured a razor's edge political acumen –, he turned
back and reached down for the device. He opened the incoming email and
read the concise message.

And then again.

His face did not change expression. It wasn't the first time he'd been
reminded.

The Reverend Monsignor John Stuart Miles raised his head as his attention was drawn to the young woman stepping seductively into the kitchen
doorway just down the hall. She wore nothing but one of the tee-shirts –
since cleaned – he wore while running every morning. Her long, muscular
tanned legs came together just above the shirt's worn, tattered edges. The shoe
company's logo was hardly distinguishable though, even if it were, it hardly
could compete with the soft, firm flesh he knew rested beneath it. Her blond-
streaked chestnut hair was cut short and cropped tightly out of his way.

Just as he preferred.

The weeks since her twenty-fourth birthday had been the most unusual if
not enjoyable of her young life. She'd spent many of her weekends – if Thursday afternoons through Monday mornings actually constituted the weekend
– in his company, often in the insane luxury of this glorious Gold Coast mansion. She'd dined in the most exclusive restaurants in the city, engaged some
of the most powerful men – and women – in city, state and national politics.
She'd done countless lines of coke, sometimes with his help, other times while
he watched. The Jag was her favorite, an experience she found more exhilarat-
ing from behind the wheel than simply as a jealous passenger. He found the
same was true when she'd do him in the Bentley, as well.

He'd always been good to her, at least up until now. He was kind, gentle, the consummate gentleman. His sexual proclivities were playful, mischievous perhaps, maybe even borderline kinky. His tastes ran young, athletic and dark. Endurance was a must. And there were days he seemed ridiculously insatiable.

The young woman dropped her head and assumed her most poutful stance. "I'm hungry," she cooed.

He laid the Blackberry back down on the antique bench and walked slowly toward her, his eyes not leaving hers. She loved being pampered. As did he.

He took her face in his hands, tilted it slightly and spoke gently. "So am I."

She disappeared inside his embrace. He bent backwards a bit and raised her feet off the floor then set her down carefully.

"And where is dinner this evening?" she asked softly.

"Nomi's. But not until 8." he whispered as his eyes widened. "Not to worry, though, if you're late, they'll hold your table."

She stepped back and contently returned his smile. She didn't ask with whom she'd be dining. It hardly mattered. The Monsignor had excellent taste in all manner of things, not the least of which was his choice of her dinner guests. And whether she'd be meeting someone her age or older, either a man or woman – or, perhaps, tonight both – or even, as has happened on occasion, an inquisitive and uninhibited group of three or four, no one she'd spent time entertaining on his behalf had ever been disappointed.

A feeling he would undoubtedly share while watching her later.

As she led him up the hardwood stairs, he motioned to her to wait. He removed a long stem rose from the bouquet sitting on the entry way table in the hall just outside the foyer. He'd selected a red Peerless Rose, named for the Virgin Mother, its deep fullness and crimson color meant to depict her sorrowful mysteries during recitation of the rosary. The one he'd selected was in full bloom, its fragrance both sweet and compelling. She smiled as he held it up for her to enjoy. She took his hand as they continued up the stairs.

As they entered his private bedroom, the door to the master bath opened. A younger woman, just as athletic, almost as muscular, perhaps a bit cuter and displaying the darker tan she'd worked on earlier that afternoon, came out drying her auburn hair with a long, thick towel. Her slender body was still damp, moist from her hot shower.

The first young woman let go of his hand and, crossing her arms in front of her, pulled her tee-shirt up over her head. He watched attentively as she jumped playfully on to the unmade king-size bed, tossing the tee off behind her before he reached for the fresh twenty-one year-old now smiling invitingly. She placed her left hand on the side of his face and kissed him open-mouthed on his lips, no tongue. She pushed herself up against his heavy terrycloth robe and felt him stiffening. He stepped back, took her hand and dragged the soft, fragrant petals across her cheek. He looked at the woman now naked on his bed, lying back against the handcrafted oak headboard, her fingers having disappeared amidst the hair between her thighs. He kicked aside the shirt that rested on the floor at his feet and led the younger woman to the side of the bed, where he released her hand. She was excited at the thought of including him this time.

He walked around the foot of the bed and up along the other side where both young women, now leaning back, sat upright in a loose embrace. He passed in front of the handcrafted chest of drawers where two aging photographs and unique religious articles, a couple of rosaries among them, served to complement the chest's otherwise austere appearance. They each, in their own way, provided him a special if not lasting memory of his somewhat unique approach to spreading the Good News and how he had chosen to do the Lord's work. He gave a quick glance to the dresser's second drawer but decided now was not the right time. The timing, the mood, was just not right.

Maybe, when they were more experienced.

He sat down on the bed and smiled, first at the one, then the other. The first woman's eyes shot to his crotch, lustfully displaying a wanton look that welcomed his interest. Her lips parted slightly; the thought of all of him inside her made her wetter.

He touched her cheek with the rose and slowly brought it across her chin. She raised her head in response as it slowly worked its way down her throat to her chest. He dragged it horizontally across her breasts, circling her areolas, scaling each nipple, then shared it with her friend. Its fragrance was as inviting as his method was arousing. He turned it slightly to one side as he traveled across the auburn woman's breasts, applying more pressure with each pass above her areolas. Finally, as it approached her left nipple, one of its larger thorns broke her tender, soft skin. A thin scratch revealed a pale red line.

She winced momentarily from the sudden, sharp pain. Together, the three of them watched a lean trail of blood trickle down her breast, a drop slowly forming at the end of its crescent trail, about to fall onto her tight abdomen. The first young woman shifted and ducked her head down and over. Her warm, wet tongue caught the drop as its weight brought it to falling. She dragged her tongue up the side of the younger woman's flesh who, shifting slightly, laid back her head, closed her eyes and moaned agreeably.

The good Monsignor watched as time slowed down, their sensuality organizing his most ravenous intentions. He gently helped the first young woman sit back, placing her shoulders where they'd once been, against the headboard. He took the rose, probably sixteen inches in length, and twisted it, snapping the stem in two. He held the flowered stem in his right hand while, with the broken remainder in his left, he firmly separated her legs. As they opened, her younger companion reached down and began massaging her friend's wet, delicate tissue. Their prey leaned back. She brushed the chestnut hair from her face and began enjoying her turn.

With his left hand, he took the stem, thorns pointing back towards him, and slowly slipped it inside her. It entered her easily. She moaned softly but excitedly. A few inches later, he gently began to withdraw it, twisting it slightly. Her expression tightened though her eyes remained closed. Her young friend took her face in her hands and kissed her deeply as the Monsignor withdrew the stem almost completely, then repeated the motion. Slowly, deliberately, his pace methodically quickened.

Each time he withdrew it, a growing number of thin red lines on her thighs grew darker. He motioned the younger woman to move aside and watched as his sacrificial lamb's face was streaked with the tracks of her tears, her glistening eyes now open in response to the increasing pain. He smiled to the young woman beside her, who dragged her tongue across the woman's cheeks. He slowly shoved the stem inward one more time. The woman's pain looked at him through clouds of welling tears.

"It is only through suffering, my child, that we can hope to be deemed worthy..."

He removed a petal from the blooming rose and seductively wiped her eyes, then parted her lips and placed it on her tongue. He nodded to the younger woman watching them, who dutifully laid back and spread her legs. He dragged the flower across her taut belly and, as she parted her tender fold, began massaging her with its petals. Her auburn hair fell across her eyes and she raised her head, her mouth opening at his beneficence if not the pleasure the flower's soft moistness brought her. He watched her expression gain strength as her fingers added to her pleasure. He then repeated the same bloodletting routine with her. Her opened eyes met his. He expected her to continue on her own.

He rose from the bed and removed his robe, his eyes fixated back on his chestnut haired lamb, the broken stem still firmly inside her. She felt drops from a small bottle of lubricant in her hand, on her fingers, which he brought over to apply on him. She had trouble seeing through the burning tears and the flashes of pain.

He reached down and pulled the stem out quickly. She spasmed and cried out in sudden agony. Throbbing, he ignored her as he positioned himself on the bed in front of her and, with his arms wrapped securely around her thighs, pulled her easily towards him. He rubbed himself against her, inside her hair, then glided himself into her wet invitation, sliding perfectly into her, surrounding himself within her warm, tight treasure.

He grinned, his eyes widening, as she vainly cried out against his size.

The younger woman rolled toward her and covered her mouth with her own.

His pleasure gained momentum. As his rhythm developed, he looked to her auburn haired companion now fondling his penitent. He pushed apart her legs to see the trickles of blood that now spotted her inner thighs. She suddenly tightened, reacting to a shifting thorn. The stem remained deeply embedded, its flower's petals still in bloom. It was as if her womanhood had provided the fertile soil from which the rose had opened, reaching out through her, in her, with her to embrace life itself. He grinned lasciviously.

Her moment of redemption would follow soon.

The next ninety minutes brought with it immense pleasure and intolerable pain. The stamina that he'd counted among his many blessings had proven to his young supple guests to be a curse unto itself. When he'd finally finished, still not having climaxed, he left them both lying prone, drained but unsatisfied. He moved to the reclining swivel chair, positioned in a corner of the room just off to the side of the bed. He reached down, picked up his robe and put it back on. He sat down and pulled back the chair's rocker arm. Adjusting the position until he was comfortable, his sightline perfect, he was now ready to continue. The sides of his robes fell away as he nodded and waved to proceed.

His hands began immediately to wander as he watched their tongues slowly if not enthusiastically wrap themselves inside a deepening sensual dance. He watched intently as their taut, firm bodies summoned the strength to continue and the incentive to become entwined, their soft, smooth flesh reacting in the early moments of the trembling pleasure his participation would soon bring.

In the coming hour, they would both righteously know the fullness of his strength. He would opt, though, for something a bit more humbling – maybe, even demeaning – and definitely more demanding of their limber, athletic bodies. But absolutely, almost certainly more delightful, at least for him. From their knees they would each know the relentless invasion behind his pounding, splitting presence. Each would have their turn to absorb the full measure of purification that only holy pain can bring, a spirituality that only their suffering could adequately teach. His pleasure would defeat their demons.

They would become worthy. No matter how long – or how often – it took.

His imagination raced as he pictured the three of them as one, serving God's most intimate pleasures from his altar behind his bent chestnut lamb, her companion willingly improvising on her lesson plan. He could almost feel his blood pulsating through his veins. It pleased him to see them eagerly – or, even better, reluctantly – submit to his licentious will. He didn't consider it so much sadistic as creative. His experience had taught him that surprises could be the most generous of all his gifts. He'd taken his time, grooming them, as he had so many others, to share these moments so that, by indulging his appetites, they'd embrace their sinful pain as justification for their rightful penance. That they'd understand his forgiveness as necessary. His absolution as cleansing.

Perhaps even redemptive.

His will be done.

* * *

Chapter 10

THE SPANISH LYRICS to Selena's "I Could Fall in Love" still provided Sandy's ring tone as the current incoming call served to remind him. Teresa's memory no longer reached out for him every hour of every day as it once had. Still, it was comforting to know that, whenever he felt the need to return to those warm summer nights, she was always there. Waiting for him.

He flipped open his phone as he wandered into an empty family room where a distinguishably steamy, musky mix still wafted in the humid air. Before he could wonder where Miguel had taken Caridád, he heard Raúl's voice.

"Where you at?"

"I'm at the house, where –"

He suddenly was speaking into silence. He turned to hear Raúl walk though the front door and into the living room, followed closely by a seething Carlos. A gauze bandage, approximately 1½" square, covered the wound he'd received just a few short hours ago in the street. It would be generous to describe Raúl as being in a somber mood. Carlos, on the other hand, seemed only interested in beating an explanation out of Sandy.

"Carlos," Sandy said, taking the offensive, "what the fuck happened, man? What were you doin'? Jesus, you were just supposed to bring them over to the car. That was it! How fuckin' simple –"

Carlos pushed his way around Raúl, who chose to let the rampage begin.

A moment later, Sandy was pinned up against a kitchen wall, his feet dangling above the floor. Carlos had Sandy's shirt wrapped tightly around his closed fists.

"You fuckin' son of a bitch," he screamed in Sandy's face. "You watched it go down, you saw it go bad, you cut me loose and you fuckin' ran. You pussy little bitch!"

Sandy struggled to speak.

"Like hell I did," he countered, hoping that the volume of his tone could mask the fear in his voice. "I looked for you, I couldn't find you!"

"The fuck you did…" Carlos angrily responded. He shoved him back one more time, bouncing Sandy's head up against the well. "…and Luís, what about him?"

"What about him? Shit, he can take care of himself. Nobody got caught. Everything's cool."

With that, Carlos stepped back, pulled back his right arm now wrapped in gauze, and landed a fist, with as much force as he could muster, into Sandy's stomach. Sandy doubled over. He tried to make a sound but the lack of oxygen left him breathless. He instinctively tried to balance himself against a nearby chair. Carlos backed away and let him fall to the floor. Sandy curled up in a fetal position.

"Everything's cool? Is that right, mother fucka? They've got my fuckin' knife, asshole! And they've got my fuckin' prints! *Everything's cool?*"

Carlos kicked him once, then again, in his stomach and chest.

"They're not coming for you, dumbass, they're coming for me!"

Sandy rolled over, groveling and moaning from the sudden, sharp pain. Carlos reached down and dragged him to his feet. He winced dramatically. He tasted blood inside his mouth. Carlos may have broken a rib, maybe even two. Unsympathetically, he hurled Sandy across the kitchen floor. He slid hard into the stove and banged his head and shoulder. Carlos began to advance on him again when Raúl stepped in front of him.

"Enough!" Raúl finally said, dispassionately.

Carlos relented, doing as he was told, though his eyes still burned with rage.

Raúl turned to Carlos and asked about his younger brother.

"Do you know where he is now?"

"No," Carlos responded, catching his breath. "I've got to go look for him."

He looked Carlos straight in the eye.

"Take Sandy with you."

"What?!?!"

"You heard me," Raúl commanded. "Things got fucked up, yes, but we resolve our problems in this family and we move on."

Carlos rejected that idea immediately.

"Nothin's been resolved until I beat him so bad he's beggin' me to kill him."

Raúl smiled as Sandy lay on the floor, desperately trying to breathe. He understood Carlos' rage as well as his vengeance. But what he also understood – what he valued most and tried to teach those around him – was the need to control it. The key to effective rage was to use it and not allow it to use you.

"I cannot allow that to happen, *amigo*…"

Raúl turned and looked down at Sandy.

"…Carlos, clean him up, then take him to go look for Luís."

Carlos respectfully if begrudgingly moved around Raúl until he stood over a groaning Sandy. With one hand he reached down and roughly pulled him to his feet, choosing not to hide his enjoyment of Sandy's pain.

Raúl stepped out of the kitchen and retreated back into the living room. He noticed the vacant family room as he opened his cell phone to a blank text message. Two characters and a couple of clicks later, it was on its way into cyberspace. He flipped the phone shut and returned it to his back pocket. He pushed his way through the front door on his way to the park. He wondered where Miguel was, where he'd had taken Caridád.

Sandy howled as Carlos shoved him toward the bathroom.

Some minutes later, having walked a few blocks further south, Raúl felt his cell phone vibrate. He flipped it open to read an incoming three character text message: "n15." He decided to slow down his pace a bit on his way to the playground park on Sangamon, between 36th and 37th Street, and take a few minutes to enjoy the warm summer evening. The park was bound to be busy tonight. It would make things easier.

His attention was drawn to a frail old man near the bus stop at 35th Street. He stood behind a pushcart, with wheelbarrow handles, fitted with a small freezer complete with chiming bells, sort of a Good Humor man on foot. He was a local vender, one he'd seen around the neighborhood before. And not just this summer. He'd been around for years, working the same neighborhood sidewalks. He sold *paletas*, a Mexican ice pop made with fresh fruit. They were outrageously good, much better than that processed, commercial crap you get in the *whetto* supermarkets. And, for only a buck, you could hardly find a better way to cool down on this or any other hot, humid August afternoon.

Raúl chose banana. Not his favorite but, toward the end of the day, the selection was a bit sparse. The gaunt, elderly man took Raúl's ten dollar bill with some reluctance. He hated making change by parting with his singles. Raúl waved him off as he peeled the cellophane wrapping away from the treat. The old man smiled, tipped his worn, dirty, sweat-stained White Sox cap, circa 1983, and went on his way back down the sidewalk.

Raúl turned and watched him hobble away, those silly damn bells announcing those same silly damn treats he'd been selling for years. And for which he could charge five times as much and still sell out. He couldn't help wonder how this one old man survived. What he told his children or their children about his day. What he thought about his own dignity, as a man, and if he found in the promise of this country the same empty future he'd left behind on the other side of the border. He wondered, when this one old man or his parents or maybe even his grandparents came to this country, what their thoughts were about of this bountiful land of endless opportunity.

Raúl was no one's fool. He knew the American Dream for what it was. George Carlin used to say people called it that because you had to be asleep to believe in it. But being born white, in this country, the comedian couldn't know the half of it.

Raúl was nothing if not keenly, if not crudely, observant and he saw the Mexican community as next in line to supplant blacks as America's latest invisible second class. Those who had a financial stake in how America runs – and who runs it – would never again sit by and watch any individual or any organized movement threaten their country's economic stability.

Which is to say, their personal fortunes.

His logic bordered on the conspiratorial, as confirmed through the lense of history: he reasoned that those whose economic interests were at stake would not again ignore the threat that organized civil disobedience could mount. If the '60s taught them nothing else, his theory went, it taught the *whettos* at least that much. So every time he got an automated voice asking him if he wanted to proceed in English or Spanish, he seethed. Every time he read packaging at the local hardware store that was written in both English and Spanish, he fumed. And when he saw Mexicans left to do jobs that no *whetto* would work, jobs like bussing tables or mowing lawns or cleaning up construction sites or shoving pushcarts around neighborhoods, he felt personally offended.

To Raúl, this land of opportunity was, and always has been, meant for Americans. Not "Mexican-Americans", not "African-Americans", not

"Asian-Americans." And every *whetto* knew what those terms — what the code — meant. It was the way Wall Street types — the investment bankers, the moneychangers, the power brokers — the people who *really* ran this fuckin' country kept everyone neatly in their place. The religion of those who bought and paid for their politics worshipped the stability and security of the status quo because it was good business. The chaos, upheaval and uncertainty of social change eventually meant nothing more than making room for more seats at the table, more hands outstretched looking for theirs. In the end, when the music inevitably would stop — that moment when a social movement would eventually get absorbed into the culture —, those left standing were, well, left standing. Still, the advantage in identifying the "haves" was that it made it easier to discern the "have-nots." Who was now considered entitled.

And who wasn't.

But that wasn't the way Raúl ever planned to go. His "career" was his choice, the result of his own American entrepreneurial spirit. He had no use for any economy, any livelihood, that dictated to him what opportunities were deemed appropriate for his class, his color, his ethnicity. No, he'd prefer to find — to make — his own way. And his own rules. He'd carved out a living as someone who, at least in his own mind, not only provided employment opportunities to people who might not otherwise have any. He'd also specialized in bringing people together, those having specific needs with those possessing specific attributes designed to meet those needs. In truth, he thought of himself as a temp agency of sorts, someone who managed his own economic growth, who gained market share through occasionally hostile mergers and acquisitions, and who offered his customers personally valuable if not uniquely creative goods and services.

Now, if that wasn't an American success story, what was?

Either way, it beat mopping floors or washing dishes or cleaning toilets or even selling frozen popsicles on hot, humid August Saturday afternoons.

Raúl's walk to the park had been a bit slower than he'd realized.

He entered the park from 36th Street, walking over to a nearby water fountain where he bent over to take a short drink. Christ, even the water was warm. He straightened up and eyed a double wooden bench, the kind with the support beam in the middle and the benches running parallel on either side. It was located strategically between two asphalt basketball courts that were in desperate need of new paint lines. A well-built man, with square shoulders and an ongoing if unacknowledged drinking problem, was seated, one leg crossed over the other, with his back toward Raúl, facing the late afternoon sun. Raúl used his hand as a visor against his forehead and strained to see that it was his old friend. He saw the seated man was wearing what resembled a yellow Corona tee-shirt, complete with dark blue shorts and shoe company sandals, just as he said he would when he'd talked to Sandy on the phone earlier in the day.

Estéban Sanchez Calderón was both a former Marine and ex-employee of the Department of Homeland Security. He left DHS before he was asked to and now freelanced as an independent security consultant. Standing just under six foot tall and considered handsome in most circles, he'd managed to keep in shape, in part due to his hectic professional schedule. He'd also recently taken up jogging the Lakefront as an addendum to his normal workout routine although that was mostly due to his latest client. A growing list of impressive political connections, both inside and outside the Beltway, along with the welcomed ongoing if often vague threat of al-Qaeda and other lesser-known splinter groups afforded him a very lucrative living. Fear, it turned out, was not an asset reserved only for the White House from which dividends could flow.

Since his departure from DHS, Estéban consulted on the coordination of security efforts for different high profile politicians throughout the country and, in certain specific cases, around the world. Earlier this spring, he'd been contacted by the Archdiocese of Chicago concerning a close personal friend of the Mayor's, a local Church dignitary of sorts, who would be returning home to Chicago for the summer. And while it sounded more like a baby-sitting job than a security detail, Estéban welcomed the opportunity to return to his hometown. He no longer had any family in the area but seeing Raúl again after so many years brought back a flood of memories. Being here for the summer gave him a chance to reconnect with the old neighborhood and with one of his oldest friends.

Raúl walked over to the bench opposite the one his friend occupied and sat down.

"Good to see you again, Raúl," Estéban said without turning to face him, "how've you been?"

"It's good to see you again, *mi hermano*, it's been too long."

"Yes, it has." Estéban uncrossed his legs, and, with both feet on the ground, leaned forward. He looked forward, across the basketball court opposite him.

"How is your man's arm?" Raúl inquired.

"Fine, just a scratch really. He got careless," he responded, understating the severity of the man's wound. "It's a good thing that young man of yours doesn't know how to use a knife correctly. Someone could have gotten hurt!"

"Yes," Raúl said, sadly agreeing, "a good thing, I suppose."

"Did you get what you needed from him?" Estéban asked unsolicitedly.

"As much as he knew," Raúl said. "Is there something more you can tell me?"

"I have people looking into it, *hermano*, but nothing yet. But it shouldn't take too long. He was able to provide a friend of mine with a partial plate number and description of his car. We should probably know something by tomorrow, I would think."

Raúl nodded. "Thank you, my friend, I apologize for putting you in harm's way."

Estéban grinned.

"Not a problem, it's what I do. Besides, I have no doubt we'll find a very comfortable form of compensation. Of this I am certain."

Raúl dropped his head and smiled.

"So, what is it I can do for you, *mi amigo*?" Estéban asked.

"I need your help, Estéban. You may be the only one I can turn to."

Estéban was not unfamiliar with playing such a role.

"I need you to find out something for me… about a cop."

Estéban pulled out a small spiral notepad and pen.

"His name is Colavito, Bobby Colavito. He's a local, a detective, out of Area 1."

Estéban stopped writing.

"Colavito you say?"

"Yes," Raúl responded, "why?"

Estéban just shrugged. Raúl continued.

"He's a freelancer, he came recommended, he's done a few jobs for me. The last one was with Sandy a couple of nights ago. Seems reliable. But I need to find out more about him. Whatever you can do for me, I would be very grateful."

"Consider it done," Estéban replied.

Estéban repeated Bobby's name to Raúl. He flipped his pad shut and returned it and his pen to his back pants pocket.

"And speaking of which," Estéban continued, "does that lovely young lady that I met last winter… I wonder, is she still around? What was her name again?"

"You mean Caridád, yes," Raul responded, looking off into the distance, "she's still around, though for how much longer I'm not sure."

"That's a shame," Estéban countered, "As I recall, you seemed to enjoy her company. Something to do with her sister, perhaps?"

Raúl dropped his head and gazed at his feet.

"She's outlived her usefulness," Raúl said, opting to say nothing more. "She's the other reason I wanted to speak with you."

"Really?" Estéban offered, poorly hiding his interest.

"Yes," Raúl started, "I need you to make arrangements for her, some-where overseas, some place where she will disappear."

"I see," Estéban said, realizing an opportunity. "It's time for her to move on?"

Raúl watched the sand beneath his shoes kick up.

"She's disappointed me," he said, "and I no longer can trust her."

Estéban waited to hear more.

"She's behind that little scuffle in the street this afternoon," he continued, "and now that she knows what happened to her sister –"

"Are you sure that was wise?" Estéban wondered, interrupting.

Raúl showed little reaction.

"I mean, did you ever find out who her sister'd been talking to?"

Raúl seemed uncomfortable talking about that night now almost four years ago.

"I did get a name, yes," he told Estéban, "a journalist, as I recall…"

Raúl could not see Estéban was already nodding his head in agreement.

"…but I don't know where it went from there. I don't remember seeing anything about him – or what her sister may have told him, for that matter – in the paper, so –"

Estéban sat back and smiled.

"There was a reason for that, *hermano*…"

Raúl's interest was piqued.

"…As it happened, my work took me to Iraq right around the time this journalist was there. I was working as a military subcontractor, providing the army with 'creative alternatives' – what my employers called 'enhanced interrogation techniques' – to aid them in obtaining more critical and very sensitive intelligence."

He pushed aside some loose gravel at his feet as he shifted crossing his legs.

"I was able to offer them some direction on a little device that seemed to serve their purposes nicely. Maybe you recall which one I'm referring to?"

Raúl could still picture the last hapless victim he'd submitted to the mer-ciless, medieval grip of the Scavenger's Daughter.

"Yes, I do, Estéban," he said, "and, you're right, it has continued to serve our purposes quite nicely on occasion."

"Well, as it turned out," Estéban continued, "I became aware of the work our journalist friend was doing in the desert. It seemed he was asking questions about some rather sensitive activities that my employers there had little interest in answering. Since he seemed so intrigued by my employer's interrogation methods, I offered him the opportunity to become acquainted with the device, thinking it might help his research."

Estéban's caustic sense of humor was not lost on Raúl.

"As it turned out, he was eventually able to offer us much of what he learned as a result of his first-hand experience. Until, that is, he unfortunately succumbed to what we later learned was natural causes. A stroke, I believe it was…"

Raúl laughed.

"…Men his age need to be more mindful when it comes to their health."

His smile widened as he nodded in agreement with Estéban.

"As luck would have it, the insurgents were only too glad to take credit for his 'abduction'," Estéban continued, "even if he was missing his head."

Some things made even Raúl cringe.

"And that would have been the end of it…"

Raúl's waited for the other shoe to drop.

"…if we hadn't learned that he'd been providing information to someone back here in the states."

"This comes as news to me," Raúl said, wondering where this was going.

"That surprises me, my friend," Estéban answered, "since it appears, from what I have been able to piece together, that the woman he'd been contacting…"

Raúl listened intently to his every word.

"…was the same FBI agent found in that van on the expressway the other night."

"You *know* this?" Raúl asked.

"*Sí, hermano*," Estéban replied. "Might this have anything to do with this Bobby Colavito, this detective friend of yours?"

"I don't know," Raúl said, nodding his head slowly. "So, what does this mean?"

"Hard to say," Estéban responded carefully, "I continue to reach out to my contacts at the FBI but her murder has left few people willing to talk."

"But," Raúl reacted, "the journalist guy and Caridád's sister… that was, what, four years ago now?"

Estéban nodded his head again.

"Why bring it up now?"

Estéban sat up and, leaning forward, placed his elbows on his knees.

"I do not know," Estéban said, "but Caridád's sister – Maria, I believe her name was? –, the connection between her and our journalist friend was definitely there."

Raúl listened carefully, his mind running through different scenarios.

"But it does seem more than coincidence that your suspicious detective was involved the other night with the same FBI agent who was herself a contact of his."

Estéban continued

"I am concerned because I suspect that this matter didn't die with her in that van. There would seem to be more to this that, perhaps, your dear Caridád may shed light on."

Raúl thought back to that summer night when he learned Maria had been talking to someone. And he recalled the loose ends her death created.

"But why am I just hearing about this now?"

Estéban tilted his head slightly in Raúl's direction.

"Are you serious, Raúl?" Estéban asked incredulously. "Are you trying to tell me you didn't know she was meeting with someone?"

Raúl was always impressed with how Estéban always seemed to be in the know.

"Besides, what was there to tell?" Estéban countered. "What we learned from our journalist friend's computer wasn't much. We only discovered his connection to the woman agent because of the email history we were able to recover. And, even though he'd mentioned Caridád's sister as a source in his emails – never by name, by the way –, we had nothing to put her together with Caridád. Had I known that you had dealt with Maria when you did…"

Raúl sat quietly, listening closely.

"…At first, we thought the big FBI sting on the east coast a few months back was connected to all of this. And, for all we know, it might have been. We learned that his contact – this woman agent – was an undercover part of their operation. What we don't know is what Caridád may have been told by her sister or, for that matter, what Caridád might have said or done to help the FBI."

Raúl could hardly believe his ears.

"Caridád? *My* Caridád? Working with the Feds?" Raúl stood up and glared directly at the ground. "That's not possible!"

But the events of the last twenty-four hours made him wonder if he was now trying more to convince Estéban – or himself.

"I understand, *amigo*," Estéban offered, "but the reality is Caridád is Maria's sister. And we know Maria talked to our journalist friend who we know supplied information to that dead woman agent who, not so coincidentally it would now seem, worked undercover as part of their east coast sting."

Raúl stood still and waited.

"If you were in my position, what would you take away from all of this?"

Raúl sat back down. Estéban's logic was difficult to argue with.

"It would seem," Estéban concluded, "that the prudent course of action would be to convince Caridád that she should cooperate with your curiosity. Would you agree?"

Raúl slowly nodded in response.

"She's at the house. I'll talk with her as soon as I get back."

"Good," Estéban said as he stood up. "I will wait to hear from you about that."

Raúl again nodded in response.

"And I will get back to you," Estéban continued, "as soon as I know something about the partial plate on the car…"

"And the cop, Colavito, the detective…" Raúl reminded him.

Estéban nodded.

"I haven't forgotten, my friend, I will get back to you with what I find out."

Raúl stood up again, this time somewhat more relaxed.

"Good," Raúl said. "And I hope you will let me know if your compensation fails to meet your expectations."

"I have no doubt she will live up to your very high standards," he replied, smiling.

Estéban now stood up as well.

"I will be in touch, *mi hermano*, just give me a day or two," he said, still not making eye contact with Raúl.

"The sooner the better, Estéban," Raúl reminded him, "for us both."

"Ah, Rolando," he said, using the name by which his mother used to call him, "the years have not changed you a bit."

Hearing that name caused Raúl to smile widely.

As he watched Estéban walk away, he felt his phone vibrate. It was Sandy. As he listened, Raúl's expression grew colder.

* * *

Jack came down the street toward the "T" intersection in front of his split-level house. He made a left toward his driveway and was surprised to see Alex sitting on the concrete stoop to his front door, working on her laptop. He pulled into the driveway and brought the car to a slow stop, leaving the three of them still asleep in the backseat.

As quietly as he could, he closed the car door behind him and walked up the short sidewalk toward the front door. Her eyes were focused on him as she closed her laptop and set it to one side next to her backpack. She stood up to greet him.

"Hi," he said, still surprised to see her.

"Hi yourself," she responded, sensing something was up. She immediately wondered, by showing up unannounced, if she was interrupting his plans for the evening.

"God, am I glad to see you… I really need your help!" He didn't even think to ask how she got here.

Her mood suddenly changed.

"Why, what's up?"

"It's a very long story but…"

Alex liked it already.

"…I've got some company in my car and I could really use your help getting them settled."

"Them?" she asked, and then again, "Settled?"

"Like I said, it's a long story."

Ana and Daniel fell back asleep quickly. Ana got the family room couch, Daniel the matching love seat. Jack wasn't really worried about whether they'd sleep through the night, not at this point. It gave Alex time to keep an eye on Caridád, who was still sleeping herself in the empty second bedroom upstairs. Jack thought it would be smarter, and Alex agreed, to keep a close eye on Caridád throughout the night.

Alex walked out of Caridád's room, pulled the door partially closed, then walked slowly down the stairs. She stopped about halfway as she saw Jack, seated on the couch – the one piece of furniture in an otherwise echoingly empty living room –, staring out the aging bow window into oblivion. She knew almost nothing of his story but something told her she was about to get to know an honest-to-goodness hero.

She reached the base of the stairs and walked softly across the hardwood floor.

"Got room for me?" she asked.

Jack looked up, his hands still folded in his lap, and smiled.

"Yeah," he said invitingly, "I've got plenty of room for you."

She pulled her left leg up and sat down on top of it, close to him but not too close. She joined his gaze out the eastern exposure of the window before them. The bright blue sky was cloudless.

After a few seconds of welcomed silence, he spoke.

"I thought you had a date tonight."

She laughed.

"Turns out I actually did," she said, "an investment banker, some friend of the guy my roommate's seeing. He seemed like a nice guy –"

"Wait," Jack said, "he was a nice guy *despite* being an investment banker?"

"Yeah, well," she said, "From what she'd told me about him, he sounded nice until I learned he worked in the financial district. A real Wall Street type. And you've heard the joke, right?"

"Joke?"

"Yeah," she continued, "the two types of guys who work on Wall Street?"

"And those would be…"

"Standard and Poor!"

Jack smiled. It really was clever though not particularly original.

"Yeah," he said, "I think I heard that line before."

"Well, I thought it was cute," she offered in her defense.

"Anyway," she continued, "I talked with him on the phone this afternoon. He sounded really sweet and genuinely disappointed. I had to tell him I couldn't make it tonight. He was heartbroken."

Jack turned to her, twisting a bit on the cushion.

"Only to be expected."

She smiled gratefully.

"Honestly, Jack, I wanted to be here with you. Everything you told me today, everything you said, it just kept bouncing around in my brain."

"I see," he said, with more than a bit of excitement underlying his tone.

"I didn't realize we wouldn't be alone tonight, but –"

"It couldn't be helped, Alex." he said, shifting back to face the window.

"I'm sure," she said understandingly, dropping her head on the back of the couch and her arm around his shoulder. "You want to talk about it?"

He turned back toward her, took her hand in his and smiled thankfully.

"It was just like before, just like when I was in the field. It's the same god-damned thing. Nothing has changed!"

She stayed attentively silent.

"I was heading home, after dropping you off, and I couldn't stand sitting in that lousy expressway traffic. I took the first exit I could find and worked my way to Halsted. When I came up to 18th Street, there was this fight going, literally in the middle of the street. I couldn't see Ana and Daniel then. I could only see the one big guy with a knife and the other guy, who I assumed was simply trying to help them."

"Anyway, the big guy with the knife sees me come running up the street and decides it ain't worth, so he runs off. The other guy starts to help the kids but he's been cut. Soon sirens are everywhere. The paramedics show up and treat the guy with the cut. Nothing real serious, from what I could tell…"

"…the kids were crying and screaming for their friend, the priest."

"The priest?"

"I'll get to him in a second."

She nodded.

"Anyway, the guy tries to help the kids to the curb, but they won't go. By then, the police and paramedics are there. The paramedics take one look at the guy and help him back toward their truck. I step in to talk with the police and tell them I'm a friend of the priest, who I see coming up 18th Street kind of frantic, looking for them. The cop lets me take the kids to him, which I do. I pick up Daniel in one arm and take Ana by the hand and walk her back to my car. I cut around the traffic and head up 18th Street where they see Father Mac…"

"Father Mac, being the priest –" she filled in.

"…Yes, I'm sorry," Jack said, "he's at St. Jerome's on the southwest side, not too far from where all of this is going on. He got involved in this whole thing because he found Ana and Daniel in the choir loft of his church this morning. Apparently, they snuck in last night and stayed there overnight. They escaped from a house, a mile or so from the church, with Caridád's help. They were about to get delivered, where I don't –"

"Delivered?"

"Yeah, they'd been trafficked out of Mexico and were apparently, from what Ana told me, the last two waiting at the house."

Alex was incredulous.

"Anyway, Ana told me that Caridád helped them escape and they found Father Mac's church. They were on their way to the police at 18th and State when, apparently, the traffickers found out they were missing and tracked them down to get them back."

"So, I'm heading down 18th Street, pick up Father Mac, and we're out of there. Until Father Mac mentions Caridád. Ana and Daniel told him all about her."

"Ok," she said slowly, trying to keep the story – and all the players – straight.

"Well, then they start telling me about Caridád, Alex, and I –"

"Lemme guess, Jack," Alex interrupted, "Time for Superman to step up?"

She leaned into him, took his face in both hands, and kissed him.

Long seconds passed. She slowly moved away. They opened their eyes together. Jack smiled. Alex leaned back and took his hands in hers.

"I couldn't leave her, Alex, I had to go back for her. I know I put Father Mac and the kids in danger and that bothered me. But I couldn't let her stay there. They would've killed her but not before…" He sounded almost apologetic.

She couldn't hide the pride her eyes displayed.

"…So, we drove back into the neighborhood where Father Mac said the kids told him they'd been held. I knew we were taking a big chance but… Anyway, they recognized something about an alley off 35th Street – how, I don't know, I thought they all looked the same – but they both yelled to me 'that's it, that's it… that's where we were!' So, I told Father Mac to stay with them. I left the car running – he was in the driver's seat, Ana and Daniel shared the passenger side and I dropped the back deck of the hatch down – so, if I did find her, we could both hop in and go. I told them to wait no more than fifteen minutes, then drive to the police station if I'm not back by then."

"That was smart."

He smiled briefly.

"Anyway, I go up the alley way and, sure enough, just like the kids described, there's the house. The overgrown shrubs, the big shade tree, the small wooden deck, all of it. As I'm walking into the back yard, I hear crying, then a scream. I work my way up the deck – I have no idea how many people are in there, I have no weapon, I'm realizing just how stupid all of this really is – and I look through the screen of an open window and see him with her. She's on this ratty old couch, crying, struggling, fighting him off the best she can. This guy's got one leg on the couch, forcing himself on top of her. He's standing over her with a hard-on, holding both her hands above her pinned against the wall. And he's forcing himself on her. She was really beaten up."

Alex shook her head slowly as she listened.

"There's a broken lawn chair next to me, so I grab it and throw it against the other side of the deck. The banging noise gets his attention. I want to know if he calls to anyone, if anyone else comes around the side of the house."

"Anyway, he stops what he's doing. It appears he's alone. He's a young guy, maybe early twenties. He pulls on a tee-shirt and a pair of gym shorts and gives Caridád a hard slap, which knocks her over, back onto the couch."

"Prick," she coldly said.

"He then turns and walks over to the screen door. He doesn't stop to pick up a weapon. I see him look out the door. He sees the lawn chair. He steps outside and onto the deck. As he does that, I slip around the corner and hunch down but I'm still on the deck. And I'm checking my watch."

"He walks around the deck and decides everything's fine. I know if he heads back toward the screen door, I won't be able to surprise him. So, when he bends over to pick up the lawn chair, I make my move. He must have sensed something because he started to turn around just as I got to him."

Alex gripped his hands even tighter.

"We tussle back and forth a bit but I'm able to get a clean hold on him."

Her eyes smiled through glistening tears.

"Anyway," Jack continued, "I get him turned around. We're both facing the back yard. I get my left arm across his chest, just below his throat. I reach around and grab my right arm. My right hand is open and flat against the back of his head. I twist his head and apply pressure on his windpipe and carotid artery. A standard 'sleeper hold' they teach at the Academy. I can feel him weakening. He's just about out. And then…"

She pushed the fingers of both hands away from her eyes, wiping away her tears before he saw them run down her face.

"…and then I snapped his neck."

She looked directly into his eyes.

"I broke the little asshole's neck, Alex," he said, almost apologetically.

"All I could think about was how none of these assholes ever answer for all the pain and misery and broken families and ruined lives…"

He stopped for a moment to regain his composure.

"…And, honestly, I thought of Carmen."

She simply smiled.

"So I killed the little shit."

She reached for him and hugged his neck.

"I'm just glad you're alive," she said gently.

Jack held a vacant expression.

Alex leaned back again so he could go on with his story.

"I went in to see how Caridád was. She was scared, of course, crying and upset. She has no idea who I am or what I want. I try to calm her down. I mention Ana and Daniel, and that helped. She starts to get dressed while I went back out onto the deck and dump the guy's body into the overgrown bushes, next to the deck. She wasn't in the best of shape so I picked her up and carried her back down the alley to the car."

She couldn't prevent all of her tears from falling.

"With about two minutes to spare!"

She laughed in a broken voice.

He dropped his head, wondering if her opinion of him would now change.

"I have to tell you, Alex, I hated him, I truly did. I felt that power, the strength it gave me. I remembered what it felt like. And I felt like that again. I couldn't stop all of it. But I could stop him. And I enjoyed it, Alex. I really did."

She brought her arms up around his neck again. She rested her head on his.

"You did good, Jack…" she whispered, with a catch in her throat. "… You did real good."

She thanked God the little bastard was dead. She only wished he'd suffered more.

Ana and Daniel woke up long enough to share some pizza and root beer with Alex and Jack. They watched a little television – some cartoons on one of the cable stations – before they fell back asleep. It was good to actually hear the two of them laugh a little. Caridád woke up, too, but only to have a little soup and another couple of ibuprofen. Alex had borrowed some of Jack's workout clothes – just sweats and a tee-shirt, really, but at least they were clean – to get Caridád out of what she'd been wearing.

Jack had scrounged up a couple of extra pillows he could use for himself as he made up the living room couch. He'd just walked up the six steps from the family room after checking on Ana and Daniel. He placed a small nightlight in the far corner of the room, away from the where they were sleeping, just in case they woke up. He brought with him one of the afghans his mother had crocheted for him many years ago. It was made of heavy white and blue yarn with small fringes adorning the edges. She'd made it longer than the usual ones she spent crafting to sell at her parish's fundraising bazaars. It was one way she found worked in reminding him how much she worried about him.

Alex came downstairs from checking on Caridád.

"She's resting now. She'll probably be out 'til morning."

He smiled and tossed the afghan onto the couch across the throw pillows.

"I can't thank you enough for everything you've done to –"

She put a finger to his lips.

"No need to thank me, Jack, really."

She moved her open left hand to the side of his face. He closed his eyes as his head tilted against it. She stepped forward and kissed him as he was hoping she would.

Her tongue was warm, wet, exciting. She moaned softly, almost inaudibly, as he took her face gently into his hands. He turned her head slightly. He'd almost forgotten how good it felt. She moved up against him and into his arms. They quickly embraced as their lips parted. She dropped her head up against his shoulders.

She felt very safe.

He opened his hands wide and massaged her shoulder blades firmly. She relaxed almost immediately. She wanted his touch. And she didn't want to stop here. She wrapped her arms around his waist and pulled him close. She felt him grow against her. She smiled a silly grin.

Suddenly, he pushed her back.

"By the way," he said unexpectedly, "how *did* you get here this afternoon? I never did ask you…"

Alex looked incredulous.

"*This* is what you want to know… *Now?*"

"I'm sorry," he said, realizing his bad timing was a comment on his lack of anything resembling a current social life.

"I'll have you know I'm a very resourceful girl, Mr. Sturdevant. I took the train out from downtown and walked here."

The mile and a half from the train station to Jack's house was hardly a trek although, for someone unfamiliar with the area, that wouldn't be necessary to get lost.

"You *walked* here, seriously? From the train station?"

She looked at him like he'd forgotten she was old enough to take care of herself.

"Yeah, why? I mean, I had to ask for directions a couple of times but, believe me, I've had to overcome greater obstacles!"

He smiled, impressed.

"No, I mean… I'm just glad you ran into people willing to help you out."

"Why?" she said, "this area doesn't seem all that tough a place."

He gave her one of the "you never know" looks.

"Besides," she said, "I keep a fully charged stun gun in my purse, just in case." She smiled and placed her arms around his neck.

"A girl can never be too careful these days, ya' know," she said.

He looked into her sparkling green eyes.

"I'm actually very glad to hear you say that."

"Well," she replied, "I've been to a few rough places and I've learned."

Jack pulled her to him and hugged her, lifting her up off her feet. Alex tightened her grip around his neck. She lowered her head against his shoulder.

Seconds past before her feet touched the floor again. She stepped back and smiled before she continued her story.

"And, I figured, I could either head out here and spend time with someone I'd like to get to know, someone who's kind and gentle and strong and *heroic…*"

Jack could hardly hide his gratitude.

"…or go on some interminable double date tonight with some international bond trader whose most-likely-insider-traded investment advice undoubtedly helped make his already far-too-wealthy clients yet more millions while supporting the very third world governments who use those investments to subjugate human rights and violate –"

He'd heard enough.

"I thought you said he was an investment bank –"

She reached her hands behind his head and pulled him to her. He willingly bent over slightly, took her face in his hands and kissed her. And while he was as impressed with her communication skills as he was with her comprehension of the social impact of global economics, it seemed only right that such a discussion be shelved for another day.

Perhaps in the morning. Or not.

Alex stepped back and dropped her head, leaning into his chest.

"You know," Alex said softly, "it's not everyday that I throw myself at a man."

Jack lay still, his feet outside the top sheet, his right leg bent. A full moon shone on a clear, still night through both open casement windows above his bed. It was cooler and less humid tonight than in evenings past though not by much. And, given it was early August in Chicago, any relief – real or imagined – was sure to be temporary.

It was just after 1:00 AM. And he was wide awake.

Alex lay against his chest, inside his left arm, which was comfortably wrapped around her, cradling her head and shoulders. Her body was as magnificent as he imagined it would be. And with everything that had happened since he'd met her, now less than thirty-six hours ago, she remained a distraction for him. Or maybe it was more of a respite. Their connection was undeniable. She was a kind and considerate lover. And, fortunately for him, forgiving, as well. Jack, sadly, was more than a bit rusty.

Like riding a bike, my ass!

Still, if she'd minded, she had shown no signs of it.

He couldn't stop smiling. He felt it. It was back. It was here. And it was real. Something unique and very special had happened – *was* happening – to him. And he didn't want to ruin it. Not like he had before. He fought the compulsion he knew so well, that he'd never felt worthy, that he didn't deserved her. His heart was so open to giving, wanting to share, so willing to take the chance to maybe love and to be loved. Yet it always seemed, for reasons he still could not understand, he just didn't measure up. He wanted to think for the longest time it wasn't him, that it couldn't be him.

Until a couple of days ago, he'd begun to wonder.

Alex rolled out his embrace and onto her back, barely stirring. He smiled when he thought he heard her snore. He turned and swung his legs over the side of the bed. He gave his back a moment to adjust then stood up. He moved slowly to his left, toward the closed bedroom door. Then he remembered.

Shit! The kids!

He quickly turned around and went back to his side of the bed. He slipped cautiously into a pair of gym shorts and had just pushed his arms through a sleeveless workout tee-shirt when the sight of her lying in his bed stopped him cold.

She lay motionless in the bathing shadows. Her right arm lay still off to her side, her left hand had just moved up near her head. Her hair was crumpled beneath her. She'd be embarrassed at how it looked. His eyes scanned her symmetrical body, each curve, every line. He'd taken his time over the past few hours to learn every inch of her. She'd responded to his touch and his feel just as he had to hers. From her soft, square shoulders to her firm, shapely calves, it all seemed so unreal to him. *She* seemed so unreal to him. Yes, making love to her had, at some point, crossed over into something more hardcore, something more uninhibited, where pleasure was all that mattered. First hers, but then his, and hers again but then also his. He happily shoved aside his demons, denying their impact, dismissing their existence, convincing himself they were illusions.

A convicted, sentenced defendant exonerated by a beautiful woman's touch. His vindication – his triumph – welled up from inside him.

But he resisted the urge to congratulate himself. Or to objectify her. She was already too important to him to treat so impersonally. But he remained amazed. All he wanted to do was simply look. His eyes absorbed her with each passing second.

He smiled and thought it odd that her very presence here tonight – and his feelings, as strange and chaotic and colliding as they all were right now – might well be the closest thing he'd found in a very long time of the existence of some cosmic force. Or was it destiny? Who the fuck knew? Or maybe some other complicated – not to mention manufactured – theory to explain what he'd long discovered was all too simple to explain. His work no longer provided a place for his father's religion or even his faith. Over the course of his career, he'd stopped counting the reasons to believe otherwise.

And, right now, right here, that made him sad. But not too sad.

Alex's sleepy voice broke his contemplative stare.

"Where are you going?"

He sat down on the bed next to her and brushed the hair away from her eyes. He answered her question with one of his own.

"How long have you been awake?"

She smiled, her eyes still closed.

"I'm not," she said, making him smile.

"Then, how did you –"

She reached a hand up to take his.

"I felt you looking at me," she said gently, "like you were watching over me."

He saw her eyes open slowly in the moonlight. He couldn't stop looking at her.

"You did, did you?"

Alex smiled in response and closed her eyes again. She snuggled next to him.

"You didn't answer my question," she said. "Where are you going?"

"Just downstairs to get something to drink. Want something?"

"Okay," she said in a faint voice.

His hand rested on the side of her face.

"I'll be right back," he whispered.

"I'll be here," she said, rolling over.

Jack reached and squeezed her hand as he slowly stood up. He wanted her again. Right now! He walked over and carefully opened the bedroom door, closing it quietly behind him. One of the steps at the top of the stairs squeaked as he made his way down toward the kitchen. He cringed as he thought it echoed throughout the silent house.

He walked into the dark kitchen, opened the refrigerator and pulled out a half-empty bottle of Gatorade. He closed the door as he turned toward the window over the sink. He looked into the vastness of the night and thought of nothing.

His cell phone, sitting on the countertop next to the sink, disturbed his solitude. He'd plugged it in last night to recharge the battery. Its small window now lit up the surrounding darkness as it vibrated with an incoming call. He saw that it was Laura.

He reached over, unplugged the phone and flipped it open.

"Laura, hi, how are you?" he said quietly, mindful of his sleeping houseguests.

"Hey Jack," she said, apparently still enjoying the buzz she'd spent the better part of the evening acquiring, "what's going on?"

"Not too much. How was your evening?"

"Interesting, to say the least... I know you said to call when I got home but, if this is too late, we can talk later this morning?"

"No, that's ok, no problem here. Tell me, how was your evening?"

"I'm coming to Chicago tomorrow, er, I mean, tonight I guess it is now, Sunday night. It is Sunday, right?"

"Yes, it is... And, seriously, you're coming into town?"

"Yep."

"Why's that?"

"Wallace asked me to personally sit in on Carmen's investigation."

"Really?"

"Yeah."

"Is there more?"

"Yep, there sure is."

"Ok," he said leadingly.

"I'll be in late, depending on what flight I can get. I gotta get some sleep."

"Good."

He finally caught on.

"So, I'll give you a call when I get in. Any chance you can pick me up?"

"If I can, sure. Just let me know where and when."

"It'll be O'Hare. Probably late-ish, maybe 7 or 8 before I can get in."

"Ok, well, just let me know and, if I can –"

Laura hesitated.

"Do you have company, Jack?" she asked bluntly.

He thought fast on his feet.

"In a matter of speaking," he replied, "yes."

"Ahhh," she said almost callously, "sorry to disturb you."

"You didn't disturb me," he insisted, attributing her tone to her buzz. "I'll tell you all about it tomorrow night when I see you."

"I bet you will," she countered sarcastically.

Jack took a second.

"It's not quite what you think, Laura," he replied.

He suddenly felt two strong hands slide across his shoulders and run down his arms. Alex's sleepy head turned and found a comfortable spot between his shoulder blades. She pushed her hands through, between his arms and his sides, then curled them up from behind him and gripped his shoulders. She closed her eyes and stood there holding him. Or, more precisely, being held up *by* him.

"Ok, you'll give me a call when you're ready to board?"

"Will do," she said. "Talk with you then."

"Count on it. G'night, Laura."

"Don't do anything I wouldn't do, Jack," she said loud enough for Alex to hear.

Jack snapped his phone shut, turned it off and plugged it back into the charger. He turned his head slightly to his left to touch hers. He brought his arms around behind him to feel her as best he could.

"I thought you were coming down to get a drink?" she said, trying to stay asleep.

"I did but I saw my phone ringing. I'm sorry." He said, just before he yawned.

"Who was that, Laura?"

"Yeah," he said almost apologetically. "She's a bit buzzed."

"Is it possible they don't have working clocks in D.C.?"

He couldn't help laughing.

"No, I asked her to call when she got in tonight. She met Wallace for drinks tonight... well, I guess that would be last night, now."

Alex raised her head off his back, strands of her hair falling into her face.

"As in Deputy Director of the FBI Wallace?"

"Yeah, that's the one. But she couldn't talk with me over the phone about it. Whatever he told her, he wants her to tell me in person."

She dropped her head drowsily again into his back.

"That's nice."

He turned his head slightly toward her again.

"You still want something to drink?"

"Ok," she said.

She reached her right hand out to take the plastic bottle. He raised his arm to release hers. Her left hand unexpectedly slid up beneath his tee-shirt and into his shorts.

Her touch shut his eyes.

She stepped to one side and took a drink as he turned around inside her arms. He felt her hand moving slowly but deliberately. She was wearing his Billy Williams Cubs jersey, the throwback home jersey from the '69 team that first broke his heart as a kid. It had Sweet Swingin' Billy's number 26 sewn on the back in Cubbie blue and the Hall of Famer's signature across the vintage Cubs logo on the front. And, unlike today's pullover jerseys, Jack's prized piece of Chicago's storied baseball past displayed the team's traditional blue pinstripes by buttoning up the front.

Or not.

She'd chosen to wear it open. Along with nothing else.

He opened his eyes and swallowed slowly as he watched her allow drops of fruit punch to trickle across her chin, down her throat and slide in place of his tongue into the valley between her breasts. Her eyes never left his, watching him watching her excite him. A long moment passed before she put down the bottle, ran the back of her hand across her mouth and comically smacked her lips, giving out a quiet "ahhhhhhh..."

Jack stepped back as her hand slipped out of his shorts, leaving his obvious interest in its wake. He tried to think of the last time a virtually naked woman – never mind one who looked this good – stood in his kitchen. He paid close attention to the seductive trails now gleaming in the streaming moonlight.

"Just what are you up to?" she cooed playfully.

"Nothing," he replied hornily, "just looking."

Her eyes were still partially closed. She stepped forward into his arms. He heard a soft, pleasant sigh.

"I have an idea," she whispered. Jack snickered.

She moved her head to one side and dropped it against his chest as he hugged her.

"But just once more or, maybe, twice," she cooed, "A girl's gotta get her rest."

"Ok," he said, his hand caressing her hair, "no more than twice."

She nodded and turned around inside his embrace. Her left hand slithered against his belly, returning between them. She found him hard, dripping, ready. She leaned back, dropping her head inside his shoulder beside his chin. He pressed himself forward against her, raising his hips to the pace of her slow, steady stroke. He reached around her, his hands moving hungrily inside the open jersey, clutching rabidly for her firm, heavy breasts. Her nipples grew defiantly against his tight, pinching twists.

Some seconds passed before she brought up her other hand to cover one of his. He immediately stopped, thinking she might still be too tender.

"No," she whispered between staggered breaths.

She shifted her head against his chest and dragged his right hand, guiding his fingers to replace her own, searching through her hair, reaching between her legs, slipping inside her fold. Her low moans, gaining momentum, became his roadmap.

He massaged her slowly, at first with one finger then with two, laying siege to the her glazed delicate tissue, surrounding its helplessness, then trapping it firmly, refusing to relinquish the rhythm she now so willing succumbed to. Surrendering to visions of his tongue tirelessly dancing on her, in and around her, she embraced the tensions building from his relentless invasion. Lightheaded, the rush from her last dizzying climax she'd so exhaustedly reached now immersing her, she was baptized again in a tangled freefall of sensations that left her to the primal frenzy of her next, somehow more powerful, release. Her hollow attempts to muffle the crescendo of her thin, contesting cries only encouraged his fervid ravenings.

Her vigorous grip on him tightened as she felt his size pierce her lower back, his guttural breaths shortening in response. Images of him now on top of her, beneath her, behind her, pounding her mercilessly left her weak, willing, defenseless, complicit.

Her free hand wrapped behind his neck, seizing him as he felt her squeezing him, tightening, resisting yet so unwilling to escape his sweet, commanding, determined touch.

She was moist, swollen, ready.

"We should really go," she said, swallowing hard, her words barely audible through halting breaths.

She gingerly stepped forward, took his hand and led him back upstairs.

* * *

Part Two

Chapter 11

"**S**O, EXACTLY WHAT are you saying?"

The Monsignor rose from the executive leather chair in his study that doubled as his permanent office. He stepped away from his roll top desk, crafted from imported Jatoba cherry hardwood. He walked over to the solid oak entry door and closed it slowly. He began walking in wide concentric circles within the living space carefully appointed to accent the room's solid knotty pine tongue-and-groove paneling. He held a cordless phone in one hand as the wire attached to his headset dangled to one side. He'd learned, whenever possible, to talk business on his private landline. His meticulous nature didn't allow for leaving things to chance.

And he was in no mood for games.

"Just what I wrote. The situation will be resolved shortly. That's all you need to know. As a matter of fact, that's all you really *should* know."

The Monsignor did not try to hide his impatience.

"The 'situation'?"

"Please, Monsignor, do not insult us both by pretending you don't understand how much exposure you can have here."

The voice paused.

"No pun intended, your grace…"

The priest ignored him, took a moment, searching for a different angle.

"And you see this problem going away then?"

"Yes, I do."

The Monsignor seemed to capitulate.

"Then that should do it, wouldn't you say?"

"For the time being, yes."

He was becoming annoyed.

"For the time being?" the priest said somewhat sarcastically.

"Well, yes, Monsignor, your somewhat..." the voice responded, pausing to choose his next words carefully, "...'unconventional' approach to fulfilling your vocation comes not without its unique challenges."

"I'm sure I don't know what you are talking about."

"Mutual friends have been in touch with me, John," the voice advised him, suddenly becoming familiar without permission. "May I call you, John?"

The Monsignor allowed his silence to convey his answer.

"As I was saying, John, our mutual friends have relayed their concerns that you've been working so tirelessly on their behalf that you may well be ready for a well-deserved and *extended* vacation."

"I see," he replied coldly.

"Perhaps someplace with sandy beaches, comfortable seas breezes," the voice quipped, "and, of course, plenty of young women in need of spiritual education."

The Monsignor was not amused.

"Assuming I take your suggestion under advisement –"

"I'm sorry, Monsignor, maybe I didn't make myself clear," he interrupted the priest caustically, "I may have you confused with some other politically connected church official whose careless penchant for illegally obtained controlled substances and a debilitating weakness for the company of very attractive, very willing and very young women..."

Despite being put on the defensive, Monsignor Miles was nonetheless pleased that this call had come through on his landline. His private line was monitored with digital audio recording software that automatically fed password-protected transcripts directly into his workstation's computer located inside his secured roll-top desk.

"...I was wondering, Monsignor, is it difficult to find such willing young women who are eager to be taught the more difficult catechistic lessons you specialize in?"

The tone of the caller's voice changed dramatically.

"I was hoping nothing I've said would have be mistaken for a suggestion."

The Monsignor had heard enough. In a cold, taskmaster voice, he countered.

"Does *he* know that you're speaking to me?"

The caller paused for a bit of dramatic effect.

"Who's idea do you think it was, John?" the caller said flippantly.

Monsignor Miles realized he was running out of options.

"Look, it's simple, really. Your friend and mine believe it's time for you to leave town," the voice concluded. "It would probably be better, John, if you chose to leave the country. At least for a while, anyway. We have a few things that need to be settled and no one wants to see you be a part of it. We don't believe it's a good idea for –"

He decided to end this right now.

"That's very considerate of you and, please, thank your friend for his concern but, if it's all the same to both of you, I still have much work to do here on behalf of the Archdiocese as well as the Mayor and –"

"Do we have a bad connection, Monsignor, I –" he said impatiently.

"I'm sorry," the Monsignor continued. "I'm expecting someone shortly. Please, tell him that I will be contacting him shortly to discuss my future plans and –"

"No need, Monsignor," the caller said. "The Mayor is hosting a function downtown next week. Perhaps there'll be time then to discuss things further then?"

"As you wish," he replied.

"Until then, John," the caller said casually if not abruptly.

The Monsignor heard nothing but silence. He disconnected the call and put the handset back into its cradle secured to the wall. He pulled his headset off and angrily tossed it onto the glass panel protecting the desktop. He'd spent too much time and invested too much energy in cultivating his political lifelines to run for cover now. True, the Mayor was staunch, committed political ally, such as they come. And his friend.

But he was not his only friend.

He began to descend the custom-designed oak staircase when he heard the doorbell. It was the private entrance. He checked his watch – it was just past noon – as he reached the bottom of the stairs and walked into the kitchen. He opened the cabinet doors to the hidden security console installed above the antique post office desk. He immediately recognized his guest in one of the four closet circuit television monitors. He closed the cabinet doors and headed downstairs.

He walked up to the heavy security door and punched in the access code on the digital display panel. The red LED flipped to green. The locks clicked as they automatically released. The Monsignor pulled down on the solid metal door handle and the door automatically opened up slowly.

A digital clock began counting down from thirty.

The Monsignor greeted him warmly, extending an open hand. His guest shook it heartily and returned a broad smile.

"I am well, Monsignor, quite well, thank you. And yourself, sir?"

"Very well, indeed, thank you. Please, come in, won't you?"

"Thank you."

Monsignor Miles closed the door as the tall, well-dressed handsome man maybe fifteen years his junior entered the small mudroom. Polished white-framed Oakley sunglasses hung from one temple slipped inside the open collar of his pastel blue knit shirt. His khakis were double pleated and freshly pressed. They walked together back upstairs as the security locks clicked obviously back into place. The clock reset.

"I wanted to come by as soon as you called, Monsignor," he said, looking to get right down to business. "I do have a couple of other business appointments this afternoon but I know you wouldn't call unless it was important."

"Working on a Sunday?" the priest kiddingly replied.

His guest just smiled.

"But, thank you, I appreciate that," the priest said. "There are a couple of rather pressing matters I wanted to discuss with you. May I offer you something cold to drink, a soft drink or something stronger, perhaps?"

"No, thank you. Monsignor, I'm fine."

The prelate showed him the way toward the family room just off the kitchen.

"Why don't we sit in here, we'll be more comfortable."

He smiled graciously as he followed the Monsignor down a short flight of stairs and into a very comfortable chair. He was eager to get down to business.

"It's good to see you again, Monsignor," the man offered. "Now, what can I do for you?"

The Monsignor smiled, appreciating his friend's busy schedule.

"All right then. First, my recent companion doesn't seem to be working out."

The gentleman's face did not change expression as he'd heard it all before.

"Her friend was by last night and, to be honest, they're a bit older than I'm –"

"Not a problem, Monsignor, I'll take care of it."

"Good," he replied, "I'm attending a function at the InterContinental this coming Tuesday evening. Is there any chance we could have some fresh faces around here, say, by later that evening? Monday would, of course, be better."

The man nodded and smiled as only someone of discretion in possession of incriminating information could. He noticed the Monsignor spoke in the plural. Observing such subtleties was just one more reason his services were in such demand.

"Anything special you'd like, Monsignor?"

The Monsignor looked out of the air-conditioned room into the heat and humidity of the bleak early August afternoon.

"She seemed a bit seasoned, too be truthful. I would like my next guests to be, perhaps, much more – shall we say – unencumbered by experience. The more innocent the better, I would think. And, of course, they won't be attending any public functions. I grew tired of the last one complaining about her dates to those fundraisers and the dinner parties. She began to embarrass me, watching her act the way she did in public."

He nodded his understanding, trying not to react to the Monsignor's somewhat unconvincing attempts at hiding his voyeuristic gratification at watching the young woman perform such intimate acts on those he intended for his viewing pleasure.

"And I don't feel comfortable putting myself in that position again."

"I completely understand, sir."

"May I assume that I need not be concerned that I will hear her from again?"

The gentleman understood precisely what his client expected. He'd become one of a growing list of higher-end clients and his wishes, quickly addressed, translated into immediate consideration. Some times it was cash, other times business or political connections. In truth, there was little difference. Currency was currency. And the relationship had always proven to be mutually profitable. The Monsignor's twenty-four year-old young companion of recent weeks had simply outlived her usefulness. It really wasn't anymore complicated than that. Just simply too old.

Being a good businessman, he'd reduced it all to a science. There was very little he left to chance. It was another reason the Monsignor had employed his discretion. It would be handled quickly, effectively and, most important of all, quietly. It was always best for everyone that it be as painless as possible though, naturally, that part depended on her. After that, all that remained was collecting his fee and shipping the merchandise.

Just like buying anything else over the web.

By tonight, the Monsignor's chestnut lamb could count Chicago among her many travel spots, another distant memory for the young woman. She would be on her way out of the city toward to any number of hubs in the Midwest. Indianapolis, Detroit, Iowa City, St. Louis, Peoria, Milwaukee… Which destination was hers this evening would be determined by client demands. And where she'd be sold from there, who could say?

It hardly mattered.

"Consider it done, Monsignor."

"Good. Now, we had the pleasure of entertaining a companion of hers last evening, I don't know if she was a friend of hers or not. Naturally, I don't know her name. A younger woman, athletic, attractive, dark skinned…"

The man said nothing as his better judgment closed ranks around a "no kidding" remark that would've served no useful purpose. The Monsignor's self-described healthy sense of humor notwithstanding, it remained a comment best left unsaid.

"…She may have said her name was Shana or Shauna, something like that. It was hard to understand her some of the time. She may have been Jamaican, I can't be certain, you understand."

"Of course, Monsignor."

"Should we have any problems with her companion –"

"There won't be any problems, Monsignor," he expectedly assured him.

"Good, that's what I like to hear. Naturally, you will use the same underground entrance and parking garage."

"Naturally."

"Good. I do so enjoy counting on your usual discretion and, particularly, your consistently good taste," the Monsignor acknowledged.

He gratefully nodded in response. Sensing this topic had been exhausted, he looked to close on something more upbeat.

"Before we move on, Monsignor, is there anything else you'd like beyond what you've already told me?"

"No," he responded, "you've so rarely disappointed me in the past, I've come to rely on your better judgment. I'm sure that, whatever you end up bringing me, I have no doubt it will more than suffice."

He acknowledged the compliment though he preferred to think of himself as providing more valuable services to the Monsignor than simply being his pimp.

"Now, as for this other matter," he continued.

"Yes?" he replied inquiringly.

"I'm afraid this is something of a more delicate matter."

The gentleman controlled his reaction.

A more delicate matter? You're fuckin' kiddin' me, right? What could be more delicate than a monsignor participating in a three-way after snorting enough coke to bring down an African Cape Buffalo? Or maybe the spiritual advisor to the

Mayor with a steady supply of young women brought into this country illegally and delivered to the doorstep of a Gold Coast mansion provided to you by the Archdiocese? Or how 'bout...

"Please, continue, Monsignor."

"I received a rather disturbing phone call just before you arrived this afternoon."

He listened attentively as Monsignor Miles related the conversation, almost verbatim, with a running commentary tossed in for his own amusement.

"Do you have any idea who it was?" he asked.

The Monsignor took a cautious moment.

"I'm not sure," he replied unconvincingly. "Does it really matter?"

"I'd be lying if I said 'no' but," he responded, realizing the parameters had been set. "what is it you would like me to do for you, Monsignor?"

"My concern is that this situation appears to be getting out of hand."

He understood the Monsignor's message. The priest continued.

"What I am anticipating is that there may be some ramifications from this afternoon's 'unpleasantness.' I have the conversation recorded. It's on my computer upstairs. I can download it for you so that you can review it at your convenience."

"That'd be fine, Monsignor."

He remembered the priest's fondness for the advantages technology could afford.

"I'd be interested in hearing any thoughts you might have on any safety measures you think should be increased as a result or any other thoughts, for that matter."

"I'd be glad to, Monsignor."

"Very good, then. Let us adjourn upstairs and I'll get you a file of that phone conversation."

The gentleman rose with Monsignor Miles and walked behind him up the short stairway into the foyer then up the custom-made oak staircase. The fragrance of white, red and yellow roses was as compelling as it was aromatic. He watched as the priest reached into his pocket for keys to the dual locks on the door to his private study.

The Monsignor was nothing if not cautious.

It wasn't until the 2008 Melbourne red metallic BMW M3 convertible made its way up LaSalle toward Lake Shore Drive's southbound entrance that his voice-activated handsfree cell phone was able to find a signal. He left the top up for the time being so he could be heard clearly. He watched through his white-framed Oakley's sporty red lenses as the number of an associate with contacts inside the Chicago Police Department appeared on the screen.

"*Hómbre*," the welcoming voice said through the dashboard loudspeaker.

"*Buenos tardes, amigo*," the man replied.

"*Como está, señor?*"

"Very well, my friend, and you?"

"I'm good. *Qué pasa?*"

"Just touching base to see if you've made any progress on that matter I sent you."

"Hang on, let me check."

He turned on to Lake Shore Drive heading south while he was on hold. As he approached the Oak Street exit, the voice returned.

"Yeah, I think I've got something for you."

"That is very good news, my friend. Could you please send it to me?"

"Your Blackberry?"

"Yes, please."

"Not a problem."

"Thank you, my friend. I am in your debt."

"You're very welcome, *mi hermano*. I hope you stay well."

"And you also, my friend. I must go now but I will be in touch you soon. I may have a job for you, maybe something you and your friends might find interesting."

"Sounds good. Then we'll talk again soon."

"Yes, we will, *muchacho*. Thank you again."

He heard the click as the connection went silent. With a press of his thumb on the steering wheel's remote control, he turned off the phone. He engaged the convertible top and, moments later, he was basking in the glorious August sunshine of a Chicago Sunday afternoon. His day was just beginning. He shifted into sixth gear and slipped across two lanes of traffic into the far left lane.

Less than a mile later, his Blackberry vibrated with an incoming message.

* * *

Jack paced slowly in the upstairs bedroom as he waited on the phone for Laura to find her flight information.

"I had it here – just a sec – wait, here it is."

He smiled, thinking about how anyone could be so disciplined to be a federal agent and yet be so seriously challenged when it came to organizing her own handbag.

"Ok, I'll be coming in on United flight 17," she read directly from her e-ticket. "Scheduled to arrive Sunday, August 10, Chicago-O'Hare at 8:50 PM."

"Got it." He repeated the flight information and scribbled it down on a yellow Post-It note to put in his wallet.

"Any check-in or just carry-on?"

Jack could feel the "you are fuckin' kidding me, right?" look through the phone.

"Sorry, Laura, stupid question."

"Hey, Jack, we female agents travel light, but not compact. I've got baggage –"

She suddenly realized what she was saying and stopped herself.

He laughed.

"Not for as long as I've known you."

He could see her smiling.

"Well, hey, dude, just 'cuz I'm working doesn't mean I shouldn't look good."

Jack paused a moment, remember how good she could really look.

"As I recall, you didn't need that much."

Laura was glad to think he'd remembered. "Flattery will only get you everywhere, Jack. Hey, I gotta run. I'll see you at baggage claim around 9-ish or so?"

"I'll be there, Laura."

"Cool, see you in a few hours then."

"Count on it!"

Jack flipped shut his phone and shoved it into his pocket. He thought about Father Mac and that he hadn't heard from him yet. That wasn't necessarily bad news, he reasoned.

But still…

Just a few minutes ago, he almost said something to Laura about what had happened here in the last twenty-four hours. But, once he started, he quickly realized how wrong it sounded to discuss it over an open line. Once again, his training seemed to kick in, treating the last several months as if they had never happened. He thought better of telling her and now he was glad he did. Once they were in his car, he could tell her, when he knew no one else could be listening.

Jack bounded down the stairs, into the living room, swung around the banister's oak newel post and down the short flight of steps into the family room. He smiled when he saw Caridád sitting on the couch, Daniel under one arm and Ana sitting next to her. She looked tired but still much improved over yesterday. Alex's nursing skills, along with the pharmacist down the street, had helped get her back on the road to recovery. She'd need every ounce of whatever rest she could get.

As would they all.

Ana and Daniel faced similar issues as well, though the expressions on their faces seemed to be unconcerned with those now. Caridád had, quite literally, saved their lives. And they believed that, with Jack's help, they had saved hers. Theirs was a quiet sense of shared happiness at simply being together – and safe – that reminded Jack that, every once in awhile, the good guys can still win.

Alex was in the kitchen at the counter, employing some of her most advanced culinary skills when she realized the English muffins were burning. Jack walked up closely next to her and whispered a soft hello. At the moment, she found his newly released and rampantly running levels of testosterone less interesting than providing something the children could eat without adding food poisoning to their list of ailments.

"English muffins for dinner?" Jack quipped, straddling the line between sarcasm and appreciation.

Without even looking at him, Alex quietly whispered "go fuck yourself…"

"Already?" he joked back.

She turned her head to look at him and just smiled. She tried blowing the few strands of hair that had fallen across her face. Jack looked at her and simply beamed.

He could hardly imagine a more beautiful creature. Her hair was pinned up, off her square shoulders. Her eyes returned his smile as he felt himself melting into her. She was wearing one of his remaining clean pair of boxers and another of his tee-shirts, this one forest green, he'd bought during the ten days he'd spent in and around Whitefish during his most recent hiking trip in northwestern Montana. He could hardly have imagined it would look so good on anyone.

And certainly not in his own kitchen!

Alex wanted to ask why he was just looking at her. But she already knew.

"I'll tell you what," Jack offered, "I don't have time to get us all out for dinner but I can run across the street and pick up some subs. Would that work for you?"

She dropped her head against his shoulder. He put an arm around her shoulder and pulled her to him.

"Thank you," she said quietly. "I'm just not good at *everything*!"

"Yes, well," Jack replied, keeping it short as to escape the kitchen without feeling the effects of the knife Alex was using to scrape the burnt black stuff off the muffins.

"Ok, then, let's see what the kids have to say."

With Caridád's help, Jack as able to get everyone to agree that subs were a perfectly nutritious and balanced meal that everyone would enjoy at least as much as they did last night's pizza. And, with that, he was out the door.

"Ok, you have the emergency numbers I gave you, right?"

Alex nodded.

"I won't be gone too long. I'll try to make it as short as possible but I need to know what Laura knows."

"I understand, Jack," she countered, "but I really think we'll be fine. I've survived everything from Croatian militia to Sudanese death squads – I'd like to think I could handle three kids for a couple of hours."

He smiled. His famous smothering technique, known around the area for destroying budding relationships, was working to perfection.

He turned to get into his car when he suddenly stopped.

"Oh, shit..."

She stopped, waiting for his other shoe to drop.

"Father Mac," he uttered. "Did he call?"

Alex smiled then walked up over to him as he stood inside the open car door. She took his face in her hands and kissed him deeply. He tossed his keys onto the front seat and kissed her back. He wrapped his arms around her slender waist. She buried her head into his shoulder and hugged his neck tightly. He lifted her feet off the ground and swung her gently from side to side.

"My phone's recharging," she said, somehow making even that sound sexy. "I'll check it as soon as you leave."

It was like high school all over again with him.

"You know, I was thinking," he quipped, staying in the moment, "I'd like to see you again tonight, that is, if you don't have any other plans."

She stepped back but stayed in his embrace.

"Well, I was planning on rescheduling that blind date but –"

He smiled and looked at her. Her beautiful green eyes lit up, dancing with her inviting smile.

"Lucky guy," he said, playing along.

"Lucky girl," she softly replied.

A moment later, she waved to him as she watched him head down the street and out of the subdivision.

* * *

Special Agent Marc Cauldwell sat at the end of the bar actively working his way through his third scotch rocks. He expected things to be slow on a Sunday evening in a backwater, one-horse town like Morris. And it would work well to his advantage. As he took a slow sip, he congratulated himself once again on his use of the technology that led him here.

And to her.

He placed his drink down on the damp napkin as his eyes were glued to the slim hourglass figure behind the bar.

There she stood, drying her hands with a bar rag, maybe twenty-five, twenty-six years old at most, wasting her life in a roadside dump like this. She wore a loosely fitting soft pink camisole top with a plunging lace neckline and thin, narrow straps spanning those richly tanned shoulders. It fell short by a couple inches of reaching the top of her shorts, which revealed a seductively delicious pair of thighs and long, shapely, slender legs and a pierced navel. Her smooth lines ran contrary to her athletic build. Her soft blonde hair, streaked almost white from the summer sun, ran down her back, coming to a "v" just below her shoulder blades. As she leaned forward to wash the empty glasses, he couldn't help staring down the curves inside her shirt. Her breasts seemed almost too perfect. They weren't large by any stretch. They were simply spectacular, roundly proportionate and demanding attention. The frigid air-conditioning resulted in a firm if not pervasive "nip" in the air, a display she seemed only too comfortable providing.

Her shorts were white, skintight and *very* short. They were thin, not a heavy denim, and his eyes were drawn to the smooth lines accenting her hips. They were the perfect offset to her tan which he suddenly noticed had no lines. He shot a glance to her chest and realized the same was also true. As she stood bent over the sink, one of the straps from her top slipped down the side of her arm. Her color was a consistent mocha. Almost like milk chocolate. He vividly imagined her lying there, sweating form every pore beneath a relentless sun as her flesh slowly turning a deep, sweet, luscious bronze.

He felt himself grow just thinking about it.

But as much as he coveted the very thought of touching her – in a way that she'd know he'd possess her, control her, even own her –, the longer he watched her the more incensed he became. For she was precisely the kind of woman he could never have. The kind of woman who was never interested in him. The kind of woman who insulted him by looking past his inviting smile or ignoring his unsolicited little quips or finding his unique brand of humor something less than funny. The kind of woman who would rather spend her life serving drunks and lowlifes than take a chance on living the good life with him. It constantly pissed him off. Not only was he a nice guy, his logic typically ran, he had an important job, a valuable career, a hot car and a sophisticated style about him that any woman should swoon over. He had thought about it a lot lately and had concluded, after much introspection, that it wasn't him.

No, it was definitely not him.

He hadn't had a date in months. *That* was her type's fault. He hadn't had sex (at least, that he hadn't paid for) in weeks. *That* also was her fault. He hadn't been out with friends or spent time after-hours with colleagues or been on vacation in longer than he could remember. And *that* was her fault as well.

He thought back to just hours ago, to the transcripts he read from the conversations she'd had with Bobby earlier in the day. That she would allow him to do such things to her, to satiate his vile demands and expectations. That she would allow him to defile her in such ways, to violate her while she pretended to enjoy his animalistic behavior, his voracious appetite, his deviant desires. Christ, only a whore acts that way. Only a whore enjoys being treated that way. Only a whore believes she's not worthy.

And *he's* not even worthy of a woman like that?

What the fuck, man?

Then again, he reasoned, maybe that's how she liked it. That must be it. In some perverted, godless way she enjoyed her unworthiness. She reveled in her worthlessness. She obviously had no moral center, he concluded, no real Christian values. She *was* the slut she dressed like. She enjoyed being treated that way because she *was* that way.

Yeah, that's it. That must be it. She couldn't fool him. Not a professional like him. Besides, who else but a whore would enjoy the company of a cop like Colavito?

He took a long sip from his drink as his anger simmered.

With nothing left to do, she finally walked over to talk with him.

"Ok, I've got a few minutes. You wanted to know about some cop?"

Cauldwell grinned. *Did they always have to start off saying such stupid things?* The ice shifted in his glass as he raised his empty drink one last time to his waiting lips.

"Let's stop the bullshit, can we, sweetheart? Ok? I'm not interested in just 'some cop'…" He took his time pulling out his ID and flashing it on the bar.

"I'm Special Agent Cauldwell. I'm with the FBI. We're investigating the murders of two people just about five miles east of here. Up along I-80, this past week."

She looked bored and disinterested. Cauldwell continued.

And took his time.

"Maybe you read about it in the paper? One of the people murdered was a veteran FBI agent. She was not only a decorated agent, she was working undercover trying to break-up a white slavery ring."

He personalized Carmen's work.

"*White* slavery?" the young woman asked incredulously, as if the two words hardly belonged together.

"Let me see if I can put this in terms you can relate to," he said patronizingly.

"With *white* slavery, girls like yourself, often pretty, young white women, are taken against their will – they simply disappear one day. It's often referred to these days as 'trafficking.' They are terrorized and gang-raped and beaten to break their will to escape. They live in horrible conditions and in constant fear. They exist only for sex. They are sold, usually over and over again, just like a farm animal. And, like a farm animal, they're worked, often for years, until they're no longer useful, until they no longer make their owners money."

He'd gotten her attention.

"And, then, just like any other that farm implement that's outlived its usefulness, they're typically disposed of. Usually from intentional drug overdoses or simple physical abuse – just beaten to death. Or, what's becoming more popular, they are either sold or traded for drugs to motorcycle gangs. Other times they're just given away. And when that happens, that's pretty much it. Assuming they're ever found…"

"Ok, ok, I get it!" she conceded impatiently. "Whaddya want?"

Cauldwell relished her new cooperative attitude.

"Well, I'd like to find out what you know about that night."

"Which night was it?"

"This past Tuesday, the 5th…"

She thought for a second.

"Yeah, I worked that night."

"And?"

"Well, I really don't know very much to tell you." she stammered out slowly.

"How about we start with your name, miss."

"Jamie," she said, "Jamie Simone."

"Ms. Simone. May I call you 'Jamie'?"

She nodded her head.

Cauldwell peeled off a ten dollar bill and placed it on the bar as he slid his empty glass toward her. Jamie watched then looked at him like he was kidding. They both knew that would barely cover the scotch he'd just finished let alone the first two he'd had.

"Why don't we go some place where we can talk?"

"I really can't leave, I –"

"Please," Cauldwell responded, looking directly into her eyes with an abiding sense of charm. "I think we can cover everything we need to in just a few minutes."

"Well, if it's only for a few minutes," she capitulated. "Ok, I'll meet you out back. Give me a couple of minutes to get somebody to cover the bar."

Cauldwell slowly turned and surveyed the handful of paying customers whose friends must have decided to come tonight dressed like empty tables and chairs.

"Yah," he said sarcastically, "I can see why you're worried."

His eyes were fixed on her shorts as he watched her walk away. They were tight and narrow. Like he imaged she would be. His mind raced. His mouth watered. He wiped his lips dry as he swiveled out of his bar chair and toward the men's room.

The sun was already hidden behind a couple of nearby abandoned buildings, casting shadows across an alleyway behind some awkwardly stacked large wooden crates and a dumpster in serious need of emptying. Another warm and muggy August day had given way to another goddamned warm and muggy August evening. Cauldwell felt flushed walking out of the deep freezer that was the climate-controlled bar into the evening's oppressive humidity. He looked around quickly, conspicuously.

The place seemed deserted.

A minute or two later, Jamie came through a large and heavy metal-framed door. A cigarette dangled from her long fingers. Her hair was now pulled up off her shoulders and clipped above her head. Loose strands fell down past her ears and around her face. The strap from her top had slipped down the side of her arm again.

He looked at her and swallowed hard.

* * *

Jack loaded Laura's one large suitcase along with her single carryon into his Honda Civic through the back hatch door and slammed it shut. He walked her over to the passenger-side door and held it for her as she gracefully slipped into the cloth bucket seat. Her svelte legs were evident even within the confines of her perfectly fitted jeans as she swung them around and into the car. Jack couldn't help but realize he was noticing her as he closed the car door after her.

"You look wonderful, Laura," he said as the key kept searching for the ignition.

"Why, thank you, Jack, that's very kind of you to say."

She wore a collared pink blouse on the plane, the two top buttons undone providing all the effect they were intended to have. Special Agent Laura Kallinger was, even she would admit, someone who never suffered even under the most stringent of admiring measures.

Sunday evening's airport traffic had been predictable heavy. Jack had just left I-190 off of Bessie Coleman Drive was heading east on I-90 into downtown. They had just about finished the requisite preliminary catch-up conversation.

"Where are you staying?" he inquired.

"The InterContinental."

Jack was impressed. He didn't remember being offered such accommodations when he was with the Bureau. Then, again, he was never invited to drink with the Deputy Director, either.

"So," he inarticulately began.

"So," she responded in kind.

"Ok, I'll start. Tell me how things went with Wallace."

She laughed a bit nervously.

"I'm not quite sure where to begin so I'll just jump right in."

"Sounds like a plan to me," he unnecessarily said.

"Ok, we'll skip his phone call. That was pretty uneventful, other than he asked me out for drinks."

"That would seem eventful in and of itself, wouldn't you think?" he said dryly.

"Yeah, well, I got guys hitting on me all the time, so," she replied half-kiddingly.

Jack cleared his throat.

"Anyway…"

"Anyway," she continued, "Wallace wants to meet with you."

"Me?" he said, authentically surprised. "What the hell for?"

"He told me that he wants to talk with you directly, about what he wouldn't say. He's flying to San Francisco – as a matter of fact, he should be in the air right now – to give some kind of address at some political luncheon on Monday. He's supposed to be in meetings the rest of the day and is flying here early afternoon on Tuesday. He has some affair Tuesday evening at the InterContinental."

Jack listened as he waited for the first shoe to finish dropping.

"He changed his return flight so he would have time to meet with you Tuesday afternoon. He's scheduled to get in at O'Hare sometime around 2:00 PM."

He began thinking through what Wallace's rationale might be as Laura searched through her purse.

"Yeah, here it is." She pulled out a bar napkin.

He looked at her facetiously. She just shrugged.

"Not to worry, I'll write it all down for you once we get to the hotel."

"He did ask about one thing, though…"

Jack turned and looked at Laura as she got his attention.

"…He wondered if you were familiar with a field agent named Marc Cauldwell."

Laura laid her purse in her lap. Her thoughts began to wander as the expressway miles drifted by. Carmen, her cryptic email, the missing package. It was all weighing heavier on her mind. She knew she had to say something. She looked over at Jack.

She knew it had to be now.

"There is something else, Jack."

She waited a quiet moment and then decided to just say it, to just tell him.

"Laura, what is it?"

Jack knew her body language well enough to know something wasn't right.

"Jack, there's something I have to tell you," she started, without looking at him.

"Ok," he said leadingly.

She paused a moment, still not having forgiven herself. She took a deep breath.

"It's about Carmen," she finally said.

Jack took his eyes from the road for a moment and looked at her, quizzically. "What about her?"

He could see she was becoming upset.

"Laura?" he asked again. "What is it?"

She finally turned and looked at him. He saw the tears welling up in her eyes.

"I'm afraid I really fucked up this time, Jack."

Jack turned north off Wabash up Michigan Avenue and across the bridge spanning the Chicago River. The InterContinental was up about a quarter mile on their right, complete with a drop-off lane and doormen in top hats. But his attention was focused squarely on the road ahead. Of all the things he needed to hear right now, what Laura had just told him about Carmen wasn't one of them. There was little time to process any of it. He had trouble making sense of what he'd heard.

Why did she send a text message to Laura's email account? And what tipped her off that her own phone wasn't safe? What did she know about Wallace? And where's the envelope she'd mailed to Laura? And how could Laura've been so fuckin' careless to –

He blinked hard. He couldn't let Laura see him reacting that way.

What was important now is their next step. They'd have to think like her, see her choices as she must have seen them, understand her options as only time would have allowed her to. Carmen was smart. He knew her well enough to know she'd have had a backup plan, some way of ensuring the envelope would reach Laura. Then again, her being undercover, alone, on the road, concerned she may've been compromised…

Maybe not.

It really didn't matter at this point. If it turned out the opportunity had passed – if the envelope was gone – and there was nothing more to be done about it, then they'd deal with it and move on. But if Carmen was right – if Wallace was dirty – and the envelope was out in the open or, worse yet, had somehow found its way to Wallace, then all bets were off. There may be critical, incriminating information floating around out there somewhere. And Jack knew the Deputy Director had a vested interest in both containing it as well as concealing it. Worst-case scenarios flooded Jack's thoughts.

As did Tuesday afternoon's meeting with Wallace.

He felt his phone vibrating. He reached into his back pocket. It was Alex. "Give me a minute, will you?"

Laura smiled as Jack pulled into the drop-off lane and came to a stop.

She waited as the doorman politely opened her car door and they exchanged greetings. Jack popped open the hatch door and stepped out of his car, now wearing a look of concern.

"What, exactly, did he say, Alex?"

"He said that they'd been to see him," she said excitedly.

"They? Who's they?"

"He didn't say, Jack. He only said that they were asking questions about a girl and a little boy. They claimed they were relatives and that they were looking for them."

Jack listened intently. Laura watched from the curb as her bags were loaded onto a six-wheel cart.

"They said the kids were missing and that they were looking for them. They said they'd heard that he'd found them and that they'd been to his rectory."

"Ok, ok, Alex," he said, trying to reassure her in a tone neither believed was working. He looked across at Laura, who knew the look of an agent in distress.

"Let's start again. When did he leave the message?"

"I don't know, Jack," she said, wondering what difference that made. "After you left, I checked and saw my cell phone needed charging. I plugged it in right away and, just a few minutes ago, I was able to check my messages. That's when I found his. He said just what you said he would, that he was calling on behalf of Mar-*teen's* sister. But when I heard everything he said, I really got scared, Jack."

Alex tried to remain calm. She didn't want the kids to hear and get worried.

"What if they know they're here, Jack? What'll we do? We've got no way to –"

Jack looked at Laura.

"Make sure all the doors are locked. Call the police. Tell them you saw some kids hanging around the house and you're scared. Tell them you're alone with three children and ask if they could just come by and check it out."

"Ok," Alex said anxiously.

"I'll be there as quickly as I can. I'm leaving now."

"Ok, Jack," she replied, feeling reassured. She was worried, clearly, but not for herself. She'd been in more dire circumstances in much more remote hellholes around the world. But she'd always been alone.

The children changed everything.

"I should be there in less than forty-five minutes."

"Ok."

"And listen, Alex, this is very important. Here's what I want you to do. After you call the police, get everyone together. Take them where you went last night."

"You mean to the pharm—"

"Yes, Alex!" he shouted into the phone, "There!" Jack wasn't taking any chances. He didn't know *if* they knew where the kids where or *how* they could have found out. But he couldn't assume they weren't listening.

"Yes, take them there. Go inside. You'll be safe there. I'll find you!"

"Ok, I'll get everybody ready."

"Good. And, Alex, I want you to call me every ten minutes, I don't care where you are. Do you understand?"

"Yes, I understand."

"Ok, check your watch. Ten minutes from right now!"

"Ok, ten minutes."

"Stay calm, call the police and get the kids going. I'm on my way."

"Ok, Jack… Bye…" she said quietly.

"Wait!" he yelled into the phone. "Alex? Alex, are you still there?"

"Jack?"

"Yes, Alex! Good. Listen, can you tell me the last number that called you? The number that Father Mac called from."

"Yeah, sure, just a sec —"

A moment later Alex read back the number that preceded Father Mac's message.

"Ok, let me read it back to you."

Alex listened then told him he'd gotten it right.

"Ok, I'm on my way."

"Ok," she said.

"Ten minutes!" he reminded her.

"Ten minutes," she confirmed.

With that, the connection went dead.

Jack immediately called the number Alex gave him.

No answer. No voice mail. Nothing.

Laura stopped the doorman from moving her bags. She knew instinctively from Jack's harried expression that something was terribly wrong. She gave the gentleman her name and asked him to leave her bags at the front desk.

"Laura, I gotta go, something's come up and —"

She was already getting back into the car.

Jack slipped back into the driver's seat and shut the door.

"Where are *you* going?"

"Just shut up and drive," she said.

As he began to pull away, she suddenly yelled out.

"Wait! Stop!"

Jack hit the brakes, thinking he was pulling in front of some unseen taxi or handsome cab clip-clopping up Michigan Avenue.

Laura jumped out of his car and quickly moved toward the man handling her bags. Her had just begun to enter the automatic door leading into the lobby. She called out to him. He stopped the cart as soon as he passed through the door.

Jack impatiently watched as she disappeared for a moment.

Laura entered the lobby and immediately pulled her checked luggage from the cart. She removed her firearms and stuffed them inside her carry-on bag. A few seconds later, she returned to the car with her bag swung across her shoulder, rushing past the doorman who had just helped her. He tipped his cap to her and smiled.

"Good luck," he said, noticing the hurry she was in.

Laura turned and slid back into his car.

"Let's go," she said as the door closed behind her.

Jack handed Laura his cell phone.

"Here, she'll be calling in less than ten minutes and every ten after that."

Laura checked the time in the cell phone's window and nodded. She set the phone down inside a recessed opening in the molded plastic door handle. She unzipped her carry-on and pulled out a leather shoulder holster with her loaded .45 caliber SIG-Sauer P220 duty-issued service weapon still snapped securely in place. Three additional seven round clips also left her bag. She checked to make sure the safety was on then placed the weapon and the clips carefully on the floorboard near her feet.

Jack smiled gratefully.

She then reached in and pulled out a second weapon, an FBI-issued .40 Glock 23 semiautomatic revolver with a standard thirteen round clip, designed to be her backup. It was also secured inside a leather holster, this one made with a single four inch-wide Velcro strap designed for securing around her ankle. It, too, remained in place by a small leather strap across the handle that straddled the weapon just beneath the hammer. Along with it came a box of Smith & Wesson service ammunition.

She engaged Jack's eyes with the look of a partner and grinned.

"Hey, you might need something, too."

She quickly zipped the bag closed and tossed it into the backseat side.

"Thanks," he said with rolling eyes, feeling like Sundance to her Butch.

Chapter 12

ALEX STOOD WORRIED in front of a weak and listless Caridád as she sat in one of the three chairs across from the pharmacy counter that Walavender's Drug store provided for their customers awaiting their prescriptions. Alex told both Ana and Daniel, seated on either side of her, to keep a watchful eye on her. She'd be right back. She walked down the back aisle that spanned the width of the store until she reached the opposite corner, turning to keep an eye on the children after every few steps. She saw Ana and Daniel each stroking one of Caridád's hands, trying to comfort her, hoping to convince her – and probably themselves – that somehow everything would be ok.

Alex approached the perpendicular wall and stopped. She peered left around the corner and looked up the store's long cosmetic aisle. From her vantage point, the automatic sliding front doors were clearly visible. As were the three imposing young men, their threatening presence still hovering as they stood waiting on the sidewalk just outside the doors. Behind them, in a well-lit but otherwise empty parking lot, she could see two parked cars, one a sports car, the other a sedan, sitting at conspicuously odd angles. She only assumed they'd brought reinforcements.

Alex didn't notice the elderly woman just a few feet up the aisle, bent down stocking supplies on to a half-empty shelf.

"Can I help you?" the woman said in a tired voice.

Alex looked at her oddly, with an abnormal feeling of vulnerability. She smiled, if somewhat nervously, in response and laughed sarcastically to herself.

Not unless you know Krav Maga, she thought.

"No, thank you…" she said graciously.

She checked her watch and realized it had been almost ten minutes since the fourth time she'd spoken with Jack. He knew about the three amigos outside the store's front door. He'd told her to stay put, not to worry and that they were now only blocks away, just down the street. A couple more minutes. That's all it would be now. Jack knew the store was closing; he'd heard the woman's voice, in the background, making the announcement a minute or two ago.

Alex decided to find a Plan B in case the store closed first. She knew the three men outside the store were probably not alone. She didn't try to make sense of how they could have found them. Or how they could have known to look here. Or even if those were the men Jack said could be looking for them. Or, for that matter, if *any* men were looking for them.

But her instincts screamed better. And she knew, right or wrong, she could not take any chances. Alone, that's one thing. Her life to this point had been spent reaping the personal and professional rewards of putting herself in harm's way. But, she realized now, in this single moment, how easy it all had truly been. How simple. How most of life really wasn't like that.

She'd never had anyone else to worry about.

She stepped back away from the corner and out of the view of the young men standing guard outside the store. She turned back to check on the kids. They looked tired. And for good reason.

She had to think.

She turned back and faced the corner. Obviously, leaving through the front door wasn't an option. The back door? Maybe, but even if they could get out that way, what if more men were waiting there? But, even if they weren't, then what? What would she and kids do? Where could they go? She knew they couldn't go back to the house. At least she didn't think they could. And Alex had no way of knowing where she was. All she knew for certain was that Jack told her he would meet them here. She thought about calling the paramedics, telling them that Caridád needed help. But they might start asking questions she couldn't answer. They would either want to get her to a hospital or contact the police. Probably both. Neither option seemed particular good. She stepped forward once more to check on the men outside the door.

She couldn't believe it.

There was no one there. No one she could see, anyway. Through the glass sliding doors, Alex could see out into the illuminated parking lot. She scanned it quickly. The cars were gone, too.

Her heart jumped.

Maybe she'd been right. Maybe it wasn't at all what she thought. Maybe she could just take the kids and wait for Jack outside. Maybe…

Suddenly, the overhead lights throughout the store began to shut off.

Alex started to freak. Time had run out. She had to decide. Now.

Just then, she felt her phone vibrate.

"Alex, where are you?"

Jack's voice was no match for the overhead announcement that the store was now closed. She held the phone tightly to her ear. She moved slowly against the back wall, past the first inside aisle, on her way back to the kids. She bent over and placed a finger to her other ear.

"Jack, we're still here, in the pharmacy. They're closing. Jack, what'll we –"

"I know, I know… Alex, listen to –"

"Where are you?" she said frantically. "The three guys hanging around outside the door, they're not –"

As she spoke, she turned to make her way back. She looked through the darkening store toward the pharmacy.

The chairs were empty!

"Oh, shit, Jack! They're gone! The kids, Jack… they're gone. What'll I do? They were just here a moment ago but they're –"

Suddenly, an arm reached around her while a hand extended a six-inch long serrated blade across her throat. Her cell phone slipped from her hand and dropped to the floor.

"Alex?" she heard Jack say. "Alex!!"

"Not to worry, *chiquita*," the strange, harsh voice whispered, "we'll take good care of them… And you, too maybe, huh?"

She felt the scratchy hard calluses from his left hand strongly grip her shoulder as his right arm pressed hard against her chest. The razor edge of the inch-wide blade was pinched against her throat. Her mind raced with everything that had, somehow, gone so terribly wrong. And everything that now seemed headed that way.

"You think we wouldn't find you here? You thought you were really smart, eh?"

Where the fuck was Jack?

"But we have them," he said, his hot breath reeking of beer, "and we have you."

Her eyes burned with fear for what had already happened to the children.

"C'mon, *chiquita*, we gotta go… Don't want to be late for the party."

He looked quickly around him as the store's lights continued to shut down. He moved the knife from her throat, bringing the tip of the blade in against her side. He grabbed her roughly by the arm and pushed it in and up.

"Now, you won't scream, will you, *chica*?"

She winced in pain. He turned her in toward him and looked into her frightened eyes. He grinned with the look of a man who realized his plans for the evening had just changed for the better.

"C'mon… My friends will want to get to know you, too…"

He pulled Alex with him as he awkwardly stepped backwards toward the main aisle. It was then that he felt the steel of the handgun's .45 caliber muzzle settle coldly against his cheek.

"Drop the knife, asshole," Jack said calmly, "and let her go. Right now…"

The man just laughed. He couldn't turn his head. His eyes strained in their sockets, as far over as they could, struggling to see who dared be so stupid. There was no surprise, no panic in his voice.

"What are you going to do, shoot me here, *gringo*?"

Jack slid the mouth of his firearm firmly up against the man's temple.

"Yes, as a matter of fact, I will…" he said assuredly. "You can keep breathing, *amigo*, if you let her go. Now."

"We are not *amigos*," the man said snidely. "But we do have them…"

"What you have," Jack corrected him in a cool, deliberate manner, "is until the count of three to let her go. Or I will put a bullet in your head. Right here. Right now."

"You won't do it, *gringo*, you won't shoot me…" the man said confidently.

"One…" he started.

"Not here, no fuckin' way…"

"Two…"

"We have them, you won't –"

"Alex, turn away," he said calmly, interrupting him, "and close your eyes…"

He then turned his attention back to her assailant. He pressed the gun against the young man's temple, angling it toward the back of his head, away from Alex.

"I don't want his brains splattered all over you." Jack said coldly.

Alex ducked her head away from the knife as best she could and closed her eyes.

The man gulped hard. He struggled at laughing again as he pressed the knife against her throat.

"Three…"

"Go fuck your–"

Alex shrieked at the single dull, staccato pop.

The man's hand fell lifelessly from Alex's arm, the knife dropping harmlessly to the floor. He crumpled on the tile at their feet then slumped backwards, his head turning to one side, hiding the single bullet hole. Blood began slowly pooling around his head.

Alex reached out and wrapped her arms around Jack's neck. She started crying.

"Jack, I'm so sorry…" she said nervously.

"Alex, it's –"

Through her tears she tried to apologize, to explain.

"Jack, I don't know what happened to them, I –"

He tried to calm her down as Laura came out from behind the pharmacist's counter, gun drawn.

"You ok, Jack?"

He opened his eyes and, through swelling tears, nodded as best he could with Alex's arms still fitted securely around his neck.

"Alex, look…" he said gently. And he pointed her back down the end aisle, toward the pharmacy's counter.

She loosened her grip enough to turn and see Laura kneeling next to a seated Caridád, Ana and Daniel beside them. She started crying again.

Laura left the kids there and went back behind the counter and into the pharmacy where the employees were safely waiting. She asked the pharmacist to call both the paramedics and the police. She then gave him her badge number and an FBI phone number where the police could reach her.

Jack walked over with Alex and hugged the kids, then asked for a couple of paper towels and a large plastic zip lock bag. He returned with Laura to where the man lay dead, carefully picked up his knife and rolled it up inside the paper towels. He placed it inside the zip lock bag, removed the air and zipped it shut. He handed it to her.

"Evidence," he said in a focused tone. "Maybe you get something on this mutt."

She took the knife and placed it in a bag she had slung over her shoulder.

"Did you get the surveillance tape?" Jack asked.

Laura looked at him as if they were partners.

"No need," she replied matter-of-factly, "the police'll want it. Besides, I can get my hands on it if we decide we want it."

Jack nodded, recalling how effective a couple of well-placed phone calls could be.

Together with Caridád, Ana and Daniel, Jack, Alex and Laura left the store using the back door, where Jack's car was waiting. It was a tight squeeze. Daniel sat on Ana's lap in the back seat on one side of Caridád while Laura gave Alex the passenger seat, squeezing in next to Caridád to sit on the other.

Jack exited the back alley and headed east. In five minutes time, they were headed east on I-80 toward the I-57 north entrance. On their way to the pharmacy, Jack and Laura had decided that the best course of action now was to bring the kids back to her hotel room at the InterContinental. They agreed the security there would be enough to give them time to figure out their next move. It seemed to be the safest place they could go. Given their lack of other options, it pretty much was the only place.

Once they got onto the expressway, Alex finally gave in to her curiosity.

"Ok, tell me, how'd you guys do it?" she asked, shifting in her seat. "What happened in there? Where were you when you called?"

The questions rattled off one after another.

Jack turned to her and smiled.

"What do you mean?" he said unassumingly.

"Cut the sh –," she said, stopping herself. "I mean, gimme' a break, Jack! How did you guys know when you got there what was going on?"

"It's not really that big of a deal. We can talk later and I'll tell you all about it."

Laura smiled remembering Jack's penchant for self-deprecation.

But there was one thing Alex had to know.

"But, there were three of them, Jack…" she said insistently.

"Yeah, well, when we came in through the back door, the pharmacist showed us the video monitor. And since you were good enough to keep the guy with the knife occupied…"

Alex feigned the expected outrage at Jack's teasing.

"…that gave me time to circle around the store."

"But how did you get passed the other two guys?"

"I, uhhh, didn't…"

"But…"

Jack glanced back at Laura.

"When you told the pharmacist about how many 'injured' there were in his store, what did you tell him?"

Laura grinned.

"One," she said innocently, "why, were there more?"

Jack's silence said more than his words could.

Alex jumped in.

"Did you…" she stopped short of asking. "But you only shot the one guy?"

He turned toward Alex and agreed.

"You're right," he admitted, "I only shot the one guy."

"But then how did you –"

"Never mind," Laura interjected.

Laura then turned her attention to Jack.

"Not as rusty as you thought, eh, Dirty Harry?"

Alex turned and looked at Laura as she spoke, then shifted her eyes back to Jack.

"So, did you… I mean, are the other guys…" Alex tried to ask without asking.

Jack turned to her with an almost apologetic look.

She sat back in her seat.

"God, you're a freakin' Rambo…" she said.

"Not quite," he responded humbly.

"I'm sure glad you're on our side," she said. "Sometime you'll have to tell me how you did it."

He smiled, embarrassed.

"It's not so hard when you take them one at a time, really."

Alex smiled back while her mind raced. She was no stranger to the remnants of violence. From the repressive slaughter in Tiananmen Square to Saddam's mass graves during Desert Storm. She'd been to refugee camps from Rwanda to Palestine, witnessed the casualties of rebellion in Chechnya and the crimes of religious retribution in Kosovo. She'd chased away vultures stalking the ethnically cleansed on their treks out of Darfur. She'd stood over dying soldiers and maimed civilians, even assisting with triage for those awaiting transports, with arms and legs scattered over checkpoints, markets and mosques from the indiscriminate carnage wrought by IEDs, RPGs and suicide bombers in Iraq and Afghanistan. But she'd never actually *watched* someone kill. Or *seen* someone killed.

Until a few minutes ago.

By the man she'd given herself to just hours ago.

Her confusion was real, rampant, impulsive, even somehow strangely sensual. And all she knew to be true was that she was here and the children were safe. Her assailant and his friends were dead, nothing more now than a nightmarish memory, and Jack, without so much as a moment's hesitation, doubt or lingering regret, had killed each one of them. One after the other Beyond that, nothing seemed to make sense.

But, beyond that, nothing seemed to really matter.

She reached over and put her hand on his thigh and squeezed gently. He covered her hand with his. He looked at her and smiled.

Laura turned away and looked out the window.

It wasn't until Jack reached the on ramp to the westbound expressway heading into the city that it finally dawned on him.

Christ! They knew. They fuckin' knew!

They knew where he lived. They knew he had the children. By now, they had to know his car. And if they knew his details, they may already know Father Mac had called Alex. There was only one way they could have learned so much so quickly.

He checked his rear view mirror again. Traffic was light, typical for a Sunday night heading into the city and despite the overnight roadwork, they were making good time. He looked over to Alex, who seemed lost in the city's brilliantly lit skyline.

"Alex, can you pull up that cell phone message that Father Mac left for you?"

"Sure," she said.

A moment later, Jack was holding her cell phone to his ear, listening to the anxious message Father Mac had left. He heard the part where Father Mac said they were asking questions about Ana and Daniel. And the part where they claimed they were the kid's relatives and that they were looking for them. He listened carefully how Father Mac explained how they told him they'd been looking for them, that they were worried because Ana and Daniel been missing for so long. Father Mac also related how they told him that they'd heard that he'd found Ana and Daniel and that they'd been to his rectory.

His rectory.

Jack could understand why they'd go to rectory to find Father Mac. But how would they know that Ana and Daniel had *been* to the rectory? And how did relatives of *both* Ana and Daniel show up at Father Mac's rectory when Ana hadn't even met Daniel until their van ride to Chicago from Denver? And how did they go from Father Mac finding the kids Saturday morning to being at Jack's house tonight?

Jack theorized of one way, maybe two, that could explain it. He feared concluding that either could be true. Both spelled very bad news. He now had another reason to be glad they didn't wait for the police to arrive tonight.

He glanced into the back seat and saw Laura looking at him.

"What are you thinking?" she asked, her tone revealing what she already knew.

"Do you have anything of value in that suitcase at the your hotel?"

"Just everything that's important to being the best-dressed female field agent in the Bureau, that's all," she said half-jokingly.

"Is that it?" he asked, ignoring her humor.

"And the sealed file that Wallace wanted me to hand to you personally." She got his attention with that.

"Ok, we'll have to get back there sometime tomorrow but I'm thinking we don't want to go back there tonight."

Alex just listened.

"Why's that? They can't possibly know I'm staying there…"

"Laura, until I figure out how they knew where *my* place was – and how they figured it out so quickly – I don't think it's a good idea to go back there."

"Ok," she agreed carefully.

"We can figure out how to get your things back tomorrow. Right now, I think we ought to find a place to get these kids parked somewhere."

Truth be told, Ana, Daniel and Caridád had already begun to fall asleep. He looked over to Alex, who'd been listening while watching him.

"Alex, do you have any credit cards on you?"

"Yeah, sure, of course."

His eyes settled into the rear view mirror then made eye contact with Laura.

"Laura, how 'bout you? Do you have any of the Bureau's cards with you?"

"Yes, why?"

"I've got an idea."

Jack passed up the downtown Ohio Street exit that would have led them to the InterContinental and headed up the Kennedy toward the airport instead.

The red 2002 Pontiac Firebird two-door coup remained a safe distance behind. The blue four-door 1998 Chevy Impala with the primer-gray quarter panel veered off the expressway and took the exit toward Michigan Avenue and the hotel InterContinental.

* * *

It was just after 11:00 PM when Special Agent Cauldwell felt his Blackberry vibrate inside his shirt pocket. He was tired. On his way back into the city, he was eastbound on I-80 toward the I-355 interchange. He immediately reached across to the passenger seat and popped open his laptop. He heard the cooling fan run and the disk drive begin spinning as it awoke it from its slumber and sprang back to life at his touch.

He'd been expecting Bobby's call.

Cauldwell smiled at knowing Bobby's every move. Technology can be good that way. That he was calling now, at this late hour, was hardly a surprise either. As a matter of fact, Cauldwell would have been disappointed if Bobby *hadn't* called. That was the thing about Detective Colavito. He was just too predictable. It was his biggest inherent weakness. And it was what would keep him nothing more than a city cop. What would keep him bouncing around the minor leagues his entire career, such as it was, instead of playing in Cauldwell's league with the big boys.

That and his temper. Or, more accurately, his emotions. And his consistently proven inability to get out from under them.

At least, according to the CPD personnel files Cauldwell had seen.

Bobby always wore them on his sleeve. Even going back to when they first met in Iraq. Cauldwell's memories of his time in the desert were selective at best. But so much of what happened there, what he witnessed there, what he became there, was due in large part to the complete lack of restraint – the total preoccupation for vengeance – that the world ignored. It was like that line from that movie Cauldwell liked so much, the one about conflict diamonds and how they were used to finance the brutal civil wars and decades of revolving-door governments in places like Sierra Leone.

"Sometimes I wonder," one main character says, "will God ever forgive us for what we've done…? Then I look around and I realize – God left this place a long time ago."

That was Iraq. This generation's Vietnam, with sand instead of rice paddies.

The tales, the comparisons, came as no surprise to those who'd spent any time in Iraq. Living there had to be bad enough. But going there to fight? And, for a guy like Bobby, it was a gasoline pool waiting to be introduced to his matchstick temperament.

To Cauldwell, Bobby's problem was that he was just another angry American who took 9/11 too personally. Just another grunt who'd been convinced that justice was best served – and America's integrity might best be restored – with an iron fist. That enough patriotism meant the eagle would eventually fly again. That the big dog's cage, once rattled, would bring the righteous fight to the enemy like hell unleashed. And the boot up their ass would have his name written all over it. At least, that's what the politicians, and their willing if not complicit partnership with the media, were selling.

And, Christ, there were more than enough buyers.

But Bobby had always tried to give people the impression he was above it all. Whether it was the summer months he spent surviving 120 degree heat in full gear – or the camel spiders and scorpions, some larger than footballs, that came to visit his tent at night or the blinding sandstorms that shredded *literally* everything he wore, owned or used – or any of the other countless reasons that fuckin' country gave him and every other GI over there to go Son of Sam on any sand nigger they found, Bobby often found himself close to, and at times straddling over, the edge.

Most GI's and civilian contractors Cauldwell'd met in Iraq had certainly spent time flirting with the abyss when they weren't calling it home. Hell, even some of the Bureau's guys had a little fun going crazy while they were in country. Their hitch, though, was nothing compared to the government-issued boots on the ground, the same ones who the Army's new policy "encouraged" to accept their invitations to do two or, like Bobby, even three tours in that human dumpster.

In some ways, Cauldwell admired Bobby's devotion to his duty and the reciprocal loyalty he enjoyed with his men. And whether he was conducting late night raids on suspected caches of stockpiled weapons used to arm local militias; or executing neighborhood sweeps outside of Baghdad's Green Zone for suicide bomb and IED factories; or loading flatbeds with less-than-high value target detainees, most if not all of whom would eventually "disappear" into the desert darkness along with any evidence of overzealous enhanced interrogation techniques, Bobby saw his first duty as ensuring the safety and survival of his men. Cauldwell respected him for that though he found little application of such admirable virtues in the real world.

It was in the gospel according to Marc Cauldwell that "every man for himself" played much more reasonably. And, from what he'd learned of the incident that eventually led to his discharge, Bobby would have been better served seeing the military that way as well. The run-up to the war had left most of America, still discovering body parts in the smoldering debris of the World Trade Center and the Pentagon, with a patriotic hangover they were only too happy to relieve in a post-Saddam Iraq. The President spoke of being "driven with a mission from God" and everything was working according to his – or was it the Almighty's? – shocking, awe-filled plan, though no one certainly wanted the party to be spoiled by a few raped and butchered Iraqi civilians.

From what Cauldwell was able to piece together from personal contacts and the vaguely written reports he was able to obtain, while caught up in euphoria of the victory of righteous might over Saddam's despotic rule one late April evening, five members of Bobby's unit kidnapped and gang-raped three young Iraqi girls – reportedly ranging in age from twelve to seventeen – then murdered them along with their families who, the soldiers incredibly alleged, they believed to be members of Saddam's Republican Guard. Their collective defense would have been laughable had the consequences of their actions not been so despicably horrific. All eventually were given dishonorable discharges after being brought up on conduct unbecoming and other equally nebulous charges. The men agreed to quietly leave the service in exchange for minimal brig time.

Bobby, however, perhaps because of his rank, was subjected to a battery of psychological tests, the results of which concluded that the events of that day could be reasonably explained by a recurring "dissociative amnestic state" from which the Second Lieutenant now suffered. He counted his blessings, agreed he was crazy and put Iraq in his rear view mirror on the first available transport home, comfortable in the knowledge that he'd helped light up their world like the fuckin' Fourth of the July!

Courtesy of his own red, white and blue...

For a moment, Cauldwell thought about not answering the call. He waited until the last ring before picking up.

"Bobby, what a pleasant surprise," he said in a tone equal parts dull surprise and sarcasm. "How's your weekend?"

"We need to meet... right now!" he responded, much more in control than Cauldwell expected.

"I'm sorry, Bobby, but that's just not possible. Hang on, just a second, I'm going to put you on speaker..."

Cauldwell reached across the steering wheel and touched the remote control button activating the speakerphone.

"That's better... Bobby, you there?"

From the background sounds, he assumed he was.

"Why don't we try to set something up for later in the week, say Wednes –"
The line went dead.

"–day..."

How rude, Cauldwell thought as he laughed out loud.

Knowing Bobby, he'd probably do something irrational, maybe even something stupid. Cauldwell reached across into the oversized glove compartment and pulled out his service weapon. His car drifted across the center stripe on the two-lane highway as he released the clip to remind himself he'd loaded it earlier that evening. He snapped it back in place, returned it to the glove compartment and slapped the hinged door shut.

He checked the digital clock on the dashboard. He'd be home around midnight.

He sat back and smiled.

Not too late to welcome a friend…

Cauldwell carefully, almost gently, backed his car into his reserved spot in the parking garage immediately adjacent to his apartment building in the South Loop, situating it evenly within the space as best he could. He'd relocated to the Printer's Row area going on two years now, impressed by the renaissance the area had experienced, particularly when it came to the renovated buildings that had been converted into lofts, one of which he now owned. He had grown a bit tiresome of the social scene in Lincoln Park. He still felt he could run with the young stuff but, in the end, he did have an image to maintain.

As he stepped out of his sedan, he secured his service weapon in the waistband of his pants against the small of his back. He was tired but his adrenaline had already kicked in. His eyes tightened, becoming aware of everything around him. His finely tuned investigative sense told him he wasn't alone, even though he saw no signs of anyone. He could be hiding behind any concrete pillar or crouched beside any parked car. There were any number of places and shadows where a resourceful person could hide. And if Bobby had proven nothing else, he'd shown himself to be resourceful.

As he shut the driver's side door, that solid sound that all finely engineered cars make echoed throughout the sixth level of the parking garage. He stood still for a moment. Waiting. Listening. Looking.

Nothing.

He pressed the remote control on his key chain to automatically lock the car and enable the security system, his headlights once flashing as the horn sounded. The echo quickly died away, swallowed into the late night stillness. His eyes searched the floor rapidly for any movement. His ears were attuned to any noise. He began walking slowly, deliberately, through the open, dimly lit area between his parking space and the elevator bay doors. He played out one scene after another in his head about where he would appear. Where he could appear.

That's what a good agent does. Always have your response ready.

He felt the weight of his service weapon securely tucked behind him with each step. He turned around every few steps as he walked, looking for anything out of place. He stopped once when he heard an approaching car's screeching tires as it turned on ramps probably floors below him. He waited a moment. When the squealing stopped, he felt comfortable, assuming the car had parked on a lower level, having probably found its way to its own reserved spot. Cauldwell was almost amused. It had elements of a game to it, the cat-and-mouse type he believed himself quite adept at playing.

He reached the elevators, trying to keep a watchful if not somewhat nervous eye on everything around him. He turned around and stood still, surveying the parking garage floor in front of him. He'd expected Bobby to have made an appearance by now.

Could the predictable Detective Colavito suddenly be not so predictable after all? He laughed as he considered the possibility. He still didn't believe he'd misjudged Bobby, not after everything he'd learned about him. He conceded he may have been wrong about tonight. But who knows? Maybe he was back with his whore, licking her wounds. Trying to find out what she'd given up tonight. Beating as much out of her as Cauldwell had threatened to, before things really got interesting. He reached over to press the down elevator button.

It was already lit.

He quickly pivoted, searching the floor once more for any movement.

Nothing.

His mind raced through the possibilities. Maybe the last guy just got tired of waiting? He hadn't heard the stairway door open, or even close for that matter. Maybe the fuckin' light was just broken. Or there was something wrong with the elevator.

Or maybe...

He listened for the elevator. There was no movement. He pressed the down arrow a couple of times.

Nothing.

It must be broken.

He pressed the up button, which lit up with his touch. He heard an elevator car begin moving on its way to the sixth floor. He quietly breathed a sigh of relief.

Of course it's broken... goddamned things, they've never worked right anyway...

He kept his back to the elevators until he heard it arrive and the door start to open. He walked in slowly and pressed the button for the ground floor. The door did not close. He pressed it again. And again. The door remained open. Then he remembered.

He had pressed the up button just to call the damn thing, to get it moving. He pressed the button for the next floor up. The seventh floor was the top floor. It also served as the roof to this abbreviated portion of his building. Cars would park there but there were no reserved spots. Exposed to the elements, it was mainly used for overflow parking for guests of residents.

Cauldwell waited impatiently as the elevator car reached the top floor and the door slowly opened. He leaned forward and pushed the button for the ground floor, again and again. It seemed like an eternity before the doors began to close. He stepped back as they finally shut. He felt the elevator begin its slow descent before stopping on six.

"God *damn* it," yelled Cauldwell as the door repeated its lazy routine.

He stepped over to the control panel and pushed the "Close Door" button repeatedly. Three, four times, maybe more. As he heard the doors finally jolt in response to his impatience, he stepped back. He never saw the open hand reach through the closing door and grip him just beneath his throat.

Cauldwell was stunned. He instinctively reached with both hands and grabbed the arm shoving him back and up against the elevator wall. A second man in a ski mask entered the elevator and immediately reached around Cauldwell for his service weapon. He then kneed Cauldwell in the stomach, doubling him over. The first man shoved a sock into Cauldwell's mouth and a burlap bag over Cauldwell's head. His companion applied plastic cuffs to Cauldwell's wrists that had been pulled behind his back. Together, they shoved him out of the elevator as the warning buzzer began sounding. The closing elevator door would not take "no" for answer.

Their execution was flawless. Like they'd done this before.

As they exited the elevator, one of the two men reached roughly into Cauldwell's pants pockets. The agent tried to regain some semblance of his senses but a tightening hand beneath his throat made that all but impossible. The first assailant quickly pulled Cauldwell's keys from his right hand pocket. He nodded to a third man, standing by Cauldwell's sedan, and tossed the set of keys underhand to him. He pressed the remote control button, disengaging the car's locks and security system. He got in, adjusted the leather seat and turned the ignition. He quickly pulled the car out of the parking space, turned toward the exit ramp and stopped hard. He reached across to the armrest on the driver's side door and pulled the trunk release.

The first two men dragged Cauldwell to the back of the car. They lifted him up and dumped him roughly into the trunk. His first assailant removed a stocking cap from his back pocket and fitted in tightly over the burlap bag covering

Cauldwell's flailing head. He pulled it down hard to his neck. The two of them searched him quickly, one of them finding his cell phone in his shirt pocket. The first man stepped back as the second man slammed the trunk closed.

The entire operation took less than sixty seconds.

The three men said nothing as the sedan negotiated each of the exit ramps on their way to the gate. The one sitting shotgun had located Cauldwell's electronic access card in one of the compartments inside the center leather console. The automatic garage door closed behind them as they pulled out onto the side street and up Dearborn Avenue. They were safely out of range of any security cameras when they pulled off their ski masks. They barely beat the red light at Jackson and Columbus on their way to Lake Shore Drive. They were headed south to I-55 then west out of town.

In literally a matter of minutes, Cauldwell went from expecting to relax in front of the latest late-night feature on his favorite pay-per-view adult cable channel to being bound, gagged and sightless inside the trunk of his car heading Christ only knows where.

He knew of only one person who would try something like this.

He had no way of gauging how much time had passed. And with the stereo blaring, he could not even hear voices inside his own car let alone himself think. He did feel the car slow down as it left the paved road and slid easily onto what he assumed was the shoulder. The crunching and snapping of gravel beneath his performance tires told him he was, most likely, out in the middle of nowhere. He couldn't believe this was it.

Or that Bobby could possibly be this stupid.

The sedan came to a stop. The stereo continued to play as the engine idled quietly. He felt what he thought were two car doors closing. Then the trunk popped open. His advanced investigative skills told him he'd reached his destination, wherever that might be.

Two men in ski masks pulled him out of the trunk and into the damp, early morning darkness and stood him up on gravel shoulder. He felt the force of a fist to his stomach, doubling him over and bringing him to his knees. He couldn't breathe. The sock shoved in his mouth kept him from in-haling. He coughed hard but made little sound. He didn't hear the slamming car doors. Suddenly, he was choking on the dust kicked up as his car took off ahead of him into the blackness. He fell forward then rolled over onto the ground, his hands still bound behind him.

A few seconds later, the stocking cap and burlap bag were pulled off his head. A hand reached across his face and pulled the sock from his mouth. Another man stood behind him and cut through the nylon handcuffs. Cauldwell tried to stand up but had trouble finding his equilibrium. He watched the two men walk away in no particular hurry, up the shoulder. He struggled slowly to his feet, trying rapidly to gather his wits.

As he made it upright, a flood of light blinded him. He raised an arm to his face, trying to see, as he fought to breathe normally.

"What do you want with the Monsignor?" a voice out of the darkness asked.

Cauldwell was dumbfounded.

He started walking forward slowly. He heard the glides on two automatic weapons click into place. He stopped in his tracks.

"What?" Cauldwell responded.

"I will ask you once more and only once more," the voice said calmly. "What do you want with the Monsignor?"

Cauldwell tried to think of what he was talking about.

"Monsignor?" he asked innocently.

"Understand something, Special Agent Cauldwell," the voice responded. "Killing you means nothing more to me than swatting down a bothersome fly. Now, you called the Monsignor Sunday afternoon. And there are two things I want you to tell me tonight. How long it takes me to learn these answers – and how much you suffer until I do – is entirely up to you."

Cauldwell was still stumped.

"First, I want to know why you are threatening to blackmail the Monsignor, and, secondly, why are you insisting that he leave the country?"

"I don't know what the fuck you're talking about…"

"I'm disappointed, Special Agent Cauldwell, you are not telling me the truth. And you should know that I am someone who takes such feelings very personally. You should also know that I tolerate lies just as poorly."

Cauldwell stood crippled, still bathed in blinding headlights, wondering what kind of joke Bobby was playing.

"I know that you called him Sunday afternoon. I also know that are expecting an answer from him…"

"Look," Cauldwell pleaded, "I don't know who you are or why you think I know this monsignor friend of yours but, if you just give me my car back, we can forget this whole thing ever happened and you won't have to worry about being arrested tonight."

The voice in the darkness laughed.

Suddenly, a quick strafe of bullets pockmarked the gravel shoulder directly in front of him. Cauldwell fell to the ground and curled up.

"All right, all right," he cried out as he cowered on the sharp gravel.

"Now, answer my questions and you might just see the sun rise this morning."

Cauldwell tried to think as he got back to his feet. He brought his arm back above his eyes, trying to shield his eyes.

"Look, I only did what I was told to do."

"And who was it that told you?" the voice inquired.

"I don't know, I –"

Another couple of rounds spit the loose gravel up around his legs.

"OK, OK!" he cried out.

The shooting stopped. He knew it was time for a different approach.

"I don't know who it was, I only know what I was told... I was contacted and told who to call and what to say. That's all I know. I swear, that's all I know!"

The voice in the darkness remained silent.

"Look, kill me if you're going to but I can't tell you what I don't know," he said in a hopefully convincing whine.

The voice waited a moment.

"When were you contacted?"

"I don't remember..."

He heard the glides click into place again.

"...Ok, ok... last night, late last night."

"How?"

Cauldwell had trouble concentrating. He tried to think of anything he could.

"By phone."

"From whom?" the voice demanded.

"I don't know, I didn't recognize the number."

The voice took a moment, wondering how naïve this agent thought he was.

"Now, which part of that is actually true, Special Agent Cauldwell?"

He opened his eyes slightly and tried looking in the direction of the voice.

"What do you mean?" he asked feebly.

"I mean," the voice asked confidently, "that you didn't recognize the number?"

He paused for effect.

"Or the person you spoke with?"

Cauldwell wasn't sure where else to go. He was dancing as fast as he could.

Suddenly, the voice changed the direction for their conversation.

"Special Agent Cauldwell, it is important that you understand two things."

Cauldwell stood still, holding his breath.

"First, if you have lied to me, I will find out. And, second, as evidenced by your company on this evening's relaxing drive to the country, should I find it necessary to meet with you to discuss this matter again, rest assured that meeting will not end nearly as pleasantly for you as this one will."

Cauldwell realized the voice must have gone through his cell phone and found the incoming call he mentioned. Maybe he'd recognized the phone number it had come from, maybe he didn't. It didn't really matter. What mattered is the voice believed him.

An increasingly relieved Cauldwell then found his own sense of humor.

"You call this pleasant, do ya'?"

The voice laughed.

"Yes, I would if I were you. After all, Special Agent Cauldwell, you are leaving this evening with the same number of holes in your head as when you arrived."

He couldn't really argue with that logic.

"I don't suppose I could have my phone back. Since I won't be driving out of here, you could at least let me call for help. I don't even know where the fuck I am!"

Suddenly, his cellphone came skidding across the gravel to his feet.

"I only hope you can get a signal…" the voice said in jest.

Cauldwell looked at his cell phone lying on the ground and waited.

"Should we need to talk again, I know where to find to you."

He bent down to pick it up.

"Oh, by the way, you'll find your car on the shoulder of this road, up just a ways. Your keys will be in the ignition. You are on I-80, just west of highway marker 93. A couple of miles west of here is Highway 23. Just in case your car's GPS system, for some reason, fails to work."

"Technology can, sometimes, be so maddeningly unreliable, would you agree?"

Cauldwell wondered what he meant though he was more relieved to know his car was not on its way to some chop shop by now.

"Tonight, Special Agent Cauldwell, you were only temporarily inconvenienced. And I do apologize for the inhospitable treatment. But I hope you understand that it was necessary for us to get your attention. Should there be a next time, I can assure you, that will *not* be one of our concerns."

Cauldwell stood still, trying to deflect the bright headlights, as he heard the car doors shut ahead of him. Suddenly, everything went dark. His eyes saw nothing but shades of black and gray blending before him. He shut his eyes and squeezed them tightly closed. He heard the car's tires spin in the gravel. He opened them to watch it fishtail onto the road and head east. Assuming his friend was telling him truth.

He covered his mouth as he coughed on a cloud of dust settling past him as he stood in the muggy August darkness. He slowly, somewhat painfully, began walking west toward where he hoped his car was waiting for him.

He still wanted to believe Bobby had something to do with all of this.

His instincts, though, were less certain.

* * *

Chapter 13

SHE ROLLED OVER in the king-size bed and lay there motionless before realizing she was alone. Alex struggled to open her eyes which burned from lack of sleep. The digital display on her nightstand's clock radio remained bleary. And recognizing it was Monday morning proved a task unto itself. By time they'd gotten to bed, it was well after 2:00 AM. She was exhausted. But the evening's unscripted dangers she'd suddenly faced – a petrifying glimpse into the nightmare that Caridád, Ana and Daniel had been brought here to live, one surely awaiting her, beginning with the perverted amusement of those sick animals – only to be rescued by her daring prince: It'd left her shamelessly wanton, irrepressibly driven by a vulnerable prurience she could not control nor choose to deny.

It would take every sensual moment over the next hour-plus to fully unleash her unabashed passion for her own romance novelist hero before she finally collapsed, spent, once again sheltered in the safety of her savior's arms.

They'd gotten to the O'Hare Hilton just before midnight. She couldn't believe, after *everything* they'd been through, that he'd wanted to drive all the way back to the southwest suburbs. Truth be told, he didn't see any other good alternative. Perhaps overly cautious by nature – or, more likely, as a result of his training –, he was concerned they'd been followed. Laura had to reluctantly agree.

The thing was, with Jack, being cautious hardly seemed like a bad thing.

When they reached the airport, Jack intentionally entered the multi-level parking garage attached to the hotel, trying to create some space between themselves and anyone who might be tailing them. And that part had worked better than they'd hoped. He'd driven all the way up to the top level of the garage – the parking level named for the Chicago Cubs, as it turned out – before dropping them off at the elevators and going to park on a lower level. He knew that the extra seconds he could gain by making anybody following him wonder which level he'd chosen could only work to his advantage.

Jack had asked Alex to rent the room, chivalrous soul that he was. In truth, he had an excellent reason: Alex had kept a credit card in Jimmy's name that he had given her, one he'd had with him when they'd first started working together. She never really thought to cancel it. Thinking back, she realized she'd always assumed that, someday, Jimmy would simply show up.

For all intents and purposes, the card was all but untraceable to her. Jack quickly realized his choice between Jimmy's Visa and Laura's FBI account was a no-brainer. After all, it was the primary reason Jack had decided against returning to Laura's hotel, the InterContinental. If they knew Laura was in town, then they may well have access to her credit card activity. The fact that it was an FBI-issued card didn't seem to matter. It was another piece in a rapidly changing puzzle that was morphing into simply opting for the best possible option. And, as Jack liked to point out from time to time, "it ain't paranoia if they're really out to get you."

So, as Alex secured a suite with a connecting door, Laura went to the terminal and rented a car. Jack wanted her to drive something with four doors, a mid-size, maybe a Toyota Camry or a Honda Accord or even a Ford Taurus, if necessary. He wanted the rental to be one of the most popular models, making it that much more difficult to spot on the road. He also asked her to use a personal credit card for the rental. This way, if they did find her car, it might validate his theory about tracking her movements through her transaction activity.

He'd asked Laura to take the kids upstairs and get them to bed. The suite Alex rented was spacious, with two queen-size beds in one room and one king-size bed in the adjoining room. Laura volunteered to sleep in the room with the kids, insisting that Jack and Alex take the other room.

She also suggested to Jack that they consider the children material witnesses for purposes of providing them round-the-clock protection. Jack first responded positively to the idea, knowing that she could make the necessary arrangements at the Bureau's office first thing in the morning. And, on the surface, it sounded like the idea had no real downside. Still, he wanted to give it a little more thought. The more people in the loop, the greater the exposure. They still weren't sure who they could – and couldn't – trust.

As Laura and the kids got settled in their room, Jack asked Alex to use Jimmy's card to rent a car as well. He told her the same thing, try and get something that was four doors and, if possible, a similar make and model as the one Laura rented. His plan was for Alex to follow him in her rental car back to the southwest suburbs. After giving her directions, he asked her to send him the same two-letter text message – "ok" – every ten minutes to let him know she was fine. He would reply with the same message.

Jack headed toward the expressway, south to Interstate 80, then west to Harlem Avenue, where he exited going north. He knew there were literally a dozen hotels and motels in the shadow of the Convention Center right off the interstate. It was a highly concentrated commercial area residents popularly referred to as the "I-80 corridor." He would park his Honda Civic in a not-too-conspicuous area in the centrally located outdoor lot. He knew that, if anyone had been or still was following him, seeing his car there would mean they would have multiple places where he and kids could be staying. It might be days before they realized they were chasing a ghost. And that would have bought him the time he needed.

At that time of the night – the morning, actually –, traffic was very light. Jack arrived first and waited in the lobby of the Holiday Inn. He'd even taken a room, under his own name, intentionally leaving a trail of breadcrumbs he knew even those mopes would find. He smiled recalling a line he'd heard a character say on one of those law and order crime shows: "Thank God they're stupid."

It was one of their traits he'd learned he could depend on.

When Alex arrived, she picked him up behind the hotel, at the employee entrance, just as Jack had instructed her. She was driving a maroon 2005 Nissan Maxima, a four-door sedan with a kick-ass stereo and leather bucket seats whose lumbar support was remote-controlled. One thing he was learning about Alex was that she had good taste. Riding back to the airport hotel, he realized just how easily he could get used to this. It certainly beat the shit out of his '93 Civic hatchback. Then again, what didn't?

As she lay there some hours later – a feint smile irresistibly emerging as she recalled his as well as her own voracious appetites, not regretting a moment yet, at the same time, unable to deny wondering what she'd gotten herself into –, Alex suddenly realized something wasn't right.

The sheets were damp. Almost wet. She immediately reached for Jack's pillow.

It was soaked.

She quickly climbed out of bed, stepping on underwear that she didn't recall removing. She glanced at the digital clock, seeing it change to 8:36 AM. She looked to the corner of the room where the connecting door remained locked. She saw the rest of her clothes, her blouse and tee-shirt tossed across a nearby chair, her jeans on the floor close by. She walked around the bed in search of a robe.

Finding it at the foot of the bed and, as she bent down to pick it up, she noticed the door to the bathroom was closed. She slipped into the soft, plush bamboo terrycloth, leaving it open, pushing her hair out of her face as she walked slowly toward the door.

She rapped gently on the door.

"Hey, you ok in there?"

Alex heard water running.

"Jack, you ok?"

She tried the doorknob and found it locked.

"Jack, open the door. Please?"

Nothing.

"Jack?" She started pounding on the heavy door with her fist. "Jack, you're scaring me. Are you all right? Open the door, please."

She pounded louder.

"Jack? Jack! Are you –"

She heard the knob turn as the door opened. She pushed through and saw him bent over the sink, naked, cold water running.

"Jack, what's wrong? Are you ok?"

He looked to her with blurry eyes, his hair soaking wet, his body glistening with heavy perspiration, as if he'd just stepped out of the shower. He looked desperately tired.

She placed her arm around him, pulling his head to hers. He only leaned into her.

She reached down and turned off the water. She felt him trembling.

Seconds passed before he finally spoke.

"I, I saw her, Alex," he stammered out. "I saw her again!"

"Saw who? Who did you see?" she asked, now as worried as she was confused.

Jack struggled to collect himself as he tried to overcome the vivid images of a child he'd never met, of the horrific crime scene photos that tormented him all these years later – and of her killer that haunted him still.

"Annie," he said softly, his voice breaking. "Jesus, help me, Alex – it's Annie."

Alex opened her oversized robe and brought him in. He turned into her embrace as her naked body formed one with his. The wet, clammy, cold sweat seemed to pervade his entire spirit. She was unable to move, adhered to his flesh, her body absorbing the agony his psyche was releasing. She withstood the flood of emotions it had forced to the surface as she saw a weakness, a vulnerability, which would have taken years to uncover.

Her tears were uncontrollable.

"Oh, Jack…" she said compassionately.

She raised her head and brought his in against her chest.

"What have they done to you?"

Annie's given name was Andría Cristina Maria Concepción, the daughter of an American businessman and his Colombian wife living outside of Bogotá. The brutal truth was she'd simply gone missing one day. Within twenty-four hours, she was already in the United States and her life – as she knew it, as her parents had known it – was over.

She was all of eleven at the time, just weeks shy of her twelfth birthday.

Jack was first introduced to her through crime scene photos he'd reviewed weeks after her murder. She was a little younger than Ana was now. And from the pictures Annie's parents had shared with him, she could've been Ana's younger sister. A playful smile, sparkling hazel blue eyes. And the most beautiful head of platinum blond hair.

The third week in August 2006 found Jack already in Denver as part of the FBI's follow-up on a ten year-old cold case involving the Christmas night murder of another young girl. Some schmuck looking for his fifteen minutes confessed to killing her and, before the prick's plane from Thailand could touch down at LAX, the piranha-like media feeding frenzy, having gone unabated for days since news of his arrest was leaked, was at a fever pitch. It wasn't long, though, before the lemming press was reluctantly forced to accept what Jack instinctively knew from day one: That this pitiful clown was to that poor child's murder investigation what Geraldo had been to Al Capone's vault.

It wasn't lost on Jack that Annie's murder, conversely, had received virtually no media coverage whatsoever. Of course, it wasn't like she was from a wealthy family with plenty of connections living in a gated neighborhood in some upper-crust, lily-white community like, say, Boulder, for example.

Annie's naked body had been found buried inside an overflowing dumpster in one of Denver's public housing projects. She'd been brutalized – repeatedly – the last time with a piece of wood broken off from a nearby pallet. The word "whore" had been scraped across her back with the splintered piece's jagged edge. A white blanket, heavily stained with her blood and somebody's – or somebodies' – semen, was near her. A pearl white rosary was intertwined between her fingers and wrapped around her wrists. What message the killer – or killers – sought to impart mystified law enforcement officers. To no one's great surprise, local LEOs quickly ran out of leads and questions eventually just stopped getting asked. As task force resources were eventually reassigned, the case not unexpectedly went cold.

And the Bureau had succeeded in doing little more. Jack had sent Laura what little information he'd piece together from the locals as well as the photos he'd been given by Annie's parents. Laura offered to reach out to some of her contacts who could follow up on the cold case, maybe reexamine the crime scene photos and old evidence, even reopen the investigation as part of an ongoing federal trafficking conspiracy case.

But it all went nowhere.

Still, for reasons he'd long ago accepted, he'd found himself living ever since in the drifting shadows of her memory. She'd somehow become more than just another child he couldn't save. Another child he'd never met.

And one he never would.

Alex placed a towel around his shoulders that matched the one wrapped around his waist and led him out of the bathroom. They sat down on the side of the bed. He was no longer shaking. His head was bowed.

"Alex," he said painfully.

"I know," she responding without knowing at all.

He raised his head and looked directly into her eyes.

"I can't explain it, I wish I could," he continued. "She won't let me be."

Jack noticed tears again welling in her eyes.

"I used to think she was here to remind me, to motivate me, to keep me going, to tell me, when it all seemed so useless, to fight back and not to give up."

Alex rested a hand comfortably across his neck.

"But, now," he said in resignation, "all she does is remind me of how I've failed, of the ones I couldn't find. Like I'm supposed to feel guilty for that? What the fuck sense does that make?"

She leaned across and embraced him, her strength belying her ability to answer.

They were still seated on the side of the bed when they heard a knock on the suite's heavy connecting door.

"You guys decent?" Laura called out from the other side.

"Just a sec…" Alex called back. She turned her attention back to him.

"…You ok, Jack?" she said gently.

He seemed to be doing much better. He'd gotten some color back and he was no longer perspiring. She stood up and helped him to his feet. She pulled the towel off his shoulders and dried his hair then wrapped her arms tightly around his neck. He opened her robe, pulled her closely to him and felt the warmth of her strong, naked body. He turned his head, laying it against her shoulder. His hands stroked the back of her head.

"Thank you," he whispered.

She smiled through her tears then felt him growing through his towel.

"C'mon, stud," she told him gently, "Laura's waiting."

She stepped out of his embrace and picked up the towel lying on the bed.

"Here, put this on," she told him.

He declined.

"I'll get my robe, it's in the bathroom."

Watching him walk away, she felt herself indescribably drawn to him. It had been such a long time. And she hadn't yet had time to process the last twelve hours. That he came out of nowhere to save her from an unspeakable fate was amazing enough by itself. But Jack had taken it one step further – the men he killed truly deserved to die. She'd watched as he'd made a higher moral choice, to act where others couldn't – or wouldn't. The civilized alternative, of course, was for Laura to read them their rights so some low-rent shyster could negotiate some insultingly inadequate plea deal with some overburdened hump of a deputy prosecutor that some indifferent, calendar-clogged judge would rubber-stamp, sentencing them to some pointless prison term they'd undoubtedly, inevitably, ridiculously outlast. No, as Alex saw it, facing them down as Jack'd done not only rescued Ana, Daniel and Caridád, he'd saved countless other children; unsuspecting, innocent victims these soulless carnivores would've kidnapped and brutalized, enslaved for profit, bartered, bought and sold. It was God's own Judgment Day, a swift, avenging justice that measured their savage crimes with a reckoning worthy of the wrath of angels.

For while it's true, she reasoned, that a person can become evil, the more difficult truth to tell is that, all too often, evil itself can become a person.

And all that is necessary for evil to triumph is for good men to do nothing.

She only hoped that, for these mutts, hell itself would never burn hot enough.

Truth be told, she was actually glad that *cabrón* with the knife to her throat didn't back down. The bullet Jack put into his brain left her seeing things differently, with hope of a kind like nothing else she'd known had ever done. Despite everywhere she'd been, everything she'd seen – having traveled across every continent, written about victims enduring deprivation and persecution and endless violence, photographed the faces of the helpless, the powerless, the thousands displaced from their homelands by the confluence of ruthless politics and even more ruthless power – despite all that, she'd never watched anyone *do* anything about it, ever do something – *anything!* – to change it, find some way – *any goddamned way!* – to stop it. She realized as much this morning while the two of them, finally alone, drove back to the hotel: There was so much more to him than she could possibly understand, let alone appreciate, right now. And despite everything she'd seen or heard or felt over the last forty-eight hours – or maybe because of it –, she couldn't help coming back to the only thing she knew to be true.

She wanted the chance – she wanted to take the time – to learn.

With all the crosses he bore, all the demons that walked side-by-side with him day in and day out, it was his heroism that spoke to her about the heart of this man. Jack had killed four men in the last two days, three with his bare hands; and Alex realized that standing in harm's way – not only the children's sake but for her's as well – meant more than just risking his life to rescue them from living out their lives as sexual property. It was about living his choice, a deeply courageous, willful choice, to stand and confront this insidious evil wherever he found it, in whomever he found it, every time he found it. And bringing an uncompromising, single-minded commitment to destroy it.

Once – and for all of them. Maybe that was what being a real hero truly meant.

It seemed his demons wouldn't have it any other way.

She smiled affectionately, appreciating her heart's good fortune, as she walked around the end of the bed, tying up her robe before unlocking the connecting door.

"Hey, what's up?" she greeted Laura.

"You guys are going to want to see this," she said, impatiently entering the room.

"Where's your remote?"

"Still with the TV. What's up?"

Laura walked over to the armoire and opened the cabinet doors. She grabbed the remote, turned on the television and punched up the local Chicagoland news station.

"Listen to this."

The news was just coming back from a commercial break. An attractive, late twenty-something young woman, with flowing auburn hair and wearing the requisite somber expression, sat behind the anchor desk and spoke directly into the camera, the live picture of the on-scene reporter superimposed above her left shoulder.

"And, to recap, as we've been reporting all morning…" she started.

Jack came out of the bathroom in his robe, a dry towel around his neck. His eyes met Alex's with a confirming smile.

"Hey, Laura," he said, "I was just about to get in the shower."

"Shhhh…" she responded, "…hold on. Listen!" as she motioned to the television. A well-groomed, good-looking Hispanic man with a thin beard, probably in his late twenties as well and outfitted comfortably for the early morning heat in an open collared shirt, stood strategically in front of Wa-lavender's Pharmacy about to speak into a hand-held microphone. A lone cameraman, careful to keep the pharmacy's name out of the frame, stood before him in the strip mall parking lot now overflowing with local media types, state and local police, coroner trucks and curious onlookers.

The anchorwoman continued.

"…there was a triple homicide in the southwest suburbs last night. For more on the story, let's go to our…"

Jack interjected again.

"Laura, it's not like we don't know about this. We were there, remember?"

"Shhhh," she loudly reminded everyone again.

The handsome on-scene reporter was now speaking.

"…and a spokesperson for the police department here has told us there is a press conference scheduled for 10:00 AM this morning, about an hour from now, where we –"

Jack couldn't resist.

"When else would 10:00 AM be but in the morning?"

Laura couldn't help herself.

"Alex, throw something at him, please?"

Alex tossed a pillow playfully at him and put a single finger to her mouth.

Jack grinned then mouthed, "ok, ok" and relented.

The on-scene reporter was still enjoying his face time.

"What we do know so far, Amy, is that there are three known fatalities, all male Hispanics, reported to be in their late teens or early twenties. Two men apparently died of neck injuries although the exact nature of those injuries is unknown at this point. The third young man, I've been told by an unnamed source, died of a single gunshot wound to the head. From the information we've been able to gather, the killings occurred last night around closing time, which would have been 10:00 PM."

Jack raised his hands as if to say "Again? Seriously, when else would 10:00 PM be but –"

Anticipating Laura's response, Alex discouraged him with a look.

The anchor kicked their previously rehearsed give-and-take into gear.

"Juan-Carlos, what can you tell us, as far as the police are concerned, if they are saying anything about any possible witnesses at this point?"

The on-scene reporter responded on cue.

"Amy, according to sources close to the investigation, witnesses have been identified and their statements are in the process of being taken. To our knowledge, though, there are no suspects or persons-of-interest at this time."

And Jack had always wanted to be a person of interest!

He looked at Alex with a feigned look of a fugitive on the run. She had trouble controlling her reaction.

The ball was now back in the anchorwoman's court.

"Juan-Carlos, do we know if local law enforcement officials are reaching out to any other agencies for assistance?"

Both Jack and Laura fixed their attention on the reporter's next words.

"Yes, Amy, we do have an unconfirmed report that local law enforcement have unofficially asked the FBI to join this investigation, even at this early stage."

Game. Set. And match.

"And while it is unusual for the FBI to be asked to join a local investigation, particularly at such an early stage, Amy, it's certainly not unprecedented," the young on-air reporter explained into the camera. "As you'll recall, in January 1993, both the Chicago Police and the FBI were formerly asked to join the investigation of the Brown's Chicken massacre in the northwest suburb of Palatine where seven people were gunned down in cold blood. Hopefully, we'll learn more at the press conference this morning, which, as I mentioned, is set for 10:00 AM. This is Juan-Carlos Her–"

Laura muted the television. She turned around and looked at them both. "Ok, so now what?"

Jack looked at Alex and flashed that "don't start worrying now" smile of his. Then he looked over to Laura.

"Do either of you happen to know what the Cubs did yesterday?"

"Jack, this shit's serious!" Laura yelled.

Jack stopped grinning long enough to say, "I know, I know, of course it is."
He looked at Alex, who appreciated his change of mood, and smiled.
He looked back at Laura and got a bit more serious.
"Your phone working?" he asked her.
"Yeah, why?" she said hesitantly, wondering what she was committing to.
"Maybe it's time we invited your friend Wallace to join this party."

* * *

Raúl's cobalt blue Chevy Camaro waited silently at the far end of the shopping center off Clark Street just north of Roosevelt Road. Other than a spattering of employee cars, the parking lot was empty. The stores wouldn't open for another couple of hours. He reached across the console and changed the station to the local twenty-four hour news, hoping for any updates on the three dead *chicos* it had been reporting were found last night inside the southwest suburban pharmacy.

Just hours earlier on this humid Sunday evening, he'd sent Sandy and Manuel, Luís' cousin, to visit the priest at the rectory at St. Jerome's, making up some story about being the kids' relatives. He originally wanted Carlos to go with Sandy – he was a much more imposing presence – but he couldn't take the chance the priest might recognize him from the street. But, just as importantly, from the beatdown he'd given Sandy after being left to fend for himself at that intersection, Raúl couldn't take the chance that Carlos wouldn't return alone!

Raúl didn't really expect the two of them would find out much, if anything, about where the kids were, who they were with, what they'd told him or even how the priest became involved. No, to Raúl, the cleric was, at least for the time being, simply a means to an end – sending the two of them was meant to rattle him, to make him react, maybe see who he'd contact and, with any luck, lead Raúl to whoever had taken from him.

What was rightfully his.

Late that same afternoon, Raúl had heard from one of Estéban's contacts in the Chicago Police Department with a solid lead on the car's owner, based on the description and a partial plate number, the one driven by the mystery man who left the intersection with the girl, the boy and the priest. But, beyond matching the driver's general features, the most intriguing news he'd received was the owner's résumé: The blue Honda was registered to a former FBI agent!

The ex-Fed lived in a house in the southwest suburbs, just minutes from I-80. Raúl had Carlos pull together a half-dozen guys and sent them down there to find out whatever they could, maybe even bring him back into the city if things looked promising. Raul knew that, if an FBI guy really was involved, former or otherwise, it could mean connections to getting Caridád witness protection. And that meant that things could get out of hand very quickly. He called Sandy and brought him up to speed. Carlos would send a car to stop by and pick him up on their way heading south toward the suburbs.

Raúl waited patiently, his car facing the retail outlets, his eyes trained on the mall's main entrance waiting for Estéban, who was running uncharacteristically late.

Apparently, he'd been out late last night.

Raúl kept wondering how it could have come to this, how things could've gotten so fucked up so quickly. When Sandy'd called him in the park Saturday afternoon to say he'd found Miguel's body in the bushes at the house, his first reaction was for Caridád. But knowing what he knew now, he began to think that Estéban may have had a point: What *if* she'd been working with the Feds all along? And though he still found the whole idea almost too ridiculous to believe – he hadn't noticed any signs from her that anything was wrong, nothing she'd said or done, nothing in how she'd acted lately that might have given him a clue – the reality was Miguel was dead and she was nowhere to be found.

He had to think clearly now. His business was at stake.

Not to mention his life.

He'd let his guard down. He'd been sloppy. Trusting her had resulted in putting everything he'd built at risk. What she knew – and, by now, who she was telling it to – were all that mattered. He didn't believe for a moment she was missing. Nor did he believe that, somehow, she'd gotten over on Miguel. Ricky, that was different. He'd been careless; his dick had gotten him killed. Raúl could understand how Caridád could do that to a kid like Ricky. But Miguel, with his neck broken the way it was? No fuckin' way. That wasn't something Caridád would do, could do, something she'd be capable of.

No, the only explanation was that someone else had been there. Someone who *was* capable, someone who had a reason to get involved – who knew how to kill a man, quickly, quietly, cleanly. Someone who knew to take the time to hide Miguel's body.

Someone like that fuckin' ex-FBI guy!

That the girl and boy went missing the same day Caridád disappeared could not be a coincidence. And while he didn't consider them to be nearly as important, certainly not nearly the threat Caridád was right now, they were still a loose end. But he couldn't discount that someone – maybe *one* someone – had them all. Maybe the same someone who left three of his men lying dead on the floor of the pharmacy.

Someone like that fuckin' ex-FBI guy!

But, as he waited, an even more unsettling thought continued to circle inside his head like some hungry vulture. Even if this ex-Fed was somehow involved – how did he know to come by the house, to take Caridád, at the one time when Miguel was alone with her? The question left him managing a slow, simmering rage, forcing him to confront a conclusion he had no choice but to concede: That it might be someone from the inside, someone he's trusted – someone he still trusts – who might be responsible for all of this.

Or maybe *more* than just one someone.

Estéban considered himself ahead of the curve when it came to navigating the digital age's ever-changing landscape. But, along the way, he'd learned the advantages of discretion, the importance of knowing when to avoid emails, text messages or tweets and the intrinsic value of personal contact when the subject matter included "personal" content. His work in the intelligence community helped him appreciate better than most how the PATRIOT Act made the surreptitious monitoring of electronic communications ridiculously simple. Privacy had become the first in a growing line of civil liberties that Americans were only too willing to compromise in exchange for their security. He'd once told Raúl how the Feds had begun using the warrantless search authority from antiterrorist laws, originally passed in the aftermath of September 11th, to bring cases against much more mundane criminals, mostly mob-related indictments like racketeering, money laundering, wire fraud and conspiracy-to-commit charges, nickel-and-dime shit like that. The FBI was nothing if not creative. And Raúl gave him his due, believing Estéban was in a position to know. His business – which is to say, his political – connections allowed him to travel in circles where Raúl simply neither would nor ever could be welcomed.

So, while he was surprised to hear from Raúl again so quickly, he was careful not to immediately respond in kind. After receiving a brief, intriguing text message from Raúl to meet this morning, Estéban reached out to Sandy, the one who'd first contacted him about meeting Raúl in the park Saturday afternoon. He knew that, if Raúl had asked Sandy to contact him directly, Raúl trusted him. Which meant Estéban could trust him. And, besides, he'd remembered Sandy from the old neighborhood, a friend of Teresa's. He'd been a close friend of hers, as he recalled now. A *very* close friend.

He hadn't thought of Teresa in years. Not since his days in Denver, anyway, a restless time, before he enlisted. He'd made his peace with what had happened. Some memories, he'd decided to believe, are simply best left forever in life's rearview mirror.

Live and let live.

Raúl shifted with a growing impatience when his attention was suddenly drawn to a special report on last night's murders. He reached over and turned up the volume as the news anchor offered little additional information on the investigation's progress other than to announce this morning's 10:00 AM press conference would be carried live. As he listened, Raúl spied Estéban's metallic red BMW M3 making its way into the shopping center's parking lot. He watched it maneuver slowly as it approached, circling around the outer drive. Raúl flashed his headlights twice. The two-door convertible worked its way around and eventually drove up next to him, coming to a gentle stop facing the opposite direction. Estéban shifted into first gear and turned off the ignition.

Raúl didn't take time for pleasantries.

"Things have suddenly become a bit more unsettled, *amigo*..." he began.

Estéban was hardy surprised. Raúl was not one for small talk.

"Yes, so I've heard. I can imagine this morning's news has been unsettling."

Raúl nodded in agreement as Estéban continued.

"I was a bit surprised to hear from you again so quickly, *hermano*. I haven't had time to gather the information you requested on your detective friend quite yet but –"

"No, I understand," Raúl interrupted, "that's not the reason I wanted to see you."

Respect was everything in their world.

"Ahhh, you have something else you would like me to do for you?"

Raúl nodded and gazed through his sunglasses out his windshield.

"Those three young men from last night –"

"They belonged to you?" Estéban interrupted.

"Yes, indirectly," Raúl answered. "They were part of a crew looking to get back some personal items that belong to me."

"That were taken," he corrected himself, "from me."

"And I am assuming that we are here because their failure made the news?"
Raúl nodded again.

"That they failed to bring them back was bad enough; but the attention their failure brought..." he assessed.

"I would agree, my friend," Estéban said. "It has put you in a difficult position."

Raúl's expression turned colder.

"I also lost another of my men the day before – my nephew's cousin – on Saturday, as a matter of fact."

"I'm sorry to hear that, my friend," Estéban said.

Raúl nodded an acknowledgment of the condolence.

"The person he was watching for me is missing, as well. It's important to me to get her back. Very important."

"I understand," said Estéban. "I have some additional information on the driver of the car, our former FBI agent. Perhaps you will find something inside that will help you in your search."

He reached over to the passenger seat and picked up an envelope that contained a manila folder of information and handed it through Raúl's open car window to him. Raúl smiled appreciatively as he took the envelope and set it down next to him.

"The information your contact gave me yesterday has given me much to think about," Raúl responded. "It's possible you may have been right all along..."

It wasn't anything that Estéban hadn't heard before.

"About..."

"About the possibility of Caridád working with the Feds," Raúl said resignedly.

"Information is currency," Estéban assured him, "but nothing beats intuition."

Raúl was in little mood to acknowledge anything more.

"The pharmacy where my three dead *chicos* were found," Raúl started, "is just two blocks from this ex-FBI agent's house."

Estéban dropped his head, smiled subtly and nodded.

"In our business, *hermano*," he opined, "we do well to believe there are no such things as coincidences."

"Obviously," he continued, "this puts matters in a whole new light."
Raúl agreed.

"I need to make an example of this guy," Raúl concluded.

"Of course. How can I help?"

Raúl was getting angry just thinking about it.

"Everything you've already given me has been very helpful," Raúl began. "But what I need to know now is who his contacts were – and are – at the Bureau. Where he will go for help, who he will turn to, who he can still count on, things like that...."

"I see," Estéban concurred.

"I know someone from the FBI – a woman friend of his – flew in last night from D.C. Why, I do not yet know. She may have something to do with him, she may not. She took a room downtown. I have a man there right now, at her hotel."

"I need to learn everything I can about him, Estéban. And I need it fast!"

"Hmmm," Estéban said, implying premium service demands premium pricing.

Raúl was no fool.

"I was thinking that perhaps you could reach out to some of your closest friends."

"*Amigo*, I was with Homeland Security, not the Bureau. The FBI still works for the Department of Justice," Estéban said, trying to build in some wiggle room. "Many of my contacts have moved on or are in the process of moving on. But –"

"I understand," Raúl interrupted, "and I realize it may take a few days. But I'll take whatever you can get for me. It's very important to me."

"Very well then," Estéban agreed. "Let me see what I can find out."

"That's all I ask," Raúl responded.

"I understand your men went to visit the priest Saturday evening," Estéban said changing the subject.

"Yes, he didn't offer us much, though. If he knows anything, that is."

"Do you want me to talk with him?"

"No, another visit won't get us anywhere. He says he only met them by accident, in his church. He probably doesn't know where there are anymore. If he does, he'll reach out to them. I've got someone keeping an eye on the rectory but, other than the church on Sunday, he's gone nowhere since he got home Saturday evening."

"That's all well and good, *amigo*, but you may not be able to wait for him to send our ex-agent friend a message," Estéban concluded.

Raúl agreed.

"The important thing," Raúl said in summing up, "is to get everything we can on this guy. He'll need resources, to reach out to someone. And I must know who that is."

"I'll get things moving as soon as I leave here," Estéban assured him.

Raúl nodded appreciatively.

"You may want to let someone else get started researching him for me, *hermano*," Raúl said with a smile.

Estéban picked up on his meaning very quickly. But he left Raúl to his surprise.

"Allow me to extend to you an expression of my gratitude for what you've done for me already," he offered.

With that, Raúl flashed his headlights twice. A car directly ahead of him flashed its headlights in response. It slowly pulled away from its parking space and turned towards them. It pulled up along side of Raúl, to his right, a few spaces away. Both back doors opened and two burly men exited, one of which was followed by a striking albeit shy young woman of not quite twenty that had him thinking Raúl was true to his word.

Estéban was immediately impressed, watching intriguingly if not lasciviously as she was escorted around the front of his BMW. She stood almost 5' 8" tall, though that included the three-inch heels of her sandals whose ties wrapped seductively up her smooth, richly tanned calves. She wore a pastel yellow tank dress, sleeveless and slim-fitting her hourglass figure, its scooped neck and mid-thigh hemline vying equally for his attention. Her nutmeg hair was pulled up off her shoulders, strands seductively lingering down both sides of her face. The mirrored sunglasses were a nice touch but totally unnecessary. She smiled nervously, maybe even reluctantly, as her eyes met Estéban's. He imagined it was the kind of deliberate smile an attractive woman usually offers in response to the attention she's made such obvious efforts to attain.

He could hardly have been more wrong.

She straightened, arching her back as she turned toward the passenger-side door. Estéban's eyes were fixed on her as one of the young men opened the car door for her. She sat down on soft, smooth silver novillo leather seat, warm from the morning sunshine, without saying a word. He watched her position her long, silky legs with growing anticipation.

He turned to Raúl and nodded.

"No need, my friend," Raúl said.

Estéban smiled back in appreciation as Raúl motioned to her escorts returning to their car. It wasted no time continuing on its way out of the parking lot.

"Keep her as long as you like," Raúl said, returning his attention to Estéban. "When you have what I need, let me know and we'll see what we can do about getting you with a wider selection for you to choose from."

Estéban grinned.

"You have given me a great incentive, *hermano.*"

Raúl grinned in return.

"That was my intention, my friend."

Estéban nodded and started the ignition. Raúl did likewise.

Then they drove off in opposite directions.

* * *

The Monsignor was typically running late, this time for his one o'clock meeting with Father Mac. It had been set up some weeks ago. The Archdiocese was interested in helping St. Jerome Emiliani parish with plans for its upcoming diamond anniversary. The Cardinal, in recognition of the Monsignor's talent for fundraising as well as having an appreciation for his political acumen in bringing together high-profile wallets for worthy causes, had asked him to take the lead on this project and to recommend any assistance the Archdiocese might provide.

They'd chosen to meet at the newly renovated though not quite completed Archbishop Quigley Center, formerly the Archbishop Quigley Preparatory Seminary. The Seminary was officially closed in June 2007. And while the ribbon-cutting ceremony for the new pastoral center and Archdiocesan headquarters was not scheduled until mid-November, enough of the interior work had been completed to allow some of the offices to be used. Not coincidentally, the Monsignor found it more convenient to meet Father Mac on this Monday afternoon at the soon-to-be christened Center. It was a comfortable walk from his residence on Dearborn Parkway as opposed to Archdiocese's current headquarters a cab ride away on the near west side near the expressway.

And to neither's surprise, the Monsignor's convenience resulted in Father Mac's journey being a bit more involved. From his residence at the rectory, the Pastoral Center was a CTA bus ride and seven El stops away. Fortunately, Jack's prepaid CTA card had more than a couple rides left on it. The priest exited the subway at Grand Avenue, walked up the uneven steps to street level and headed east toward Rush Street.

The last couple of days were weighing heavily on Father Mac's mind. From finding Ana and Daniel Saturday morning to almost losing them that same afternoon to helping Jack rescue Caridád from that terrible place, it had been an unsettling time, to say the least. Meeting those two men, who claimed to be Ana and Daniel's relatives, was equally unnerving. It was all Father Mac could do to keep his mind on saying Mass Sunday morning. It was usually the one place he could go to regain his focus and attain a semblance of peace. The one avenue that led to his own personal sanctuary.

As he walked slowly up Rush Street beneath an overcast sky, it began to feel like it was going to rain. He decided, as long as he was early, to visit the Chapel of St. James, located inside the Quigley Center building adjacent to the new Archdiocesan offices. He was ashamed to admit he hadn't visited the chapel since his seminary days. Attending mass there held some of his most enduring spiritual memories, where each celebration was bathed in a rainbow array of colors beneath the magnificently handcrafted stained-glass windows that towered above them within the almost basilica-like structure.

As he entered the chapel of his alma mater through a side entrance, he was immediately overwhelmed by a sense of humility. Dedicated on June 10, 1920, the seventy-fifth anniversary of the Archdiocese of Chicago, the chapel was modeled after Sainte-Chapelle in Paris. The windows at the front of the chapel, recessed into the curved wall encircling the altar, stood thirty feet high and seven feet wide. Each window was divided into two vertical columns containing five medallions. Scenes from the life of Christ as well as his parables were depicted in trifoliate panels. He slowly walked the length of the chapel, down a side aisle, to the main entrance, trying to take it all in again.

To the south, the windows were enclosed within limestone frames. Each stood forty feet high and ten feet wide and were subdivided into twenty-two distinct panels of various shapes where stories from the Old Testament were told in glorious depiction.

On the opposite wall, to the north, were scenes from the New Testament's Acts of the Apostles as well as moments in the lives of church-honored martyrs and founders of different Catholic religious orders. The cinquefoil medallions displayed in the windows identified some of the most significant moments in the history of the Church, from its earliest inception down through the Middle Ages and the founding of the New World.

Finally, he came to the rear of the chapel where he found himself standing beneath the famous Rose Window, spanning an almost unbelievable twenty-eight feet in diameter. Sixteen triangular pedals extended equidistantly from the window's center. Along with eight outer medallions that encircled the window, the life story of the Virgin Mary was recalled in breathtaking splendor. It was as if through this window he was allowed to gaze upon heaven itself. Humbled, he stood in almost wondrous awe, admiring the Michelangelesque artistry of the divinely inspired minds who'd conceived it's magnificence and the skillful hands who had crafted it when, as if on cue, sunbeams dramatically broke through the overcast afternoon, bathing the vestibule as well as the priest in a shaft of white light surrounded by a spectrum of glorious color.

He suddenly felt himself fortunate just to be standing in this moment.

Over the years, the sheer weight of the windows themselves, in addition to simple pollution and the passage of time, threatened to bring irreparable damage to the treasured creations. In response to this growing need, a group of Chicago natives, Catholics and non-Catholics alike, formed a volunteer organization to solicit the financial aid to pay for the professional services to perform the ongoing and necessary work.

It had been, within the splendor of these walls, in the presence of a tradition steeped in all that he'd come to know as holy, that Father Mac learned the nature of his true calling. This chapel seemed to represent the very best to which the human spirit could aspire. He felt as grateful as he did unworthy to know again the full strength of the faith to which it bore witness, its impact as captivating as it was transcendent. Surely, Father Mac reflected, if a man could not bring himself to believe in the goodness of God after spending time in this environment, he should probably check to make sure he still had a pulse.

And yet...

Father Mac had lost track of time. He'd been sitting in contemplative silence, in a pew just off the main aisle, for almost half an hour. He'd checked in with the Center's main receptionist, telling her that he would be spending a few minutes here, and had asked her to let him know when the Monsignor arrived. He sat, adrift in his own silence, until he became aware of a single pair of footsteps walking up the side aisle toward the pew. He turned slowly, his smile welcoming the Monsignor to join him.

"Good afternoon, Father."

Father Mac smiled. He remembered the Monsignor's well-intentioned efforts at phonetically pronouncing his name on the couple of previous occasions they'd met.

"Monsignor Miles!" Father Mac said, beginning an apology. "I'm so sorry. I asked the receptionist to come get me when you arrived."

"Not to worry," the Monsignor replied as he worked his way through the aisle to where Father Mac was now standing. "When she told me she was going to get you, I told her not to bother, that I would come to you."

The two men shook hands. The Monsignor took a seat next to Father Mac.

"I didn't realize how much I've missed this chapel," Father Mac conceded.

"Yes," the Monsignor agreed, "it is truly a remarkable building."

"I went to school here when it was still a minor seminary," Father Mac allowed.

"Ahhh, I can understand, then," the Monsignor responded, hoping to avoid a vague and protracted trip down memory lane.

Father Mac dropped his head.

"You seemed troubled, Father," the Monsignor noticed.

"I have had," Father Mac began, "a most interesting weekend."

Sensing his younger colleague's mood, the Monsignor reconsidered this afternoon's agenda.

"In what way?" he asked.

Father Mac raised his head and took in the splendor of his surroundings. He was having trouble control his emotions.

"I look around us, Monsignor, and I see the wonder of what we can be, what we can create. I see the beauty that reflects man's soul and the image of his Creator. I marvel at his imagination and see in his vision a spiritual, maybe even a sacrosanct, quality, something that is left for others to appreciate and through which we are brought closer to our God as well as our true nature."

The Monsignor listened patiently, waiting for the other shoe to drop.

"And then," Father Mac said, "when I see what evil we are capable of, when I hear from children – innocent, young, guileless children – what dastardly and despicable things our minds can conceive of and our lack of conscience, our amoral ways, will allow us to do, it simply staggers me, Monsignor. It leaves me shaken to my core."

The Monsignor sat quietly but attentively.

"I cannot help but feel that my faith needs to respond."

Father Mac turned to the Monsignor, who looked him directly in the eyes.

"My faith must respond to such an assault on our human dignity. And yet I find myself with few answers and even more questions. I find myself contributing, however indirectly, to the problem."

The Monsignor's interest was piqued.

"In what ways, my friend?"

Father Mac took a moment to compose himself and looked away.

"I'm sorry, Monsignor, perhaps this isn't the time or place for this."

The Monsignor returned a knowing smile.

"My son," he said paternally without being patronizing, "if we can neither find the time nor the strength in this blessed place, of all places, when shall we?"

Father Mac gratefully smiled in response as his eyes found the altar.

"Monsignor, how does one combat evil when good is not enough?"

The Monsignor laughed softly.

"I'm sorry, Father," the Monsignor replied, "it's been a while since I taught my last class in the philosophy of religion. Resolving such a conundrum would require – "

Father Mac turned to him.

"It's hardly some ethical issue suitable for classroom debate, Monsignor."

The Monsignor's expression allowed him to continue.

"This weekend I came face-to-face with evil. And I helped someone save a child. Three children, actually. But in the process, I may've helped take another man's life."

The Monsignor continued listened without reacting.

"And I know that the longer I stay silent, the more men may die."

Father Mac began to lose his composure again.

"But I also know that the longer I stay silent, the more innocent people may be saved."

The Monsignor spoke up.

"And the more who may die, what of them?"

Father Mac turned to him with a pained expression.

"Given the evil they do," the priest said, "perhaps it's good that they should."

Their discussion took on more the feeling of a confession than a conversation. Over the course of the next hour plus, the Monsignor learned the details of Father Mac's weekend. Although he hadn't had much time to process everything he'd seen and heard over the past forty-eight hours, sharing his experiences with the Monsignor did leave him feeling less burdened. His ultimate dilemma still unresolved, Father Mac felt better having opened up to someone in whose confidence he felt comfortable confiding. Over the last sixty minutes, the Monsignor had provided him little in the way of guidance or advice. He'd simply listened, for the most part without being judgmental, and, where he could, he tried to reassure the younger priest that, in the end, God's enigmatic will remains a mystery to us all. That when we are caught up in the moment, it can be all but impossible to see right or to know right let alone to do what was right. All we have, the Monsignor assured him, is our innate goodness to help us find the right path.

Father Mac was grateful for the mini-homily. He didn't expect that anything the Monsignor would say would provide him with any answers. Nor did he think that any answers were necessarily right. It occurred to Father Mac, after revisiting the events of the past forty-eight hours with the Monsignor, that perhaps the sad truth was that it's not that some actions are more right than others but, rather, they may just simply be less wrong.

Some minutes later, the emotional nature of their conversation having given way to lighter topics, Father Mac and Monsignor Miles agreed to reschedule their meeting on St. Jerome's diamond anniversary for another time, maybe for later in the week. For now, though, Father Mac would remain behind in the chapel to think and to pray. The Monsignor excused himself and wished him well, assuring his colleague that he would keep him in his thoughts.

The two men shook hands. Father Mac watched as the Monsignor left the way he came in, passing beneath the overhead Rose Window on his way into the vestibule.

Father Mac couldn't help but noticed the shaft of light had disappeared.

He felt his phone vibrate as he walked up Rush Street, approaching his neighborhood near Division Street, as the midafternoon traffic began building on the crowded side streets.

"Good afternoon, Monsignor."

"Good afternoon."

"I received your voice mail message. I agree, I think we should meet. What's good for you?"

"I'll be home in the next ten minutes or so. Anytime after that would be fine."

"As it happens, I'm just leaving a meeting now. I'm probably twenty minutes or so from your place. Would that work for you?"

"That would be fine."

"Great, I'll see you then, Monsignor."

"Thank you, Estéban."

The Monsignor was about to hang up when he recalled the second reason he'd called earlier.

"Wait! Estéban? Are you still there?" he called into his phone.

He wondered if the moment of silence was a dropped connection.

"Monsignor?" he finally heard in response.

"Estéban?"

"Yes, Monsignor. I'm still here," he responded. "Was there something else?"

"Yes, thank you, there is, yes," the Monsignor replied. "I realize we spoke only yesterday of my upcoming plans for Tuesday but, I was wondering, have any arrangements been made for Wednesday evening?"

Can you believe this horny little bastard?

Estéban held his tongue.

"Yes, Monsignor," he responded. "As a matter of fact, arrangements are being made today and will be finalized in time for your plans Wednesday evening. I will let you know the time."

The Monsignor smiled. Estéban continued.

"I recall you mentioned some things you did and did not want but I think you will be pleasantly surprised."

"Estéban," the Monsignor said, "you continue to meet all my expectations."

"Thank you, Monsignor," Estéban said graciously.

"No, Estéban," the Monsignor said as thoughts of the evening after tomorrow's already began stirring his creative interest.

"Thank *you*."

Monsignor Miles returned his Blackberry to his back pocket. The weather had begun to change noticeably. The humidity was dropping and the breeze off of Lake Michigan seemed to be getting stronger. It promised to be a much more comfortable evening than in recent days. And he couldn't help but think, knowing what he now knew, that Divine Providence was again at work.

And, as usual, it was to his advantage.

* * *

Chapter 14

"A MATERIAL WITNESS?" BOBBY said deliberately, "You threatened her with a fuckin' material witness warrant?"

Special Agent Cauldwell held the phone away from his ear as Bobby's voice carried throughout his office. He wondered if Jamie had told him everything that had happened last evening at the bar. Or only what wouldn't get her smacked around.

His eyes wandered across his office and settled comfortably on Special Agent Laura Kallinger, whose unexpected appearance just before lunch, was, as it turned out, not really all that unexpected. Now, a couple of hours after the conference call had ended, she was seated at a small round table just inside the window wall in a white blouse and blazer with a matching skirt. He ignored Bobby's onslaught in favor of an overactive imagination that was losing itself exploring her firm but soft, subtly scented flesh before settling in, hungrily wrapping himself inside and between those incredibly smooth legs.

He'd taken Bobby's call in an overt if shallow attempt to interrupt his efforts at bringing her up to speed on the evidence pertaining to Carmen's murder. Cauldwell wanted to play the first card. He wanted Laura to know where *he* thought she could fit in to *his* investigation. Earlier in the day, Cauldwell had heard from the Deputy Director's office looking to confirm a lunch hour conference call – 10:00 AM San Francisco time – when Wallace would inform the Chicago staff of his decision to have Laura act as his personal liaison in Chicago concerning the ongoing investigation.

Cauldwell was many things to many people but, in the end, he was no-body's fool. At least two, maybe even three, things were true that the Deputy Director's decision left conspicuously unsaid. The first, and most obvious, was not so much Wallace's interest in a having a spy in the Chicago office; what Cauldwell found so interesting was Wallace's choice of spies. That the Deputy Director of the FBI would opt to send a demoted and internally-disgraced agent, relegated of late to pushing paper in the Office of Tribal Justice, one whose loyalty to the Bureau, as a result of her involvement in the New York Times leak investigation, could be considered suspect at best was, in itself, quite curious.

And it hadn't gone unnoticed that Special Agent Kallinger had a "personal history" with the deceased Agent Eyas' former lover – one ex-Senior Special Agent Andrew Jackson Sturdevant –, a relationship that an FBI's Internal Affairs formal inquiry concluded most likely contributed to the cover-up of the leak. And while the most serious recommendations by the panel's report to pursue possible obstruction of justice charges against Special Agent Kallinger were ultimately dismissed, it appeared to all involved that her exile to the Office of Tribal Justice would quietly serve the same ends.

Finally, Cauldwell found Wallace's premise completely speculative, if not totally unwarranted, that the three bodies found by state and local police the same day Carmen's body turned up in a burned-out van were somehow connected. Toss into the mix that the Deputy Director announced his intention to have the Bureau take the lead investigative role into those murders to determine their connection to Special Agent Eyas' death, and Cauldwell saw more red flags than a drunken fifteen year-old prom date.

Timing is more than just everything. It more often than not points to the only thing. The politics of the FBI now being in play, that Special Agent Kallinger appeared this morning in advance of the noon conference call should not have been completely unexpected. But Wallace's interest in "determining" how these murders were connected assumed, as lawyers often say, "facts not in evidence." Cauldwell couldn't help thinking that Wallace already had his reasons for concluding the four murders were linked.

And Special Agent Kallinger provided the perfect means toward that end.

What Cauldwell suspected Laura might know about last night's events – the three dead Hispanics at the southwest suburban pharmacy, just blocks from her former lover's house – gave him even more reason to pause. That Wallace oddly refrained from naming a lead investigator only added another curi-

ous layer to an already volatile situation that he conceded was now rapidly spiraling beyond his control. Cauldwell learned long ago that, where the Bureau
was concerned, it wasn't always what you knew that made your cases. Often, it
was what you weren't told – what you never saw coming – that mattered most.

And his instincts told him what he didn't know here was dangerous, indeed.

He'd pressed the issue with Wallace during the conference call, claiming
a need to coordinate efforts concerning his ongoing investigation. But Wallace's reticence, combined with Laura's seat at the table, was a signal that no
one could ignore. Cauldwell had always loathed sharing information with
anyone – Bobby was a good case in point – but he especially hated doing
so under orders. Sharing information on – and, ultimately, responsibility for
– joint investigations was a little bit like living with your in-laws: everyone
had their own ideas about who's opinion mattered most and no matter what
anyone said, at the end of the day, everyone thought it was theirs.

In the couple of hours since the conference call, Laura had worked to
get up to speed on Carmen's investigation. She had taken up temporary residence in a small conference room just down the hall from Cauldwell's office.
It was her choice, actually. The room had a door. And the door had a lock.
But after their conference call with the Deputy Director, Laura had spent
much of the afternoon in Cauldwell's office gaining access to evidence files
and field agent reports. She studied the website data along with a small stack
of investigator notes all the while aware of Cauldwell studying her.

During the course of her review, Laura noticed that the original working theory supported Wallace's theory that Carmen's murder was somehow
related to the three dead bodies found around the time her body was discovered. The victims were described as:

- A young Hispanic male, early twenties, found in a ditch along the Interstate I-80 with five bullets in the back of his head, execution-style.
  Ballistics has matched the rounds to a Beretta Tomcat 32 Automatic.
  Bullets from the same gun were removed from Carmen's head, although the preliminary autopsy report indicated it was most probable
  that she died from the knife wound she sustained to her abdomen.
- Two as-of-yet unidentified black males, also early twenties, with assorted gang affiliations, were found at a safe house being used for
  running illegal immigrants. Both were shot multiple times, though
  not with the murder weapon that killed Carmen and the kid from
  the ditch. And their kneecaps were broken. Tortured, it appeared.

Forensics was able to match the composition of a wet spot of radiator fluid found on the floor of the attached garage to a similar spot found under a white van some blocks away, the one in which Carmen's body was found. Preliminary analysis indicated a similar coolant-to-water ratio. Final results had yet to come in but, as the report noted, it was simply too coincidental to ignore. Interestingly enough, she saw a note in the file that the forensics team hadn't yet completed processing the I-80 crime scene for some discolored gravel they'd discovered on the shoulder of the road. Should the ratios match, that would be conclusive evidence that the white van had been at both crime scenes.

To Laura, nothing else made sense. This had Carmen's name written all over it. Working a long-term assignment, deep undercover. Infiltrating human trafficking routes out of Central America. Identifying a network of safe houses used to distribute them throughout the lower forty-eight. It was Jack's "Operation Homeward Bound," the very same one Carmen had worked. What she'd learned she would've found valuable, even necessary, to resurfacing alive. But a couple of things jumped out at her.

The first was the ballistics. The same gun was determined to have killed both Carmen and the young Hispanic man found in the ditch on I-80. But she didn't find any fingerprint analysis of the bullets. There wasn't one note referencing any results from IAFIS – the FBI's Integrated Automated Fingerprint Identification System. Not one request to IAFIS for analysis. Laura found that more than a bit puzzling.

Killers, particularly professionals, who used guns as their weapon of choice are often smart enough to remember to wipe the murder weapon clean. That was a no-brainer. Any cop show on television tells criminals that much. And if that weapon used clips, such as in this case, maybe, though not always, they'd remember to wipe that clean as well. So, it was understandable if nothing definitive was found either on the weapon itself or the spent clip. But, in her experience, shooters universally tend to overlook the bullets. When the Beretta's ten round clip was loaded, it could not be assumed that it was done so with the killer wearing latex gloves. Yet there was no report even remotely suggesting that fingerprints from either crime scene – either from the white van where Carmen was found or the ditch where young man was murdered along I-80 – were requested of IAFIS concerning the bullets used in murdering the victims.

And something else of interest jumped out at her. As she read further, she learned that terminal ballistics had identified the type of bullets as hollow point. This told Laura that the killer intended to shoot the victims at close range. The reason behind using hollow point bullets was to allow for maximum expansion of the projectile as it enters its target. The inside leading edge of the bullet, typically made of lead, expands outward as the projectile's force met the target's resistance. As it passes through the target, it inevitably begins to slow, resulting in a widening, or flattening, of the bullet's cone-shaped nose. As force decelerates, it not only decreases penetration but, in the process of expanding its mass, it creates greater damage. The perfect bullet for the perfect occasion, ideally suited for shooting someone at close range. Thus, the shooter, by controlling the depth of the bullet's penetration, ensured that it would remain in the victim's head.

Laura knew that gave the killer another distinct advantage. Leaving the bullets in the body also served to dramatically decrease the possibility of identification upon examination. The more damage the bullet eventually would do, the greater the possibility the resulting chemical reactions within the body – in this case, the brain – would act upon it, lessening the chance forensics could eventually tie it to a specific weapon for use later as evidence. And since the bullet flattened as it entered its target, very little was left for the lab to adequately test.

Maybe that was what the lead investigator was thinking when it came to ballistic analysis of the bullets themselves. Or what fragments of the bullets remained once they'd been retrieved from the victims during autopsy. Still, not having submitted them for testing, that was more than just puzzling.

That was troubling.

But the weird thing was the shooter intentionally left the murder weapon behind. It had been placed inside Carmen's hand before she was wrapped in the plastic tarp. It seemed obvious the shooter – or, at the very least, someone at the scene – *intended* for the police to find the weapon. That meant ballistics wasn't something the shooter was concerned about. Given that theory, it made sense that the choice of hollow point bullets was solely intended to leave no physical evidence on the bullets themselves.

Which is precisely why they should be examined for fingerprints.

Then there was the fact that the murder weapon was used found in Carmen's *right* hand. It seemed to be an amateurish, even clumsy attempt at bringing Carmen herself under suspicion. Certainly, the killer would have – or at least should have – realized that the gun would be tied to both murders, not just young man in the ditch. So why leave the gun? And why leave it in Carmen's possession?

That the killer didn't know she was left-handed also told a story. It seemed most likely that he – or she – had not met Carmen before killing her, simply assuming she was right-handed. A safe assumption, perhaps, but a telling one. Laura couldn't know at this point how that fact might be important but her experience told her that obtaining and interpreting *all* the facts during a homicide investigation meant exactly that. Recreating a crime scene during a homicide investigation was literally like fitting together pieces of a jigsaw puzzle. The smallest piece could provide the most revealing part of the picture.

And she knew those pieces only fit together one way.

Which brought her to the knife. The coroner had a choice when it came to ruling an official cause of death: either the five gunshot wounds sustained by her head or the knife wound in her abdomen. Serology test results proved conclusive: While her death would have been an inevitable consequence of the stomach wound and intestinal damage inflicted by the knife, blood tests identified the more immediate cause of her death was from the gun shots. Carmen's death was officially ruled a homicide resulting from gunfire. And the Bureau conveniently had the murder weapon in its possession.

But while the autopsy definitively ruled it out as inflicting the fatal wound, Laura wanted to know more about the knife. The report she read online was very informative. The knife was special issue, a military knife. The kind used in special ops, by underwater demolition teams and SEALs, groups like that. Its' six-inch blade was made of stainless steel. It had a flat, black finish and a double-edge point. A non-slip resin grip formed the handle, which had a serrated back and a solid steel cap on the butt end.

Laura found the IAFIS request concerning the knife. What she didn't find were the results. There was no responding report referencing either a positive or negative match for prints.

That didn't seem possible. From her knowledge of the FBI's automated system, results could typically expected within twenty-four hours. It had been five days since her murder. Laura quickly realized something was wrong. She saw only two possibilities: either the lab had failed to send the knife for analysis or the results, which would have been updated and linked directly to the evidence files online, had been altered. That the status on the IAFIS file still indicated "open" at this point in the investigation she found as implausible as it was inexcusable.

She made a note of the file number.

Laura looked up from her laptop as Cauldwell's phone conversation invaded her concentration. Her initial review of the Chicago office's computer files left her with enough open questions that she could not rule out the possibility, if not probability, that Carmen's murder was somehow connected to that of the three other young men. But, as for last night's pharmacy killings, nothing was jumping out at her. It would take time for field agents, working that crime scene with local police, to update the various file locations with their notes and specific reports. She added her name to an email list that would send her a notice when files at the secured web page were updated. And she would access the online shared file repository every couple of hours using the FBI's secured intranet connection, one she had no doubt was being monitored. The files were supposed to be updated no later than every two-to-three hours, particularly during the first seventy-two hours an ongoing investigation. At least that was procedure at the Chicago office, Cauldwell had assured her. While she had no reason yet to doubt his insights, her first impression of Special Agent Marc Cauldwell was that he was the type of guy whose assurances she could trust about as far as she could kick a bathtub barefoot.

In truth, her commute into the Loop this morning with Jack helped her prepare for meeting with Cauldwell. He'd taken time to tell her about his "conversation" with him after identifying Carmen's body at the morgue. She understood what Jack thought of him and, quite frankly, now that she'd met him, she realized Jack's perspective was probably a bit too generous. But the more interesting aspect to her was the relationship Cauldwell had with Deputy Director Wallace.

And where she fit into how Wallace was playing him. Or her, for that matter.

On their way into the Chicago Office, Jack had driven to the InterContinental though he chose to keep to the side streets as a precaution. Laura's phone call to the hotel's head of security allowed them to use the service entrance below street level to gain access to the lobby undetected. Jack had parked at a meter on North Cityfront Plaza, one block east of the hotel off Illinois Street running parallel to Michigan Avenue. He insisted on escorting Laura upstairs after she'd picked up her access card from the front desk. Upon entering the room, they discovered her single suitcase on the bed had been opened, the small lock having been broken. Virtually all of the contents of her luggage had been strewn across the bed as well as the floor. It came as no surprise to Jack that, whomever they were dealing with, they not only knew where she was staying but they'd found someone to let them in.

The curious thing to Jack was why they would search her luggage. What would they be looking for? Or were they simply sending a message that there was nothing about her movements they couldn't find out?

It seemed Laura could no longer consider that one of his fears as irrational. And she was totally pissed. She didn't think about how Jack's foresight may well have saved her life. She wanted to get her hands on the mutts who pawed through her things like some Arbor Day sale at J.C. Penney's. Before long, Jack wondered out loud about the sealed file. Laura capped her outrage long enough to point him to the empty suitcase where she directed him a small zipper hidden deftly beneath a sealed false bottom Velcroed in place. Inside he found a heavy overnight envelope, still sealed. A quick inspection told him it had not been tampered with. He watched Laura finish repacking her things and zipped her suitcase shut. Her anger simmered on the back burner as he took the envelope and shoved it inside his shirt and against his back.

They'd left the hotel separately. He'd taken her suitcase down through the service entrance. Laura walked out the back and north, up St. Claire Avenue a couple of blocks toward the hospital. He watched her catch a cab to the FBI building at 21st and Roosevelt Road, then made his way to the car and back to the airport hotel via the expressway. He'd told Laura to email him when she was ready to leave. He suggested she take the CTA's Blue Line back to the airport. He didn't have to remind her that she might be followed but he did suggest that she switch to another line at least twice on her way there. Under no circumstances should she take a cab back to the hotel.

He needn't have wasted his breath.

Laura couldn't help but notice that Cauldwell's conspicuous attention had again drifted from the somewhat one-sided phone conversation he was having to leering at the shapely legs she'd just crossed. The guy was as lecherous as his manner was obvious, not to mention obnoxious. She laughed, thinking he really was a walking advertisement for why it's such a long and winding road from *redheaded* stepchild to favorite son.

"And what about the access to the evidence locker? Do I have access yet?"

Bobby's forceful tone had Cauldwell rapidly losing patience. His greater concern now was that Laura being within earshot. Having had enough, he tossed Bobby a bone.

"Look, I've got someone in my office. Can I either call you back or maybe we could meet somewhere this evening to talk about this some more?"

He waited for a moment while Bobby decided.

"Eight o'clock. Parking garage. Oak and Clark. Fifth floor." he said brusquely.

Cauldwell smiled. Bobby was *so* predictable.

"I know it," Cauldwell said snidely. He'd been there Saturday afternoon. It was the same place Bobby had met Raúl.

"You shouldn't have done it this way this, Marc."

"Oh?" Cauldwell remarked "How's that?"

"You've made a very serious mistake."

The line went silent. Cauldwell smiled, though it was a nervous smile just the same. Maybe Bobby was right. Maybe he did come off a bit heavy-handed with the bartender. Still, it hardly mattered. He was covered. Wallace was still securely in his corner. At least he was as of Friday, when he called about Jack's request to get in on the investigation. He was open to the possibility that Laura's sudden appearance may be an indication of Wallace's change of heart, at least the beginning of one. Of course, for all Cauldwell knew, he could be banging her and all of this could be nothing but reciprocity. Besides, what Wallace knew about Cauldwell's more playful side in Iraq – and, more importantly for Cauldwell, that other direction Wallace chose to look – convinced him that the Deputy Director's allegiance to his own self-interest would dictate events going forward, events Cauldwell remained confident would continue to unfold to his personal and professional advantage. If he stayed alert. And if he played his cards right.

Which only made him fixate on Laura all the more intently. And when she asked if he had time to go over some things she had questions about, he was only too happy to walk over and sit down next to her.

But whatever anyone could conclude about Special Agent Marc Cauldwell, it was *not* that he was stupid. He'd always prided himself with knowing which head to think with. At least most of the time. Given the confrontation he'd had with Jack at the morgue, he reasoned that anything she learned about Carmen's homicide investigation would go straight to him. A blind man could see she was his conduit. Why Wallace would allow that remained a mystery. But he would figure it out. Because he was that good. It was just a matter of time.

He pulled a chair up next to her and was immediately allured by the charismatic fragrance of her perfume. He heard her talking but he wasn't really listening. It was all he could do *not* to react to the stark images of her flooding his imagination – naked, wet and moaning, her clothes scattered in stages across the floor. He saw her bent over his desk, heard her begging him through the pain for more, crying out she can take all he has. He watched her body quivering as her last thundering orgasm collided head-on with the growing intensity of her next one. He grinned as her insolence berated him, taunted him, invited him to pound her even harder, grip her hips even tighter, hit her even faster. At first she'd have naturally resisted, been enjoyably combative, struggled to fend off advances she'd so secretly desired. But, in the end, like all the rest, she'd submit, become compliant, at some point even willing and, of course, appreciative.

He so hated to disappoint.

He realized he was smiling when he wondered out loud if they wouldn't be more comfortable at one of his favorite martini bars, a few blocks north in the Printer's Row section of the south Loop.

It was just past 4:30 PM.

Laura's first reaction was to tell him to go fuck himself. She found him repulsive. The red hair, the bushy eyebrows, the allergies and that cocky, shit-eating grin he flashed.

Yeah, like the women are lining up to get a piece of that every weekend!

But she knew he could be useful. He might help her with something, maybe fill in some of the blanks, if he was properly motivated. Especially with a couple of drinks in him. *You never know.* She stopped thinking as an agent and started thinking like a woman. And if she let him think he had a chance, who knows?

She realized how dangerous that could be. How dangerous all of this could be. But no one else knew what she knew. How it all was coming together. And she knew what Jack would say.

That sealed the deal. She mustered the best flirtatious smile she could.

"Sure, just let me check my email."

* * *

As Jack entered their room at the O'Hare Hilton, his eyes were immediately drawn to Alex sitting cross-legged on the bed in her robe, working from her laptop. Her hair pinned up off her shoulders, she'd taken her contacts out, opting instead for her eyeglasses, sturdy black designer frames holding thin six-sided lenses. His first thought – well, in truth, his second thought – was that she looked positively academic. It was a dressed-down look that became her, an intellectual look of sorts, and it succeeded in stirring him immediately. She made the whole scholarly thing work perfectly!

Then again, Alex could make compression stockings and a hairnet provocative.

He smiled reflexively as he tossed the overnight envelope on the bed. Alex slipped across the comforter and walked over to greet him. A soft kiss and a big bear hug later, she reluctantly stepped back out of his embrace and picked up the envelope.

"What's this?"

"It's the file that Wallace gave Laura for me to review before I meet with him tomorrow afternoon."

"Think it will add to my story?"

He grinned thinking it might easily end up *being* her story.

"Probably… I'll let you know once I get through it."

Alex smiled and tossed it back on the bed.

"What 'cha been up to?" he asked.

Alex sat down on the end of the bed and pulled the open laptop toward her, the cable providing her Internet connection snaking behind it.

"I've been putting some of notes together, trying to make sense of everything you told me about Cauldwell and Wallace and Anderson Scott and …"

She lost her train of thought as her browser slowed to a snail's pace.

"…And I went back to our secured intranet website that Jimmy and I used to use. We'd send each other photos we posted, information on articles we were researching, stuff we were working on. We also used it to blog messages to each other, sorta like a way to send secured IMs to each other, stuff like that."

"Ok," Jack replied, wondering where all this was leading.

"Anyway, I came across this one link in the site that was kinda weird. When I click on it, it doesn't take me anywhere. Just when I thought the screen was frozen, a popup came up and prompted me for a password. Then, when I wait too long to enter a valid password – maybe ten seconds or so –, it times out and the browser shuts down."

"That is kinda weird," he said, hoping his agreement would hide his lack of Internet acumen.

"And when I *do* type in something for a password, the same thing happens."

Jack stood there not knowing what to tell her.

"Sounds like the equivalent to that opening scene from 'Raiders,' he commented.

Alex looked back at him, completely puzzled.

"Raiders?"

Jack smiled sheepishly.

"Yeah, ya' know," he started, "'Raiders,' the one where he's looking for the Lost Ark?"

She waited, really wanting to hear his line of logic. He kicked it into gear.

"When he went into the cave, with the guide, looking for the golden idol?"

A growing blank expression was her only response.

"Remember, there was only one way he could take to get in there and find it?"

"Ohhhhhh," she finally replied, with an exaggerated vowel.

"All the booby traps and death traps and all that he had to –"

He suddenly stopped talking, noticing the glint in her eye and her growing smile.

"Soooo," he decided to start again, "any idea what his password could be?"

"No," she said returning to reality, "I have no idea what it is."

Jack offered what he hoped would be a more practical thought.

"Sounds like he wanted to discourage anyone who didn't know his password from trying to gain access to his hidden website."

"Yeah, I'm sure you're right," she said, pushing her laptop aside to focus her attention on Jack. "Anyway, everything ok downtown?"

He sat down on the end of the bed next to her.

"Well, we were right about not going back to her hotel last night."

Alex was learning that Jack said things like that when he tried to share the credit.

"Whoever's watching the hotel got into Laura's room. They went through her stuff. Made a mess of things."

"No way!" she said in sincere surprise. "Seriously?"

"Yeah, she was *really* pissed!"

Alex just shook her head.

"Yeah, whoever these guys are, they're well connected."

"So, what did you guys do?"

"I helped her pack her things up and we got her out of there."

He looked around.

"Where are the kids?"

"They're ok, Jack, they're right in the next room," she said, "I was going to take them down to the pool."

He thought for a moment.

She read his mind.

"Don't worry, I think it'll be fine. There's security right outside the door by the pool – I checked – and there's a lifeguard on duty during the daytime hours. And there were kids already down there."

"Besides," she continued," they've been cooped up with nothing but television and video games, which seems all right with them. I bought them some books to read but that'll only go so far. Caridád's feeling better so I figured, as long as the feds are footing the bill for this little vacation, we should try and have some fun. Wanna come?"

Jack was pleased at the thought of the kids getting a little down time and trying to relax, maybe even acting a little normally.

"I'd love to, Alex but I've got some work to do."

"Ok, but," she replied as she walked back around the bed and closed her laptop.

He surprised her.

"No, I was thinking they didn't have suits."

"Not to worry, I am nothing if not resourceful," Alex countered. "We went downstairs while you guys were out, when we were checking out the pool, and I picked up some suits for them. And for me, too. Wanna see?"

Jack smiled as he nodded instinctively.

Alex stood up, dropped her robe and stepped back. She pulled the clasp from her hair and tossed it on the bed next to him. Her glasses followed suit. She shook her head and ran her right hand off her forehead through her hair, seemingly trying to shake it loose. She stood before him as if she'd just stepped off a runway.

He could not take his eyes from her.

She was wearing a black one piece. The suit was soft and molded itself around her every curve. The fabric was advertised to fit like a second skin and it certainly did not disappoint. A mesh inset decorated a plunging tankini neckline of nylon and spandex that cut just above her navel and connected it to a low-rise scoop bottom. Deliciously thin straps crisscrossed the middle of her back. His interest was unavoidably obvious.

"And check this out," she said, as if he could believe it would get any better.

Alex disappeared for a moment into the bathroom then just as quickly reappeared in the doorway. She'd added a white fishnet tunic as a cover-up to her ensemble topped off by a pair of bronze designer sunglasses with graduated dark brown lenses that somehow matched the highlights in her hair.

Jack's smile was only one demonstration of his approval.

"Like I said," she said smiling, bowing her head as she looked over the top of her sunglasses. "I can be very resourceful"

He got up from the bed and walked over to her. She smiled in anticipation.

His eyes danced as they met hers. He leaned forward, took her face in his hands, and kissed her. Long. And deep. Their tongues darted and danced across each other in a warm, wet, erotic game of tag. She pushed herself forward into him. She felt so safe.

He buried his head against her shoulder and lifted her into his arms. Her feet left the floor as he hugged her tightly.

"You are so beautiful," he whispered. "And I am so lucky!""

He put her back down and she stepped back from his arms. She propped her sunglasses on top of her head and smiled as her eyes connected with his. She wanted him to take her. Right now.

He cupped her cheek in his hand. Their eyes saw nothing but each other.

"Alex," he said gently. She smiled again.

"I love it when you say my name," she said, invitingly.

She turned her hips into him. She felt how he hard he wanted her.

"Why don't you give me a moment," she whispered, running her hand across him.

"Alex," he said, thinking he should object but finding no reason to.

She reached a hand around his neck and drew his mouth into hers. She kissed his slowly, softly at first, before her tongue gained a certain momentum. Her other hand continued rubbing him, wrapping itself around the vertical form grown inside his pants.

She pulled herself away from him without taking her eyes from his.

"Just need a minute, Jack" she said, her eyes twinkling. "Or maybe two."

She slowly, gracefully dropped to her knees as his hands ran through her hair. He closed his eyes and drew a deep breath as he felt the button on his jeans become undone.

Just then, a knock came on the connecting door. The kids were giggling and laughing and calling out her name.

She stood up and glared at the sound coming through the door.

"Sonuvabitch!" she said quietly.

Jack took another deep breath and laughed.

"Not to worry, Alex," he said. "We'll remember where we left off."

Alex pouted for a moment then started to laugh.

"I know, I know…" she said as she walked over to the bed to put on her robe.

Jack walked up from behind her and hugged her. She noticed his interest was still piquing. She reached back and her hands disappeared between them. Jack lowered his head and pulled her hair from across her neck. He bit her gently and flattened his tongue against her throat. She moaned audibly.

The chorus of voices from the other side of the door grew only louder.

"Damn!" she said, trying to catch her breath.

Jack stepped back and turned her around to face him.

"Like I said," he reassured her.

She nodded and smiled, then started walking over to unlock the connecting door.

"Hey," he asked, "are you taking your laptop downstairs with you?"

"No, you need it?"

"If you don't mind, yes, I'd like to check my email."

"Sure, no problem. I'm already connected."

A telecommunications cable ran across the comforter and down along the floor, beneath an open wooden desk, and into a wall outlet.

"Great, thanks."

He picked up her laptop off the bed and sat it carefully on the desk. He sat down in a nearby office chair and wheeled himself over. A moment later he was inside his email account. Alex put her robe back on and walked over behind him. She placed her arm around his shoulder.

"Ok, I'll probably keep them down for maybe an hour or so. I'll have my cell with me if you need to reach me."

"Sounds great, mine'll be on too," he said, not taking his eyes off his work.

She leaned forward and pushed the screen closed.

He lifted his head and turned toward her, ready to apologize, when he felt her mouth meet his. He closed his eyes and welcomed her hand as it reached around the back of his neck and gently massaged his head. Her tongue shot inside his mouth, teasing him, playing with him, reminding him. Just as he reached for her, she pulled back.

"Nope," she said, "you've got work to do."

"Uh-huh…" he said not so cooperatively.

Jack watched her turn away, out of his grasp, and walk through the open connecting door. He smiled knowing the kids would be safe with her.

"You guys ready to go?" she called out.

Three resounding "yeses" responded.

"If you change your mind, we'll be downstairs," her fading voice reminded him from the adjoining room. He pulled the screen back up and returned to his email as he heard the door close behind them.

The tab from the empty overnight envelope lay curled up next to Alex's laptop on the bed behind him. The contents of the second of two manila folders the envelope contained were spread out on the desk before him. Jack sat back in the room's only comfortable chair as he skimmed through the handwritten summary Deputy Director Wallace had prepared for him. The accompanying dossier on Special Agent Marc Anthony Cauldwell seemed as impressive as it was extensive. But before focusing his attention to this folder's more detailed information, his eyes wandered back to the first file still lying open at the corner of the desk.

It was considerably thinner and, to his experienced eye, heavily edited.

There were numerous redactions which he didn't necessarily find all that un-usual. But there also appeared to be paragraphs, even pages, missing, which he found not only strange but troubling. What drew his interest was not the little it said but the awareness it implied. The sparse documentation was just enough to be confusing. To Jack, nothing in it would warrant having it hand-delivered to him. Nothing at all.

He thought back to last evening's conversation with Laura, in the car on the way to the hotel from the airport. Their conversation about the package that Carmen had mailed to Laura to give to him. The cryptic email Carmen sent her from an unidentified phone number because hers wasn't safe. How Carmen knew Wallace was dirty.

Jack opened his cell phone and pulled up his text messages. Laura had emailed Carmen's message to him and had copied his cell phone. He read it slowly once more.

Laura, it's me. Haven't much time. Sending u this from a private #, my #'s not safe. Mailed u docs, get them to Jack. Wallace is dirty. Call u l8r. Carmen

Call u l8r?

That made no sense. Carmen would never break cover to contact an FBI agent directly. And she would never have written a message like that. None of the language in that message was hers. And she would not simply use just anyone's cell phone to send an incriminating message like that, especially while she was undercover. That is, unless she had no choice. Besides, she *never* signed her text messages that way! At least, none she'd ever sent to him. Jack's mind started to wander. And he was getting a bad feeling.

What if somebody else had sent Laura that message?

Somebody who knew Carmen's assignment. Somebody who knew Lau-ra. And somebody who knew Wallace was involved. And, most importantly, *wanted* it known.

And who specifically wanted Jack to know.

He sat up and reached across the desk for the open file, quickly skimming through the few redacted pages it contained.

He suddenly realized he'd been reading it all wrong.

He stopped and looked up into the eyes of his own reflection in the outside-facing window. A moment of clarity washed over him. This file had nothing to do with Cauldwell. There wasn't a trace of information in it about Cauldwell. No, sending Jack this file had a completely different purpose. Wallace included it in the package for a very special reason. Maybe even a very personal one. He was sending Jack a message. And suddenly that message seemed unmistakable.

The stakes had changed.

Or maybe Jack was finally learning what the real stakes had been all along.

For the first time, he wondered if he was in over his head. His first thought was for Carmen. She had to have been set up. That's the only way any of this made sense. But even Wallace wouldn't have authorized the murder of one of his own agents.

Would he?

Jack played out different scenarios in his head. He tried making sense of what now seemed so evidently true. But, no matter where he started, everything came back to the person – or persons – who wanted Wallace exposed. Why else would the author of that text message tell Laura to get the "docs" to Jack?

Whoever sent that message did so with more than just the intent of getting Jack involved – it was to ensure the hell that would be coming with him. He would be relentless. He would search into the Second Coming to find Carmen's killer. There would be – there could be – no stopping him. It all fit. He realized that was *precisely* what the text message was designed to do. He stared out the window into the massing cloud cover of the early evening's sky. His thoughts drifted, struggling to understand the shit storm in which he suddenly now found himself.

Jack returned to the desk after taking a few minutes to wander around the suite. He tried to clear his head as best he could. He decided to focus on the Deputy Director's handwritten summary on Cauldwell's dossier lying open before him. But with what he knew – with what he *thought* he knew – he'd do so from an entirely different perspective. He cleared his throat and returned his attention to Special Agent Marc Cauldwell.

Cauldwell was recruited by the FBI after graduating from Eastern Michigan University in 1990 with a degree in computer science. It was during the mid-90's that the Bureau began looking to expand the development of its Behavioral Sciences program to include combating cyberterrorism, specifically profiling suspected terrorist web sites, both foreign and domestic. Over time, Cauldwell's computer expertise distinguished itself and served to overcome what his personnel file quantified as a highly arrogant and self-serving personality. His service record was otherwise clean up until Jack got to the timeframe that Wallace had begun highlighting with personal comments.

In the immediate aftermath of September 11th, the FBI, not unlike most other governmental agencies, began bracing for the inevitable crises. Internally, word was spreading that the Bureau had working knowledge of suspected terrorists taking aviation-related training at flight schools around the country. But, due to "logistical difficulties" perceived by the Bureau in investigating civil aviation schools, it chose not to act on recommendations such as those detailed in the now infamous July 2001 memo from its Phoenix office. The FBI had not only failed to see the forest for the trees, it was now forced to publicly explain how it had willfully turned a blind eye.

Wallace understood the political gamesmanship the Director had to play even, or perhaps especially, in the post-September 11th world. But there could be no excuse for being asleep at the wheel during such a cataclysmic event. Coupled with the other shoe that dropped shortly thereafter – the President's Daily Brief given to the Chief Executive on August 6, 2001 entitled "Bin Ladin Determined To Strike in US" – damning evidence had been uncovered that two specific, high-level warnings of the impending attacks had, at best, been bungled or, at worst, been simply ignored. It was all but impossible to spin the dual realities that our government had reason to suspect terrorist threats and, in fact, knew of specific terrorist activity two months prior to September 11th and failed to react.

But Wallace had long ago chosen to serve only one master. Despite accepting the appointment to his position only weeks after the attacks, he had no political ambitions. He had but one agenda: he would not allow the Bureau to ever be exposed that way again. So, lack of Congressional authorization notwithstanding, he opted to do what he perceived his superiors did not have the political will to suggest. In the euphoria that erupted in the aftermath of the fall of Baghdad, Wallace realized the timing was right. He created a strike force of sorts – the intelligence community's equivalent to the Navy SEALs – and sent them unofficially into Iraq. They had only one objective: to obtain raw, unvarnished and unfiltered information directly from specific high-valued sources already identified as terrorist suspects, possibly even al-Qaeda operatives, which were safely in the custody of the U.S. Army.

What could be simpler?

Active intelligence would now be *the* priority for the FBI in the world of bin Laden and active global terrorism. The Bureau had failed to anticipate this threat largely because it lacked forward-thinking. But Wallace would ensure that it never again stumble under the weight of its own hubris. He knew human intelligence was the key. To know what they know. To Wallace, it was the *only* way. It was the one missing component, the one piece of the puzzle that would bring the entire picture into focus.

And it was the one piece the FBI was entirely unprepared to recognize.

Wallace was single-minded in his focus. Never again was the Bureau going to be embarrassed by failing to act. Never again would it be reduced to paper chases, piecing together bits of unsubstantiated reports, only to end up chasing its own tail based on information whose foundations were later determined to be "flawed." And never again would the Bureau find itself faced with uninformed choices because of a lack of dedicated resources.

Not on his watch.

Their mission statement would now include it's own doctrine of preemption.

Toward those ends, Wallace solicited interpretations of existing law from the Office of Legal Counsel, the same entity in the Department of Justice that gave the President the legal authority to dismiss Common Article III of the Geneva Convention prohibiting torture of "detainees." In his view, the President had successfully led a willing nation to accept his "struggle against global extremism" as an unconventional war, one in which "enemy combatants" were not considered prisoners of war. In this sudden new world, the brave would euphemistically redefine torture to make it not only palatable but acceptable, enthusiastically embracing such methods as critical if unspoken means toward achieving ends necessary to preserving the American way of life. And patriotic Americans would line up to support the White House at every turn. Hell, the Administration even argued before the Supreme Court that the American system of jurisprudence – specifically, habeas corpus – didn't apply to detainee military tribunals because the U.S. Naval Base at Guantánamo Bay wasn't located on American soil!

Deputy Director Wallace decided to take a similar tack. He had no intention of allowing statutes enacted by Congress while the Twin Towers were still standing to shackle or otherwise inhibit what he saw as his constitutionally-charged responsibility to preempt domestic terrorist activity in a post-September 11th world. Human intelligence was the straw that stirred that drink. He was committed that the FBI would not fall victim to the same smoke and mirrors campaign that the CIA so desperately either wanted to fall in love with – or was conveniently told to. No, Wallace would ensure that there would be no "Curveball" in the FBI's future.

And the one way to ensure that was to do it himself.

Jack found that Wallace's most extensive notes pertained to Cauldwell's time in post-invasion Iraq. He found himself slowing down, absorbing every word carefully, trying to relate the handwritten notes with the summary

reports they commented on. Much of what he read to this point he already
knew or at the very least suspected:

- The covert FBI teams sent to Abu Ghraib and other Iraqi detention
  sites, where the open use of torture and other "enhanced interrogation techniques" resulted in the deaths of an unknown number of
  detainees, most of who were buried in unmarked mass graves in the
  desert. Jack tried not to nod in disgust when he noticed "Saddam?"
  scribbled in Wallace's handwriting in the margin.
- According to both the report and Wallace's comments, Cauldwell
  and other FBI personnel were present during interrogations where
  such methods were employed. In certain unspecified cases, with detainees being identified only by code names, witnesses identified
  Cauldwell as volunteering to participate in the execution of those
  methods "with undue enthusiasm."
- The sealed report submitted to Wallace and forward on to the Attorney General was, as Jack had suspected, never opened. Cauldwell,
  along with other members of the covert team, contributed to the
  report that was written over a series of weeks as he was being interviewed by everyone from Homeland Security to the CIA to the
  National Security Administration.
- Cauldwell's time after he left Iraq was chronicled. Jack's information was right-on here. Cauldwell had traveled to Egypt, Israel and
  Turkey as well as Kuwait and Qatar. On his way home, he also spent
  time in Italy, Romania and Kosovo. The reasons for the visits were
  twofold: to personally gather useable intelligence obtained from
  suspected terrorists held in CIA black-op prisons and to determine
  which "enhanced interrogation techniques" had proven to be most
  successful when "interviewing" extraordinarily renditioned detainees.

Jack learned that, at any one time, there could be as many as two dozen
field agents on rotation in Iraq. And since their time there was officially
"unofficial", Wallace soon realized he would need some way to monitor their
activities. He revealed in his comments that each FBI team in Iraq was shad-
owed by what he termed "JAFOs" – Just Another Fuckin' Observer! These
"observers" were either members of defense contractor teams or, in some case,
subcontractors, charged with working directly with FBI personnel and were
considered part of their security details.

Cauldwell's trips to Syria, Jordan and Palestine were noted in a hand-written memo as an addendum to the file. Wallace was receiving regular, and in some cases daily, electronic updates on Cauldwell's unusual choice of vacation destinations by his JAFOs. It was here that Wallace reflected on Cauldwell's involvement in trafficking.

It was a time of lawlessness and complete mob rule in Iraq. Militias rose up over night. Imams and tribal lords alike armed their zealot followers with weapons that rivaled occupying coalition forces. Most importantly, where the press was concerned, the Sunni insurgency was gaining both strength and acceptance. Fallujah had given the loosely organized resistance exactly what it needed. The perceived defeat of U.S.-led coalition forces there gave it a be-lief in itself and the legitimacy it needed to gain the support of the populace at large. And it served to get the attention of the bin Laden's newly formed al-Qaeda in Mesopotamia.

As a result, families, neighborhoods, entire communities began a mass exodus. Violence seemed to be everywhere. Suicide bombings in and around Baghdad numbered in excess of forty per day, almost two an hour, every hour, every day. Hospitals and morgues were overrun. The bombers were at-tacking day care centers, schools, mosques, open markets and family celebra-tions such as weddings. Even those mourning at the funerals of loved ones, in many cases burying those who themselves were victims of random mass murderers, were not exempt from the insanity.

It was in the vacuum created by this anarchy that Special Agent Cauldwell first saw his opportunity. As Wallace's notes related it, both Sunnis and Shi'ites were fleeing the violence, emigrating from Iraq in droves. Syria and Jordan were overwhelmed. Believing himself to be as much a humanist as an astute businessman, Cauldwell's initial efforts were not entirely motivated by personal profit. However, as the chaos descended into madness, Cauldwell's altruistic motives succumbed to more practical concerns.

It began crudely enough. According to the report, Cauldwell would use government contacts – from the DOJ to the Pentagon to the State Depart-ment – in and throughout the Middle East to broker arrangements for those seeking "special consideration or accommodations" in resettling outside of Iraq. In return, Cauldwell would be paid in cash, specifically American dollars.

Soon, as word spread throughout the underground of his connections, their demand overwhelmed his supply. Cauldwell's entrepreneurial talents had introduced a remarkably simple business plan into a rapidly expanding marketplace. The business had exploded and was growing exponentially. It was getting harder and harder to manage all of that cash quietly. And, over time, it gave way to more electronic means of payment. Almost unbelievably, Wallace's notes identified bank records, wire transfers and account numbers. Cauldwell had created a partnership with an existing shadow organization specializing in trafficking Iraqi immigrants. It was only a small step from there that he became involved in the sale of those same immigrants. Where desperate families had no other means of compensation, other arrangements were often negotiated. Children – girls and young women, specifically – were often the typical form of currency. Age was hardly relevant. And in a butchered land – in a time of unabated madness – when the only rules that applied were surviving one more day's insanity, Cauldwell himself would eventual become immersed in this carnal form of payment.

Wallace's private, handwritten addenda revealed that Cauldwell reveled his new role as both hero and savior. An American with money and the power to change lives and decide futures. It fed his massive ego as strongly as it stimulated an almost insatiable sex drive. Life was good. At least his was. War had proven once again to be no different than any other business enterprise. The approach was simple: provide a quality product in meeting consumer demand by manipulating supply through controlled distribution. For those who did it right, waging war could prove to be hugely profitable.

Of course, not everyone did it right.

Cauldwell perceived himself as providing a valuable service. He'd watched the American-led coalition forces supposedly bring democracy to Iraq and had discovered in its wake a very lucrative opportunity. He'd succeeded in finding a way to tolerate this insufferable country and their fanatical ideas. And everything would have been just fine.

Then, for the first time, Jimmy's name appeared in the margin.

Jack closed the file and tossed it aside, as much in anger as disgust, and walked away from the desk. His emotions weren't wasted on Cauldwell. There would be time enough for him. No, he knew what he was about to read. He also knew that, once he read it, he would have no choice. He would have to tell Alex.

He thought about Carmen, about how numb he'd felt when Laura broke the news to him the other morning. Her words released the trapdoor beneath his emotional feet. He felt the bottom fall out of his heart at that very moment.

Even now.

He wondered about Alex as he stared out the window across the nondescript landscape surrounding him. He cursed Cauldwell and his like, a type

Jack had seen too many times before. He'd spent the majority of his adult life staring down and beating back the evil that assholes like Cauldwell spread like some hideous viral contagion. Guys like Cauldwell infected everything they came in contact with. He invaded their lives, ambushing the unsuspecting, robbing them of their innocence, permanently disabling their future if he left them any at all. A destroyer of families, he disfigured parents' hopes for their children, obliterating their dreams and creating only ugliness and fear. It is their belief in the wonder of life, in the boundless possibilities that only a child's heart has room enough to hold, that he stalks. That he terrorizes. That he kills. And it would continue. And the pain would go on. Until it was stopped.

Or the virus itself was neutralized.

He looked into the eyes looking back at him in the window's reflection. But after what he'd just read, and knowing what awaited him, Cauldwell's time would surely come. And if there, indeed, was a God, Jack would be given the chance to see to it personally. He turned to the open connecting door to the room next door. He thought of Ana and Daniel and that intersection on the south side, how he'd found them fighting for their very lives. He thought of Caridád, abused for years in almost unimaginable ways yet defiant against insurmountable odds. He thought about Laura working Wallace and the system, a system that bred guys like Cauldwell, fighting to bring him out into the open, to bring him down, to prove that right does matter in the end. He swore to himself that Special Agent Cauldwell would soon know righteousness. Judgment. Vengeance.

If not God's, than surely his own. Once – and for all of them.

He solemnly walked back to the desk, picked up the report and was about to sit down to continue reading when he noticed a flashing message announcing an incoming email. He clicked on the icon.

It was from Laura.

* * *

Raúl shielded his eyes from the evening sun as he snapped his phone shut and held it tightly in his hand. Estéban hadn't even reached his car after meeting with the Monsignor before he'd call. He related what Father Mac had told the Monsignor, much of which Raúl either already knew or had good reason to suspect. The one new piece of information was Father Mac's contact, the woman Father Mac had called after Raúl's friends paid him a visit. Estéban had said the Monsignor had been explicit about the fact Father Mac had spoken with a woman, or at least left her a message. If Raúl could find this woman, odds were he would find his missing items. It had only been a couple of days. He could still contain this thing. And he could send a message in the process.

But the woman was the key.

He'd asked Estéban to find out what he could about Father Mac's outgoing phone calls. If Raúl learned who the priest had called since Saturday evening, he would at least have something to work with. Since the raid early Wednesday morning, he'd had to relocate from the south side neighborhood to a house in the southern suburbs. He wanted to keep the location as close to I-80 as he could, knowing more deliveries were expected later in the week.

Raúl didn't expect Estéban would have anything for him until maybe Tuesday evening at the earliest. Raúl knew better than to press him. Besides, he needed time to think, to plan, to react carefully and deliberately. The trail of dead bodies this ex-FBI guy was leaving made Raúl wonder if this Rambo-wannabe was working his up to the top. Or maybe he was just thinning the herd, removing any obstacles that stood in the way of him getting more involved in a piece of the action.

After all, that's what the other FBI guy had done.

But if Raúl understood nothing else, he understood this was a business. And he was nothing if not a good businessman. He wondered if the ex-FBI guy would be willing to talk, maybe even cut a deal. There was no need for any more killing. Maybe if they could talk. If they could arrange something through a third-party. Maybe there might be some wriggle room there. Given the guy's habit of killing anyone from Raúl's crew that he came in contact with, that didn't seem likely. But you never know. Negotiation doesn't have to always end in somebody being pissed off. It's all in the way you look at it. Reasonable men can disagree. Maybe something could be worked out.

Except for Caridád.

There could be no discussion about her. He would get her back, no matter what it took. And who knows what she's already told the ex-FBI guy about the organization. Perhaps Estéban was right. The coincidences were adding up. Caridád is – was –, after all, Maria's sister. That Maria died before she could provide any information about what she'd told that freelance journalist complicated matters. And, from what Estéban said, it seemed reasonable to assume that the dead woman agent knew everything the journalist knew. That made sense when he thought of how she was able to infiltrate and eventually help bring down the east coast operation.

The decision as to whether Caridád would die quickly or spend the rest of her life dying slowly, that would come later. If she was still able to make the organization money after he was finished with her, well, so much the better.

If not, then not.

To Raúl, it all began and ended with one thing: respect. It's what drove him from his earliest days back in the neighborhood to where he'd gotten today. Nobody does what the ex-FBI guy did and simply walks away. That crossed the line, it simply cannot be allowed. There was already precious little room for error in this business. But, after losing four men and three deliveries over the past couple of days, he knew his people – and most likely the street, by now – were watching. The command of his organization had its legs in their respect. And in his willingness to create the fear that gave rise to it.

He knew it. They knew it.

Now, what mattered most is that former Special Agent Jack Sturdevant knew it.

* * *

Alex closed her laptop and pushed it to the side of the bed. She was frustrated. And losing her temper over that damned browser continually shutting down each time she tried to access Jimmy's blog on his secret web page. She settled in on the bed, her back compressing a couple of pillows as she propped herself up against the headboard. She wanted to be alone when she read Wallace's file. She needed to be. The part about Jimmy. And that rat bastard Cauldwell.

Jack had at least wanted to be in the room next door. He'd even tried to get her to go with him, along with Ana, Daniel and Caridád, to dinner. He had no chance. And he knew it. He understood. Closure is something that, by it's very nature, is personal. To some extent, he'd still been experiencing his own. And he knew all he could to do for her was be there when she reached out. It was a journey that only she could take alone.

He'd promised the kids that, after dinner, they could tour the new United Airlines terminal. The modern terminal was the latest addition in the O'Hare Expansion Project, one that seemed to be going on continuously since the early 1950s. And at least it was something for them to do, a way to escape the boredom of their very comfortable but somewhat confining quarters. After all, despite everything they'd been through, they were still children. It was easy to forget that, given all was happening around – and all that had happened to – them.

Jack didn't see any real danger in walking the kids around the airport. The precautions he and Laura had taken appeared solid, though he made a mental note to follow-up with her about getting the kids federal witness protection. He wasn't sure how open-ended their situation was staying at the hotel. Having a couple of marshals outside their hotel room door might prove necessary if not convenient. He didn't want to start underestimating things now.

Alex had seen something in Jack's face when they'd returned from the pool an hour or so earlier. Before she'd brought them upstairs, she took them for some ice cream and a shake for Daniel. They also had made a couple of stops at the myriad souvenir shops around the hotel. She thought it would be fun for the kids to have something uniquely Chicago, maybe help them smile a bit. And it would be something that they could share with their families.

When they see them again.

Tee-shirts, post cards, jewelry, even books about this beautiful city. It didn't really matter. Whatever it was, it would carry with it better memories of their time here, even if it were only as they were leaving, than those they'd had before finding Father Mac. Of course, no souvenirs since that moment – either of the priest's altruism, or of Jack's heroism, or of Laura's self-sacrifice and or of Alex's kindness – would be necessary for Ana, Daniel or Caridád to keep those memories alive.

Everything else seemed best left forgotten. Assuming they ever could.

Jack had explained to Alex what he'd read though offered little in the way of detail. He tried to prepare her for it as best he could, well-meaning but pointless as his efforts were. She had to read it for herself, this much he knew. The most significant information about Jimmy was found in notes made by JAFOs responsible for tracking Cauldwell's movements. There were interviews, mostly Army personnel, particularly with grunts who were friends of Jimmy's and had become increasingly concerned about his disappearance. Wallace, after reviewing the reports, provided his own thoughts on what seemed to have happened. Some were theories he projected based on circumstances he'd pieced together, others conjecture after he factored in what he'd learned about Cauldwell's more discreet dealings during the agent's travels throughout the Middle East.

Alex was understandably both anxious and apprehensive. She wanted to know yet, at some level not surprisingly, she feared letting go of the comfort of not knowing. It had been so long. And though there would not be any official declaration by the military about Jimmy's ultimate fate – independent journalists weren't counted among any of their statistical categories – she'd always assumed he had died somewhere, somehow, in or around Baghdad. Maybe in an explosion, a roadside bomb encountered while he was embedded with some unlucky patrol. Or in the crossfire of some ambush staged by al-Qaeda and filmed for their own sick propaganda purposes. Or even friendly fire. It'd been known to happen. After all, that's how that football player died, the one who quit his professional football team to become an Army Ranger. Accidents happen. As the Secretary of Defense had so correctly pointed out, it's "untidy" over there.

She had stopped trying to imagine the scenarios. It was a path that only led to a descent into her own personal freefall she'd always chosen not to take. What she knew for certain, what she'd learned to accept, was that he was gone. The reality was they'd had no contact for almost four years. She'd only hoped, however he met his fate, that it had been quick. And mercifully painless. She opened the file and began to read.

She couldn't stop her hands from shaking.

A little over an hour later, Alex closed the file and laid it in her lap. She wiped away tears still collecting in her eyes. She felt her anger rising to a level that rivaled her emptiness. She hurt all over again. It all was so goddamned real again, it was almost palpable. She put the file down, grabbed the nearest pillow and clutched it to her chest.

And walked deliberately once more back into her past.

Her mind pinballed across the history they'd written together. She'd grown up with Jimmy and, in large part, because of him. Much of the professional who she was, of the woman she'd become, and the things that mattered most to her, were due to him. Thinking back to their first real work together – Tiananmen Square – brought a smile. It had been so goddamned hot in Kuwait, so fuckin' cold in Chechnya. The Kosovo farm country was still some of the most beautiful she'd ever seen. Darfur provided the stage for which the world would not only begin to notice the senseless plight of countless refugees and the conditions under which they lived but also, for the first time, *her* work. She couldn't recall, for the life of her, why she wouldn't go to him in Iraq when he'd pleaded with her so many times. She wondered why that was.

Realizing she couldn't made her saddest of all.

She pulled back the file and read the part again about the last room he'd rented, what he'd left behind. True to Jimmy's nature, there was precious little for his friends to collect. His work allowed for few luxuries and even fewer mementos. But she smiled when she read again the one thing that was with him, remembering how, no matter the assignment, Jimmy'd always found room to bring with him that stupid ball and glove.

The ball was an official game ball, a Rawlings baseball, scuffed and scarred from being relentlessly jettisoned into play during batting practice. It was indelibly marked from skimming across the infield dirt like a smooth stone over a still pond. It had also picked up a distinct and permanent shade of green from its travels through the tall outfield grass of the old Sportsman's Park in St. Louis.

His best friend went with him and his dad to the game that glorious fall afternoon. Jimmy was in middle school, eleven or twelve at the time, his friend the same age. They had arrived at the park early, in time to see the players on the field taking batting practice and infield fungoes. Jimmy and his friend wandered the outfield bleachers, hoping to get any attention they could from the Cardinal players stretching and shagging flies. Suddenly, almost unbelievably, one of the players picked up a ball rolling toward him and, after spotting the two boys, called out to them. They both jumped at his notice and raised their gloves as he lazily tossed it in their direction.

His friend actually caught the ball. But, almost immediately, he turned to Jimmy and handed it to him. Jimmy was thrilled beyond words. He kept that ball in his grasp throughout the entire game. And no matter how many times Alex had heard him tell the story, Jimmy could not recall if the Cardinals won the game. Or who pitched that day. Or who made the plays or hit the home runs he remembered cheering.

But he remembered the ball and his best friend who'd given it so selflessly to him.

Hal Smith.

The baseball glove he treasured was old and worn, a Wilson, pro-style twin action catcher's mitt with nylon stitching and a Grip-Tite pocket. It was assembled with long strings of rawhide leather that hung so impressively from it's Tru-Trap webbing. When he was just a boy of eight, maybe nine years old, he'd gone with his parents one Thanksgiving to a fundraiser held by an order of nuns for a local church. There, at the raffle, he'd won the chance to choose his prize. But from among everything he could choose, he'd already decided – the glove was all he wanted. And even though Jimmy wasn't a catcher on his little league team, he'd chosen the glove because it reminded him of his best friend. And the gift his best friend had given him.

The glove was autographed by the catcher for his beloved St. Louis Cardinals. Hal Smith.

When Jimmy got home that night, he took the baseball and placed it carefully, the sweet spot facing up, inside the baby-bottom soft pocket of the catcher's mitt he now coveted. He kept them on top of his dresser where he could see them from any place in his room. And it stayed that way from that day on.

Jimmy enjoyed recalling the novel he'd first read years ago. It told the story of an author reminiscing about his childhood and the time he and his three closest friends decided to go hiking one Labor Day weekend to find the dead body of a boy who, rumor had it, was struck and killed by a train. Jimmy loved the way the story ended, with the book's narrator recalling, now that he was married, with kids of his own, how he never again had any friends like he did when he was twelve, then asking, "does anyone?"

For Jimmy, the answer was obvious. For no matter where he traveled, memories from that early autumn day at the old ballpark went with him. And every time he looked at that mitt's fading, drying leather that somehow, almost miraculously, still smelled of glove oil and sandlot summer afternoons. When his eyes settled on the ball snuggled safely in its webbing, it's bruised cover now discolored with age and its red stitching finally beginning to fray. Or when he saw the dimming machine-etched signature still visible on the heel of the glove's well-worn pocket, it wasn't Hal Smith, the big-league ball player or the All-Star catcher or Stan Musial's teammate, who came to mind. Rather, it was his best friend, Hal Smith, the closest friend he'd ever have, that he thought of.

That author's insight was simple but powerful. And, for Jimmy, unequivocal.

In her mind's eye, Alex could still picture that damned glove and the ball it safeguarded. She had all but forgotten that, no matter where they went on assignment, no matter what story they were covering, no matter what conditions they encountered, that stupid ball and glove was always there. Now that she thought about it, it seemed like he was never without it. And no matter how little space he might have had for his clothes, his equipment or anything else he was carrying with him to some of the most inhospitable places on this earth, that stupid glove, with the freakin' ball still shoved inside it, came along for the ride.

Suddenly, she froze.

Her thoughts stood still. For a moment she was afraid to even breathe. She had a look of startled insight. She stopped reading. Her eyes pulled away from the page and settled on the horizon outside the room's window. She was overcome with an abiding sense of his presence. A moment of clarity brought with it a serene feeling that only certain knowledge can provide. She quickly closed the file and tossed it aside. She sat up, reached across the bed and rapidly crossed her legs. She excitedly pulled the laptop toward her, wiped away her last tears and pushed open the computer screen.

Shit!

It could NOT be that simple!

* * *

Chapter 15

JIMMY'S PERSONAL BLOG told how he'd been trying for the last couple of days to get in touch with Alex, with no luck. His phone was charged and seemed to be working fine. Why neither his outgoing calls nor his text messages were getting through was a mystery to him. True, the weather there had not been cooperating. As a matter of fact, it'd been down right shitty. December in Iraq was much like early March in Chicago. Damp, wet, cold to the bone and mud… everywhere!

And it rained – every fuckin' day.

He hadn't given up on when she was coming – or maybe, at this point, whether she was coming –, but the truth was there was work to be done: photos to shoot, copy to write, deadlines to meet. His blog told about the last time they chatted, via a webcam connection that was anything but an advertisement for state-of-the-art technology. He felt more than the miles between them. He'd always admired her commitment to her work and the passion she brought to it. And he shared her dedication that their work should send a message to the world. Hell, he'd taught her that much. His career, his life, had been spent doing just that. So he had only respect for her and the time she'd spent in the Sudan with the international aid groups. He wrote at length how the world's awareness of the growing refugee crisis there was due in no small part to her efforts. He was proud of the journalist, not to mention the person, he'd helped her become.

313

Alex grabbed a tissue from the box on the nightstand and wiped her eyes before she continued reading from one of the last entries he'd made.

It was dated Wednesday, 22-Dec-2004 at 7:50 AM, Baghdad time.

He'd expected her in Baghdad weeks ago. He needed her here. And though their deal had always been that the work came first, in recent times that meant different assignments in different time zones on different continents. And it would be a mistake to think his additional workload was all that made him anxious about her absence. She'd told him she would be there, in Baghdad, by September, October at the latest.

And here it was, three days until Christmas.

As she read the lines he'd written almost four years ago, Alex could still hear Jimmy's baritone voice as if he were whispering in her ear. Their work, he was fond of saying, allowed them to spend most of their adult lives documenting some of the world's greatest human calamities. And whether those tragedies were born of natural causes or owed their genesis to more man-made intentions, to do it right – to tell the world the truth, as he would say – their credibility as journalists was essential. And the one way to preserve their credibility was to maintain a professional distance. Knowing where – and when – to draw the line was the difference between reporting the story and becoming the story. Making the mistake of becoming emotionally involved with any of his subjects or assignments was almost always contrary to his professional interests. And, with a lingering sadness in his words that seemed almost palpable, he wrote that, as gifted as she was, he'd long since began wondering if she'd lost that perspective.

Alex stopped and removed her glasses. She ran her fingers against her eyes that had turned red from rubbing and wiping away tears. Part of her wanted to stop. As difficult as it was to listen to the voice of his memory, it was brutal to read how she'd failed in his eyes. And it's not that he wasn't right. Jimmy usually was. That was thing about Jimmy. He could be counted on to remain detached from any assignment he was covering. Perhaps it was that standard that had created the widening gulf between them then. She'd spent hours debating the hows and whys since. But the cold truth was she didn't go to Iraq in the fall of 2004 for reasons other than her work. Which meant she wasn't there when he disappeared. But it also meant she didn't disappear with him.

And she hadn't quite forgiven herself for that.

Baghdad in December 2004 was madness masquerading as insanity. Jimmy wrote that the military seemed powerless to stop the growing insurgency. The U.S.-led coalition forces were suffering up to forty attacks per day, the majority of which were occurring around, and sometimes in, the Green Zone. In the ensuing chaos, the bizarre began passing for the norm, the absurd for the average. He saw neighborhoods and open markets littered with scattered limbs. He watched mosques become no safer than coalition checkpoints. And in the wake of rising body counts, suicide bombings had sent the city, if not the country, spiraling toward the very brink of civil war. The reality was Iraq existed in the vacuum of any legitimate authority. And its freefall into anarchy was not only consuming the region. It threatened to undermine what fragile stability the entire Middle East enjoyed.

But Alex was no less a stranger to the truth than Jimmy. Putting herself in harm's way was often part of the story. It was to be expected. And it was anything but an excuse. The hard truth was, for all the good she'd been doing in Darfur at the time, it wasn't the reason – hell, it wasn't even *a* reason – why she really stayed. And pursuing the truth, consequences be damned, was the choice Alex had when she chose her career. It seemed the truth was now pursuing her.

An all-too-familiar rush of guilt washed over her again, bursting through the gaping wounds his words from Baghdad now four years removed had re-opened. She noticed that he'd made his last blog entry at 9:02 PM, Baghdad time,on 22-Dec-2004. He wrote of a meeting he was going to with one of Cauldwell's JAFOs. The man had contacted Jimmy via email to say he'd found something he needed to share with him. The message went on to say that he'd found relatives of a family living outside the Green Zone who claimed to have evidence that Cauldwell had sold the emigrating family to traffickers working through Kuwait. In addition, the man wrote that the relatives of the family claimed to have cell phone video of Cauldwell having sex with a twelve year-old girl, and implied that the child was some kind of de facto compensation for delivering the family. But while Jimmy's notebooks were rapidly filling up with corroborating stories telling similar tales, he had virtually no physical evidence to support the series of articles he had already begun selling.

Until, he wrote, maybe now.

He did not identify the name of the JAFO who was acting as his primary source. Maybe he didn't know, maybe the guy's name appeared somewhere else. And, strangely enough, there was no mention in Wallace's file of Jimmy's notebooks ever being found in his Baghdad apartment. The same was true concerning his laptop and most of his equipment. Like him, they'd simply vanished.

But of all the embedded links in this page of his blog, two in particular stood out. The first was entitled *carmen-thescavengersdaughter-december2004*, which seemed as interesting as it was oddly named. But she'd wait to open it. The link that intrigued her more was one she'd found further down the page: *marialastmeeting-july2004*. Alex clicked on the link and watched as a pop-up window immediately displayed before her. It was his journal, thoughts he was polishing that would become his best work yet.

She nervously began reading.

Over the next hour and few minutes, Maria Engañada answered all my questions, sometimes directly, sometimes rambling, but I felt always as honestly as she could. The heartwrenching story she told, and the emotion that surfaced with it, has put a human face on my research into trafficking and the slave trade industry. That Maria and her sister had been so randomly selected – that their lives been ripped inside out beyond any recognition – spoke as much to the evil nature of their predators as it did to the horrific efficiency with which these organizations so easily operate.

I remember her telling me in one of our very first conversations how, almost three years ago – it was Labor Day weekend, literally days before September 11th –, another fun-in-the-Albuquerque-sun carefree afternoon at a local outdoor mall for her and her then-ten year-old sister, Caridád, had become a horrifying and abject lesson in the brutal business of human trafficking. The two playful young women – girls, actually – had inadvertently attracted the attention of a handsome young man and his older friend he introduced to them as his cousin. Maria'd described how the four of them spent part of the afternoon together, playing video games, laughing and sharing some slices of pizza. It was then she remembered suddenly feeling lightheaded, tired and lethargic, weak to the point of almost being sick. It sounded to me like one of them had probably laced their soft drinks with Rohypnol, an odorless, tasteless date-rape drug, when the girls were distracted. It was hardly original. But it proved to be highly effective.

Hours later, when Maria'd finally come to, she was naked and on her knees, held tightly in the grip of a sweating old man having his violent way with her in a room of half-dozen men of various ages watching them anxiously, waiting their turns. Caridád was nowhere to be seen. As the indescribable torment wore on, as she submitted to him there, contorted into various positions, she was terrorized beyond the point of making a sound. Paralyzed by a surreal numbness that prevented her from feeling the degradation her body was experiencing, she could not know that her sister was just down the hall, providing similar entertainment for an equal number of eager participants.

Their induction into their new life had begun.

On the other occasions over the past couple of months when we'd met, Maria always talked about how that first night seemed to go on for an eternity. And how for days afterwards – or maybe it had been weeks, she had no way of knowing –, she had little concept of time. During that time, she'd been moved often, from one house to another, usually in the dead of night. She'd seen firsthand what happened to those who would mistakenly find the will to resist, how they were beaten, often drugged, and raped repeatedly until they lost consciousness. At almost any time during any night, they would be rounded up, with no notice, and herded into vans. Ten, twelve at a time, including children. They would be driven for what seemed like hours only to find they were at another location where everything seemed exactly like the place they'd just left. At some point, she could tell by the damp, humid weather that Albuquerque was now a distant memory. Only later would she learn, and only then by accident, that she was in Chicago.

Maria told me that, at first, she was always kept in darkened, barren rooms. Any windows were always shuttered. Sometimes an old mattress would be provided though she seldom chose to sleep on it. Most nights, she slept on the floor, curled up in the corner. Every so often, she would share a room with others, most like herself and about her age. New arrivals, she assumed. Their captors frowned upon conversation. She told me she couldn't recall ever seeing the same women or children more than once.

It became normal for men of all ages, sometimes as many as three or four of them, to walk into her room at any time. Sometimes she would be dragged to another room. Other times, they would take her where she was, in front of anyone who was there. The screams, the tears, the pleading, the begging seemed only to entice them, to encourage them. It seemed to invite their depraved creativity and heighten their sadistic pleasure.

Maria recalled that, in some ways, the hardest part was never knowing where she was. Nothing ever seemed familiar. Buildings, landmarks, street signs. Nothing. Those first weeks and months, she was always confused and disoriented. She didn't know who any of these men were or why she was here or what she had done to deserve this. All she knew was the wicked, degrading pain they always brought with them.

And the constant fear.

At some point, she remembered, it became evident to her that something had changed. The seemingly endless stream of men that had used her seemed somehow different. They dressed differently. They smelled differently. They acted differently. They were only given a short time with her. And, every so often, one of them would mutter something about getting what he was paying for, especially when she didn't act exactly like he demanded or did exactly what he expected her to do.

If there had been any doubt, she now knew why she was here.

She recalled feeling completely abandoned. When she was alone, when she would try to eat or sleep, she would tremble uncontrollably. She could not stop asking herself why, how this could be happening here, in America? Sometimes she wondered if she was even still in America. She cried most every night, many nights so hard her stomach ached. Finally, when she was too exhausted to stay awake, she would close her eyes though sleep offered her little respite. In her dreams she saw the faces of those who had violated her and those who had paid for the privilege. She heard their derisive laughter, their foul language, their demeaning demands. There was no place she could go — nowhere she could turn — to escape the living hell that had become her life.

Hers and her sister's.

But amidst the hopelessness, the powerlessness, the almost unimaginable existence of living solely for the sexual pleasure and sadistic appetites of strangers, it was Caridád that provided the single thread that kept her tied to the fabric of her sanity. Finding her became all that mattered, seeing her again all she cared about. But that seemed all but impossible. Until the day she met the young man who wanted to be known only as "Snake-Eyes." Looking back, it was meeting him that Maria slowly began to realize she might not be as powerless as her circumstance insisted she was.

His given name was Santos, "Sandy" for short. And aside from the artfully done spiraling cobra tattoo that stretched up his left arm to his neck, her first impression of him was a kindness she saw in his eyes. Maybe it was wishful thinking, who knows? But, over the coming months, as her situation began to stabilize and she wasn't moved as often, she would see him from time to time. At first, it was only to notice her, maybe even to say hello. But she saw he had that look guys get, the one a woman seems to intuitively understand. The one every guy gets when he's met someone he likes. And Snake-Eyes seemed very interested.

As long as she didn't call him "Sandy."

As she spent time with him, she slowly began to understand the dark world into which she had descended. Her survival instincts had kicked in during those first weeks. And as the months came and went, she learned how to separate herself from her body. She even came to no longer think of it as rape. Most if not all of her innocence had been strangled out of her. What little was left fermented into an empowering hatred that fed not only her daily survival but the hope that had lain dormant for so long. Breathing life into that hope was where Snake-Eyes would prove invaluable.

Over time, the constant threats their captors had used so freely against them and the families they'd left behind became less necessary. In most ways, Maria was no different than many of the other young woman and children they'd taken. Their captors told them that escape was impossible, that they knew where their families lived. And that, from now on, their lives were no longer their own.

They were very convincing.

And, after a while, the physical and mental assault inflicted on their innocence had begun having the desired effect. The logic was simple, really: the operation was safest when it hid in plain sight. And, in truth, their pathology was no different than subjugating any population, whether it was slaves working the land on a pre-Civil War southern plantation or an entire race of people enduring ethnic cleansing in Hitler's Germany.

All that was required was the death of hope.

Once they no longer believed they could return to their former lives – that there was no more reason to hope –, it became unnecessary to keep them under lock and key, to constantly stand watch over them or to control their every movement. It was then that the process had become complete. It was almost like brainwashing, like reprogramming the way they would, or even could, think. When they reached that point, there would be no turning back. Their lives were now the property of someone else. It was then that they could start earning their captors the money they'd been brought here to make.

But as most would eventually come to accept their fate, Maria quietly decided on another path. She told me how she'd carefully nurtured her "relationship" with Snake-Eyes. Slowly, she developed a trust between them that allowed her to learn more about the cell-based trafficking organization that his half brother, Raúl, ran so profitably. And, over the months of patient determination, it was that knowledge which would gain her a critical advantage, one that ultimately led her to her first conversation with me.

The first time we met, Maria was understandably uncomfortable. That first day at the coffeehouse, she offered nothing about what she did or where she was from. She steered the conversation toward his career as a photojournalist and the places he'd been, the events he'd covered and the people he'd met. She was leery about trusting him. Or anyone, for that matter. It was a painful struggle for Maria just to find the inclination, let alone the strength, to talk about her ordeal. But over time that changed.

And that moment came almost three months ago. I'd given her my card that very first day. She later told me she'd memorized my numbers and then left it on the table. She knew, even then, that, at some point, she'd have to trust someone to help her. But she'd first have to believe enough in the possibility that there might actually be a way out. When the time came, when she'd finally decided to reach out *to someone, she knew there would be no turning back. She told me she just hoped I would reach back.*

Knowing that Caridád's life had been hers since that one horrible afternoon made Maria see the risks as almost reasonable. And as I met with her earlier this evening, seeing her sitting on the cold, concrete floor in that dank and dark downtown parking garage, listening to her go over again everything she knew and the nightmarish life she'd led, I sensed an odd, even peaceful, feeling seemed to come over her. She'd traveled an almost unimaginable path to get here. And she told me that, thinking back to our chance meeting that morning at that coffeehouse, it was that one small gentlemanly gesture — offering my seat to her in the crowded coffee bar — that first let her feel comfortable with me. That first brought a smile to her face. She told me it'd reminded her that strangers need not always bring with them a fear of the unknown.

Sometimes they could bring help, she once told him.
Or so she'd finally dared to hope.

More than two hours after she'd first cracked Jimmy's hidden web page, Alex pushed the laptop off to one side, slid down a bit and pulled a pillow up to her chin. She hadn't even been aware that Jimmy had been researching articles on human trafficking, let alone his inside source was Caridád's sister, Maria. What she'd read left her scared, feeling helpless and noticeably empty. Maybe, even oddly, somehow responsible.

And strangely cold.

Her mind dialed back to early February 2005, when she'd finally arrived in Baghdad. It was unlike Jimmy, even when he was mad at her, not to communicate for so long. Granted, much of her time in the Sudan she was incommunicado. But just as much of it she wasn't. And as her time in Iraq slowly began being numbered more easily in weeks than in days, as her emails continued to go without responses in the same way her voice mails and text messages did, Alex found herself with few good options. She eventually came to the only conclusions she could: she didn't know what happened to him and she hadn't one clue as to where he was.

She didn't know if he were alive or dead, if he was safe or suffering, if he was being treated well or if he was gravely wounded. Maybe he'd found himself embedded with a patrol that found itself in some firefight with a local militia. Maybe he'd simply traveled north to work with the Kurds in northern Iraq and he'd eventually contact her. Or maybe some faction of al-Qaeda in Mesopotamia was holding him captive, and one day soon she'd see some videotaped released over the Internet showing him sitting in front of some Arabic flag screaming "Death to The Great Satan" with armed, hooded terrorists behind him threatening to decapitate him. She simply didn't know. And no one she spoke with offered her any reason to hope that would change anytime soon.

Neither his body nor his head nor any other part of him had been discovered. That, in itself, she tried to take as a good sign. But all it ultimately did was allow her to continue living in some heartwrenching limbo, wondering whether she'd ever see him again alive. Or if the hope she was clinging to was simply wasted torment.

She eventually realized she had no choice but to accept the reality that, whatever had happened to Jimmy, there was nothing more she could do for him in Iraq. After following up on what few leads his emptied apartment left her for her – what units he'd spent time with, what towns he'd written about and photographed, what friends were still willing to talk with her –, Alex went to the Coalition Provisional Authority and completed a missing persons report.

Her attempts at filing Jimmy's paperwork met with a healthy dose of Army bureaucracy, in more knowledgeable circles known as SNAFU – Situation Normal All Fucked Up. She was told that, short of him walking through their front door with his name tattooed to his forehead, they offered Alex no reason to expect they'd have any resources to expend on finding him. After all, she was told bitingly, there *is* a civil war going on! The best advice they could offer was to consider hiring a private contractor who specialized in finding missing civilians. The partial list she was given was of mercenaries and subcontractors who did just that. Life here was truly upside down; the world this country lived in had literally been ripped inside out. And, apparently, there were people lining up to profit from it.

Shortly thereafter, Alex remembered packing up her gear and quietly leaving Iraq. Funny thing was, no matter how hard she tried, as she lie here now, alone, she couldn't recall what her next assignment was or where she even went from Iraq.

Really... What did it matter?

A sense of urgency helped her find the energy to roll out of bed and walk over to her purse. She pulled out her cell phone and punched up her Gold Coast friend's number.

"Jules, hi, it's me," Alex said.

Julie was surprised to hear from her.

"Everything ok, sweetie?"

Alex swallowed hard.

"Yeah," she said, "everything's fine. I was wondering if you could do something for me?"

"Sure, whaddya need?"

Alex took a moment to breathe.

"Could you check my bag for me? I think I left something in there I need."

"Sure, hon, just a sec…" Julie said as she started for the back bedroom. "You sure you're doin' ok? You sound a bit strange."

"No," Alex insisted, "really, I'm fine."

Alex waited the few seconds it took for Julie to walk there.

"Ok," Julie said, "checked luggage or carry on?"

"The big bag," Alex replied, "The one I had checked."

"Ok," Julie said again, "what am I looking for?"

"A blue nylon carry-all, looks like a large fanny pack almost."

"Just a sec…" Julie repeated. A few seconds passed as Alex heard Alison Krauss's latest CD playing on the stereo in the background.

"Alex?"

"Yeah, Jules?"

"I'm not sure what you're looking for but –"

"What do you mean?" Alex asked.

"All that's in there is some ratty old baseball glove and a dirty baseball."

Alex closed her eyes and smiled as a tear escaped down her cheek.

Jack knocked softly on the closed connecting door before entering. Alex stirred as she lay on her side on top of the covers. He heard her laptop humming quietly though it was nowhere in sight.

He walked slowly over to the bed and sat down next to her. She didn't move.

"Hey," he asked softly as he brushed her hair away from the side of her face. "You ok?"

No response. She was asleep though he wasn't sure she was resting.

He wore a look of concern as he ran the back of his hand down the side of her arm then stood up. He thought better of waking her. Whatever rest she was getting was well-deserved. Walking around the foot of the bed he found her laptop on its side, closed, leaning up against the nightstand, still on. Like her, it, too, had slipped into sleep mode. Jack reached down, and picked it up then brought it back to the desk.

As he placed the computer carefully on the desk, he opened it and slid one thumb across the mouse pad. The screen, its image faded and light, suddenly appeared. Thinking the battery was running low, Jack sat down and reached back behind the desk for the computer's AC adapter. Plugging it in, a clean, crisp definition suddenly displayed brightly before him, catching his attention.

Almost intuitively, Jack realized what he was looking at. It was Jimmy's hidden website page, the one Alex had been trying so hard to access, the same one she'd complained had kept freezing up her computer. That she'd somehow figured out Jimmy's password came as no real surprise. She was nothing if not tenacious. He smiled at the thought of her relentless nature.

The last page she'd been viewing was one of the blogs Jimmy had been maintaining, this one a collection of random thoughts he'd recorded, perhaps article ideas only he expected to access. The page's design was predictably organized not unlike the man Jack had once known. Assorted links to related topics Jimmy'd found relevant were neatly listed in a column to the left. To the right was narrative. But as he lightly skimmed the text, complete with the embedded links to other web pages underlined and colored in blue, he suddenly realized what he was reading. He slowly scrolled down the lengthy page as Jimmy's world unfolded before him. This blog recalled a conversation.

And Carmen's name seemed everywhere.

The narrative played out in Jack's imagination as he anxiously started reading.

"What about the photo? Did you get it?" she heard him ask again through their intermittent webcam connection. Jimmy'd finally gotten online just past 5:30 AM, Baghdad time, eight hours ahead of Chicago where the unusually warm early December weather was in stark contrast to the more seasonable temperatures accompanying the approaching winter storm. The cold front brought a hard, icy rain from thunderheads silhouetted outside her motel window. Flashes of lightning snaked across the night sky.

"The photo, right," she responded. "I think it's in my inbox. Give me a sec —"

A moment later, Carmen looked up, directly into the webcam.

"How are things over there?" she asked matter-of-factly to fill the void.

"It's everything you've heard, believe me," he said, "It's been six months since Abu Ghraib; it feels like six days! This freakin' place is certifiable, seriously! Nobody knows what's going on. Or what's going to happen next! Everything's so raw here, I —"

"Ok, it just came up," she interrupted him. She studied the picture for a few seconds. He quickly shifted his attention, realizing by her reaction that she'd just launched the photo he'd sent.

"What the hell is this thing?" she asked.

"You mean the picture?" he said. He watched her digitized nodding head temporarily freeze across the video feed as her eyes remained fixed on her screen.

"Yeah, it's something, ain't it?" he said. "It took me awhile but I ran it down. This thing is so bizarre. I think it's what she was talking about, what Maria saw them —"

"Maria," she repeated, recalling her as soon as she heard herself say her name.

"Yeah, you remember me telling you about her?" he asked.

The name was not lost on her.

"Yeah, I think I do," she answered. "She was one of your sources for that article you wrote?"

Jimmy looked back into the webcam.

"Yeah, that's her," he said optimistically. "Were you able to reach out to her with what I gave you?"

She thought for a moment.

"I'd sent you the photo she gave me of her and her sister," Jimmy said, hoping his reminder could somehow still mean the ball didn't get dropped.

"Anything happen there?"

"Yeah," she responded, the pieces beginning to fall back into place. "I remember now. You'd been meeting with her over the spring and summer. Yeah, we talked about her and her sister just before you left."

"Right," he replied. "Did the photo help?"

"I think so," she said, "I tried reaching out to her a couple of times but don't remember ever connecting with her."

"So, you didn't talk with her?"

"No, I mean, I was never able to reach her. I called her to set up a time to meet — that's right, her voice mail mailbox was full, I couldn't even leave a message —"

He knew Maria was never without a cellphone although she wasn't allowed to keep the same one for more than a few weeks at a time. He wouldn't dwell now on what that could mean.

"But I passed the photo of her and her sister along with her contact information on to Missing Persons. I figured they could at least get a file opened on them, maybe get some background information that could help. Now that I think about it, though, I don't recall ever getting a follow-up from them. I'm sorry, Jimmy, I —"

He was hoping for better news.

"I'll get someone on it. I'll make a call tonight…"

He listened through the distorted voice connection to every word he could. He wanted to lash out but knew Carmen had issues of her own to deal with. He should have had a backup plan. He should have followed-up. It had been six months now since he'd last seen Maria. And he knew he could not blame Carmen. He knew it was – it always had been – his choice, his commitment, his responsibility.

He closed his eyes as tightly as he could.

"Thanks, Carmen," he said with as much enthusiasm as he could muster. "I appreciate that."

"I'm sorry, Jimmy," she repeated.

He said nothing and waited. There was no place else to go with it.

"Now, as far as this thing you just sent me is concerned…" she said.

She looked back on the photograph displayed on the screen in front of he, lost as to even what she was most confused about

"…what the hell am I looking at?" she asked.

He worked to refocus his attention on the image he'd just sent her.

"It's a torture device," he said, changing gears. "It's from the Middle Ages. It's called the Scavenger's Daughter."

"The Scavenger's what?"

"The Scavenger's Daughter."

"Why a 'daughter'?" she indignantly replied.

"Christ, I don't know, Carmen," Jimmy responded. "Maybe it has something to do with the guy – this guy, what's his name…"

Jimmy took a second to refer to his notes. He was nothing if not precise.

"…yeah, this guy Skevington – Sir Leonard Skevington – who invented it. Maybe that's why they called it his 'daughter'? Who the hell cares? That's not important…"

Carmen listened attentively as she waited for Jimmy to get back to the point. She watched as he continued glancing back to his notes.

"…Anyway, this Skevington character was the Lieutenant of the Tower of London for Henry the VIII. Apparently, this guy's career path blossomed when he demonstrated a particularly useful talent for extracting confessions. Or, more precisely, inventing new and uniquely painful ways for entertaining his guests."

Carmen glanced back at the picture and tried imagining how depraved this Skevington character must have been.

Jimmy continued.

"It works on the opposite principle of the rack. Instead of stretching a person, this thing squeezes its victim into the smallest possible space. And the longer you're in this thing, the more compressed your body becomes."

"Seriously?" she replied displaying an incredulous look tinged with disgust.

"Yeah, it was something Maria said that started me thinking. It was a little while ago, during one of our first meetings. She talked about what she'd seen them use on this woman. I remember how she said it made her feel. From what Maria

told me, these guys chose this poor woman at random. Everybody in the house was made to watch..."

The photo he'd sent her was of this woman — bent forward on the floor, her knees forced up against her chest, her arms tightly pressed against her sides — locked inside a device that looked like a wishbone fastened at both ends to a wide, oval metal plate.

Carmen listened intently. Her eyes were riveted to what she saw.

"Oh, my god..." she said, uncertain of what revulsed her more: that such a device existed or how it was used.

"...Yeah, she said they got everyone together in the basement of this house she was at. This thing is brought in and placed in the middle of the room. Then these two guys just walked up to this one young woman and grabbed her. Maria said the young woman was screaming, begging them to let her go. But, once she was put into this thing, she could barely make a sound..."

"What do you mean?" Carmen asked, thinking she hadn't heard him right.

"I was wondering what she meant by that, too. But, remember what I said, it's made for constriction. When I read more about this thing I realized what Maria was talking about. To fit into it, the woman would've had her knees shoved up against her chest, just like in the picture. Once they locked her in, it would put pressure on her lungs. In that position, she would have had a helluva time trying to breathe, let alone scream."

"Jeee-zus," Carmen said slowly.

Jimmy continued.

"So, maybe five, ten minutes go by. Maria couldn't be sure. Everyone is forced to stay in the basement and just watch this poor woman endure this torture. Then, suddenly, everyone is herded over to one side of the room in front of this poor woman. Maria said one of the guys there walked over and pulled the woman's head up by her hair. And you could see the blood oozing from her eyes and her nose and her mouth."

It made even an experienced federal agent like Carmen Eyas shudder.

"Holy shit," she said quietly.

Carmen nodded unable to take her eyes off the photo.

"The position would have impacted the woman's lungs almost immediately, which, like I said, would prevent her from screaming. If the downward pressure on her body became intense enough — meaning, if she were left in this thing long enough for the pressure to build on her spine — most of her vertebrae would gradually begin to splinter and fracture. But that wouldn't kill."

"No?" she asked.

"No, that was the beauty of this thing's design. Maria didn't know if the woman survived. Everyone left the room before they took her out of the device. But, if she did die, it was because of the damage done to her circulatory system."

"Say that again?" Carmen asked.

"What would have killed her was the lack of blood circulation. Instead of circulating normally, her blood would've backed up at different parts of the body. And with her circulation interrupted, the woman's blood pressure would have begun to rise rapidly. It's that increasing pressure that would force her arteries and blood vessels to burst. It would look for any way to relieve the pressure. The blood trapped in her head, for instance –"

"Which would explain how her face was covered with blood," Carmen replied.

"Exactly," Jimmy agreed. "She'd been left in that thing long enough that the rising blood pressure caused her eyes, ears and nose to bleed…"

"You've got to be kidding me, Jimmy…"

"Eventually, she would've died from either a stroke – brought on by the high blood pressure –, major organ failure or…"

Carmen looked up at Jimmy through the webcam as he finished.

"…her heart would have simply exploded. Literally!"

"Holy shit," she softly repeated. "What the hell is this, somethin' out of Pablo Escobar and the Colombian cartels?"

Jimmy went back to his notes he'd made from his web research.

"Yeah, but it seems our boy Darth Skevington and his pals in the Tower would sometimes pull a victim out of the device only to put him back in later, depending on the point of the torture. If they didn't want the prisoner dead just yet – if they needed more information from him or weren't convinced he was telling the truth –, they would release him from the device for a while before putting him back in it."

She cringed at the thought.

"Other times…"

"…they didn't." Carmen replied.

"Yeah, devices like these have storied histories," he responded.

"I see, she said.

"But get this, it gets better," he said.

"Better?" Carmen said sarcastically.

"Maria told me this guy she's been getting close to – this 'Snake-Eyes' character – told her about this one guy he knows named…"

Jimmy referred again to his notes.

"…Just a minute, here it is. Sanchez, something Sanchez, she couldn't remember his first name…"

He continued reading from his notes.

"…Apparently, this guy Sanchez used to work in the government – Homeland Security, she thought it was – and had, coincidentally enough, has been to Iraq."

Carmen knew Jimmy long enough to know where this was heading.

"It sounds like he's some kind of consultant to contractors on the short list at the Pentagon. I remember she said this guy does something in security now."

"Are you saying this guy Sanchez is working for the government now?"

"I don't know that for certain," Jimmy said. "She only told me that the guy was a consultant. I'm not certain of any Iraqi connections yet."

Carmen wasn't making sense of what she was hearing.

"Anyway, according to Maria, Snake-Eyes said this guy Sanchez is the one who provided this technique."

"Wait," she said. "What are you telling me?"

"I'm not sure," Jimmy said, "but I'm wondering, knowing what I know about what's going on over there – you have to know Abu Ghraib is just the tip of the iceberg –, if certain people in Homeland Security or maybe the Pentagon want to talk to this guy Sanchez and possibly get their hands on this Scavenger's Daughter thing because –"

Carmen finished his sentence for her.

"Because they think it's an enhanced interrogation technique? That's crazy, Jimmy, even for the goddamned Republicans."

She tried to get comfortable in her cramped motel room's single chair.

"Think about it, Carm," Jimmy insisted, unwilling to let go of the idea. "This thing leaves no visible marks on the victim. From what I've read, if the victim's only in it for a few minutes, it leaves no lasting physical problems. It's quiet; the prisoner wouldn't be able to scream. It's quick; the pain is almost immediate. And, most of all, I imagine it would be effective. I mean, do you really think anybody put in this thing wouldn't be highly motivated to talk, no matter how many virgins are sitting there waiting for him?"

"Jesus Christ," she said softly, looking back into the webcam.

"I'm guessing the intelligence would be pretty reliable from this baby," he said.

He continued making his obvious point.

"Hey, what has the Secretary of Defense and the Army and everybody else over there been telling us about how they're leaving detainees in uncomfortable positions for extended periods of time?"

Jimmy just shrugged his shoulders.

"Seriously, Jimmy, do you honestly think they could really be using this thing?"

"Why not?" he offered. "Who'd be there to stop them?"

Carmen's silence told him she considered the possibility that he might be right.

"Oh, and one more thing," Jimmy added.

"What's that?" Carmen asked.

"Our friend, Dr. No, the genius who dreamed up this little bad boy?"

"Yeah?"

"The motto on his family's coat of arms?"

"Yeah?"

"Per augusta ad augusta."

"Which I'm sure you'll tell me means —"

"Through dangers to honor…"

Jimmy swiveled his chair in the direction of a 1½" thick gusset folder snuggly packed with a dozen or so tabbed manila folders. The setting Baghdad sun did little to relieve the day's heat. He pulled out the first one in line which contained what he hoped was the final draft of the article on human trafficking his editor had submitted just weeks ago for fact checking before it went for publication. They'd been negotiating with the magazine for the cover.

Inside the folder, in front of the typewritten pages, was the photograph Maria had given him. It was creased and worn. The corners curled up as he carefully removed it from the folder. It was of Maria and her younger sister, Caridád, in happier times, arm-in-arm, among family and friends, at a barbeque on the 4th of July. It was taken some three and a half years ago. Exactly sixty-one days before they would both disappear.

They were together. They were smiling and happy. They seemed carefree.

But, most of all, they were safe.

Jimmy slowly closed the folder and laid it on the desk in front of him. He recalled vividly the last time he'd spoken with Maria. He remembered thinking even then about the risks she'd taken just talking to him. And what would happen to her if —

He abruptly stood up and walked over to a small, badly built chest of drawers. He unplugged his cell phone from the travel charger and desperately punched up the last number he had for her.

That it rang gave him hope. That it didn't stop ringing —

It never went to voice mail.

He ended the call and tried again with the same results. Something was obviously very wrong. His first thought was that it was his fault. He couldn't have realized it then on that summer evening he'd last seen her. He hadn't even considered it since. But he did now. He'd let her down. All this time had passed. Everything he'd told her he would do for her. And not a goddamned thing had gotten done to help her. Not one.

He'd contacted Carmen the same night with everything he'd learned. He'd read to her from his notes. He'd even scanned the photograph Maria had given him and sent it to her. But tonight, for the first time, he faced the harsh reality that nothing he'd promised Maria had happened. Help hadn't come. No one had reached out to her. He suddenly felt in free fall as a growing emptiness inside of him took hold.

And a strange damp chill settled in.

Carmen clearly hadn't made any serious progress toward finding them. He was angry, pissed-off actually. As much with himself as with her. This was his fault. There was no escaping that.

He'd failed her. He'd committed himself to Maria then disappeared. An unforgiving sadness pervaded him as he thought about her all alone. How she had to have begun to wonder if he'd forgotten about her. If he'd simply used her for his story. And that first horrible moment when she must have realized that everything she'd risked, everything he'd said to make her believe, even the promise he'd given her... All of it.

It had all been for nothing.

He slumped backwards onto his bed. He winced as the lumpy mattress sent a sharp pain across his lower back that shot up his spine and behind his shoulder blades. When he finally, slowly, opened his eyes, his eyes remained transfixed on the plaster cracks that snaked across the ceiling, staring disinterestedly back at him.

The sound of Maria's voice echoed across his memory. He could not escape her words or the feeling that this was all on him, that it was only on him. He couldn't ignore the ugly truth that he hadn't kept his word. That he'd been like all the rest.

Or the brutal reality that, for Maria, it may no longer matter.

* * *

Special Agent Cauldwell's Tuesday morning was late getting started which only made Bobby's uninvited presence as he exited the elevator that much less appealing.

"Bobby, what a surprise. What brings you here this morning?" he said as he continued walking past him. He proceeded to his office door where, as he stood unlocking it, he felt the weight of Bobby's glare on his back. Cauldwell welcomed him in as the door swung open and the lights flickered on. He walked around to the back of his desk and sat down. He finally acknowledged Bobby hadn't said anything.

"What can I do for you today, Detective Colavito?" he said dryly.

Bobby took a seat across from Cauldwell's desk and looked directly at him, wondering what new heights of stupidity Cauldwell was seeking to scale.

"You must be swamped with the work since you didn't bother to show up last night. So, if you want to do this here, that's fine with me."

Cauldwell wasn't amused.

"Detective, I have quite a busy day today, I don't have time for your –"

Bobby's steel expression did not change at all.

"Perhaps you could make an appointment for later in the week?"

Bobby stood up, turned and pushed the door shut.

"What I've got to say won't take long, Cauldwell," he said, glaring down at him while he stood.

"Bobby, I –"

"Shut up and listen, you stupid shit," Bobby said, the tone in his voice belying his level of self-control.

Cauldwell sat back like the cat eavesdropping on the canary.

"Why did you feel it was important to speak with her?" Bobby started.

"I'm investigating the murder of a federal agent, Detective, would you prefer that I wait for you to give me direction as to whom I should and should not interview?"

"I don't know how you found her, Cauldwell, but that doesn't matter. You're not to go near her again, do you understand me?"

"Yes, Detective, I think I understand you completely. You seem to be informing me that you are attempting to impede an official federal investigation."

Bobby sensed that something had changed. He wondered what Cauldwell knew. And how he'd suddenly developed a backbone.

"Would that be an accurate statement, Detective?"

"You shouldn't be fucking with me, Cauldwell. You –"

"Oh, and, while we're on the subject…" Cauldwell calmly, arrogantly interrupted.

"…You should know that I've decided against allowing you to have personal access to the physical evidence file. As a matter of fact, I've decided that, should we be in need of a liaison with the Chicago Police Department, we will be asking the CPD to provide us with someone who has *no* prior involvement with the case, who *wouldn't* qualify as a 'person of interest' and who may *not* ultimately become a target of our investigation as a suspect in the murder of our agent as well as her companion."

Bobby was stunned. *Who the fuck does this guy think he is?*

"Also, Detective," Cauldwell said with a cold confidence, "you should be aware that we believe it is only appropriate, as we more fully determine your involvement with Special Agent Eyas, that, throughout the course of our investigation, we will be providing the CPD's Internal Affairs Division's with updated reports pertinent to their open and ongoing inquiry into prior allegations concerning your professional conduct."

Bobby could not believe what he was hearing. The dumb sonuvabitch was slitting his own throat!

"You and I both know that IAD investigation found nothing," he blurted out.

"And how the fuck do you know about it anyway?"

Cauldwell ignored him, rose from his desk and walked around to his office door.

"Now, if there's nothing else, Detective," he said as he opened the door.

Bobby noticed Cauldwell's confident body language.

"You just cut your own fuckin' throat, Cauldwell. You can't know the kind of hell I can rain down on you. You –"

"Enough, already, Detective, "Cauldwell said, staying in character.

"If you would like to file an official complaint, I can –"

"Don't bother, Cauldwell, "Bobby interrupted. "When I file my 'complaint,' you'll know it. And you'll remember it for the rest of your miserable life."

Cauldwell only grinned.

"Is that some sort of threat, Detective?"

"No, Special Agent Cauldwell, it's not a threat. What could I possibly do or say that might be interpreted as threatening to someone like you?" he asked sarcastically.

"Look, Detective, the integrity of our investigation is paramount. If you have any evidence or 'collateral information,' either in the form of hearsay or of a physical nature, say like a CD or a DVD, that you believe is germane to this case, I would urge you to come forward with it so that we can evaluate it's significance with re– "

"Can you *really* be this fuckin' stupid?" Bobby said, almost in amazement. He wasn't finished.

"What is it you think you know, Cauldwell?" Bobby continued. "Do you think your 'friends' will keep what I know from getting out? Or maybe you think they'll get to me before I can cut a deal? Is that it?"

"As I said, Detective, if you believe you have –"

Bobby'd heard enough. He started out the open door then stopped and turned.

"What did you think, Cauldwell? That guys like you end up in some silly ass federal white-collar prison? Is that what you think you'll get for extortion, for raping children and selling their families? No, no... you get hard time, in general population with the broth'as and the beaners, with the gangbangers and the other lowlifes who pound white boys like you into midday snacks..."

Cauldwell refused to look him in the eye as Bobby stood glaring at him.

"...Do you really think you will survive what I know?"

Bobby leaned forward and whispered harshly.

"Or who I know?"

That Cauldwell hadn't expected.

He tried to keep his face from turning as red as his hair.

Bobby walked out of the office but turned as he exited.

"I'll be seeing you again soon, Special Agent Cauldwell," he said, winking at him. He curled the bottom three fingers of his right hand closed and pointed his index finger at Cauldwell while raising his thumb, then dropping it like the hammer of a pistol.

Cauldwell pushed the door closed in response.

Bobby watched as Cauldwell chose to ignore him, turning his back on the detective to retreat to his desk. Bobby swore under his breath as he glared through the glass wall. He began walking slowly down the narrow hall, passing a sea of neatly aligned cubicles, toward the elevators. Bobby was nothing if not about getting even. And revenge was, indeed, a dish best served cold. His time in the desert had taught him that anger proved most effective when properly harnessed. Indulging his emotions, while maybe gratifying, gained him nothing. This wasn't Abu Ghraib. He had to remain focused and allow events to unfold. The time would come when Cauldwell would understand the mistakes his arrogance had just made. And it would be sooner rather than later. He allowed himself to smile as he pressed the down arrow button and waited.

Moments later, the illuminated button went dark. As he heard the rush of air exiting the elevator shaft announce its arrival on his floor, Bobby heard a voice from behind him.

"Detective, I was wondering if we might have a word?"

The elevator doors opened as Bobby turned and immediately liked what he saw.

"Would you have a few minutes? Maybe I could buy you a cup of coffee?"

Bobby grinned as if she'd just invited him up to her place. He stepped into the open elevator and placed his hand against the door to prevent it from closing.

"Yeah, an Irish coffee would be good right now," he said with a nod while flashing a bad Tom Cruise-like grin, apparently in the pathetically sad belief that a sorry pickup line somehow could compensate for a lack of personal oral hygiene.

"I'm afraid it's a bit early in the day for me, Detective..." she responded, wondering how this guy ever got laid.

"...but, if you have a few minutes," she continued, holding it there.

"That'd be fine. It could only improve my day, believe me," he said, settling for whatever opportunity she'd left open to him.

"I'm going down. How 'bout you?" he asked, thinking his suggestively subtle-as-a-sledge-hammer style was still somehow cute.

"Yes, please," Laura responded as she stepped into the elevator behind him, his lack of gentlemanly manners as expected as the now sounding buzzer was annoying. She wondered if she wouldn't have to shoot him before they reached the lobby.

* * *

Jack looked at his watch as he waited alone at the bar in the lounge of the O'Hare Hilton. Wallace's incoming flight from San Francisco was scheduled to land almost thirty minutes ago. Jack had checked the departure time flight number on the web and found it had left on time. Laura had confirmed with Wallace's secretary earlier this morning that the meeting with Jack was still on for this afternoon. Wallace would find him, he didn't have to worry. Jack sensed something odd about this meeting, beyond the obvious. Why the Deputy Director would go out of his way to talk with a disgraced, former FBI whistle-blower seemed more than a bit unusual. Laura thought he was being a bit paranoid, though typical of the Jack she remembered. And she made a point of telling him so before she left to head downtown earlier in the morning.

Laura appeared fine, a little tired but no noticeable or lingering aftereffects from her evening spent with Cauldwell ignoring his insufferable double enténdres. She was looking to do some follow-up work on the forensic results from the I-80 crime scene as well as Carmen's autopsy. She had also agreed with Jack, for her own safety and his peace of mind, to set up a GPS locater on the FBI's personnel website page, one he could access from Alex's laptop. That way, no matter where she was, he could find her.

She told him she would email her unique user ID and today's password to Jack's account when she received it later today. Jack had realized, after thinking about it while she was gone last night, that she was too vulnerable, particularly knowing what he knew about Cauldwell. He wanted to take no chances. Laura wasn't as concerned but decided it couldn't hurt.

As a result of the travel itinerary Jack had suggested, Laura now had to allow extra time to get downtown. She hated taking the El but the Blue Line to and from the airport allowed her to keep an eye open for anything – and anyone – suspicious. She'd get off at Congress and walk over to State Street and catch the Red Line south a couple of stops south to the FBI building on Roosevelt Road.

Jack had met Laura downstairs last night for an update after she'd returned from her "date" with Cauldwell. She couldn't decide which word best described her evening: dreadful or interminable. Keeping with her attractive nature, Laura was all too familiar with the subtleties of the dance. How to let a man know she either was – or, in Cauldwell's case, nauseatingly wasn't – interested. How to gracefully encourage his pursuit or unmistakingly ensure that it come to a screeching halt.

And it wasn't that he just didn't seem to take the hint. The thing with Cauldwell was, it simply didn't seem possible she *wouldn't* be interested! The guy was either the most socially "challenged" forty-something male whose company she'd ever had the misfortune of tolerating or he was simply as dumb as a stump. Of course, there was a third and perhaps even more viable option – that he was just an asshole. Their drinks had barely been served last evening when Laura realized she'd start from door number three.

And she never looked back.

The evening itself was uneventful if not downright boring. Undoubtedly much like being between the sheets with this self-absorbed law enforcement version of Ronald McDonald. The most interesting moment of the evening came when it was time to pick up the check, particularly after Laura made it known that she was more than just a little bit uninterested. She wondered if "revulsed" was a real word but she kept reminding herself she was still on the job. And the job *always* came first.

What she learned most was that, if his actions were anything like his words, she pitied the next – or perhaps maybe it would be the first? – woman to spend an evening subjected to what he so probably if not arrogantly considered his sexual prowess. Jack actually felt sorry for her though he was hoping she would have at least something more to show for her evening of protracted suffering besides getting even with him.

She left no doubt that Jack owed her. Big time.

As they were knocking off for the night, Jack asked Laura what she thought about Father Mac coming out to visit the kids. Ana and Daniel were asking about him during dinner and again back at the room. Laura did raise two valid points: getting him here and back without being followed and, should they succeed in doing so, dealing with the reality that someone else would now know where they were staying.

Jack thought about what Laura said and quickly realized she was right. He did remember to ask her about getting the kids federal witness protection. She thought that might just work. The more they talked it through, the more she liked the idea. The kids certainly qualified for protection and, with Wallace coming into town, a call from him would eliminate any resistance she might encounter in the Chicago office. Yeah, she told him, that made a lot of sense. She'd get on it when she got to the office in the morning.

Laura was impressed: Jack hadn't lost a step in his time away from the Bureau. And owing perhaps more to the evening's alcoholic consumption than she cared to admit, she reluctantly conceded it only partly absolved her of the attraction that, all these years later, still haunted her. Despite everything she'd done to convince herself that she'd moved on – all the memories she'd come to terms with, all the raw, kicked-to-the-curb feelings she'd buried or left for dead – nothing had changed. They were back. They'd somehow survived. And they were breathing heavily. With the opening elevator doors beckoning them, she warmly welcomed Jack's hand on her back, directing her into the empty car. He didn't notice the impish smile or her inhibitions buckling beneath the impatient weight of her racing heart's anxious reach, her better judgment now relegated to an irrelevant if somewhat jealous voyeur. As the gently closing doors silenced the real world safely behind them, she instinctively responded by turning and drawing him close.

And immediately kissing him.

With the moment blossoming, her hands moved from his shoulders, her arms wrapping themselves slowly, securely around his bent neck. As their tongues engaged, it was like stepping back in time. Suddenly, the choices they'd once so defiantly followed – the uncompromising reasons that had sent their lives in such opposite directions – now seemed undefined, so unintelligible, blurring together into a dissipating mist. As she first advanced then teasingly retreated, he willingly, hungrily pursued her. And, finding her, he became her predator and she his prey. His lips sealed around her, imprisoning her, sucking her tongue back into his mouth, stretching her into his throat to the groans that admitted her undeniable pleasure, leaving her wanting, seeking, demanding more, all the while hiding inside his arms from the knowledge that any second it would all have to end.

As the elevator gently came to a stop, she felt his lips relent, releasing his grip on her. Her arms retreated, her hands meeting flush against the side of his face. She tilted his head slightly, trying to gain greater leverage as she sent her tongue once more deeply into his mouth, searching for his one last time. She recognized the immediate emptiness of their moment as it ended, as it evaporated like the morning fog sacrificed before the unforgiving August sun. She fought to hide her sadness as she stepped out of their embrace and into the light of the hallway leading to their separate rooms.

Laura walked ahead of him out of the elevator. She smiled at their awkward silence. She stopped outside her room and pulled out the cardkey.

"This is me," she said, hoping some last-second cosmic event would change where she knew all this was heading.

Jack smiled.

"I'll see you in the morning, ok?" he said gently.

She nodded, trying hard to swallow.

He turned and walked towards his room. He didn't hear her door latch release or her door open and close. He stopped as he got to his room then turned to look back into a now empty hallway.

"Just fuckin' great," he mumbled.

After grabbing the first tee-shirt she could find from the chest of drawers near her bed, Laura made her way back carefully, quietly through the dark room toward the illuminated light switch just inside the bathroom door. On her way she slipped out of her shoes and blazer and placed her purse on the small round table near the door. She stepped lightly into the bathroom and gently closed the door behind her. She stopped as she went to flip on the switch, noticing her image in the double-sink wide mirror through the shadows of an almost romantic glow. She shook out her silky chestnut brown hair that curled just below her shoulders when the full-length mirror on the back of the bathroom door attracted her attention. She removed her clothes and moved curiously toward her naked image, searching through the dim light into her reflection's blue eyes for several long seconds before stepping back, wondering what the fuck she'd just done.

She was remarkably toned – never mind for someone her age – but the image that looked back to her left her feeling oddly apathetic, almost to the point of wondering what did it matter. She watched herself raise her arms in anger then press the palms of her hands against the sides of her head. She'd *kissed* him! *For Christ's sake*! What the fuck was she thinking? How could she have done something so stupid? Never mind they were working together again – sort of. Never mind that she knew better than to let her heart have the final say. And that it was Jack, of all people, that she'd allowed to pick at the scars she'd thought – or was it hoped? – had finally healed. And, as if that wasn't enough, knowing he was right next-door, sleeping – or maybe not! – at this very moment with another woman! An accomplished, attractive, sexy-as-hell woman she was forced to admit she actually liked! How fucked up is that? It was moments like this that reminded her just how weak she truly was.

When it came to him.

She inched closer to the mirror and again found her reflection's eyes. Her memories of him – of them – flashed like lightening across the clearing skies in her heart, like so many highlights from a play she'd inexplicably chosen to leave at intermission. Their issues, what few they honestly had, never did emanate from the intimate times they shared together. And whether it was during an unexpected autumn getaway in rustic Galena Territory. Or on a cliff overlooking the ocean in the glow of a Mendocino sunset. Or that secluded alcove beneath the picturesque lookout point at the Colorado National Monument. Those splendid moments – and countless others when their passions had so unexpectedly flared – were not what had given Laura reason to pause. No, it was rather how often they'd connected with their clothes *on* that tended to complicate things.

Laura's career, as much as it meant to her, was ultimately just that. She'd consistently sought a positive work balance that enabled her to walk away from her professional life, to take time off, particularly when her sanity was at issue. She had used her "lateral promotion" to her current position in The Office of Tribal Justice as an opportunity to reassess her life's goals. A former assistant prosecuting attorney, she had considered other options before accepting the internal move offered by the Bureau. Truth be told, she would have been equally comfortable with being dismissed, a reaction Jack never quite understood.

Jack's career, on the other hand, had evolved into his life's work, a passion often treading upon obsession. A significant aspect to the driving force behind his unrelenting nature was his belief in the linear relationship between the truth and reality. At least, in his interpretation of both. Toward that end, he demanded of himself – and others closest to him – a self-awareness that, at times, bordered on the fanatical. Since being invited to leave the Bureau, he'd come to realize that working within the system – and the culture that gave rise to it – to effect real change seemed patently absurd. What Jack lacked in diplomacy and tact he more than made-up for with a work ethic that embraced nothing short of correcting and, where he could, preventing the evil that men do.

Laura maintained more of a corporate mentality. She understood and, on a good day, appreciated if not always respected the need for a chain of command. Jack was more of a maverick. He'd come to believe that everyday was an opportunity to change the world for someone. And you couldn't do that entertaining management that had not only long ago outlived its usefulness but served to inhibit, and in some cases prevent, making the life-and-death decisions that could impact so many helpless victims.

She enjoyed crowds and being around people. The Air and Water Show at the Chicago's North Avenue beach, highlighted by a heart-stopping performance by her favorite Blue Angels, was something she looked forward to every summer. She was approaching a time in her life when she liked leaving her job behind each day she could and, on occasion, even being pampered. Jack understood people from a very different perspective. He saw most of them as, essentially, occupying the same common ground: people, at least in this country, were generally more greedy than they were hungry. They were more focused on themselves and their own problems than those facing their communities, their cities, their states or even their country. They'd sooner find it easier to master Portuguese than take the time to understand climate change. To get them to care about something as foreign as human trafficking was almost beyond their capacity for cognition. And, for Jack, therein lie the problem.

And, ultimately, the source of his contempt.

So when Laura mentioned that she was considering accepting a transfer to D.C. during their time together in the Chicago office, Jack was hardly surprised. In truth, he was almost relieved. As respect was never an issue with them, personal and otherwise, it was an easy decision to recognize that their professional relationship was much too important to relegate it to the dumpster. So they became allies, often each other's strongest advocates and staunchest supporters. And, in the aftermath of the inquiry investigating the leaks that had led to the Attorney General's resignation and Laura's inadvertent contribution to Jack's dismissal, eventually back to being friends again.

Which is why none of this made *any* fucking sense!

But as she stared at the nude image looking back at her, draped in the shadows of the room's only light, the thought of him – of them – left her vulnerable, unable to resist succumbing once again to the one weakness that she'd nearly raised to an art form since they'd went their separate ways. She could admit anything to herself – except the reason why she could not forget him. And now, as she relived the electricity of his tender but relentless stroke, as she felt her pulse quickening, her desire flaring, its embers floating uninhibited on her soft desert's breeze, her imagination ignited like a wild brushfire. And she descended into the sublime madness that had always been so necessary to loving him.

She closed her eyes and turned, leaning to her left against the wall, to face the mirror above the vanity. Her fingers traveled lightly, almost without notice, taking only a moment for her to become lost in the sensuous memories she guarded so jealously. Any perception, any awareness of her quivering legs, her pounding heart, her staggered, halting breaths had subtly disappeared, her touch having indiscernibly become his.

Her hips rotated slowly, repeatedly forward then back again, as each advancing rush brought his body that much closer. Every prolonged sensation brought vivid images that eagerly incented her growing intensity. She arched her back as she gradually opened her tearful eyes, watching her reflection spasm in sharp contractions, their intentions now having strengthened beyond her control. One moment she was shuddering, his tongue blazing a scorching trail across her smoldering, aching flesh; the next, convulsing to the competing tensions that were now multiplying as he greedily assailed her delicate fold without mercy or moderation. She opened her thighs to welcome him, stretching herself apart, wantonly inviting what would surely be his full, deep if depredating presence even as she had yet to forgive him for conquering her so completely.

Suddenly, her head shot back. Her eyes closed one last time as her lips parted slightly, a thin, solicitous moan building alongside the heightening tensions that left her dizzy, almost faint. Entrapped, she was no longer able to escape. She began to tremble as her body rose to seek its own pleasure, culminating in one final seizure that engulfed her, leaving her helpless in the path of the surging tremors that now consumed what was left of her will to deny them. Finally surrendering to its loathsome ecstasy, she unleashed her rage as it acquiesced in kind, releasing her torment amidst the muffled cries and climaxing senses that refused to subside until she'd acquiesced to whispering his name.

Softly. Lustfully. Regretfully.

While he waited for Wallace, Jack was still nursing his Chivas neat, continuing to replay the events of last night. He wasn't so much upset about

Laura kissing him as he was disappointed how much he enjoyed kissing her back. It was a no-win situation. Naïve as he seemingly always was when it came to matters of the heart, he never saw it coming. Not from Laura. He kept going over the last couple of days, trying to figure out if he'd said or done anything to lead her to think he was interested in her again.

He loved Laura. He had no doubt about that. Truth be told, he'd never stopped loving her. But he hadn't thought of her romantically for quite some time though, in his more honest moments, even Carmen had to compete with her memory. As a matter of fact, Laura taking that transfer to D.C. was probably one of the few things they could agree on as things continued to unravel between them. And, even though he and Alex had slept together the last couple of nights, the reality was he'd only known her since Friday! He could hardly be certain where *that* was heading.

The one thing Jack *did* know was that he needed a clear head right now to deal with everything that was going on around him – and them. Focus was everything right now. From everyone. Especially with this meeting with Wallace today. For the sake of everyone involved, he decided it was best to back burner this whole issue.

Laura would be onboard with that, he thought. There's simply too much at stake.

He sat on the barstool, still lost in his feelings about last night. He stared at some imaginary point on one of the many television screens behind the bar. Both his hands were wrapped around the half-empty drink that he hadn't touched for the past few minutes. He paid no attention to the well-groomed man walking up next to him. He appeared to be a classy gentleman, maybe in his early sixties, slim and in good shape. He wore a white shirt and navy blue tie and a gray windowpane suit that somehow showed no signs of the three-hour plus airplane ride in from the west coast. And an American flag lapel pin, the requisite calling card of any politician these days regardless of profile.

When Jack heard the bartender ask the man standing next to him what he'd like to drink, he suddenly realized he was no longer alone. And his meeting was about to begin.

"Bourbon and branch, if you would, please, sir," the man said.

Jack turned to greet his guest.

"Jack," the man said, assuming permission to call him by his first name.

The Deputy Director of the FBI, L. Stephen Wallace, stood next to him, his right hand open and extended to him, a carryon bag draped across his left shoulder. Jack was surprised to see Wallace was without his bodyguards.

"Deputy Director Wallace," Jack said respectfully as he got up from his barstool. "It's a privilege to meet you, sir."

"Please, Jack," he said graciously, "call me Stephen."

Jack nodded in response.

"Let's grab a booth, get ourselves a bit of privacy, hmm?" Wallace suggested.

The bartender finished pouring Wallace's bourbon and motioned to the waitress to bring him his drink.

The two men adjourned to a booth at the far end of the bar. They had just sat down and gotten comfortable when the waitress brought Wallace his bourbon and water on ice in a highball glass. She was young, probably just old enough to be serving drinks, blonde, tanned and athletically slender. She was personable and very attractive, the kind bars love to hire, though the black fishnet stockings and heels were a bit over the top. Only made her look cheap, in Jack's opinion. But perhaps that was the intention. Her black skirt was tight and very short. She wore a frilly white French peasant top, dropped down off her shoulders, which, even in the dimly lit lounge, notice-ably offset her richly tanned skin and provided the intended effect.

And while Wallace chose to disguise his leer, Jack couldn't help but notice how the young woman's square shoulders, which sported no tan lines, wasn't lost on him.

"Jack, if I were twenty years younger…"

Yeah, then you could be her father instead of her fuckin' grandfather, you lecherous bastard!

Jack look down at his drink and wondered what the fuck he'd gotten himself into, then decided to get the ball rolling.

"How was your time in San Francisco, sir?"

"Fine, Jack, it was very nice. I was only out there a couple of days. Just long enough to give a couple of speeches, shake a few hands and head on back," he said. "And I've got another dinner to attend this evening at the InterContinental downtown."

Jack nodded, pretending he understood the demands on a high profile law enforcement politician.

"So, I understand you've been a bit busy, Jack," Wallace said, leading the conversation in the direction he wanted it to go.

"Yes, sir," Jack self-effacingly agreed, "it's been a rather hectic couple of days."

"So I've been told," Wallace responded. "I was contacted by Special Agent Kallinger about the need for federal witness protection. It seems she has three children in custody that she's looking to have guarded. Do you know anything about that, Jack?"

"Yes, sir, I do. We rescued them from a trafficking organization operating out of a safe house on the south side. They've already begun providing Laura – I'm sorry, I mean, Special Agent Kallinger – with details of their confinement and subsequent abuse."

Wallace remained quiet, making eye contact with Jack as he listened carefully.

"Apparently, this organization has a main artery that runs directly in from Denver. This particular group, from what we've been able to gather so far, appears to use Chicago as the hub for the entire surrounding area – Iowa, Wisconsin, Indiana, Michigan, –"

"Sounds just like the Big Ten conference, eh, Jack?" Wallace said callously.

Jack was beginning to realize it really is true: You can dress 'em up but you just can't take 'em anywhere.

"Something like that, sir," Jack said intentionally without emotion.

"Well," Wallace said to conclude this topic, "I have no issue with the protection request. I instructed my admin to get the appropriate authorizations and expedite the request. From what Laura told me, you'll be needing those marshals right away?"

"Yes sir, that's correct."

"Good," he responded, "you should see them by later this afternoon, tonight at the latest. If you don't, or if she gets any blowback, have her call me immediately. She knows how to get in touch with me."

"Yes sir," Jack responded gratefully if not sincerely, "thank you, sir."

Wallace nodded then turned his attention to more current if not important matters.

"Ok, may I assume that Laura provided you with the envelope I gave her?"

"Yes sir, she did."

"And may I further assume that you've read the file I compiled in that envelope?"

"Yes sir, I have," Jack responded. "Both of them."

He watched Wallace's reaction, which remained calm and polished. The Deputy Director was nothing if not a seasoned and professional political animal. Jack could tell he anticipated the remark at some point. Wallace didn't miss a step.

"And do you have any questions for me, Jack?"

As Jack sat back and sized up his options, the young woman returned to their table, asking if everything was all right and if there was anything she could do for them. Jack cringed in expectation of what Wallace's creativity could do with such an innocent question as that. Thankfully, he acted his age.

"Yes sir, I was wondering about a couple of matters."

"Good."

"First, if you could help me understand why you've chosen me, of all people, to share this information with."

Wallace sat back and took a sip of his bourbon and water.

"Jack, I read your file. I think I have a fairly good understanding of who you are and what you're about. When I learned of Special Agent Cauldwell's alleged activities while in Iraq, I was mortified. I simply could not believe it. Not only is that behavior – I'm sorry, *alleged* behavior – reprehensible on a purely professional level, it violates laws on both a national and international level."

Jack listened to what could easily have been the prepared remarks Wallace offered his audience last night.

"But, more than that," Wallace continued, "it violates precepts of the most fundamental human moral behavior. If I could prosecute Cauldwell today, I would. But, with what I have…"

Wallace took another sip of his drink.

"…with what I have, all I can do is allow it to lead me in the direction of searching for more evidence. You see, the problem is that – "

"Forgive me, sir," Jack interrupted, "but what you have here is more than sufficient to remove Cauldwell from his position. You could suspend him without pay. You could use what you have as leverage in gaining admission to other charges. He obviously didn't act alone. He undoubtedly was involved with others, perhaps Americans, maybe even FBI or Army personnel."

"So, I'm confused, sir," Jack decided to say directly, "what are you waiting for?"

Wallace looked down at his drinks as both of his hands held it firmly. He slowly smiled, the look of a man who knows not only when but where the other shoe will drop.

"Jack, allow me to be blunt."

Jack finished his drink, carefully set his glass back on the table and sat back.

"If you've read my comments carefully, you know that our activities in Iraq were not only unofficial, they could be construed by some not-so-bipartisan and influential members on the Hill as technically outside our legal province, that is, beyond the scope of our jurisdiction as constitutionally provided by Congressional mandate."

In other words, you broke the law! Just fuckin' say it, for Christ sake!

As the thought crawled across his mind, Jack smiled since, from his reading of the file and his knowledge of the original timeline, there was nothing technical about it.

"But we need to keep in mind that, in the post-invasion environment, human intelligence was key. There was no priority beyond learning what our enemy knew."

Here it comes. Next should be 9/11 something, something, yada, yada, yada…

"We could not allow another 9/11 to happen and we were to determined to turn over every grain of sand in that country to find out what their next plan of attack was."

Wallace continued.

"It was in this environment that we decided that Iraq was simply too valuable to be left to anyone else, particularly civilian contractors with virtually no investigative or interrogative experience."

Jack wondered if he wasn't getting a preview of Wallace's opening remarks to the joint committee that would eventually be investigating him.

"But even with everything we planned and the safeguards we put in place –"

"Safeguards?" Jack finally had heard enough.

Wallace had sense from Jack's tone that Wallace was losing him.

"Yes, despite the horrific and almost inhuman conditions over there, we were not only counting on the professionalism of our agents but the individuals we contracted to shadow them and to report back to us on a regularly basis. We wanted to take every measure we could to avoid this very thing."

"I see," Jack replied, trying to keep a straight face.

"As I said, though, it was under the most inhospitable of conditions –"

"I'm sorry, sir," Jack interrupted again, "are you referring to the country or to the 'enhanced interrogation techniques' they use?"

Wallace ignored Jack's intentionally poor attempt at hiding his skepticism.

"Both, actually, Jack," he countered, "there can be no doubt that mistakes were made and one could even make the case that a cover-up of sorts ensued."

"Of sorts?" Jack inquired.

"Yes, I mean, we found ourselves in a position of balancing the useable, valuable and necessary human intelligence we obtained from high-value targets we interviewed with a respect for human life and dignity –"

"Forgive me, sir," Jack interjected, "but I saw nothing in either of those files or in any of your handwritten comments, for that matter, that would allow me to conclude that respect for human life and dignity was a priority for *any* of those field agents."

Wallace realized Jack was saluting what he'd just run up the flagpole.

"The reality was – and still is –, sir," Jack continued, "that there were no rules over there. All that mattered, at least from what I could piece together, was that we were allowed to gain some measure of revenge against defenseless and, as it turned out, mostly innocent Iraqis, more than a few of whom ended up dead as a result."

Wallace sat back and shook his head.

"Jack, if that's what you want to see."

"Sir, it is *not* what I did or did not want to see. But, unfortunately, it appears to be exactly what happened."

"Jack," Wallace countered in an almost patronizing tone, "we can argue ad nauseum about the hows and whys and wherefores about the war and end up precisely where we are now..."

Jack's emotional temperature was still rising.

"...or we can do something about it."

The attractive young woman returned at that moment take an order for another round. She returned Jack's smile and ignored Wallace's grin as she walked away.

"I'm sorry, sir," Jack picked up, "you were saying about *doing* something about this 'situation'?"

"Yes, my problem – our problem, and by that I mean the Bureau's problem – is one of perception right now. No one is interested, now that the war has finally turned the corner, in bringing up issues that could only serve to relive the past. Nor is anyone in this Administration lining up to be the target of additional investigation – and, thus additional blame – for its displacement policies concerning Iraqi nationals. What's done is done and we must move on now to do what we can to help the Iraqi government bring its people back together, from wherever they may be."

"I see," Jack said, feeling like he'd wished he wore his hip boots.

"My concern, Jack, is focused only on Special Agent Cauldwell and his unique knowledge about our involvement over there. His participation in various interrogations that ended with both unfortunate and regrettable results certainly is a significant part of the perception issue I will deal with. However..."

Jack thought he should duck to avoid that second shoe.

"...his disturbing involvement in the apparent trafficking of innocent Iraqis, in many cases entire families, seeking to emigrate to other countries and his somewhat creative albeit disgusting ways of accepting compensation not only cannot be condoned by the Bureau, they can neither be acknowledged nor allowed to be made public."

The young woman returned with their drinks. They waited until she'd left.

"If you don't mind my asking, sir," Jack responded now with less respect than sarcasm, "if that is, in fact, the case, why don't you simply have him taken him out?"

Wallace was taking a sip of his second bourbon and water when he began to reveal the look of someone who'd finally gotten his point across.

"Funny you should mention that, Jack, for that is precisely what brings me in from San Francisco to see you here today."

Jack knew he could not afford to react with any great surprise.

"I'm sorry, sir," Jack said in an effort to clarify Wallace's remark, "but what is it, exactly, that you're hoping I can do for you?"

Wallace moved his drink and leaned against the table, clasping his hands together.

"Are we off the record, Jack?

Jack waited a moment, only imagining what was next, then nodded affirmatively.

Wallace dropped his head, then raised it and looked directly into Jack's eyes.

"Then let me ask you something, reinstated Special Agent Sturdevant..."

* * *

Chapter 16

JACK WAS JUST beginning to process his conversation with Wallace on his way back to the room when he came upon Father Mac in the hotel lobby waiting for him.

"Father," Jack said, extending his right hand trying to hide his surprise.

"Jack," Father Mac replied, shaking his hand, "it's good to see you again."

"I'm glad you were able to rearrange your schedule so quickly," Jack admitted, "Ana and Daniel both have been asking about you!"

Father Mac dropped his head and laughed.

"Well," he allowed, "I had a couple of home visits I had to shuffle around but, when Alex called and asked if I'd like to come out and visit the children, well, she only had to ask me once."

Jack reacted with a broad smile.

"Well, we're certainly glad you were able to, Father."

Father Mac was gratified to hear he hadn't been forgotten in everything that had happened since Saturday afternoon.

"Have you been waiting long?" Jack asked politely.

"No," he replied, "I only got here a few minutes ago. Your timing is perfect."

"Good!" Jack said, as he escorted Father Mac to the elevator. He hadn't been upstairs since he'd left to meet Wallace a couple of hours earlier and he was hoping against hope that the federal marshals were already in place outside their rooms. His mind raced with what possible problems the priest's premature arrival could create.

"How was your ride out here?" Jack asked.

"Well, it was pretty long. But I don't get a chance to take the Blue Line that often so it was a nice change of pace."

Jack smiled, happy to hear the priest had at least used public transportation.

But as he feared, when the two men exited the elevator after reaching their floor, no federal marshals were within sight. Jack had asked Laura to request two armed officers, in plainclothes, be assigned to the detail but, since he hadn't heard from her since she left this morning for FBI headquarters, he couldn't be sure who to expect – and, just as importantly, when he could expect them.

Jack welcomed Father Mac into the room he shared with Alex, who was in the adjoining room spending time with Ana, Daniel and Caridád. They heard them talking and laughing as they circled around the room and headed toward the connecting door. Jack saw the open laptop on the desk. He recognized the web page Alex had been reading. His thoughts stopped at the memory of Carmen.

The kids were bonding quickly. No surprise there. Caridád's spirits had picked up considerably. It appeared that Ana and Daniel had something significant to do with that. She enjoyed being their big sister. And they liked her in that role. Together, they were busy creating their own safe places for each other. It was a small step.

But it *was* a step.

Caridád couldn't help thinking of Maria, wondering if, wherever she was, she was somehow doing the same.

Father Mac walked through the door and was immediately swamped by the three of them. In all the excitement, Jack was able to introduce him to Alex but that's about all the kids were allowing for. As he got comfortable in a nearby chair with the kids surrounding him, laughing and being silly, Jack motioned to Alex. They stepped back into their room to talk.

"Any news from Laura yet?" Jack worriedly asked.

"No, I haven't heard anything and nothing's showed up in my inbox."

"Does she have your address?"

"Yeah, I left it for her last night, just in case she wanted to 'cc:' me on anything."

"Good idea," Jack said. "I'm gonna check my email, maybe it's there by now."

As Jack went to open up a new window in the browser, he turned to Alex. "You doing ok?"

"Yeah," she said, "why?"

"No, just wondering, that's all," he said gently.

He watched as she smiled while walking up to him. She looked amazing. She was wearing a pair of white denim shorts that only enhanced her svelte and soft brown thighs. She had on a thin, very feminine, pink blouse, unbuttoned down her chest, exposing a smooth snow-white sports bra. Her hair draped across her square, athletic shoulders. Jack thought how she could pass for one of the models in a shampoo ad. She leaned over and wrapped her arms around his neck.

"I'm ok, thank you," she said softly, then gave him a kiss.

He leaned into her and kissed her back.

Jack sat at the desk as he opened his web mail account in a new window. He's inbox had many incoming emails but none were from Laura. He wondered if perhaps the new spam filter his Internet Service Provider had recently installed on his account might prevent her message from being delivered. He checked the "Suspect Email" folder.

Nothing.

It wasn't like her. She knew he was waiting to hear from her. Something was obviously wrong. And without her GPS user ID and password, he couldn't track her. He didn't know where she was.

"Alex, does your email account have a spam filter?"

She was standing by the bed, folding some clothes.

"Yeah, probably. Why?"

He sat back and thought.

Fuckin' technology.

"Nothing," he said reluctantly.

Alex tried to change the subject.

"How was your meeting with Wallace?" Alex asked.

He remained lost contemplating what he could do next to contact Laura. She waited for a moment then asked again.

"Jack?"

"Huh?"

"I was just wondering how things went with Wallace."

"Oh, I'm sorry, Alex."

He looked up from her laptop and turned to face her. She immediately knew something wasn't right. She stopped what she was doing and sat down on the side of the bed just across from him.

"Ok," he said distractedly.

She looked at him, knowing he was somewhere else, wondering what Wallace could've said to him.

"You ok, Jack?"

"Yeah, I was expecting to hear from Laura by now."

"Well, maybe, she's –"

"No, something's not right," his instincts said.

"Maybe you could call her?"

He checked his watch. It was just past five o'clock.

"Yeah," he thought out loud, "maybe I should."

His thoughts about Laura kept getting interrupted by replays of his conversation with Wallace. Not only what Wallace had to say to him about Cauldwell. But what he'd said about Laura. What he said about helping to get her the security detail.

"I'm sorry, Alex," he finally answered, "you were asking about my meeting with Wallace?"

She could see he was still distracted.

"It can wait."

"No, no," he insisted, "it was very interesting, maybe more than I first thought."

"What do you mean?"

He paused for a moment and thought about what he was going to say.

"Ok, I know this is gonna sound dumb but, first, before I say anything, whatever I share with you, I have to know you will keep it in the absolute strictest confidence."

"Ok," she said cautiously.

He turned away from the laptop and looked directly at her.

"No, this is really important. If I tell you what I learned today, I need your word that you will not divulge it to anyone. And I mean, anyone!"

"Ok," she repeated a little more slowly, wondering what she was agreeing to.

"If you can agree with that, I will tell you. If you don't think –"

Alex stopped him right there. She stood up and took the couple of steps from the bed to the desk and knelt down in front of him. She reached up and took his face in her hands, her deep, piercing green eyes looking directly into his.

"Jack," she said gently but firmly, "you can trust me. No matter what you tell me, whatever you tell me will be strictly between us. But I would rather you not tell me anything at all than doubt that I'd use it..."

He smiled appreciatively.

She wrapped her arms around his neck and dropped her head against his chest.

"If you have any doubts at all, then don't –"

He stopped her in mid-sentence. He gently straightened her up and looked into her eyes. He brushed aside her hair then retreated and took a deep breath.

"Wallace offered me the chance to come back to the Bureau, with my senior special agent status intact. He'll guarantee me full reinstatement. I'll get my nineteen years back toward my pension. And he promised me complete back pay from the day I got let go."

Alex was duly impressed. But she was a bit surprised he wasn't more excited. As a matter of fact, the more he spoke of Wallace and their conversation, the stranger his voice was sounding. It was like the more he heard himself say it, the more some mysterious pieces were falling into place.

She listened as Jack continued.

"He even said, if I'd prefer, he'd create an internal consulting position for me, an advisory role, to raise the Bureau's visibility on trafficking. He'd create a major task force. I'd report directly to him. I could virtually be my own boss, decide my own direction. I could authorize specific investigations, handle my own press conferences, have access to all the Bureau's resources. Get a chance to do some serious work again."

Suddenly, she began to share his uncomfortable feelings.

"He said he'd put it all in writing, Alex," he said slowly, averting her attention.

What usually sounds to good to be true, she thought.

"As a matter of fact," he continued, "he said he'd put *all* of it in writing…"

Uhhh-huh.

She got to her feet and, without taking her eyes off his, stepped back and sat back down again on the side of the bed.

"Shit, Jack, you drive a hard bargain," she said in a deadpan voice. "I should use you to negotiate my –"

The look in Jack's eyes stopped her from finishing her sentence.

"All I've got to do," he said slowly, deliberately, matter-of-factly, "is kill Marc Cauldwell."

* * *

"Yeah, I just got off the phone with my guy," Raúl told Sandy. Sandy'd never heard him use Estéban's name over the phone. It was always "my guy."

"I want you to start spending some time with him," Raúl said.

"Why?" Sandy asked, resistantly.

"We can talk about this more later," Raúl said, "but he'd asked me a while ago, before this whole mess started, about providing him with a good man he can count on here for some special projects he may have coming up."

"And –" Sandy said.

"And I thought of you," Raúl said. "I think it would be a good thing to get you off the highway circuit for a while and maybe learn a different side of the business. After all, he's well connected and can get you in a few doors."

He's also the biggest asshole I've ever met, Sandy thought.

"Yeah, but the same could be said about you, man," Sandy replied. "Besides –"

"Maybe," Raúl interrupted him, "but I think it might be time for you to have a chance at trying something new. I remember what you said about stepping out on your own. Here's a chance to do that. And with someone I trust."

Trust, my ass, Sandy heard his thoughts respond, *you just don't want to know! You've never wanted to fuckin' know!*

"That's true," Sandy said, telling Raúl want he wanted to hear.

"Well," Raúl said more commandingly, "I want you to do this."

Sandy could not help but feel like he was being fired.

"Now, you got something to write with?"

"Yeah, just a sec," Sandy grabbed a nearby pencil that was nearly worn down to a nub and a section of yesterday's newspaper.

"Okay, go ahead."

Raúl continued.

"The number the priest called was a woman. She's some journalist, which means there might be a whole 'nother angle to this thing."

Sandy listened without interrupting. Raúl *hated* being interrupted.

"She hasn't used any of her own credit cards but an AmEx she's authorized to use rented two rooms at the airport as well as a car Sunday night. She's driving a maroon 2005 Nissan Maxima, a four-door sedan, plate number…"

Sandy wrote as quickly as he could though the combination of the pencil's almost worthless point and the front-page article he was trying to scribble around made legibility wishful thinking.

"What's her name?" Sandy inquired.

"Alejandra Montoneros."

"Ahh," Sandy said, "nice name."

Raúl ignored him then waited a few seconds.

"Sandy," Raúl said almost condescendingly.

"Yeah?"

"Don't you want to know the name on the credit card?"

"Yeah, sure. I was just about to ask."

"It's a corporate card though in name only. Used to belong to her boyfriend."

"Uh-huh."

"The name on the card is TSE Enterprises. The guy's name is Elliot…"

"Oh," Sandy responded, like he'd somehow recognized him, "like the poet."

"What?" Raúl replied impatiently.

"Elliot, like the poet," Sandy explained, "T.S. Eliot."

Silence was the only response. Sandy knew what was coming next.

"Sandy," Raul demanded, "get your fuckin' head in the game, ok?"

Sandy said nothing.

"Get with Carlos and a couple of his friends, no more than two, and get out there. I want them all back here tonight!"

"Got it!"

"And Sandy," Raúl said.

"Yeah?"

Raúl paused for emphasis.

"No mistakes? Ok?"

Before Sandy could respond he heard the phone connection drop.

Sandy flipped his phone shut. He felt flushed, almost humiliated. This was not at all how he wanted things to go. He loved Raúl like a brother. But right now, after that cowardly display, all he wanted to do was to hit something – or someone!

And the last thing he wanted to do was to work for Estéban Sanchez Calderón.

His thoughts predictably rushed toward Teresa. Maybe because things with Raúl had not been going so well. Maybe it was the warm summer nights. More likely, though, he admitted to himself it was something quite different.

Something very personal.

The scene replayed in his mind as vividly as if the intervening years were only minutes. When he saw Caridád lying there, naked, on the kitchen floor, it was Teresa he heard screaming for her life. And when saw Ricky advancing on her, the butcher knife in his hand, it was Estéban who meant to do her harm. He wasn't standing there, in the kitchen, a loaded gun in his hand, with the experience and courage to use it. He was back in their apartment, standing in the doorway of Teresa's room after walking in on her and Estéban. She was curled up on the bed, up against the wall, most of her clothes tossed aside to the floor, a pillow hugged against her chest, demanding through tearful eyes for Estéban to leave. Estéban stood to the side of the bed, his shirt off, his heavy breathing indicative of her resistance, a sarcastic grin across his face. Sandy stood there, not realizing his very presence was deterrence enough. But he said nothing. He did nothing. And Estéban just laughed. He bent down and grabbed his shirt from the floor. He mumbled something about Teresa being a *puta* and forced himself passed Sandy, bumping into him and pushing him against the doorframe. Sandy let him go.

All he saw was Teresa crying.

And all he felt was his heart breaking.

So now, as he thought back on the other evening, remembering standing there in the kitchen, this time in a position to do something about it, he realized it wasn't Caridád he was really protecting. And, afterwards, when he was holding her, trying to comfort her, trying to calm her down, telling her everything would be all right, he wasn't Caridád's hero. And when he heard Miguel screaming at her, watching his rage directed at her, he was back in that goddamned doorway, watching all over again. But this time it was different. Even if this time it was all too late.

Maybe Raúl was right.

Maybe it was time to try something new.

Sandy had found little reason to be reminded of T.S. Eliot, let alone his poetry, for some time. The truth was, without Teresa here to share it with him, he'd simply forgotten about it. The poet's words only held meaning for him insofar as they did for Teresa. And without her here to read them to him, well… All they were good for now was linking him to memories of her. Of how Teresa's feelings for him always came with her clothes on. Of an unrequited love that, with her death, twisted into something almost unrecognizable. Her murder ushered in a dark and difficult time for him. He shut down emotionally. He became self-centered, uncaring and provocative, almost daring the world to fight. And he chose to do without the torment that memories of her – and her reading of his poetry – held for him. Eliot was probably Teresa's favorite poet, which was something noteworthy all by itself. Not many people in their neighborhood were up on their Eliot. It wasn't a high priority where they grew up.

He wouldn't let himself remember that Teresa had a way of making it all seem so interesting, so relevant, that when she'd recite Eliot's words, it was like they were meant for them alone. Or when they'd talk about his poetry, when Sandy'd take the time to listen to her explain the words to him, a whole new way of seeing the world opened up. Most of what she read to him he never really understood. In truth, he only started listening to her read to him because he wanted to hear the sound of her voice. He wanted so much to being the center of her attention. And it was that void – that relentless black hole – that ruthlessly sucked him in, that had left his world reeling as he watched what little purpose his life held crash and burn.

The hole in his heart had been matched only by the vacuum in his soul.

In another place and time, Raúl's idea about working with estimable Mr. Calderón would probably work, maybe even welcomed. But this wasn't another place and time. Sandy had never told Raúl about what he saw that day, what Estéban had done to her. Teresa had made him promise. But, even before that brutal evening, there was nothing about Estéban Sandy liked. Or, for that matter, even respected. To him, guys like Estéban forgot where they'd come from. The neighborhood spawned people like Estéban. The career and the cars, the money and the women, the status and the lifestyle – it was insidious. But it wasn't inevitable. Estéban was a user. Anything he could. Anytime he could. And anybody he could. For him, the neighborhood proved to be an excellent teacher. He used it for what it could gain him in life. And he sought to forget, if not bury, the rest. And that pissed Sandy off. Big time. That Teresa would choose to spend time with Estéban – instead of him – only made matters worse.

From the beginning, Teresa and Estéban never made a good match. Maybe it was Sandy being jealous, who could say? But when you see two people together and there is that special something about them, the way they act with and react to each other, it's that whole "chemistry" thing. Teresa and Estéban never had that. Besides, she was so young when she went out with Estéban. Then, again, she was so young when she died.

When she was murdered.

And that was the thing. The way Estéban behaved after Teresa died. He was different. Not that everyone hadn't been affected by what happened. Certainly the neighborhood had been, probably irrevocably. But Estéban seemed to take Teresa's death almost too personally. And, unlike Sandy, for whom the anger and rage slowly began to permanently alter the course of his life, for Estéban it was much more than that, much more immediate. Estéban handled Teresa's death almost the way Raúl did. That Teresa was Raúl's sister, it was only natural for him to be the way he was. To feel the way he did. To react the way he did.

With Estéban, it didn't seem to make any sense.

Sandy remembered, just before Teresa disappeared, she had decided that she was breaking things off with him, she wasn't going to see him any more. He took it badly. Like she was somehow disrespecting him. Like she should have asked permission. Like the decision who she would spend time with, and how that time would be spent, wasn't hers alone to make. Sandy found Estéban's reaction not only strange but a bit over the top, even for the stud he considered himself to be back then. He'd always thought it more than coincidence, them breaking up and her disappearing so soon afterwards. But no one wanted to believe what Sandy had begun to suspect.

It was easier to hate an outsider.

And, after they found her they way they did, Estéban was right there, comforting Raúl like they were brothers. And when Raúl's work was done – after ensuring that those skinheads had so deservedly reaped what they had apparently so violently sown – and the final body count had been tallied, Sandy seemed to remember that Estéban just up and left town. Estéban's mother told everyone she wanted him to get away from all the violence, to have a chance at a better life. Maybe enlist in the Marines.

So she sent him to live in Denver? Yeah, like that made a lot of sense.

No, there was something weird about it all. Sandy had his suspicions, even danced around the subject once or twice with Raúl some time later. Raúl was not receptive. In his mind, the matter was closed, the issue settled. The offenders had been dealt with. Justice, as the President was wont to say, had been brought to them. That Raúl's stature in the community changed almost overnight as a result seemed incidental.

End of story.

He thought back to the lines of Teresa's favorite poem of Eliot's, *The Hollow Men*. Sandy couldn't remember the verses quite right or even the meter, for that matter. But he recalled how it talked about being among the walking dead, having lost a loved one, of watching a lover cross over into what Eliot called "death's other kingdom." How the poet wondered if she'd remember him, if she still existed at all, not as a lost or violent soul but – and this is the part he couldn't forget – as a "hollow man."

Sandy had found himself lately thinking more often of Teresa and of the years that had passed since she'd died. It tortured him to wonder, when he imagined her watching him now, what she would see, with her eyes of sunlight. Would she see a lost, violent soul, his voice as meaningless as wind in dry grass? Or would she simply see him as sightless, desperately clinging to the hope of empty men? It had come to haunt him.

He was beginning to understand. He had reflectively started asking himself how hollow he'd become, doing what he was doing. How what he'd chosen to be a part of had left his soul hollowed out. Some days he thought about what Teresa would say, if she were here, about the choices he'd made, the things that he'd done. He wondered how proud – or disappointed – she would be of what he was doing, what he'd become. Or hadn't.

Then, again, if she were here today…

He flipped open his phone once more and punched up Carlos' number.

He sniffled. And wiped tears from both his reddening eyes.

* * *

Jack had decided he couldn't wait any longer. They'd been no messages from Laura. No phone contact, no emails. Nothing. Something had happened, what he didn't know. But something *had* happened. And he couldn't sit here any longer.

Alex wanted to go with him and she wouldn't take no for answer. He tried to convince her that he was still formulating a plan, that he wasn't sure what he was going to do, what she should see him do.

She didn't care.

Besides, she'd told him, Father Mac was here. The kids were safe. And the security detail would be arriving soon. She'd only worry about him if she weren't there, watching his back. And it would be great insight for her story! She was only half-kidding about that!

Jack finally, reluctantly gave in.

Father Mac was only too happy to get to spend the evening with the kids. Jack told him to order anything they wanted from room service. He and Alex both gave him their cell numbers. Jack told him they might be back late.

Jack and Alex had nothing to go on but the last place he knew she'd been: FBI headquarters downtown. He grabbed Laura's loaded .45 SIG-Sauer P220 duty-issued service weapon, missing one round, and gave it to Alex to put in her purse. He grabbed the three additional seven round clips and shoved them into his back pocket. They went downstairs, got into her rental car and headed toward the city.

* * *

"Where do you have her?" the caller's voice said

"Right now, you mean?" his lighthearted response came back.

"Is she still safe?" the caller demanded to know.

He shifted in his chair as he swiveled the open laptop on the desk in front of him. A drop-down menu and two mouse clicks later the screen was subdivided into four quadrants, displaying a view of the motel room where the web cams had been strategically placed in each corner. The images of three of his best men keeping watch over Laura streamed in real time.

"For now, yes. She's fine. You worry too much," was the answer, "besides, what difference does it make anyway. After tonight, I mean?"

"Did you have any problem with her?" he was asked.

"No, none at all," he said. "I'm told she offered no resistance. She came quietly. Then again, we really didn't offer her many better options…"

The caller waited for an explanation.

"…She was told her that her life – and the lives of the children – depended upon her cooperation. There was no need to bring Sturdevant into it, at least not yet."

The caller's response was cautious.

"Whatever she knows she can only serve our needs if she remains alive. Once the job is done…" the caller said cryptically, "…then the job is done."

"Not a problem," came the confident response, the nonchalant attitude tossed in at no extra charge. "it's not like I haven't – like *we* haven't – done this before."

He paused a moment, waiting for a reply that obviously wasn't coming.

"I assume I collect my end in the normal manner?"

"You've always been too hasty, my friend," the caller responded, "You really need to take things a little easier, be a little more relaxed."

"Easy for you to say what I –"

"Just shut the fuck up and listen to me."

Silence was the only response.

"Now, eventually he'll figure out she never got back to the building this afternoon. Sturdevant was – and probably still is – an excellent agent. He's smart."

"I can handle him."

This time silence came from the other end of the line.

"Are you finished?" the caller asked.

"Go ahead," he responded.

"Do *not* underestimate him. Just because he's ex-FBI doesn't mean he wasn't *once* FBI. Fuck with him and he will leave you like Katrina left the Gulf. And, if it rains on you –"

"Yeah, we couldn't have that, now could we?" he interrupted.

The sarcasm hung in the air like a cold mist.

"Like I said," he followed-up, "I will handle Sturdevant."

The caller was not reassured.

"Now, once he gets here, how do you want me to handle it?"

"Make it look like a suicide, clean and simple. However you do it, get him back into his house tonight, leave him in his bed or his study or wherever makes sense to you. But get it done. Tonight!"

"And her?"

"Seems to me we have a choice there. I'd prefer nothing fatal happen to her. The fewer the explanations, the better. Perhaps we could keep her for a few days, take our time with her. Dope her up, get her hooked. Then, she could disappear into traffic. And, if she becomes too much trouble, she could easily succumb to an overdose in some back alley somewhere in Tijuana or wherever the fuck she happens to be at the time."

"You've really thought this through."

"I'd prefer not to try to explain a dead agent, yes," the caller repeated.

"Ok, we can work that out," came the affirming response.

"Thank you," the caller said, as if the opinion just expressed to him mattered.

"Just make sure you take Sturdevant out clean," the caller reiterated. "It will be much easier to dismiss him as a suicide. She leaves us with options but, with Sturdevant, there's only one. Keep your cell phone on and make sure it's charged."

"Not a problem," came the reassuring response, "we're good."

"Good... and the gun?"

The caller heard the rack of a slide action Beretta Tomcat 32 Automatic come across clearly over the phone.

"There'll be no mistakes."

"If there are, they'll be your last."

The caller waited a few seconds then punched up one more number. He held the cell phone firmly against his ear in the hall where he stood outside the noisy ballroom. The call connected but no voice immediately answered.

"It's happening tonight. You'll know when it's over."

"Thank you. Call me when it's done."

The call lasted precisely four seconds.

*   *   *

Father Mac somehow heard the knock on the door over the noise the kids were making as their attention was divided between some completely mindless cartoons on cable television and using the one bed as a miniature trampoline. The voice coming from the other side was muffled as he announced their room service order had finally arrived. Dinner this evening consisted of sandwiches, cheeseburgers, lots of French fries and sodas. Father Mac knew they weren't, perhaps, the most balanced meals the kids could have had but, hey, tonight was for having fun. Paying ten dollars for a burger just didn't seem all that important.

He peered through the spy hole then opened the door and welcomed in a young, well-groomed Hispanic man in a white Eton jacket and black bow tie pushing a dinner cart. The kids paid no mind as the young man took each tray off the cart and placed them carefully, in turn, on the small round table near the door. Father Mac checked each dinner to make sure what they'd ordered is what they'd received, then signed the bill after adding a substantial tip. He decided the government could afford giving the young man a little extra. The young man took a moment to look around the room. He saw Ana, Daniel and Caridád enjoying themselves and, besides the priest, he saw no one else.

Just the four of them.

He smiled and nodded as he took the receipt back from Father Mac. He thanked the priest, turned his cart around, and began to leave. The kids yelled goodbye and waved as they bounced on the bed. All that pent up energy and no place to release it.

Father Mac closed and locked the door behind the young man then called everyone over for dinner. And though they all said they weren't hungry yet, he told them it was time to eat, while their dinners are still hot. The kids encircled the table where the trays had been placed.

Ana and Daniel pleaded with Father Mac to take their trays over to the bed so they could watch the television. He reluctantly agreed as long as they sat on the floor, which they obediently did. He and Caridád opted to pull up chairs and eat at the table.

It wasn't long until the inevitable spill occurred. Daniel looked up from the overturned drink and immediately blamed Ana. Father Mac hurriedly got up, grabbed some napkins and moved quickly to help clean up the mess. He heard a knock again at the door as he got to where Daniel had spilled his drink.

"I'll get it," Caridád said as she got up and headed for the door.

Father Mac was handing the napkins to Daniel and Ana when he turned around and told her, "No, Caridád, wait, I'll –"

But it was too late.

As Caridád pushed down on the handle, the door burst opened. Three young Hispanic men entered, none of whom Father Mac recognized. Two were slightly built and younger than the third who followed them, a heavyset young man with a scar across his cheek and down the right side of his face.

Father Mac yelled out to Caridád, who was struggling with the first young man as he forced his way through the open door. Ana and Daniel screamed. The scene quickly turned surreal. Father Mac fought with the second young man through the door and was able to wrestle him to the ground. He shouted to Ana and Daniel to run into the next room and close the door. The kids were screaming, scared and crying. Father Mac yelled again as the second young man fought back. Finally, the priest broke away and grabbed both children and rushed them into the adjoining room.

"Lock the door," he yelled to Ana. *"Now!"*

The second young man grabbed Father Mac again and began hitting him from behind. As the priest turned to defend himself, he heard the sliding deadbolt on the door behind him click into place. He looked back toward the opened front door and tried to shout to Caridád but she was nowhere to be seen. The third, heavyset young man with the scar on his face walked quickly toward the struggling two men.

Father Mac never saw the knife.

Carlos tried the handle on the locked connecting door but it would not turn. He put the full weight of his body up against it, banging into it one time after another, but it would not give. It was not going to open.

Then a single voice called to the assailants from the hallway.

For Father Mac, things went quiet – and dark – after that.

Carlos followed the two young men, dragging a disoriented Caridád, as they hurriedly walked into the service elevator, held open by the young Hispanic man in the white jacket and black bow tie. Carlos peeled off another hundred dollar bill and handed it to him. There'd be three more coming at the end of their elevator ride to the garage level, assuming they were able to reach their car safely.

Caridád was out on her feet, the chloroform having taken effect as quickly as Raúl told Carlos it would. That the kids were left behind was unforesee-able. But Raúl had said they really weren't that important anyway. After all, they were only kids and they were from across the border. What could they know, anyway? And, with all the confusion, what could they remember?

But Raúl's interest in Caridád had taken on a new dimension. Her be-trayal was simply a line no one should cross – no one who'd hoped to die of old age, anyway. He had allowed her to get away once. That mistake was being rectified. Everything that had happened in recent days demanded that Raúl send a message.

And Caridád would make an excellent messenger.

Whether the priest would live, who could say? Not like it mattered all that much.

Carlos got into the passenger side of the car. With Caridád still uncon-scious in the back seat between the two young men, Sandy headed for the street exit. Carlos pulled the five one-hundred dollar bills from his pocket and counted them one more time. They were sticking together, tacky with the remnants of smeared blood not his own.

As they pulled out of the underground parking garage, the young Hispan-ic man in the white Eton jacket and black bow tie lay crumpled and groaning in the corner opposite the far elevator bay, his pressed white shirt, soaked in a thick crimson paste, adhering to his chest. Spurts of blood gushed from the wide, open wound with every labored breath he took with what little strength he had left. With one hand on his stomach, instinctively if hopelessly trying to stop the bleeding, he set the other down in the massing pool of red un-derneath him, trying to steady himself as he bravely fought to get to his feet. As he shifted his weight, his hand suddenly slipped out from beneath him. He collapsed, falling awkwardly on to the cold, concrete floor. He slumped forward onto his side as his eyes rolled back in his head then gradually closed to the world. Now, as his life drained away, all that remained was to wonder whether he would die from the deep slit across his throat or the contents that continued to spill unimpeded from the gaping hole in his abdomen.

The slit won.

* * *

Alex unlocked the driver's side door then shielded her eyes from the brilliant setting sun as she watched Jack hurriedly jog down the wide concrete steps leading from FBI headquarters and head back toward the car.

"No one's seen her all afternoon," he said as he slid in behind the wheel. "At least, no one who's there right now."

She looked down the street of parked cars and wondered what to do next

Jack pulled out his cell phone and called Wallace. It was the only person he could think of that might be able to help. He knew Wallace was attending a dinner this evening at the InterContinental downtown, just over the river on Michigan Avenue but, after their conversation this afternoon, he thought Wallace would pick up.

It went straight to voice mail.

"What about Cauldwell?" she asked.

"He wasn't there," he replied, "and, from what I could gather, he left early today."

"Any idea where?"

"No, none at all."

Alex gave Jack a moment to think. He turned and looked out his driver's side window, desperate for a clue – *any* clue – he could run to ground. He needed to make something to happen, to shake things loose. Who knows how much time Laura had?

Alex reached out and took his hand.

"We'll figure something out, Jack."

He spoke into the window, without even turning toward her.

"I *know* Cauldwell knows something about what's happened to her, probably even where she's at. I fuckin' *know* it!"

His fist landed against the steering wheel.

"I've just to find a way to get to him."

Without even thinking, Alex said something she'd taken for granted.

"Don't you have his number?"

"No," he responded immediately. "I never had any reason to call him so I –"

Alex suddenly squeezed his hand.

"Yes, you do, Jack!"

He felt her grip and turned around to look at her.

"I do?"

"Yes," she said with a broadening smile. "Remember, Friday, when we first met in the park? Just before you asked me to dinner? You got a phone call."

He started to nod his head.

"Wasn't that him? Didn't you tell me that was an FBI guy calling you? That was Cauldwell, wasn't it?"

He smiled as he looked at her beaming face.

"You're a genius!"

He pulled his cellphone from his back pocket and flipped it open. He searched the phone's call history searching for any number with D.C.'s 202 area code, the one assigned for any cell phone issued by the Bureau to all of its field agents. He had to hope Cauldwell had not called him from his office phone. Sure enough, he found the incoming call he received just before five o'clock last Friday afternoon.

A 202 area code.

Technology, Jack thought. *Fuckin'-A.*

He turned to Alex.

"Do you have your cell with you?"

"Of course," she said, thinking him silly for even asking.

"Here, enter this number in your phone." He had an idea.

After she finished punching in Cauldwell's number, Alex looked up and saw Jack grinning.

"How are you at flirting?" he asked, as if he needed her to answer.

She gave him a feigned look of surprise.

"I don't know, Jack," she said, smiling, "why don't you tell me?"

He laughed out loud.

"C'mon, let's get outta here –"

Jack pulled out onto the empty street and did an immediate U-turn, heading east back toward Clark Street.

"Where are we going?" she asked.

He grinned again.

"You're going on a date."

Jack pulled Alex's rented Nissan Maxima into the Kinzie Street parking garage through the Wabash Avenue entrance just after eight o'clock. After listening to how Laura had described her evening last night with Cauldwell, Jack knew Alex would have no trouble at all. So, when they'd gotten a safe distance away from FBI headquarters, he had her call Cauldwell.

She'd introduced herself as the journalist she is and that she was researching an article she was writing for the New York Times Magazine about FBI counterterrorism measures involving domestic al-Qaeda sleeper cells. Though immediately enchanted by the mellifluent voice of a woman who'd fashioned a career persuading men to give her what she wants, Cauldwell listened interestedly for a moment before interrupting her. Dismissing the direction, for the time being, her subtly provocative manner suggested, he reacted firmly but professionally. Before going any further, he'd told her, he wanted to know how she gained access an FBI-issued number and why she'd chosen to contact him.

Alex had learned that the most believable lies are the simplest, the shortest distance being the straightest line. So, she explained that her sources inside the Bureau referred her to Cauldwell, spoke highly of his reputation and his work in cyberterrorism, mentioning that his success in profiling suspected terrorist websites might dovetail nicely with the point-of-view her article was taking. She'd found that Jack's take on Cauldwell was dead-on: once started, the man simply never tired of talking about himself.

Acknowledging his busy schedule, she'd asked if they could meet in the next few days when she could, perhaps, take him to long lunch to get his thoughts. Cauldwell counteroffered with dinner one night this week, leaving Alex to suggest splitting the difference: meeting for drinks this evening? It would give them both a chance to get acquainted as well as help her focus her research for when they sat down together later.

Alex mentioned that she wasn't dressed appropriately, that she'd spent most of the day running errands and was dressed more comfortably for the summer's heat than she ordinarily would be for to meet about her work. She knew he'd taken the bait by the tone in his voice. Cauldwell hardly disguised his curiosity – it was like playing Texas Hold 'em where the other guy's hole cards were showing! It brought to mind that old Billy Crystal line: women need a reason to have sex, men just need a place.

Jack had given her a location – Kavenaugh's on Hubbard near Dearborn, one of a handful of favorite after-hours hangouts for local feds. It was just down the street and a block or so over from the parking garage. Eight o'clock on a Tuesday evening found the parking garage relatively empty. Jack found a spot on the first level. It was accessible by walking up the incoming ramp, allowing Alex to avoid an elevator ride with Cauldwell. Jack pulled into a spot next to an oversized GMC Yukon sports utility vehicle on one side and a Chevy van on the other. He was thinking it might help provide necessary cover as she brought him to her car.

Alex was fashionably late for her 8:00 PM "date." When she'd called him earlier, he was already seated at the bar, which was hardly surprising to Jack. Then again, it did work to their advantage. It served to avoid any issues with Cauldwell's apartment and, having him out in the open, it made him more vulnerable to what Jack had in mind, a plan he was making up as he went along.

He would deal with Cauldwell in his own time.

Jack walked with Alex down the ramp and out of the parking garage across from Trump Tower, then headed north on Wabash. They walked the two blocks to Hubbard Street, where Alex went west two blocks past State Street to Dearborn and the bar. Jack told her if it wasn't happening by 9:30 PM, if he wasn't looking like he was interested enough to leave with her by then, to just cut him loose and walk away. They'd figure something else out. Alex laughed and tossed him a "you're kidding, right?" look.

It wouldn't take nearly that long.

Jack went back and waited on the opposite side of the street from the parking garage. He kept moving all the time he was waiting. He knew the next hour and a half was critical to gaining insight into where Laura was and if she was still alive. Knowing someone had been in her hotel room at the InterContinental made him question why he didn't do more to protect her.

His professionalism saw nothing to forgive. Laura was a big girl, a career federal law enforcement agent. She understood the risks and accepted the realities of the job. Besides, she'd be insulted to think that she needed *anyone* to worry about her or take extra measures on her account. Special Agent Laura Kallinger ran with the big dogs because the tall weeds posed no problem for her at all.

Jack's personal feelings, however, were not nearly so magnanimous.

Just before 9:15 PM, Jack's cell phone vibrated with an incoming text message: "c u n5." Jack felt Laura's service weapon safely secured in the small of his back. He also had one of the extra clips in his back pocket. He meandered around the sidewalk a little north of the garage entrance, blending in with the small crowd coming and going from the Tower. It wasn't long before he spotted them, Cauldwell walking closely and attentively next to her, as they made their way up Wabash toward the garage entrance.

Jack kept his distance as Alex and Cauldwell hurriedly walked into garage and up the ramp. He crossed the street and followed them in. He saw Alex and Cauldwell about seventy-five feet in front of him, up the first level ramp, leading to her rental car. When she realized Cauldwell was anxious to get her into the car, she slowly took his face in her hands and kissed him. Long and slow, full of expectation. Cauldwell was mesmerized.

She'd delivered just as promised.

After what seemed like an interminable moment later, she stepped backwards and made eye contact with Jack coming up the ramp. She then turned and took Cauldwell by the hand, taking him with her into the space between the passenger side of her car and the SUV parked next to them. Alex pressed the Maxima's remote access button, unlocking the front doors, then stepped forward and stood in front of Cauldwell as he reached around her to open the front passenger side door. Cauldwell grinned as he pulled up on the door handle, already rethinking his morning schedule, deciding how he could juggle his appointments and how late he could get to work. His grin widened as he imagined the pleasure that awaited him. Right up to the moment he heard the hammer's click of Laura's .45 caliber service weapon nuzzled firmly against the side of his jaw.

Cauldwell's thought he was being mugged.

"Take whatever you want, I've got money."

Then he noticed Alex smiling.

"I don't want your fucking money, dumbass," Jack replied.

Cauldwell recognized the voice but couldn't believe it.

"Sturdevant?" he asked, trying to turn his head around.

Jack pressed the muzzle of the gun forward.

"Uh, uh, uh," Jack replied, "hands on the car, Cauldwell, feet back and spread 'em. You know the drill."

As Cauldwell obeyed, Jack leaned to one side to see Alex wipe off her mouth.

Jack suddenly felt his cell phone vibrating. He turned to Alex with a surprised look and, with his weapon still resting firmly against Cauldwell's jaw, he reached into his back pocket then glanced at the phone's call window. An unidentified number appeared. And though he didn't recognize it, he noticed it was local. He handed the phone to Alex and asked her to take the call.

Jack shoved Cauldwell forward then started to roughly pat him down.

Alex flipped open the phone and quietly said hello.

"I have a message for Jack Sturdevant…"

* * *

The Monsignor John Stuart Miles welcomed FBI Deputy Director L. Stephen Wallace into his home after another political fundraiser for which the Mayor would be deeply indebted. Wallace, a former deputy superintendent for the Chicago Police Department during the almost three-decade reign of the Mayor's father, realized last week he would be able to attend and informed the Mayor's office that he would, indeed, be making room in his schedule.

It had been a sparkling event held at the InterContinental's Renaissance Ballroom this evening. Celebrities from around town as well as dignitaries from the world of state and local politics gathered to help raise money for one of the Mayor's pet projects, that being his learn-through-literacy campaign. The Monsignor had offered a stirring and eloquent invocation before dinner, taking the opportunity to display a piety generally reserved for more solemn occasions. Funds raised this evening would go to support activities throughout the city to buy books and other reading materials toward supplementing local libraries. The evening was also dedicated to honoring those volunteers who donate their time and efforts in the city-sponsored tutoring and mentoring programs as well as private corporations who contributed financially to its success.

The Deputy Director had asked the Monsignor to allow him to give the prelate a ride home from this evening's event, an offer the he graciously if not somewhat suspiciously accepted. On the short ride back to his Dearborn Parkway mansion, the Monsignor entertained questions from Wallace about the priest's upcoming travel plans, whether he was thinking of getting away anytime soon on vacation and if he had any thoughts about traveling abroad, maybe Europe or South America. The Monsignor politely deflected his queries, mentioning how busy things were and much work there was to do, particularly with a new school year just about to begin, and how the Mayor had him involved in a couple of special consulting projects. Any time away at this point, revealed the priest, would be fairly short in nature and undoubtedly local. Maybe a getaway to a family summer home in Wisconsin or perhaps a long weekend to Michigan. But that would be about it.

Wallace seemed oddly disquieted.

Upon arriving at his home and getting settled a bit, the Monsignor offered Wallace a glass of cognac, which the Deputy Director politely accepted. As they sat down in the lower level family room, Wallace checked the time. They had just taken their first sip when he rose for his chair and excused himself.

"I'm terribly sorry, John," Wallace said, "– may I call you, John?"

The Monsignor nodded his approval. Wallace continued.

"As I was saying, John, I'm very sorry but I need to make an important phone call and the battery on my cell phone is running low."

"Of course," the Monsignor responded, "my den is just upstairs, first door on the right. It should be open. Make yourself at home. Take whatever time you need."

"Thank you, John," the Deputy Director said, "I'll be just a moment."

The Monsignor smiled then directed a careful eye toward Wallace as he walked up the few steps out of the family room then turn the corner and ascended the stairs toward the study. Wallace closed the door to the room behind him then removed the cordless phone from the cradle attached to the wall. He pulled a thin cylindrical device, smaller than the size of a pen with a small clip at one end, from his inside jacket pocket. He listened for the phone's dial tone, then clicked the device once, illuminating a thin red light. He attached the device on the short antenna extending from the phone's cradle.

He dialed Jack's number and watched as the red light turned to green.

Four rings later, just ahead of going to voice mail, Wallace was surprised to hear a female voice respond to his call.

"I have a message for Jack Sturdevant," he said quietly.

"Ok," Alex responded with tentative surprise.

"If you're still looking for Special Agent Laura Kallinger, find Marc Cauldwell," Wallace said, "and he'll take you to see Detective Robert Colavito."

He disconnected his call and returned the cordless phone to its cradle then place the voice alteration device back into his jacket pocket. He pulled out his cell phone and punched up one more call, this one with a D.C. area code.

The call connected though no voice answered again.

"I spoke with him this evening. He has no travel plans for the foreseeable future."

"We shall see," was the voice's response.

The call lasted precisely four seconds.

Alex took Jack's phone slowly from her ear and looked strangely at him. He still had Cauldwell assuming the position up against the side of the car.

"Alex," he said, noticing her oddly standing there, "you ok?"

She nodded in response.

"Jack, you didn't recognize that phone number?"

Jack looked puzzled.

"No. Why?"

"It was a man on the phone. He was a little hard to understand. But he said that if you're still looking for Laura, you should have your friend here take you to see someone detective named Robert Colavito."

"What?" Jack asked.

"I don't know, Jack, that's what he said. I don't get it but that's what he said."

"Ok," Jack said, "what *exactly* did he say?"

"His precise words were 'if you're still looking for Special Agent Laura Kallinger, find Marc Cauldwell and he'll take you to see Detective Robert Colavito.'"

Jack looked at Cauldwell and realized he'd struck gold.

He looked back at Alex and smiled.

"You're sure that's exactly what he said?"

"Absolutely," she replied.

He turned his attention to Cauldwell, who now felt Laura's gun against the base of his neck.

"Ok, Special Agent Cauldwell, tell me about your detective friend."

Cauldwell just laughed.

"You ain't getting shit from me, Jack. You won't shoot me, especially here, in a public place. You won't assault a federal agent. You're too smart for that."

Jack turned to Alex. He'd seen that's same smile earlier in the evening.

He spun Cauldwell around and faced him, his left forearm pressing just beneath Cauldwell's chin as he held the gun against the side of his head.

"You know what, Cauldwell, you're right."

Jack stepped to one side as Alex walked up to Cauldwell. Her hand suddenly appeared from a small purse hanging loosely from her shoulder. With one swift and smooth motion, she shoved her personal defense stun gun in Cauldwell's groin.

And pulled the trigger.

She pulled away as Cauldwell cried out and immediately collapsed.

Jack quickly stood him up, keeping him from falling to his knees.

"Where is Robert Colavito?"

Cauldwell couldn't catch his breath. The pain was almost more than he could bear. He felt his stomach twisting in knots, turning inside out. His eyes were tearing up when they weren't feeling like jumping out of his head. He was dazed, bordering on numb. The world spun all around him.

"I don't know where he is," Cauldwell mumbled, trying desperately to conserve his breaths, "I swear, I don't." He was on the verge of crumpling to the ground.

Jack wouldn't give up.

"But you know how to contact him, don't you?"

Cauldwell kept leaning forward, against Jack, praying that the vertigo would stop.

Jack pushed him back again.

"Don't you?"

His head dropped backwards and his eyes rolled around.

Jack turned to Alex.

"Alex, care to try again?"

She grinned widely. Cauldwell begged Jack not to let her near him.

"I'll only ask you one more time, Special Agent Cauldwell. Do you know how to reach Detective Robert Colavito?"

Cauldwell's groaning was his only response.

Jack turned to Alex.

"Hit him again," he said succinctly.

Jack stood him up as she approached him again. This time, she raised the stun gun to eye level and pulled the trigger before she touched him. For the moment, the blue electrical current danced harmlessly between the two small, extended metal prongs. Cauldwell's eyes grew large, his knees giving way in anticipation of the pain. He started falling forward before she could hit him with another 100,000 volts.

"No," Cauldwell yelled out, his voice echoing throughout the empty garage. He started to double over to defend himself. "Noooooo!"

"Go fuck yourself," she said demanded.

She stepped back as Cauldwell fell forward. Jack grabbed him and pushed him backwards against the car then forced him upright.

Still trying to catch his breath, Cauldwell broke.

"We have to get to my car," he said, trying to speak. "My laptop's in my car."

Jack smiled sinisterly as he looked back to Alex.

"Who says torture doesn't work?"

She smiled back, glad to be of service.

"Why?" Jack asked forcefully, focusing his attention on Cauldwell and his laptop.

"I have a computer program that tracks his cell phone," he said in between swallowing. "If he's got her, it's because he's working on instructions. And he'll have his cell phone on."

"Who's instructions?" Jack said. He grabbed him by the collar with one hand while shoving the gun's muzzle up under his chin.

"I don't know," he cried out, "How the fuck should I know?"

Jack had trouble imagining it was a trick though he doubted Cauldwell didn't know who'd wanted Laura taken. Decision trees lit up in Jack's brain as he considered the very real possibility that the reason Laura had gone missing was not so much an incentive to remove her from the equation as it was an effort to force Jack to make his play. And he couldn't get his conversation with Wallace out of his mind. If his training had taught him nothing else, it was that, in investigations, there were no such things as coincidences.

But right here, right now, there were no options: he had to do whatever he could to get Laura out of harm's way. Assuming, of course, she was still alive. But whoever was responsible for making all of this happen, he'd revealed something very important about himself: Whoever he was, he believed he had a decided advantage over Jack.

The call to his cell phone, the one about the detective, indicated that much.

"Where's home?" he demanded of the disoriented Cauldwell.

Cauldwell had trouble talking. He felt like he was going to vomit.

"Printer's Row, south Loop. My driver's license. It's in my wallet."

Alex reached around Cauldwell and found his wallet in his back pants pocket. She opened it, pulled out his license and showed it to Jack.

Jack skimmed it quickly. "Ok," he said. "Pop the trunk, would you, Alex?"

A push of the remote brought a click from the back of the car as the trunk rose slowly in response. Alex closed his wallet and shoved it in her purse.

"Let's go for a ride, Special Agent Cauldwell."

Jack pulled Cauldwell along with him as Alex walked around them and raised the trunk hood the rest of the way. He stumbled taking each step gingerly, his legs refusing to work, his stomach still knotted in pain, his eyes rolling in his head.

"In you go," Jack said.

"Jack, wait!" Alex said quietly but hurriedly.

He looked up to see her anxious expression then turned to notice the lone figure – the owner of the SUV, a muscular, rugged, outdoorsy type, maybe in his early-to-mid thirties – walking up the ramp towards them. Jack shoved the gun into his waistband against his lower back then pulled a still groaning Cauldwell into a tight, secure embrace. Alex comfortably trained her gaze on the approaching stranger's steady, deliberate stride.

Handsome. Athletic. A few unshaven days of attractive, almost sexy, dark beard growth. A burnt red baseball cap. Asolo hiking boots.

And ocean blue eyes.

She took his square shoulders for a boxer. Or maybe the martial arts. Something about him reminded her of a young Jimmy. Or maybe it was wishful thinking.

"Everything ok?" he asked in the modest voice that completed the package.

Alex jumped in as if on cue.

"Yeah, no, ummm… My boyfriend over did it. He's not feeling very well."

Just then, Jack noticed Cauldwell was acting like he was going to vomit. He pulled him around to the driver's side and let him drop to his knees.

"See what I mean?" she said sheepishly.

Their uninvited guest didn't seem to hear a word she said. He tilted the bill of his weathered cap back up off his forehead as his engaging smile spoke of his noticeable interest.

Jack rolled Cauldwell over and pulled out his car keys then opened the back door. He shoved him inside and, as Cauldwell groaned, slumping forward across the back seat, he closed the door behind him.

He then walked back around the car and carefully closed the trunk lid.

"He'll be fine, thanks," she continued, "we don't have far to go."

Her new friend nodded. Alex smiled. Jack waited.

The moment dragged on as they all traded looks.

"Uh, sis," Jack finally interjected, "shouldn't we be getting him home?"

Alex stepped back into reality.

"Well, I gotta go, I guess," she said, almost reluctantly. "My brother's, uhhh…"

The rugged stranger just smiled back and offered to help Alex into the car. He held the passenger car door for her, closing it behind her after she'd slid in. She smiled to thank him. Jack started the car then raised an eyebrow as he shot Alex "the look."

Alex returned a *"What?!?!"* of her own.

As he backed out of the parking spot, Alex smiled again and waved as the equally courteous and smitten stranger watched them pull away. Jack noticed the late model black Toyota Four-Runner he was getting ready to open had replaced the GMC Yukon that had been there when they'd arrived. And the darkened, smoke-tinted windows all around.

And the government plates.

A couple of down ramps and thirty dollars later they were back on the street, southbound, heading toward Cauldwell's apartment building. Alex pulled out Cauldwell's driver's license again and entered the address into the car's GPS system. Jack figured they were only a few minutes away. He was right.

Alex reached over and gently touched Jack's leg. He responded by covering her hand with his. At the first red light, he turned and looked at her

"You did good, sweetie."

She smiled in response.

"That was nothing, Jack. I didn't even have to bring my "A" game with him…"

Jack just shook his head.

"Not with him!" she said, thinking he meant the rugged stranger.

Then she laughed. "You expected less?"

Jack just grinned and shook his head.

"No, not really," he replied. "But, knowing you as I do, I never had any doubts."

Alex reached into her purse and pulled out a pack of sugarless gum. Jack grinned as he declined her offer.

"Then again, I wasn't the one who had to kiss him," he said with a smile.

She nodded and squeezed his hand. And as he made his way through the downtown traffic, she wondered all the same what she'd gotten herself into.

The black Four-Runner idled quietly in its parking spot as its driver sat invisibly inside the privacy of its opaque glass. He opened his cell phone and punched up a number in the 202 area.

"They just left. They have him. What would you like me to do?"

He listened carefully to the answer.

"No, he wasn't in good shape but they need him alive, so –"

He waited for his instructions.

"Very good, sir. I'll take care of it."

Bobby flipped his phone shut and tossed it into the empty leather seat beside him.

*   *   *

Chapter 17

ALEX STUDIED THE blinking cursor carefully. Cauldwell's laptop had proven much more difficult to get their hands on than he'd led them to believe. It wasn't in his car, as he'd told them. It was in his apartment. And his building, unfortunately, had a doorman.

It was time to improvise again.

Cauldwell had told them where to find his car, what level of the parking garage it was on and what numbered spot to look for. Jack parked their car on the street across from Cauldwell's apartment and waited while Alex went to search Cauldwell's car. She took Cauldwell's keys, looked everywhere in the car she could, and returned with the bad news. Jack pulled around the corner and found meter parking on the street. Alex was not surprised he had no quarters on him, so she "offered" once again as long as he promised to pay her back. It brought a smile to his face.

Together, they helped Cauldwell from the back seat. They decided they would both help Cauldwell into the lobby of his building and tell the doorman that he was ill, that they were friends of his out for the evening with him and that they were helping him up to his apartment. But once Cauldwell was on his feet again and began regaining his balance, he started showing signs that he was recovering from having his introduced to Alex's stun gun.

So, just to play it safe, it gave her great pleasure to acquaint them once more. Cauldwell played his part perfectly. He looked horrible, like he had a particularly vicious strain of the Asian flu. He groaned with each step. He was pale and weak, like he'd spent the last hour vomiting. Alex and Jack convincingly helped him into the lobby and past the doorman. Once they were safely in the elevator, Jack winked at Alex.

"No need, Jack," she responded, "I'm enjoying every minute of this."

After entering his apartment, they helped a still-wobbly Cauldwell onto the couch in his living room and went about searching his place. Jack found his laptop plugged into a wall outlet sitting on a solid oak kitchen table in a small dining room. Thankfully, it was a Windows operating system. He began searching quickly though both the desktop icons and directory folders before realizing he'd found what they needed. He noticed an open icon: Cauldwell had been IM'ing with someone recently.

It was communication that may prove helpful later.

Alex found the backup battery fully charged still standing in the charging unit. She realized they'd need an inconspicuous way of leaving the building with both Cauldwell and his laptop.

She had an idea. She went to the back of his apartment and searched his bedroom. She opened a dresser drawer and grabbed the first clothes she found, tossing them on the king-size bed behind her. As she closed the drawer, she noticed a backpack on a chair in the corner. As she reached across to grab the backpack, she stepped on a white tee-shirt lying on the floor. She bent down and picked it up.

It appeared clean and relatively new. It sported "EMU" for his alma mater, Eastern Michigan University, in large, green Roman letters. The profile of its mascot, a bald eagle named "Swoop," strutted across the letters in a fighting stance, his chest arrogantly puffed out to match his defiantly confident expression. She laughed thinking of how it resembled Cauldwell without hair. All that was missing were those god-awful red bushy eyebrows of his. She stuffed it in the backpack along with the other clothes and went to find Jack.

Jack was waiting with Cauldwell's computer and the extra battery. He stuffed them both into the backpack and covered them up with Cauldwell's clothes. Though it was a bit heavy, Jack asked Alex to wear the backpack thinking her green eyes and new highlights would make the doorman much less likely to notice it.

When they went to help Cauldwell off the couch, she noticed a growing, red bump on his forehead.

"What happened to lover boy?" she asked.

Jack grinned.

"He tried to sit up and fell right over. He banged his head on the coffee table."

Alex looked at him sideways.

"Hey," Jack said in his defense, "I'm not the one with the stun gun!"

"At least it matches his hair!" she said.

They laughed as they got Cauldwell to his feet and headed for the door.

They knew bringing him with them created certain risks. But he left them little choice. He might still prove valuable to them. And killing him wasn't an option.

At least until Laura was freed.

As the three of them exited the elevator, the doorman noticed Cauldwell had a big bump on the side of his forehead. Alex told him the still-groaning Cauldwell had slipped and fallen in his weakened condition and that they'd decided to get him to an emergency room right away. When she noticed the doorman eyeing the backpack Jack was wearing, she told him that they were bringing along a change of clothes just in case Cauldwell illness required he get admitted. The doorman commented on how lucky Cauldwell was to have such good and caring friends.

Cauldwell had been right. Bobby's cell phone was on and the software's tracking mechanism had him in a south side neighborhood maybe thirty minutes southwest.

Jack turned the computer in Alex's lap and immediately recognized the area.

"Alex," he said, "I know that neighborhood. I've been there before."

"What? Where?"

Jack looked carefully at the streets on the grid map surrounding the blinking cursor to make sure.

"That's where I found Caridád," he said. "I'm sure of it!"

"Seriously?"

"Yeah, Ana and Daniel showed me where it was. We were here during the daytime but I'm certain this is the place."

Alex waited for a moment.

"Is that a good thing, Jack?"

He smiled.

"Yeah, I'm thinking it is."

They'd been driving only a few minutes when Alex took a moment to minimize the tracking software and began looking over the couple dozen or so icons displayed against the background wallpaper on Cauldwell's desktop display. One in particular jumped out at her. She double-clicked on it and, seconds later, a large document file appeared. It appeared to contain text conversations, probably imported from another software program, which were separated and organized by military time within date. Cauldwell was nothing if not anal.

Another reason he would have made a great Nazi, she thought.

As she began reading through the file, she realized it contained transcripts of phone conversations. The file was formatted to display changes and reference points made in the margins by Cauldwell. Detective Bobby Colavito was identified by name, initially in Cauldwell's notes he'd made in the margins. The detective was the only name indicated. Only their phone numbers identified all other parties unless a name would appear in the text translation of their conversation.

As Alex scrolled through the document, she began to notice Carmen's name appearing in Cauldwell's notes in the margins. Then, she came upon the reference Bobby made to "the Fed bitch" and where the person he was talking to spoke of the "the FBI lady." From his notes, Alex suddenly realized Cauldwell had concluded that Detective Colavito was either involved in Carmen's murder or, at the very least, knew something about it. And the text of the conversation she was reading implied both Colavito and the person he was talking with had specific knowledge of her death.

Alex couldn't believe it. She felt flushed, almost embarrassed. She started to say something to Jack then stopped. He noticed something was wrong.

"Alex?" he asked, "You ok?"

She didn't respond.

"Did you find something?" he asked.

She swallowed hard and tried to disguise her look. She quickly decided this was not the time to say anything. She tried to overcome her sudden nervous feelings. If what she'd stumbled on was true, there was no way Jack wouldn't beat everything he could out of Cauldwell. And he wouldn't stop until he'd found – and killed – Bobby Colavito, detective or not. The transcripts Cauldwell had recorded, and the notes he'd made, might well be the key to everything that's been happening. But as much as she wanted to tell him, she couldn't find the words.

And her instincts were telling her not to.

She hadn't noticed Jack reaching across for her until she felt his hand on her leg. She jumped as he startled her.

"Are you ok?" he asked. "You look as though you've just seen a ghost!"

She flashed an awkward smile.

"No, I'm fine…"

"It won't be long now," Jack said.

He couldn't know how right he was.

Jack was right about the intersection, the one at Halsted and 18th Street. It was where he'd first found Ana and Daniel in the street, fighting for their lives. Where he'd been driving, quite by accident that Saturday afternoon, all in a vain attempt to avoid the congestion on the outbound expressway. So much had happened since then. It seemed so much longer than just three days ago. And it was because of Ana and Daniel that he was able to rescue Caridád. And, of course, none of it would have been possible if it hadn't been for Father Mac. Meeting him there was…

Shit! Father Mac!

He turned a worried expression toward Alex.

"Damn, Alex," he exclaimed. "We forgot about Father Mac. He's still there with the kids!"

She looked up from the laptop.

"What can we do about it now? Should we call him?"

He thought for a long moment. His eyes jumped to the dashboard clock.

"No, it's late. He probably decided to stay the night. At least I hope he did. I know he wouldn't leave the kids alone."

"Besides," she agreed, "he has our cell numbers if he needed to contact us."

Yeah, you're right," he replied, looking for a reason to believe the priest was the least of his worries right now. "He probably took our room."

Jack looked at Alex, took her hand and smiled.

"Yeah," she said, "probably."

As they drove through the neighborhood, Jack noticed an all-night convenience store.

He had another idea.

* * *

Raúl wasn't expecting to hear from Estéban this late in the evening.

"*Hermano, como está?*"

Estéban was apologetic for calling so late.

"No worries, my friend, what can I do for you?"

"I have an important guest, Raúl, who is interested in entertaining someone very special for tomorrow evening. Though he has somewhat unorthodox tastes."

Raúl didn't need to know anymore. But he asked just the same.

"For example…"

"Well," Estéban continued, "the last two young ladies he was with disappointed him. From what he told me, they seemed resistant to what, perhaps, someone with less discriminating taste might consider a more rigorous evening's entertainment."

"I see," Raúl responded.

"What can I tell him, my friend?"

"Tell him," Raúl said slowly, "that the young one I have for him will not disappoint him."

"Ahh, thank you, *hermano*," Estéban said.

"And, Estéban," Raúl said in closing.

"Yes, my friend?"

"When he is finished with her, for however long he chooses to keep her…"

"Yes?"

"…do with her what you will. I will not be wanting her back."

"I see," Estéban replied, "if she works out for my client, perhaps I can find a place for her.'

Raúl paused for a long moment.

"That is up to you," Raúl said cryptically, "if she does or does not, it is no longer my concern. If she can make you money, so be it. If not –"

Estéban took a moment.

"I understand, *amigo*, consider it taken care of."

Neither Raúl's expression or his tone changed.

"Thank you, my friend."

"No," Estéban countered, "thank you."

"I'll have her at the regular spot at six," Raúl told him.

"Until then, *hermano*," Estéban said.

"Until then," Raúl responded.

Raúl snapped his phone shut.

The new safe house was an original one-story colonial Cape Cod that had experienced a renovation as well the addition of a family room and a third bedroom at the back of the house. The resulting design created a circular effect in the home. Where Raúl now stood in the kitchen, he could walk through the family room, follow around to his left into the back bedroom, continue through that room into a middle bedroom and exit that room into a small hallway. At that point, to his left, was the house's only bathroom, to his right, the master bedroom. Walking forward would bring him into the living room. Continuing the circular tour, around to his left, would bring him back where he started, the kitchen.

The house had three outside entry doors. The front door led into the living room. It stood at the end of a short walkway that connected the house to the driveway and served to frame the small lawn that covered the area between the house and the sidewalk. One side door, off the blacktop driveway, allowed direct entry into the kitchen. And a third door, off the back patio, led directly into the family room. A cracked and crumbling cement patio separated the back of the house from the detached one-and-half car garage.

He walked from the kitchen through the family room and toward the back bedroom where he pushed aside a sliding wooden door that disappeared into the wall to his right. The connecting door to the middle bedroom, located about ten feet to his left from where he stood, was closed.

Four of Raúl's more seasoned associates stood guard in the dim glow of the room's only lamp. Caridád was seated near the far corner of the room, her arms and legs bound to a wooden chair, her eyes covered by a black bandana wrapped tightly across her forehead that blanketed her face.

He motioned to the young men and they immediately followed one another out of the room. He stopped the last one in line and spoke to him in a whisper. A moment later he left, sliding the door closed behind him, leaving Raúl alone in the room with her. He walked slowly toward her, dragging a second ladderback chair with him. He pulled it up next to her and spun it around, sitting down in it backwards. The worn wooden joints creaked unstably as he crossed his arms across the top slat and slowly leaned forward.

"When will you tell me what I want to know?" he said softly, knowing better.

She turned her head toward the sound of his voice.

"There is nothing to tell, Raúl," she insisted, "I can't tell you what I don't know."

Her tone was strong though unmistakably tinged with the anticipation of her fate.

Raúl tenderly placed his open hand against the side of her face. She immediately jumped, reacting to his unexpected touch.

"Caridád," he asked gently, "who are these people that turned you against me?"

He looked at her carefully, waiting for an answer he again knew wasn't coming. But he asked nonetheless.

"And this man – this FBI agent, the one who took the girl and the boy, who puts you up in such expensive hotel rooms, the one who is killing my men and disrespecting me so openly – who is this man to you?"

Raúl took back his hand and stood up next to her, pulling the chair out from under him. She turned her head and faced forward, unwilling to compromise the man who'd already rescued her once, whose bare hands had snapped Miguel's neck and spared her from any more of his cruel degradation, the man she'd been begging Jesus to send her one more time. But, no matter how this evening would end, she would tell Raúl nothing. Whatever path it took, she'd decided to face what he had in mind for her in silence.

There was no way she could know the tortuous agony her silence would mean.

It was now her turn to keep Jack safe. And though she'd prayed, when her time came it would come swiftly, maybe even mercifully, her years spent with Raúl watching him time after time settle things with those he believed had betrayed him spoke to a completely different experience.

She'd seen firsthand just how creative – and sadistic – his imagination could be.

He paced slowly in front of her.

"I want to know about this man, Caridád. I know it is late and we are both very tired. So, the sooner you tell me what I want to know, the sooner we can both put an end to this silliness."

Caridád showed no reaction at all. She just continued to pray silently.

"Now, what could be more fair than that, hmmm?"

Caridád remained silent. Raúl let out a noticeable sigh.

"You will talk to me, Caridád," he said resolutely. "I promise you that much."

His passion for her had dissolved in the acid of her betrayal.

"The longer you convince yourself otherwise, the more uncomfortable it will be."

Caridád took a deep breath, raising her square shoulders. She exhaled nervously.

Raúl waited a few more seconds.

"As you wish," he said and turned, walking toward the door. And though she'd wanted so desperately to brave, Caridád quietly began to cry.

As she trembled.

Raúl called out in response to the soft knock on the closed entry door. It made a distinctive sound as it slid open, allowing four sets of footsteps to return. Two of them passed by him as they walked directly over to her, untying her from the chair. They pulled off her blindfold but left her ankles bound together as well as her hands tied behind her. They stood her up and shoved her chair to one side then forced her to the floor on top of a flat, oval solid base plate made of inch-and-a-quarter thick red oak, about the size of a fireplace grate. She was shoved forward into a tight crouching position, her arms pinned against her sides. Her knees burned from rubbing across the lacquered wood while two sets of hands positioned her, holding her in place. A third man standing in front of her lowered his knee against the top of her back, just below her neck.

She exhaled hard as she strained to resist his overwhelming strength. She scraped her chin against the floor as two large hands forced her head against her chest and back into her knees, compressing her into the smallest possible space her body could occupy.

Raúl nodded in approval as the fourth young man brought the remaining two parts of the medieval torture device over to those holding her in place. Each was handed an inch-and-a-quarter thick wooden semi-circular bow, about three inches wide, which were originally milled to fit the thickness of the oak base. They were secured to the plate with open compression fittings that snapped firmly into place. Each bow was then bent across her flattened back until the two arches met above her. At the top of what now resembled a wishbone, short extensions rising from the two wooden bows were brought flush to one another. The two young men held the pieces in place while a third inserted a large, threaded dowel rod through the aligned openings. He then attached wooden nuts, one on each end, and spun them toward one another until the wishbone's extensions were snuggly connected.

Caridád couldn't swallow; she could barely inhale. She was unable to make a sound. It took just seconds for the pain to begin. Her lower back, curved and frozen in place, had already begun to spasm. The same was true of the pain climbing up her thighs and calves. Her shoulders were tightening up, as was the base of her neck. She couldn't catch her breath. In fact, she could hardly breathe at all. She felt the pressure building in her head, the throbbing in her neck, as her blood flow immediately began to restrict. She felt like she was going to black out.

Raúl motioned to one of the young men to take a seat then walked over and bent down next to Caridád. He ran his hand across the smooth finish of one side of the wishbone that the constructed device formed. He wrapped his fingers around it and tried to shake the frame. It was solid. It wasn't going anywhere. The wonder of this device – the ingenious simplicity behind the almost inconceivable torture it was engineered to inflict – was found in the efficiency of its design that displayed the single-minded nature of its purpose. And that purpose had not changed since the sixteenth century days of Henry the VIII: to prevent anyone confined within its grip from moving. And, ultimately, if left in it long enough, from breathing.

"I received this device as a gift from a very good friend of mine, someone I've known since I was a child." Raúl said softly to her over the sounds of her struggle. "He himself had received it as a gratuity, a souvenir of sorts from a client he did some work for in Colombia, in Cali. It seems this client was interested in finding a very special way of repaying those who had betrayed him. My friend was instrumental in discovering who those people were."

Caridád tried taking smaller breaths but the spasms in her lungs wouldn't allow it.

Raúl continued.

"In gratitude, his client had this device handcrafted for him by a local woodsmith, a cabinetmaker by trade. He found that this device was popular long ago, during the Middle Ages. It's called 'the Scavenger's Daughter.' An odd name, don't you think? It was invented by a man named Skevington. He was responsible for helping 'guests' of the King who resided in the Tower of London to remember certain things, maybe motivate them to confess their crimes against their host. And some of his guests could be quite obstinate. But my friend found that as old as the idea for this device was it remained a very effective means of obtaining information."

He placed his hand on her head and stroked her wet, matted hair. Her muscles were convulsing. She was sweating profusely. Her eyes, bulging from the increase in her blood pressure, burned from sweat and tears.

"My friend told me that his client saved this special treat for people he had once considered his friends, Caridád, people whom he had trusted, who he had shared his life with and the profits from his business, who he had counted on to be there for him. People to whom he had gone to for support and advice, perhaps even guidance, some who shared his most intimate secrets."

He wondered how long she could last. He found her vulnerability amusing.

"You should know, Caridád, that, at some point, you will feel blood begin to trickle from your ears, your nose, maybe your mouth and, eventually, even from the corners of your eyes. The discomfort you feel now is nothing compared to what you will feel five minutes from now. And, that, nothing compared to the five minutes after that."

Caridád was unable to speak. Her anguish was beyond anything she could have imagined.

"You see, the wonder of this device is that it will not leave a single mark on you. Yet the pain that awaits you will be greater than anything you could believe possible."

He waited a moment and decided now was time.

"You know, your sister, Maria," he started, "she knew something about pain."

Caridád struggled to turn her head toward him. It was the first time she'd ever heard Raúl speak of Maria.

"Apparently, you have a lot in common with her. It seems, like you, she felt it was important to tell people about what she knew, about what she saw, probably thinking she would eventually find her way out, maybe even find you, and somehow leave me."

Caridád tried to concentrate over the pain, hardly believing what she was hearing.

"Sadly, though, with her," he continued, "we were not able to find out what she'd said, though she did eventually lead us to the man that she'd been talking to."

Caridád tried to talk but her words "what did you do to her?" were hardly audible.

"Too bad, really," Raúl feigningly conceded, running his hand again over her head, "she had so much potential, your sister. It really was such a shame…"

He took out his cell phone and pulled up the video Carlos had taken in the parking garage stairwell on that warm and muggy July Chicago evening, more than four years ago. He opened the file, turned up the volume and set the phone down in front of her.

"Here," he said caustically, "maybe something to help you pass the time…"

As Raúl rose to his feet, he thought he heard Caridád summon the strength for a "you bastard!" He laughed, shaking his head as he turned and walked toward the door. He nodded to the young man seated across from the open door.

"I'll be back in a few minutes."

The young man nodded and sat back in the chair that Caridád once occupied.

She'd always believed in Maria's presence. She felt her there, despite everything she'd been through. And she somehow believed, despite the years that had passed, that one day they'd see each other again. Images and memories of her sister competed with the waves of unbearable pain now made even more tortuous by knowing she was gone.

She wanted to give up. She prayed that Jesus would take her now. That He would spare her the ordeal that only grew greater with each passing second. She begged Him for compassion. She recited The Lord's Prayer, over and over again, until she could no longer concentrate, her thoughts succumbing to the almost indescribable agony.

But the only name that escaped her lips was Jack's.

* * *

Jack drove slowly into the back alley he remembered using to bring Caridád to safety. He pulled into a short driveway to turn the car around then parked across a concrete walkway near one of the many garages that lined the alleyway. They were only a matter of yards from the safe house. Alex closed the laptop and left it on her seat as she got out of the car. She opened the glove compartment and removed Laura's service weapon. She opened the center console and grabbed the additional seven round clips. She placed them in the plastic bag of items they'd bought just minutes before at the convenience store. With the bag in hand, she stepped out of the car and closed the door behind her.

Jack met her at the trunk. He pressed the button on the remote control and popped it open to see Cauldwell still curled up in pain. Jack reached into the plastic bag and grabbed the first of the two bungee cords he'd purchased. It was approximately sixteen inches long with bendable rubbed-coated metal hooks on each end. He rolled Cauldwell over inside the truck and pulled his arms behind him. He fashioned the bungee cord around his wrists tightly, knotted it, connected the two metal hooks then compressed both hooks around each other.

He then reached into the bag and pulled out a second bungee cord, this one a little longer, maybe twenty-four inches. He repeated the same routine around Cauldwell's ankles, though he left some slack between his feet to allow him some ability to move. He then untied Cauldwell's shoelaces and knotted them around the confining cord.

Finally, he reached into the sack and pulled out a pair of athletic socks, an oversized knit cap and a pair of sewing scissors. He handed the scissors to Alex, who placed them in her back pocket. He separated the socks, leaving one still in the bag while stuffing the other inside Cauldwell's mouth. He placed the knit cap over Cauldwell's head and pulled it down past his eyes and across his mouth. Alex handed Jack the gun and the additional clips. He put the clips in his back pocket and shoved the gun into the small of his back.

Together, they lifted Cauldwell from the trunk.

Jack held the gun in his right hand as they half-walked, half-dragged, Cauldwell up the back alley to the house. As they approached the house's back-yard, everything began looking very familiar to him. The big shade tree, the overgrown shrubs, the small wooden deck. All of it. He noticed a single back-door light shining across the back yard. That was the first thing that had to go.

They pulled Cauldwell up to the shrubs lining the wooden deck. Alex helped Jack get Cauldwell on the ground then, together, they shoved him headfirst halfway underneath the wooden staircase leading up to the deck.

He whispered to Alex to stay with Cauldwell. He told her to make sure her phone's ring tone was turned off and to check it every couple of minutes. If he needed to contact her but couldn't talk, he would send a text message. She smiled, grabbed his neck and gave him a kiss.

"Good luck, "she whispered, "and *be* careful."

Jack smiled then winked. He drew his weapon. It felt like old times.

He worked his way slowly up the stairs and up to the back door where he remembered watching that punk kid assaulting Caridád. He looked carefully for any kind of trip wires but saw nothing. He slowly loosened the setscrews that held the outdoor lamp's cylindrical glass enclosure in place, then carefully unscrewed the hot light bulb. He placed the bulb gently on the deck underneath a nearby lawn chair. He waited a few seconds, listening for footsteps or any other movement that would tell him that Colavito was coming to see why the light had gone out.

Nothing.

Jack slowly opened the creaking screen door and disappeared into the house.

Alex waited until Jack was out of sight. She felt for the pair of sewing scissors in her back pocket. She leaned over and started pulling Cauldwell out from underneath the slowly rotting staircase. Cauldwell was shifting and bending forward. A few seconds later, Cauldwell's head appeared. Alex grabbed the kit cap and pulled it off his head. She took the scissors from her back pocket and held them to the side of his throat.

"I'm going to ask you two questions. All you have to do is blink. Once for 'yes', twice for 'no'."

He felt the scissors open slightly as they pressed against his throat.

"Just so we are clear, I have used lesser weapons to kill men in places you've probably never heard of, dirt bag," she said, lying through her teeth. "I have no problem wasting your fucking life right here. My first question is, do we understand each other?"

Cauldwell blinked once.

"Good."

He lay there on his side, trying in vain to shift his weight to get more comfortable.

"Ok, now, question number two…"

Alex looked directly into Cauldwell's in his eyes and leaned forward.

"…Did Detective Colavito murder Special Agent Eyas?"

Cauldwell's eyes remained fixed on Alex. He tried to speak but Alex wasn't interested in anything he had to say.

"Perhaps we didn't understand each other after all, Special Agent Cauldwell. Allow me to repeat the question," she said.

"Did Detective Colavito kill –"

Just then, she felt a body fall against her, knocking her over to her left side. She banged her head against the faded gray pine staircase. The scissors dropped from her hand as she reached for the back of her head. She tried to get up but her momentum had driven her between Cauldwell and the wooden steps.

As she struggled to regain her balance, she saw Laura lying across from her.

Alex's eyes grew wide and fear overtook her senses. She reached for Laura's limp body which was not moving at all.

"The answer to your question," a confident male voice said out of the darkness, "is 'yes, he most certainly did'."

Alex finally got to her knees and reached for Laura. Blood was trickling down her left temple. Alex couldn't tell if she was alive or dead. She pulled Laura to her. At least she still felt warm.

"Where is he?" the stranger asked.

Alex looked up toward the figure standing in the shadow of the big shade tree.

"Where's who?" she replied, cradling Laura.

Alex heard the click as he pulled back the hammer on his revolver.

"Must we play this game? Tell me where he is or I will shoot your pretty friend."

Alex tried to buy some time.

"I really don't know where he is."

Cauldwell was fighting to talk through the sock still stuck in his mouth. The stranger found it amusing.

"Who is that next to you?"

Alex moved slowly away from the staircase.

"I won't ask you again."

Alex finally relented.

"His name is Cauldwell. He's an FBI agent."

The stranger laughed. It was too delicious, simply too good to be true. And it could not be coincidence.

"Please," he asked Alex politely, "remove the sock from his mouth."

Alex slowly did as she was told.

"Bobby, that you? Thank God. Sturdevant's in the house. He's in there looking for you right now."

"Well, Special Agent Cauldwell, this is, indeed, a surprise. What a pleasure it is seeing you again."

Cauldwell had heard that inflection before. The other night. The side of the road.

"Who the fuck are you?"

The stranger was content to leave him guessing.

"You don't remember me, Special Agent Cauldwell?"

Cauldwell was panicky knowing Jack was in the house.

"Shit, he's in the house looking for Bobby. He's armed but just one weapon, I think. Whoever you are, untie me, for Christ sakes, and we –"

The stranger remained still.

"I'm sorry, Special Agent Cauldwell, but that simply won't be possible."

Cauldwell reacted.

"What the fuck is wrong with –"

"Please," the stranger said calmly, "there's no need for that. Part of the reason I'm here this evening, Special Agent Cauldwell, is to tie up some loose ends. One of which, it just so happens, is you."

It was hard to imagine that Deputy Director Wallace could have had the foresight to set all of this up so neatly, so conveniently. Still, with Bobby becoming as angry as he was after learning that Cauldwell had gone out of his way to involve the girl from the roadside diner, the only conclusion Wallace could reasonably infer was that Cauldwell was looking to make Bobby the target of the investigation. And after what happened this morning in Cauldwell's office between them, well, things could hardly have worked out better. Wallace knew this mess had reached critical mass. It was time to play his hole card. And he had played his hand, as he had done so often in the past, almost flawlessly. Sending a short fuse like Cauldwell to Iraq was, indeed, in hindsight a mistake, no question about it. But he had counted on Sturdevant – and Jack's reputation for making things happen – to do just that. The opportunity presented itself and Wallace simply had no choice.

After all, timing is how historians remember patriots.

It was truly unfortunate that a good field agent like Carmen had to die. Wallace regretted that. But serving the greater good was what made public service a career worth pursuing. Agent Eyas would be a martyr to the cause. He would accept that. Sacrifices were always having to be made. But, more importantly, Wallace knew that her death would bring Sturdevant charging back into the picture. Perhaps, if his approach had a flaw, it was that he had forgotten just how efficient Jack could be. But Cauldwell had simply become more trouble than he was worth. And Sturdevant, as much as he admired him, had played his role perfectly. He'd just outlived his usefulness.

Everything seemed to becoming together.

Cauldwell was becoming anxious.

"C'mon, untie me... Let's get –"

"I'm sorry, Special Agent Cauldwell, but it seems, again, you weren't listening."

Cauldwell looked up incredulously.

"What the fuck are you talking about? Didn't you hear what I –"

The commanding voice coming out of the darkness offered little sympathy.

"The reason we are here tonight is more than simply eliminating Mr. Sturdevant. It is, as I said, also because of you."

Alex cradled Laura gently in her arms as she began to stir. Cauldwell looked honestly confused.

"What are you talking about?" he said, still wondering who he was talking to.

"It's really quite simple. I'm honestly surprised someone of your vast investigative skills didn't figure this out much earlier. We weren't sure we could make this happen. You can be unpredictable at times, Special Agent Cauldwell. But it was satisfying to know that you eventually could be brought along so easily."

"We? Who's we?" Cauldwell asked impatiently. "What the fuck are you talk–"

The voice paused, not so surprised that Cauldwell needed to be drawn a picture.

"You really don't get it, do you? Did you honestly think you were going to get away with it? Did you really think that the Deputy Director of the FBI would allow you to tell him what your career path would be? That he would allow you to call the shots? Even someone like you should have understood the limits of your own arrogance! Your time in Iraq, it was a mistake, no question about it. Sending you there was expecting the fox to keep an eye on the hen house. He should've seen that coming. And we've had more than a few conversations about that move, believe me. But hindsight can be such a terrible waste of time and effort, don't you think? Foresight is such a smarter way of making decisions."

Now Cauldwell was getting angry. But all he could do was listen.

"But the one decision the Deputy Director regretted most, even more than sending all those agents into Iraq illegally regardless of how noble the cause, was involving you in any of it. All those trips into the desert to bury all those dead detainees whose only crime, it tuned out, was that they couldn't withstand your sadistic 'enhanced interrogation techniques.' All that black market money you made selling all those families whose only fault was their own naïveté, trusting you because you were an American. And if you'd only juiced them and sent them on their way, well, who there *wasn't* doing that? But you had to take it another step further, didn't you? You decided to take their money but what they couldn't have known was that you were actually selling them, not helping them emigrate. That they were paying you to do it to them must have given you a good laugh."

Cauldwell began feeling like this was some macabre "This Is Your Life!"

"And when they couldn't pay, or couldn't pay enough, you bartered for their daughters. All those young girls you raped and molested. All those lives you twisted into so much wreckage. It wasn't enough that Iraq had become your personal ATM. No, you wanted a piece of every young woman – every young *girl* –you could get your degrading and deviate hands on."

Alex glared at Cauldwell with a look of disgust.

"And, of course, there was that pesky journalist you had murdered."

Alex's head shot back to the voice in the darkness.

What'd he say?

"How did you really think the Deputy Director was going to react to that stupid and completely avoidable turn of events? Did you think he was simply going to continue to turn a favorable blind eye? Did you believe he'd simply let you walk away?"

Alex turned again toward Cauldwell. Laura was now conscious again.

"You?" Alex said, her voice cracking. "You *killed* him?"

Cauldwell look at her but paid her no mind. He finally realized the true nature of the game tonight.

"No, *he* didn't kill him," the voice corrected Alex. "He never did have what it took to do his own dirty work. He proved that when he was over there. Unless, of course, he was surround by military police and regular Army! Then, he was a fuckin' Captain America!"

"No," the voice continued, "*he* may not have murdered him. But he might just as well have. Cauldwell, you see, set him up."

"That's a lie!" Cauldwell protested. "I had nothing to do with it."

Alex eyes were frozen on Cauldwell as she drank in every word coming from the lone, dark figure. Laura sat up, trying to clear her head and listen as well.

"Cauldwell put him – what was name again? – "

"Jimmy," Alex slowly and deliberately recounted. "Timothy St. James Elliot."

"Yes, that was it, Elliot. Well, it seems our friend Cauldwell here put Mr. Elliot in touch with someone Cauldwell paid to lead Mr. Elliot into the Sunni Triangle, supposedly to research a story on the trafficking of Iraqi émigrés that, ironically enough, would have led him directly back to Cauldwell!"

"NO!" Cauldwell yelled.

"Imagine that!" the stranger's voice said sarcastically. He continued.

"Mr. Elliot really should have known better, in all honesty. I mean, seriously, an American, using unreliable locals on the take, going into that fuckin' death trap? Those burnt offerings hung from the bridge in Fallujah stood a better chance!"

"As I recall," the voice said finishing up, "Mr. Elliot – or, at least, some part of him – was eventually found some weeks later."

The tears in Alex's eyes, now beginning to run down her cheeks, were borne of her deepening pain listening to him describe Jimmy's fate. And her growing rage about Cauldwell's immediate future.

"I'm not sure they ever found his head."

Alex couldn't believe what she was hearing.

"You sonuvabitch!" Alex screamed out.

"He's lying," Cauldwell exclaimed, "I didn't do any –"

Without thinking, she lunged at Cauldwell's neck, her hands wrapping around his throat. Cauldwell tried yelling but she quickly moved her left hand over, choking him, while she began pummeling him with the fist she'd made of her right hand. Laura reached for her from behind, trying to calm her down. The figure stood quietly in the dark, enjoying the show, as Laura eventually pulled her off and away from Cauldwell. She placed arm around Alex and comforted her as she cried openly.

"Keep her the fuck away from me," Cauldwell yelled as he turned away. "I didn't kill him! I swear, I didn't *kill* him! I had nothing to do with it."

He took a moment to regain his composure.

"I never saw him again after he left for the Triangle."

He looked at Alex as if defending himself mattered.

"Last I'd heard, he was alive! I swear it!"

Laura grabbed Alex and held her back from lunging at him again.

Cauldwell turned his attention to the man standing before him.

"Look," he started, "whatever happened in the desert, that's ancient history. What's important now is that we use it to our advantage. I know Wallace found out about what I was doing. But so what? What could he say?

What could he do about it? I had everything documented about our vis-
its over there. The Bureau's, I mean. *Everything* documented. Besides, after
awhile, he took a more personal interest in what was going on over there.
Shit, eventually, he even bought in. He fuckin' helped with the contacts, for
Christ's sake! He used to joke about being both a silent partner *and* a client!
I've got all of this on him. And he knows it!"

The voice grew impatient.

"Unfortunately for you, Special Agent Cauldwell, this is not about what
Deputy Director did or did not know. Nor what he did or did not do. That is
of no consequence for us here tonight. What I *am* interested in is finishing
the job he is paying me to do."

"You?" Cauldwell said in mock surprise. Then he shook his head slowly
and grinned. "You're forgetting one thing, aren't you?"

While the figure remained with the shadow cast by the big shade tree,
the barrel of a revolver he trained on Cauldwell's head now reflected the
partial moonlight. He'd heard quite enough. It was time for tonight's lesson
to be concluded.

It was time to get down to business.

"You're forgetting about Sturdevant. He knows," Cauldwell said. He then
tossed his head in the direction of Alex and Laura. "They know, too. Bobby
killed that woman agent. Because Wallace told him to!"

"And you know it!" Cauldwell's accusation demanded but received no
response.

So he continued.

"The evidence I have, everything I've seen, points to him. Bobby was on
that highway that night to do the job for him. I have the proof. I have the
file. That's why Wallace wanted him in on our investigation. He authorized
a CPD liaison to work with us on the case. That way, Bobby could get his
hands on the physical evidence. The fingerprint report that came back on
the knife – the information that never made into the online file. Nobody
else knows, nobody else saw it –, those were Bobby's prints on the knife and
Wallace knew it!"

Laura listened carefully as things began making sense. And the inconsis-
tencies in the reports she'd noted began coming together.

Cauldwell continued spilling everything.

"I have the file and if anything happens to me, Wallace won't be able to
control its release. He can't protect you, no matter what he's promised you.
Don't you get it? He's setting you up, too! Just like he set up Bobby! Think

about it! How did Sturdevant know how to come here tonight looking for Bobby? How did he know where to find me? Wallace is double-crossing us both, he's tying up loose ends tonight and he's using Sturdevant to do it. He gets rid of me and what I know. He gets rid of Bobby because he knows he killed one of his agents. How long do you think it will be before he'll have you hunted down? Sturdevant was the perfect choice because he's a disgraced agent. He's the perfect patsy. The only reason that Fed bitch is dead is so Wallace could get Sturdevant to be his hit man! Bobby killed her to bring Sturdevant into the picture so he could lead him to me. I'm the guy he wants taken out! And Sturdevant's the guy Wallace chose to do it! He probably even promised Sturdevant he'd let him back in the Bureau, some shit like that."

Having now gained control of herself, Alex listened and realized Cauldwell was right. That her intuition had been right all along. Jack had been set up.

"I don't know who you are but, if we stick together," Cauldwell pleaded, "we can both come out of this thing alive *and* ahead. We can handle Wallace *and* Bobby. With what I know alone, we can handle him. I'm telling you, if you just listen to me, I can –"

Just then, Cauldwell went silent. His head fell straight back. A dark red hole, about the size of a dime, suddenly opened his forehead, directly above his nose. Both his eyes and his mouth were still open.

It was as if Cauldwell were frozen in fear.

Alex grabbed Laura and hugged her tight. She'd seen men die before, in ways much more gruesome than a single gunshot to the head. But never had she felt so vulnerable, so fearful, watching someone die and believing that she was next. She couldn't stop shaking. Laura held her tightly. They were both thinking the same thing.

Where the hell was Jack?

Without warning, a second staccato pop created another dull echo in the heavy, late night air. Alex felt a spray across the side of her face. She held Laura as close as she could. And shut her eyes tightly.

The man in the shadows reached back to grab his right thigh, dropping his gun to the ground. Twisting around, he fell to his knees, his face contorted in pain. Jack stepped out from behind the big shade tree and walked carefully, both hands holding the gun now trained on the prone, wounded man. He kicked the assailant's weapon aside, past the staircase, and into the dried, browned-out grass well out of the man's reach.

"Alex, Laura," Jack said, "you both all right?"

Alex could hardly believe what she was hearing. She started to cry as she turned to see Jack standing over the man face down and contorted on the ground, writhing in pain. She suddenly felt Laura struggling in her arms.

"You think maybe you could let me breathe," Laura said. "Please?"

"Oh my God, you're ok!" Alex cried out and tried to give Laura another big hug.

Laura leaned back and winced when she touched the side of her head, where she'd been struck earlier with his gun butt. She felt the tacky blood and wondered aloud if stitches would leave a scar.

Alex watched her and started laughing almost as hard as she had been crying.

Jack called to them both then tossed his gun over to them.

He then bent down and rolled over the man he'd just shot, facing him. He looked him directly in the eyes for what seemed like more than just the few seconds it was.

"You killed her, didn't you?"

The man just grinned.

Jack grabbed him by the shirt and pulled the man's chest up off the ground.

"You fuckin' maggot, you stabbed her with her own knife and you blew the back of her head off, didn't you?"

The man just laughed as he coughed.

"No," he said, struggling to talk, "I didn't kill your friend."

Jack was confused. The man grinned between grimaces.

"I'm not the one!"

What? Jack thought.

The man struggled to speak.

"I didn't kill your friend, the woman agent."

Jack shook him again.

"Who the hell are you?"

"His name is Estéban," an unexpected voice said from behind Jack.

Jack quickly twisted around and saw a thin young man in his twenties standing behind him.

"Estéban Calderón. Estéban *Sanchez* Calderón!"

Jack looked back and saw the man beneath him display a look of recognition.

Sanchez! Jimmy's words echoed through Jack's memory.

"Sandy, how good of you to join us this evening," Estéban glibly remarked.

Alex shot a look in the direction of the stranger's voice. Jimmy's words resounded in her head.

Sandy? As in Maria's Sandy? Maria's "Snake-Eyes"?

Sandy looked at Jack on top of Estéban.

"He's right, he didn't kill the woman agent." Sandy said. "It was the cop."

"Cop?" Laura interjected. "How do you know?"

Sandy looked at her apologetically.

"Because I was there," he said almost mournfully.

Jack looked at Sandy then looked back at Estéban still in his grasp. His confusion relented to the thunder now crashing in his head. Jack released his grip on Estéban, who fell relieved back to the ground with a deadening thud.

Estéban took a moment to regain his focus.

"You see?" Estéban confidently if not artfully said, "I told you. I didn't kill her. I didn't kill your friend. I haven't killed anyone."

"Except Teresa," Sandy responded coldly if unexpectedly.

Jack looked quietly at Sandy, his face barely visible in the midnight darkness.

Estéban lifted his head and looked in the direction of Sandy's voice. He laughed in denial. Sandy's eyes remained laser-fixed on Estéban's lying eyes.

"Say what you want, Estéban, it doesn't matter. You know and I know." Sandy's voice rose with his temper. "You killed her. You fuckin' killed her. Then you ran away. You comforted Raúl, you consoled him, you even helped him take his revenge. And all the time it was you."

Jack turned back and watched Estéban avert his eyes and drop his head back to the ground.

"You were always such a jealous little prick, Sandy."

"NO!" Sandy screamed in response.

Everyone waited to see what Sandy would do next. He calmed down a bit.

"I mean, yes, I was jealous of you, Estéban. You, at least, had a chance to spend time with her the way I'd wanted –"

Sandy took a moment and a deep breath

"But now I know I was stupid for being jealous. We both wanted to be with her, that much was true. But she rejected you, Estéban. She never rejected me. She cared about me. Maybe she even loved me. She shared her poetry with me."

Sandy's voice started to crack. Jack turned to see a look of disdain showing on Estéban's face.

"She wouldn't be what you wanted her to be. She wouldn't do what you wanted her to. She couldn't care about you. Not like you wanted. And she was never anything but nice to you. She was always good to you. But that wasn't enough for you, was it? You couldn't have her. She wouldn't let you. So you killed her for it."

Sandy's voice broke.

"*YOU FUCKING KILLED HER FOR IT!*"

Sandy tried to catch his breath as his chest started heaving.

"No," he said to Estéban, slowing regaining his composure "you didn't kill the woman agent..."

He looked at Jack.

"...He didn't kill your friend. I saw the cop do it. It wasn't Estéban..."

Jack looked back at Sandy still standing in the dark.

"...but he *did* murder Teresa. And he didn't settle for just killing her."

Jack watched as Sandy struggle to tell the story.

"We found her, naked, thrown into some wooden crate next to a dumpster. He beat her so badly. He did terrible things to her. He even carved *puta* into her stomach. He intentionally misspelled it so that we would think it was someone else! He left a metal pipe he used to rape her with, just left it there, inside her..."

Sandy dropped his head to his chest. He was close to breaking down. Alex got up and went over to him. She placed her arm around him gently.

"...He butchered her, he tortured her," Sandy said, raising his head, "just because she wouldn't let him touch her. Just because she told him 'no.' And then he framed a bunch of goddamned skinheads so he could get away with it."

Jack's virulent attention shifted to Estéban still cringing from the gunshot wound to his leg.

"Is that true?" Jack asked Estéban, calmly and dispassionately.

Sandy looked at Jack straddled across Estéban.

"He killed her. I know it! I knew it then. Shit, his own goddamned mother knew it. That's why she sent him to Denver! If he would've stayed, we would've found –"

Jack's glare intensified. He bent forward as Estéban winced, a sharp pain shooting up his leg.

"When were you in Denver?" he asked, talking over what Sandy said.

Estéban lay there silently, a smirk still painted across his face.

"When the fuck were you in Denver?" Jack repeated more loudly.

Laura struggled to get to her feet. She nervously knew what Jack was thinking. She could hardly believe what she was hearing.

Estéban returned a cavalier look of someone who'd found the entire conversation – not to mention the young man's feelings – meaningless.

"Go fuck yourself, *gringo*."

Estéban just laughed, both knowing and dismissing the direction Jack question was heading.

"There is no proof. There couldn't be. But, you see," Estéban said, "the boy just told you. I didn't kill your woman friend. I told you the truth. I'm not the one you –"

Estéban suddenly went quiet. The dull sound from a low, sharp snap – like the crack of a thick dead branch – hung in the heavy midnight air. No one moved. Estéban's head was positioned at an odd, dramatic angle. It was awkwardly pointed to his left, his chin turned unnaturally perpendicular to his chest. Jack's left hand lay flat, his palm and open fingers flush against the back of Estéban's head, the heel of his right hand still opposite his left, still pressing down hard against the jaw line of Estéban's face whose lifeless eyes were open and staring directly at Cauldwell.

"Maybe not," Jack whispered harshly. "But you'll do."

He pulled his hands back and looked over at a stunned Laura, the tears pooling in her eyes already overflowing down her cheeks. Neither of them said a word. Neither of them spoke Annie's name. But both of them knew. Both of them felt it. And while the truth may not have set him free, for Jack it seemed enough that it lit the path to forgiving himself.

"He deserved a lot worse, Jack," Laura assured him.

Alex nodded in agreement.

"Much worse."

Jack rose and stood over Estéban's body. He turned to the young man still composing himself, standing behind him next to Alex.

"Raúl's got Caridád," Sandy blurted out.

"What?" they echoed in unison, their attention raptly drawn to the young man.

"How?" Jack wanted to know.

Sandy looked at Jack. He ignored his question.

"And I know where she is."

* * *

They listened as Sandy explained what happened earlier in the evening at the airport hotel. He didn't know how Ana and Daniel were. They'd been left behind. Sandy had stayed with the car but from what the three guys who'd gone upstairs told him, the kids weren't hurt. According to Carlos, Ana and Daniel were able to lock themselves in the next room – Alex and Jack's room – and the guys simply ran out of time to worry about them.

Father Mac, on the other hand, was a different story. Sandy said that Carlos had told him that he'd cut the priest but didn't know any of the details. He didn't really know how the priest was or even if he'd survived.

Caridád was Raúl's primary objective and they were successful in grabbing her. She hadn't been hurt, other than maybe a couple of bumps and bruises bringing her downstairs and getting her into the car. Sandy said he drove the group to Raúl's new safe house in the southern suburbs, east of the I-80 and I-57 interchange. Raúl had chosen to relocate his base of operation, pretty much due to Jack, after finding Manuel lying dead in the bushes. Since Raúl was expecting more "packages" to be delivered later this week, he wanted to keep the safe house as close to Interstate 80 as he could.

Sandy hadn't finish his story before Alex was on the phone with the hotel. She told them that she'd heard about a break-in on her floor and she asked about her niece and nephew, Ana and Daniel. She was transferred to the hotel manager, who told her that both kids were safe and were temporarily being cared for by hotel security. Because they'd been found alone, the Department of Children and Family Services had been contacted. The hotel was still waiting for a representative to arrive to take the children.

Alex asked about Father Mac. The manager told her that he only knew what the paramedics on the scene had told him, which was that they had determined that his knife wound, while serious, did not appear life threatening. They stabilized him and transported him to a local hospital. Alex learned that another person, a member of the hotel staff, had also suffered knife wounds that, unfortunately, had proven fatal. Though she inquired about the circumstances around his death, all the manager would tell her is that his body had been found in the hotel parking garage.

Sandy wasn't aware the young man had even been attacked.

While listening to Sandy's story, Laura took the time to begin checking their weapons. She had thought enough to grab Estéban's gun as they were leaving the house. With her backup revolver and her service weapon that Jack was using, they had three firearms with them. Estéban's Beretta Tomcat 32 Automatic had a full clip of ammunition, as did Laura's backup revolver. Jack still had three additional full clips beside the five rounds that remained loaded in the gun.

Alex took the time to contact the local hospital where Father Mac had been taken. It seemed the paramedics' diagnosis was spot on. The duty nurse would only tell Alex that he was stable and would be transferred to a nearby Catholic hospital some time later this morning, which it now was. Once Jack learned that Father Mac appeared to be out of danger, his attention quickly turned to finding Caridád.

Sandy gave very specific instructions. Jack took the southbound express-way to Interstate 57 and head south to the 167th Street exit. There he went east to Kedzie Avenue then into the neighborhood.

Their plan seemed simple enough. Jack, Alex and Laura were all con-vinced that Sandy was committed to helping Caridád. Jack didn't like the idea of trusting him, particularly someone who had not only been an active participant in Raúl's trafficking business but had, as recently as a couple of hours ago, helped kidnap Caridád from their hotel room! Add to that the not-so-incidental matter of Sandy being there the night Carmen was mur-dered and his concerns appeared completely justified. He took part of the time on their way to the safe house coming up with different "Plan B's" just in the event his gut feeling proved right.

Their "Plan A" was simple: Sandy would show up at the safe house, in-tentionally unexpected. If Raúl asked about tonight or Estéban, Sandy would tell him two things: first, that Sandy was not part of the execution tonight, just part of the cleanup, but that it appeared to him that everything went according to plan and, second, that Estéban would be calling him tomorrow. Why Estéban would be calling, Sandy wouldn't know.

Sandy's only job in the safe house was reconnaissance. Jack wanted to know three things: first, where Caridád was being held; second, how many men Raúl had with him in the house; and, third, the basic layout of the house. After that, Sandy was free to meld into the group and disappear as soon as they made their move. He didn't care where Sandy went.

He didn't expect there would be a need for him to testify at any trial.

Jack, Laura and Alex all agreed it made no sense to formulate a plan until they knew better what they were dealing with. And since they had no idea how Caridád was being treated, they knew that, whatever shape their plan would eventually take, urgency could quickly become a significant part of it.

They were still a few miles from the 167th Street exit when Jack finally asked Sandy how it was he happened to be at the house tonight.

It turned out it had been Raúl's idea. He'd decided that Sandy needed a change of pace, to learn a new side of the business, and he'd reached out to Estéban about bringing Sandy onboard. As a favor to Raúl, Estéban agreed. Sandy had met up with Estéban earlier in the evening.

Though Estéban was not particularly forthcoming about the details, the plan seemed simple enough. Two of Estéban's men were at the FBI building this morning looking for Laura. Their original plan was to grab her up either at lunchtime or leaving to go home. When she appeared going for a cup of coffee midmorning with some guy, they saw their opportunity. They approached her as she left the coffee shop, a couple of blocks from headquarters.

Laura took it from there.

"They took me to this motel room somewhere on the south side, I think, it was near Midway airport. They stayed with me in the room. And they were certainly pleasant enough. But the fact that they didn't care that I knew where I was or that I had seen their faces made me think that this probably wasn't going to end well for me. They were kind enough to bring me both lunch and dinner. Right around 8:00 PM, they brought me to the south side safe house, where Estéban and Sandy were waiting for me."

"That's right," Sandy concurred speaking to Jack, "from what Estéban told me, there was never any intention to do her any harm. The plan was to get *you* there."

Jack turned and looked at Sandy.

"Me?" he said, "Why me?"

"You and Cauldwell," Sandy finished.

Jack was a bit stumped.

"Help me understand," Jack said, "how was grabbing Laura going to get you Cauldwell?"

Sandy looked across the backseat at Laura and smiled.

"I'm not sure," he said, "All I know is that Estéban told me he'd been given a job to do tonight. And whoever brought him in knew that grabbing Laura would get you there with Cauldwell."

Jack stopped and thought for a second.

Whoever brought him in? Who would've – That made no sense! Unless…

"What did Estéban say about Cauldwell?" Jack asked, looking at Sandy in the rearview mirror.

"Just that we had to take him out clean, take you both out clean."

"So," Jack realized, "taking out Cauldwell was part of the plan from the beginning?"

"No, from what Estéban told me, Cauldwell *was* the plan," Sandy replied. "When he learned you would be bringing him to the house, that's when things changed."

"But," Jack responded, "how would anyone know Cauldwell would be with us?"

Alex jumped in.

"Remember, Jack," she said, "where was the first place we went to look for Laura?"

"You're right, Alex," Jack said, recalling their visit to FBI headquarters.

"As a matter of fact, who's idea was it to start with Cauldwell, Jack?" Alex said, walking him through the not-yet-evident logic.

"Any reason why that was?" Alex asked him.

Jack thought for a moment.

Because I knew Cauldwell knew something about what had happened to Laura.

"Because I knew," Jack said, "that Cauldwell knew –"

"Precisely," she said. Laura was impressed with how quickly she'd learned the way Jack's mind worked.

"And who else have you talked to, Jack?" Alex asked in that dull surprise voice that told Jack she'd already figured it out.

Jack paused for a moment before the light went on.

Shit, she's right!

"When Estéban and Cauldwell were talking, before you got there," Alex continued, "he told Cauldwell that the reason everything came together to-night was more than simply getting rid of you, Jack. He said it was largely because of Cauldwell."

The elevator had finally reached the top floor.

"So, if tonight was about him as well as me, that means –" he said.

"Yep," Laura interjected, "it was all about tying up some very loose ends."

"And the only one who was missing…" Alex started.

"…was Colavito!" Jack finished.

"So, the obvious question" Laura asked, "is why wasn't he there tonight?"

Jack nodded as his smile grew wider.

"Seems to me," Jack concluded, "there's only one person who can know that."

* * *

Chapter 18

SANDY SHOVED ASIDE the sliding door and walked into the back bedroom. He saw Caridád, lying on the floor in the far corner, motionless. To her left lay the dismantled torture device. He immediately made the connection. He didn't want to believe that Raúl would be that cruel. Not to Caridád. He'd seen the device work before. He thought of the indescribable suffering she must have endured over the past couple of hours. He watched the young man sitting in the opposite corner get up from his chair and walked past him, without making eye contact.

"She ain't goin' anywhere," he mumbled in broken English.

Sandy walked over and knelt down next to her. He saw the tacky blood on her face, down her chin, in her ears. He heard her wheezing as she struggled to breathe, a sound that was both labored and shallow.

He thought of Teresa. His eyes became clouded with tears.

She appeared unconscious or so he thought. He could actually see the muscles in her legs and arms react in sporadic spasm. He could only imagine the pain she must be in. Sandy touched her gently, to see if she'd react. She groaned, not having the strength to cry out. He couldn't know the courage it must have taken to survive the device's grip.

He felt a cold chill. He sensed he was in the presence of something evil. Then a voice called to him from the family room doorway.

"What are you doing here, Sandy," Raúl said as he stood behind him.

"You shouldn't be here."

Sandy stood and turned to face him. He was fighting to keep his rising anger under control.

"What have you done, Raúl?"

Raúl laughed and looked directly at him.

"What do you care?" he responded. "After all, you brought her here."

"Because you told me to, Raúl," Sandy reacted in self-defense.

"What difference does it make?" Raúl said. "She's here and she will soon tell me what I want to know." He began strolling into the room, toward the two of them. "I will admit, though," he continued, "she is highly motivated. I am surprised that she hasn't said anything… at least, she hasn't yet."

Sandy began to tear up again.

"But she will," Raúl assured him as well as himself. "She will."

Sandy felt Teresa's presence.

"I can't watch you do this anymore, Raúl," Sandy told him.

Raúl ignored him.

"Actually, I'm more impressed than surprised. Whoever she's protecting, she –"

"Raúl –" Sandy started.

"Besides, like I said, you shouldn't be here," Raúl interrupted. "I spoke with Estéban yesterday." Suddenly it dawned on him. "Why aren't you with –"

"Estéban's dead, Raúl," Sandy blurted out.

Raúl laughed in response to something so ridiculous.

"What are you talking about?"

Sandy realized it was too late.

"I… I saw him die…" Sandy confessed, "…tonight."

Raúl just looked at him with a growing crooked smiling. Sandy grew bolder.

"As a matter of fact," Sandy said, "I would've killed him myself if it hadn't –"

Raúl walked up to the young man whom he'd raised, whom he watched over like an older, wiser brother, someone he'd come to count on, despite the boy's obvious flaws and weaknesses. Not the least of which was the stomach he lacked for the "rougher" side of this business. Raúl gave him with a steely look.

"What the fuck are you talking about?"

Sandy swallowed hard then continued.

"I was at the house tonight, Raúl, I watched him die."

"You were what?" he demanded, staring a hole into his eyes.

A long moment passed as Sandy began to give way to his nervousness. Raúl turned away in disbelief.

Sandy walked passed him toward the family room before Raúl physically turned him around. He tried to place his hands on Sandy's shoulders, who shook them loose.

"Listen to me, Raúl," Sandy said, "You've got to get out of here. Right now!"

Raúl looked at him like he was crazy. He started to turn away again when, this time, Sandy grabbed his shoulders and pulled him back.

"You don't understand," Sandy pleaded. "You've got to go. There's no time."

Raúl indignantly scanned the hands that gripped his shoulders. The boy was making no sense at all.

"Let go of me, Sandy," Raúl said slowly and deliberately.

Sandy dropped his hands.

"I'm sorry, Raúl, but you've got to –," Sandy started. "If you don't –"

Raúl shot him a quick look.

"If I don't," Raúl countered, "what?"

Sandy dropped his head and turned away from him. Raúl had seen him act stupid before but this was unusual, even for Sandy. Something had obviously happened tonight with Estéban. But he couldn't be dead. What sense did that make?

Raúl pulled his phone from his back pocket and punched up Estéban's number.

"Whatever happened tonight," Raúl thought out loud, "I'm going to find out –"

Without turning around, Sandy repeated himself.

"I told you – Estéban's dead."

As his call eventually went to voice mail, Raúl suddenly had a sense that Sandy wasn't wrong after all. He flipped his phone shut, cutting the connection.

"Tell me what happened, *hermano*," Raúl said, "You said you were at the house?"

Sandy was fighting back tears. He heard Caridád softly groan again and watched her move slightly.

"This is over," Sandy said defiantly. "Did you hear me, Raúl?"

He turned around and faced Raúl directly.

"This is fuckin' over. It ends here. Right now. Tonight!"

Raúl was stunned. Sandy didn't seem drunk. And he'd never seen him act this way when he was high. He decided to beat back his initial reaction.

"What's over? Why you acting so crazy? What the fuck are you talking about?"

Sandy wiped away a tear running down his cheek.

"You can't treat her this way, Raúl. Teresa doesn't deserve this. She –"

Raúl was stunned.

"Teresa?" he said almost incredulously. "Teresa? What the hell does Teresa have to do with any of this?"

Sandy regained his composure and walked back up to Raúl. He placed his hands on Raúl's forearms. He wore an expression of urgency.

"Look, you've got get out of here. They're coming. You've got to go. *NOW!*"

Raúl was getting more and more uncomfortable with Sandy's antics.

"Who's coming?" Raúl asked. "What are you talking about, man? And what does Teresa have to do with any of this?"

Without warning, a third voice entered the conversation.

"She's the one reason why you're still alive, asswipe."

Raúl reacted immediately but it was too late. He turned directly into the muzzle of Laura's .45 caliber pistol Jack was holding flush against his neck just beneath his jaw.

"Now who the fuck are *you*?" Raúl said, completely confused.

Jack sarcastically laughed.

"You know, for a guy who runs such a sophisticated operation, you ask the dumbest goddamned questions."

Jack reached around in front of Raúl and grabbed the .38 Special from under his tee-shirt then shoved it behind him against the small of his back.

Sandy was in meltdown.

"Look," Sandy said looking at Jack, "you wanted Caridád. There she is." Sandy tossed a glance in the prone young woman's direction. "Take her. The deal was for her. You didn't say anything about Raúl or anybody else."

Raúl began piecing things together. Sandy had buyer's remorse. He'd sold him out and now was having second thoughts. Raúl's anger was becoming palpable.

"Sandy," Raúl demanded, "who the fuck is this guy?"

Before he could answer, Jack pushed the gun harder up against his throat.

"Who I am hardly matters. What does matter, though, is that, as of tonight – as of right now, asshole – you're out of business!"

Raúl looked directly into the tears welling up in Sandy's eyes.

"I don't know, *amigo*," Raúl said, regaining his trademark cool and cocky tone, "you shouldn't count your *pollos* –"

Jack's gut told him Sandy was turning. He had a sense that Sandy's conviction to help them tonight had been the result of a temporary attack of conscience. That's why he decided to follow him into the house, to count on him only for the honest distraction he knew Sandy would provide. Laura was busy with Alex securing the opposite end of the house, bounding and gagging the four tough guys that had hurt Caridád. Including Raúl, Jack had counted only the five of them in the house though, from what his outdated Spanish could ascertain, they could expect company. When was anyone's guess.

Just then, the door at the other end of the room suddenly opened.

"Jack, are you –"

Jack's attention to Alex was all Raúl needed. He leaned back and turned quickly, grabbing Jack's right arm, twisting it. The gun sounded, the bullet entering the opposite wall where Caridád was lying, just below the ceiling line. As Raúl wrestled Jack for his gun, Alex saw Caridád on the floor to her left. Instinctively, she ran to her and knelt down, shielding the young girl's body with her own. Sandy took one step back through the doorway and into the family room, unsure of what to do next.

The gun in Jack's hand was pointed toward the ceiling as Raúl's large arms forced him backwards. Alex yelled for Laura then picked up Caridád as best she could, half-carrying, half-dragging her out of the room and into middle bedroom. Sandy stood fixed as he watched them leave. Alex pulled her to the far corner of the room before feeling the floor shake from a large thud in the next room. She quickly returned to the door to see Raúl wrestling with Jack on the ground for his gun. Alex saw another gun – Raúl's .38 Special – on the floor near the doorway.

Without thinking, she moved toward the gun, trying to get past the two of them on the floor, to reach the weapon.

"Sandy!" Raúl yelled out. "The gun!"

He pulled himself away from Jack long enough to trip Alex as she tried to get by them. As she fell forward and hit the floor, she reached for the gun but succeeded only in shoving it forward away from her and into the family room.

Sandy was frozen in place, indecisive, unable or unwilling to respond. Realizing he wasn't going to help, Raúl worked his way out of Jack's grip. He scrambled away on all fours away, lunging toward Alex. Before Jack could get to his feet, Raúl pulled Alex up and slapped her hard, sending her reeling. She crashed against the wall opposite the doorway. He then turned toward the family room, searching the floor for his gun.

Jack lunged at Raúl's legs and tackled him. Raúl kicked at him, first with one foot, then with the other. He caught Jack flush against the side of his face, turning him over. He spied the gun lying underneath a chair just a few yards to the left of him. He crawled across the floor as Jack scrambled back toward him. Raúl reached for the gun just as Jack landed on his legs, rolling him over. Jack felt a sudden pain shoot up his neck from his shoulder. He grimaced noticeably. The gun slipped from his grasp as Raúl continued kicking him.

Jack fought through Raúl's pumping legs and climbed his way up past

Raúl's knees as Raúl began pummeling him with his fists. Jack dug his head down, against his chest, and continued inching forward. Raúl tried to roll-over, to reach the gun now just a foot or two from his grasp. But he couldn't overcome Jack's weight on his legs. Jack worked his way up against Raúl's flailing arms and pinned him against the floor. Raúl spit his face as Jack maneuvered on top of him.

Jack fell forward, landing against Raúl's chest. They both reached for the gun, Jack's left hand now engaged in its own battle with Raúl's right hand for the weapon. Jack tilted left and was moving closer. Raúl was pinned beneath him. Raúl worked his left hand free and reached around Jack's head, grabbing the side of Jack's mouth and nose, pulling him sideways away from the gun. Jack rolled back over across Raúl's body and onto the floor, bringing with him Raúl's left arm he now had securely in his grip.

Jack pushed himself upwards until he felt Raúl's nose behind his head. He raised his head then violently thrashed it backwards, breaking Raúl's nose. Blood spurted from Raúl's face. The moment of sudden sharp pain was all the time Jack needed. He made a fist in his right hand, covered it with his left hand and slammed his pointed elbow directly into Raúl's gut. An explosion of exhaled air accompanied a wrenching sound from behind Jack. He rolled across Raúl again and reached for the gun. Raúl desperately pushed at Jack, shoving him off balance and rolling past the gun.

They both turned and simultaneously reached the weapon with their right hands. Raúl, bloodied and having trouble seeing, tried reaching across his body to grab at Jack. The cramps in his stomach made that all but impossible. Raúl's fingers were wrapped around the gun handle. Jack's hand was wrapped over Raúl's fingers as well as the gun's cylinder. Jack regained some of his balance and reached around with his left hand to help his right control the weapon. He leaned forward, raised himself up as high as he could, then landed on Raúl's right arm.

Raúl yelled out. Jack positioned himself on top of Raúl's right forearm as he worked with both hands to free the gun from Raúl's fingers. Raúl reached around with his left hand and started pulling at Jack's neck, trying to get his arm around Jack's throat.

Suddenly, a bullet thundered throughout the room as it burrowed into the wall just above their heads. Jack looked up and saw Sandy standing in the family room, holding Jack's gun, both his hands training the barrel directly on them.

"Enough," Sandy cried out. "Stop it!"

Raúl and Jack stopped fighting and lay still for a moment.

"Get up, both of you," Sandy commanded. "Raúl, grab your gun."

As Raúl crawled to his pistol, Laura came running into family room from the third bedroom, gun in hand, stopping in the doorway.

"*STOP!*" Sandy demanded. "Stop or I'll kill him, I swear!"

Laura stopped and assumed the position, leveling her .40 Glock semi-automatic directly at Sandy's chest.

"Drop your weapon, Sandy," Laura responded firmly. "And do it now."

Jack and Raúl slowly got to their feet, catching their breath. Raúl held his .38 Special in his right hand as he wiped the blood from his nose with other.

"NO!" Sandy yelled back. "You drop your fuckin' gun! *RIGHT NOW!*"

Laura looked to Jack, who looked directly back at her and nodded slowly.

"*DO IT NOW!*" Sandy demanded more loudly.

"Ok, Sandy, ok," she said calmly, maintaining eye contact with him as she bent down, put her gun on the floor and slowly stood back up.

"Now, kick it over to me," Sandy said.

Laura's foot hit the gun's handle first, sending it spinning away behind her.

"Good job, Sandy," Raúl said as he pulled away from Jack.

Sandy heard him but didn't respond.

"Look, you guys came for Caridád," he said. "She's in the other room. She's alive. That's enough. That was our deal. Just take her and get out. Leave us alone."

Jack stepped forward.

"We can't do that, Sandy," he said. "We can't walk away from here. Too many innocent people have been hurt."

Jack watched Sandy's reaction carefully then went for the jugular.

"Too many innocent people like Teresa –"

Sandy suddenly raised his weapon at Jack.

"You don't fuckin' know shit about her. Don't you *even* say her name!"

Jack wouldn't back off.

"Sandy, you know and I know that you loved her. We know what Estéban did to her. We both know how she died. You stood there tonight, you watched me kill him. And he knew you knew, Sandy. He killed her and he knew you knew he'd killed her. What I did tonight I did as much for Teresa as I did it for you."

Raúl couldn't listen to him any more.

"You? *You* killed Estéban?" Raúl countered.

Jack ignored Raúl, just like Sandy did.

"You knew Estéban killed her, don't you, Sandy?" Jack responded. "You loved her. And he killed her. Just like you told us at the house. He couldn't have what you had with her. She wouldn't share her life with him the way she did with you. She returned your love, Sandy, you know she did. You know in your heart that she did."

Sandy eyes began welling up. Jack kept going.

"Innocent people like Teresa are being victimized and brutalized every day here, Sandy. You know that! But you can stop it. Right now! You can put an end to it all."

"You can't stop shit, asshole," Raúl interjected. "You think you can stop us? You can't stop shit! And you know why? 'Cuz nobody cares! *Nobody fuckin' cares!*"

Raúl's confidence began to swell.

"Nobody but idiot assholes like you! And you know why nobody cares? 'Cuz they don't *want* to care. 'Cuz nobody *wants* to know. They look the other way! They think all we do is pimp out a bunch of whores! And, the best part is, they think it's their own fault! It's perfect, when you think about it. You think we could do what we do – right out in the open – if anybody really gave a shit? It's them; it's their fault! Nobody wants to know what we do. People don't; cops sure don't; even politicians don't!"

Raúl felt a sudden if odd rush of pride as he decided to correct himself.

"There are only three kinds of people who care about what we do…"

He raised the fist in his left hand, opened his thumb and began counting.

"…those who get paid…"

Next up was his index finger

"…those who get careless…"

And then one more.

"…and those who get delivered."

He then grinned widely.

"That's it. That's all there is. So, go fuck yourself, tough guy."

But then he nodded in Laura's direction and began to grin.

"But you, *chiquita*…" he said, leering at her, drawing her attention, "maybe we can work something out? I mean, maybe you don't have to die like your boyfriend, eh? Maybe we let you live… eh, Sandy?"

Jack glared back at Raúl but spoke directly to Sandy.

"Don't listen to him, Sandy. Teresa would be so proud of what you did tonight!"

"Shut the fuck up." Raúl said. "Just waste him, Sandy, get it over with."

Sandy made this mess, he thought, *he'll clean it up.*

But Laura picked up Jack's approach.

"Sandy," Laura said, "Honor her memory, respect the love she felt for you. The love you know you felt for her. What you did tonight – bringing us here to rescue Caridád – took courage and strength. The same courage and strength she saw in you."

Sandy looked at her and listened.

"Make her proud of you again, Sandy. Would Teresa want you involved in what goes on here? Would she want young, innocent, courageous women like Caridád to suffer so horribly? Ask yourself, Sandy... what would Teresa want you to do?"

Thinking of Teresa – and what he could only imagine had happened to Caridád – was more than Sandy could bear. He looked at Raúl almost apologetically as tears started running down his face.

"You said nobody cares, Raúl," he said slowly, "but I care... I'm sorry, but I do."

Raúl turned a disappointed eye toward Sandy then shot a look back to Laura.

"Why don't you shut the fuck up, bitch," he said as he calmly raised his gun. And fired.

Laura let out a stifled cry, dropping her weapon as she collapsed to the floor.

The single gunshot shattered the room's heightening tension. Jack's eyes froze in disbelief as he watched Laura twist in agony, a deep crimson spot growing on her blouse.

"*JACK!*" she tried to call out, fighting to make a sound through the agony.

He sprang to her side, immediately putting pressure on the gushing wound. He desperately tried to think of what he could use – something, anything – to wrap it, to try and slow if not stop the bleeding. He had no way of knowing if it was a through-and-through or if the bullet was still embedded in her muscle, whether it had shattered bone or struck a major artery. Laura was conscious but fading in and out. She was taking short breaths, hard and labored. She fought to push herself passed the searing, blinding pain as, in her mind, she repeated every word he said, listening to him talk, trying to focus on him through eyes that stung with perspiration and were now clouded with welling tears.

Raúl self-assuredly trained his weapon on Jack. He shifted the gun butt in his palm – he wanted a firm, more comfortable grip for the bullets that had Jack's name on them. His grin widened confidently as his eyes flared with a fatal payback, his ready finger curled snuggly around the trigger. Jack raised his head but didn't turn around.

Three rapid staccato bursts suddenly thundered in succession. Jack instantly fell across Laura, yelling out in a garbled voice as his body smothered hers. A debilitating spasm streaked from his shoulder up his neck and down his back. He lay there perfectly still, unable to feel, wondering if Laura had been hit again.

Sandy lowered his gun slowly. He watched a flush Raúl, his eyes wide in blazing disbelief, take a staggered step then remove a bloody hand from the two bullet holes in his abdomen. A dark red stain quickly spread from the third bullet that entered his left side, puncturing his spleen. Dizzy and disoriented, sirens erupting in his head, he didn't notice the gun fall harmlessly from his hand. He looked past Sandy, struggling to keep his balance, when, suddenly, his body was launched backward, violently contorting in a helpless, spastic dance that only ended when his dead weight finally crashed to the floor.

Four more shots had rapidly followed, leaving seven bullets from the now half-empty magazine lodged fatally in the blood-soaked chest of her sister's killer.

Caridád slumped into Alex's arms as her hands opened, releasing Laura's gun. "He killed Maria," she kept repeating, out of breath. "He killed my sister…"

"I know, sweetheart," Alex reassured her softly. "I know…"

She pulled her close and caressed her as Caridád had only the strength to cry.

"…he's dead now, *querida*. You did it. He can't hurt you ever again."

Alex looked up to see Raúl's riddled body lying moribund and unconscious, his clothes drenched from soaking up his splattered blood, his life draining further away with every weakening heartbeat.

"He won't hurt *anyone*," she said softly, "ever again."

Sandy turned to see Alex comforting Caridád as she lay crying in Alex's embrace on the floor then looked over at Jack, who was still attending to Laura. He turned back to Raúl, bleeding out on the family room floor. He'd watched the vengeance that had taken his life play out in front of him. He thought of Miguel and how Raúl had fostered in him the hate and indifference he'd so casually come to embrace. He thought of Estéban and the smugness with which he rationalized all the pain, all the hurt, he'd caused in the name of all the money he made and the power that had consumed him.

Not that any of it mattered now.

And then he thought of Teresa.

He gazed out of the large family room window and into the deep, sullen morning darkness. He suddenly saw her face before him, smiling, his head filled with the rhythms and sounds of the Tejano music she loved so much. He heard the songs they'd sang together, sitting outside on the balcony all those hot, humid summer nights. He listened as he heard her reciting those haunting lines from her favorite T.S. Eliot's poem.

And realized just how hollow a man he'd truly become.

"I really do care," he told her, repeating himself again.

He swallowed hard. He nodded as he watched her smile back at him, her face beaming, her eyes bright and twinkling like stars in the black emptiness of the night sky.

"I miss you so much," he said to her.

She looked at him and opened her arms. Her smile beckoned him.

His eyes glistened with collecting tears as he smiled back, trembling. He nodded.

He shoved the gun up under his chin and fired.

Jack and Alex jumped, startled at the sound of the gunshot. He looked to Alex before turning to see Sandy's limp, lifeless body lying on the floor near Raúl. Suddenly, he noticed the swirling red, white and blue lights from outside the house now casting flashes against the family room walls. Laura struggled, trying to push herself up. Jack turned back toward her and tried to keep her still. She lay back and painfully reached for the left side of her chest – the bullet had torn through the muscles just above and to the side of her breast. She heard the additional sirens in the distance gaining strength.

And sighed heavily.

Alex sat on the floor with Caridád. She wrapped an arm around her and pulled her close into a tight embrace. A moment later, Alex raised her head looked at Jack as tears slid down her cheeks. She waited for his eyes to meet hers.

She stretched out her hand until her fingers could reach no further.

Jack smiled easily, gratefully, then reached back, entwining his fingers with hers.

As he felt Laura taking every breath, squeezing his hand.

* * *

Alex lay quietly on Jack's chest as the sound of the television from the adjoining room finally stirred them. They'd barely gotten four hours sleep, if that much. It was close to 5:00 AM before they'd gotten to bed. Laura had spent what was left of Tuesday night under observation in a local hospital on the south side. Caridád would be there for some time longer, most likely receiving physical therapy while doctors looked to determine if there would be any lasting effects from the time she'd spent inside the grip of the Scavenger's Daughter. She would also be receiving visits from counselors on staff at the hospital. Her testimony would prove invaluable in helping Laura assist federal prosecutors in obtaining human trafficking indictments in the Chicago area as well as connecting states.

The four mutts that Alex and Laura had bound and gagged in the living room would be arraigned some time today in federal court on multiple gun and sexual assault charges as well as unlawful restraint and assorted human trafficking felonies. The state court would get their chance on kidnapping and attempted murder charges at a later date.

Even though Alex had gotten her to safety, Caridád had somehow crawled her way into the back bedroom. She saw Alex slumped against the wall and Laura's gun lying near the doorway. She'd heard the gunshot and saw Jack attending to Laura on the floor. She'd heard Raúl, bragging in the next room. And all she could think of was killing him. She'd willed herself to the gun but struggled painfully to raise it. Raúl simply didn't notice her as he leveled his gun at Jack's back. But Jack had noticed.

And though it felt as if her burning hatred for Raúl somehow had given her the strength to point Laura's gun, it was, in actuality, Alex who had crawled up behind her, to help her train the weapon. She'd held Caridád's arm steady as, together, they'd carefully taken aim then calmly proceeded to empty seven rounds into Raúl's chest.

Caridád had taken the first three shots, Alex the last four.

And all of them found their target.

None of them had had any illusions that it would take very long for the vacuum created by Raúl's sudden departure to be filled. But, for the time being, the more urgent matter requiring their attention was the Deputy Director. And Alex had come up with a good idea. Wallace was here in Chicago. Chances were good that, if Cauldwell was right and Wallace was actually behind everything that went down last night, he'd want to stick around to know for himself that all his loose ends have been cleaned up.

And that meant, at some point, he'd have to be in contact with the mysteriously elusive but seemingly omnipresent Detective Bobby Colavito.

Jack's mind wandered as he held Alex close. He realized that all Wallace can know, at this point, is that Estéban is unavailable, that he isn't answering his phone calls. He probably doesn't know that Calderón's dead. For that matter, he probably doesn't know Cauldwell is dead, either. And thanks to Alex's computer acumen, Jack knew that Cauldwell had been tracking Colavito all the while Cauldwell had been, for all intents and purposes, blackmailing Wallace. Since Cauldwell confessed that he had evidence that Colavito had murdered Carmen, chances were good that Colavito would be in touch with Wallace. But Estéban was the one who ended up being tracked last night on Cauldwell's laptop. How could that have happened unless Wallace made it happen? Unless the tracking software was given a new cell number? And, if that was the way it happened, who could have made that happen other than the Deputy Director?

It made sense. Cauldwell had nothing to gain from lying last night. He was pleading for his life. And he made a convincing argument that Wallace was behind it all.

And Alex's idea made sense: Laura should be the one to make contact with Wallace, especially since Jack was supposed to be dead and Wallace would have no reason to take a call from Alex. Wallace would certainly take Laura's call if, for no other reason, than to find out how she unexpectedly survived last night's ordeal.

Jack was intrigued and was restless to get things moving. Alex turned out of his embrace and reached across the nightstand for her cell phone. Some ten minutes later, Laura called Alex back to say she had a meeting setup with Wallace at 6:00 PM in Millennium Park. Wallace had decided to delay his return to D.C. until Thursday. Laura spoke with Jack and told him she was fine, that her prognosis was, for all intents and purposes, excellent and that, one way or another, she would be released sometime early this afternoon. Jack knew better but, after checking with Alex to make sure that she'd stay with the kids, he told Laura he would be there to pick her up. And while he had her on the phone, he asked her to help him with a couple of housekeeping items that might prove valuable for the meeting this evening with Wallace.

As Jack moved to get out of bed, Alex grabbed him and pulled him back. He lay there in front of her as she sat up next to him, one leg curled up beneath her. She wore one of his old Cubs tank top, as loose-fitting as his boxers. Her eyes looked directly at him as her emotions stirred, building quickly. Her eyes began to water.

"Jack," she started seriously, "I want you to tell me the truth."

Jack smiled and squeezed her hand.

"Of course. Why?"

She nodded and cleared her throat.

"Ok, I want you to tell me," she said. "Do you really know how Jimmy died?"

Jack thought back to the first of two files that Wallace had Laura deliver to him.

"Yes, Alex, I'm certain," he said gently but confidently. He placed his open hand against her face and brushed away a tear slipping down her cheek.

"Jimmy didn't die the way Estéban said he did," Jack told her. "He didn't die in the Sunni Triangle."

She reached behind her for the box of tissues on the nightstand.

"From everything I got from Wallace," Jack said, "he didn't die that way."

The truth was Wallace's notes weren't very specific about Jimmy's fate though it did appear, from what Jack could piece together, that Estéban had been lying. There was no evidence that Jimmy had been kidnapped. There had been no videotape, no demands for his life, no press coverage whatsoever of his disappearance. For all of their ideals, jihadists loved publicity. Selling terrorism was not unlike any other consumer product.

It owed its market share to heavy advertising.

Jack believed that Jimmy simply learned more than allowed him to live. How he died hardly mattered, really. If it helped to know it was quick and painless, so be it. Chances were he didn't. Chances are he did suffer. And Alex probably knew that, in her heart of hearts. But, in the end, he saw nothing to be gained from trying to find out more. Jimmy lost his life pursuing the truth trying to save innocent people.

Beyond that, what else really mattered?

But he felt he had to offer her the chance, if she wanted to read it for herself.

"Alex," he said tenderly, "if you want to read Wallace's file, I'll show you what he wrote about him."

Alex smiled back, tears welling up again in her eyes.

"No," she said softly, returning to her place against his chest, "I believe you."

She released a heavy sigh and closed her eyes. She stroked the hair on his chest.

"I honestly do," she said.

He pulled her close and kissed her forehead, through her hair.

"Jack," she said hesitantly, "I suppose it would be stupid now, after everything that's happened, to tell you that I think I might be – I mean,"

"I know," Jack said slowly, interrupting her.

Her fingers slowly stroked the side of his face. She stretched out and laid back down next to him, snuggling tightly up against him.

"I know," he repeated, softly.

He closed his eyes and smiled as he pulled her close.

And found himself back in that damned elevator.

Something Cauldwell said last night had been bouncing around in Jack's head. He said he had a file on Wallace. That, if anything happened to him, Wallace would be unable to control its release. He implied it proved Wallace had Colavito murder Carmen.

He wouldn't be bluffing, Jack realized. *Not begging for his life.*

I've got to find that file!

The only sense Jack could make of Cauldwell's statement – that Wallace would be unable to control its release – led him to believe the file had to be stored locally. Cauldwell wouldn't have kept it on the FBI's shared web server or even on their secured site. No, keeping it on his local drive would guarantee Wallace could not get to it directly. That meant it had to be somewhere on Cauldwell's laptop. Or downloaded to a CD or flash drive or some other form of media that Wallace would know nothing about.

There had to be some clue on Cauldwell's computer.

When Ana and Daniel learned that Jack was going to the hospital, they begged to go, too. They wanted to visit Caridád while Jack was there to pick up Laura. And Jack could hardly say no. But they decided to take separate cars to the hospital. Alex brought Ana and, though Daniel had wanted to go with Jack, he asked Alex to bring him with her as well. He wanted to make a couple of phone calls on the way there.

Alex offered to stay at the hospital with the kids and visit Caridád, hoping she was up to receiving visitors, so Jack could take Laura into the city to FBI headquarters. Jack knew Wallace had plans to leave for D.C. and he assumed that flight was for tonight. A couple of things had to come together if they were going to move on him before then.

As they'd hoped, the kids and Alex were able to spend time with Caridád, who, though still sedated, was already showing some very positive signs of improvement. Perhaps knowing that her nightmare had finally ended was enough unto itself. While the kids spent time with her, Alex took the time to make notes on everything that had happened. The last few days had Pulitzer written all over it!

One Jimmy would be especially proud of.

A thought occurred to Jack on the drive in to pick up Laura. The phone call he took in the parking garage – the one he gave to Alex to answer that eventually led them to the south side safe house – got him thinking. He called Laura and gave the number to her over the phone in the hopes that she could get it tracked down. But there was something else about that call that just didn't add up, about what Alex said the voice told her:

"If you're still looking for Special Agent Kallinger, find Marc Cauldwell and have him take you to see Detective Robert Colavito."

Now, Jack reasoned, the voice could not know they'd already found Cauldwell. But why would the voice intentionally lead them to Detective Colavito? Jack wondered why Colavito wasn't at the safe house last night. Was Wallace protecting him? Maybe whoever made the call – and given Cauldwell's deathbed confession last night, it seemed a safe assumption it had been Wallace himself – only needed Colavito's name to get Cauldwell to bring Jack to the safe house, where Estéban was waiting. But that only made sense if Colavito had a bargaining chip with Wallace.

Then Jack smiled.

What bigger chip could there be than what Cauldwell said about Wallace being "both a silent partner *and* a client." If Cauldwell was telling the truth, which not only meant what Detective Colavito learned during his time in Iraq might eventually be used to against Wallace, it also meant that Alex was right. There was at least one more loose end Wallace needed to tie up.

Which would explain why he delayed his flight home until tomorrow.

How Estéban fit into the picture, why he was the triggerman last night, was still a problem for Jack. But what Cauldwell said last night, though, about why Carmen was murdered in the first place – that it was to bring Jack into the investigation with the intent of *not* catching her killer so much as ridding Wallace of Cauldwell – had stuck with him. And, given what Jack now knew, it all seemed to make sense. Wallace knew Jack would get back in, somehow. Even after Wallace himself told Cauldwell to stand in his way, Wallace knew. Jack realized Cauldwell was right!

Jack had been Wallace's hit man!

He reached for his cell and pulled up Laura's number one more time.

It was time to play the hand they'd been dealt!

* * *

Laura had been at her desk in her conference room office for only a few minutes, having already discarded the sling from her left arm her doctors had advised her to wear, when the information Jack had asked her to get came through. She'd made inquiries from her hospital bed, even as Jack arrived at her room to check her out. Online local usage details – what was commonly known by the acronym LUDs – confirmed that the call to Jack's cell phone last evening was placed from the home number of Monsignor John Stuart Miles. Laura grabbed this morning's local newspaper and opened it to the social page. She dropped it in Jack's lap and pointed to the photo accompanying the story. There was the Monsignor, attending the fundraiser last night for the Mayor's literacy campaign. Which was the function Wallace was in town to attend.

There it was. Wallace goes back to the Monsignor's place and makes the call to Jack's cell Wallace *knows* can be traced. But why the Monsignor? What could the priest possibly have anything to do with this?

Laura made a quick check of her inbox. After seeing Detective Colavito in Cauldwell's office yesterday, Laura had asked one of the clerks in the office to do some digging. An email that summarized Detective Colavito's service record waited to be opened. Laura double-clicked on the item and up popped the officer's information, highlighted by the most recent Independent Review Board action still pending. Though the email did not allude to contents that comprised the investigation file or the specific details surrounding the allegations against Detective Colavito, it did identify the board members investigating the case against him.

Laura read the names then leaned back in her chair. She motioned for Jack to take a look. The very last name listed was the Monsignor John Stuart Miles, the Mayor's personal appointee. That he was serving on the IRB hardly came as a surprise. That he was adjudicating preliminary aspects of an official departmental investigation into Detective Colavito actions, unclear as those might be, seemed a bit too coincidental.

The detective's name seemed to be crawling out under every rock. Sandy claimed he witnessed Colavito murder Carmen while Cauldwell claimed he had evidence to prove Sandy right. The mysterious caller from the Monsignor's home told Alex that Cauldwell would lead them to Colavito. And the Monsignor was assisting in the IRB investigation of Colavito. If nothing else, that should be enough to have a sit-down with the detective. All they needed now was to tie Wallace to Colavito. Confirming that Wallace made that call from the Monsignor's home would do that nicely.

Laura picked up the phone and dialed the Monsignor's number.

Jack returned with a bottle of artesian spring water for Laura and a rain berry Gatorade for himself. He was hardly surprised that she was unable to get the Monsignor on the phone. She was told she would have to go through the Archdiocese's main office, the former Quigley Prep Seminary, in order to reach him. But Laura wasn't about to put up with that bullshit. She was nothing if not resourceful.

In the meantime, she'd received responses from the FBI's tech group concerning Cauldwell's laptop. Alex had told Jack, then later informed Laura, about the document file she found behind the icon on Cauldwell's desktop display. Apparently, Cauldwell had exported certain incoming email messages, complete with domain names and address headings, directly into a single document. He continued appending each day's messages to the existing ones, creating one very large file. Cauldwell was nothing if not organized, an attribute which helped make Laura's work that much easier.

Not that it made much difference to him now.

The email messages reflected conversations between Colavito and any number of individuals, only identified by their specific phone number. Laura had the idea that Cauldwell's email account may be currently backlogging new incoming emails. So she made a call to a friend of hers in the tech group. She originally had requested his email logon and password but that, she was told, was a technical violation of security protocol. However, what *was* possible was to have copies of every incoming email received by Cauldwell's account sent to Laura's email account. In addition, in an hour's time, she could have two programs downloaded onto her laptop. The first would automatically search her incoming email for the message code identifying Cauldwell's emails that were generated by the transcript program he was using. The second would collect those emails and append them into a specific file name of her choosing.

All it would cost her was a couple of drinks after work.

While she was running the programs, her tech guy called on a couple of matters. Laura had dropped off Cauldwell's laptop to search for any hidden files or password-protected files. They'd found several. It would take a little time, maybe a day or two, but tech guy thought that the files they couldn't crack might possibly be able replicated using a "backdoor" program, which would allow them to at least be opened as read-only files.

Jack's eyes lit up. He wondered if he'd found what he'd been searching for.

The other issue involved the program that had been installed on his computer that allowed him to track a specific phone number. The so-called "roving bug" program's activity log indicated that the number had been altered. When her tech friend brought Cauldwell's laptop back upstairs to Laura and Jack, he showed them how the program worked and where the number had been changed. Interestingly enough, the geek pointed out, the number wasn't changed locally. It had been changed remotely. The tracking software that Cauldwell used required web-based technology in addition to locally installed files. What this allowed, the techie explained, was that someone could access his computer, assuming it was running, even through a wireless web connection, and alter the phone number it was tracking.

Sure enough, that's precisely what had happened. The tech guy, while he could identify the original computer as the source for the change request, said it would be next to impossible to determine who specifically requested the change. He did say he would run it to ground. He just didn't want Laura to keep her hopes up.

It wasn't long before Laura was in a position to not only receive copies of Cauldwell's incoming emails but those subject to his transcript program would automatically append the content of those emails to a local file for her review. In addition, Laura and Jack could now alter the program to begin tracking the original number – Colavito's cell phone – again.

When her tech friend would crack the Cauldwell's password-protected files was anybody's guess. And nobody knew what a review of the email transcripts would turn up. But, even if they had to bluff, Jack and Laura realized they had enough to move on Wallace. It was a calculated gamble but one they knew they had no choice but to take.

It was approaching five o'clock.

* * *

Bobby slowly paced around his apartment as the thought resurrected in the back of his mind that taking this call might not have been the smartest thing he could've done.

"How much longer will you be in town, Deputy Director?" he asked.

"Right now, I'm scheduled to fly out Thursday morning to D.C. I've got a dinner meeting tonight but the rest of my evening is open."

"Good, we should talk," Bobby said.

"Anything in particular, Detective, or were you just interested in how the Redskins were going to be this season?" the Deputy Director responded.

"No, not much of a football guy, sir. After all, living in Chicago, you tend to recognize limits when you see them."

Wallace laughed.

"No, I heard from Cauldwell about some information he either planned to provide, or maybe already has provided, the IRB concerning my case."

"I see," Wallace said.

"He also made somewhat of a veiled threat concerning my involvement with the death of your special agent last week."

"I see," came the repeated response.

Bobby waited and but heard nothing but silence.

"I'm sorry, did you hear me, sir?"

"Yes, Detective, I heard you. Are you finished?" Wallace asked.

"Yeah, that's about it," Bobby said.

"So, what would you like me to help you with?"

What the fuck is with these feds? Bobby thought. *Jesus!*

"I was hoping you might be able to reach out to one of the IRB members, sir."

"Ahhh, I see," Wallace responded. "And – if you could help me out here again, Detective – why would I want to do that?"

Bobby was getting pissed. He hated being jerked around.

"It's really very simple, sir," Bobby said sarcastically, "Either you make this little unpleasantness go away for me or I will create a lot of unpleasantness for you."

"I see," Wallace said, grateful that the dance had finally ended. "Detective, perhaps I've failed to make something clear throughout the duration of our somewhat brief but nonetheless mutually beneficial relationship. Threatening me is something that can only result in regret for you."

"Look, I don't need this sh–"

"I'm not quite finished, Detective."

Bobby listened silently if not impatiently.

"Last evening, I spared your life. You may not know it yet or even believe it. That's of little consequence to me. The fact is, you are only alive today because of a phone call I made yesterday afternoon."

Bobby couldn't help but wonder.

"You are the only one, Detective, who believes his knowledge of certain specific events can create – how did you put it, 'a lot of unpleasantness' – for me. I can assure you, at this very moment, Detective, that is *not* the case. What you think you know is both unsubstantiated and uncorroborated. When the time is right, should the time ever be right, I will contact you. Until then, perhaps it would be a good idea if we not communicate with one another."

"What is with you arrogant FBI pricks, anyway?" Bobby retaliated.

"I'm sorry, Detective," Wallace continued toward winding things down. "I appreciate that you originally reached out to me. And I'm grateful that you provided me with all of the physical evidence you did concerning Special Agent Cauldwell's activities during his time in the Middle East. But, the truth is none of that is important any more. None of that mat –"

"Look, I'm through fuckin' around with you," Bobby finally said, giving in to his temper, "if you want to roll the dice, that's your call. The bottom line is you either reach out to the IRB or I go to the press with what I know. It's a simple choice, really. Even someone who's risen to your level of stupidity ought to be able to figure it out."

"Detective," Wallace dryly replied, "I don't see that we're making any progress here. As I mentioned earlier, perhaps it would be a good idea if we not communicate with one another for the foreseeable future."

"You really don't think I can hurt you, do you?" Bobby asked incredulously. "Do you realize how easy it is for me to take out your agent? How I didn't even give it a second thought when I sliced her open and spilled her guts on the side of the road?"

Wallace decided to wait him out.

"It was no different there than in any of your 'undisclosed locations' in Iraq, sir," he said caustically. "Killing her was no different than killing any of them. Not at all. You see, the thing is, Deputy Director, once you get used to killing people – when you know how to do it silently, without making a sound, so they never know its coming – it's something that you don't forget. Oddly, it's a skill you tend to enjoy, even take pride in."

"Why, Detective," Wallace said arrogantly, "that sounds like a threat."

"Take it anyway you'd like, Deputy Dir–"

Bobby found himself speaking across a dead line.

* * *

From where Laura was seated she could see Jack on the end of a recently painted if not personally familiar wooden bench, just across from the open-air restaurant, outside of Chicago's Millennium Park. When she'd spoken with Wallace earlier in the day, she said nothing about Jack being there. For all Wallace knew, Jack was dead. But, then again, the same was supposed to be true of her.

Wallace was predictably late, in part due to his security detail and their concerns about the Deputy Director meeting with anyone in such an open area. But he was also entertaining concerns of his own: what went wrong last night that Laura somehow survived and what, if anything, did she know about the role he played in it. That she suggested a public place offered a tantalizing clue to the reason for the meeting. All she'd told him this morning was that she'd solved Carmen's murder and would be ready by tonight to give him a personal update. Wallace was nobody's fool. But whatever she knew, he had to be the first to find out. For him, containment was always the first option.

What form it would take depended entirely upon what she had to say.

Four physically fit men in their late thirties and early forties, looking almost like clones in their dark suits, white shirts, dark ties and black sunglasses, approached Jack for the customary once-over. Jack was unarmed. Laura had secured her service weapon as well as her backup in the trunk of her rental car. The Beretta Tomcat she'd taken off of Estéban Calderón was locked up with them.

After completing their search, the four men took up their positions in a guarded square, each standing approximately thirty feet apart from one other, with the park bench in the center. On cue, two more agents escorted the Deputy Director up until he reached the secured area, which he then walked through alone to reach the park bench. The two agents then began their surveillance, floating around the secured perimeter.

Wallace was visibly surprised to see Jack.

"Why, Deputy Director," Jack quipped with a hint of sarcasm, "perhaps you weren't expecting me?"

Wallace quickly reassessed.

"I was expecting Special Agent Kallinger, Jack. I don't understand. What's going on here?"

He turned and began to motion to one of his agents.

"Deputy Director, please," Jack asked, "allow me just a couple minutes of your time. I believe it's in your best interests to hear what I have to say."

Wallace quickly sized up his options. He decided he'd find out more about what happened last night. Maybe pick up some clues as to why Jack wasn't wearing a toe tag right now in the morgue at Northwestern Memorial Hospital next to his beloved Carmen. He sat down next to Jack on the opposite side of the bench. They did not shake hands.

"Deputy Director, if I may," Jack began, "I'd like to get right to the point."

Wallace nodded coldly in response.

"We have a problem, sir, and by 'we' I mean, specifically, you and I."

"How's that, Jack?" Wallace asked innocently.

"Sir, I am in possession of information that implicates you in a conspiracy of ongoing illegal activities. Some of these activities you are already aware of: deploying FBI personnel to a foreign country without benefit of Constitutionally-required Congressional authorization; authorizing the participation of FBI personnel in the illegal use of enhanced interrogation techniques on foreign soil that, in certain cases, resulted in the deaths of Iraqi citizens and detainees at various prison locations throughout Iraq; and, participating in and personally profiting from the trafficking of émigrés from Iraq to Kuwait, Syria, Jordan and Palestine."

Wallace sat stone-faced, his expression unchanged. He appeared to be less than impressed if not completely disinterested.

"Finally, sir, we also have evidence that you obstructed justice and took specific steps to impede the investigation into the murder of Special Agent Carmen Eyas. And, on a personal note, sir," Jack added with that 'cat-inviting-the-mouse-to-dinner' deadpan flair of his, "I can't even begin to tell you how many laws you violated when you solicited me to murder Special Agent Marc Cauldwell."

Wallace sat up straight and displayed a look of profound incredulity.

"By the way, as per your earlier request," Jack said, pausing for effect, "Special Agent Cauldwell is dead."

"Special Agent Cauldwell is dead?" Wallace asked.

"Yes, Deputy Director, he's dead. As is Estéban Calderón who, we have reason to believe, was responsible not only for one of the largest organized human trafficking rings operating in the midwestern United States, we also consider him suspects in at least two murders: The rape and murder of Andría Cristina Concepción in Denver in the fall of 2006 and the death of Teresa Maria DeJesús here in Chicago. We've determined an identifiable pattern we are now pursuing in other similar crimes occurring in other cities. And we have been able to establish a relationship between Monsignor John Stuart Miles and Mr. Calderón, who we now believe provided the Monsignor with trafficked young women and girls, one of whom was Ms. Concepción, during his time in Denver which, we believe, resulted in her murder."

"Jack, I don't know what you're talking about." Wallace objected. "What does any of this have to do with me? I don't know any –"

"Deputy Director, it would save us all a lot of time not to mention wear on my patience if we could simply take a break from all the bullshit and allow me to finish what I came here to say. I don't enjoy being this close to you, sir, and the sooner we can get through this, the sooner I can get back to my room and shower."

Wallace appeared annoyed.

"I'll give you two more minutes."

Jack smiled knowingly.

"Sir, we not only have transcripts of telephone conversations wherein you hired Calderón to murder Cauldwell, Special Agent Kallinger and myself, we also have password-protected files from Agent Cauldwell's personal computer which directly implicates you in specific criminal activity in Iraq as well as here in this country."

Wallace had no response. But Jack's formal tone left him wondering where Jack was wearing the wire.

"Now, you should know, Deputy Director Wallace, that I am prepared to take what I have to the U.S. Attorney General and allow him to ascertain the nature of the criminal charges that should be filed."

"Or –" Wallace interjected, sensing that Jack was about to begin negotiations.

"Or," Jack responded, "you can immediately place Special Agent Kallinger back on active duty within the Criminal Section of the Civil Rights Division of the Bureau."

"And –" Wallace continued, awaiting the proverbial other shoe.

"And then tender your resignation."

Wallace remained silent.

"The choice," Jack concluded, "is yours, Deputy Director Wallace."

After what seemed like an interminable few seconds, Wallace responded.

"Jack," he said softly, "why are you doing this? What are you hoping to gain?"

"Deputy Director, before you continue," Jack interrupted, "you should know that we identified, as you might have guessed, the phone call you made to my cell phone last evening from the Monsignor's home. That was the phone call where you spoke to a colleague of mine and told her that, if we were still looking for Special Agent Kallinger, who was missing at the time, we should first find Marc Cauldwell and have him take us to see a Detective Robert Colavito of the Chicago Police Department."

Jack continued.

"What you may not have realized, Deputy Director, is that the Monsignor records all of his incoming and outgoing phone calls made using his landline."

Jack waited for a moment.

"You did use his landline, didn't you?"

Wallace shifted uncomfortably.

"Deputy Director?"

Wallace continued splashing about.

"Jack, I don't know what information you think you have but –"

"Sir, please," Jack asked, "we also have transcripts of a phone conversation you had just this afternoon with Detective Colavito. It was in the course of that conversation that you told him that he was only alive today because of a phone call you made Tuesday afternoon."

Wallace waited as Jack went on.

"That phone call, sir," Jack continued, "we believe was the one you made to Estéban Calderón. It was then that you contracted him to murder Special Agents Cauldwell and Kallinger as well as myself."

Wallace comfortably if not confidently rested his arm across the back of the bench, turned slightly and crossed his legs.

"Now, Jack," Wallace objected, "why would I do such a thing?"

Jack leaned forward, his feet flat on the ground, his elbows forward on his knees. He turned and looked Wallace directly in his eyes.

"For the same reason others in your position have been seduced, Deputy Director. At one point, you probably believed what you were doing was right, that it was in the best interests of the country. In the aftermath of September 11th, countless sins were committed in the guise of our best intentions. But the times, no matter how uncivilized, cannot be used as an excuse to ratify relinquishing our civility, sir. That was the problem Iraq posed for you, Deputy Director, one you and your agents were completely unprepared to manage. But, in for a dime, in for a dollar, sir. But once you began walking down that path, there was no turning back."

Wallace listened, expressionless.

"And a rogue agent like Cauldwell, he offered you a choice. He could be seen as creating either a problem or an opportunity for you. For as long as he was useful, the latter made sense. As he pursued his own greedy ends, your hunger for the sake of this country became corrupted, was transcended. We even have Cauldwell's own words, sir – a dying declaration, if you will, Deputy Director – that you became 'both a silent partner *and* a client.' It was when you finally understood your exposure that you invited Detective Colavito into your plan to eliminate Cauldwell. But you couldn't simply kill Cauldwell. He was, after all, active FBI. You knew murdering Carmen meant I would find a way to get back in. And you knew that, if you could point me in Cauldwell's direction, your problems would go away."

Wallace dropped his head as he sat nonchalantly, a grin widening on his face.

"This is all very nice, Jack, but –"

"Ahhh," Jack interrupted. "Here's Laura now."

Jack stood and looked beyond the secured perimeter to see Laura standing near the park's entrance. Wallace turned in his seat to see her there with the Monsignor.

"You see, Deputy Director," Jack said without looking at him, "we also have another conversation you asked Special Agent Cauldwell to have with the Monsignor that he recorded. One where he describes, in somewhat nauseating detail, his fetish for particularly young women and your interest in his travel plans. That the Monsignor chose to ignore your advice to leave town made us wonder why someone at your level of government, with your immense responsibilities and obligations, would be so concerned about when and where the Monsignor opts to vacation."

The Deputy Director was now visibly upset.

"The mistake you made, Deputy Director," Jack said, unable to resist the irony, "was in the package you gave Laura to have me review prior to our meeting at the hotel."

Deputy Director Wallace remembered the meeting vividly.

"In it you included a second, thinner file, which summarized the research that Carmen and Timothy St. James Elliot, her friend and a photojournalist working in Iraq, had compiled on trafficking activity occurring throughout the Midwest…"

Wallace showed no indication he recalled who Timothy St. James Elliot was.

"…and it's connection to the 'enhanced interrogation techniques' you authorized be used by Cauldwell and other FBI personnel in Iraq."

Jack continued.

"Jimmy was murdered in Iraq when he learned of the connection, how Cauldwell was acting on your instructions. Calderón – one of your subcontractors in Iraq, as it turned out – actually killed him though Cauldwell was also in on the planning. It served to protect not only your political initiatives in Iraq but their business interests, interests which became uniquely lucrative during the insurgency."

Wallace's face was beginning to turn a decidedly whiter shade of pale.

"But murdering Mr. Elliot only meant that you had to also murder Carmen. After all, she knew what he knew. And you knew that killing her meant that I would find a way to get back in, that I'd become the answer to all your problems, sir."

Jack looked directly into Wallace's eyes.

"And so I shall, though perhaps not in the way you'd originally planned."
The wind he'd so meticulously sown had reaped a fateful whirlwind.

"Jack," Wallace said in denial mode, "we have nothing more to discuss."

Jack rose as Wallace stood up, turned and began to walk away.

"Understand this, Deputy Director," he said, speaking to the back of the man's head, "if I'm not reading of your resignation by Saturday's New York Times, start watching your inbox for a Congressional subpoena."

Wallace stopped abruptly and turned to look back at Jack. He grinned slightly, wondering if Jack had what it took to run with the big dogs. Jack stared into Wallace's eyes with the look of a stone-cold killer. Wallace laughed and walked out of the secured perimeter followed in tow by each of the six dark suits.

Jack watched him for a moment then turned and walked over to Laura as the Monsignor stood somewhat uncomfortably next to her.

He extended his hand to Jack

"If it's all the same to you, I'd like to leave now."

Jack looked directly into the Monsignor's eyes as he grasped the priest's hand and squeezed it firmly. He pulled the Monsignor up next to him, appearing as if to offer him a hug or a pat on the back. He tried to back away but Jack's grip wouldn't allow it.

He leaned forward, whispering harshly into the priest's ear a prophesy from the words of the Book of Ezekiel. Laura listened, her fierce expression unchanged, as Jack repeated one of her favorite Old Testament verses.

"And I will execute my vengeance upon them, by the hand of my own people... and they shall do there according to my anger and my fury. And they shall know my righteous might."

Jack then stepped back and glared deeply into the Monsignor's eyes. And smiled.

* * *

Epilogue

THEY SAT AT a small round table in the outdoor restaurant at Millennium Park, not far from where Jack had thrown down the gauntlet to the Deputy Director only a couple of hours earlier. Laura was successfully working her way through her second glass of St. Pauli Girl. Jack kept with an old favorite, Johnnie Walker Black neat. He was glad to hear she'd be staying through the weekend.

The setting sun cast a picturesque glow across the high-rise buildings lining the downtown area. The sky was a canvas of watercolors, a portrait of pastels and twilight deftly blended. There was even a cool breeze coming off the lake, driving the humidity down. A shadow stretched far enough across their table for Laura to remove her sunglasses. This Wednesday evening found Jack, his back now to the sunset, feeling comfortable for the first time in a long time. Things were far from resolved. But where justice hadn't already been served, he was confident it would be shortly.

Lost in all that had happened over the last few days, he appeared distant, almost disconsolate. Instinctively, Laura seemed to appreciate if not understand where he was at and what he needed to hear. She moved her glass, leaned forward and, with some discomfort, rested her folded arms on the table. She lowered her head and, without warning, offered her unsolicited thoughts.

"And his disciples came to him," she began, "and asked, 'Who then, Lord, is greatest in the kingdom of heaven?'"

Jack suddenly, if oddly, found himself paying attention. She raised her head, shook back her hair and smiled as her glistening eyes found his anticipating her next words.

"And Jesus called a little child to him and set the child in their midst and said, 'See that you not despise one of these little ones; for I tell you, their angels in heaven always behold the face of my Father. Let the little children come to me and do not hinder them for such is the Kingdom of Heaven.'"

Laura teared up as she looked back into eyes that had already started to soften.

"For whosoever causes even one of these little ones who believe in me to sin, it would better for him if a great millstone were hung about his neck and he were thrown into the sea."

He maintained eye contact with her as he settled back into his chair.

"I didn't remember you as being such an authority on Scripture."

She, likewise, sat back and crossed her legs.

"You forget, Jack," she said, "all those catechism classes I had growing up. And all the bible study. I was a good Catholic girl, Jack..."

She lowered her beer slowly from her lips, her eyes never leaving his.

"...once upon a time."

Jack smiled hesitantly as only someone with such vividly intimate images of her ever could.

"Yeah," he agreed, "I know what justice you did that school girl uniform."

She lowered her head slightly as her eyes remained fixed on his.

"You never know," she said in mock shyness, "it might still fit."

He nodded easily, his memories of her slender figure still very much alive.

"I have no doubt it probably does..."

And he couldn't stop grinning at the thought.

"Just like I have no doubt that you're still quite the good Catholic girl..."

She had a look of mock horror at hearing him make such a statement.

He decided to finish his thought.

"...Though I think you're a better person now," he concluded shyly.

Laura shifted gears as she started to blush. The look in his eyes got stronger.

"Yeah," she said, unnecessarily explaining herself, "no matter how hard you try, no matter how long you ignore it, it's there. Just when I think I've left it all behind me –"

"I know," Jack added, watching her nod her approval, "it's like some insidious form of indoctrination, like some kind of drug. And once it has you, then it really has you. Nothin' you can do or say. There's no turning back. The best you can try to do is convince yourself you can resist it, you can somehow get past it. But you really can't, not once it's a part of you. You can spend a lifetime telling yourself –"

Laura took another sip of her beer and thought out loud.

"Are we still talking about –"

"But the memories are always there," Jack said deliberately interrupting her, "good and bad. Whether we like it or not."

"Yeah," she agreed, speaking slowly while maintaining eye contact, "whether we like it. Or even if we don't."

He felt at ease as he returned her look, knowing he'd not so unintentionally shown his hand. He'd always believed that, when it came to matters of the heart, Laura always appealed any conviction to the cool logic of her head.

Except when it came to them.

A long but somewhat comfortable moment later he changed the subject.

"But you confused the two different verses," he said with a grin. "One's from Matthew, the other's from Mark."

"The what?" she clumsily asked.

"The bible quotes you mentioned," he answered, "the New Testament verses."

"Maybe in your bible," she said, not willing to acquiesce.

"It's not like you got them wrong," he said now in his own defense, "you just got them confused. I should know. I was an altar boy. I was fed my share."

She shot him a "give me a freakin' break" look. But she wouldn't back down.

"Christ, it's not enough I remember them," she shot back playfully. "Jesus, you sound like the nuns I had in school."

He took another slow sip of his scotch.

"No, I'm just saying that, of everything I thought I knew about you, Laura, I didn't know that," he said. "That's all."

She dropped her head and smiled.

"Of all people, Jack," she said without hesitation, "you should know how deep my still waters run."

"I suppose so," he said cautiously.

She sat up and leaned forward again, deciding it was time to change the subject.

"So, what do you think he'll do?"

Jack was just removing the glass from his lips.

"Who, Wallace, you mean?" he said coyly just after swallowing.

"Of course, Wallace," she answered.

"He'd be a fool if he doesn't retire but I can tell you this, it'd make Alex a much better story if he tries to stay on! Personally, I hope he tries it. Nixon had better odds!"

Laura laughed and reached for her beer. Like she wanted to be reminded of Alex.

"Besides, if he stays, the fight will help bring the issue front and center. Imagine, the Deputy Director of the FBI involved in human trafficking. Either way, once the papers get hold of this…"

He just wagged his head in mock disbelief.

"Jesus, I still can't believe how stupid he was!"

"Men are so fuckin' shameless," she authoritatively concluded. "If you're not thinking with that goddamned thing, you're acting directly on its behalf."

Jack smiled.

"Minnie Driver," he said, as if answering a question, "'Good Will Hunting.'"

She nodded, smiling.

"Yeah," she responded, "I paraphrased it a bit but still one of the best lines ever!"

He just grinned. *What else could he do? When she's right, she's right!*

"How's the shoulder?" he asked.

Laura just shook her head.

"It didn't hit my shoulder, Jack."

He knew it hadn't. She met his attempt at discretion head on.

"Christ, Jack, another couple of inches and I'd have had a free mastectomy!"

He shook his head, smiling, remembering what a shame that truly would've been.

"Besides, it'll take a helluva lot more than some dumbass loser's lousy aim to keep me off the job."

"No argument here," he said.

She took a longer drink of her beer then started again.

"Jack," she said, her tone changing, "about that envelope that Carmen sent me –"

"Not to worry, Laura," he said without letting her finish, "As it turned out, Wallace getting his hands on it was the best thing that could have happened to us. Once he decided he could use it to force me to help him, he couldn't resist tipping his hand. He underestimated how I – how *we* – would react to seeing it, how we would end up using it to piece things together. Especially about Jimmy. Looking back, I honestly believe it ended up being what made the difference."

Laura smiled but didn't want to let it go. Jack leaned forward and took her hand across the table. He couldn't escape her look. He didn't want to. Her eyes caught what light remained from the fading sunset. A gentle breeze stirred her hair.

She suddenly cleared her throat then winced as she instinctively reached up her hand and waved. Jack watched her with mixed emotions, comfortable with calling a temporary truce. He put down his drink and turned to look behind him and see Alex, hand-in-hand with Ana and Daniel, walking their way. And she could hardly have looked better! But it was also good to see the kids finally able to leave that lousy hotel room. Laura's slender fingers pushed quickly across her cheeks as they approached.

"Hi," Alex said as she brought the kids to the table.

"Hi," Laura said, clearing her throat.

Jack looked at Alex and just smiled. He pushed back the chair and got to his feet. He picked Ana up in his arms and drew Daniel close, his hand resting on his head.

"So how's everyone today? What did you guys do today?"

Daniel stepped back as Ana squirmed to get down before both started talking about their day visiting with Caridád at the hospital then all the things they saw walking around downtown. But on such a comfortable evening, there was still one thing missing.

"Hey, whaddya say we go get some ice cream? Anybody in the mood for –"

He wasn't able to finish his sentence. Alex snuggled up against him and gave him a big hug. She stepped back and kissed him then hugged him again. She stepped into his embrace and against his chest as he turned with helpless eyes to see Laura look away.

Jack left cash on the table inside the small leather folder containing the check and off they went. As they walked into what remained of the evening sunshine, he pulled his sunglasses from his shirt pocket and slipped them one. Alex couldn't help but snicker in response to his outdated eyewear. He flinched from the tightness in his still sore shoulder as Ana and Daniel asked in unison if they could bring some ice cream to Caridád tonight.

They could hardly have had a better idea!

* * *

Bobby lay there with his eyes closed, spent. Again. He felt her begin to roll out of the other side of the bed. He instinctively tightened his arm around her neck and hugged her back toward him. When it came to her and her delicious body, he was all but insatiable. She groaned agreeably in response as she crawled on top of him. He openly welcomed her smooth, moist skin pressing against him as his head left the pillow. His tongue invaded her mouth as he wrapped his legs around her. A long moment later, she opened her eyes and spied the digital clock on the nightstand.

It was three minutes to 10:00 AM.

She pushed away from him wearing nothing but a wistful smile.

"Hold that thought," she whispered insistently. "Gotta make a stop."

"Fuckin' prick teaser," he said caustically underneath his breath.

She leaned back into him, dragging her tongue across his throat. With both hands he pulled her face to his and opened his mouth. The simple taste of her made him hard.

Giggling, she slid provocatively across him and out of bed. She began to slip into a long, heavy pastel yellow robe that had been draped across a nearby chair when she felt his hand grip her arm. She looked to see his eyes traveling slowly from her chest down to her thighs, following the map of her body without a single tan line to guide him. He watched as she dropped the robe to the floor then dragged it behind her as she walked toward the bathroom with an almost runway-like seductiveness. When she reached the door, she turned a sparkling eye over a deeply rich, milk chocolate shoulder to see his leering eyes still reaching for her, noticeably scanning her hourglass shape. Every inch of her tight, smooth, lavender and violet-scented flesh – from her perfectly-shaped calves to her perfectly-formed ass to her firm, delightfully resilient breasts that could withstand his most wanton assaults to the wet, smothering warmth of a tongue that danced with a prima ballerina-like artistry – every inch of her left him having surrendered his religion to the one true faith which delivered on its promise that God – or was it the devil? – is only truly found in the details.

He heard the door close behind her and the water soon run. He reached across to the nightstand and relit the joint he'd started over an hour ago. He took a long drag and held his breath. He shut his eyes tightly then exhaled slowly.

His mind quickly wandered. He wondered how things had gotten so fucked up. He knew Wallace posed a formidable problem. The man was hallowed ground on which Bobby had to be sure to tread lightly. But what could he do? Still, one thing was certain: He wasn't going to let him walk away. He wasn't going to let this thing go with Wallace coming out ahead. That simply wasn't going to fuckin' happen. He thought he might reach out to some of his old Iraq buddies, guys who worked with the FBI at the detainee sites at Camp Bucca or Camp Cropper. There probably still were some Abu Ghraib buddies around he could talk up. Nothing too violent. Just something to wake Wallace up. Something to remind him about just where he stood. About where right stood.

The IAD investigation now only promised to get worse. If Cauldwell was telling the truth – something that Bobby'd learned not to take for granted – things were bound to get messy. He needed leverage. He just wasn't sure any more where he could find it.

And he needed time.

Suddenly, there was a loud pounding on the door of her apartment.

"FBI, MS. SIMONE! OPEN THE DOOR! WE HAVE AN ARREST WARRANT!"

Bobby hardly reacted or moved at all; he didn't even sit up. His eyes opened slowly as he showed no sign of surprise that they'd finally arrived. He watched calmly – almost too calmly – as she quickly came out of the bathroom, as if on cue, wrapped completely inside her knee-length robe, her hair down, wiping her face with a hand towel so as to avoid making eye contact with him. He heard the door open and a confluence of determined male voices as they entered. They weren't here for Jamie. Fuck Cauldwell's material witness warrant.

Abu Ghraib suddenly didn't feel so far away.

* * *

The Monsignor lay silently in his bed on top of the handsewn comforter he'd had flown in after one of his visits to Latin America. He was dressed in a purple-trimmed black cassock with a deep purple sash. A silk, purple cape trimmed in amaranth red laid neatly beneath him, curling around his thighs, its tassels almost reaching his knees. A black *zucchetto* – a skullcap denoting his ecclesiastical position – matching his cassock sat tilted comfortably on the back his head. His hands were clasped together, as if in prayer, across his chest. It was just before midnight when a latex-gloved hand extended its fingers across his bluish-gray face and gently closed his vacant, distant eyes.

A custom-made chest of drawers stood across from the foot of the king-size bed. It was four feet high and three feet wide. A series of three additional pull drawers of equal width, 9"deep, sat atop the chest accenting its design. Displayed on top of the pull drawers, at opposite ends, were two photographs. To the left was an 8" x 12" black-and-white matted portrait of his parents taken on their wedding day. A rosary of polished amber beads, blessed by

Pope John Paul II during his Holiness's visit to Chicago in 1979, was draped across the upper corners of the traditionally ornate old-world frame.

They remained two of his most prized possessions.

To the right was a 4" x 6" color photograph, matted and framed modestly in hand-rubbed Philippine mahogany. It was of the Monsignor posing with a group of school children, probably ranging in ages from as young as seven or eight to as old as thirteen. Snowcapped mountains provided a majestic backdrop beneath a brilliant sapphire blue Colorado sky. A young girl, a child of maybe twelve with short cropped brunette hair, sat in his lap wearing a forced smile, her sparkling hazel blue eyes betraying her sadness.

Next to the framed photograph stood a wooden chalice, milled from solid maple. It was handcrafted, turned on a lathe by his grandfather for him when he was just a boy. It was painted gold, a finish that had long ago faded into a dull brown. It had been a gift from his grandparents for his confirmation. For even then, as a seventh grader at Santa Terisita Middle School, a young John Stuart Miles believed he'd heard his calling.

Inside the chalice lay a curled-up, inexpensive – some might say even cheap – pearl white rosary, its crucifix dangling outside the carefully beveled cup. The stranger reverently removed it from its resting place and carefully intertwined it inside the fingers of the dead prelate's hands.

The gloved hands then pulled opened the top dresser drawer and removed the Monsignor's personal bible. A gift from his mother upon his ordination, the book was placed respectfully on top of the chest, the old and brittle binding cracking as it was slowly opened. A holy card commemorating his father's life slipped out from inside the front cover. Another acted as a bookmark inside the Gospel of Matthew, Chapter 7. The Sermon on the Mount. Apparently a favorite of the Monsignor's. The card was old, it's edges creased. It was printed in remembrance of his mother's passing.

Carefully thumbing through the yellowed and fragile pages, once lined in 14k gold, determined eyes scanned through the books of the Old Testament until the search settled on the elusive page. A single finger slid carefully to find both chapter and verse.

The Book of Ezekiel. Chapter 25. Verse 14.

The stranger pulled out a small photograph of the young Colombian girl, then eleven years old, playfully smiling, her platinum blond hair windswept across her soccer jersey, her sparkling hazel blue eyes loving life. Written on the back was Judgment Day.

"And I will execute my vengeance upon them, by the hand of my own people...

and they shall do there according to my anger and my fury. And they shall know my righteous might."

The solitary figure pulled both holy cards from the book and laid them in place, one just above and the other just below the bible verse, then fit the child's picture snuggly inside the photograph's picture frame, against the glass.

The rubber-gloved hand carefully brought a cell phone to one ear as the number in the 202 area code rang. Looking directly into the dark glasses of the image reflected in the full-length mirror that stood as silent witness in the corner of the room, the stranger's black stocking cap provided a menacing touch. This Saturday morning's New York Times lay on a reclining chair, positioned in a corner of the room off to the side. The headline in the far right column, above the fold, told of the unexpected resignation the day before of the Deputy Director of the FBI, L. Stephen Wallace, owing to health reasons. The article said he would be leaving office in a month to enjoy his retirement. The mirror across the room reflected an approving nod.

An abrupt connection brought the stranger back to the task at hand.

"Yes?" a distant voice said.

"It's done."

"Thank you."

The call lasted precisely four seconds.

* * *

Jack's Tuesday morning class was enjoying as many students as this fall semester was likely to provide. It was the last week of September and, by now, most of them had settled into their normal class schedules. And while teaching part-time at a junior college in the southwest suburbs was one of the more enriching ways Jack had found to get out his message, the size of his class on human trafficking – Introduction to the Basic Principles of Human Rights –, a 100 level class in the School of Social Sciences, spoke to a not totally unexpected but nonetheless truly sad reality.

The thought that rabid vermin like Raúl could have been so perceptive – that there truly are only three kinds of people who cared about the business of buying and selling human beings – seemed even more accurate today than Jack was willing to admit.

It had been just over six weeks since the Monsignor's untimely passing.

The fall semester had begun the last full week of August. Jack's class was offered from 9:30 AM to 10:50 AM every Tuesday and Thursday in a lecture hall with an auditorium-like setting that was nothing if not overkill. Jack's lectern, desk and whiteboard at the front of the class were down thirteen semicircular steps from the doors leading into the classroom. Each step held approximately twenty student chair desks. On that first day of class less than one-quarter of the auditorium's seats were filled.

This morning found slightly less in attendance.

Still, despite the sparsely attended semester hours, discussions were often lively though the most interesting moments were when Jack would share his own personal experiences, either from his FBI days or his work as a freelancer. Whenever possible, Jack would bring in guest speakers who often found the allotted class time so insufficient they would be asked to return. Those in attendance this morning were of all ages, from all walks of life and from all fields of major studies. And, as was again the case this morning, the class's hour and twenty minutes was not nearly long enough!

So it was not unusual for Jack to find himself in the middle of a small gathering once class let out, seeking more resources, more information or deeper discussion on specific topics. Since this was his only class at the junior college this semester, he often stayed afterwards to spend time encouraging his students to explore issues more deeply.

And today was no different. For more than twenty minutes after class had ended, a handful of students surrounded him as discussions brought impassioned interest in somehow making a difference. Slowly the crowd dwindled until just one person was left. And she was seated among the vast sea of desks.

Alex.

Her work at the Democratic Convention proved more successful than she had hoped. The nomination of the first African-American from a major party to run for the presidency was an historic event she felt privileged to be a part of. From the convention she'd spent a week in London documenting the plight of British Muslims. In the past ten days, she'd begun interviewing detainees who had been renditioned to secret CIA-run prisons in various parts of the world. The angle her story was pursuing involved the legal battles, citizens and non-citizens alike, were waging against the federal government to bring the issue of extraordinary rendition and unlawful detention to light. She also had somehow found time to meet with a publisher who was interested in an idea she was developing for a book on her experiences as a journalist. But she'd made a special point of taking some time off to surprise Jack and maybe spend a few days together.

Though they'd talked on the phone frequently, it had been a little more than a month since he'd last seen her. And much had happened in between.

Detective Bobby Colavito had been indicted on a series of charges, including two counts of first-degree murder. He'd been denied bail awaiting his trial. Then the Feds suddenly asserted jurisdiction, ostensibly to charge him with federal civil rights violations in Carmen's murder. Soon after, rumors began to swirl concerning specific knowledge he claimed to have involving key members of the Bureau, going as high up as the deputy director's office, and their activities in post-Saddam Iraq. Nothing concrete had yet broken. But, oddly enough, Detective Colavito had yet to see the inside of a courtroom.

Laura was back in Washington. And back in the Criminal Section of the Civil Rights Division of the Department of Justice. Wallace had at least come through on that much. And she'd already begun lobbying to get Jack back on the payroll.

Father Mac recovered without any long-lasting side effects and returned to the pulpit. The parish school at St. Jerome Emiliani was saved, at least for another year due, in no small part to the priest's newly-found celebrity that Jack's interviews had secured.

Ana, Daniel and Caridád had all returned home safely – Jack had seen to it. They all flew home together. Their first stop was Albuquerque where Caridád was welcomed home. The local press ate it up – a young girl kidnapped into prostitution and sold as a sex slave gone missing for seven years somehow miraculously reunited with her family – and gave it a lot of play. It wasn't long before the network affiliates picked up the story, with cable news not far behind. Caridád handled it all with a maturity beyond her age. And in a move Jack helped orchestrate, designed to take full advantage of the publicity the press had generated, the neighborhood where they'd once lived renamed a local children's park for her sister, dedicating it to the peaceful memory of Maria Engañada.

Jack continued on to escort Ana and Daniel on to their homes, though they were greeted with much less fanfare. Ana was reunited with her family on her grandparents' hacienda in small village outside of San Miguel de Allende. Daniel returned to his family in the border town of Laredo, Texas. Laura arranged for the Department of Justice to pay the bulk of their expenses but what the DOJ was unwilling or unable to pickup, Jack willingly did so out of his own pocket. And, before leaving each of them, he promised, on behalf of Father Mac, Laura and Alex, that they would all see each other again.

And they both knew from experience Jack was nothing if not a man of his word.

The FBI completed its investigation concerning the deaths of the three young men at the Walavender Drug Store. It pointed to the professionalism of and interdepartmental cooperation between the local police and the Chicago Police Department that led to the conclusion that the murders were gang and drug-related. The deaths of Special Agent Marc Cauldwell and Department of Defense contractor Estéban Sanchez Calderón were also considered gang-involved murders although there was increased speculation that trafficking was one of the major forces at play. Cauldwell was *not* considered in the line of duty at the time of his death. And Alex, now armed with Deputy Director Wallace's notes and personal observations concerning Cauldwell's activities while "unofficially" in Iraq, had been invited by the New York Times to write a series of investigative articles.

Seeing her this Tuesday morning in his classroom allowed Jack to come full circle. But the sudden rush of adrenalin almost made him nervous. He'd only returned yesterday from a longer than planned weekend trip to D.C. and hadn't yet begun to work through what he was feeling. He knew it didn't make any sense. It couldn't. But he also knew he felt guilty. And responsible. But he decided, until he could sort it all out, he wouldn't say anything to Alex about what had happened.

Or who he'd been with.

Jack had flown out five days ago – last Thursday afternoon – to spend Friday meeting with members of the FBI Service Martyr Review Board. He was invited to testify in support of Carmen's nomination as both a member of the D.C. office's Hall of Honor as well as a member to be permanently enshrined in the Bureau's Wall of Honor in the J. Edgar Hoover Building. Special Agents killed in the line of duty as the result of what the FBI officially terms "direct adversarial force at, or by, the hand of an adversary" are deemed "Service Martyrs." Names of those agents are included on a plaque as the FBI's official tribute, in perpetuity. As the morning-long interview came to a close, it was apparent to Jack that Carmen's ultimate sacrifice would be memorialized in honoring her service to the Bureau and her commitment to the work that mattered so deeply to her.

While visiting the Hoover Building, he'd had the opportunity to see Carmen's Special Agent badge, draped with a black sash, on display in the lobby. And he had a chance to speak with some of her friends in the local office as well as to catch up with some of his old friends and former colleagues. Some he sought out; others not so much.

He'd called Laura before he flew in that Thursday afternoon. They'd made plans for dinner the following night. Spending time together on Saturday seemed a forgone conclusion until he found himself missing his Sunday evening flight home.

Alex was hoping to spend a few days just kicking back with Jack. She had to be in New York at the beginning of next week for a meeting with her literary agent. Jack cleared his schedule, such as it was. She even asked if she could attend his lecture on Thursday, as if she needed permission. Jack said he'd invite her to talk for a few minutes as a guest lecturer. Their time together was uniquely special, even apart from all the excitement they'd shared and the string of bodies Jack had left in their wake. And in ways neither could possibly yet appreciate, their lives had been irrevocably altered. They would look back at their chance meeting that August Friday afternoon in Millenium Park and know that they'd learned from each other some of life's most valuable lessons.

Alex learned to believe in heroes again. And to risk all of the vulnerability that doing so implied. She'd watched, almost like an innocent bystander, as Jack awoke feelings in her that had long since gone dormant. Since Jimmy – and, in all honesty, even before he went missing – her heart existed in the emotional equivalent of a persistent vegetative state. With Jack, slumbering embers had erupted into an unencumbered passion from which had risen the hope she so carefully now wanted to nourish for many tomorrows to come. A deeply special place in her heart was now his and his alone.

What Jack had learned was that his heart had finally started to heal.

Now, as Alex lay asleep next to him, her soft, familiar naked curves warm up against him, her head nestled snuggly against his chest, Jack's eyes were glued to the ceiling. Despite it being almost 3:00 AM, he couldn't sleep. His dinner with Laura last Friday night kept spinning through his head. He wanted to believe he didn't understand how it could have happened. Or, more to the point, how he could have let it come to this, what he could have done to stop it. He wondered if he simply found greater comfort in not wanting to understand. And, for a while, his tortured logic tempted him to absolve it all with a trite if not altogether unreasonable "it is what it is." But he could no sooner hide from the feelings that stirred in him anymore than he could from the passion that ruled his life. And that included Alex.

Truth be told, he was nothing if not introspective. It was where he drew his strength, even as he preferred to be weak. But it was moments like this when he appreciated how deeply perceptive Annie Savoy really was.

The world truly is made for people who aren't cursed with self-awareness. But he closed his eyes and decided he'd try one more time.

He checked his watch and grinned expectantly knowing that, for Laura, being twenty minutes late meant she was right on-time. He was glad he'd taken a seat at the bar to wait for her. The lounge at the downtown D.C. hotel where he was staying was doing a brisk business this Friday night. The high-definition plasma screens behind the bar were all tuned to the same closed-captioned cable news show. Talking heads were offering ad hoc commentary on a taped interview with the Attorney General from earlier in the day while awaiting a live press conference with the Director of the FBI. Jack swirled his Chivas Regal neat slowly as he read along with the ongoing discussion, trying unsuccessfully to make sense of the script scrolling across the bottom of the screen.

"Hey there, sailor," a soft voice cooed from behind him, "buy a girl a drink?"

Jack turned, smiling as he rose from his barstool to give Laura a warm hug. As they exchanged small talk, he marveled at her style, her look, thinking how she had a way of wearing a business suit that would make even Claudia Schiffer take notice.

While it had been a long day for both of them, Laura's day had been no less eventful. She'd spent it managing rumors concerning the latest accusations to come from the legal representatives of Detective Bobby Colavito. And, between that and today's breaking news, little else mattered. Which left little time for anything productive.

Jack turned Laura's attention to the televisions behind the bar.

"Do you know what's going on? Something's up but I'm not exactly sure what—"

Laura took a sip from her lemon drop martini then interrupted, mumbling something that resembled "not really sure" and "who really cares."

"C'mon, Jack," she said, "I don't want to sit at the bar." She gestured toward a small couch and an armchair off in the corner, away from the big screens.

"Here's a spot, let's go over there," she encouraged, "we'll be more comfortable."

Jack reluctantly agreed as they began to work their way through the crowd.

It had been almost two months since they'd last seen each other though they'd talked on the phone once a week or so. But tonight, here in this hotel's lounge, they comfortably picked up where their conversation had left off that cool, breezy game changing summer evening in Millennium Park. Their easy give-and-take, combined with a couple of additional rounds, inevitably gave way to the latest news out of Chicago.

Laura decided to step up to the plate first.

"So," she began, "it appears our favorite prelate met a decidedly just end, eh?"

Jack placed his drink down on the table beside him.

"Yeah," he said, "the Chicago press is really tap dancing around the whole thing."

Laura looked at him inquisitively as he continued.

"The Archdiocese vaguely referred to some kind of coronary condition he supposedly had. And the press has let it be. I've checked around – asked a few people I still trust – but I haven't been able to find out much more, other than the rosary he was supposedly saying at the time. Who knows if the truth will ever come out."

Laura held her drink and took a long sip.

"The truth? Really?" she asked, offering him an out. "Why would you say that? I mean, maybe there's nothing more to it. Sometimes things just turn out neat and tidy."

"True 'dat," he said in his best Chicago accent, showing a willingness to take it.

"Still," she continued on, "I would've thought the photo would have given them a clue. I can understand they didn't get the pearl rosary – but her picture? Seriously?"

Jack had his glass to his lips but suddenly stopped drinking.

"But what a story that would make, eh? The Catholic Church involved in a cover-up," she said with a dangling if dull surprise, returning to her martini. "Imagine that!"

"Yeah," he replied with a cautious, nervous smile. "Imagine that."

Laura caught herself grinning. His eyes, trained on her, had already sought to escape the mood. She giggled as she clumsily set her third empty martini glass down hard on the small round table in front of them.

He watched and wondered.

"You didn't think you're the only one with sources, did you, Jack?" she asked cutely. She opened her clutch purse then suddenly stopped and looked directly at him.

"But it's like you always say – it's never simply about *being* right, is it, Jack…"

He waited and listened. She'd proven to be both his student and his teacher.

"…In the end, all that matters is *doing* right."

Their eyes met, his look one of worry, hers one of coy satisfaction.

"Isn't it, Jack?"

He finally nodded slightly before leaning forward and placing his drink down on the table in front of them. He was about to say something when she took a deep breath and began to stand up.

"Now, if you'll excuse me, sir," she said first, "I'll be right back."

He immediately stood up with her.

She leaned forward and seemed to lose her balance. He grabbed her and held her for a long moment.

"You ok?" he finally whispered.

"Yeah I'm fine, really," she said. "I guess I should have eaten something earlier."

"Can I walk you?" he offered chivalrously.

"No, I'll be fine, really, it's ok," she insisted.

"But, you know, Jack," she offered in a supplicant voice. "Would it be so terrible if the good Monsignor's demise was something other than natural causes?"

Her eyes betrayed her usual self-confidence.

"Would it, Jack?"

He listened without trying to show any emotion.

"I mean," she continued, her logic befitting a former prosecutor arguing an exculpatory motion, "what a miscarriage of justice that would've been, right?"

There were no visible signs of the gunshot wound she'd sustained as she raised her left arm easily between them before firmly shaking it. A bracelet of polished amber beads slid haltingly down her forearm.

"And, wouldn't ya' know it," she started, gazing at her wrist as if trying to focus, "I really used to like this bracelet."

"Used to?" Jack asked innocently.

"Yeah," she replied, "I used to... but he had something just like it."

Jack had the sense he really didn't want to know what she was talking about.

"Had something like..." he conceded to ask leadingly.

"Yeah," she replied, "he had a fuckin' rosary that looks just like it. Now I just don't think I can wear this anymore." Then she whispered lowly, "God *damn* him!"

Laura looked up at Jack with glazing eyes.

"God *damn* them all to hell, Jack."

He couldn't help wondering what she wasn't saying.

"It never will burn hot enough for them," she asked, "will it, Jack?"

She started to smile a bit as she placed her hands on his arms.

"Anyway, I'll be right back," she said seductively. "Then we'll go eat."

She stepped back and turned to leave, stopping to turn her attention to the Director's image now displayed on every plasma screen above the bar. After carefully navigating the chairs, tables and people around her, she turned her head slowly back to see him watching her. She smiled as her eyes met his in the romantically lit atmosphere.

He somberly watched her walk away, her words still ricocheting inside his head.

She disappeared down a hallway as he downed the rest of his scotch. He picked up her empty glass and worked his way to the bar to pay the tab. Dinner would be later than expected. It was then that he noticed that the news program had gone live to a press conference at the Justice Department with the Director of the FBI, who had just finished making his statement and was now taking questions. Jack asked the bartender to raise the volume on the screen nearest him and tried to listen as the Director was asked about an unconfirmed report that the Deputy Director's family bible was opened to a highlighted verse from the Old Testament, the Book of Ezekiel – chapter 25, verse 14 – to be exact.

His stomach dropped.

He slumped onto the nearest barstool then rested his elbows on the bar as he folded his hands tightly. The Director's comments continued as he leaned forward and lowered his head. He listened to the Bureau chief's politically correct recollections of the Deputy Director's career, ones that seemed safely rehearsed while sufficiently sincere.

Jesus, God! Laura! NO! What have you fuckin' –

"I thought we weren't going to sit at the bar."

Jack raised his head, looked up at the screen then slowly turned an eye to her.

"He's dead," he said sternly, his rising anger colliding with his deepening regret. She felt his drilling look but chose to ignore him, focusing instead on the Director as he lamented his late Deputy's untimely heart attack – he'd been found in his home earlier this morning, hardly a week after beginning such a well-deserved if overdue retirement, one he'd earned through decades of selfless devotion to the many causes of justice.

"What a shame," she began, borderline caustically. "How tragic is that, really?"

His eyes clouded as his heart buckled beneath the crushing weight of a moment of frightening clarity.

See that you not despise even one of these little ones… and do not hinder them for such is the Kingdom of Heaven.

The brutal reality came into focus, leaving him helpless but to watch play out the deal she'd struck with God's own avenging angels, a covenant from which there could be no turning back.

For whosoever causes one of these little ones who believe in me to sin, it would better for him if a great millstone were hung about his neck and he were thrown into the sea.

It was a price he understood, one he knew all too well. One he himself had decided long ago to mortgage his very soul to pay.

And I will execute my vengeance upon them… according to my anger and my fury. And they shall know my righteous might.

"Just, tell me, how did you come to –" he started curtly. "Christ, why would –"

She firmly placed a hand on his shoulder and squeezed it gently as she moved to stand closer to him. Her eyes widened as a thin smile graced her expression.

The bartender came by with the check.

A few long moments later, as the Director again digressed to Wallace's career achievements, she finally turned to him, slowly and deliberately, a disarming grin now incorrigibly trying to emerge. His expression grew harder. But it was no match for her own fierce, determined look that had already evolved in response, a look of someone who, not unlike him, saw the world in almost naïvely clear and uncompromising terms, someone who would accept his judgment – even withstand it, if necessary – while neither regretting nor renouncing a duty she'd willingly accepted and executed so methodically.

After all, true justice carries with it no burden of apology.

Eventually, she'd come to appreciate Jack's view that the Administration's proactive stance against terrorism must apply equally to the invisible threats from within our borders as well as to the visible ones outside of them. The President's words in the aftermath of September 11th were no less hollow for acknowledging the difficult truth that this new enemy wore a face as unrecognizable as any suicide bomber. She admired that Jack had dedicated his life to, as the President once intoned, either bringing those responsible to justice or bringing justice, ultimately, to them. But, regardless of how it was affected, one reality would remain non-negotiable.

Justice would, indeed, be served.

Not unlike the Monsignor just a few short weeks ago, former Deputy Director L. Stephen Wallace was home when justice had come calling.

Silently. Quickly.

And most certainly with more compassion than he deserved.

It hadn't been twenty-four hours since his date with vengeance at his estate just outside Alexandria, VA. And unlike the countless, nameless, faceless victims whose interminable suffering he'd so richly profited from, he died at home. But like each of them, he'd died alone, with no one to help him, to take pity on him, no one he could reach out to for mercy or a safe haven, only his confessor, his ex-

ecutioner, standing there before him, smiling upon his fate, ushering him into his eternal reward.

Such as it was.

He'd faced his final terrifying moments devoid of any hope, not unlike every one of the myriad lives he had destroyed.

The lingering memories of those whose innocence wasn't so much lost as stolen had at long last brought with them truth without equivocation, righteousness without compromise, judgment without mercy. Their angels in heaven had seen to that.

No less than she.

And the phone call lasted precisely four seconds.

www.ingramcontent.com/pod-product-compliance
Lightning Source LLC
Chambersburg PA
CBHW020920020726
47495CB00002B/273